Out of the Blue

Bouquet

cross𝕊Roads
c o l l e c t i o n
1

Published by

Olivia Kimbrell Press™

Olivia Kimbrell Press™

CONTENTS

Out of the Blue Bouquet: Crossroads Collection 1

INTRODUCING

When I was young, my sisters and I loved to read those Christian collections where multiple authors each contributed a story. We called them "potato chip" books because once you started, they were difficult to stop, but they didn't have any real nutritional value, so to speak. Of course, back then, they were hefty paperback collections that rivaled the Bible in weight. While I remember enjoying the stories, I honestly can't remember the plot to a single book I read in one of those anthology collections.

Earlier this year, I was talking to a friend about putting together a collection of new stories. Right now, these multi-author collections are a pretty big deal in the world of ebooks. I am often asked to write books for collections, and I usually refuse, simply because I don't have the time to write something completely separate from my other series to fit the narrow theme of a collection, whatever that may be. But after my conversation with my friend, I got to wondering if it was possible to put together a collection that was different than the usual and didn't include the parts I don't like.

As often happens, the "what ifs" lead me down a path to something better than I would have thought possible. What if I could arrange a multi-author collection so that all of the books were independent and could be part of each author's universe, yet they had a point of intersection drawing everything together? What if the reader didn't understand how they were all connected until they read the last book? (Hehehe!) What if it was a unique collection, unlike any that has been done before? And... what if it was memorable and more than a set of potato chips?

And thus, the idea for a *Crossroads Collection* was born. A few minutes, and a nice hot shower, later, I had the idea for the "Out of the Blue Bouquet." I thought about it for several weeks without mentioning anything. I frequently have great ideas that never go anywhere. Then I told my friend. She loved the idea, and from there, the rest is history. I recruited some other fabulous authors who loved the idea as well, and we worked to create a collection unlike any that has been done before.

Now it's your turn to read and enjoy. Each story is a brand-new, never-before-published, complete, independent story. It may be part of the author's other series or have a part in one of their fictional universes, but it is also a stand-alone story. For instance, *A Kærasti for Clari*, by Carol Moncado takes place in the universe of her fictional country, complete with modern-day royalty. Other stories take place in a variety of settings, with no two in the same place. *Seoul in Love* takes place in Seoul, South Korea and has a more serious angle, while *Premeditated Serendipity*, by Chautona Havig includes a more humorous set-up. *Courting Calla*, by Hallee Bridgeman is first in the line-up and involves deception and a dark secret that threatens to destroy a budding romance.

All of the books are Contemporary Christian Romances, but all told in the styles of the individual author. Finally, the last book, *Out of the Blue Bouquet*, penned by me, ties all of the books together while telling its own story. (I'm so thrilled that I got to write that last book!) It is a mixture of fun and serious and may make you both laugh and cry at times. So read each individual story, but make sure you read them all to understand the *full* story!

The good news is that after you read this collection and love it, you don't have to feel sad that it's over. You get a glimpse of the worlds of five wonderful authors who each have a full "playlist" of books for you to check out and enjoy. Each author has listed her books at the end of her individual book, or another easy way is to type the author's name into the search of whatever retailer where you got this collection.

Also, this isn't the only *Crossroads Collection* that will be published. At the end of the collection, you will find a link to sign up for my newsletter. If you enjoy this unique set, I encourage you to sign up for the newsletter to find out when the next Crossroads Collection will be released. I have some exciting plans with a variety of different authors for 2018!

I encourage you to help spread the word about *Out of the Blue Bouquet*, Crossroads Collection 1. This is a limited-time collection, at a limited-time price. Eventually, the collection will be disbanded, and the titles will only be available on an individual basis. If you love it, talk about it so others can enjoy it too.

Finally, it is my hope and prayer that, as a reader of this collection, you come away with more than the fleeting enjoyment of a potato chip. May you escape into a world of enjoyable fiction, but may you also find something touching that gives you a different perspective. It is my prayer that you may recognize the good things that God has planned for all of life's "out-of-the-blue bouquets."

Happy Reading!

Amanda Tru

INTRODUCING

I t is my very great pleasure to introduce the first book in this collection. I have been very blessed to call Hallee Bridgeman a true friend of mine for several years now. She has been a blessing in my life and is an author and a woman I admire.

My story, *Out of the Blue Bouquet*, finishes up this Crossroads Collection of stories and ties all of these stories together. Hallee's story has a little more serious flavor than mine, which works perfectly because she is awesome at suspense and writing exciting parts! *Courting Calla* is a Christian Contemporary Romance, but it also involves deception and a dark secret that threatens to destroy all trust and any chance for a future.

As authors, it is really thrilling for us to think about how readers experience the stories we write. I am excited for you as you begin your journey through all of these stories. Thanks again for reading! May God use all your trials for good, turning life's accidents into "out of the blue bouquets."

Happy Reading!

Amanda Tru

Author of *Out of the Blue Bouquet*

Out of the Blue Bouquet

Courting Calla

a Dixon Brothers Novella

by

HALLEE BRIDGEMAN

Published by

Olivia Kimbrell Press™

Olivia Kimbrell Press™

Courting Calla by Hallee Bridgeman

Copyright © 2017. All rights reserved.

Some scripture quotations courtesy of the King James Version of the Holy Bible.

Some scripture quotations courtesy of the New King James Version of the Holy Bible, Copyright © 1979, 1980, 1982 by Thomas-Nelson, Inc. Used by permission. All rights reserved.

Library Cataloging Data

Bridgeman, Hallee (Hallee A. Bridgeman) 1972-

Courting Calla / Hallee Bridgeman

Summary: Ian knows Calla is the woman God has chosen for him, but Calla is hiding something big. Can Calla trust Ian with her secret, or will she let it destroy any possible hope for a future they may have?

ISBN: 978-1-68190-034-6 (ebook) ISBN: 978-1-68190-035-3 (trade paperback) ISBN: 978-1-68190-036-0 (Print on Demand) Library of Congress Control Number (LCCN): 2016911766

1. Christian fiction 2. man-woman relationships 3. suspenseful romance 4. romantic thriller 5. family relationships

CONTENTS

CHAPTER 1

Calla Vaughn felt the telltale shudder of the car through her seat just as she started to pull through the gate. "No, no, no," she said out loud, as if the machine might actually hear and decide not to die in the middle of the post-lunch rush to the parking deck. Despite the feeble attempt to stop it, with a lurch and a cough and a cloud of black exhaust, her car sputtered to a stop.

Resigned, Calla slipped her glasses off and lay her forehead on the steering wheel, closing her eyes, the smell of burning oil stinging her nose. If this week would just end, if she could just get through this afternoon, then tomorrow, and make it to the weekend, everything would turn out fine. It had to. Surely, the domino effect of her life would still and cease if she could just shut the door to her little apartment and hide from the rest of the world until Monday.

The tapping on her window startled her, and she hastily sat up, slipping her black-framed glasses back on. She knew with her black hair and dark brown eyes the thick black frames made her face stand out. She'd resisted buying them, but Sami, her best friend and confidante, had insisted, claiming they gave her a striking appearance. She said the glasses made her look like she just needed a nearby phone booth to transform into a courageous and strong heroine in primary colors. Calla knew nothing could help her not ugly but certainly not beautiful features, but she kind of wanted to see if the new frames would change her life in any way. They hadn't, of course. They were just glasses. So much for wanting to look like a superhero in disguise.

As she rolled down her window, her face flooded with uncomfortable heat. Of course, the car behind her would belong to Ian Jones, one of the mechanical engineers in the Dixon Contracting firm where she worked as a file clerk. She saw his signature a dozen times a day in her job but hadn't ever spoken to him beyond an uncomfortable hello whenever they passed in the halls. He had bushy brown hair, light hazel eyes that shifted from gold to brown to green, and a face better suited to some rakish Duke in one of her favorite Regency romance novels. She'd carried a crush for him since her second day on the job three years ago, though he barely glanced at her whenever their paths happened to cross.

Trying to keep from actually crying out of embarrassment, something that would make this whole horrible moment a thousand times worse, she simply drawled out, "Hi there."

His right eyebrow rose and his lips twitched up into a half grin. He had a dimple. "Need some help?"

If he only knew. The fish and chips lunch she had just wolfed down started to feel like bad sushi. She smiled weakly and asked, "Do you have a tow truck handy?"

He looked at her little Geo Storm that had rolled off the assembly line the year she was born and tapped the sun faded yellow roof. "Put her in neutral. We'll just move it out of the way of the gate." He gestured with his head, and she looked in the rearview mirror to see the growing line of cars behind them. She watched him wave an arm, and another man got out of a car three cars back.

With a sinking, burning feeling in her chest, she recognized him as one of the Dixon sons. She suddenly started wishing she believed in portals that would open up and suck someone into another dimension. Mr. Dixon, owner of the massive Dixon

Contracting construction and architectural firm, had three identical sons. Triplets. No one could really tell them apart, so they were all simply "Mr. Dixon." She guessed this was Jon from his pickup truck but honestly had no idea whether maybe one of his brothers, Brad or Ken, had borrowed Jon's truck this morning.

The little Storm shifted when Calla felt Mr. Dixon's hands grip the sooty back bumper. Following Ian's directions from the driver's window, she put her car in neutral and glanced out the window in time to see Ian's biceps bulge and bunch beneath his shirt as he maneuvered the car while Mr. Dixon pushed. "Let's get it to that spot there," he said, and she turned the steering wheel as they propelled her into the senior Mr. Dixon's space.

As soon as she set the parking brake, she hopped out of the car. "I can't park here. Mr. Dixon—"

"Is nowhere near Atlanta today. He's inspecting the New Orleans job for at least another three days. You're fine. Don't worry about a thing," the young Dixon said. He smiled, clearly trying to put her at ease. Turning to the man next to him, he said, "Hey, Ian? You're next, bro."

As the two of them rushed back to their cars that still sat blocking the entrance through the gate, she lifted a hand at their retreating backs. "Thanks." It sounded weak even to her own ears.

Sighing, cheeks burning with embarrassed heat, she pulled her phone out of her purse intending to call a garage. Her hands shook slightly from chagrin and, as the phone cleared the purse, it slipped from her fingers and crashed to the concrete parking deck floor. A flood of tears blurred her vision, making the cracks that appeared on the screen all blur together.

"Calla!" She looked up with tear-stained cheeks as Sami's zippy little convertible pulled up next to her and her best friend put her head out of her open window. Sami's eyes went from Calla's face to the ground next to her feet, then she put her car in park, and hopped out. "Oh, Calla, honey, let me help." She bent and picked up the broken phone, slipping it into her own pocket. She had on a brightly flowered shirt, mustard yellow leggings, and red boots.

Somehow, with her blue fedora sitting on top of perfectly curled black hair, it worked. "I'll call my uncle. He has a garage in Decatur."

"Don't bother. I couldn't pay to fix it, anyway. I'll just get it towed to a junk-yard. It's where it belongs."

Sami raised an eyebrow. "And then what?"

Realizing she had started to grit her teeth, she intentionally relaxed as she closed her eyes and took a deep breath and held it. In with the good, out with the bad. Letting out a long, slow sigh, she said, "Then I ride the Metro until I can get out of the hole my stepmother has so graciously dug for me." She reached into the pocket of Sami's shirt and snatched her phone. "I'll be fine."

"You'll get out of that hole faster once you press charges," Sami said. When Calla opened her mouth to protest, Sami held up her hand. "I know. I won't say it again. That's between you and God and the local police." She looked at her watch. "Get back to work. No reason to add trouble at work to your load. I'll take care of this. I have personal time saved, and you don't."

Calla hugged her, tightly, knowing God had blessed her with a true friend. She retrieved her bag from the back seat, made sure she didn't have anything in the glove box she didn't need, and rushed to the elevator just as Ian Jones reached it. Feeling the clumsy awkwardness that he always invoked overtake her, she smiled an uncomfortable smile and pressed the button for the second floor. "Thank you. Sorry to block your way."

He turned to look directly at her. "Glad you had a small enough car that it was easy to move. What brings you to Dixon this morning Ms...?"

She stammered a reply, "Vaughn. Calla. Calla Vaughn." Realizing Ian didn't even know her name made it even worse. Did he think she was married? "It's, uh, Miss. Not Mrs." Had she really just said that? "Not Miss, either. Don't call me Miss Vaughn. It's just that I hate that Ms. nonsense and I'm not married. So I'm not Mrs. Vaughn. But don't call me Miss Vaughn. I mean..." She closed her eyes one heartbeat after she shut her mouth. She took a breath, exhaled through her nose, raised her head, smiled, and said, "Call me Calla. And I, uh, file."

The dimple had reappeared. Throughout her entire babbling introduction, he hadn't so much as moved. He cleared his throat and nodded. "You file?"

"Here. I file here. At Dixon. I, uh, work in the file room."

"Ah." He nodded as the elevator stopped on her floor. When she just stood there, he held the elevator door open with his left hand and gestured with his right hand. "I believe the files are that-a-way."

She glanced through the open doors and saw the oversized glass doorway that provided access to the rows and rows of filing cabinets surrounding the cluster of cubicles. "Right," she said, stepping off the elevator. "Thanks. Uh, thanks for everything."

He extended his right hand toward her and said, "My name is…" but when she placed her fingers lightly into his right palm he stopped speaking.

"I know who you are, sir," Calla whispered, trying not to think about how nice his fingers felt beneath hers, though staring at his dimple didn't distract her from that thought very much. She jerked her hand back and stepped further out of the way of the elevator doors. "I see your name all the time."

"Right." He acknowledged. "Well, you're welcome. No problem at all." He gave her a single wave goodbye just as the doors slid shut.

After the doors slid closed, Calla took a final deep breath. In with the good and out with the bad. After she slowly released it, she reluctantly headed to her little cubicle and put her purse in the bottom drawer of her desk. Next to her desk, a large cart from the architectural division sat, piled with papers, plans, and files. Knowing that would take up the rest of the afternoon, she slipped earbuds into her ears, maneuvered through the broken screen on her phone to access her favorite radio station's app, and started sorting files.

Samuel Ian Jones thought about Miss Calla Vaughn
and her big brown eyes the entire trip from where she left him on
the second floor all the way up to the seventh floor. As he walked
off the elevator, he tried to rid his mind of the worry and stress he
saw in her eyes and focus instead on the amount of work he had to
do in the next three hours before his four o'clock meeting. He
crossed through the empty conference room that took up the center
of the floor then maneuvered through the cubicles used by the
interns and assistants. He went straight to his office on the far side
from the elevators. He left the door open, knowing his assistant
Penny would arrive bare seconds behind him.

Pulling his phone out of his pocket, Ian set it on the wireless
charger, then used the remote control sitting next to the charger to
turn on his favorite classical radio station. Only then did he allow
himself to go to his coffee maker, choosing an English tea over a
coffee pod. After confirming that he had no messages waiting in
either office voice mail form or email form, he grabbed his fresh
brewed tea and sat on the stool at his drafting table. Before he even
picked up his pencil, Penny slipped inside and shut the door behind
her.

"Your four o'clock canceled. The incoming storm has them
closing down the site early."

"Do I need to go now?" he asked, thinking of the twenty-story
building in the heart of downtown. The weekly job site meeting
was a vital part of the construction process at this point in the
schedule.

"No. They want to try to arrange a phone meeting with you
and the architect first thing tomorrow morning. The full job
meeting stays at the regular time next week."

"So just fast-tracking this week? Good." He felt an immediate
release of stress over what he needed to accomplish since he'd just
added two extra hours of useful work time to his schedule.

She gestured at him. "You have something black on your
shirt."

He looked down at the white golf shirt he'd worn to work and saw the streak of oily black dirt. "Hmph. Must have been the Storm."

Puzzled, Penny asked, "I beg your pardon? The storm's miles away. Where did you eat lunch, exactly?"

"No, not that storm." Unbidden, his thoughts once again returned to Calla Vaughn. She'd come across as utterly hopeless, which was silly considering they got the car moved within seconds of it breaking down. Maybe she just didn't know what to do next. The Mister-Fix-It inside of him thought about looking her up in the company directory and calling her, making sure she could handle the arrangements. Maybe he could give her a ride home. Maybe they could stop for a bite on the way. He quickly talked himself out of it. That would ruin his self-imposed moratorium on helping any people under the age of sixty. Well, unless said people happened to have a broken-down car blocking the path to his parking spot. "Never mind. Anything else?"

"Yes. You received a phone call from someone who claimed it was important but addressed you as Sam. Since only your grandmother ever calls you anything but Ian, I figured it was a vendor. I took the number, anyway." She held out a slip of paper.

As he took the note from her, he chuckled. One nice thing about going by his middle name, he always knew when someone actually knew him or when they looked at his name in some directory and tried to pretend. "Thanks, Penny."

"Sure. Let me know if you need anything. I'm leaving at two, today, don't forget. And I'll be out all day tomorrow."

"Right. Long weekend at the beach with the potential husband. I remember." His own moral compass never entered his relationship with Penny, who happened to be a fantastic secretary despite her personal lack of faith and resoundingly secular worldview.

As Penny shut the door behind her, he looked down at the dark streak on his shirt one more time then shook his head, reminding...no, telling... telling himself to stay out of it. Instead, he unrolled a set of plans onto his drafting table and focused on the mechanical engineering for the shopping mall Dixon Brothers had contracted to convert into a megachurch.

By the time three o'clock arrived, the sky outside Calla's cubicle window had darkened, and it looked more like nighttime than afternoon. She could see the branches of the trees across the street bending and bowing in the wind. Her phone had alerted her twice about thunderstorm warnings, and she thought about the wet walk from the metro station to her apartment she faced this evening. Resigned, she punched holes in the papers in her hand and fastened them to the prongs of the file folder in front of her. Inevitably, she would get soaking wet tonight. She tried to remember if she had an umbrella somewhere in her apartment; not that it would do her any good tonight. Still, since she had to ride the train for a while, she should probably have one on hand.

Even through the love song playing in her ears, she could hear the rain pelting against the windows. She began praying that the storm would move quickly through the area and completely dissipate before she had to go home. Maybe she could put in some overtime work. She certainly had enough work to do, and she really could use the extra hours.

Before she could go to her supervisor Francine and ask, her desk phone chirped. She slipped the earbud out of her ear as she answered the phone. "File room, Calla Vaughn," she said by way of greeting.

"Hey, girl," Sami said. "I'm driving you home tonight, but first we're going to get loaded on nachos and *pollo* enchiladas," she announced, accentuating the word *pollo*. "My treat. No arguing. See you at five."

Before Calla could reply, Sami hung up. Relief at not having to walk in the weather warred with the desire not to take Sami up on what was clearly a charity offering.

Wait, silly, she thought to herself. This is Sami. It's not charity. It's a friend acting like a friend. You'd do the same thing.

Just as those thoughts left her, the DJ on the radio announced,

"Next week is Thanksgiving. Crossroads Florists has teamed up with us here at Q103 to let you send someone special in your life a beautiful fall bouquet. Caller number ten will be our winner this hour. Four-oh-four, five-five-five, Q-one-oh-three. Caller ten."

Phone still in hand, she dialed the number. Her heart leaped when she heard it ring. "Q103, you're caller four. Good luck next time!"

They hung up without another word. Calla hit redial. To her surprise, she could hear the phone ring again. "Q103. You're caller ten! Congratulations! Who do we have on the line?"

Mouth dry, heart pounding in excitement, she said, "Calla."

"Well, Calla, you've won a bouquet of fall flowers from Crossroads florists. Who do you think you'll send them to?"

Calla smiled. "Actually, I know exactly who deserves a bouquet."

CHAPTER 2

Ian listened to his desk phone ring but ignored it while he typed details about the limitations of the customer requested heating system into the project's specifications. He had a two o'clock meeting about this project and didn't have time to do Penny's job. As he had pulled in this morning, he felt somehow unexplainably disappointed that Mr. Dixon's parking space sat empty. He had sort of hoped to catch a glimpse of a faded yellow Geo Storm parked there, which made no sense and had him wondering exactly where that thought even came from.

He had made it all the way up to the seventh floor today before remembering that Penny had the day off. The morning hours jumped from one crisis to another. For some reason, everything always erupted on Friday morning, as if everyone had sudden onset panic attacks over the prospect of no one working for the next two days. With Penny out, it made everything outside his office door feel like chaos.

As he finished typing, he didn't even look up at the sound of a tap on his door. "Come," he called, sending the print order for the specifications he'd just written to the print department before closing the lid of his laptop. He expected an intern or even his friend Al. When a large bouquet of flowers in the colors of fall came through his door, he raised an eyebrow, confident the person belonging to the legs he could see under the arrangement had come to the wrong office.

"May I help you?"

"Delivery for Sam Jones," a squeaky teenage boy's voice said.

Curious, he got up from his desk and removed the mammoth bouquet from the boy's arms. "Okay. Well, thank you," he said absently.

"Happy Thanksgiving," the young man said as he ducked out of the office.

Who would send him flowers? More importantly, who would send flowers for him addressed to Sam? His grandmother? Definitely not her style, but maybe her assistant did it without guidance? She usually wouldn't send such an elaborate bouquet full of sunflowers, mums, chrysanthemums, roses, dahlias, and gerbera daisies. He dug through the stems until he found the envelope that contained the card clutched in the prongs of a transparent plastic fork. The scent of the roses filled his senses as he opened the envelope and read the typed note.

CAN'T THANK YOU ENOUGH FOR YESTERDAY. YOU WERE A LIFESAVER. DINNER AT MY PLACE. SIX TOMORROW NIGHT. WON'T TAKE NO FOR AN ANSWER. WANT TO THANK YOU PROPERLY. CALLA

Ian cleared his throat, a little embarrassed and uncomfortable at what he had just read. The last time a girl had so boldly asked him out was for high school homecoming dance senior year. How did he even respond? Should he respond? Should he just not show up?

Then again, maybe he should show up. Admittedly, he had thought of her more than once since their encounter and elevator ride yesterday afternoon. He had fleetingly entertained the notion of asking to give Calla a ride home and maybe treating her to dinner last night. Still, this seemed very forward on her part, much more forward than he would have expected based on their brief conversation. Highly unexpected, surprising, and a little bit unsettling.

What did one do with something like this?

Should he just ignore it all together? That felt rude. Should he return the flowers? Even more rude. She didn't deserve rude. Maybe just shoot her a short email, or give her a quick call down in filing. Just let her know that he had appreciated the offer, but that the flowers and the gratitude they expressed were thanks enough. No. She had sent him flowers. His response had to be equal to that gesture and an email or even a phone call would seem too impersonal, really.

Besides, did he really want to decline? He found Calla very attractive. Also, and of equal importance in his mind, he assessed her as a genuinely nice person. What would be the harm in accepting her invitation? Even if things didn't work out, it might get Al off his back for a while. That would be nice. Of course, she worked for the same employer as he did, and that could spell trouble in the future. Interoffice romances always came with extra challenges. He really didn't have the time to deal with interoffice drama, much less any inclination.

Deciding he would have to speak to her in person, he glanced at his watch. He had a few minutes before his meeting began. He would stop by the file room on his way to the print department and politely respond to her invitation.

Even as he walked out of his office, though, he had no idea what he would actually say to Miss Calla Vaughn. As the elevator arrived on his floor, he decided that unless he saw some very compelling reason to join her for dinner, he would smile and politely let her down. Hopefully, she would take it well.

Calla strode, skipped, and hopped to the beat of the song playing in her ears, holding a file folder in each hand as she hummed, spun, and swayed to the tempo. Her eyes closed as she performed a stage-worthy pirouette then popped open a file drawer with a hum and a low whistle. She expertly inserted a red file folder into the drawer then rhythmically bumped the drawer closed with her hip and a Rockette flourish before dancing further down the aisle.

Halfway through a turn, she faltered, and stopped moving entirely when she identified Ian Jones standing at the end of the row of filing cabinets. She must have looked even more odd standing there in a frozen vignette pose with just her eyes widening and no other discernable movement, like a New Orleans street mime, maybe. How long had he stood there, watching her? Feeling her face flush with heat, she straightened, yanked the earbuds out of her ears, and cleared her throat. "Uh, sorry. Just, you know, keeping it fun."

His right eyebrow sat higher on his forehead than his left, but the left side of his mouth curled into a dimpled half-grin. "Fun, huh?"

Her voice sounded weak to her own ears. "It's, uh, kind of quiet and a little cave-like in here. Music makes the day go a little faster." She shoved the earbuds into the shirt pocket that contained her phone and adjusted her glasses on her face. He just stared at her with that half a smile on his face.

"I see."

She set the file folders on top of the closest cabinet and walked toward him. Thankfully, he hadn't come three hours ago when papers, hole punchers, and files had covered the floor. "Oh! Can I do something for you? Penny usually comes for files, but I just remembered she's out today."

His eyes widened slightly. "You know Penny?"

She shrugged. "Well, I know all the assistants. They come here to get files and, you know, there's just the four of us down here." She kept a thin pad of paper in her skirt pocket and pulled it out with a pencil. "What can I pull for you?"

As she reached him, nervousness came over her that made her hand tremble a little around the pencil. Why, oh why, did she become such a bumbling, stuttering, fumbling idiot around this man? Why couldn't she act poised and calm? Why couldn't she look three inches taller and twenty pounds thinner? And maybe more classically beautiful. Without the glasses.

Ugh.

He just stared at her, with his head slightly tilted. She began to wonder if she had something on her face. Finally, she said, "Mr. Jones?"

He cleared his throat. "Ian. Please, just Ian. So, about dinner."

She tilted her head slightly toward him, unconsciously mirroring the angle of his gaze, and raised her eyebrows as if trying to hear what he said better. Was he? No. She must not be understanding him. "Dinner?"

"Yeah, dinner. Tomorrow. Your place. Remember? Flowers? Invite? Won't take no for an answer dinner?"

Flowers? Invite? Dinner? "Uh…" Suddenly, she realized.

Samuel Ian Jones. Sami Jones.

Oh no! Remembering what she'd put on that card, her whole face flashed with molten heat and she carefully set the pencil down on the counter before she dropped it. Oh no! "I, uh…"

"I just need your address. Not sure I can make six, but I can do my best to make six-thirty or so if you're on this side of town."

He was accepting an invitation to dinner from her? Not that she had actually invited him to dinner. Well, he thought she had invited him. Still. Why in the world?

Deciding not to sound like more of an idiot than she already had every time they'd spoken, she mumbled her address and confirmed that six-thirty would be great. He had the grace not to cringe about her wrong side of the tracks address. Out of habit she asked, "Is there anything you won't eat?"

Ian's face lit up in a smile. It made Calla's heart thump against her chest so hard she thought he might hear it. "That's really nice of you to ask. How about this? I promise I'll eat whatever you put on the table. I'm not what you would call a picky eater. But I've never really been a huge fan of shellfish."

Calla nodded and said, "Okay, so omakase is for sure off the menu."

"Oma-what?"

"Omakase." Calla said, carefully pronouncing the Japanese

and bowing slightly. "It's, like, the most expensive shellfish dish on earth. You can only get it in this one place in Tokyo… you know what? Chef joke. Never mind. No shellfish. Got it."

She hadn't thought his smile could get bigger, but somehow it did. He had very straight, very white teeth. He glanced at his watch and took a step back. "Can't stay and chat. Gotta run by the print department and pick up some plans for a meeting I'm nearly late for. I'll see you tomorrow, though. We can talk more then?"

"Sure," she said weakly, "tomorrow. Dinner. My place. Looking forward to it."

As soon as she was sure he wasn't going to return, she rushed out of the row and told her supervisor she was taking a late lunch. Forget that hour of overtime she'd planned on, she needed to talk to someone!

In no time, she found herself on the eighth floor ensconced in Sami's little office outside Brad Dixon's office door. The big boss was with his dad in New Orleans, so she felt safe sitting down across from her desk. "You'll never believe what just happened."

Sami rolled her chair closer to the edge of her desk and leaned forward. Her bright green eyes shone out from under a metallic green gypsy scarf that she'd tied around her head. "Spill."

"So, yesterday I called in and won flowers from Q103."

Sami's eyes widened. "Seriously? Cool! I won a gift card, once."

"Yeah? Anyway, perfect timing because you'd just called me, offered to buy me dinner, and arranged for my car to be towed to the junkyard. You totally saved my life last night. Really. And I knew you would. So, I preemptively sent you a thank you bouquet."

"Me?" Sami grinned. "Wow! Thanks! I hope I get them today!"

"That's the thing. They were already delivered." Nervous and edgy again, she said in a voice barely above a whisper, "To Sam Jones."

A frown appeared between Sami's eyes. "Sam Jones? Sam?"

"Yeah. Sam. Samuel Ian Jones."

With wide eyes, Sami said, "Ian? The hot guy on seventh you've had a slightly obvious crush on since you started working here three years ago?"

Mouth dry, she cleared her throat. "Yeah. That Ian."

Sami threw her head back and laughed. "So, he got your flowers. What happened next?"

"You mean after he read the card thanking 'him' for his help yesterday and demanding that 'he' come to dinner at my place tomorrow so I could thank him properly?" Calla used air quotes for the him and he. "Why, he came down to my little forest of metal filing cabinets to ask me for my address so he could come have dinner and get properly thanked."

Sami's mouth opened and closed twice before she said, "Seriously? Calla!" she said her name on a gasp. "Isn't God good? That is amazing!"

"What am I going to do?"

"What do you mean, what are you going to do? You're going to do what you do in the kitchen and make something amazing. I have no doubt."

"Yeah. Sure. In my dinky one-bedroom apartment that doesn't even have a table! I was planning on making you spaghetti and garlic bread. Cheap. Easy. Filled with love and gratitude that you would have understood. Him? He wears a watch that cost more than my car is worth! How am I supposed to cook for him?"

Sami started to answer, but her phone rang. She held up a finger and answered the call. She scribbled a few notes and said, "Yes, Mr. Dixon," she paused, "right. Give me five minutes."

She hung up the phone and turned to her computer, bringing it out of hibernation. "I can't think right now, Calla, but I have a table you can borrow. We'll cover it with a beautiful cloth, and you'll do something amazing. I'll be over at ten in the morning."

"Sami!" Calla pleaded.

Sami shook her head. "Honey, this is a good thing. A very good thing. Stop worrying. It'll be fine. Now shoo. Let me work."

Calla stood as Sami began maneuvering through the files on her computer. She lifted a hand to wave goodbye as she left the office.

Ian shifted under the weight of his end of the dresser and waited for Al to guide the way. His feet remained steady on the gold-colored shag carpet as they maneuvered the massive chest through the little World War II era cottage.

"Step at the door," Al announced, and Ian started expecting the feel of the metal threshold that would clue him to take a step down. As soon as they cleared the doorway, they turned sideways and moved with more precision and speed, soon setting the dresser into the moving van.

Al, a well-muscled six-five electrical engineer who dedicated four mornings a week to the gym, looked like he'd barely broken a sweat. Four inches shorter and a good thirty pounds lighter, Ian felt the strain in his arms as he rolled his head on his shoulders.

"Bedroom's done," he said to Daniel, the leader of his church's men's ministry. "Are the guys ready to start loading the kitchen boxes?"

"Pretty sure," Daniel said, using a handkerchief to wipe the sweat at his white hairline. "Let me go check with Marlene and I'll let you know. Why don't you two get some water and take five?"

Ian wouldn't admit to how relieved he felt at the suggestion. He followed Al over to Daniel's truck and grabbed a bottle of water out of the cooler in the back. As he twisted the cap open, he sat on the open tailgate. He looked up through the branches of the live oak tree and saw the vivid blue of the Atlanta sky. The dry seventy-degree temperature made it a really lovely November day.

"Want to grab a pizza after?" Al asked. "Georgia's playing at seven, and that place in Decatur's going to show it on every screen."

Fast friends since the first day of engineering school at Georgia Tech, Ian and Al spent most weekends doing something together, either sharing a meal or two, catching a movie or a football game, or something casual and relaxing of the sort. However, right now Miss Calla Vaughn dancing to the tune in her ears floated across his mind. "Actually, I have a date."

"A date?" Al's teeth looked bright white against his chocolate colored skin as he grinned at his friend. "Well, well, well. About time. With whom, may I ask?"

"Calla Vaughn. From work."

Al frowned and muttered, "Calla Vaughn? Is she in the architectural division?"

"No. She's one of the file clerks down on the second floor." He took a long pull of water. "I helped Jon push her dead car out of the way of the gate reader Thursday afternoon. She's cooking me dinner to thank me all proper like."

Al threw his head back and laughed. "Your grandma would love that one."

Ian pressed his lips together as his rather blue blood heated. His grandmother, old member of Atlanta high society, would certainly not find amusement at Ian's dating anyone other than a crowned princess, perhaps. Or maybe a president's daughter. Depending, of course, on whether said president drank red or blue Kool-Aid.

"It's not that bad," he lied.

"Oh, please," Al said, "she's the reason you don't ever date."

Ian raised an eyebrow. He couldn't deny it. It was just easier not to date than to try to find someone who would pass inspection and gain the reluctant approval of the family matriarch. "Yeah? What's your excuse, then?"

Al's face sobered, and he cleared his throat. "Like you don't know."

Feeling like a cad, especially as the brother of the woman who so thoroughly broke his best friend's heart two years ago, he immediately apologized. "Dude, sorry."

"No sweat." Al looked up when the door to the house opened, and a very small, frail woman carefully maneuvered her doorway with her walker. "Need help Mrs. Manchester?" The church men's group had volunteered to help move Mrs. Manchester's belongings into storage while her son got her settled into his spare bedroom.

"You boys get on in here and get yourselves a sandwich," she ordered. "I made egg salad. Even managed to toast the bread before the toaster got packed."

"Yes, ma'am," Ian replied, standing.

"Did you make some of your sweet tea?" Al asked, a hopeful sound in his voice.

"You better believe it." She turned and carefully lifted her walker back into the house. "Ain't nothing like egg salad and sweet tea."

"No, ma'am," Al agreed. Ian laughed while he followed them slowly into the house.

CHAPTER 3

"Beautiful," Sami assured, surveying the rust-colored tablecloth covering the little square table, the short round vase filled with bright sunflowers, and the white plates perched atop gold chargers. She arranged one of the rust-colored napkins more carefully in the sunflower napkin ring and stepped back, putting her hand on the back of the folding chair. "Thank goodness for the dollar store. Who knew, huh?"

"You did," Calla smiled, looking at her living room transformed into a very welcoming dining room. "You do so well with this kind of thing."

"It's not hard. You just find a theme or a color scheme and go with it." She turned and looked around the room, nodding at the throw pillows she'd tossed onto the worn brown couch. Their colors perfectly matched the tablecloth and napkins. "I'll pick the card table and pillows up tomorrow after church," she said, "where I intend to get the full scoop about every word that gets spoken tonight."

Calla's stomach dropped in a nervous flutter that had grown in intensity since waking up this morning. "Maybe he won't show," her voice sounded weak. "He's a gentleman, after all. So polite all the time. Maybe he'll spare me the humiliation of acting like a total idiot tonight."

"Nonsense," Sami replied. She followed Calla into the

kitchen. As Calla pulled an onion out of the grocery bag on the counter, Sami rummaged in the refrigerator then shut the door and looked at her. "Okay, bread is rising, I see chicken and spinach in the fridge. What else is on the menu?"

Calla looked at her watch and calculated the time she had left in the day. "Chicken Florentine served on a bed of wild rice and some fresh green beans." She lifted the towel covering the loaf of bread and pressed into it lightly with a knuckle of her little finger, deciding to preheat the oven. As she turned the dial to the right temperature, she added, "I'm just doing some fresh berries and whipped cream for dessert."

"That sounds lovely." Sami picked up her purse and pulled her car key out of the side pocket. "I can't wait to consume leftovers after church tomorrow."

Calla walked over to her and hugged her. "Thank you for your help. You have calmed me considerably."

"I loved the project. I especially loved the project on such a budget. It was a challenge and kind of exciting."

After she left, Calla went back into the kitchen and pulled a skillet out of her cabinet. She ran her finger over the ceramic coating on the inside of it and felt a small smile. Her couch might have seen better days ten years ago, and her car might have died completely, but no one looking at her kitchen accouterments would ever think that she bought anything but the very best for herself. She thought about the three semesters of culinary school she'd attended, where she had never felt so alive and free in her life. One day she would go back. As soon as she got everything in order in her life, she'd have the freedom to walk back into the school and don her apron.

She heated some olive oil in the skillet while she quickly sliced an onion and some garlic. When she heard the oven signal that it had reached the desired temperature, she slid the bread inside and set the timer. As she did, she marked the time and knew everything was right on schedule.

Ian approached the apartment, looking around as he walked along the concrete breezeway. From the second floor, he could glance down over the metal railing and see the dirty swimming pool with a few faded plastic chairs scattered around it. He passed apartment 2C taking in the broken blinds hanging crooked in the window. He reached 2D, Calla's apartment according to the address she gave him. Light cotton curtains adorned her windows.

The area in front of her door looked swept clean, and a mat bid a "Welcome Friends" greeting. On either side of the door, pots filled with fresh herbs covered tiered plant stands. Some he recognized, like the massive bush of rosemary. He smelled mint and parsley among other scents he could only guess at. Oregano, maybe. All of the scents mingled and filled his senses with such a pleasant aroma that he wanted to just stand there and breathe it in deeply. He held his finger over the doorbell and hesitated only slightly before pressing it. Within seconds, Calla opened the door, and the first impression he had was the tantalizing smells coming from the apartment that even overpowered the scent of the herbs.

Then he took in the sight of her. Calla wore an oversized rust-colored shirt that buttoned with brass buttons all the way down to her thighs, dark leggings in a geometric design with rust, mustard yellow, and forest green colors, and knee-high brown leather boots. Yesterday, she'd worn her sleek black hair down, swinging to her shoulders. Today, she had it pulled back in a ponytail, which made those rich brown eyes behind those large black framed lenses stand out even more.

"Hi," she said, smiling, "welcome. You're exactly on time."

She opened the door wider, and he stepped in, quickly surveying the room. Bright pillows on the couch and the small table covered with an autumn flare gave the room a happy, homey feel. He spotted a little desk in the corner with a laptop, lid closed, sitting on top. With the flustered way she'd acted when her car broke down and the way she floundered and fumbled when he went to see her in her department yesterday, he halfway expected a little bit of chaos in her environment. Not so. Even the desk looked neat and ordered.

"Part of me wondered if you would even come." She shut the door behind him, and he noticed that she almost absently locked the deadbolt.

"I thought about it. It's not every day I'm invited in such a fashion." He slipped his hands into his pockets. "The table's beautiful."

"Thank you." She touched the back of a chair. "My friend Sami came over and helped. She has an eye I don't have. I'm better in the kitchen than in the drawing room, I'm afraid."

His stomach gave a slight rumble of hunger and his mouth watered at the thought of the heavenly smells. "I can't wait to compare."

She walked into the kitchen, but it didn't place her out of his sight or hearing. He moved to the small bar that separated the two rooms and watched her use a kitchen towel to pull a pan out of the oven. He saw roasted chicken breasts bulging with a spinach stuffing. "That looks amazing," he said.

"I hope you like spinach. I probably should have checked." She took two plates out of her cupboard and set them side-by-side on the counter. After lifting the lid of a pot on the stove, he watched as she scooped wild rice onto each plate, then placed one of the chicken breasts on top of the rice. Using tongs, she artfully arranged green beans alongside the chicken. He couldn't help but notice the confidence and smoothness with which she moved while she handled the food. She picked up each plate and walked back into the room, setting them on the little table. "I hope water's okay. It's really all I drink after six," she said, picking up a clear pitcher of ice water off of the bar. "I can make coffee or tea? I have decaf."

He shook his head. "Ice water's perfect."

Where did these nerves come from? He was twenty-eight years old. It's not like he'd never had dinner with a beautiful woman before. But suddenly, he found himself anxious, worried he'd say the wrong thing, move the wrong way. He suddenly longed for that moment when the initial awkwardness passed, and he'd relax around her.

She gestured toward the chair nearest him, and he waited for her to settle into her chair before taking his. Following her lead, he pulled the napkin out of the flowered napkin ring and laid the cotton cloth across his lap, setting the ring to the side of his silverware. She started to pick up her fork then set it back down. "I'm sorry. I feel wrong eating without praying. Do you mind if we pray first?"

He smiled in reaction to the question, a smile that revealed his straight white teeth. "I'm actually relieved to hear you say that." Automatically, he held out his hand to her, palm up. She didn't so much as hesitate as she lay her hand in his and bowed her head. His fingers enveloped her slim hand gently, and she gave his hand a little prompting squeeze. Waiting for half a second to make sure she didn't intend to lead the blessing, he spoke, listening to his voice fill the otherwise silent room. "Father, we thank You for this food. We ask that You bless it, bless the hands that made it, and let our fellowship be pleasing to You. Amen."

As soon as they lifted their heads, he felt himself relax, somewhat surprised that his initial attraction to this woman just increased with her desire to pray before the meal. "This looks really good," he said, slicing into the bird with his knife. The aroma and the juicy tenderness of the perfectly prepared and well-portioned entree compared to the finest meals he had ever enjoyed. "I could smell it as soon as you opened the door."

She smiled, conspicuously pleased with the compliment. "I'm glad. This is a favorite dish of mine." Her eyes widened, and she tossed her napkin atop the table and quickly stood. "Bread!"

She rushed into the kitchen and returned with a basket that she set on the table in front of him. When he opened the napkin on top, he revealed a pile of steaming hot sliced homemade bread. He selected a piece and smiled. "Bread is a good thing."

"It felt good to knead it this morning. It's one of the ways I like to relax. Is it good?"

Amazed that she'd made her own bread, he took a bite and almost closed his eyes in wonder. As he savored the light yet hearty perfection of the bread, he shook his head slowly from side to side. Finally, he swallowed and answered, "No." Calla looked slightly panicked until he said, "No, I would describe it as excellent. Not just good."

Relief washed over her expression, and her shoulders relaxed as she reached for a slice of bread for herself. "This is a really good whole grain flour. It's better with fresh ground flour, but I don't have my own grain mill yet. Saving up for it, though. There's a wonderful place to get grain over on the west side of town."

"Fresh ground or not, it's delicious. Anytime you feel stressed and need to work it out by kneading some bread dough, please know that I'll happily take any extra loaves off your hands."

Her laugh rang around the room. "Deal."

He took a few bites of the amazing chicken dish before he spoke again. "How's your car doing?"

The frown that crossed her face made him wish he hadn't asked the question. "Totally dead. I'm car-less for a while. Thankfully, there's a MARTA station on this block and one near the office, so I'll be okay."

"I think it would be hard to function in Atlanta without a car."

"Unless there's a wreck on the 300. Then it's hard to function in Atlanta with a car." She grinned.

He chuckled, thinking of the main road dead stop traffic of every weekday rush hour in and around Atlanta. The bigger Atlanta grew in any direction, the more improved the infrastructure, the worse it seemed to get.

She shrugged. "Not much I can do about it anyway." She poured herself more water. He noticed she didn't eat with the same enthusiasm he felt for the meal. "Sami will give me a ride wherever I need to go, if there's somewhere I can't get to by train or bus. I'm totally fine with it. Besides, it'll save me the insurance payment every month, so there's that."

He considered her words, wondering if he could help her in any way. Then he had to remind himself that he'd officially given up on helping people not formally classified as an elderly person in his church. Not even a sabbatical anymore. More like a life choice. Officially. Period. End of story.

Still…

Calla sat against the opposite arm of the couch with her legs pulled up under her, her body turned toward Ian, cradling her coffee cup in her hand. He sat on the other end. When he'd arrived hours before, she thought she'd come out of her skin with nerves. She'd opened the door, and there he stood, like something she'd dreamed about since the first time she saw him walking the halls at Dixon Contracting. His hair had shown damp traces of a recent shower, and she could smell his aftershave when he'd walked into the apartment. Tonight, the dark-green button-down shirt made his hazel eyes shine a bright green.

Despite her initial nerves, they enjoyed such a relaxed and enjoyable meal. She felt relief she never gave in to her weak impulse to cancel the dinner and just admit to Ian wires had crossed and she never intended to invite him in the first place. After finishing the chicken, she served them fresh berries with a basil infused whipped cream. She probably should have toned down the cheffy foodie-ness of the meal, but the look on his face when he took the first bite made her glad that she'd stepped outside of what most would consider a normal boundary.

They enjoyed their dessert on the couch—much more comfortable seating than the metal chairs at the card table.

"My best friend, Al, and I are the young, single, and in shape men in our church. So, we call it volen-told. We get volen-told a lot. We get *told* that we *volunteered* for most tasks that involve heavy lifting. I think I've had a free Saturday morning twice in the last four months."

"What was this morning?"

"Helping an elderly widow move into her son's place. We packed her house up into a storage container. So, we had one truck going to the son's, and another to the storage facility." He set his coffee cup down on the table next to them, and she noticed he hadn't had more than a sip or two. "She's a sweet woman. Her son is quite old himself, and they have no other local family, so the church stepped up to help her."

"What would you do on a normal Saturday if you didn't have to help an elderly widow move? Rescue cats from trees? Feed orphans?"

He grinned and shrugged. "In the spring, I'm on a baseball team. We always play on Saturdays. Al's talked about wanting to find a basketball team for the winter months. But, I'd rather just stick with baseball. I tend to hole up in the winter. It's about the only time I allow myself to indulge in long stretches of reading for pleasure and not for work or education. I have a hoop at my house, and Al and I play one-on-one every so often, but I'm not really into being on a team."

Thinking of the bulging bookshelf in her bedroom, she perked up. "I love to read! I wish I had more time to do it. What do you like to read?"

"Fiction? I like thrillers. Medical mysteries." He smiled. "Sometimes Biblical fiction, if I like the author."

"I like cozy mysteries. You know, the kind where the sweet old woman who owns the little tea parlor somehow stumbles upon a murder and works out the killer by having one-sided conversations with her cat?"

He stared at her blankly for a moment then threw his head back and laughed. "I can honestly say that I have never read anything like that."

"They're brilliant. I cut my teeth on Agatha Christie novels, and the insight and intelligence of Miss Marple always stuck with me. Whenever I come across a good character like that in a series, I'll read every book the author has written in just a few days. It's crazy." She gestured toward the desk. "I work a lot. Evenings and weekends, I caption movies and television shows, so when I intentionally take off to read, it's about all I do."

She watched him look at her desk and back at her. "Caption movies?"

"Yeah, you know. Like the closed captioning."

"Huh. How'd you get into that?"

Remembering the process, she decided not to bore him with the details. "I wanted something I could do early mornings or late nights to earn a little extra money. A friend told me about this website, so I applied. I type really fast, so that helps."

"That's actually kind of fascinating." He looked at his watch and shifted forward. "It's later than I want it to be. Better call it a night. Thank you for an amazing meal, Calla."

She set her coffee cup down and stood as he stood, then gestured toward the door in a nervous movement—as if he may have forgotten how to find the front door. He unlocked the deadbolt and turned to face her. "I really enjoyed talking with you. I'd love to take you to lunch tomorrow. Maybe you could go to church with me, and we could have lunch afterward? I'm happy to give you a ride."

Her heart beat a little bit faster. He wanted to spend more time with her? "I ah, have a church. I teach the preschool Sunday School, so I can't come to church with you. But lunch would be very nice."

They discussed where and when to meet, and then he opened the door. Did she see hesitation in his eyes? A reluctance in his movements? For just a fraction of a second, it looked as if he might reach for her, but the moment passed. She put her hand on the doorknob and smiled. "I really enjoyed cooking for you, Ian. Good night."

CHAPTER 4

Calla sat in the back row of her church and felt her cheeks burn with shame. She hated the sermons about offerings, tithing, and giving. No matter what she knew in her heart or her internal desire to tithe, she struggled to the point of drowning in debt so she couldn't possibly do it. How could she give ten percent of what she had when what she had was negative forty-six thousand, seven hundred according to last week's calculations? She looked around feeling like everyone knew this about her, even though no one possibly could.

If only she could fix it. She thought about her situation and felt anger brimming on the edge of rage burn in her heart, the kind of anger she hadn't felt in a long time. Maybe it burned because she had such a good night last night, perhaps because she knew that, eventually, Ian would find out. He'd find out and then what? What would he think? He certainly wouldn't want to have anything to do with her afterward.

Trying to push back the anger, grief pushed through, and sad tears pricked her eyes. She pulled off her glasses and pressed her fingers against her eyes. Her father's death had come as a surprise. Her stepmother's betrayal came as more of a shock in the wake of his death.

Three years had passed. One might think she would have recovered from the shock and accepted the reality of the situation by now. However, sitting here in the back of the church with all of these thoughts running through her head, her heart suddenly overwhelmed, she found herself on her knees in front of her pew sobbing. She felt hands on her shoulders and heard whispered prayers, but she didn't look up to see who ministered to her. She just started praying from deep inside her soul asking for God's help and release from this pain. Petitioning to Him as Jehovah Jireh, God her Provider, for provision to fix it and make it go away, begging Him for wisdom to know how to help herself through this trying time.

When the storm of emotions passed, she felt empty. Not exactly empty, more like hollowed out. Her stomach felt cold, swirling with a winter wind, and a cold sweat covered her skin. Her hair clung to the back of her neck, and she reached back and lifted it off, feeling the cool air conditioning. She stood and hugged the woman who had prayed with her, knowing she knew her name but unable to retrieve it from the chaotic thoughts swirling in her mind. She thanked the woman for her prayers then snatched up her Bible and purse and slipped out the door.

Calla had planned to meet Ian for lunch, but she wanted to cool off first. She didn't want him to see the evidence of her crying jag. She walked down the street to the restaurant a full thirty minutes before they arranged to meet and slipped into the bathroom. She saw her reflection in the mirror and realized she looked as bad as she thought she would with her bright red nose, puffy lips, and swollen and red eyes. A little trickle of a tear slipped out of the corner of her right eye and slid down her cheek. She frowned with impatience at the fact that she still had more tears inside. Thankful for the little makeup kit she carried in her purse, she turned the cold water on in the sink and let it wash over her wrists, cooling her down.

Her text tone sounded as she finished drying her face. She slipped her glasses back on and glanced at the sender. Sami. She would have seen her escape from the church from her position in the choir loft. The message read:

FIGURED THAT SERMON WOULD GET YOU. CALL WHEN YOU

CAN. ENJOY YOUR LUNCH.

Calla typed out a quick reply thanking Sami and glanced at her face in the mirror again. She had cooled off a little. The cold water helped. The ugly cry face had started to fade away. After reapplying her makeup, she brushed her hair then pulled the sides of her hair back from her face and clipped them with barrettes. Her bright red dress and polka dot red and white scarf had made her feel happy this morning. Thinking of her lunch date with Ian, she chose bright colors over more muted fall tones. She smoothed her hands down the side of her dress and checked her reflection in the mirror, turning this and that way, then grabbed her purse and Bible and walked out of the ladies room.

She entered the lobby area of the restaurant just as she saw Ian come to the door. Since she'd just seen him last night, the joy at seeing him walk through the door surprised her. She'd walked him to the door of her apartment about twelve hours ago, but for some reason, it felt like a lifetime had passed. He wore khaki pants, a blue dress shirt, and a dark blue blazer. The blue turned his eyes a brown-gray. He'd unbuttoned his top button, and she could see the end of his tie hanging out of his jacket pocket.

Maybe God had done something in reply to her desperate plea earlier. Maybe something inside of her head changed. Whatever the case, she felt a big grin appear on her face the moment she saw him. When he saw her, his eyes lit up with a smile, and she easily went into his arms for a hug.

"For some reason, I feel like it's been a lifetime since I saw you last," he said.

Her eyes widened as she grinned and said, "I was just thinking that exact same thing. I had a very ugly crying deep prayer at church and wondered if it was just something that happened to me there, or something else."

She waited while he spoke to the hostess then stepped forward as he gestured toward her. He put a light hand on the small of her back as they followed the hostess to the little table next to the window. She felt acutely aware of the feel of his fingers through the fabric of her dress. As he pulled out her chair, she glanced out the window to see a family walking down the street pushing a baby carriage. Despite the late November day, the mid-sixties temperature outside made a Sunday stroll in the downtown area a pleasant time.

Ian studied her for a few moments before he remarked, "Ugly cry at church, huh?"

She felt a tiny bit of emotion creeping back into her throat, so she took a sip of her water to get herself back in control. She gave a small shrug of her shoulders. "Sometimes sermons get the best of me. It's hard to know the right thing to do is if you don't happen to be doing the right thing at this exact moment."

He raised a questioning eyebrow. "Like what?"

"Like anything." She paused then paraphrased the book of Romans. "There's not one righteous. No, not one."

Just in time, the waitress approached. She was blonde and young and very bubbly with a sparkling green bow in her hair and bright pink lipstick. "What can I get y'all?"

She hadn't even glanced at the menu. Ian never even opened his. He said, "I'm ready. Do you need a few minutes?"

"No." Looking at the waitress, she said, "I'll take a turkey sandwich and a side salad with the house dressing on the side."

Ian scooped up her menu and handed them both to the waitress as he said, "Burger, medium well, extra mayo. Fresh veggies on the side. No fries."

The waitress nodded, wrote down the orders, and asked, "Anything more than water to drink?"

Calla shook her head. "I'm good if you can bring me some lemon."

Ian smiled. "I would love some of that good iced tea." As the perky blonde walked away, he looked at Calla again. "What is your testimony?"

She could have thought of a dozen questions beyond that one. It stumped her. "I beg your pardon?"

He sat back in his chair. "Your testimony. What has God brought you from? Where is He taking you?"

A server brought a small dish of lemons, and she took the opportunity to contemplate her answer as she added two slices to her water. "I went to a youth group with a friend when I was fifteen. I knew when I left there that night that I'd changed. My home life was hard. My mom died when I was three, and my dad remarried when I was fourteen. His new wife was one of his college students. She acted like a bratty stepsister instead of a stepmother. So, I went to this youth group party, and my friend introduced me to Jesus. Home life changed overnight."

Ian smiled. "I like that."

She waited, but he didn't say anything else, so she finally asked him. "What about you? What's your testimony?"

"Orphaned as a teen. Fourteen. My paternal grandmother finished raising me. She's old money, so, like my father before me, I grew up in a staffed household and attended private boarding schools. But, she is also a devoted follower of Christ and serves Him like no one I've ever seen. All of my uncles work with her, and their various businesses help support her in whatever she needs for her ministries. Our family Christmas vacations are spent in Haiti at an orphanage, and Easter is down in Ecuador. We don't do a lot of traditional American holiday things save Thanksgiving and Fourth of July.

"As I entered adulthood and realized the true uniqueness of my upbringing, I found myself in awe of my family's faithfulness and often pray I can live up to it." He sat forward and folded his arms on the table in front of him. "I love Dixon Brothers Contracting because they're as mission-minded as my grandmother. But, I also like going to my own church, away from my family, and creating my own legacy instead of living in the shadow of hers."

She let what he said sink in, then slowly nodded. "I can see that, even if I have no actual experience with it." The tension from leaving the church service dissipated as she leaned forward with her elbows propped on the table and put her chin in her hands. "I wish my dad had come to know God before he died. But, he never did. Not that I know of, anyway. And, I assume if he did, I'd have known."

Ian's eyes sobered. "That would be hard. I'm sorry."

"It made everything about his death harder." She smiled warmly. "Two orphans. Too bad it's not raining out there. I'd make some poetic reference about finding each other in a storm."

He reached forward and put a hand on top of her arm, giving her a gentle squeeze. "There are all different kinds of storms. I'd say that would be accurate despite how warm and bright it is outside. After all, it was a Storm that brought us together."

Knowing he referred to her car, she smiled warmly. A server approached with their meal, and they both sat back to give room for their plates. As soon as she refilled waters and walked away, Calla put both of her hands in his. He asked, "Would you like to bless the food?"

Clearing her throat, she bowed her head and felt heat flood her cheeks as she softly thanked God for providing safe harbors in the storms of life, and for their food. When she said, "Amen," he gave her hands a warm squeeze before releasing her fingers.

Cold wind and rain drove Calla into the building. As the glass doors shut behind her with a whooshing sound, she shook her umbrella over the rubber mat and pulled the damp collar of her coat closer to her. She couldn't feel the heat in the building until she walked further away from the doors and into the lobby. She couldn't believe how fast the weather had changed from yesterday to this morning. Thankfully, she'd found an umbrella in the back of her closet and hadn't had to walk from the train station without one. As she approached the elevator, she felt a hand on her elbow and looked to see Ian standing right next to her. Immediately, a bright smile covered her face as the joy in seeing him lit her up from the inside. Her reaction surprised her, considering she'd seen him just yesterday at lunch.

He wore a cream dress shirt with black and yellow grid lines and a tie covered in the Georgia Tech yellow jacket mascots. Somehow, he made that look classy and stylish. Even in the crowded lobby, the scent of his aftershave tingled her nose.

"I was hoping I'd catch you early," he said with a warm smile.

"Good morning," she greeted. She pulled her glasses off to wipe the rain from the lenses.

"I know your shift starts at eight, which means you still have about twenty minutes. Would you like a cup of coffee?"

He'd sought her out—waited for her in the busy lobby on a Monday morning. She knew he typically began work at six-thirty, so his presence in the lobby could only be intentional. A warm rush of emotion moved from her chest through her whole body, making her face flush.

"Coffee would be heaven right now," she agreed, wondering if she might have said it a little too enthusiastically. They got into the elevator, and he pushed the button for his floor. As they moved up, stopping at floor after floor, the crowd gradually thinned until just a few people shared the car with them. When they stepped off the elevator on his floor, he put a light hand on the small of her back to guide her. They strolled through the empty conference room in the middle of the floor to the sea of cubicles and desks, then on to the other side, where he unlocked an office door and she stepped into his realm.

Motion sensors caused the fluorescent lights to flicker on. On the far wall, bookshelves on either side of a credenza held thick tomes of books on engineering and architecture. His desk sat in front of it, empty except for a phone and a black leather desk pad. Next to the window, she saw a small counter that contained a single cup coffee maker and a water filtering pitcher. Across from the window on the other wall, she saw his drafting table with a closed set of plans sitting on top of it. A rack of plans sat on one side of the table, and a low shelf full of bound specifications sat on the other side. A whiteboard with various columns and notes written in different colors hung above the table on the wall. She recognized job numbers, dates, and some codes.

He moved directly to the coffee pot on a counter and put a ceramic mug under the spout. With efficient movements, he placed a coffee pod into the machine and, within seconds, the smell of brewing coffee filled the small room and made her mouth water. She already felt warmer.

"How was your Sunday evening?" she asked as she slipped off her damp coat. Underneath, she wore camel colored wool pants and a brown sweater. She wiggled her toes in her boots, thankful that her feet hadn't gotten too wet.

"It was quiet," Ian said. "I watched highlights of the ball game and readied myself for the week. Yours?"

"The exciting life of laundry." She grinned. "I don't know why I always put it off until Sunday night. I captioned a thirty-minute television show in between loads."

She noticed the massive arrangement of flowers sitting on the credenza behind his desk. Immediately, she felt a little guilt and walked over to it, running a finger over the petal of a mum the color of the richest wine. "Ian, I have a little confession to make," she said quickly before she could talk herself out of it.

He brought her the steaming mug of coffee, and then went back to the coffee maker to wait for his cup to brew. "A confession? That sounds interesting."

She cleared her throat and took a sip of the coffee, hoping the hot drink might give her a little bit of courage. "Yeah, a confession. I hope you're not, ah, angry."

"Impossible to tell with this much information. I'm going to have to digest it." His teasing tone helped boost her fortitude. His coffee finished brewing and he pulled the cup out from under the spout and took a careful sip.

She took a deep breath deciding that the longer she kept from telling him, the worse it would be. "These flowers," she said, then she stopped, cleared her throat, and continued, "the flowers were meant for my friend Sami." With his blank stare, she elaborated.

"Sami Jones. Brad Dixon's secretary. I don't know how the delivery company got them to you, except it may be because your first name is Samuel. Anyway, I'm sorry I didn't tell you when you came to my office Friday, but I was kind of in shock and really, really wanted to have dinner with you."

He stared at her for several seconds, not moving, and she couldn't read his thoughts behind his stoic expression. Finally, he sent his coffee cut down and walked toward her. "I think," he began his voice low and deep, "that if you had said this to me on Friday afternoon, I would have been annoyed and embarrassed. But because I have spent so much time with you this weekend, all that I can say is I'm thankful to God for that mistake and believe very sincerely that this must be something He orchestrated."

With everything he could have said, she did not expect *that*. He reached down and took her hand and didn't say anything. He stood close enough that she could feel the heat from his body, and just looked up at him, staring into his hazel eyes. He reached up and slipped the glasses off her face.

A tap-tap on his door made her step quickly away. She clasped her hands behind her back and watched annoyance creep into his eyes at the interruption.

"Hey, Ian? Just got word that the 9:00 got moved to 8:30," Ian's secretary Penny announced as she came through the door. She stopped short when she saw Calla standing next to Ian behind his desk. He very casually handed her glasses back to her. She fumbled and almost dropped them, but finally got them back on her face.

Comically, Penny didn't speak until Calla had her glasses back in place as if she didn't recognize her without them. "Oh, hi, Calla."

Heat flooded Calla's face, and she stepped even further away from Ian. "Hi, Penny. Good morning."

She wanted to escape, but she still had almost ten minutes left and didn't want to miss the time with him. Instead, she scooped up her coffee cup and clasped both hands around it.

"Thanks, Penny," Ian said. He paused. Penny paused, looking back and forth between him and Calla. Finally, he asked, "Anything else?"

Penny smiled and stepped back out the doorway. "Nothing that can't wait," she said through her grin.

Ian turned and looked at Calla as the door shut. "Sounds like the day has to begin," he said.

"Pity that." At his grin, she burst out laughing. "I hope there comes a time when I'm not so nervous around you."

"Well, I'm terrifying. I don't blame you for feeling nervous." The dimple appeared.

"Not terrified. But I am nervous. I admit it."

"You'll get used to me. We just have to spend more time together." The cell phone on his desk began vibrating at the same time his desk phone started chirping. "Lunch?"

"I brought mine, but I'm happy to share." He had a hand on each phone, so she set her cup on the credenza next to the flowers and waved at him. "Get to work. Come get me when you're free." As she slipped out the door, she found Penny hovering, obviously waiting for her.

"Do tell," Penny said, grinning. "I'm dying to know."

"Penny," Calla whispered, looking around, "Shh." She knew all of the secretaries well because they all constantly communicated with her about files. She and Penny had hit it off as friends almost immediately. "I can't. Really. Too new." But she stopped and leaned her back against the door and put a hand over her heart. "But, I have to say, I feel like I'm walking on air."

Penny waved her forward and grabbed her hand, pulling her into an empty conference room.

"I interrupted something, didn't I?"

"Maybe." She thought about what might have happened after he took her glasses off. "Fine. Yes. But, really, it's so early. Please..."

"Girlfriend, I love Ian second only to my boyfriend. And,

well, maybe my brothers and dad. But he's up there. I wouldn't hurt him or gossip about him to save my life." She laughed and brought her clasped hands up to her chest. "But I feel so happy right now! It's like perfection to me."

Calla looked at her watch. "I have to get downstairs. Catch up with you later. You still need to tell me about your weekend getaway."

Penny grinned like someone clutching a secret. "Oh, I do. I can't wait."

Calla laughed and rushed to the elevator, making her way down to her floor. As she walked to her desk and slipped her purse into her drawer, she watched the digital clock on her radio switch to 8:00 exactly.

"Good morning," Francine, her boss, greeted, coming up behind her with a stack of requests. "How was your weekend?"

"Wonderful," Calla sincerely replied. "Best one I've had in a long time."

"That's fantastic." Francine held out the papers. "Best get to it. The short Thanksgiving week has everyone trying to cram the world into three days, and Meredith and Becky are both out this week."

Calla took the papers and walked over to the empty counter that spanned the length of the room. She started sorting requests. With dozens of rows of filing cabinets, documents cabinets, and plans racks, she needed to sort by department—legal, accounting, residential, commercial—and by location inside the filing system. Once she had everything in order, she pulled the plans, blueprints, and specifications first, and loaded them into the large cubicles right inside the doorway to the department. Then she marked the request with the cubicle number.

She carried the papers to the reception area. Normally, the college student Meredith would then contact the person who submitted the request and let him or her know from what cubby to pull the items. But, she had gone home for Thanksgiving break, so Calla slipped into the desk chair and sent several interoffice emails then went back to her stack of requests and started pulling files. By the time she felt like she'd made a dent in the work, Francine brought her several more requests. With just the two of them working in a department usually staffed by four, and at busy times, five or six, they worked quickly, not talking, just trying to stay on top of the requests. As the morning faded, they slowed down, giving them a chance to tackle the baskets of "to be filed" and the returned plans and specifications that had come in since the morning.

Slipping earbuds into her ears, she found an upbeat 80's music station on her phone and turned the volume up so that she could drown out the world and just file.

✳

Ian leaned against the filing cabinet and watched Calla dance to the music pumping out of her earbuds. He could faintly hear it even from several feet away. It fascinated him how efficiently she worked while bopping her head around and shifting her shoulders to the rhythmic beat. He felt a silly grin cross his face while he waited for her to spin or turn and twist and see him, in a way hoping that it took a little bit longer so he could continue the sheer enjoyment of just watching her.

However, within seconds of that thought, she hit a file drawer with her hip to shut it, and turned and spotted him, halting mid-swing. She immediately stopped moving and yanked the earbuds out of her ears.

"You're really going to have to quit sneaking up on me like that," she mumbled, obviously embarrassed.

"Well, for one thing, I like what I see and," he watched her cheeks turn cherry red, "for another thing, I wasn't sneaking."

"You were sneaking. A little."

He laughed. "Maybe you shouldn't have your music so loud. How do you know when someone is here?"

She tapped the pocket of her pants. He could see the outline of her phone. "We normally have a receptionist, and she texts me."

She looked at her watch. "Is it seriously 12:30? Wow, we've been so busy this morning that the time has flown by."

"Yes, and I only have about twenty minutes." With the Thanksgiving holiday this week, he had a last-minute meeting piled on top of a crisis meeting as people prepared to take a four-day holiday. "I just wanted to stop by and beg out of lunch. How about tomorrow?"

He could see the disappointment on her face and wondered why that filled him with some sort of male pride. "I would love that. Can I bring it?"

"I'm happy to take you out."

"You took me out last time. Yesterday. Remember? I'd like to think it's my turn."

Deciding not to argue, yet, he nodded. "Okay. Sounds good. I have to go. I'm very sorry. I'll see you tomorrow and make it up to you."

As he turned to leave, she said, "Where?"

Already thinking about the agenda for his upcoming meeting, he frowned when he looked back at her. "What?"

"See me where? Where do you want to meet? What time?"

"Ah, uh, coffee shop downstairs? Eleven-thirty? I'll check with Penny and confirm."

He turned away again and headed back to the elevator. As he stepped in, the phone in his hand vibrated. He answered it almost immediately. "Hi, Al."

"Hey. You coming to the one o'clock?"

He pressed the button for the seventh floor. "Yes. Headed to get my tablet now."

"I have Reubens from that place on Peachtree."

Wishing he could enjoy what Calla had packed this morning instead of corned beef and sauerkraut on rye, he nevertheless thanked him. "Sounds great. I'll grab cash when I go to my office, too."

"Get a couple bottles of water, too."

"Water, too, got it."

Five minutes later, they sat alone in the conference room and bit into their sandwiches. Ian ate quickly, knowing that within ten minutes, the room would fill with people. "How was that dinner Saturday?" Al asked in-between bites. "With the flower girl?"

Ian contemplated the question as he chewed. "Tell you the truth? Incredible."

"And, did she properly thank you?"

Ian caught the tone of the question and answered the question Al didn't ask. "Not like that at all. The first time we even held hands was to bless the meal. She's something else."

"I see." Al grinned. "Do go on."

How much to elaborate? How did he explain to his best friend that he felt like he'd waited for someone like Calla Vaughn his entire life? "She's an amazing cook. She went to culinary school a few years ago. And, honestly, I feel like I'll never get tired of having conversations with her. She's bright, funny, kind of vivacious." He paused and caught Al staring at him with a huge grin on his face. "What?"

"Brother, I've known you since I was seventeen. I have never heard you talk like that about any girl, ever."

Ian set his sandwich down and wiped his buttery fingers on a paper napkin. "I never felt like this about any girl, ever. We had lunch yesterday after church, coffee this morning..." He picked up his water bottle and sat back in the conference room chair. "I've had a heck of a time concentrating today. All I want to do is go down to files and talk with her. Listen to her. Talk with her some more."

"Mmm hmm." Al nodded, rather knowingly. "I hear you. Can't wait to meet her myself."

"I bet you'll recognize her when you see her. You'll like her."

"Doesn't matter if I like her. She just has to pass the grandma test."

Ian's expression turned sharp. "That isn't funny."

"Oh, I know it's not funny," Al agreed. "It's not funny at all. I failed the grandma test. Remember?"

Ian opened his mouth to reply, but the conference door swung open and Brian, an architect in the firm, entered. "Smells like sauerkraut in here," he observed as he pushed a cart full of four-inch bound specifications for an upcoming central Alabama sports arena. As he reached the end of the table, he started placing a specifications book at each seat. "Those from that new place on Peachtree?"

Al nodded as he took his last bite. "They are."

"I hit them up last week. Man, I haven't had sandwiches that good since I left Miami."

"Word's getting out, too. Line was twenty minutes long today." He wrapped up his paper and balled it up. "Worth every minute."

"I hear you."

Ian finished his sandwich and pushed away from the table. "I need to check in with Penny. Be back by one." He stepped out through the door on the side of his office into the sea of cubicles and, thankfully, saw Penny at her desk. "Penny, am I free tomorrow at 11:30? My calendar looks good. I want to make sure there's been nothing last minute that hasn't propagated to me yet."

She pulled up the program on her computer and looked up at him. "Clear."

"Great. Schedule me in firm for lunch at 11:30. Unless Daddy Dixon appears, grab that half hour and growl. Okay?"

She smiled as if she knew he had lunch plans with Calla Vaughn tomorrow at eleven-thirty. "Sure. Where?"

"Coffee shop downstairs." He looked at his watch. "Have to get back to the meeting."

"You have a two-thirty after this one," she reminded him. He gave her a thumb's up as he went back to the conference room.

CHAPTER 5

A s she pulled her bag out of her desk drawer, the phone at her elbow rang. Answering it almost absently, Calla checked in her bag to make sure she had the keys to lock the file room door. "File room, Calla Vaughn," she answered.

"Hello, Callie." At the sound of her stepmother, Becky Vaughn's voice mispronouncing her name, Calla's hands turned ice cold.

Trying to keep her voice from shaking, she demanded, "What do you want?"

"Oh, I'm just calling to let you know that if you were planning on coming home to daddy's house for Thanksgiving, I'll be in Cozumel. Jimmy, my boyfriend—you've met Jimmy, haven't you?—we're leaving tomorrow."

She'd met Jimmy. At her father's funeral. "Cozumel? Did Jimmy suddenly win the lottery?"

"No, silly. I got a new credit card last week. It's just dying for me to use it up. Ta!"

Becky didn't call her to keep her from coming "home" for Thanksgiving. She had no home. She'd sold that house before the headstone even came in for her father's grave. Becky called to make sure that Calla knew about another credit card in Calla's name.

Putting her head on her desk, a sob that she'd held back for far too long escaped her. No matter how hard she worked or how hard she tried, she would never get out of this pit. Her father's marriage to Becky had ruined her entire life, destroyed any possible good future. She just didn't realize the extent of it until after her father died.

After his funeral, Calla had taken a semester and a summer off from school, during which time Becky had gone through her father's savings in a matter of months. By the time it came time to pay her school bill, there was no money left. Calla tried to get a student loan, but apparently, she had tens of thousands of dollars of credit card debt, and the loan got declined.

That was when Calla discovered that Becky had used her name and social security number during her entire stint as step-mommy.

She'd never win. Another sob escaped and, with a wail, she let the tears fall. She ripped her glasses off her face and threw them on her desk. Anger made her ball her fists until her fingernails dug into her palms. She brought them up to her forehead violently, hitting herself so hard it nearly hurt. She pressed her fists hard into her head and battled the desire to break something, rip something, screech out loud.

"Calla?"

Startled, she whirled around in her chair, horrified to see Ian standing there. Immediately, she wiped her cheeks with both palms, wondering about the level of eye makeup leaving streaks along her cheeks. "Ian," she hiccupped. "I didn't hear you."

A confused frown marred his face. "Are you okay? What happened?"

She cleared her throat and stood quickly, grabbing her bag and the key to the door. "It's nothing. It's..." He pulled her to him and his arms came around her. She hadn't expected that, but without warning, she felt safer, freer, less like the world was closing in on her. "I'm sorry. I just fielded a phone call from my stepmother. She tends to have this kind of effect on me."

He shifted back so he could frame her wet face with his hands. "Is there something I can do?"

A joke about loaning her fifty-thousand dollars froze on her tongue. Even in this overemotional state, she knew it wouldn't have gone over well. Instead, she shook her head. "I think I just need to build a bigger shell where she's concerned. Dad's been dead for three years. It shouldn't still hurt this bad."

She could see he didn't quite believe her but could tell when he decided not to push. He released her and stepped back far enough that she couldn't feel his body heat anymore. "I came down to see if you'd like a ride home? The weather is just as nasty as this morning."

Even though her knee-jerk answer would be to thank him and turn him down, she really wanted a ride home. "Thanks," she said, feeling calmer. "I would really like that. I appreciate you thinking about me."

They walked to the door together, and she pulled the double doors closed, locking them and setting the alarm. "What are you doing for Thanksgiving?" she asked.

"My family will all be at my grandmother's." He pressed the down button on the elevator. "You?"

"Sami invited me to dinner at her parents'. I'm making pies and veggies." They stepped into the empty elevator car, and Ian pressed the appropriate parking garage button. "Speaking of cooking, I'm looking forward to lunch tomorrow. I hope you like chili."

"That sounds wonderful, especially in this weather." She followed half a step behind him as they walked to his car, trying desperately to shake the emotional overload assaulting her right now from Becky's phone call.

He remotely unlocked the door to his car so that, by the time they reached it, he could open her door for her.

As she settled into the seat and fastened her seatbelt, she wondered how to act with him. Part of her felt like she'd known him her whole life and should feel completely at ease. The other part of her knew they'd barely scratched the surface of what they could learn about each other and perhaps the almost kiss this morning was a little preemptive. Her mind went back and forth with all of the do's and don'ts and what's, and all of it swirled with the conversation she'd just had with Becky.

Ian opened the back door and set his backpack on the floorboard, then slid into the driver's seat. As he started the car, he rubbed his hands together. "Can't believe how fast the temperature dropped since this morning."

The safe conversation about weather gave her a little more time to shed all the negative emotions and find some balance again. "It should warm up again by next week. That's definitely one nice thing about living in the south—you only have to take tastes of fall and winter then everything goes back to right again."

He laughed. "Have you ever lived anywhere other than Atlanta?"

"No. Born and raised in the A-T-L. But, my dad came from Wisconsin. I spent many a white Christmas on the lake with my grandfather before he died. I don't think I'd enjoy living up there."

"I've always spent Christmas in Haiti, so I don't know about anything but mosquito nets and bags of tepid water."

"Bags? Not bottles?"

"Yeah. They come in bags, and you buy them in a big bag." He maneuvered his way out of the garage and turned in the direction of her apartment. For the next twenty minutes, they enjoyed easy conversation, remembering childhood Christmases and sharing stories. She told him about ice fishing, and he told her about bringing new soccer balls to a village. All too soon, he pulled into a spot near the front door and put the car in park, but did not turn off the engine.

"I'm sorry your stepmother hurt you so much," he said, shifting so he could partially face her. "If you need to talk about anything, let me know." He surprised her by reaching out and taking her hand. "No one should cause such an emotional reaction. Just know that you're not alone."

Her breath hitched, and she fought another surprising wave of emotion. "Thanks," she said, her voice hoarse. "I appreciate your concern, and I'm sorry that you saw me in such a state."

He raised an eyebrow. "Sorry? What does that mean?"

Her laugh sounded a little rough, despite its sincerity. "It means that right now, I still hope I look my best when you see me. I want my lipstick on and my hair straight. I changed clothes three times before church yesterday and twice before work this morning." She opened the door and grinned at him. "Ugly crying at my desk at six-fifteen on a Monday night does not constitute my best, and I'm truly sorry that happened."

He closed his eyes and gave a brief shake of his head. "Hey, Calla? For the record, I don't even understand what you just said."

"That's okay, Ian. You're a guy. There's no reason you would understand." She slid out of the car and leaned down to face him. "Thanks for the ride. I appreciate it more than you know."

Pulling her legs under her, Calla settled more comfortably on the couch with her notebook computer in her lap. The last pie for tomorrow's Thanksgiving dinner had just come out of the oven, and the fragrance of cinnamon and nutmeg mixed with Granny Smith apples wafted through the room, filling her with a feeling of comfort and happiness.

Since she didn't have to go into the office tomorrow, she could work as far into the night as she wanted. She had earbuds in her ears and typed as fast as her fingers could go, transcribing the video that played. She'd picked this one because as an instructor doing a voice-over for a presentation, he spoke clearly and concisely, and when he said words she didn't understand, most of the time they appeared on the screen. She barely had to pause.

An hour into the ninety-minute video when her cell phone chirped. Pausing the video, she picked it up and read the message from Sami.

SISTER'S WATER BROKE. HEADING UP TO CHARLOTTE WITH MY

PARENTS. SORRY TO CANCEL THANKSGIVING! TALK SOON.

A smile crossed her face. She didn't think she'd ever met any sister more excited about a coming baby and wished she could go with her to Charlotte just to experience Sami meeting the baby for the first time.

Resuming her transcribing, she pressed play and started typing, then paused again. On an impulse, she picked up her phone and shot a quick text to Ian.

THANKSGIVING PLANS CANCELED. WANT TO COME BY FOR PIE TOMORROW EVENING? HATE TO SEE MY ALL MY WORK GO TO WASTE.

They'd enjoyed lunch together on Tuesday, but she hadn't seen him today. He had warned her of his full and busy schedule all day Wednesday. In fact, she hadn't even heard from him since the end of lunch today.

By the time she finished transcribing the video, formatted the captioning, and submitted it for billing, another two hours had gone by, and she still hadn't heard from him. Purposefully not letting that bother her, she went ahead and got ready for bed. She felt her energy draining from a long day at work and figured she could get up really early tomorrow in lieu of staying up late tonight.

When her alarm woke her at four on Thanksgiving morning, she saw a text from Ian time-stamped at two in the morning.

PICK YOU UP AT THREE. NOT TOO DRESSY.

A silly grin covered her face, and she held her phone to her chest as if she held a love letter. Did he truly plan to take her to his family Thanksgiving? Since no one could hear her, she went ahead and let the gleeful laugh out before texting him back.

I HAVE PIES AND SOME VEGGIES, TOO. DON'T FORGET.

Ten minutes later, she settled comfortably into the corner of her couch, a cup of coffee steaming at her elbow, the silly grin still on her face. As she accessed the site where she worked as a transcriber, she pulled up the list of available jobs. Seeing an upcoming episode of her favorite television show, she claimed it. While the video loaded in the interface, she put both of her hands on her cheeks and felt the smile. The sound of the opening credits pulled her out of her happy glow, and she paused the video to take a sip of coffee before getting to work.

A few minutes into transcribing, she got a new text.

PICK YOU AND THE PIES UP AT THREE. BREAD TOO? HOPE SO. SEE YOU THEN.

Ian entered the large house using his key. On the table that sat between the bottom steps of the double staircase sat a colossal vase of fall flowers lit by the ornate crystal chandelier. He walked across the gleaming tile, passed the leftmost staircase and through the door to his grandmother's sitting room.

He could see a low fire in the fireplace. That's where he found her, standing next to the marble mantle, looking at a picture of his parents. She had a very distant and wistful look on her face, and he cleared his throat before walking all the way over to her. As soon as she saw him, her eyes cleared and she smiled. He reached her and kissed both of her cheeks, breathing in the scent of roses that her lotions and sprays always smelled like.

"Grandmother," he greeted, "Happy Thanksgiving."

"Samuel," Annabelle Jones replied, patting the side of his arm, "you are early." She called him Ian until the day his father, her middle son, died. Then she began calling him Samuel, after his father.

"No, ma'am. I just stopped by to let you know I'm bringing a guest today."

"A guest?" Annabelle raised a perfectly plucked eyebrow. "And will this guest be a lady or a gentleman?"

He smiled, knowing she had immediately started praying that he planned to bring a guest of the romantic female persuasion, and not just a friend who found himself without a table this Thanksgiving. "A lady. Miss Calla Vaughn. I apologize for the last-minute invite, but she had her plans canceled late yesterday and has no family."

"No apologies necessary. You know my table is always open." She pursed her lips and looked him up and down. "You've never brought a young lady to our table before. I'd remember."

He threw his head back and laughed. "You'd remember, yes, ma'am." As he slipped his hands into his pockets, he thought back to the last five days, to the vibrant and fun woman with eyes as dark as the richest chocolates. "I've had one dinner, two lunches, and a coffee with her, grandmother. No wedding bells yet, please. I've only invited her because she found herself unexpectedly with nowhere else to go."

He cleared his throat and stopped himself from fidgeting. He knew he'd just spoken what amounted to a very small fib. Okay, a lie. He invited her because the text he read from her last night filled him with hopeful anticipation. He invited her because he couldn't stand the thought of not seeing her all day long. He invited her because he wanted to spend the day with her. "I like her, though. I do. She's really something. I hope you think so, too."

"Another first. Be still my heart." She walked over to a large arrangement of burgundy roses and picked a dying leaf off of a stem. "I won't make a big deal of it. Don't fret. Your old grandma-ma won't embarrass you today."

"You, dear lady, would have to try really hard to embarrass me in any way." He let a breath escape that he didn't realize he'd held. "I will warn you, though, you won't know her family. She's not exactly—"

The waving of her hand cut him off. "You assume too much about me. Always have. I disapprove of one girlfriend back in high school…"

When he realized that she didn't intend to finish the sentence, he did it for her. "The one you embarrassed to the point of tears? After that, she wouldn't even look at me."

Annabelle sat on her flowered settee and patted the cushion next to her. "You obviously don't have a clue what happened. That girl, I don't remember her name—"

"Melissa Posner." He pictured the athletic blonde who led the cheerleading squad. "Missy."

"Okay, Missy." She cleared her throat and straightened the gold watch on her wrist. "I walked in on her talking to the maid Bea in such a tone that I couldn't believe a teenager was speaking. I was appalled. So, I tested her, and she failed." Her hazel eyes met his, and he could see no regret in them. "I know that was the last time you brought someone home. But, it had nothing to do with my snobbery and everything to do with not wanting you to end up with a woman like her."

He tried to remember the incident, the exact words that his grandmother had spoken, anything at all, but so much time had passed, and he couldn't grab all of the details from his very hazy memory. "I've always resisted bringing anyone else home because I assumed you wouldn't approve, that's true. I wish you'd said something to me before."

"There was no need before." She patted his hand. "Now, if you have someone you feel would survive my scrutiny, however mistaken that thought is, this must be someone incredibly special. Because, I imagine if she weren't, you would have simply made plans with her after coming here or something of the sort. Bringing her here, with your uncles and me, now, tells me that she is someone I need to pay attention to."

Ian closed his eyes then demanded, "What about Al, Grandma?"

His grandmother froze. She turned slowly and met his eyes. "Samuel, that is between your sister and me. I understand you may feel protective of your sister and your best friend, but you do not know the details, and I will not gossip. So, I would appreciate your trust in this matter, and I will thank you if you never bring that subject up with me again in the future."

Ian tasted copper on his tongue. He swallowed and said. "All right, Grandma. But it doesn't make me feel better about bringing my friend over for Thanksgiving dinner."

She crossed her arms, then said, "Then perhaps you should tell me about her, Samuel."

His mind drifted to Calla and pictured her hitting the filing cabinet drawer with her hip. A silly smile crossed his face at the image. "She loves Jesus. And she's really fun to be around. I think you'll like her." He looked at his watch. "I have to go. She is bringing food, by the way."

She frowned. "Food?" She said the word as if it felt foreign to her tongue. "I'm not sure I understand."

"Trained chef, grandmother. Trust me. You'll be happy."

"What kind of food?"

"Pies." He smiled and winked. "And some kind of vegetable."

"I have a caterer, Samuel. Our Thanksgiving dinner table is not some country tent meeting potluck." Again, she said the word potluck as if pronouncing a foreign phrase attached to an equally foreign concept.

He loved his grandmother. She'd sell her family jewelry if it meant helping someone in need. She could also don the upper-crust snob mantle whenever she felt the need. "I understand. But, like I said, trained chef. You asked me to trust you? Trust me. You'll be happy. And," he said in a slightly warning tone, "you'll be thankful because I'm saying please."

The sigh she heaved gave the impression that she just conceded a hard-fought battle. "Very well. Go into the kitchen and get the appropriate dishes for your lady friend. My table will be set with matching dinnerware, even if it's put together hodgepodge."

"Hardly fair, grandmother," Ian said with a smile as he leaned forward to kiss her cheek. "I'll see you in a few hours."

CHAPTER 6

Calla stared at the reflection of her third wardrobe change in the mirror and smoothed down the sides of her dark green jacket. She wore a suede skirt the color of rich caramel, dark brown boots, and a scarf that pulled all the colors together. As she examined her outfit, she worried that she had overdressed. He did say not too dressy in his text, right? Was this too dressy? What if everyone there wore blue jeans and football jerseys?

Before she could change outfits yet again, her doorbell rang. This outfit would have to do, she thought, as she rushed through her apartment and opened the door. She smiled when she saw Ian in a dark blue button-down shirt and a pair of khaki pants. Perfect. She hadn't overdressed.

"Hi there," she greeted with a grin, stepping forward to hug him. "I'm ready. I just need to grab the food."

He brushed his lips over her cheek as he hugged her back, then stepped fully into the apartment. She gestured at the serving dish in his hand. "What's that?"

He cleared his throat. "My grandmother is sort of set in her ways. She doesn't like a mismatched table. She sent me with a serving dish for your vegetables." He held it out. "I feel like I should preface that with an apology."

"Nonsense." She took the dish and went into the kitchen,

pulling the pan of roasted Brussels sprouts and butternut squash out of the oven. "It makes perfect sense. Appearance is actually a huge part of dining."

Ian walked over to the counter where she had an apple pie and a pecan pie. He leaned down and sniffed the apple pie. She'd sliced Granny Smith apples and arranged them in a pattern to look like a rose in full bloom. She'd scalloped the crust so that it looked like the edge of a lace doily. Over the top of the fruit, she'd sprinkled cinnamon, a sauce made from brown sugar and butter, and then grated fresh nutmeg. "This looks incredible," he remarked, smelling the rosette pie again. "Apple pie is my favorite."

"If I'd known that, I would have made two," Calla said, and immediately felt her cheeks heat. Where did such a flirtatious comment come from?

"The way to a man's heart," he teased as she packed the pies into the portable carrier, carefully not damaging the crust she had painstakingly designed.

"That's the rumor." She scooped the vegetables into the casserole dish and pulled the box of plastic wrap out of the drawer. "I have an arsenal if that's the case. You might consider yourself warned."

She moved around the kitchen with a grace and poise that looked different from her movements in the file room. Her movements there looked improvised. Here she looked contained, practiced, disciplined, and smooth. She moved with confidence and mastery. He felt like he was watching a professional ice skater or prima ballerina. The entire time she arranged the food, she continued talking about food though she captured his eyes and his heart more than his ears.

"You know how in the Bible it talks about how Eve saw that the apple was pleasing to the eye? Isn't that interesting? Even the first people on earth desired food that looked good. You know?"

"I think *you* look good," Ian said.

"What?"

Ian grinned. "I said I think you look good, Calla Vaughn.

Beautiful, even."

Calla leaned against her counter, pausing in her practiced movements long enough to blush and grin. "Well, I'm not food, Mr. Jones."

Ian shook his head. "No, ma'am." He smiled as he stared into her eyes. "You are not food. You are something else."

She broke eye contact first, turning back to care for her vegetables. Quietly, she said, "Thank you, Ian."

"Tell me something, Calla Vaughn."

"What would you like to know, Ian Jones?"

"Why did you leave culinary school?"

The question threw her off, and she momentarily lost her poise. She found her hands fumbling on the plastic wrap, tangling it and making it rip. With her back to him, she closed her eyes, breathed deeply through her nose, then carefully covered the casserole dish with a sheet of plastic, this time very smooth and perfect.

Knowing she smiled an overly bright smile, but unable to do anything about it, she turned to him and said, "That's a long story. Can we talk about it later, when I'm not a nervous wreck on my way to your family's house?"

He stared at her with serious eyes for several seconds before finally nodding. "Sure." He cleared his throat. "I'm not trying to be nosy. I just want to get to know you better."

With an uncommon boldness, she stepped toward him. "Here's something about me you don't know, but that Sami and Penny and probably half a dozen other assistants know about me. I've had somewhat of a schoolgirl crush on you since I started working at Dixon Contracting. That's three years. The reason I know Penny so well is that if it was for you, I did it first and foremost, and she started noticing. It feels really weird to say it out loud, especially to you, but it's the truth. I didn't tell you about the flowers the first night because you accepted my dinner invitation, and being able to cook for you was like a dream come true."

Suddenly very uncomfortable and self-conscious, she picked up the serving dish and started out of the kitchen. "I'm ready to go if you can grab that pie container."

"Hey," he said, stopping her as she walked past him. When she turned to ask him what, he took the dish from her hands and set it on the counter next to him before he cupped her face with his hands. He looked into her eyes for several seconds before he slipped the glasses off of her face and lowered his lips to hers. The smell of his aftershave overwhelmed her as his soft, warm lips covered hers. She hesitated only a second before sliding her hand along his smooth cheek and stepping just a little closer, rising up on her toes to get that much nearer to him. It lasted just long enough to have her catching her breath, then he lifted his head and took half a step back.

"Thanks for making apple pie." His voice was deep, hoarse.

Clearing her throat and trying to do the mental shift back to pie, she took her glasses from him and straightened her jacket. Somehow, she managed to get her brain to form a response, and then communicate with her mouth - the same mouth still tingling from the kiss. "Glad I didn't like the look of the pumpkins at the market."

An hour later, Calla observed the dynamics of his family at the table. Ian's grandmother, Annabelle, sat at the head of the table, with Ian to her left. Calla sat between him and Ian's sister, Heidi. Ian's uncle Dwayne sat at the foot of the table, with his wife Beth to his left. To finish off the circle, his other uncle Theodore and his wife Donna, who sat to Annabelle's right. Over hors-d'oeuvres, Annabelle had explained to Calla that the children, all of Ian's cousins, spent Thanksgiving with their in-laws every year so the entire family could be together for their annual Christmas mission trip to Haiti.

Ian's sister, an engineer who designed roadways for the city of Atlanta, had dark brown hair and hazel eyes that seemed to shift between green and brown. Calla really enjoyed talking to her.

They chatted comfortably, like old friends. The anxiety Calla had felt about what awaited her at this dinner faded with every passing moment. Despite the luxurious surroundings in the old plantation mansion and the presence of a uniformed staff, every family member treated her in a manner that she found very welcoming and kind. In no time, she felt like they had enfolded her into the family.

"You met Ian at work?" Heidi asked.

"Yes. He had to push my car out of the way in the parking garage," Calla said, laughing. "It hasn't been hard to find the silver lining in that cloud."

Ian took a swallow of his water and leaned over Calla to speak to his sister. "It was really over a misdelivered flower arrangement. She sent flowers to her friend, Sami, to thank her for helping her with the car. But the florist delivered them to me since father insisted I be called Samuel instead of Ian. So, I guess there's a silver lining to that as well." Everyone laughed, and Ian took Calla's hand under the table. He gave her palm a gentle and reassuring squeeze, either to convey support or just because he needed to have that momentary contact with her, she didn't know. All she knew was that she liked it and missed his touch as soon as he let go of her hand.

Ian sat next to Calla and watched her interact with his family, listening to stories he'd heard a dozen times in his lifetime. He laughed at the appropriate times, interjected when things got a little exaggerated, and generally enjoyed every single moment of this Thanksgiving more than he thought he'd ever enjoyed the holiday before.

Calla was fun and had a good sense of humor, and a laugh that brought a smile to his lips. She charmed his uncles, made friends with his sister and his aunts, and he could tell she impressed his grandmother. He loved the fact that the dish that had held her roasted vegetables left the table empty, and that the beautiful works of art she created in her pies caused compliments to come from all parts of the table.

He tried to remind himself that he had only officially met Calla less than a week ago and that these kinds of feelings didn't just appear out of nowhere. The more his mind tried to tell his heart that, the less his heart listened or believed. Ian felt something special about his attraction for her. He could only hope and pray that she felt the same way.

As the maid served the pie, he put an arm around the back of her chair and leaned toward her. She finished saying something to Heidi and turned toward him, half a smile on her lips. It took considerable restraint to keep from kissing her then and there in front of God and everyone, but she must have read his mind because the smile slowly faded and she glanced at his lips.

Her voice touched his ears like a gentle caress. "You know what I'm most thankful for today, Ian?"

"What's that, Calla?"

"I'm so thankful you invited me today," she said very softly, her words only for his ears, only for him.

He reached out and took the hand she'd set in her lap. "And I am very thankful you agreed to come. You have certainly brightened up this table."

"Which pie, Mr. Samuel?" the maid at his elbow asked.

He straightened and let go of Calla's hand. "Apple, if you please, Velma. And bring another slice after everyone else is served. Thank you so much." On top of the pie sat a perfectly formed football shaped quenelle of cinnamon ice cream. It had started to melt and dribbled down the sides of the pie in a perfect formation. His mouth watered at the sight of it as he picked up his fork. At the first bite, the tartness of apples warred with the sweetness of the caramel sauce, accentuated by the spices and his tongue could barely keep up with the amazing experience of the taste. He closed his eyes and slowly chewed, wanting to savor every bite.

After dessert, Annabelle stood up and addressed the family. "This has been a delightful meal," she said with a smile. "It is always a treasure to have all my children available to me. I am especially happy that Ian brought a guest because I have tremendously enjoyed getting to know her and I'm sure I've not had vegetables that well prepared in a very long time." She looked at Ian with a mischievous smile. "We won't tell her this is the first time you've ever brought a girl home to dinner." Ian barked out a laugh and glanced at Calla, who looked surprised. He took her hand and laced his fingers through hers, enjoying the feel of her smooth skin against his.

"With sincere thankfulness," his grandmother continued, "I pray for each of you daily, and hope that you have a beautiful holiday season. Now, regarding Haiti. If you are filling a container for me to ship ahead of our trip this year, I have a list at the front table in the hall for you to use as your guide for supplies. After the hurricanes this year, I know that one vital need is powdered milk." She stepped away from the table and pushed her chair in. "You are now released from your family obligation," she said with a smile, making the whole table laugh, "and I love you all."

As everyone got up from the table, Ian led Calla to his grandmother's sitting room. They found Annabelle sitting next to Dwayne with a tablet in her lap, discussing packing lists. "I've already sent the money, ready to pay the customs officials' extortion," Dwayne said. "The containers should get there about a week before you do. I have a team of Haitian workers who are already contracted to unload the containers and truck them up the mountain."

"Perfect," Annabelle said, "Are you sure you sent enough?"

"With the hurricanes this year, we're thinking the extortion won't be so bad. But, yes, we're sure we sent enough."

Ian glanced at Calla and saw the confusion on her face. "Usually, containers filled with things like building materials require a bribe to get through customs. The extortion is almost a standard operating procedure." He looked back at his grandmother. "Calla and I are going to head out, grandma."

She stood in a fluid motion and hugged him. He breathed in the smell of roses that lingered even after she stepped over to

Calla. "It was such a pleasure to meet you. I hope to see you again."

Calla smiled and didn't hesitate to hug Annabelle. "It was wonderful. Thank you so much for inviting me."

"You are welcome any time."

As they stepped outside into the dusk, Ian took Calla's hand and led her along the circular driveway. "You certainly made an impression," he said quietly, stopping at his car to open the passenger's door for her.

When he settled into the driver's seat, she looked over at him and surprised him by asking, "If you've never brought a girl home, how do you know that's not how they would treat any female guest of yours?"

He could see her grin in the dim light and grinned back. "Despite orphanages and mission's trips, there's still a very superior air about my family. I can assure you that if you had not passed muster, so to speak, you would have very much realized it."

After a moment of silence, she said, "I'm just glad they liked my food."

Surprised, he asked, "What do you mean? Of course, they liked your food."

He saw her slight shrug. "I'm afraid that's part of the creative brain. I'm riddled with insecurities about my food. Every time. I wonder why I even cook until someone eats something and they love it so much. Then I get filled with creative energy and can't wait until I get to cook again."

"That sounds absolutely exhausting."

She laughed. "Why do you think I'm tired all the time?"

He found that he rather liked her brain. They enjoyed comfortable conversation all the way back to her apartment. When he walked to the door, he leaned down and brushed his lips against her cheek. "Let me know when you're feeling up to making another apple pie," he teased.

Despite his intentional teasing tone, she said, "How about

Sunday? After church?"

Knowing he had the whole weekend free, he nodded. "I can do that."

"Perfect." She unlocked her door then turned back to face him. "I very much look forward to it." After staring up at him with eyes that looked very nearly black in the dim corridor light, she softly said, "Goodnight, Ian."

He closed his eyes and took a deep breath through his nose. Then he opened his eyes, turned, and purposefully put one foot in front of the other all the way down the corridor to his car.

Calla sat in Ian's desk chair and pulled her legs up underneath her. She'd worn a long skirt today so she could wear long underwear underneath it. The temperature had chilled this week before Christmas, and the morning walk to the train station in thirty-three degrees made her thankful for warm boots and foresight. She blew on the surface of the hot cup of coffee in her hand and watched her breath create ripples in the dark liquid.

Ian perched on the chair in front of his drafting table, his eyes narrowing as he looked at a set of plans and spoke to the contractor on the phone. She enjoyed watching him when he worked, admired the intensity of his concentration. She didn't feel a need to interject, to remind him of her presence, to try to get his attention. No, she just wanted to watch him, watch the expressions cross his face, watch his brain work through whatever problem the person on the other end of the line had presented to him.

He hung up the phone and made several notations on a notepad in front of him before looking at her. His face gradually softened as his eyes focused on her. "Sorry about that."

"No reason to be sorry," she claimed, straightening her legs and sitting properly in the chair. "Your work day starts way earlier than mine."

"Yeah, I have to get to it, really."

"I understand." She held up the coffee cup. "I'm taking this with me."

"Please do." His phone chirped with a text, and she stood, grabbing her coat and her bag. He had the phone to his ear when she started to walk by him, but he grabbed her arm and pulled her to him for a very quiet, brief kiss. When she pulled away, he winked at her, then his eyes grew serious again, and he started talking on the phone.

As she slipped out of his office and closed the door behind her, she paused at Penny's desk. "Any big plans for Christmas?" Penny asked, cutting her eyes to Ian's door then back at Calla with a mischievous grin.

Calla smiled and settled into the chair next to Penny's desk. She spoke in a quiet tone, not wanting to have any of the other assistants or interns in the cubicle area overhear. "Yesterday, he told me that his cousin couldn't go to Haiti this year. So, he asked if I wanted to go since the plane ticket was already bought."

"Haiti is hardly a romantic getaway," Penny said. "You should push for Cancun or something."

Calla cheeks flooded with color. "It's not intended to be a romantic getaway. It's supposed to be a mission trip."

"Nevertheless." Her phone sounded a tone, and immediately Calla heard Ian's voice coming through the speaker. "Penny, I need you."

"Yes, sir." As Penny stood, she leaned down toward Calla and whispered, "Seriously, he could take you anywhere."

Calla understood that she and Penny had a different moral compass, especially when it came to men and relationships…and relationship boundaries. Instead of arguing purity over temptation, she just smiled and said, "Penny, anywhere on earth would feel romantic with him. Have a great day."

A few minutes later, she sat at Sami's desk. Sami gave her a half grin. "Haiti, huh?"

"It's an annual Christmas tradition." She thought of the news footage she'd seen of the island country when she'd transcribed a news report. "It was pretty much destroyed when that big hurricane hit it in September."

"I know. I remember." She took a sip of her tea. "Seems kind of soon to be asking you out on a trip out of the country, though."

"One month." Calla sat back and held her mug with both hands. She couldn't remember a time when she didn't spend time with Ian on a daily basis. She smiled and thought back to the very first time she opened her apartment door to him. "Only one month? How is that possible?"

"Works that way sometimes," Sami said. She blinked, and Calla could see the gold glitter of her eyeshadow - the same gold that matched the ornaments painted with glittery fabric paint on her dark green dress. She'd obviously worn it for the evening's annual Dixon Contracting Christmas party. "You've never been more relaxed, though, honestly. I think it's great." Calla glanced at her watch as Sami fielded a call. She had another five minutes before she had to head down to the file room. When Sami hung up, she asked, "Have you told Ian about your stepmom?"

Instantly, her stomach knotted painfully. She pressed her lips together and slowly shook her head. "No. Not yet."

"Calla," Sami chided.

"How do I, even?"

Sami leaned forward as if someone could overhear them. "Calla, you have to tell him. He has to know the mess that woman created before he develops any deeper feelings for you. Keeping it from him is not fair to him."

She was right. She knew it. She sighed. "I know. I'm just so afraid that I'll lose him."

Sami narrowed her eyes. "I hear you. But, better now than a month from now, or a year. You two, you're like this perfection in a couple. Even Al Carpenter thinks so, and he's super defensive about Ian."

Calla sighed. "I think I've decided to press formal charges."

Sami, who had spent years trying to convince Calla to do just that widened her eyes in surprise. "Shut up. Really?"

Thinking about Ian, how ordered and careful he kept his life, and how chaotic and out of control hers had become, she nodded. "I think it's the right thing to do. And, I think it will be easier to tell him about it when I've done exactly what I should have done three years ago."

"Good for you." Sami leaned forward. "But, this is something that the longer you go without saying something, the more it's going to seem like deceit. You don't want that."

She didn't want that. Hours later, in her sea of filing cabinets and drawers, she resolved to tell Ian about it. After Christmas. After she filed charges.

CHAPTER 7

Ian sat next to a dozing Calla as the jet airplane entered Atlanta airspace. He leaned forward and looked out the window, analyzing the last two weeks. He'd spent the first week in Ti Peligre helping with the rebuilding of a footbridge over the Thomonde River that the hurricane in September had wiped out. When Calla arrived on Christmas Eve, he'd met her at the airport in Port-au-Prince. They spent the night on two-inch mattresses covered by mosquito netting on the flat roof of a church, which provided a refreshing respite from the tropical heat. The next morning, they had driven two hours to Cariesse to catch the ferry to Anse-à-Galets on La Gonâve Island.

Emmanuel Danos, a Haitian neighbor of the orphanage and the fiancé of his cousin, Hettie, had met them at the ferry in a small four-wheel drive all-terrain vehicle. They proceeded to drive for hours on the worn paths of lava rock the locals referred to as roads through narrow passages of rough terrain up the mountain to the village of Ti Palmiste. Finally, they arrived at the orphanage his family's mission ran.

The first time he'd taken this journey, his mother had carried him as a six-month-old in a sling made out of a large sheet of cloth fastened with a ring, allowing her to hold him hands-free while she worked and walked. By contrast, as he experienced everything with Calla, he felt like he experienced it for the first time in his life. The excitement, wonder, fear, and exhaustion that she felt radiated from her, and he felt all of those things, too. It breathed new life into something that had at some point become rote to him. Seeing the mission through her eyes made him seek to serve God on this trip with a renewed heart and spirit. It deepened his prayer life in a way he couldn't begin to have fathomed. It excited him and made him want to tell her everything about this island, its people, the language.

When his grandmother had met them at the gates of the orphanage, she'd hugged Calla enthusiastically. For the next three days, they'd worked nonstop, rebuilding a fence that had blown down, fixing a wall and roof at the school that had collapsed under a falling palm tree, and shopping for chickens and goats at the marketplace to replace those that disappeared in the storm.

He'd watched her interact with the children, had observed the sheer joy on her face when she watched them open their Christmas presents his grandmother had brought. He watched the sorrow overtake her as they tried on shoes and socks and accepted them with the same enthusiasm an American child would show for a new laptop or smartphone. She'd sat for hours while a teenager had braided her hair, playing marbles with some younger kids the whole time. And then, in the daylight hours, watched her work until her palms bled.

She cried when they left. He had a feeling that some part of her considered staying there permanently. The way the children responded to her, he knew his cousin who lived there full-time wouldn't have hesitated to bring her on as a member of the staff.

Unfortunately, Calla had limited time available to take off from work, so he left early with her, leaving his family behind so he could accompany her home. Retracing their steps, they went back down the mountain to the ferry, back to spend the night on the roof of the church, then to catch an early flight back to Atlanta. As they boarded the plane in Port-au-Prince, he wanted to warn her about reintegration and the hard time she could have reconciling the American way of life with what she left behind. He knew from experience, though, that no words would or could explain the pain and heartbreak she would feel. She would have to go through it, and she would know next time how to begin to steel her heart against the culture shock she'll feel just getting off the plane.

For now, though, she rested with her braided head on his shoulder and her hand in his. He wondered how something as simple as her holding his hand could possibly feel so right. He'd known for days now that he had fallen very deeply in love with her. But, they'd had that first dinner just six weeks ago. Hardly enough time for such declarations or talk of a future. Best to wait. Give her time.

As he looked out the window and watched the pavement rise up to meet the plane, then felt the pull of force as his body tried to keep going forward when the pilot applied the brakes, she sat up. He watched her as she slipped her glasses on and ran her palms over the braids in her hair before she looked at him. When her eyes met his, he felt a rush of emotion, and it took all his willpower to keep from saying the words out loud. Instead, he just cupped her face with his palm and leaned forward to give her a slow kiss as the plane came to a stop at the gate.

"Thanks for coming this week," he said as they stood and pulled bags out of the overhead compartment.

"I feel like coming back was the wrong thing to do," she admitted, putting the strap of her bag over her head so that the bag crossed her body. She started inching forward out of the plane. "I feel like I left a part of me back there in Haiti."

"Imagine how it is for my family. We do Haiti every Christmas, and then an orphanage in Ecuador every summer. I keep waiting for my grandmother to announce she's taking up permanent residence at one or the other. I think the fundraising she regularly does for the missions is what keeps her here."

She stood in front of him, and he fingered one of her dark braids. "I could get used to this look," he said, remembering the way she'd just sat and let the girls minister to her.

She put a hand on her head almost self-consciously. "When I looked in the mirror in the airport restroom back in Haiti, I didn't really recognize myself," she said with a smile. "It took so long to put in that I'm loathe to take them out. But I will soon. They're already looking a little messy."

"They'll be fine for a couple more days. I'll help you take them out if you want."

He watched her cheeks fuse with color before she looked up at him with surprise in her eyes. He immediately wanted to know what thought had crossed her mind, but didn't ask. She just said, "Thank you, Ian," very quietly.

In no time they strolled up the jetway toward the red-coated stewards directing the passengers toward US Customs. They held hands naturally, like they'd done it all their lives. They chose a line and, in a way, Ian wanted to pick the longest one. He knew real life would pick back up again on the other side of that checkpoint. Work, church obligations, more work—things that would keep them apart for good chunks of the time.

When they got to the front of the line, Calla went forward first. She handed her passport to the Customs agent. From his place several feet away, Ian watched Calla's frown as the agent stood up from his chair. Calla looked over at Ian with a worried expression on her face, but when he stepped forward, the agent held a hand out, palm up.

"Stay right there, sir."

Seconds later, two uniformed security agents approached. One took Calla by her arm and led her away. The other retrieved her bag and accepted her passport from the Customs agent. She looked over her shoulder at Ian, but the guard kept propelling her forward relentlessly.

Ian rushed to the Customs agent. "What's going on? Where are they taking her?" he demanded.

"Sir? Calm down. Hand me your passport, please," the agent directed, looking at him with measuring eyes.

As he handed over his passport and his declaration form, Ian pleaded with him. "Please. What's going on?"

The agent looked over his shoulder as a door closed behind Calla and her armed escort. Then he looked back at Ian and said, "Her passport was flagged. There was an arrest warrant for her. That's all I can tell you." He looked down at the passport and back at Ian and began the brief interview to allow him back into the country. "What was the purpose of your trip to Haiti?"

Calla sat in the cold metal chair at a dark gray metal table in a room with no color and bad lighting. Scuff marks from countless shoes broke up the monotony of the dull green floor. A mirror reflected the gray room back at her, and she wondered who, if anyone, stood on the other side watching her. A chill in the air made her want to rub her arms, but she didn't want to look defensive. She'd planned on changing clothes at the airport, and her thin cotton dress worn for the tropical climate of Haiti did little to shield her from the cold chair or the cold air.

Where was Ian? What could he possibly think of her now? All the happy, comforting, familiar relationship she'd felt until now had probably dissolved the second the officer put the handcuffs on her in the interview room outside the Customs area.

She stared at the detective sitting in front of her. He had dark hair and olive skin but spoke with a southern Georgia accent. "Miss Vaughn," he drawled, "let's go over this one more time."

Calla sat back in the metal chair and tried to not look as scared as she felt. "Sir, I don't know what else you want me to say. I know that my father's widow did this. But I don't know where she is. She called me right before Thanksgiving and said she was going to Mexico."

"Right. Mexico. That's what you said. What I'm trying to understand is that if you dislike her as much as you clearly do, why would you have let this go on for as long as you have?"

Calla took a deep breath and slowly let it out of her mouth. "I've asked myself that a hundred times a day for three years. I…" she felt her throat constricting, and she paused long enough to clear her throat and fight back tears. "I think originally it was grief over my father's death. And then, I don't know, it was almost a sense of disbelief like, surely, I was wrong about everything I was finding out. At some point, I think I adopted a victim mentality. I felt like a victim, I thought like a victim. She used it. She used me. She lorded it over me like she knew exactly how I felt and thought. And I just took it. Like some whipped dog. Does that make sense?"

He inclined his head as if to agree with her, but his lips pursed and he said, "I just don't understand, Miss Vaughn, how anyone can allow another person to put them in debt close to $60,000. And that's not even counting another $10,000 in bad checks from last week. So, I'm just trying to understand how you let this happen, and really trying to ascertain how complicit you were in the entire thing."

"I wasn't!" She slapped her hand on the table so hard the sound echoed around the room. Her voice stayed raised. "I had nothing to do with it. She started when I was fourteen years old. I live in a one-room apartment, I don't own a car, I work two jobs, and more than half of all of my income goes to service debt that she made in my name, and I have nothing. Nothing!" She took her glasses off and rubbed her eyes. "I had planned to talk to the police about her tomorrow. Seriously. I talked to my friend Sami about it before I went on my mission's trip."

He turned a page in the open file folder. "We have no record of her going to Mexico. Where would she have gone?"

"Sir," her voice sounded tired, ragged, hoarse. "I have no idea. I really don't. I don't know anything about her. I don't even know if the man that's with her is actually named Jimmy."

"Do you have an address for her?"

He'd asked these questions four other times. "I haven't seen her since the day of my father's funeral. The funeral she attended on Jimmy's arm. The funeral where she laughed about his death and sent everyone home." She hadn't said any of that out loud before, and that caused the detective to raise an eyebrow.

She wearily rubbed the back of her neck. "She called me right before Thanksgiving. She called my work extension. I can tell you the day. Maybe you can get a phone number from the phone records."

A knock on the door interrupted them. The uniformed police officer standing by the door opened it, and a youngish woman in a blue business suit walked in. She had brown hair cut to her chin and striking green eyes. "Hello. I'm Miss Vaughn's attorney. I'd like a moment with my client please," she said to the detective. He looked at her for several seconds before shutting the file folder in front of him and getting up. The men left without another word. As soon as the door shut behind him and the officer, the woman spoke to Calla as she pulled a yellow legal pad out of her bag and sat down in the metal chair across from her. "My name is Mary Ann. Sam—," she paused and corrected herself, "Ian is my cousin. He called me."

Hot tears filled her eyes for the first time since the Customs agent took her passport from her. "I don't—"

Mary Ann reached over and took her hand. "Don't worry. Okay? I need to know what's going on so I can know what we need to do. Ian didn't have any information for me."

Calla took a deep, shaky breath. "When I was fourteen, my father's wife used my identity for the first time. That was almost ten years ago. In that time, she has put me into almost $60,000 in debt. This arrest was for $10,000 in bad checks that she's written in the last couple of weeks. The checking account was in my name and was a closed account. The police think we're in cahoots."

Mary Ann rapidly made notes on her yellow legal pad. "Okay," she said. "Have you ever pressed charges? Filed a civil suit? Reported her to law enforcement at any time?"

Calla shook her head.

"Why have you not pressed charges against your stepmother? Is it because your father doesn't want you to?"

"My father died when I was twenty. But, I don't think he ever knew anything about any of it. I think she's a con artist and I think that my father was her victim. What do they call it? Her mark?"

"If that's the case, why have you never even once gone to the police?"

With a sigh, Calla answered, "I don't know. I'm sure a psychiatrist would have a field day analyzing my psyche right now. But I'll honestly tell you that my relationship with Ian made me realize that going to the police was exactly what I needed to do and I planned to go this week."

Marianne made notes. For several minutes, the sound of the scratch of her pen on the paper resonated in the otherwise silent room. Finally, she nodded. "Okay. Don't say another word unless I'm in the room with you. I'll get you out of here, and we'll talk some more."

"That's it? Will this go away?"

Marianne shut the lid to her pen and laced her fingers together, resting her hands on top of her notepad. "I think that, eventually, we can prove you were not complicit. As long as you're not hiding material merchandise or something like that. No expensive trips or lifestyle. I think if we can find out if the stepmother has a past, maybe charges pending in another state or something, it will go further toward proving your innocence. Your lack of pursuing legal matters might have something to do with your stepmother being someone in authority, and then you having a victim mindset. It's hard to say what the D.A. will accept as fact. But we'll give him everything and then see what happens. I know him. He's fair, and he's not going to pursue charges if there's nothing substantial there."

Tears poured out of Calla's eyes. "I can't pay you."

Marianne reached over and covered her hand with her own. "Actually, we can work it out but that's something we'll worry about much later. One thing at a time." She stood up and said, "Right now. I'll go up and see about getting you released."

CHAPTER 8

Ian sat with his back to the arm of the couch and looked at Calla. In the two weeks since he'd seen her last, she'd taken the braids out of her hair and the tan she'd gotten while in Haiti had faded. She had dark circles under her eyes, and her cheeks looked sallow, as if she had lost weight.

He'd come here because Al thought talking to her face-to-face would help him. But, as he stared at her, he found himself growing angry as the hurt tried to infiltrate his heart again.

She'd let him in then sat on the other end of the couch, legs pulled up to her chest, tears sliding down her cheeks. It took a lot not to reach out to her and try to comfort her. He reminded himself of the two weeks of silence and unanswered texts and phone calls.

She didn't speak, so he finally broke the silence. "At what point were you going to tell me what was going on with you?"

Calla rested her temple against her knees as she turned her head to look at him. "I'd promised myself after Christmas. I wanted to press charges against her before I told you about it. Plus, I had a feeling you wouldn't want to be with me anymore, and I didn't want to spoil your holiday."

He took a deep breath through his nose and slowly closed his eyes. "Well, having you arrested at the airport was probably better than just telling me the truth. I can see that."

The sound of her breath hitching made him open his eyes

again. "Obviously, I didn't know…"

"Right. Because if there was a chance you might be arrested upon your return to American soil, why you might have just considered staying in Haiti? Like you told me you wanted to do?" He surged to his feet and walked across the carpet, feeling like a caged animal in the small room. "I asked you, Calla, flat-out why you quit culinary school. That first week of our relationship, I gave you an opportunity to be honest with me."

"On our way to your family's Thanksgiving dinner!" She ripped her glasses off her face and threw them on the coffee table, then dug her palms into her eyes. "How am I supposed to start that conversation, huh? 'Sorry, Ian. You probably don't want to continue to see me because my stepmother is a con artist—wanted in three states it turns out—and she has destroyed my name and credit to the tune of tens of thousands of dollars.' Yeah, you would have helped me pack up those pies and taken me right on over to grandma's house."

Rage burned behind his eyes and he spoke without thinking. "So, you just bring me in deeper, make me fall in love with you, and then what? I bail you out? Write a big fat check, and you're in the clear? Taking your cues from your stepmom now?"

As soon as he spoke the words, he knew he didn't believe them. He opened his mouth to retract them, but Calla gasped and surged to her feet. "Get out!" She raced across the room and threw the deadbolt on her door. "Get out of my house. Get out of my life."

Immediately, the rage dissipated, like air from a balloon. His shoulders slumped forward. "I'm sorry, Calla. That was—"

"That was exactly what you think of me. Get out. Leave. Just go. I'll find another job, so you don't have to worry about running into me anymore."

She opened the door and crossed her arms over her chest. For the first time since he walked into her apartment, no tears fell from her eyes. Resigned, he walked to the door but stopped in front of her. "Calla, I didn't mean that. I'm sorry."

She stared at the ground and didn't say a word, so he finally walked out the door. He went to his car and slipped into the driver's seat, but didn't start it. Instead, he lay his head back against the headrest of the seat and closed his eyes. That was a mistake, because every time he closed his eyes for the last two weeks, he saw Calla in handcuffs getting escorted out of the airport by two police officers.

Just as he started to reach for the ignition, his phone vibrated. Seeing Mary Anne's number, he answered. "Hey, there, Mary Ann."

"Hello, Samuel." No member of his family ever called him Ian. "I just got off the phone with Calla. I wanted to let you know that the D.A. isn't going to indict her. Now, she and I can go to work clearing her credit and getting her life back."

He clenched his teeth. "Thank you. Thank you for all you've done. That's great news, Mary Ann. Definitely an answer to prayer."

"Amen." She paused before continuing, "This wasn't her fault, you know."

He heaved a heavy sigh. "I know." A flood of emotion had him closing his eyes. "I don't think it's her fault. I just think she should have told me about it before she got arrested."

"It's not easy for a woman to admit to being a victim. We females don't want to appear weak or needy."

He cleared his throat. "I get that, but I think it becomes a matter of trust at some point. And, I don't think that I can have feelings for someone who doesn't trust me. I have to go. I love you." He hung up the phone before she could reply, and started his car.

Sami scooted closer to Calla in the pew. They looked at the front of the church and not at each other.

"It's finally over," Calla whispered.

"This is good, right?" Sami reached over and took Calla's

hand. "We've been praying that it would be over. Why are we sad?" Calla bowed her head. Her body shook with emotion, and Sami squeezed her hand. "I'm sorry that it had to be an arrest, honey, but honestly, you needed a catalyst to make her stop, to make it go away. I think this was honestly the answer to your prayers. You're free now."

She was free. Mary Ann worked on clearing her credit, writing letters and sending documentation. She planned to go back to school in the fall. And yet, instead of relief and joy, she kept hearing Ian's words from last week. "Ian thinks I was with him so he could clear my debt."

Sami let go of her hand and turned to face her fully. "No, he doesn't." She spoke firmly, with conviction in the simple three words.

Calla shrugged with one shoulder. "He said it himself." Sami didn't speak, so Calla raised her head and looked at her. She had a shocked look on her face. "I could have taken him breaking up with me because I wasn't honest and I was hiding what happened. But to have him say that I made him fall in love with me so that he would write me one big check was horrible. I just—" her breath hitched as she stopped talking. She was so tired of the negative feelings, the tears, the despair.

She surged to her feet and reached behind her to pick her Bible and purse up off the pew. Services had ended more than forty minutes ago. As she left the sanctuary and entered the annex, Sami ran up behind her. "Wait!"

She paused and looked at her best friend. "I just need to work everything out in my head, Sami. I'll be okay. I promise." She hugged her friend. "Thank you."

Sami looped her arm through Calla's as they walked through the church doors. Calla paused and made sure the door locked behind them and slipped a crocheted cap onto her head. Cold January wind blew straight at them, and Calla pulled her wool coat closer around her. Sami gestured at her lone car in the parking lot. "Want a ride?"

Calla considered it, then shook her head. "No. But thanks. I'm going to go get something to eat. I haven't eaten since yesterday."

"Okay. I want to say something." She slipped her hands into the pockets of her fuchsia trench coat and looked up at the sky. "I feel like what you and Ian had was real. I feel like he was really hurt by you not being honest with him and he must have lashed out to say such a fool thing as that. I think you need to consider forgiving him and letting him know that you have." She spoke quickly, saying it all in one breath.

Calla felt a stirring of annoyance at her friend. "I appreciate your honesty. I'll see you tomorrow." She hugged her and turned to walk away without saying anything else.

The cold wind blew into her back, making her rush forward down the sidewalk. A couple blocks away, she pushed into a restaurant and paused for a moment in the warm air while she waited for her glasses to defog. She pulled the hat off her head, and the smells immediately made her realize she'd come to the restaurant where she and Ian had met every Sunday after church throughout their short courtship.

She contemplated leaving, but thinking of the cold wind and the warm interior, she decided to stay. With a smile, she walked toward the hostess stand.

"Hi! Haven't seen you in a couple of weeks," the hostess greeted.

Suddenly missing Ian, she nodded. "I went out of the country for Christmas."

"Well, hon, I hope you had a great time. Your young man is here. Been here about fifteen minutes, I think."

Her stomach fell but, despite the apprehension, she put one foot in front of the other and walked into the restaurant. She spotted Ian at the window table where they always sat. He had a cup of coffee in front of him and stared out of the window.

She slipped into the chair across from him before speaking. "Hi."

Immediately, he whipped his head around, and his eyes widened when he saw her. "Calla!" His head turned to look out the window before looking at her again. "I was watching for you."

Surprised, she said, "What?"

"I knew you'd walk past here on your way home." He straightened the coffee cup so the handle was perfectly perpendicular to the line of the table. "I, uh, planned to persuade you to come eat with me."

She looked at her watch. "If you've been here long enough for that coffee to be cold, you must have skipped church."

He looked down then back at her. "I was at your church this morning. I wanted to approach you there, but…"

Calla waited then raised an eyebrow. "But?"

He cleared his throat. "But I noticed that you were praying and saw Sami with you. Didn't seem right to intrude."

She felt the broken halves of her heart start to come back together. Ian cared enough about her to not interrupt a time of prayer and meditation. The consideration he'd shown her, that he'd almost always shown her, humbled her. "I see."

"I was about to leave and go to your apartment. When I didn't see you walk by, I thought maybe she'd given you a ride home."

"No. I just stayed for a while." The waitress approached, and Calla ordered food even though she didn't feel hungry. "Do you have something like a beef soup?"

"We have a vegetable beef. It's terrific."

"I'll take a cup. With a roll and some water. Thanks."

The waitress looked at Ian. "You, hon?"

"I'm good with just the coffee. Thanks."

Calla sat back as the waitress left and intentionally kept herself from crossing her arms defensively. "So," she began, toying with the bundle of silverware wrapped in a blue cloth napkin, "you were at my church, and then you were going to come to my apartment? What for, Ian?"

He looked at the coffee in his cup for a long time before looking at her. His eyes looked dull gray-green and red-rimmed with dark circles underneath. Finally, he said, "I sincerely apologize for speaking to you that way. I've spent the last week trying to figure out how to word it so that you would believe me, but all I can say is that I'm sorry."

The waitress brought the water, and Calla asked her, "Can I get some hot tea, too?"

"Sure thing, hon." She looked at Ian. "Want a warm up?"

He didn't speak, but he shook his head and kept his eyes on Calla. When she left, he said, "I don't know why I said what I did, but I didn't mean it, and I don't believe it. I was just really mad at you, I think."

Calla slowly ripped the paper covering off of her straw then tore it into tiny pieces. Using the tip of her finger, she brushed all the pieces into a pile on her placemat. "I knew I should treasure every moment I spent with you because once you found out what had happened to me, you'd not want to be with me anymore."

Ian let out a long sigh. "Calla, you've said that before. But, the truth is, I want to be with you. What hurt me more than anything was that you didn't trust me with the truth."

"Not trust you? It wasn't a lack of trust, Ian. It was a lack of confidence. Confidence in who I am, confidence in who I could be to you. I was embarrassed. No. Not embarrassed." She thought about it. "I was ashamed."

"Ashamed?" He reached forward and took her hand. "Why?"

She stared at their joined hands. "I had spent the last three years paying twenty thousand dollars off of debt that wasn't mine, and prayed daily that she would just die so I didn't have to do it anymore. That day you came and found me crying, she'd just called me to brag about getting a new credit card in my name. I should have recorded the phone call and called the police right then. But I didn't do anything. Except feel sorry for myself and cry."

"Calla—"

She held up a hand to cut off what whatever he planned to say and raised her head to look at him. "I know. Intellectually, I know a lot of things that I'm not able to emotionally face." She took a sip of the water and said without thinking, "Sami said I need to forgive you for saying that to me."

He squeezed her hand and let it go, sitting back so the waitress could bring her soup and tea. She set the heavy soup mug in front of her, made sure she didn't need anything else, then walked away. Calla didn't pick up her spoon. "That wasn't really what I thought. I was just angry and hurt," he admitted, "I'd really appreciate your forgiveness, but I'm not expecting it."

She used the round soup spoon to stir the soup, leaning in to smell the richness of the broth. "I don't think I need to forgive you." At his raised eyebrow, she explained, "I don't think you're the problem. She is. I need to forgive her. I need to forgive her, and I need to learn just what's broken inside of me that allowed me to roll over and let her do what she did since I was a teenager, to just take it and keep taking it the whole time." She dropped the spoon and sat back. "I worked eighty hours a week for two years so I could pay for her thievery, and it was done with such passiveness that the police actually thought I was her partner."

She pushed the soup away, unwilling to risk trying to eat right now. "Why did you use the word broken?" Ian asked.

"What?"

"You said something was broken inside of you. Why did you use that word?"

In her mind, she pictured herself, fractured, colorless, in a gray room without windows. "Isn't that what it is? Whole people don't let someone do that to them without fighting back or at least standing up for themselves, right?"

He sat back, resting his elbows on the arms of the chair and lacing his fingers together. "Hard to say. She catapulted off of your grief. You were an orphan, and she was supposed to have been someone who loved your father."

"Maybe." She considered her father. "But I should have been

strong enough to defend him and his memory. Instead, I just—"
She cleared her throat. "I need to go."

As she pushed away from the table, he stood with her. "Please
stay and talk to me."

She knew if she stepped forward, he would put his arms
around her. Instead, she stepped backward, retrieving her coat from
the back of her chair. "I don't think I can, right now." She slipped
her coat on and pulled her hat out of her pocket. "I appreciate you
wanting to defend me and champion me in my circumstances. But,
I'm realistically looking at it and don't agree with you. I need to
work on me. I need to let God work on me. And I really think I
need to do that without the distraction of you trying to work on
me." She slipped her purse strap over her head, letting the strap fall
across her body. "Goodbye, Ian."

Halfway across the room, she heard him call her name, but
she did not stop. "Calla!"

Calla laughed as she chased a soccer ball down the dirt
hill. She grabbed it just before it rolled into a thorny brush and held
it on her hip as she climbed back up the hill. A group of teenagers
waited for her, jabbering to each other in Creole. Calla tossed them
the ball and pantomimed to let them know she needed to get a
drink of water.

For five months, she'd worked at the little island orphanage in
Haiti. She arrived in late February, free from any legal issues and
ready to pay Mary Ann back in the most expedient way she could,
with her talents and skills. She worked hard cooking for the
orphanage, taking local produce and meats and learning from the
Haitian cook how to turn them into nutritious meals for the twenty-
two children and six adults they fed daily. She'd learned how to
operate in a kitchen that had only generator powered electricity,
using only products she could obtain regionally. She learned how
to prepare foods the kids knew instead of the gourmet fare she'd
studied years ago in school. And every day, she'd healed and
grown until she could think back to the last four years of her life

without feeling persistent pain in her stomach or sharp shame in her heart.

She'd prayed, studied her Bible, prayed, worshiped, prayed, and cooked. The hurricane season had come, and she'd survived a strong category four storm that knocked the school flat and destroyed the generator, leaving them without power for three weeks and a day.

When she had good Internet, she downloaded work projects then transcribed videos and movies and uploaded the finished captions. She made more than enough income to support herself here. Now she faced the end of her time in this beautiful place. She'd received her acceptance back into culinary school. She would start classes in August. It took her a full week to decide that she needed to go back to the United States. Leaving this place behind would hurt. She lessened the pain by promising herself she'd come back again.

She stepped onto the porch and grabbed a bag of water, ripping the corner off with her teeth and drinking all five ounces of the water with three long swallows.

"You're getting better at that game," Hettie Jones remarked from her plastic chair. "One day they might not smear you all over the field."

Calla laughed. "I doubt it, but thanks for the vote of confidence." She looked at her watch. "I should finish getting packed. The truck will be here soon."

Hettie frowned. "I wish you could stay through July. School doesn't start for you until mid-August."

"I need to get settled in Atlanta," Calla said. "It's going to take me some time to reintegrate. I don't want to start school right after coming back. It's going to be hard enough."

"I know. I'm just being selfish. I get to do that sometimes." She stood and hugged her. "I have enjoyed getting to know you better. I hope you come back."

"You would have to try hard to keep me away." She went into the building and walked through the common area to the room she shared with another staff member. She had packed almost everything. Now she added her toothbrush and her laptop. As she zipped the bag closed, she heard the truck pull into the yard.

Taking one last look around the room, at the two cots shrouded with mosquito netting, the small mirror hanging by a rusty nail above a wash basin, and the narrow closet the two women shared, she felt a sense of sorrow at leaving. She had known though, that God brought her here for a short time, not forever. Whatever He had planned for her next waited in Atlanta, not here. Still, she looked forward to returning as soon as possible.

Heaving a sigh, she slung her backpack over one shoulder by a single strap then picked up her duffle bag and walked out of the room, back through the common area, and out onto the porch. She expected to see Emmanuel Danos chatting with his Hettie about their upcoming Christmas wedding as they unloaded supplies he'd picked up at the mainland. She did not expect to see Ian Jones lifting a fifty-pound bag of cornmeal out of the back of the truck.

She resisted the urge to duck back inside the building. Instead, she set her bags down like she originally intended to do and walked over to the truck to help unload.

"Hi, Ian," she greeted as he turned, slinging the heavy bag up onto his shoulder.

He stopped moving and stared at her, from her braided hair to her leather sandals. "Sounds like I almost missed you," he said by way of greeting, banishing any thought that he didn't know about her presence here for the last several months.

"A day later and you would have." She felt nerves, familiar nerves, like the kind that had assaulted her the first time she cooked dinner for him.

They unloaded the truck in silence with Hettie and Emmanuel. A million things she wanted to say to him ran through her mind, but she couldn't find the right opening, so she just lifted, carried, and stacked bags and boxes in the storeroom. Once they had emptied the truck, Ian collected her bags from the porch and put her tote bag into the bed and her backpack into the cab of the truck. Calla hugged Hettie, tight. "I can't wait until next time," she said.

"Looking forward to it. Next time I'm in Atlanta, I hope to be able to experience what you do with your own ingredients in a modern kitchen. You've been an amazing help here, and we will miss you like you can't even know."

She turned toward Ian and extended her hand. "I'd love to stay and spend time with you, but I can't."

He smiled a half smile and shook her hand perfunctorily. "I know." He turned to Emmanuel and said something in Creole. The men shook hands warmly, and Emmanuel tossed Ian the keys. Emmanuel waved at Calla and put his arm over Hettie's shoulders, leading her into the building.

Calla frowned as Ian turned to her. "Ready?"

"For?"

"To leave." He walked to the truck and climbed into the driver's seat. Calla began to understand that he would drive her to the ferry. It took her several minutes to get to the truck, though, because as she walked forward, the children surrounded her. She took the time to speak to each one, hug everyone, and make a personal connection with every child. By the time she disengaged from them, she had tears pouring down her face. How could she leave?

Knowing she must, she slipped into the passenger's seat. Ian started the truck, and she shifted her backpack to rest behind the seat as she snapped her seatbelt into place. "This is harder than I thought."

"Every time." He slowly drove down the dirt lane, carefully avoiding potholes. "I spent a year here in between high school and college. I'm still not sure how I managed to leave willingly."

The truck bounced over a rut, so he slowed down even more. "You're not supposed to be here," she finally said. "It's July."

He spared her a quick but serious glance. "I wanted to see you. I didn't want to wait anymore. I had no idea you'd leave so soon."

He wanted to see her? Her heart started pounding, and she licked dry lips. "I..." She looked out the window and watched the island jungle crawl slowly by as Ian navigated over the lava rock path.

"You wish I'd never come." The truck jostled roughly, and he hit the brakes, stopping it entirely. He turned his body toward her. "If you didn't want to have anything at all to do with me, you would have found another place to work, another orphanage, another mission, another country even. The fact is, you needed the connection with my family."

"Leaving engineering behind to become a shrink?" She crossed her arms over her chest. Not because she wanted to shield herself from him, but because she knew he spoke the truth and it made her feel defensive. "I'm here because I spent the last five months paying Mary Ann back for her brilliant legal services. That was our deal. She represented me and will continue to fight collection agencies and credit reporting agencies, and I cook for Hettie and Emmanuel. So what?"

"So what is I'm here. That's what," He lay his arm over the steering wheel and his other arm over the back of the seat, boxing her in. She wanted to reach forward and touch him, but kept her arms tight around her chest. "And I've missed you. This month is the eight-month anniversary of the day you sent me flowers—the day I began the journey of falling in love with you." Her breath hitched, and she opened her mouth to speak, but no words came out. He'd mentioned love twice now. "Don't you tell me that wasn't God's providence. You and I both know otherwise."

She unbuckled the seatbelt and leaned back against the door, pulling her legs up. Her forehead fell forward and rested on her knees. "I know," she whispered. "I needed to come here. I needed to get close to God and work my way through the years since my father died. I had to come to a place of forgiveness for Becky, or whatever her real name is, and I had to mean it. I didn't want it to be a hollow promise because God would know the difference."

Several seconds went by in silence. She raised her head and found him staring at her, his hazel eyes serious and searching. Finally, he said, "And me?"

"Ian, I don't know about you, or us. I wanted to talk to you when I got home, but I didn't even think you'd want to see me. I need to get home and figure things out."

He started the truck again and slowly inched forward. She straightened in the seat and latched her seatbelt. After a few seconds, he said, "I appreciate that, but I feel like that's what you've been doing, here. I took off work and made a two-day trip to see you. I've given you space, and I've given you time. I honestly don't know how much more space and time I'm willing to give you."

She sat in silence for several minutes and finally said, "I respect that. Thanks for your honesty."

They didn't speak again until they finished the descent down the mountain and pulled onto the coastal road. Too soon, he pulled into the parking lot for the ferry.

"Pastor Jeremy Banks will meet you at the ferry," he said, opening the driver's door. She slipped out of the truck and reached back into the cab to get her backpack. "He's made arrangements for you to stay at the mission in Port-au-Prince overnight, and he'll give you a ride to the airport tomorrow."

He handed her the tote bag. She set it on the ground and stepped closer to him, putting her arms around him. She could feel his hesitation before he hugged her back. "I miss you," she said quietly. "Thank you for the ride."

"Bye, Calla." She picked up her tote and walked to the ferry, unwilling to look behind her.

CHAPTER 9

C alla **heard her alarm going** off, but tried to bury under the covers and ignore it. No luck. Ignoring it didn't make it stop.

As she sat up, she grabbed her phone and turned the alarm off. 5:32. Had she seriously managed to ignore it for two whole minutes?

It didn't take long to throw on a pair of jeans and a long-sleeved T-shirt. She went into the bathroom and washed her face, leaning close to the mirror to stare into her own eyes as she dried her skin. She'd stayed up late studying and her red-rimmed eyes showed it. This fatigue, though, compared to the fatigue she'd felt a year ago, felt good, productive, like she could look forward to a good end after all of her hard work.

She braided her hair into a tight plait, then walked back through her bedroom, scooping her glasses off of the dresser and slipping them on her face. In the living room, she went to her desk and pulled the stack of papers off her printer, then punched holes in them to put them in her binder. Today, she had an exam, and she knew that the chef would check the binders to make sure that they contained all of the recipes, properly written, neatly typed with clear instructions.

While she sat on the couch to tie her shoes, she mentally went through the lessons the day before and the recipes she'd typed up.

They'd served a venison medallion with three different purees: chestnut, carrot, and celery root. She'd fallen in love with the chestnut puree, and so very much wanted to take the time to perfect it in her home kitchen. Maybe she could do something at Thanksgiving with it.

Thoughts of Thanksgiving immediately brought Ian to mind. She thought about how relaxed and happy he'd been, sitting at Annabelle's table while she got to know his family. Her stomach fluttered with nerves at the thought of him. She'd wanted to call him for weeks now. Why did she keep hesitating? Fear of rejection?

She sat back against the cushions and closed her eyes, leaning her head back until it rested on the back of the couch. She had regretted leaving Ian in Haiti the moment she stepped onto the deck of the ferry. It had taken all of her will to not turn around and go back to the island and beg his forgiveness for doubting herself for even a moment. Yet, despite regrets, she constantly felt like she truly had needed to leave. She needed to discover the true Calla Vaughn.

She'd worn the hats of an adored child of a single parent, a despised step-daughter, an exhausted culinary student working her way through her first year as an independent adult, a grieving orphan, and a victim of a con artist who currently faced charges in three states. She'd never had an opportunity to live, on her own, without suffocating under grief or fear. It felt like God-given wisdom to allow herself to take time alone, back in familiar surroundings, older and much wiser.

It didn't take long for her to realize that the Calla she knew still existed—only this Calla had much more confidence and faith. She should have called Ian right away, but had just not. Why?

Had God kept her from reaching out? How many times had she walked past his church on a Sunday morning, wanting to go in and slide into the chair next to him? How often had she considered just ringing his doorbell? Despite this constant wanting to contact him, she had always pulled back.

This morning, though, more than ever, she felt a pull to call him. "God," she said softly, "this is the part where I need to hear Your voice. I need to know what to do next."

Her phone vibrated and she saw the notice for her daily Bible thought that came at 5:45 every day. Today's verse said:

And no one puts new wine into old wineskins; or else the new wine will burst the wineskins and be spilled, and the wineskins will be ruined. But new wine must be put into new wineskins, and both are preserved. Luke 5:37-38

Pursing her lips, she considered the words. An answer to prayer, or was she reading into it?

As she gathered her knife bag and put her binder and clean uniform into her backpack, she thought about the verse. What did it mean? What could it mean to her in this present circumstance?

She lived just a few blocks from the school, so she walked in the predawn darkness along the quiet street, meditating about Ian. The few weeks they spent as a couple, they received constant affirmation from people around them—Christians and non-Christians alike. Despite age differences, background differences, and other things, they had made a good couple, a strong couple, a mission-minded couple with a love for people and God. How could anyone consider that a bad thing?

But she'd waited so long. Should she have stayed in Haiti with him, or begged him to come back with her?

No. No time for regrets. Right now, she faced a new start. She had long considered this school year the beginning of the beginning.

"In the beginning, Calla shed her insecurities and fear and stepped boldly forward to accomplish her goals and dreams." She'd said that out loud as she walked out of the Atlanta airport in late July, fresh from her time in Haiti. And, she'd meant it. She said it again this morning to remind herself of her forward motion.

No insecurities or fears.

She entered the side door of the school and nodded to fellow culinary students. In the locker room, she put on her uniform and wrapped a hot-pink bandana around her head. She spent the next hour and a half prepping the chef's *mis en place* for the coming lesson, peeling head after head of garlic, chopping shallots, and gathering supplies and equipment from the commissary. The entire time she worked, she kept saying that Bible verse over and over again in her head. *But new wine must be put into new wineskins, and both are preserved.*

Hours later, after serving the head of the school a medallion of lamb served with roasted Brussels sprouts and a potato dish called *pommes roesti*, she joined the other students outside at the picnic tables. Despite the hot sun, the wind picked up and blew cool air. Calla quickly moved her plate out of the shade and into full sun, taking another small bite and analyzing the sauce she'd put on the lamb. An oak leaf floated past her plate, reminding her again of Ian, of autumn, of the time they'd spent through Christmas.

She'd kept in touch with Mary Ann, hoping that the attorney would pass along her new address and her new phone number. She knew he knew she was at school right there in Atlanta. However, she'd heard nothing from him. She'd hoped that he might reach out to her just one more time, even though the two prior times he had, she'd turned him away. While she hadn't flat out rejected him, she had asked him to wait until she was ready. He'd told her very point blank that he didn't know how long he could wait. Now she worried too much time had gone by, and what stretched between them now was a chasm that she didn't know if she had the strength or the tools to cross.

A chasm that he may not want her to cross.

She had to consider that he might have closed his mind and heart to her forever. She also had to consider that he might have found someone else by now. If it was true, then she only had herself to blame. Accepting that didn't make the thought any easier to bear, didn't make the ache in her heart at the thought lessen in any way. But, the idea of him fully rejecting her hurt worse with a pain that seared through her heart and deep into her soul.

That was what kept her from reaching out. However, the longer she gave into that hesitation, that insecurity, the more likely an outcome that ended in Ian turning her away. Every minute she held herself back was a minute lost to them together. She could see that and hated the reluctance born of an insecure persona she purposefully shed months ago. Stepping forward boldly—she intentionally used those words to strengthen her resolve in everything in life. So why hesitate now?

She mulled that question over as she pushed her plate away. She only hesitated out of fear. She would not stand for that. Time to span that chasm.

Knowing full well that she must contact him, she thought about how to go about doing just that. If she called, would he answer the phone? If she rang his doorbell, would he open the door to her? She thought about the first time he came to her home for dinner, about the administrative mistake at a flower shop that brought them together—that they both believed that God used to bring them together. What would he do if a bouquet of flowers walked through his doorway with a note on them asking him to dinner?

She gasped out loud, then looked around to see if anyone noticed. Should she? What if—

What if she sent him flowers and he ignored her? What if he didn't, though? What if he felt a nostalgic pull to the idea of her stepping boldly out in faith and restarting their relationship, or even the possibility of restarting their relationship?

Doing something so fantastically crazy might be exactly what he needed her to do. It would give him time alone to process the idea of her invitation, without the pressure of her standing in front of him or waiting for a word form him on the other end of the telephone. He could think about it, pray about it, and determine if he had the desire in his heart to accept the hand she reached out to him letting him know that she wanted to be with him, that she wanted a reset.

He could choose to toss the flowers into the trash and ignore the invite, but he could also choose to accept at the invitation and show up with their future in his hands.

Giving in to the impulse, she pulled her phone out of her pocket and looked up the number for Crossroads Florists. Calling the toll-free number, she turned so that her back was to her fellow students.

"Out of the Blue Bouquet," a woman with a very happy and pleasant voice said, "this is Brooke. How may I help you?"

Calla's stomach nervously twisted. "Hi. Didn't I call Crossroads?"

"Yes, ma'am. You sure did. How can I help you?"

Calla cleared her throat, "I, uh, sent flowers a year ago today. Could, um, could you maybe look them up and re-send the same bouquet?"

She could hear the clicking of keys on the keyboard as Brooke answered her. "Absolutely. Let's see if we can find you. What phone number would those have been ordered under?"

Ian tossed the pencil down and closed his eyes, rolling his head on his neck. He couldn't concentrate, and he grew steadily impatient with it all. Before Calla, he could always shut out the world and just work. Not anymore. For months now, he had to battle thoughts of dark brown eyes.

Last week, the long Georgia summer had finally released the reins of sunshine and the air reluctantly started cooling down. With a cold wind, the leaves began falling from trees. Immediately, he thought of Calla Vaughn and her mustard-colored scarf and earth brown boots.

He wondered if she'd settled back into the student routine at the culinary school. He wondered what her days looked like and what her heart felt like and whether she had worked her way through all the stuff going on in her brain that kept her from just allowing something good to happen in her life. He felt impatient, and a little bit angry, but mostly just done with waiting.

No one would ever know how often he drove past the school, hoping for a chance meeting. He'd watched with rapt attention at a bid that Dixon Brothers put in to build a new building for the college. When they didn't get it, he felt personally affected. Now, he stared down the unsatisfying time of the coming week before Thanksgiving and realized that he had a season full of memories to experience and get past so he could hopefully start to get over her.

He heard the knock on his door and looked at his watch. Penny wasn't due back from lunch for another fifteen minutes. "Come in," he called, not moving from his perch at his drafting table.

When a large bouquet of flowers in the colors of fall came through his door, his stomach fell, and he immediately got up to intercept them.

"Let me," he said, relieving them from the teenager's arms.

"Delivery for Ian Jones," the boy said.

"Thanks," Ian replied, quickly setting the flowers on his desk and digging through the fall colored blooms to find the card.

"Happy Thanksgiving," the boy said as he ducked out of the office.

Ian retrieved the note from the plastic prongs, his heart racing.

DINNER AT 6:30 TONIGHT. MY PLACE. WON'T TAKE NO. CALLA

He read her new address, recognizing a street close to the school. He hadn't bothered to look up her new address upon his return from Haiti. Mary Ann had informed him that Calla had moved but Ian hadn't asked to where and she hadn't volunteered the information. He suspected Mary Ann just wanted him to know she had Calla's new address in the event Ian ever wanted to look her up again. Fine and good, but in the nearly four months since Calla had returned to Atlanta, Ian had not wanted to see her, and she had not made any effort to reach out to him.

Until today.

Almost like one of those sappy climactic scenes in a romantic movie where the guy flashes back to the pivotal moments he and the heroine have shared, a private movie played out in his memory. He remembered the first time he really took notice of her that day they shared the elevator after her car died. He remembered the way she moved as she hummed and danced in the filing room. He remembered her cheeks blushing the first time they held hands which happened to also be the first time they prayed together, asking God to bless their first shared meal. He remembered the taste of that first meal and he could not erase the image of her chocolate eyes or her uncensored smile.

He remembered how she loved on every single child at the orphanage. He watched as her heart nearly broke leaving Haiti behind when returning from that first mission trip. He imagined just how she would pour love and nurturing care into her own children one day.

He remembered the way she smelled when they hugged. He remembered the first time he had kissed her, the feel of her soft lips beneath his, and the scent of homemade apple pie when the kiss ended.

He also remembered her shocked pale face as she was introduced to handcuffs at the Atlanta airport. In that moment more than any other, he felt a giant fracture crack through any future plans that may have involved her. Up until that moment, his plans involved flirting with her and courting her in a way far superior to any other men who may have come into her life before. He never had any idea he might end up forking over bail money or writing out a sworn statement for the Superior Court. He never could have imagined courting Calla might involve actual courts of law.

He remembered her angry, defensive words as she tried to justify her deception. Shamefully, he also remembered his own angry words, and wished for the hundredth time he had never spoken them into the world. He remembered asking for her forgiveness, trying to mend fences. He had hoped she would see the sincerity in his heart and lean on him and his strength. He had hoped they could continue to build on their relationship and rebuild the trust. Instead, she had left him cooling his heels. She fled to Haiti for five months, which may as well have been a lifetime on the moon.

He had reached out to her so many times, only to get silence or some blow off response. He had decided that when he went to Haiti weeks early so they could have some one-on-one time to see what, if anything, could happen next between them, that would be the end of it. One way or another, he would know if they had a future before he came back home. If anything, the way Calla left things between them the last time he saw her should have decided it once and for all.

So, what was the deal with this invitation? The flowers? The won't take no for an answer when all she had given him for nearly a year now was no kind of answer at all? Did she think he was some kind of safety net? Come over and play boyfriend but only when it was convenient?

Or did he dare hope she might have really changed? Had she come to some kind of realization after all this time? At this point, with so much water under the bridge, could they have a future? Was this her idea of a let's settle this thing once-and-for-all like Haiti had been for him?

If so, did she deserve one more chance? Or not. Won't take no? What if he just went home and forgot all about Calla Vaughn? What then? Would his life finally resume without visions of chocolate brown eyes constantly distracting him?

As he tossed the card on the desk, his door opened again, and Al came striding in. "You up for some lunch?" He stopped when he saw the flowers on the desk. "I'm feeling a bit of a déjà vu."

"Yeah. Me, too." Ian ran a finger over the petal of a mum. "The only real question is, do I go or not?"

"I think you know the answer to that, brother." Al slapped him on the back of his shoulders. "I think all of us in your life right now pray that you go and that things get worked out one way or the other."

"What does that mean?"

"That means our dinner plans are officially canceled, and I'll see you tomorrow."

Ian took a deep breath. "I don't think so, man."

Al crossed his arms. "What does that mean?"

Ian shrugged. "I don't think I'm willing to go, to open back up."

Al sat on the stool at Ian's drafting table. "Let me tell you something, brother. I know her lack of trust hurt you. I get that from here to tomorrow. But, I also respect the fact that she very openly told you about her need to find out who she really is before she could be with you. She didn't ask for five years, and she didn't even wait six months. You ask me? I think this is a good thing."

Knowing that Al had suffered a broken heart made him narrow his eyes. "You say that knowing how it feels…" his voice trailed off, unable or unwilling to delve into the intricacies of Al's tumultuous relationship with his sister.

"How it feels to have my heart cut out of my chest?" Al barked a short, humorless laugh. "Yeah, bro. I am. You and Calla, man, you two fit. I think you just need to let last year go and start fresh, you know. Begin again, with all the hurt and pain and angst that has driven you into the ground since the New Year just gone, not to return."

Ian unconsciously mimicked Al by crossing his arms. "A fresh start, huh?"

Al walked across the office and pulled the chair out from Ian's drafting table. He rotated it around and straddled it, resting his arms across the back of the chair. "Sometimes you have to forgive and forget. Start over. Think about this, man. What if…?"

Ian waited but Al didn't finish the sentence. After a few seconds he looked up to meet his friend's gaze. The look in Al's eye made it clear that he was about to ask something he felt was important. Al nodded. "What if God made her for you and made you for her? You still up for standing her up then?"

Ian's gaze fell and he studied the toes of his shoes. "I thought that before, you know. That first time we went to Haiti? How she was with the kids? I thought to myself, this is the one for me. I praised God that he could make someone so beautiful and kind and all I had to do was make her mine." He smiled at the memory. "Then we came back from Haiti and everything changed."

"Well," Al chuckled. "Every relationship has its ups and downs."

"Funny." Ian didn't laugh.

"Oh, so you think you're some prize? Brother, let me just drop a few truth bombs on you. You have momma and daddy issues a mile high from losing your folks so young. You're moody. You can get way too focused on things. And you're just a little bit judgmental of the blue-collar types in that oh-so-special old money kind of way. Did you know that?"

"That's raw, man."

"Hey, I love you. But you have to know you have your own baggage, too. This girl was terrorized by her stepmother. She didn't have a rich grandmother to take her in." Al held up a halting hand when he saw Ian tense up, realizing he was dancing on a line he didn't want to cross. "The point is that she's reaching out to you, now. Something made her do that. Maybe she just feels sorry for you, I don't know. Or maybe God has been working on her, too. A lot of people have been praying for her."

Ian thought about that. Could he possibly forgive and forget like nothing had happened? Did he want to? "That's what I need to do."

"What? Go to dinner?"

Ian grinned a toothless grin. "Maybe. But right now, I need to pray. I need to ask God to speak to my heart." He looked up and met Al's eyes. "Pray with me?"

"Thought you'd never ask."

"Are you sure about this?" Sami asked. She stood in the middle of Calla's apartment wearing a maroon jumper miniskirt over a blouse covered in gold and maroon cartoon turkeys. She had a beanie cap perched on the back of her head and ankle-high black boots. "He's not the same person he was a year ago."

"Neither am I." Calla spread the tablecloth over her little round table and brushed her hand across the top, smoothing out a wrinkle here and a fold there. She'd hoped that the tablecloth she'd used on the card table almost precisely a year ago would fit on her table. It almost did, well enough to use it.

"No. You've really gained some confidence I've never seen before. I like it."

They set out chargers, plates, and napkins secured with sunflower rings. When the table looked perfect, Sami picked up the box she'd brought over. "I'm just going to set this in your room. Load everything back up, and I'll pick it up after church Sunday."

Calla met her at the bedroom door. "I really appreciate your help. I wish I had a way to repay you for all the times you've been right there, helping me."

Sami laughed and hugged Calla. "You say that like you've never cooked for me in your life. Girl, you've got it backward." She pulled away and looked at Calla with serious eyes. "I'm worried tonight won't go well."

Calla's stomach turned and twisted. She walked into the kitchen and Sami followed. Here, she had confidence. Here, she could excel and not fail. Outside of the kitchen, she'd made a shamble of her life. In here, though...

She pulled the towel off of the loaf of bread and pressed her finger into it, checking to see if it had risen long enough. The indentation remained, so she set the oven to heat up. As she worked, she considered her words.

"I know that I hurt Ian. But I also know that I needed this time. It's up to him to accept that." She looked at her friend. "Or not. But I have to give him a chance to definitively end it."

"And if he doesn't show?"

"That would be rather definitive, would it not?" The idea hurt her heart, but in all fairness, she half expected that to happen. "I prayed for an end to my problems. God provided it. Now I'm praying for God's guidance here, and he gave me this verse, *But new wine must be put into new wineskins, and both are preserved.* I can only rest in the hope that God is telling me that Ian and I should start fresh, start over, not go back." She smiled. "Whatever happens, reaching out was the right thing to do."

"Seeing how God worked out the thing with your stepmother makes me believe that if you asked for a word from Him, He'd totally give it to you. Some people would just take any sign that pointed in the direction they wanted to go as the word from God. You? I think you're something special." Sami picked her purse up off of the kitchen counter. "I can't wait to see you at church Sunday. Do me a favor and shoot me a text tonight before bed. Give me a little glimpse of what happened?"

"Deal."

After walking Sami to the door, she slipped the bread into the oven then went into her bedroom and opened the closet door. Since she wore a uniform to school, she had so few items to wear. She settled on a cotton, long-sleeved dress the color of sage that fell to just above the knee, camel-colored knee-high boots, and a lilac and sage scarf. Before she could put her makeup on, the timer for the bread went off. She looked at her watch. 6:25. Rushing through the apartment, she pulled the bread out of the oven and set it on the stove to cool, then went to her bathroom to put on makeup.

Just as she applied the coat of pink lip-gloss, the doorbell rang promptly at 6:30. Calla looked around the apartment one last time, seeing everything still in order. Would he notice how much everything resembled their dinner a year ago, down to the cushions on the couch?

She put a hand on her fluttering stomach, breathed out through her nose, then opened the door. He wore a pair of khaki pants and a dark green button-down shirt that made his eyes shine with a green light. A smile broke across her face at the sight of him, but his expression remained stoic in response.

"Hi there," she said, opening the door so that he could come in. "I wondered if you'd come."

"That right? Well, I reckon I did too." He kept his hands in his pockets as he entered the apartment. She watched him look around, with his eyes resting several spare moments on the table decorated with sunflowers. She wondered if he could recognize the smell of chicken Florentine cooking in the oven. "Still not sure I wanted to, but I'm here."

She gestured at the couch and said, "We have about ten minutes before dinner's ready."

"I can come back," Ian turned back toward the door.

"I'd like to talk if that's okay," Calla said quickly.

A muscle ticked in his jaw, and he stiffly stalked across the room and sat at the end of the couch. She sat at the other end, turning toward him. She had worked out what she wanted to say all day, but she didn't know how to begin. Did she just start by apologizing, maybe begging, maybe pleading? Would throwing herself at his feet fix the ache in his heart that had to mirror the pain in her soul?

Not knowing where to start, she began with, "I spent the few weeks we were together knowing that it would eventually end. I wouldn't burden you with my debt, and I didn't see a way out of it. I feel like my desperate prayer to God about it is what led to my arrest. I say that in hindsight because, in the midst of it, I was overcome with despair. But the arrest was the catalyst to free me from it all, which was exactly my prayer."

He kept his eyes forward, staring at a spot on the wall, not even looking at her, so she kept speaking. "Keeping that to myself the entire time wasn't fair to you. I've spent the last several months remembering every word, every touch, every expression. And, again, separated from it, in hindsight, I can believe that you would have seen me through anything. Not giving you that opportunity to lead me through it wasn't fair to you, and I would like to ask you for your forgiveness."

At her words, his head whipped around, and he stared at her in stony silence for a long time, his lips thin, his eyes hard. She held her breath, desperately wishing he would relax and smile and open his arms. Finally, he said, "I don't know."

"That's fair." She gestured at the table. "I would very much like a reset. I want you to be able to get to know me without a sixty-thousand-dollar secret affecting my every thought and word. I want you to let the real Calla Vaughn into your life, and maybe you'll fall in love with the real me the same way I fell in love with the real you." She paused, and her breath hitched. She clasped her hands tightly together.

He closed his eyes as if looking at her fatigued him. She held her breath, worried that he'd just flat out reject her and then where would she be? Lost. Without direction. Hopeless.

When he opened his eyes again, his expression had softened. He slowly lifted his arm and held out his hand, palm up. Without hesitation, she placed her hand in his and let him pull her close. She breathed in the familiar smell of him as his arms came around her. "I think I would like that very much," he said, his voice vibrating against her ear. She lifted her face to look at him and caught a glimpse of a promise of a beautiful future in his eyes as his lips covered hers.

THE END

LUNCHEON MENU

S uggested luncheon menu to enjoy when hosting a group discussion for *Courting Calla*.

Those who followed my Hallee the Homemaker website know that one thing I am passionate about in life is selecting, cooking, and savoring good whole real food. A special luncheon just goes hand in hand with hospitality and ministry.

For those planning a discussion group about this book, I offer some humble suggestions to help your special luncheon conversation come off as a success.

Chicken Florentine

Calla is a trained chef, but working with an extremely limited budget. She makes Chicken Florentine for Ian for their first date. This recipe will impress anyone without breaking the bank. It's delicious, hearty, and beautiful on the plate.

INGREDIENTS

2 chicken breasts, skinned, boned, cut into halves

$1/2$ tsp salt (Kosher or sea salt is best)

$1/4$ tsp ground white pepper

1 TBS Extra virgin olive oil

$1/2$ cup chopped onion

$^1/_2$ cup chopped baby bella mushrooms

$^1/_2$ of 10 oz. pkg. frozen chopped spinach, thawed, well drained

1/3 cup ricotta cheese

A few grates of nutmeg (no more than $^1/_4$ tsp)

1 egg, lightly beaten

$^1/_2$ cup bread crumbs

PREPARATION

Slice the chicken breasts in half - like opening a book (so that you've reduced the thickness by half and not the length or width by half). Using a rolling pin or mallet, pound each half thin until about $^1/_3$ to $^1/_2$ inch thick. Sprinkle with salt and pepper.

Chop the onions.

Chop the mushrooms.

Place the thawed spinach in a towel and squeeze it dry.

Preheat oven to 350° degrees F (180° degrees C)

Beat egg.

DIRECTIONS

Heat the olive oil in a skillet. Add the onions and mushrooms. Sauté until onions are translucent, about 5-6 minutes.

Stir in the cheese and nutmeg. Stir just until heated.

Divide the mixture between the four breasts. Starting with the short end, roll up the breasts. (If necessary, you can secure them closed with wooden toothpicks.)

Dip each breast in the egg, then roll in breadcrumbs.

Place on baking pan, seam side down. Cover tightly with aluminum foil.

Back at 350° degrees F (180° degrees C) for 15 minutes. Remove the foil covering and bake for an additional 10-15 minutes, or until browned.

French Bread

French bread is the perfect accompaniment to Chicken Florentine. It's a simple recipe and can easily be turned into garlic bread.

INGREDIENTS

2 $^1/_4$ tsp (or 1 packet) dry years

1 $^1/_4$ cup warm filtered water -no hotter than 120° degrees F (48° degrees C).

3 $^1/_2$ cups flour (I use fresh ground mixture of hard red wheat and hard white wheat - unbleached flour will work if you don't have fresh ground)

1 tsp salt (Kosher or sea salt is best)

1 TBS extra virgin olive oil

PREPARATION

Heat the mixing bowl by filling it with hot tap water.

Drain the bowl. Add the warm water and yeast. Let stand 5 minutes.

Lightly grease a large bowl to use for rising the dough.

DIRECTIONS

Mix all ingredients in bowl with the water and yeast.

Knead with the stand mixer for 2 minutes, or knead by hand for 10 minutes.

Once the dough becomes smooth and elastic, put it into a lightly greased bowl. Turn it once and cover with a light towel. Let it sit in a warm spot until it doubles in bulk. It will take about an hour.

Punch the dough down. Roll dough into a rectangle and roll up tightly. Pinch the ends and place on a greased baking sheet (you can sprinkle the baking sheet with cornmeal if you desire). Cover and let rise in a warm place until nearly double in size.

Bake at 400° degrees F (205° degrees C) for 20-25 minutes. When you tap the loaf, if it sounds hollow, it's done.

Sautéed Green Beans

Even though the Spinach Florentine is stuffed with spinach, fresh green beans help the plate look like a work of art.

INGREDIENTS

¹/₂ lbs fresh green beans.

1 TBS extra virgin olive oil

1 clove garlic, minced

2 TBS sliced almonds

PREPARATION

Wash the green beans. Cut off the stems.

DIRECTIONS

Heat olive oil in skillet over medium-high heat. Add the garlic and sauté for about 2 minutes, stirring constantly. Stir in the green beans and almonds.

Reduce heat to medium-low and cover the pan and cook for about 10 minutes, stirring the beans regularly.

Wild Rice

I use a packaged organic wild-rice and brown rice blend.

INGREDIENTS

2 cups vegetable broth
1 cup wild-rice/brown rice blend
$^1/_2$ tsp salt
2 tsp extra virgin olive oil

DIRECTIONS

In a medium saucepan, combine all ingredients. Bring to a boil. Cover pan tightly and reduce heat to low. Simmer for 45 minutes or until the brown rice is tender.

Basil Infused Whipped Cream

Calla wanted to serve a dessert that would be light and easy, but didn't want to serve "just plain" whipped cream. So, she infused her cream with basil and served that over berries.

INGREDIENTS

1 cup heavy whipping cream
$^1/_3$ cup fresh basil leaves
1 TBS powdered sugar

PREPARATION

In a small saucepan, heat the cream over medium heat until almost boiling (do not boil) - just until it stars to simmer. Remove from heat and toss in the basil.

Sit at room temperature for 30 minutes. Strain the cream through a mesh strainer into a clean bowl. Refrigerate for at least 3 hours.

DIRECTIONS

Mix the powdered sugar into the infused cream. Beat with a mixer until stiff peaks form.

Serve over fresh berries.

DISCUSSION QUESTIONS

S uggested discussion group questions for *Courting Calla* by Hallee Bridgeman.

When asking ourselves how important the truth is to our Creator, we can look to the reason Jesus said he was born. In the book of John 18:37, Jesus explains that *for this reason He was born and for this reason He came into the world.* The reason? To testify to the truth.

In bringing those He ministered to into an understanding of the truth, Our Lord used fiction in the form of parables to illustrate very real truths. In the same way, we can minister to one another by the use of fictional characters and situations to help us to reach logical, valid, cogent, and very sound conclusions about our real lives here on earth.

While the characters and situations in The Dixon Brothers Series are fictional, I pray that these extended parables can help readers come to a better understanding of truth. Please prayerfully consider the questions that follow, consult scripture, and pray upon your conclusions. May the Lord of the universe richly bless you.

Calla and Ian both believe that God orchestrated the mix-up in the flower delivery that brought them together.

1) Do you think that God actually plays such an active part in our lives so as to arrange people to meet in such a way?

2) Can you think of a time when that happened to you—a time when you're certain God had a hand in it?

Calla prayed for God to release her from the debt in which her stepmother had maliciously placed her. The end result was that Calla was arrested on the suspicion of passing $10,000 worth of bad checks. It caused a spiral that, despite the terrible moments, ended up freeing her from the debt—which was an answer to prayer.

3) Romans 8:28 says, *For God works together for good all things for those who love Him and are called according to His purpose.* Do you think that this is an example of God working together for good all things as they pertained to Calla?

4) Or, do you think that God answered Calla's prayer by orchestrating her arrest?

Ian believes that if Calla had been honest with him at any time during the brief beginning of their relationship, he would have supported her.

5) Given an idea of Ian's personality, do you think he would have supported her, or was he speaking in hindsight?

6) Do you think Ian's faith was strong enough to believe that if God had indeed brought them together, he *should* have supported her and therefore would have?

Calla asked Ian to give her time to get to know the "real" Calla before she would be free to pursue a relationship with him.

7) What do you think her real motivation was?

8) Do you think this was fair to Ian considering he'd come so far to show her how much he cared?

9) Do you think that Calla's decision showed a lack of her own faith in trusting God's answers to her prayers?

Calla did not file charges against her stepmother and instead subjected herself to tens of thousands of dollars of debt that SHE chose to pay off.

10) What do you think you would do in the event that a family member stole your identity?

11) Do you think that filing charges would have been the right thing to do right away, or should Calla have given her stepmother a chance to stop what she was doing and pay her back?

12) Do you consider the theft of the identity of a family member a crime, or an inconvenience? Would you consider the relationship with the family member more important than justice?

MORE BOOKS

by Hallee Bridgeman

Find the latest information and connect with Hallee at her website:
www.halleebridgeman.com

UPCOMING FICTION

The Dixon Brothers Series:

Book 1: Courting Calla

Book 2: Valerie's Verdict

Book 3: Alexandra's Appeal

Book 4: Daisy's Decision

FICTION BOOKS BY HALLEE

Virtues and Valor series:

Book 1: Temperance's Trial

Book 2: Homeland's Hope

Book 3: Charity's Code

Book 4: A Parcel for Prudence

Book 5: Grace's Ground War

Book 6: Mission of Mercy

Book 7: Flight of Faith

Book 8: Valor's Vigil

The Jewel Series:

Book 1: Sapphire Ice,

Book 2: Greater Than Rubies

Book 3: Emerald Fire

Book 4: Topaz Heat

Book 5: Christmas Diamond

Book 6: Christmas Star Sapphire

Book 7: Silver Hearts (Coming Winter 2017)

The Song of Suspense Series:

Book 1: A Melody for James

Book 2: An Aria for Nick

Book 3: A Carol for Kent

Book 4: A Harmony for Steve

PARODY COOKBOOKS BY HALLEE

Vol 1: Fifty Shades of Gravy, a Christian gets Saucy!

Vol 2: The Walking Bread, the Bread Will Rise

Vol 3: Iron Skillet Man, the Stark Truth about Pepper and Pots

Vol 4: Hallee Crockpotter & the Chamber of Sacred Ingredients

ABOUT

www.halleebridgeman.com

With more than half a million sales, Hallee Bridgeman is a best-selling Christian author who writes action-packed romantic suspense focusing on realistic characters who face real world problems. Her work has been described as everything from refreshing to heart-stopping exciting and edgy.

An Army brat turned Floridian, Hallee finally settled in central Kentucky with her family so that she could enjoy the beautiful changing of the seasons. She enjoys the roller-coaster ride thrills that life with a National Guard husband, a teenaged daughter, and two elementary aged sons delivers.

A prolific writer, when she's not penning novels, you will find her in the kitchen, which she considers the 'heart of the home'. Her passion for cooking spurred her to launch a whole food, real food "Parody" cookbook series. In addition to nutritious, Biblically grounded recipes, readers will find that each cookbook also confronts some controversial aspect of secular pop culture.

Hallee is a member of the Published Author Network (PAN) of the Romance Writers of America (RWA) where she serves as a long time board member in the Faith, Hope, & Love chapter. She is a member of the American Christian Fiction Writers (ACFW) and the American Christian Writers (ACW) as well as being a member of Novelists, Inc. (NINC).

Hallee loves coffee, campy action movies, and regular date nights with her husband. Above all else, she loves God with all of her heart, soul, mind, and strength; has been redeemed by the blood of Christ; and relies on the presence of the Holy Spirit to guide her. She prays her work here on earth is a blessing to you and would love to hear from you. You can reach Hallee at hallee@halleebridgeman.com.

Sign up for Hallee's monthly newsletter! When you sign up, you will get a link to download Hallee's romantic suspense novella, On The Ropes. In addition, every newsletter recipient is automatically entered into a monthly giveaway! The real prize is you will never miss updates about upcoming releases, book signings, appearances, or other events.

Newsletter Sign Up: tinyurl.com/HalleeNews

Author Site: www.halleebridgeman.com

Facebook: www.facebook.com/pages/Hallee-Bridgeman/192799110825012

Twitter: twitter.com/halleeb

Google+:   /plus.google.com/105383805410764959843

Goodreads: www.goodreads.com/author/show/5815249.Hallee_Bridgeman

Homemaking Blog: www.halleethehomemaker.com

INTRODUCING

I'm so glad that you chose to read *Courting Calla*. I pray that it blessed you. I wrote *Courting Calla* to introduce the upcoming Dixon Brothers series, so look for the stories of the Dixon triplets very soon. I'd love to hear from you. Leave a comment online at the Hallee Bridgeman website. Your feedback inspires me, engages me, and keeps me writing good books.

Now, it is my very real honor to introduce the second book in this collection written by my very good friend Alana Terry. Knowing Alana for many years has personally blessed me in so many ways. I admire her God given talent as an author but she also inspires me as a true woman of faith whom I admire greatly. I admit, I have also relied on Alana to answer some research questions about life in Alaska.

Alana's story takes place in the international setting of Seoul, South Korea so get ready to take a journey there in your imagination. Her hero and heroine deal with so many topics that affect Christians today from traveling abroad, non-profits, divorce, dealing with grief, all the way to middle age second chance romance. *Seoul in Love* is a Christian Contemporary Romance that involves love lost many years ago that might have a new beginning based on a chance meeting on foreign soil.

I know *Seoul in Love* is going to bless you and challenge you!

Author of *Courting Calla*

Seoul in *Love*

a Novella

by

ALANA TERRY

Seoul in Love Alana Terry

Copyright © 2017. All rights reserved.

Library Cataloging Data

Terry, Alana (Alana Terry) 1983-

Seoul in Love / Alana Terry

Summary: >Love was lost a long time ago. A chance meeting in Seoul might change all that forever.

1. Christian fiction 2. man-woman relationships 3. second chance romance 4. seoul, south korea 5. non-profits 6. divorced couple 7. middle-aged romance 8. coping with grief

CONTENTS

CHAPTER 1

The last time Jolene was in a wedding, it had been her own.

She stared at the wine-red bridesmaid dress and the uncomfortable-looking shoes. The short skirt and the high heels both screamed *you're way too old for this.*

The only person she'd know at the ceremony would be the bride, but she still had gone on a crash diet, hoping to lose ten pounds before the big day and gaining seventeen instead.

Or maybe she was just comfort-eating after that messy break-up.

She glanced around the Korean *hanok*, looking for a place to hang her clothes. She booked a room here because she'd heard the accommodations were historically accurate. She'd never bothered to ask the manager if they'd have a closet or not.

Even though it was fall, the Seoul air was muggy, especially compared with the dry desert heat of her home back in Orchard Grove, Washington. The back of her shirt was drenched in sweat. Real appealing. She'd have to walk down to the market area and buy one of those little hand-held fans she'd seen some of the young people carrying around.

Speaking of young people, where had she put Mena's contact information? Jolene's phone didn't come with an international plan, but Mena gave her the name of some app to download. As long as she was connected to the internet, she could receive calls and texts.

Jolene was exhausted. She'd stopped trying to remember what time it would be back home. All she knew was that the sun hadn't set in Seoul, but it felt like midnight. She should be sleeping.

So many shoulds.

The story of her life for the past five years.

I shouldn't have let Chelsea go on that trip alone. I should have been with her.

I should have known something like this would happen.

I should have prayed harder.

That last one was the real kicker. If Jolene had been spending regular time in prayer with the Lord instead of fighting so much with Chelsea's dad, would anything have changed?

Questions that had plagued her for five years now.

Five years to the month.

What was she doing in Seoul? She could have backed out. Mena would have understood. Jolene was twice as old as everyone else in the wedding party, but for some reason, she'd made this martyr's journey to honor her daughter's memory. Chelsea would never find true love, never marry, never put on a wine-red bridesmaid's dress, so it was up to Jolene to stand in for her at her best friend's wedding.

At least she'd changed Mena's mind about the cut of the gown. There was no way anyone at the ceremony would want to see Jolene in a sleeveless.

She sighed and hung the dress up on the back of the bathroom door. She should have asked if there would be a closet in the *hanok* instead of snagging the online deal after glancing at a couple images.

Not that the accommodations were shabby. She had more than enough space. In addition to the large kitchen area with a sky roof were two separate bedrooms. No beds, however. Jolene wasn't sure exactly how she was supposed to arrange those flat mats stacked up in the corner, but she'd figure it out.

With as tired as she was, she could probably fall asleep in the bathroom if she had to.

She felt like she should call somebody. Let them know she'd made it safely to Seoul. But who? Garcia had tried to apologize before her flight, had tried to get back together, but she was done.

Who did that leave for her back in the States? She hadn't spoken to Chelsea's dad in years, and she couldn't remember the last time she had a meaningful conversation with anyone from church.

She should get in touch with Mena, but to do that she'd have to figure out how to connect her phone to wireless. Then she'd have to dig her cord adapter out of her suitcase, which was crammed full of stuff she'd thrown in haphazardly yesterday evening. Or was it two days ago now?

Blame it on the international date line for getting her internal calendar so messed up.

She shut her eyes for a moment, fully aware that she risked falling asleep while standing in the middle of the empty room. Her mind relentlessly replayed her last conversation with Garcia. They'd only broken up two days before her flight, and she hadn't found anyone else willing to drive her to the airport on such short notice.

"Have a good time," he told her. She was surprised his voice wasn't hoarse after all the time he spent on the road trying to convince her to take him back.

The one good thing that would come out of this trip is it would get her away from him. Clear her mind. She and Garcia had been dating for over a year. She had no idea how or when their relationship turned so toxic.

Just like her marriage to Chelsea's dad. She wasn't going to walk down that road again. Wasn't about to make those same stupid mistakes.

"I'll see you in a few days," he told her, even though Jolene had every intention of finding another way back to Orchard Grove after she flew home. He cleared his throat, unable to make eye contact. "Again, I'm really sorry."

Yeah, well, she'd heard that before too. From him, from Chelsea's dad... The male race was plagued with cheaters, and all of them were masters of apology.

She grabbed her suitcase handle and turned away. "Bye."

Funny, she thought she would have felt worse walking away from him. This was her first serious relationship after the divorce, but instead of mourning over a lost chance at love, she felt more relieved than anything else.

With all Garcia knew about her, did he honestly think she'd just open her arms and forgive him for everything he'd done?

The irony of being a divorcee who just broke up with a marriage counselor.

She should have left him months ago. Should have recognized all those telltale warning signs. Should have never gotten together with him in the first place.

More shoulds piled one on top of the other.

When Mena asked her last winter to travel all the way to Seoul and stand as her maid of honor in her daughter's place, Jolene had agreed without even thinking. It's what Chelsea would want. What more compelling reason did she need?

Maybe she should have prayed about it.

Maybe she should have spent her energy preparing herself emotionally instead of pretending like this trip wasn't going to happen.

Maybe she should have kicked Garcia out of her life months ago.

So many shoulds.

Dozens of shoulds.

Hundreds.

The irony is that she wished she hadn't traveled to Seoul

alone, not for something like this.

She should have never boarded that airplane in the first place.

CHAPTER 2

I t took Joseph at least half a dozen business trips to Seoul to learn all the nuances of the highly ritualized ordeal of drinking shots with his associates. So many rules to remember, how to hold your wrist with one hand, how to never pour your own drink or turn someone down who offered to fill your cup, how to turn your back toward your boss when you took your first sip. Who knew how these customs began or what made them so important? What mattered was not forgetting yourself for a second.

Even when, like Joseph, all you were drinking were shots of seltzer water.

When he thought back about the mess his life had spiraled into five years ago, it was something of a miracle that he was still sober.

Losing Chelsea had almost destroyed him. Almost driven him back into the clutches of alcohol and addiction and despair. Instead, it drove him into the arms of Denise, a perky intern his firm had just hired.

He wasn't proud of his failings. There was very little about that first year he wouldn't take back if he could, but life didn't work that way. You had to keep moving forward.

He'd spent months rationalizing each and every act of infidelity. Denise pulled him out of his depression like nothing else could have, except maybe for the alcohol. And so he'd justified the affair, justified ruining the marriage he'd worked a quarter of a century to build.

It wasn't until Denise dumped him that Joseph realized what he'd done.

How he'd irreparably destroyed his relationship with his wife. And for what? For a twenty-something-year-old brunette who left him the hour her ex moved back to town. He'd forgotten the pain of losing his mistress, but not his wife.

Last he heard, Jolene was dating some marriage counselor.

Nobody ever said God lacked a sense of humor.

Life was funny sometimes. Like how for twenty-five years of marriage, Jolene had always been the one nagging him about going to church, about getting serious about his faith for Chelsea's sake if nothing else. How it took losing their daughter and finally his wife before he truly repented and realized his need of a Savior.

How now that he'd finally kicked his addiction for good, now that he was finally walking in a right relationship with the Lord, Jolene wasn't around to see his improvements.

Instead, she was dating a marriage counselor.

Maybe this was her not-so-subtle way of getting back at him for refusing to go to couple's therapy.

More irony for you.

Boisterous conversations flew across the table, most of them in Korean. Twelve months of half-heartedly working with Rosetta Stone meant that Joseph could ask for simple directions and order off a menu. That was about the extent of his language skills, but he put up a good show and laughed when everybody else did.

He knew he pulled it off too.

None of his associates would know the intensity of his grief.

Nobody around him could guess the extent of his regrets.

CHAPTER 3

"**M**rs. Gregory!" **The young woman** gave a hug strong enough to put a professional wrestler to shame.

"Please, call me Jolene," she insisted, feeling decades older than forty-nine.

Mena dumped her purse onto the counter in Jolene's *hanok*. "I'm so glad you made it. How was the flight? Did everything go ok? You must be exhausted. How long were you in the air? Have you eaten dinner yet?"

Jolene stood blinking. Was this confident, boisterous woman the same gangly teenager who had spent so many sleepless nights gossiping away with her daughter back home in Orchard Grove? Where had the time gone? "I can't believe you're getting married," she croaked.

Mena was beaming. "I know. But if Jin-Sun had his way, I swear, that man would have dragged his feet until..." She stopped short. "You look exhausted. Do you need to call it a night?"

Jolene shook her head, telling herself it was ridiculous for a woman her age to be scared of spending an evening alone in a big *hanok* like this. "I'm fine. It's just that you've grown so much since I saw you last. How long's it been?"

"I was trying to figure that out too. I've been here in Seoul for a little over five years, so I'm guessing the last time we saw each other was the summer after Chelsea and I graduated." She winced when she mentioned Chelsea's name. Looked up at Jolene with uncertainty etched into every feature.

Jolene hated when people treated her like an expensive figurine in danger of cracking. She spent nearly all her mental energy lying to herself and everyone else that she wasn't nearly so fragile. She donned her most convincing smile and forced cheer into her tone. "Chelsea would be so excited for you, wouldn't she?"

There. She could talk about her daughter, talk about her as if every memory didn't hack at her spirit like shattered shards splintering her soul.

Mena didn't look as convinced as Jolene would have liked. She paused with a half frown then grabbed her purse. "Well, hey, the best news about where you're staying is there's a great market literally around the corner. Have you eaten much Korean food? I should warn you, most of it's pretty spicy. And I seriously hope you're not a vegetarian because then you'll be stuck with nothing but noodles the whole time you're here. But if you're hungry and feel ready for it, I can show you some of the places where Jin-Sun and I like to eat when we're out this way."

Jolene nodded. Her body was exhausted, but she knew enough from her ex-husband's life of international business trips that the best way to fight off jet lag was to force yourself to adjust to local time no matter how tired you felt. She'd stay up until the sun went down even if she had to prop her eyelids open with chopsticks. After grabbing her camera case, which would most definitely mark her as a tourist if by some chance her light hair and pale complexion failed to do the trick, Jolene glanced up at the sky roof. "Think it's going to rain?" she asked. "Should I bring my umbrella?"

"I've got one big enough for both of us to share," Mena answered. "So you ready?"

No, Jolene was most certainly not. She wasn't ready for any of this.

Not ready to admit that her daughter's best friend was now a grown woman with an international career, a fiancé, and a life that hadn't stopped when Chelsea died.

She wasn't ready to venture out into the city that had stolen her daughter from her.

Wasn't ready to stand in what should be her daughter's place at Mena's wedding.

She wasn't ready for any of it, but what choice did she have?

Grabbing her windbreaker, Jolene took a deep breath and forced confidence into her tone. "Sure. What are we going to eat?"

CHAPTER 4

"More soju?" **asked the vice** president of the firm's somewhat scrawny male assistant.

Joseph shook his head. "No alcohol." It was hard to explain in this company of loud, boisterous drinkers. In a culture in which the devastating impact of addiction was never openly discussed, in a work environment that placed such emphasis on doing everything—including getting dead drunk—communally, Joseph was ever aware that his status as a recovering alcoholic was a barrier to his success in the Korean field.

At least now he knew that the setback was worth the cost. There was a time when nothing, not even family, was allowed to come before his career advancement.

Which could explain in part why his wife left him and was now dating a marriage counselor.

Or maybe that wasn't a fair assessment. His career may have put a strain on their relationship, may have made things worse when he wasn't there to mourn with her over Chelsea's death, but wasn't the affair what truly destroyed their marriage?

It was hard to tell. Looking back, they had drifted apart years before Chelsea traveled to Korea to visit her best friend. Years before Joseph's firm ever hired Denise.

What made it worse was thinking about how close they'd once been. Both in college, head over heels in love. Their differences in faith were hardly cause for worry. Jolene had been raised in a Christian home, but by the time he met her at the university, she was just as ready to have fun as the next girl. Three years later, when Joseph asked her dad for his blessing to marry his daughter, the topic of religion came up briefly. Joseph had been quick to assure his future father-in-law, "I believe in God. I'm a Christian," as if the two statements were interchangeable.

There was so much he hadn't understood at the time.

Like how their first miscarriage would cause Jolene to turn to the Savior she hadn't thought seriously about in years.

Or how their daughter's birth would solidify his wife's desire to buckle down about attending church every Sunday. Before long it was daily devotions, annual prayer retreats with the other ladies from Orchard Grove... When had living a nice, comfortable, suburban life stopped being enough?

When had Joseph stopped being enough?

What kind of husband wants to feel like he's been replaced by an invisible deity, a perfectly selfless, loving, and all-powerful God you could never dream of competing against?

From the moment of Jolene's spiritual renewal shortly after their marriage, Joseph could no longer satisfy her like before.

Was it so wrong to want to come home on a Friday night and watch a movie with his wife? Soon even that became a near impossibility. This film had too much swearing, that one was too violent. Anything that even hinted at immodesty or immorality was scrutinized, judged, and condemned. And seriously, what grown man who was partner and VP of his own firm would actually want to come home and watch movies about talking animals since that appeared to be the only kind of show tame enough for Jolene's now prudish sensibilities?

And then there was the nagging. *Aren't you coming to church with us? Why don't you lead the family devotions tonight? Do you want to pray about it?* Every hour, every minute of the day.

Wasn't it enough that Joseph brought in a hefty salary, that they owned their own four-bedroom in the Heights, that their daughter never wanted for anything?

"What she wants is a spiritual leader," Jolene had told him.

As if a four-year-old cares about whether her dad does or doesn't close his eyes when the family prays around the table.

The more she nagged, the more he pushed Jolene away. For years, he pushed her away. Eventually, the nagging stopped. Maybe she gave up. Maybe she realized it wouldn't do any good. But even when the verbal bashing ended, the judgmental attitude didn't. She stopped telling him what kind of movies he could or couldn't bring into the house, but if there was a sex scene or if the scriptwriters used one too many bad phrases, she'd stand up and walk out of the room. She never said a word in complaint, but her silence was even more pointed than a dozen lectures.

She was disappointed in him.

Story of his life for over two decades.

And now he was doing all the things she'd begged him to. Now he was trying to live a righteous life. He turned to God when he was still reeling from his daughter's death and his mistress's abandonment. With the help of his recovery sponsor, he'd finally come to realize what Jolene meant when she talked about having an actual relationship with the Lord.

He wasn't just going through the motions anymore. He was reading his Bible and was excited about the content, at least when he remembered to keep up his daily devotion time. He was part of a men's group at church and had gone to a Truth Warriors conference in Seattle to hear speakers talk about how to be a godly man in the home and in the workplace.

He got it now. He wasn't perfect, not by a long shot, but he was finally starting to understand what it meant to be a selfless and loving leader.

Of course, now it was too late.

Five years too late, to be exact.

CHAPTER 5

The waitress yelled something at Jolene, gesticulating angrily.

"She's telling you to take off your shoes," Mena whispered.

When Jolene slipped out of her sneakers, the waitress's voice doubled in volume and her mannerisms grew even more furious.

"Not right here," Mena said. "Over there."

Jolene didn't need Mena's help to translate the woman's body language. *Stupid tourist.*

"It's ok." Mena smiled and led Jolene to a small cubby, apparently the proper storage place for shoes. Then they sat down on cushions beside a table low to the ground.

Jolene wondered if Chelsea had come to this same restaurant, if her first week in Seoul she'd gotten berated by an angry waitress as well. Chelsea had come out here five years ago since she and Mena couldn't bear the thought of a semester apart from one another. When Mena got her internship to work for Korea Freedom International, a non-profit helping North Korean refugees resettle in Seoul, Chelsea convinced her father to book her tickets out here that same week.

Joseph hadn't even asked for Jolene's opinion. Of course, Jolene would have agreed to the trip. Chelsea deserved it after graduating with her degrees in psychology and early childhood development. But he'd never even asked...

Still, she couldn't blame him for everything. In his own way, he grieved Chelsea's death every bit as much as she did. Of course, she hadn't thrown herself into the arms of some secretary only two years older than their dead daughter the minute sadness overtook her.

In so many ways, their marriage had been doomed years earlier. After starting off so strong, after three years of passionate, adventurous, reckless dating, she would have never pictured them turning into the kind of couple that only remained together for the sake of the children.

But that's precisely what she'd done.

She'd stayed with him through the worst of his alcoholism when his addiction nearly cost him the job he'd sacrificed so much for. She'd stayed with him through the confusing years of empty-nesting when she was terrified to discover she had no interests, no pursuits, no hobbies or aspirations that didn't somehow relate to raising her daughter. During those long, quiet months with Chelsea all the way out on the East Coast, Jolene was forced to find herself all over again, a second adolescence stuck right in the center of middle age.

She'd stayed with him even after the silence of grieving severed her heart into bloody shreds. She vividly remembered waking up one morning and realizing the man she'd gone to bed with the night before was a complete stranger.

And then came the affair.

She'd known even before the piece of incriminating evidence fell into her lap. She'd known but tried to convince herself it was something else. It was grief. It was stress. It was a mid-life crisis.

A mid-life crisis in a tight, sheer blouse and three-inch heels.

And then, just a week ago, her boyfriend had done the exact same thing, only this time with the sister of a client.

Mena was saying something to her, asking what she wanted to

order. How long had Jolene been stuck in the past?

Would she ever learn to live again in the present?

Thankfully, the menu contained some pictures, and Mena relayed their order to the waitress who seemed just as grumpy as before.

Jolene hadn't realized she was staring until Mena asked, "What are you thinking about?"

She was tempted to make up a lie. Tell Mena she was jetlagged or daydreaming about her upcoming wedding. But Mena had been part of her family's life since she and Chelsea met in middle school. There was no reason to keep secrets.

"I was just imagining how much Chelsea would have loved to be here right now."

Mena's smile was soft, appropriate for a young woman who'd lost her best friend but was about to get married and clearly expected to face nothing but happiness and bliss in the decades to come. She sometimes looked so much like her daughter Jolene was tempted to reach out and touch her hair. Stroke her cheek. The girls had always joked they must be long-lost sisters, and with as close as they remained throughout their teen and college years, Jolene almost had to agree.

"I wish she could be here too," Mena replied in a soft voice. "I miss her so much."

CHAPTER 6

J ust three more blocks and he'd be back to his room. After so many trips to and from Seoul, he should have been prepared for the amount of noise at tonight's company dinner, but he'd been fighting a headache since morning. The cacophony at the restaurant did nothing to improve matters.

Thankfully, this would be a short trip. Not even a full week in Korea, and then he'd be on his way home. Work at the office didn't slow down just because he was on the other side of the world.

He quickened his pace when the rain began to pour. Who was stupid enough to walk around Seoul without an umbrella? He'd already been sweltering in his suit. Now he was about to get drenched as well.

Why hadn't he taken a cab? It wasn't that much more expensive, and work would have paid for it either way. But he'd been hot and thought a short walk outside might help him clear his mind. As if anything was refreshing or relaxing about the polluted air in a city this crowded.

He'd developed a small cough, usual after traveling to such a smoggy part of the world. Given his track record, there was a one in four chance he'd develop bronchitis in the following weeks and end up on antibiotics.

Hurrying toward the B&B, Joseph wondered what he was

even doing in this area of Seoul. For some reason, when his office assistant booked this trip she didn't put him up in one of the usual hotels downtown. Joseph didn't know if there'd been a price special or if Misty thought he'd enjoy a more authentic Korean experience staying in a traditional *hanok*, but he didn't appreciate having to sleep on inch-thick mats instead of a regular bed or being forced to walk three or four extra blocks to the subway station.

Especially in a downpour.

There had been a time when he loved the rain. Back in college in Seattle, he and Jolene would run outside, laughing like the children they were, splashing and skipping in the spray.

A little rain never hurt nobody. How many times had he said that to her?

It had been raining when they shared their first kiss.

Raining when he got down on one knee and proposed.

Raining when they drove to the hospital the night Chelsea was born.

And yes, raining the day they got the call about her accident.

He still avoided Seoul Tower. Over a dozen trips to South Korea, and he hadn't ventured anywhere near the city's biggest tourist trap. What would be the point? The pilgrimage wouldn't bring his daughter back to him.

Usually, he was so good at burying her memory. How had he started thinking about her again?

That's right. The weather.

His memories started with him and Jolene dancing in the rain and ended with the news of his daughter's death.

A little rain never hurt nobody? Yeah, right.

No wonder he and his wife had divorced. His stupid affair aside, how could their marriage have survived if every single happy memory they once made together turned into a jagged, barbed reminder of the daughter they lost?

There was no recovering from wounds like that.

Maybe it was pessimistic. Some might listen to him and tell him he'd lost faith. Well, Joseph believed in God, believed in Jesus, believed in the Bible.

But he no longer believed in miracles.

Which is what it would have taken to keep his marriage from crumbling apart.

CHAPTER 7

Jolene couldn't remember the last time she'd gone out with a woman half her age and enjoyed herself so much. Probably never. While they waited for their food, Mena talked about everything at once—her non-profit work for Korea Freedom International, her fiancé, Jin-Sun, who was one of the staff members in her organization, the plans for their wedding, their upcoming honeymoon in Greece.

It was like talking to Chelsea's twin. Jolene was reminded in every one of Mena's smiles, every inflection in her voice, every animated story how similar the two girls had been.

"I'm sorry I haven't kept in better touch with you," she said once the food arrived. "After we lost Chelsea…"

Mena offered a smile full of warmth and sympathy. "I know. It's embarrassing to admit, but I was really nervous about asking you to be in the wedding. Like it would hurt your feelings too much."

Jolene understood that rationale all too well. How many women from church stopped talking about Chelsea altogether because they didn't want to bring up painful memories? As if ignoring the fact that Jolene's daughter had died a tragic, early death would somehow heal her brokenness. As if erasing Chelsea's memory was easier than confronting the pain of what happened.

How long had it been since she'd had a conversation with

anyone about Chelsea? She and Garcia used to talk about her. That's what made her feel so safe, so loved early on in their relationship. Garcia was a psychologist. He wasn't afraid of Jolene's grief.

But apparently, even a thriving career as a marital counselor doesn't make you the perfect partner.

Hence the fling with his client's sister.

He was remorseful. He apologized more profusely than her ex-husband had ever tried to.

But she was done. Done with him, done with dating, done with men in general.

If she thought Garcia deserved the second chance he was begging for, she was even more naïve than she'd been to marry Joseph half a lifetime ago.

CHAPTER 8

J oseph opened the door to his room and scowled at the colorful arrangement of flowers on the counter. If the men back at the Seoul office wanted to offer him a gift, they could have chosen something a little more practical and hopefully more masculine. Or maybe Misty sent it. His assistant spent half of her mental energy figuring out the flower arrangements in the Seattle office. It was a nice touch that probably made the space warmer and more inviting, but there was no way to gauge whether or not that actually translated into increased sales.

It certainly didn't make a difference here, except for the fact that one of the flowers—the purple ones with such huge petals— had such a strong smell it was sure to turn his headache into a full-fledged migraine.

Just what he needed.

A card peeked out at him. He yanked it from the envelope, wondering how soon he could dump the arrangement without offending whoever sent it to him.

I'm so sorry. Can you please forgive me for what I've done? I love you and can't stand it when we fight like this.

It was a dumb delivery mistake. That explained it all. Some pushover ordered flowers for a disgruntled lover, but they'd been sent here by accident.

Laughing at himself for actually thinking his secretary would order him such a gaudy arrangement, he checked the name on the envelope.

Joe Gregory.

Wait a minute.

He turned the paper over once. Twice. As if some clue or ink stain might explain what his name was doing on an arrangement that was clearly not meant for him.

He took a deep breath, but the flowery perfume was so strong he ended up letting out a sneeze instead of a sigh.

Great. Now some repentant or guilty lover was going to be wondering why his flowers never made it to their destination. What do you expect when you put the wrong name on an envelope like that?

But still, why was it his name, and what was it doing there?

He picked up the arrangement, holding his face away to ward off another sneeze and hoped the B&B hostess hadn't gone home for the night.

He had to get this thing out of his room.

CHAPTER 9

J olene was so tired her eyes were half shut by the time she hugged Mena goodnight. Entering the bedroom, she ignored all the unpacking and organizing she should probably start on and headed straight to the pile of thin mattress pads. Was she supposed to leave them stacked on top of each other like that and make herself a bed? Or spread them out to give herself more room?

And if nobody was there to watch, what did it matter?

She was tempted to go to sleep without taking care of any of her toiletries, a mistake she knew she'd regret when she woke up in the morning with breath rancid enough to scare off a dozen tourists.

Then again, if nobody was around but her, did it make a difference at all?

She could leave her suitcase shut, avoid the clutter it would make once she started strewing everything around. She could sleep just like she was. Start tomorrow fresh with a shower and a clean set of clothes.

She leaned back on an oversized pillow propped against the wall and shut her eyes. Just a few minutes to clear her mind. Then she'd put on her pajamas and wash her face and brush her teeth and do all those other things she was supposed to do as a responsible, self-respecting adult.

Just a few minutes' sleep first...

A knock at the door.

Had Mena forgotten something?

If it were anybody else, Jolene would make them wait. But she'd connected tonight with Mena like she hadn't with any other woman since Chelsea died. For once, Jolene didn't have to worry about making people uncomfortable by talking about her daughter too much. She didn't have to make excuses for the way her brain was still stuck in five-year-old memories that were strong enough to hold her in their clutches no matter how hard she struggled to break free.

Mena understood. Even when they weren't talking directly about Chelsea, it was like her daughter was still there. In Mena's smile. In her cheerful laughter. In the way she talked so hopefully about the future.

Where would Chelsea be right now if she were still alive? Here in Seoul, obviously, preparing to be Mena's maid of honor. But what about in her day-to-day life? Would she be a teacher? A psychologist? A grad student finishing up her studies? Would she travel the world like Mena? Would she have found her true love by now? Would she be married? Maybe even a mother?

Another knock.

Jolene snapped her eyes open and resisted the gravity that tried to keep her on the pile of bedding.

She walked to the door, hating the way each muscle was so stiff after the twelve-hour flight.

"What'd you forget?" she started to ask, except it wasn't Mena.

She saw the flowers first. Huge, purple geraniums with oversized leaves and an overpowering stench.

And then she saw Chelsea's dad.

Her ex-husband.

CHAPTER 10

"J olene?" Joseph stood staring, certain at first he was mistaken.

"Joseph." He could see the surprise in her eyes, but still, she said his name flatly.

He glanced around before finally finding the voice to ask, "What are you doing here?"

Any initial shock she displayed at seeing him was gone. "Mena's getting married." Her tone was icy. Even after all this time, the degree of pained bitterness he heard in her voice each time they spoke managed to surprise him. Make him regret his mistakes all over again, which was probably what she was aiming for.

"Who's Mena?" He realized it was the wrong question to ask the instant Jolene's eyes narrowed and her expression clouded over. As if the fact that he couldn't keep all of Jolene's friends straight was proof that he was a negligent spouse.

"Mena's been Chelsea's best friend since the time they were in seventh grade."

Memories clashed around in his gut. *That* Mena. "So she's getting married?" It was all he could think to say. What a night to have stayed away from the soju. "What's she doing in Seoul?"

"She lives here." Jolene's expression didn't change. "She's

been here for several years now."

He knew that. At least he should have known that. Mena. His daughter's bleeding-heart, world-traveling best friend. The reason Chelsea came to visit South Korea in the first place.

The reason she was no longer alive.

"What are you doing at her wedding?" He didn't mean to sound so brusque, but he'd done everything he could to move on and forget about what happened in this city five years ago. It was bad enough he had to travel here so often on business. Had to confront these memories that haunted him every step he took, but what choice did he have? It's not like he could avoid work because this city was distasteful. But why would his wife put herself through so much misery voluntarily?

Jolene was still staring at the gaudy flower arrangement and didn't answer his question.

He thrust the bouquet toward her. "This showed up in my room. I assume it was meant for you."

She took the oversized vase, opened the envelope tucked inside, and read the words.

The words of a lover apologizing.

Joseph wasn't sure what he had expected. For her to stare at the arrangement in surprise and ask who would be sending her flowers halfway around the world? She scowled at the letter.

"So you know the guy?"

Her eyes flashed. Why had he said that? What business was it of his? He was the last of all people who should ever make her feel guilty if she'd found someone else.

If she'd finally moved on...

He raised his hands as if in surrender. "Never mind. I'm sorry about the mix-up. Who would have thought there'd be two Joe Gregorys staying at the same B&B?"

His attempt at humor fell flat. No surprises there.

He probably hadn't heard her laugh once since they'd lost their daughter.

He cleared his throat. "Well, nice bumping into you." The kind of thing you'd say to a neighbor you ran into at Walmart. Not what you tell your ex-wife when you both happen to be staying at the same bed and breakfast halfway around the world. "Enjoy your flowers."

He stepped outside again to walk the thirty feet to the front door of his own room. The rain had stopped, but he hardly noticed.

CHAPTER 11

Jolene sat and stared at the flowers. What an ugly arrangement.

But she couldn't focus on that, even if she wanted to.

Joseph is here in Seoul. Of course, his travels took him all over the world, especially now that he had fast-tracked his way up the corporate ladder and headed the Seattle office. It shouldn't surprise her that he was in South Korea. Even when she'd been raising Chelsea, that man had never been home.

But what was he doing at her *hanok*? It wasn't the expensive luxury hotel she knew he was accustomed to.

Why, God? Why?

Was this some cosmic practical joke? Did God think she needed more chaos in her life?

Her phone beeped. Why had she given Garcia the name of that app?

I SENT YOU A PRESENT. DID YOU GET IT?

He was the last person she wanted to talk to right now, but if she didn't respond, he'd probably pester her all night long.

She should be asleep.

THANKS FOR THE FLOWERS, she wrote back. HAVEN'T CHANGED MY MIND.

It wasn't like her to be so terse, but she was tired and cranky and ridiculously confused. She still couldn't figure out what Joseph was doing here, why Garcia's flowers had ended up in his room…

Did he read the note? What would he think?

Garcia sent several more texts. She didn't have the energy to deal with this.

WILL YOU PLEASE FORGIVE ME?

Funny. Had her ex-husband ever said those five simple words to her before?

If she was younger, she might try to patch things up. Try to make things work. Garcia was a good listener. Sympathetic and compassionate.

But in the end, he was no different from Joseph. It was time for her to count her losses and move on.

She didn't know how, but she'd find a way.

Another text. Maybe she should feel flattered he was trying so hard, but in the end, it didn't matter.

Jolene slammed off the phone.

CHAPTER 12

O ut of all the hotels his assistant could have booked for him.

What was Misty thinking?

Joseph hadn't stopped pacing since he got back to his room.

Jolene. Here in Seoul.

The flowers. The note.

Of course, it must be from the marriage counselor. Stupid jerk. Whatever he'd done to make Jolene mad at him, he didn't deserve her forgiveness.

Why was she here? Here, when there were literally thousands of bed and breakfasts to choose from in the city of Seoul. And why right now? Why not in two days when he'd be on his flight back to Seattle?

Why not next month, when he was scheduled to be in South Africa, about as far on earth as you can feasibly get from the Korean peninsula?

And why couldn't he even think about her without remembering that terrible night?

The rain had been falling. There was a leak in the attic, a leak he'd promised to fix weeks earlier but never got around to. Jolene had been nagging him. That woman was always nagging.

And then the rain was pounding so hard he had to go up to

change the bucket, or else the water would start seeping into the master bathroom.

They'd been fighting. No real surprises there. The irony was that he didn't even remember what it had been about. His long hours at work? Something to do with Chelsea? The way Jolene had accused him of checking out the new intern at the company party?

His cell phone rang. He didn't recognize the number or the area code. Thought it might be someone from one of the international offices trying to get through.

"Dad?"

He could live to be a hundred and ten, his brain might get riddled with Alzheimer's, but he would never forget the way her voice squeaked when she made that last call. He had known even then. Something in the way his gut seized up.

"What is it?"

Jolene could tell from his tone too. She stopped whatever it was that she was doing and watched. Frozen.

"We're stuck in a cable car." Had he ever heard his daughter—his strong, courageous, spunky daughter Chelsea—with such terror in her voice?

"What do you mean a cable car?" he asked as images of San Francisco and Rice-a-Roni flitted through his head.

"Mena's taking me up to the Seoul Tower. We're hanging on a cable, but something went wrong. The attendant said…"

And then the scream. Not just from his daughter but from the forty-eight others with her that night. Forty-nine voices shrieking in terror, and he could still tell which one was hers.

Her scream, then silence.

The beeping telling him the call had been lost.

And then the waiting. The waiting until the authorities confirmed what Joseph already knew.

His daughter—bright, vivacious, energetic, and so frustratingly stubborn Chelsea—was gone.

CHAPTER 13

Jolene **felt like she should** feel guilty for ignoring
Garcia, but she didn't. Was it normal to be this relieved after a
breakup?

Or was that just a sign of how bitter she'd become?

After the divorce was finalized, she was distraught even
though she'd been the one to finally call things off. She spent
endless nights crying, begging God to change the past, trying to
figure out what she could have done differently to make their
marriage work.

She'd been plagued with guilt. Stopped spending as much
time with her friends from church. Couldn't stand the thought of
their gossip. Joseph's affair wasn't common knowledge, but it
certainly wasn't top-secret either. In a town like Orchard Grove, in
a church as small as theirs, speculation is often taken for gospel
truth.

At first, she'd tried to justify it to everyone who'd listen.

I'm divorced, but I did everything I could to make things
work.

My marriage is a failure, but I tried to get him to go with me
to counseling.

I left my husband, but I had a biblical reason.

It was so different now. Now, when she could simply turn off her cell phone and ignore her pestering ex-boyfriend. Of course, she and Garcia didn't have decades of history or the ghost of a dead daughter between them. She could forget him so much easier. Move on so much faster.

The only problem was the loneliness, but she'd been on her own before. She'd get used to it again. Even when she was married, she and Joseph ran out of things to talk about years before the divorce. What was there for them to say?

Remember the day you made our daughter nearly miss her senior prom because you got wasted and we had to pick you up at the station for driving under the influence?

Or here's a great one. How about when you showed up to her parent-teacher conferences in ninth grade dead drunk and two days late? That's a story for the history books, isn't it?

Of course, when he wasn't drinking, life wasn't nearly so hard.

Maybe even good.

Remember when we took Chelsea to the Oregon Coast and she caught a cold, and we stayed inside for three straight days cuddling and watching movies?

Remember that vacation to Disneyland when Chelsea was so little, and she was terrified of the man in the Mickey Mouse costume?

Remember that cruise we saved up for, the little cabin where our daughter was conceived?

Well, none of that mattered anymore anyway. Chelsea was gone. Joseph was gone, cut out of her life forever.

And good riddance.

Now Garcia was gone too. She really needed her sleep, but seeing Joseph had shot surges of adrenaline through her whole system. She couldn't get her brain to relax no matter how exhausted her body felt.

Stupid relationships.

Stupid romance.

Stupid men.

How was she supposed to get some rest when so much anger surged through her body? Anger at Garcia for continuing to pester her when she'd made it clear they were through. Anger at her ex-husband for having the audacity to book a room so near hers in the same *hanok*. Anger at Mena for dragging her to Seoul in the first place. And for what? For the next couple days, Mena would make Jolene feel like they'd made this great connection, then after the wedding, she and her new husband would go off and forget about her entirely.

The only reason she was in Korea was to assuage Mena's guilty conscience. Mena, who had invited Chelsea to Seoul in the first place. Mena, who had taken her to that cursed tower. Mena, who had survived the accident while her daughter...

Jolene knew she shouldn't have come here. Like picking scabs off a nearly-healed wound.

She stormed into the bathroom and turned the shower on to full heat. Then, dumping out every blasted item in her suitcase, she flung them around on the floor until she found her sweats, her pink slippers, and her mud facial cream.

If she couldn't get to sleep, she was at the very least going to give herself a proper pampering.

CHAPTER 14

"**I**t can't just be a coincidence." Joseph paced the width of his room while he yelled into the phone at his recovery sponsor.

Chuck was twelve years older than Joseph, a hundred pounds heavier, and several lifetimes wiser. "How did you feel when you saw her there?" That was his first question. Not *did you think about getting something to drink after a shock like that?* Not *did you figure out how in the world you ended up at the same B&B?* Not *who's the punk sending your wife an expensive bouquet of flowers from overseas?*

"I felt…" Joseph stopped himself before he rammed into the bedroom wall. He turned the other way and began marching in the opposite direction. "I felt…"

"Some men would see those flowers and be jealous." Chuck's quiet observation invited a response, but Joseph had none to give.

Jealous? Of some pipsqueak of a marriage counselor who had to woo his wife with gaudy floral arrangements to stand any chance with her? What was Jolene thinking? Didn't she know she deserved better than that?

Better than a man who would mess with her heart, whatever it was this jerk had done to his wife, and then have the audacity to bribe her with expensive gifts until she forgave him?

Jolene was the best thing that had ever happened in his life, and she deserved so much better.

Better than that idiot of a marriage counselor. Better than a lousy alcoholic who'd destroyed his life, who'd destroyed his family time after time again.

Destroyed his wife.

His wife...

"It's natural for you to still have feelings for her, you know." True to form, Chuck was dishing out truths that were so stinking obvious there was no need to reply.

"I'm not good enough for her." With as many times as Joseph had said those words to himself, he would have thought they'd be easier to admit out loud.

"You weren't good enough for her," Chuck corrected. "But you're a changed man now, brother."

He slowed down his pacing. Those abrupt turns each time he nearly plowed into a wall were making him dizzy. "She won't see it that way."

Chuck's response was as simple as everything else he'd said so far. "So you gotta wait for her to see it."

These platitudes would work for a recovery sponsor who was telling a man to keep away from the liquor store. Not so helpful when you were dealing with issues as complicated as Joseph's failed marriage.

Or the depth of his remorse for the ways he'd hurt Jolene.

Or how willing he'd be to do penance every single day of his life if it only meant a chance to make things right with her again.

CHAPTER 15

With her facial dried and caked onto her parched skin, a soothing eye mask blocking out the harsh overhead light, and her newly pedicured toes drying while she rested, Jolene leaned back and visualized peace and relaxation flowing into each and every part of her body. At some point tomorrow, Mena was taking her out for a three-hour trip to the spa. A hot tub for soaking, a sauna for relaxing, and a masseuse for spoiling each and every tight muscle and ligament in her body sounded like just the treatment she needed to melt her cares away.

Or at least deaden her senses.

She'd have to ask Mena how to block Garcia's number on that app. Any issues with him would have to wait until she got home to Washington. There were far more pressing things for her to focus on now.

Like the fact that her ex-husband was staying practically next door.

She tried to remember how long it had been since they last spoke. Nearly all of her other divorced friends complained about the way their kids forced them into constant communication with their exes.

That wasn't a problem for her and Joseph.

There had been a time when creating a family had been the most important of all of Jolene's life goals. So many of her other friends were settling down, having babies. With each new pregnancy announcement she received, each new baby shower she attended, she'd fought the disappointing realization that she was missing out.

It was that miscarriage halfway through her first pregnancy that finally brought her back to the Lord. Back to the God she'd never outright rejected but certainly hadn't paid much attention to during her carefree college years. Was God punishing her by taking away her child?

As she mourned the loss of that precious baby boy, she realized that what she'd really been missing wasn't a family of her own but a relationship with her Creator. The God who was big enough to shoulder all her burdens. Soothe over all her sorrows.

And then he blessed her with a second pregnancy.

They had still been so young, she and Joseph. Young and so happily in love.

It was Joseph's steadfast devotion that sustained her through her second pregnancy when the trauma of her previous miscarriage and the chaos of her raging hormones convinced her that she'd never be able to carry a healthy child to term. She still had a homemade video of Joseph cradling their newborn daughter in his arms, singing *Brown Eyed Girl* to their sweet and perfect Chelsea.

She couldn't have asked for a better father, at least not at the beginning. Joseph was doting. The way he'd babble to Chelsea, make up little nursery rhymes to whisper in her ear, the way he'd turn the stereo up and dance with her in his arms... Had Jolene ever realized how good she had it? Or had she been too busy changing diapers or turning herself into some kind of humanoid dairy cow to notice? To appreciate what was right in front of her eyes?

Then came Joseph's work promotions. The long days at the office. The weekends spent holed up in the den poring over paperwork. The good news was all that time alone, when it was just her and her daughter, gave Jolene the chance to fall in love with the heavenly Father she'd previously only known by name.

But that spiritual growth came at its own cost.

Like her dreams of a perfect marriage.

All of a sudden, Joseph's numerous shortcomings grew far more evident. The way he never prayed before meals or took any initiative in talking about spiritual matters. How he'd only go to church if Jolene made such a big fuss about it that everyone was grumpy, even the baby, by the time they arrived.

Maybe she shouldn't have pestered him the way she did. Back then, she'd thought she was encouraging her husband to do the things she knew he was supposed to be doing from the start, but all it did was tear them farther apart.

As if work hadn't done that enough.

And then, of course, the drinking.

Jolene was never going back to that kind of life. Which is why she never touched alcohol, even socially, and refused to let Garcia drink when they went out together. Not that it did anything to save their relationship.

Cursed in love. That might explain it.

Or maybe God was punishing her. Punishing her for loving her daughter so fiercely. How many times had she feared that she'd made Chelsea her idol? How many times had she asked God to forgive her because she couldn't truly say that he was the most important part of her life?

Is that why he'd taken her away? Had God murdered her daughter because Jolene was certain life would stop altogether without her?

She had been right, now that she thought about it. Life had stopped five years ago. Stopped and never resumed.

She was older now. With more gray in her roots. More wrinkles on her face. More heaviness in her heart, but she still hadn't started living again.

Meeting Garcia brought her closer than she'd been. There were times early on in their relationship that she thought she'd finally found true happiness, but those were all illusions. Illusions and wishful thinking.

She let out her breath. It was time to wash her face mask off, but she was too tired and weighed down by all these memories. Sadness and regrets that sank into her bones one by one. Whatever masseuse she ended up with when Mena took her to the spa would have her work cut out for her.

Tomorrow couldn't come fast enough.

CHAPTER 16

J oseph stopped his pacing. Chuck had been right. Chuck was always right.

He needed to tell her.

Tell Jolene how he felt. Explain how he'd changed. It sounded so simple coming out of his sponsor's mouth.

Simple until he got off the phone with Chuck and realized how terrifying that kind of conversation would actually be.

He resumed his march up and down the floorboards. If he kept his routine up much longer, he'd start the day off tomorrow with shin splints.

It didn't matter. Anything to get his mind off Jolene. Anything to get Chuck's advice out of his head.

Tell her? Tell her what?

Hey, hon. Remember when I went behind your back and slept with the company intern for five months right after our daughter died? Yeah, good times, weren't they?

He could try to explain to her how he'd changed, but what reason would she have to believe him? Besides, she was in another relationship now—and why shouldn't she be?—so what reason on earth could possibly compel her to take another chance on Joseph, the addict? Joseph, the deadbeat father, who was so stone-cold drunk he missed an entire decade of their daughter's life.

Joseph the adulterer who'd been more heartbroken when his mistress dumped him than he'd been over the fact that he'd ruined his relationship with his wife of twenty-five years.

Joseph the alcoholic, the workaholic, the man who would be forever in recovery because his mind and body were both so sick he wouldn't ever find true healing.

That was the most depressing fact to face about his sobriety. He'd never stop being in recovery. He'd never stop wanting to drown his pain in liquor. He'd never escape the temptation.

Day after day, decade after decade, he'd remain addicted to alcohol until his death.

There's some real optimism for you.

And Jolene deserved so much more than that. As much as he hated the thought of another man in her life, he had to confront the truth.

She needed someone to love. She'd wasted two and half decades already. He wasn't going to ask her to take another chance on him.

It wouldn't be right.

With newfound determination, he pulled out his phone and sent his office assistant a text. He was checking out of this B&B and spending the rest of his trip in a hotel.

He couldn't risk making Jolene's life a nightmare again. Couldn't risk running into her and letting his mouth spout off all the apologies he'd been storing up.

Jolene didn't need him hanging around like deadweight.

For her own good.

He had to let her go.

CHAPTER 17

Now that she'd taken off her eye mask, she couldn't get that ostentatious flower arrangement out of her line of vision. What had Garcia been thinking, sending her flowers like that? Didn't he know how badly geraniums would stink? Besides, their relationship was past the point of recovery. He was the one who messed around, and now he was expecting her to take him back?

Did he think she was some love-struck rookie fresh out of high school?

A college student whose infatuation clouded out her better judgment?

Disgusting. There was no way she could relax as long as that bouquet was in her room. She threw on her shoes. It didn't matter if it was still raining outside. What was it that Joseph always said? *A little rain never hurt nobody.* Nobody died from getting wet.

There were at least a dozen or more homes in this little *hanok*. They had to keep a dumpster somewhere, right?

Or maybe that had been wishful thinking, she realized after finding nothing outside. How could a city this size stay so clean without trash bins? She walked down another alleyway. Nope. Turning back toward her room, she heard someone opening a door. She kept her face buried behind the flowers. Thankfully Garcia had been feeling guilty enough that he purchased an impractically large arrangement. She wasn't in the mood to interact with anybody.

Especially not...

"Jolene?"

Not her ex. She peered out from behind the flowers, completely unprepared for his expression of surprise and then bemusement.

"What's so funny?" She hated the way she sounded so crabby. As if running into Joseph here in Seoul was anything to get riled up over. He was out of her life now. A splinter couldn't hurt you anymore once you gouged it out.

He meant nothing to her.

So why was he trying to swallow down a laugh, and why did his expression irritate her so much?

A drop of rain fell on her cheek. Why did her skin feel so scaly and dry?

She nearly dropped the bouquet when she realized what she'd done. Had she seriously stepped foot outside her *hanok* with that mud caked onto her face? Had Joseph's presence and Garcia's stupid flowers gotten her so riled up she stopped thinking clearly?

How could she not have noticed?

She held the vase closer, doing her best not to gag from the overwhelming stench. What kind of florist would willingly throw these weeds into a bouquet? Sure, they looked nice until you had to try sharing a room with them without succumbing to the migraine of the century.

"Where are you going with the flowers?" Thankfully, he didn't make any comments about her appearance, but the jocular twinkle in his eye remained.

Her ex-husband had always been an attractive man. Which was why he could easily have his choice of office interns, and did. Why was she still thinking about all this five years later? Why were such old wounds so close to the surface now? Maybe because of what she'd just gone through with Garcia.

Yeah, that must be it.

She'd cut Joseph out of her life like an infected appendix. Sure, their breakup had left its share of scars—what divorce wouldn't? But they were scars that had years ago healed over. At least that's what she'd thought.

Until now...

"You know, you've always looked great. You don't need the beauty treatments."

She tried to stammer out some sort of reply but couldn't make herself coherent.

"Is something wrong with the flowers?" Was that hopefulness in his voice? Was he jealous of Garcia? How was that for irony?

As eager as she'd been to find a trash can to dump the entire arrangement into, she was now protective of her mass of overpowering, pollen-infested, allergy-inducing flowers, geraniums and all. "They're fine. I just thought they might need water."

He raised an eyebrow. "Something wrong with the water in your room?"

She didn't have a response. It was time to deflect. "Where are you going? Are the bars even open this late?" A low shot, maybe, but he was the one who put her on the defensive all the time.

"I'm not drinking anymore. Three and a half years sober."

She shrugged. Why should his word mean anything to her after decades of lies? She glanced at his face. Tried to see if she'd wounded him by what she said. That's when she saw his suitcase and carryon. "You're leaving?"

Now it was his turn to shrug. "Misty found me a hotel closer to downtown. Saves the company some money on cabs."

There were so many things she wanted to know. Was he leaving because of her? Was this what he thought she wanted? Was he jealous about the flowers? She tried to guess the answers even as she did her best to appear indifferent. After all, why should she care what her ex-husband did on his business trip to Seoul? She hadn't seen him in over four years and could happily go the rest of her life never encountering him again.

Never having to face those unbearable memories his presence dredged up from the recesses of her mind. She'd thought she'd been making so much progress...

He squeezed his way past her even though the alleyway was hardly wide enough for two people. Out of habit, she took a sniff as he scooted by, hunting for a scent of whiskey or soju that would prove she still had every reason to detest him.

There was the smell of cigarettes, but smoking wasn't ever one of his vices, and she doubted he'd picked it up now. Not when he was so successful with drinking himself senseless and bedding cute, curvy interns who didn't care that he had a wife of twenty-five years at home. No, the smoke was probably from his work associates. She remembered back when they were married how badly his clothes would stink after he returned from his trips.

Nearly half a decade washing nobody's laundry but her own. That was a nice feeling right there. Something she'd taken for granted for far too long.

He turned around once he reached the sidewalk. "Nice running into you." He managed to get the words out so casually, as if there weren't half a lifetime of history between the two of them. She could have been an associate he met for the first time that night and would have forgotten about by morning. "Tell Mena hi, and congratulate her for me."

Jolene wanted to come up with some sort of reply. Some way to show Joseph that he couldn't just show up in her life and then leave her alone in an alleyway wearing a mud mask and holding an arrangement of sense-deadening geraniums. That there was more to be said between them.

But she never got the chance.

He turned, and without another backward glance, he was gone.

CHAPTER 18

How could a woman in a facial mask and sweatpants look so irresistibly sexy?

Joseph quickened his pace. It didn't matter that the sprinkling had turned into a deluge. It didn't matter that his dry-clean only business suit was going to be unusable for the rest of this trip.

He just had to get away. Put distance between himself and his past.

Nice, safe, comfortable distance.

Over four years. And she still looked good. Even with mud dried onto her face.

Four years. He'd been so focused on work that it only felt like a few short months. After the divorce, he'd thrown himself into his career, relocating to the Seattle office, fast-tracking his advancement, pushing for more international trips like these. A shrink like Jolene's boyfriend might tell him he was running away.

The reality was he liked to succeed. Enjoyed the respect his associates showed him at the office. Relished having his own staff to manage the way he saw fit. Nobody breathing down his neck or second-guessing his every move.

And he'd stayed sober. Work gave him something to focus on. Some higher purpose to live for than the bottle.

He clenched the sobriety coin in his pocket. He didn't always carry it with him anymore, but on business trips where he knew there'd be temptations, he brought it along as a reminder of what he'd worked so hard for. He'd managed to turn his life around, maintained his sobriety when Jolene divorced him, Denise left him, and that New York promotion he'd worked so hard for passed him by. Sure, there'd been a few relapses, but this was his longest clean spell.

His fingers ran over the grooves of his coin. As proud as he was for these three and a half years of sobriety, he knew he couldn't take the credit for them all. Chuck had been a huge factor in straightening him up. It was Chuck who told him what a fool he was for sleeping around with Denise in the first place, Chuck who took him in after the divorce, Chuck who dragged him to church and Bible studies and recovery meetings.

Chuck who would be so disappointed if he found out what Joseph was about to do.

Thankfully, his sponsor was on the other side of the world and would never know the difference.

He'd noticed the bar on his walk back to the *hanok*. Noticed the American music blaring inside, the Budweiser posters on the windows. He wouldn't even have to take a cab to Itaewon where most of the ex-pats lived. He could find everything he'd need right here.

Wheeling his suitcase into the establishment, he glanced around. It could have easily been a bar in Seattle except for the Korean staff.

"Welcome." The young waitress's accent was heavy, but Joseph had been to Korea enough times he barely noticed. "The bar? Or table?" she asked.

It was a good question. If he picked the table, he'd have a chance to change his mind. Think through the ramifications of jumping off the wagon. Then again, he'd been in recovery for over six years, fully sober for half that. Just because he'd had a problem in the past, why did that condemn him to a life of abstinence? He didn't even need to get drunk. Just a single beer. Something to get his mind off his ex-wife who was at this moment just a few blocks away in a Seoul *hanok* and his daughter who'd died in this blasted city.

Talk about a horrible family reunion.

"Table?" the waitress asked, pointing as if Joseph might not have understood the question.

He shook his head. "No. The bar." He clenched his fists and took a definitive step forward. "I'll sit at the bar. Thanks."

CHAPTER 19

How could she have been so stupid? What was she thinking waltzing around Seoul with mud dried onto her face? Especially when she knew Joseph was just a few doors down?

What made her even angrier was that she still had those stupid flowers in her room. What was she supposed to do after bumping into her ex-husband? Toss out her boyfriend's bouquet while he was watching? Besides, she still hadn't found a dumpster.

Stupid city.

Why had she come here? What had she been thinking? When she made plans to see Seoul, she'd imagined this as a pilgrimage of sorts. Visiting the country where her daughter had died. Maybe traveling here would help her find a way to come to terms with Chelsea's death.

Everyone else had moved on. Joseph certainly had. So had Mena, even though Jolene would never deny her the happiness she deserved.

Everyone else was living their lives, making the most of a world without Chelsea's bright smile, hot temper, and comforting companionship. Everyone else had found healing and closure.

Why couldn't she?

Jolene turned the water temperature up far too high and

lathered up, welcoming the scalding heat on her skin. She'd forgotten to bring soap and had to use whatever generic brand she found in the bathroom cabinet. *Fabulous Body Wash.* That's all the label said. She had no idea what was in it, but she wasn't in a position to be picky. She had a day's worth of travel and grime and sweat and frustrations to wash away.

Once she'd cleaned her body and scrubbed the mud off her face, she realized she'd left her shampoo in her suitcase. She picked up the bottle hanging up over the sink. *Spectacular Shampoo.* What was it with the Korean language and its overuse of adjectives? The shampoo might be fine, or even spectacular like the label claimed. Or it might turn her hair into a mess of dried-out frizz.

She wasn't going to take her chances. Not with a wedding coming up in just a couple more days.

She shut off the water, threw her towel around herself, and zipped into the bedroom. Where had she put her bottle? By the time she was done looking, the room looked like it had been hit by a hurricane. Still no shampoo, but at least she'd found her conditioner. Whatever odd chemicals were in that *Spectacular* stuff, she'd have to use it and trust her luck.

Why hadn't she been more careful packing? What else had she forgotten to bring with her?

It wasn't like her to feel this flustered. Had running into Joseph really thrown her off so much? Or maybe it was the city itself. Why couldn't Mena have waited five or ten more years to find the man she wanted to marry? Or brought him to Washington to tie the knot there?

The water was tepid by the time she returned to the shower. Stupid of her to leave it running so long. What did she expect?

Oh, well. Her hair was wet, which meant she was committed. She had to wash it now, or else tomorrow she'd end up with a head of oily plastic.

Back under the faucet, under the cooling water, hoping to get her hair washed and conditioned before the flow turned icy.

No such luck. She'd expected the water to continue to cool down in small spurts, but it dropped about thirty degrees in the two seconds it had taken her to smother on her conditioner.

Drying herself off as best she could with a head of lathered-up hair, she threw on her robe. She'd let the conditioner sit for five or ten minutes. Hopefully, by then, there'd be something akin to warm water to rinse it off with. She certainly wasn't going back into that waterfall of ice.

Tying the belt of her fuzzy bathrobe, she sat in one of the hard chairs in the kitchen. At least in the *hanok* they had a Western-style table instead of the floor arrangement like back at the restaurant, but she wished there was something soft she could sink into. A recliner, love-seat, oversized beanbag, she wasn't picky. Not a straight-backed chair.

But what could she do?

She sat at the table, hoping the water would heat up soon, and stared at Garcia's stupid geraniums. The fool was trying hard. But after everything Jolene had endured the past five years, she wasn't in a forgiving mood. She'd told him from the beginning. Social drinking was acceptable, even though she was only slightly comfortable with that. Drunkenness, on the other hand—totally out of the question.

Drunkenness that leads to a one-night stand with your client's sister?

Yeah, that's a deal-breaker.

And he'd been so apologetic. Hence the emotional pleas at the airport, the flowers sent all the way to Seoul.

After twenty-five years married to Joseph, Jolene could recognize a manipulator a mile away. She should have gone with her instincts and dropped Garcia months ago. But she'd wanted to believe that a marriage counselor of all people could have a little more couth.

Live and learn, right?

The water still wasn't hot when she checked, so she passed

the time plucking petals off the stupid geraniums one by smelly one.

This is for making me feel like I'm the bad guy when you drove me to the airport.

This is for getting drunk and messing around with your client's sister.

This is for not being here in Seoul when I need you.

This is for sleeping with your secretary a month after we lost our daughter.

And making her almost miss her senior prom when you got arrested.

And showing up in Seoul when I...

She stopped and stared at the geranium shreds she'd littered onto the table. How had that happened?

A knock on the door.

"Jolene? You in there?"

Joseph. What in the world was he thinking?

"Jolene? You left your key in the lock. I'm just going to open it up and..."

Her ex-husband was about to walk in on her with conditioner in her hair while she was ripping apart her ex-boyfriend's flower arrangement wearing nothing but a bathrobe. It wasn't her finest of choices, but she ducked down behind the table.

The door opened.

"What are you doing down there?"

She straightened up awkwardly and barely missed hitting her head on the corner of the counter. "Just, you know, picking up." She held a single geranium petal in her hand and immediately reminded herself that this was her room. Her territory. She had no reason to feel embarrassed, and he had no right to be here. "You need to get out. What happened to that hotel Misty booked for you?"

He stepped forward. He didn't know she'd taken self-defense

classes after the divorce. Another foot or two in her direction, and he'd get the surprise of his life. Aside from the fact that she had conditioner in her hair and a fuzzy bathrobe over an otherwise naked body, she was a formidable force.

"I came to talk. You left your key in the lock."

It was no surprise. She'd been so flustered after running into him in the alley, so embarrassed to be spotted in her mask. She held out her hand and accepted the key he offered. "Thank you. Now go away."

He kept his eyes low. Was he embarrassed for her? Did he seriously think that with as many times as he'd wounded her, she'd care whether or not he saw her looking like this? Some people were so full of themselves.

He held out his hands. "I came back." What was that supposed to mean?

"I can see you came back. Now do what I said and go away."

He didn't budge. She crept her hand closer to the vase. If she needed to, she'd bring the whole thing down on his head. At least Garcia's gift wouldn't be entirely useless.

"I wanted to talk."

One more step closer and she could smell it on his breath. Three years sober? Yeah, right.

"You're drunk." Well, that at least explained why he was brash enough to force his way into her room this late at night.

"I'm not. It's not…"

"Get out." This time, she really did pick up the vase. It was so heavy she had to use two hands, but she wasn't worried about the exertion. She could handle him.

"Listen, Jolene, I've changed. I haven't…"

"Get. Out." Each word came out like a separate entity from the core of her body, where she was storing years' worth of hatred and bitterness and unforgiveness that she hadn't even known existed.

"I didn't drink. I promise. I was just…"

His lies were too much. "You think your promise means anything to me? You think I'm impressed when you barge in here smelling like cheap beer? Haven't we been down this road enough times? I'm sick of it. So sick of it." Great. She was so worked up she was close to tears now. Her self-defense trainer told her it was normal, that female brains were wired to get emotional after a major adrenaline surge like what happens in a major fight, but she needed a good cry about as badly as she needed both her legs amputated.

She gritted her teeth, shoved her emotions down into that dark pit she'd so recently unearthed, and growled once more, "Get out. Now."

He took a step back. At least he realized she was serious. "Ok." His body deflated, but hers was still on edge. Still ready to fight him off if he tried anything else. Still holding onto the vase.

"Ok," he repeated, backing up toward her door. "I'm going. I'm sorry. I won't bother you again."

"Good." She hurled the word at him as if it'd been the vase she was aiming at his head.

"I just wanted to talk."

She wouldn't listen. They'd danced this dance before, the one where he apologized so profusely until she was left certain she was in the wrong. No more. Nobody had the right to manipulate her. Nobody. Especially not her cheating, alcoholic ex who lied through his teeth, claimed he hadn't been drinking when even someone with a sinus infection could smell the beer on his breath.

Once he was at the door, she set the vase down and crossed her arms, glaring at him. Daring him to do anything besides walk out the way he came in.

"I just wanted to talk." His voice was softer now. Soft but coherent. Funny. He was so pathetic he usually couldn't get out two or three words straight when he was drinking.

Oh, well. Not her business. Not her problem.

He lowered his gaze. "Ok. Guess I'll go."

She didn't respond. After he shut the door behind him, she marched forward, threw down the deadbolt, and then let out the breath she'd been holding in.

The water was scalding hot by the time she got back into the shower, just the way she liked it. She rinsed out her conditioner, refusing to think of how outrageous she must have looked in her bathrobe with her hair all soaped up. Even so, she'd managed to force Joseph to take her seriously, a feat she certainly had never accomplished during their twenty-five years of marriage.

Twenty-five years...

Sometimes she was tempted to think they were all wasted, but she knew better than that.

Twenty-five years...

After rinsing, she slammed off the water, dried her hair with the towel, and got dressed in her pajamas.

At least now if Joseph came back, she wouldn't look quite so ridiculous.

CHAPTER 20

Three and a half years of sobriety and he'd almost wasted it. And for what?

He knew he should call Chuck. His sponsor would want to know what happened, how close Joseph had come to diving headfirst off the wagon.

But he didn't want to.

Didn't want to admit his failure.

Settled into his new hotel room with its western-style bed, he sank into the armchair and placed the call.

"Hey, brother." Chuck's voice was laden with concern. As if he already knew what Joseph was about to say.

No use making small-talk. This was the kind of conversation you had to jump right into. No looking back. "I went to a bar tonight." He cleared his throat, hopeful that the worst part of the confession was over. "I didn't drink. I mean, I wanted to. I ordered a beer, and the waitress brought it to me. But then…"

"Did you drink?" Chuck cut him off.

"No." Joseph cleared his throat once more. "No, I mean, I took a small sip, but I spit it out. First of all, the stuff tasted rancid." He let out a nervous chuckle, a chuckle his sponsor didn't share. He toned down the jocularity. Stopped trying to diffuse his shame with humor. "I spit it out and left right after that."

"Good." Chuck spoke the word in a monotone. He may as well have been a jury declaring Joseph guilty.

"I'm not drunk now."

"I can hear that."

Joseph felt his body relax ever so slightly. It was good to have someone believe him for a change. He sat waiting for his sponsor to say something. Anything. Joseph didn't know what was supposed to happen next.

"Was it seeing Jolene that brought you so close to the edge?" Chuck asked the question so pointedly, there was no use trying to deflect or avoid the topic.

"I don't know. Probably. She was... I saw her again. She was outside with that man's flowers. Don't know what she was doing with them." He could shut his eyes and picture her so easily, mud mask and all. "And then after I left the bar, I went back. I walked by her door and saw that she'd left the keys in, and I didn't want her spending the whole night that way where anyone could let themselves in."

So he stretched the truth a little. Didn't it count that he was being so painfully honest about everything else?

"Did the two of you talk much?"

"No. I wanted to. You know, I thought I should say something. It's been five years to the month since Chelsea... I thought maybe I could try to cheer her up a little..." He was floundering. He knew it, and he was sure Chuck on the other end of the line knew it, too.

"Let me guess," Chuck butted in. "She wasn't very engaging."

"No. That's the thing. When I went back to return the key, she thought I'd been drinking. I swear that woman can smell beer a mile away." He'd meant it as a joke but realized it was entirely his fault his wife had gained such a discerning sense. "She never trusted me in the past..." he began and stopped.

"From what I understand, you didn't give her much reason

to," Chuck observed. From any other man, the comment would make Joseph jump to the defensive, but his sponsor was right, and the love Chuck had shown Joseph when he was at his lowest earned him the right to speak these truths into his life, painful as they were.

"Maybe not, but I've changed."

"She doesn't know that."

"That's why I tried telling her."

"You can't force these things, son." There was no way biologically speaking that Chuck was old enough to be Joseph's father, but he accepted the gentle rebuke without bristling.

"Where are you now?" Chuck asked.

"At my hotel. I moved to a different one, where Jolene..." With as incoherent as he was, Chuck might soon start doubting the part of the story where Joseph said he spit out the beer. "I'm in a different part of town." Knowing exactly what question his sponsor was going to ask next, he added, "I'm not planning to go out again. I don't even want to drink. Not right now."

"Why's that?" There was no judgment in Chuck's tone. Just a gentle invitation for Joseph to bare his soul.

"Because the small sip I spit out tasted terrible. Because something in my body reacted so strongly I felt like I wanted to puke." He paused, wondering if he should say everything that was on his heart. Would it just make matters worse once he admitted the truth out loud? "And because I don't want to be proven a liar. Not with Jolene somewhere in this city."

Chuck was quiet for a moment. What was he thinking? About how pathetic it was for Joseph to still act like he had anything to prove to his ex-wife? About how a grown man like him shouldn't hold onto such babyish hopes that one day she might realize he'd changed and take him back?

The next words out of Chuck's mouth weren't wise, sagacious observations about life or sobriety or lost love. No more pointed questions either. Instead, he began to pray, thanking God for helping Joseph stay sober, asking for continued strength to stand up against temptation.

Chuck was a godly man, with a spiritual strength and maturity Joseph would give up all four of his limbs to achieve.

Then Jolene would see how much I've changed.

In the back of his head was the nagging suspicion that pursuing godliness to win back your divorced wife's trust might not be the most righteous of motivations, but he was where he was, and at least he could admit to his own shortcomings.

He joined Chuck in prayer, asking God to mold him into the man he was supposed to be, the kind of man Jolene could trust and rely on, the kind of man she'd be proud to call her own.

CHAPTER 21

M ena showed up at Jolene's front door a few
minutes after nine.

"Good morning!" She was dressed in a bright pink blouse with a violet and teal scarf draped around her neck. Jolene still couldn't figure out how her daughter's fairly awkward best friend from junior high had developed into this capable, sophisticated young woman. "Sorry if I woke you up."

"Don't worry about that." Jolene shut the door behind her. "I've been awake for a few hours anyway." All the stress of running into her ex-husband made it impossible to fall asleep until after midnight, but by five in the morning, her body woke her up, convinced it was time to start her day.

Stupid jet lag.

Mena set a bag of groceries on the counter. "I brought some breakfast over. Have you ever tried an Asian pear? And this is banana milk. It's really popular here."

Jolene studied the unfamiliar items, imagining how good a nice pancake breakfast with a generous portion of syrup sounded instead. "This was really sweet of you."

"Don't worry about it. Jin-Sun's tied up all morning getting ready for a fundraising luncheon. And I've got the pre-wedding jitters, I guess. I thought it might be good to have something to focus on besides the ceremony for a change." She rummaged

193

through the grocery bag. "Oh, I don't know if you like sweets this early, but these shaved ice drinks are delicious. And after we eat, I thought we'd take a walk. Check out that spa I was telling you about."

Jolene wasn't about to argue. A short time later, after about a mile-long walk that made her grateful the rain from last night had let up, they were sitting together in a sauna. It was early enough in the day that they were the only two there.

"This is great." Jolene hadn't realized how tight her muscles were. That's what you get when you sit cramped on an airplane for twelve hours then go to sleep on a floor mat. That and running into your ex-husband in a foreign country just a few days after breaking up with your boyfriend.

Good times.

"The masseuses here are great," Mena told her. Jolene's body was already aching for a massage.

She shut her eyes, wondering what it would be like to tell Mena about last night. It's the kind of conversation she might have had with Garcia. After a year of dating him exclusively, she realized how many of her female friendships she'd failed to maintain. Was there anyone back home she'd be comfortable inviting out for a spa day? Or calling to vent after running into her ex-husband in the same foreign city where their daughter had been killed?

Even her church attendance had slipped recently. It wasn't that she was trying to distance herself from God. She just stopped getting as much out of the sermons as she used to. It didn't make her a bad Christian. She just had other obligations.

Like what?

Usually, she spent her weekends with Garcia. Maybe that explained things. It wasn't that he didn't want her to go to church, but it wasn't as much of a priority for him. Maybe he'd rubbed off on her more than she intended.

But she still prayed. Still trusted God with her future. She wasn't reading the Bible as much as she sometimes did, but for her entire Christian life, she'd gone through seasons of deeper devotion than others.

None of that meant she was a second-rate Christian or a backslidden believer.

So why did she feel guilty now?

Maybe it was just loneliness, and her recent breakup with Garcia could explain that part. Why she was sitting here in Seoul wishing she had the courage to pour out her heart to a young woman who wasn't even born when Jolene first fell in love with Joseph. Those happy, chaotic, blissful years...

"You know, you've hardly told me anything about your fiancé. What's his name again?" Why couldn't she ever remember?

"Jin-Sun."

"Yeah. Jin-Sun. Tell me about him. How did you meet?"

Mena smiled. The smile of a carefree bride-to-be who was just as much in love with her groom as Jolene had been on her own wedding day so many years ago. "Through work. He's actually from North Korea."

"Really?"

"Yeah. He came to Seoul a few years ago. He was part of the first wave of refugees we brought here with Freedom Korea International."

"Wow. So you brought him over here, helped him resettle, and fell in love?" Why did the story make Jolene's heart feel so heavy?

"Kind of. He's working for Freedom Korea now too. He was hired about a year and a half ago. That's when we started growing close."

"That's really sweet." Jolene meant what she said but hated the way she had to swallow down that unwelcome dose of envy. Why should she be sitting here half-naked in a sauna feeling jealous of a girl she'd known since she was a somewhat chubby, pimply-faced adolescent? Jolene was the adult here, the one who was supposed to have her life together. A mother figure that Mena could look up to and respect. But what's so impressive about a middle-aged divorcée with a second failed relationship to her credit and hardly anything to show for her life?

Decades. She'd invested decades into her family, into her daughter, into her marriage. And for what? For an alcoholic husband who cheated on her within a month of their daughter's death. Eighteen years being nothing but a stay-at-home mom. Not that she regretted the time she had with Chelsea, but what was all that for? So her daughter could travel to this God-forsaken corner of the globe and die here in a freak accident?

And where had God been when that cable snapped? Out of the forty-nine people on board, only three were killed. Why Chelsea?

Mena had been there that night. Jolene couldn't remember the details, but there'd been something about a broken leg. Maybe a surgery... So much about that time remained a haze in her memory. And for good reason. Why would she want to relive those horrific months of not only grieving her daughter but watching her husband bury himself into his shell of anger and bitterness...

Jolene had promised herself never to become bitter. A promise that Joseph made very difficult to keep when the details of his affair burst into the open.

A text. How clichéd and trite could you get? A text he'd meant for his mistress but sent to his wife instead.

His wife whom he'd been hiding from, avoiding intimacy with. At the time, she'd thought the grief was to blame.

Still so naïve...

While Jolene shed rivers of sweat, Mena prattled on about Ji-Hun or Jin-Bun or whatever her fiancé's name was. Talking about their hopes for the non-profit they worked for. Their plans for the future.

"He said he wants five or six or seven kids, but he's just going to have to learn to get used to disappointment." Mena laughed at her own words. Jolene longed for the time when the sum of her and

Joseph's worries was how many children they might conceive.

Before the miscarriage, before Chelsea, before the drinking and the grieving and the affair.

Jolene shut her eyes, not necessarily because she was tired—which she was—but because it was too painful to see that much happiness on Mena's face while she talked about her future.

CHAPTER 22

J oseph hated this part of his job. The charity cases, the fancy fundraising luncheons spent listening to emotionally manipulative speakers with their sob stories and sales-pitchy appeals.

But until he was the one calling all the shots in the Seoul office as well as in Seattle, he had no choice.

At least the weather was more cooperative today. This business suit hadn't gotten soaked in the rain.

Let's just get this over with.

His conversation with Chuck last night had convinced him of one thing and one thing only. He had to get out of Seoul. He'd been here dozens of times since losing Chelsea, but it was different now. Maybe because it was the five-year anniversary. Maybe because of Jolene.

He couldn't believe she'd traveled so far just to watch Chelsea's best friend get married. He still remembered Mena when she was pimple-faced wearing braces. And now she was working for some non-profit, probably getting paid a pittance, and about to get married. When did she get old enough to find a husband? He didn't want to think about it. He'd never get the chance to walk his own daughter down the aisle, and that's just the way it was. Why waste energy focusing on hypothetical impossibilities?

Why waste energy wondering what Jolene was doing, if she

was enjoying her time in Seoul or if she patched things up with the boyfriend who sent that hideous bouquet?

The problem was that as soon as lunch was over, Joseph would have nothing to do but pretend to be interested in some refugee's plea for his company's investment. It wasn't that Joseph begrudged him the funds the firm would donate. He just wished he could sign a check and be done with it. None of these dragged out charity spiels. It was like having to watch a TV commercial about starving African orphans for an hour straight.

Yeah, he was definitely ready to be done with Seoul. He'd already been brainstorming new procedures to implement back in Seattle. Get Misty to stop wasting so much blasted time on flower arrangements and actually work on client relationships, the part of her job she'd been hired for.

And how much money was the firm leaking with these overseas trips, anyway? It had been worth it a couple years ago when they were still building relationships here in Seoul, but now the return on investment was dwindling at best. Hemorrhaging money at worst.

Some accused Joseph of being an alarmist, but that's what made him good at his job. Cut out any unnecessary expenditures. Hadn't that been his policy since he started? And not just in the work field, at home too.

Unnecessary expenditures.

Like that stupid vacation he and Jolene had taken to the Oregon Coast when the weather hadn't cooperated with their plans and his wife thought Chelsea was too young to be outside in the rain. Nine hundred dollars later, all they'd gotten out of their trip was three days binging on Disney movies.

The problem was every time they talked about money, Jolene would get all self-righteous about how they should be tithing a full ten percent—ten whole percent! As if Joseph worked as hard as he did just so their church could buy new carpet.

What was wrong with the old stuff, anyway?

Even now that he'd gotten more serious about his faith, now

that he was attending church regularly and waking up early for that Thursday morning men's breakfast and prayer time, he still bristled at the thought of any man telling him what he should do with his hard-earned money.

The last thing God converts is a man's pocketbook. Who was it who said that? Joseph couldn't remember, but his pastor had used the quote more than once. Which is why if Joseph got a hint that a certain sermon would touch on the area of financial giving, he often tried to come up with some convenient excuse to be sick or traveling or golfing that particular Sunday.

The Seoul VP was up on stage now, thanking everyone for coming, *blah, blah, blah.* Which meant that he was about to introduce the speaker, which meant that Joseph would have to spend the next hour pretending to pay attention while someone else—this time someone he didn't even know—tried to tell him what to do with his finances. At least now they were talking about the firm's money and not his own.

Joseph leaned back in his chair, adjusting his waistband to make room for all the Korean barbecue he'd eaten. Too bad he didn't have those tinted glasses so he could fall asleep without anyone noticing.

Oh, well. This was just as much a part of his job as laying off workers or paying taxes. No way to get out of it.

Adopting an expression that hopefully made him appear more interested than he felt, he took a deep breath and told himself to get comfortable. This would take a while.

CHAPTER 23

Jolene **struggled to keep up** as she hurried across the street.

"We're almost there," Mena called over her shoulder.

Jolene told herself that it was the smoggy air that made her short of breath. It shouldn't be this hard to keep up with a woman half her age.

A woman who was rushing to some big conference hall to hear her fiancé speak.

When Jolene had agreed to attend the meeting with Mena, she hadn't realized it would mean jumping on three different subs and then sprinting down crowded sidewalks to make it there on time. Jolene had no idea how anyone would keep all those different subway lines straight, but apparently there was an app Mena raved about that helped her navigate the crowded city.

It still didn't get them to her fiancé's lunch on time.

Yet another common trait Mena and Chelsea shared. They were both chronically late.

How many times had Jolene had to call her daughter in college so Chelsea wouldn't miss an important lecture or test? Joseph hated it. Said that Chelsea would never learn to manage her own time if Jolene kept babysitting her schedule. Yet another reason for the near-constant strife between them.

Maybe it was this city. In Orchard Grove, Jolene stayed busy enough she didn't think about her ex that often. She'd always think of Chelsea—she'd resigned herself to that years ago. But at least back home she could think about her daughter without constant reminders of what a terrible dad Joseph had been.

How many times he'd let them down.

And Chelsea always forgave him. Always had a smile for Daddy. A kiss. A hug. Maybe that was the blessing—as well as the curse—of youth. You're able to overlook the faults of those you love...

Jolene had loved her husband. That was never the problem. The problem was his constant drinking. The affair with Miss Perky Secretary. The lies, deceit, everything that came after Chelsea died.

Maybe it was that she'd loved him too much. Enabled him to descend into the abyss of alcoholism, propped him up when what she should have done was separate sooner. Show him that she was dead serious about him changing.

Too late now.

For so many things.

"Jin-Sun's really glad you're coming today," Mena said. Even after their trek across town and their insanely fast sprint, she wasn't even winded. "I can't wait for you to hear his story."

At least listening to Mena's fiancé would give Jolene something to focus on besides the emptiness and longing, the heavy regrets and incessant sorrow, that weighed down on her soul.

CHAPTER 24

"Thank you so much for** allowing me to speak here."

Joseph shouldn't have eaten so much pork. Oh, well. At least the speaker's English was easy to understand. The beginning of the speech was hardly surprising. He'd grown up in North Korea, where of course he'd experienced hunger and oppression. What else was new? You could watch sob stories like this all day long if you wanted.

The speaker was as generic as they come. Younger than some of these charity cases, but he had no other defining characteristics.

"I was raised by my mother, who never told me who my father was." So apparently men had daddy issues all over the globe. Not exactly the most earth-shattering of revelations.

Joseph fought the waves of exhaustion that swept over him, inviting him to shut his eyes, drown out this background noise, and lose himself in dreams. Dreams of happier times. Just him and Jolene. Young, carefree. No mortgages to worry about, no miscarriages, no fights over who would say the prayers at mealtimes or why Joseph couldn't be a better spiritual leader.

Just him and his wife. Young. In love.

It was his fault things turned out the way they did. And not just the drinking either. All of it. How he hated his wife's constant nagging. *Why don't you tithe to the church? Why don't you say bedtime prayers with your daughter?* He resented her relationship with the Lord because it meant there was something in the universe more important to her than he was.

Why wasn't he enough?

And why did he still feel so guilty after all these years? He'd asked God to forgive him dozens of times. If Chelsea were still alive, he'd apologize to her as well. Beg her to forgive him for that night he'd gotten arrested and ruined her senior prom. For all those times he'd embarrassed her, forced her to make excuses to explain why she couldn't invite girls from school over like a normal teenager could because then everyone would know about her father's problem.

Mena was the only friend who spent any regular time at their home, and that was because they'd been together since junior high, before the drinking escalated into the monster it became. Mena was grandfathered into their family's dysfunction.

And now she was about to get married…

Poor young fool. She was probably just as in love with her fiancé as he and Jolene had once been. Young people never learn. Never understand.

He had to stop feeling so sorry for himself, especially since he was the one to blame for ruining his marriage. Logically, he knew how stupid it was for him to get upset with Jolene. She'd done what any self-respecting woman in her right mind would do. She gave him the choices—his marriage or the affair. His marriage or the bottle. He'd made his priorities clear on both accounts.

She wasn't wrong to leave.

So why was he so irked at her now, after so much time had passed? Was he mad that she'd found someone else? Who could blame her after nearly half a decade?

Who could blame her for moving on? For daring to live life and enjoy it?

He was a fool. He'd lost her years ago. It was stupid now to wallow in regrets. What pained him the most was that last night she thought he was drunk. It shouldn't matter so much, but it did. He hadn't realized until his conversation with Chuck that one of his driving motivations to stay sober was so she'd finally give him another chance.

The rationale was so subconscious it had taken him years to recognize. But somewhere in the back of his head was this stupid, naïve assumption that Jolene had simply put her life on hold and was waiting for him to clean up. Was he really that juvenile? Did he think that after all the turmoil they'd walked through that he could waltz into her life, claim sobriety, and demand her affection once more?

It didn't work like that. He would have never allowed Chelsea near a man like him. But here he was, after making a fool of himself, burning with jealousy, irked senseless because his wife was here in Seoul without him, was dating someone else, was living her life as if he'd never existed.

It was too late for second chances. He realized that now. But just like he'd been forced five years ago to admit his daughter was never returning home, this new realization would require an adjustment period as well.

He'd get over it. Find peace with the fact that his wife was in a relationship with someone who probably had done far more to earn her affection than Joseph ever could. At least Jolene's boyfriend had the guts to apologize when he made a mistake.

Joseph needed to accept the fact that any chance he had at reconciling with his wife was lost years ago. He'd just have to face the truth.

The sooner he understood that, the sooner he could move on.

Finally.

CHAPTER 25

"**M**y mother attended secret meetings. I was a teenager when I started wondering where she went."

Jolene leaned forward in her seat. The auditorium was so crowded when they arrived she and Mena had only managed to grab two chairs in the very back. Jin-Sun was a few minutes into his presentation by the time they got settled in, but Jolene was sucked into his story and listened in rapt attention. She didn't want to miss a word.

"Back home, children are taught that their primary loyalty is to the state. Teachers commonly ask their students to spy on their parents. That's why my mother was very careful not to let me know where she was going. It wasn't until I was a young adult that I realized she'd been attending religious meetings.

"My mother was a secret Christian, or at the very least she was a sympathizer. I say this because I don't know for sure. It's never something that could be safely discussed in a North Korean family. I was not a believer, not at first. This is one of the many difficulties Christian parents face back home. If they share their faith with their children, they risk the whole family being sent to prison camp. But according to the Bible, one of a parent's highest responsibilities is to lead their sons and daughters into a saving faith in Christ. This makes it a dilemma for Christians."

Jolene listened, surprised to hear religion spoken so freely in a public forum.

"As I said, my mother attended these meetings, even though outwardly, she was highly patriotic. She worked hard at her job. She was on good terms with those we lived near. This is also important back home since it's very common for your neighbor to denounce you to the secret police. The biggest hardships my mother faced were raising her children during the famine that unfortunately stole my baby sister's life."

Jolene glanced over at Mena, who was watching her fiancé with love beaming unmistakably from her expression.

"As a young adult, many things happened to me which it is not safe for me to speak of, but I ultimately escaped North Korea through the network of Christian helpers on Freedom Korea International's underground railroad. It is to this organization I owe my physical freedom, but it is the blood and power of Jesus Christ that set me free from my spiritual bondage.

"When I arrived in Seoul, I was broken. I had been betrayed." His voice cracked once. "Betrayed by someone very close to me."

Beside her, Jolene noticed Mena stiffen slightly.

"I was angry and hurt and confused. This is normal for refugees from the north. We are not taught back home how to compete in a capitalistic society. We do not understand the very basic methods of survival here. The first time I saw an ATM, I felt sorry for the poor worker who had to sit inside it handing people their money. I wondered why his boss wouldn't allow him more room."

Several people in the auditorium laughed, but Jolene held her breath. Somewhere in her heart was the conviction that this man held the secret she was looking for. He was filled with peace. So composed. And yet he'd faced more heartache and trauma than Jolene could fathom. What was the source of his strength? Was it something he could impart to her through a miraculous act of providence?

"I began studying Christianity in North Korea. It was dangerous, and I only learned enough to grow more curious. When

I arrived here in Seoul, I began to seek out the truth more fully. And I came to realize that Jesus Christ is the sole source of freedom and hope that this world has to offer. I weep for my compatriots who suffer under such political oppression back home, but in the same way, my heart breaks for all those—in the free world as well as those living under totalitarian regimes like North Korea—who do not know the saving power of Jesus Christ."

Jolene couldn't have stopped listening if her life depended on it. If an earthquake flattened the auditorium where she sat, she'd continue hanging onto Jin-Sun's words until the wall caved in on her and crushed her beneath its powerful weight.

"I'm here today with a message. A message of hope. North Korea as it stands today cannot persist. Such oppression will not endure in this day and age. Many North Koreans, especially along the border regions, now have cell phones smuggled in from China. They are able to use these phones to gain access to outside information that in previous generations was completely blocked out. The young men and women of my generation understand that freedom exists. They thirst for it. They long for it.

"Even more so, however, they long for the truth that comes from knowing they have a Creator, a Creator who loves them infinitely, who longs to call them his children. That, my friends, is the source of true freedom and belonging and hope."

Subdued applause broke out, but Jolene was too transfixed to join in. She stared at Jin-Sun, begging God to reveal what made him so different from her. What allowed him to suffer all that he had and remain so pure and faithful.

She asked heaven to reveal what this strange, seemingly unattainable secret of his was, but in her heart, she already knew.

CHAPTER 26

G reat. A sermon.

If Joseph wanted to be preached at, he'd download the app from his church in Seattle and listen to one of the recorded services.

His eyes darted from table to table, wondering what his more secular colleagues thought of this holy roller. If statistics were to be trusted, over half of the workers at the Seoul office claimed to be Christian, but that didn't stop any of them from drinking themselves into a loud and raucous oblivion at nearly every company dinner they attended.

Joseph was wary of anyone who tried too hard to mix work and religion. Some things were simply meant to remain in the private sphere. If you wanted to overdose on Christianity, you became a pastor or a missionary. You didn't bring it into the workplace and shove it down everyone's throat.

It wasn't that he disliked the young man's message. In fact, if Joseph went to hear this guy speak at church one Sunday, it would probably be a very memorable and uplifting sermon. But this was a work function. This wasn't the place to tell people about God or talk about their sins or try to force people through heaven's gates.

He sighed. Is this why Jolene had been so disappointed early on in their marriage? Is this the kind of man she'd hoped to turn him into? The kind of man who'd take any opportunity presented to him as a chance to force-feed the gospel into people's hearts?

No wonder he'd fallen so pitifully short.

And even now that he was sober, now that he was involved in church and finally working his way into God's good graces, he would never turn into a preacher like this.

The man had to be wrapping up soon. Did he see how restless his audience was growing? Or was he so enthralled with the chance to speak to people about his private beliefs that he wasn't paying attention to their reaction?

"I was saved shortly after arriving in Seoul. It was a young woman I met through Korea Freedom International who taught me the steps to salvation, taught me the importance of asking Jesus to forgive my sins and accepting his free gift of eternal life. But I was still far from healed. I was scarred and traumatized from what had happened to me. I was angry at the woman who betrayed me, who gave me no choice but to leave everything behind and escape.

"Perhaps you think about me, or other refugees from North Korea, and assume that we'd want nothing more than to get as far away as possible. But how can that be? North Korea is my home. I know this can be hard for some to accept, so imagine with me if you will. Imagine that someone attacks Seoul, and everyone here is forced to evacuate to Russia, for example. While perhaps we'd be grateful to the Russian government for letting us in, does that mean we would forget about the land we left behind? Not at all. North Korea will always be home to me, and I will never cease to pray for the day when freedom tears down the walls that are holding my compatriots captive.

"But even once I arrived in Seoul, even once I was free from the oppression of my homeland and the burdens of my sins after accepting Jesus Christ as my Lord and Savior, I was still trapped. Still in bondage to the hatred and bitterness and fear that had seeped its way into my spirit. I was angry at the Lord. Once I came to believe that there was a God who spun the entire universe into motion and yet remained intimately involved in every detail of our lives, I had no choice but to ask him why he left me there to suffer so much before I found my escape. Once I realized that God was powerful enough to lead me out of North Korea, I also had to confront the reality that he was powerful enough that he could have saved me years earlier. Or kept my homeland from ever growing so oppressive and dark in the first place.

"I hated him."

Something in the speaker's tone, or maybe it was his words, caught Joseph's attention. How many times had he entertained those same, seemingly futile hypotheticals? If God was powerful enough to raise Jesus from the dead, wasn't he powerful enough to keep his daughter from dying? If he could part the Red Sea, or resurrect the young man who fell out of the window listening to an all-night sermon, or heal all those lepers and the lame and the blind, couldn't he have prevented Chelsea's death?

If God was powerful enough that he could have saved her, but he still decided not to intervene that fateful night, didn't that in a way make him responsible for her death?

Joseph didn't care how close his thoughts teetered on the edge of blasphemy. When it came right down to it, isn't that exactly what happened? God killed his daughter. God knew that if she came to Seoul, if she traveled to Seoul Tower, if she got on that cable car that would lift her high up in the hills to see the city skyline in all its splendor, she would die, and he didn't do anything to stop her. How was that any different than the Almighty holding a gun to his daughter's head and blowing her brains out?

How could you love a God like that?

How could you trust someone who would allow such a tragedy?

"I prayed a lot," the speaker continued. Joseph listened, wondering if his words would contain the answers his soul so clearly needed, certain they would fall short.

"I asked God why. *Why did you let me be born in a place like North Korea? Why did you sit by when so many terrible things happened to my family and me? Why didn't you do anything?*"

His voice was so sincere, so full of the same questions that

Joseph's spirit had screamed. He leaned forward in his seat. When had his hands turned so clammy? Why was his shirt collar drenched in sweat?

"I didn't receive any answers from God."

Joseph let out his breath. *Figures.*

"At least not directly."

Joseph was about to tune him out for the rest of the afternoon when the man stopped and stared right at him. Why would he do that? Out of everyone here, out of this whole room full of hundreds of listeners, why would he single Joseph out like that?

Joseph picked up his napkin and wiped his mouth, finding a small fraction of comfort from having his face partially concealed.

"But he laid a verse on my heart. A verse from Joel. *I will restore the years the locusts have eaten.* It's talking in the Bible about a famine. We went through a famine when I was a child. I know what it's like to boil tree bark and try to swallow it down as soup. I know what it's like to grind corn cobs down and try not to chip a tooth on the cake you bake from the shavings. And in my heart, I was asking God why he let those things happen to me and my family. My little sister starved to death. I wanted answers.

"But instead, he gave me restoration. He didn't tell me why the locusts came in the first place. Why my family and I had to suffer the way we did, why my compatriots are still trapped under a dictatorship that stands ready to squash and torture and silence any opposition. My brain was looking for answers, but what my spirit needed, even more, was his promise. A promise of comfort. A promise of restoration.

"*I will restore the years the locusts have eaten,* God told me through his Word. And that's what he's done. Because of my journey, because of my struggles, I'm able to speak at events like this and let the world know what's going on in my homeland. I'm able to encourage others to pray for the day when North Korea will be open to free thinking and democracy and most importantly the gospel. And after the heartaches of my past, I've met the love of my life. A young woman I'll be marrying in just a few days."

More polite applause. Joseph took a noisy gulp of water.

Maybe platitudes and verses worked for someone like this preacher. Maybe he was so happy in his new life it didn't matter to him that all his previous questions remained unanswered.

Joseph would never be content with that. He glanced at his watch. Just a few more minutes, and then he was gone.

CHAPTER 27

M ena snuggled up against Jin-Sun's chest. "Didn't he do a great job?"

Jolene forced a smile. "That was very encouraging." As tired as she was, both physically and mentally, she truly meant what she said. If sermons back home were anything like this, it wouldn't be so difficult for her to make time for church.

Mena had her arms wrapped around his waist. "Jolene and I didn't get lunch yet. Have you had anything?"

Jin-Sun laughed. "I was too nervous."

Mena giggled. "No one would have known." It was true.

Jolene couldn't remember hearing a more polished, inspirational speaker. She felt like she should say more. "I really appreciated what you said. Especially that part about the locusts."

For as many times as she'd set out to read the Bible cover to cover, she hadn't made it to the book of Joel before. Had never read that verse. She couldn't remember hearing any sermons preached on it either. Too bad she'd forgotten to bring her Bible along on this trip.

"What do you think?" Mena asked. "Should we all get something to eat?"

Jolene stared at the couple with a melancholy ache in her soul. How long had it been since she and Joseph had been close like that? So much of her mental energy when she thought about him was spent dwelling on what a terrible father he was or how wretchedly he'd hurt her with that affair. But there had been good times too. Most of them early on, but that didn't take away from the fact that they'd started off with so much love between them.

At one point, Jolene's biggest concern was whether her daughter would or wouldn't catch a cold if she played outside too long in the rain. Even though she knew she could never go back to those times, part of her wished that she could forget all the pain, all the heartache of the past. Go back to their vacation on the Oregon Coast, snuggle up with her husband and preschooler, and watch Disney movies.

All day.

She was such a different person now. Would she even know herself if she could go back to that little cabin? She'd gained so much since then—confidence, poise, assurance. A sense of identity that didn't revolve around her family or her role as a mother and wife.

But she'd lost so much more.

"Well, should we grab some *bingsu*?" Jin-Sun asked. "There's a spot just around the corner."

"I love that place," Mena exclaimed with a girlish giggle that sent unexpected pangs shooting through Jolene's heart.

"I think I'll go back to the B&B," she said. "Take a little nap. I'm pretty tired."

Mena frowned sympathetically. "That's right. I forgot you're still jetlagged. I'll take you back to your room." She turned to her fiancé. "I don't want her getting lost on the way."

It was cute the way Mena was trying to help. As if she were the parental figure and not the other way around.

"I'll be fine. I remember how to get back to the subway station."

Jin-Sun and Mena both looked dubious.

Jolene held up her phone. "I'll just download that app to get me to where I need to go. No problem." She adjusted the strap of her purse in a way that made it clear she was taking off and didn't need a follower.

Didn't need a babysitter.

"Your rehearsal dinner's tonight at six, right?" she asked.

Mena nodded, clearly unconvinced.

"Ok, I'll call or text before then and you can tell me where to meet you. All right?" Before they could try to change her mind, Jolene turned to Mena's fiancé once more. "Thanks again for sharing your testimony with us. I can tell you and Mena are perfect together, and I'm glad you found each other."

With that, she turned and walked out of the auditorium, wondering how in the world she'd find her way back to her room in a city of over nine million, praying to God she wouldn't get lost.

CHAPTER 28

L ocusts. Locusts. Locusts.

Joseph flipped through the concordance in the back of his Bible. *Locusts.* There it was.

He turned to the book of Joel.

I will restore the years the locusts have eaten…

What did it mean?

He was supposed to be packing. Earlier in the day, he'd called Misty and told her he wouldn't need to attend that retirement party for the Seoul head of sales after all, and she booked him a red-eye flight home. He was due at the airport in six hours. But something the speaker had said grabbed hold of his psyche and wouldn't let go.

I will restore the years the locusts have eaten.

God didn't apologize for sending the devastating swarm to begin with. Didn't try to explain himself in a way that could make his actions appear justified or fair.

But he promised restoration…

How? Chelsea's accident had already happened. What was there left to restore? Unless God planned to raise a girl who'd been dead for five years from the grave, his daughter was gone. Joseph had already grown to accept it as much as a father can ever come to terms with a tragedy like that.

So what right did God have getting his hopes all worked up with impossible promises?

Restoration was a nice concept that might make certain believers feel all warm and fuzzy inside.

But it was too late for Joseph. Too late for anything now.

He shut his Bible and tossed it into his suitcase. It was time to get out of Seoul.

CHAPTER 29

The subway app that Mena had been so enthusiastic about would work great if Jolene could figure out which level she was supposed to get to. Here in Seoul, each subway station seemed to have a dozen different entrances, five different stories, and about a thousand different trains, none of them apparently being the one Jolene needed.

She took the first train and got off at what she thought was the right station, but the automated announcer said the names so fast she couldn't be entirely sure. She finally admitted defeat about half an hour after arriving at a second station she seriously doubted was anywhere close to where she needed to be. Unfortunately, the two different strangers she'd asked for help couldn't speak English. One at least tried to use gestures when Jolene pointed on her phone to explain where she needed to go, and even though she'd taken off confidently in the direction he pointed, she was still just as lost as before.

At least the subway stations were interesting. Interesting and relatively clean. It was more like an underground mall than a mass transit hub. If she'd had an appetite, she could grab herself some lunch, but all she wanted to do was get home.

Get home and figure out why Mena's fiancé had impacted her so deeply with his words. He and Jolene weren't alike. He was half her age, born under a totalitarian dictatorship on the other end of the world. He'd never been married, never lost a daughter, never experienced the humiliation of a divorce. But somehow she felt a connection to him.

He knew something she didn't. Or possessed something she didn't. Maybe that was a better way of putting it.

He had something she wanted.

Of course, she could spiritualize it all. Tell herself that if she hadn't pulled away from church recently, she'd be in a better state to handle the stress of being in Seoul, completely jetlagged and lost, having to confront unwanted memories of her daughter's death and her ex-husband's alcoholism, affair, and abandonment.

But deep in her heart, she knew there was more to it than that. Even when she was at the peak of her spiritual journey, during those spells when she was studying her Bible every day and praying regularly and investing in her church relationships, there was still something missing.

Something she wanted.

Desperately wanted.

She should have gone out to lunch with Mena and Jin-Sun after all. It was stupid to try to brave these subways alone.

But there was no choice now. Even if she wanted to get in touch with Mena, the public wifi around here didn't have enough broadband to send a text or make a call.

She was on her own.

She sank onto a bench. Tried to give her confidence a boost, give her psyche a little pep talk. But inside, she knew she was just as broken and scared and alone as ever.

And to top it off, she was completely lost.

CHAPTER 30

"You going to Namsan Tower?"

Joseph usually felt lucky when he found a cab driver who spoke some English, but right now he wasn't in the mood for any conversation.

"Namsan Tower?" the cabbie repeated. "Yes?"

"Yeah. That's right."

"You going up?"

"Mmm." Could the man take a hint? Thankfully, after a few minutes, he stopped asking questions and focused on the road ahead of him.

This was stupid. There was nothing good that could come from this ridiculous pilgrimage. That's why he'd never made his way out here the dozens of times he'd been in Seoul.

What would be the point?

Chelsea was gone. Traveling to the spot where she died wasn't going to bring her back.

It wouldn't even bring closure. How could it? Seoul Tower was just a place. Places didn't have any mystical or magical meaning unless you were some superstitious-minded simpleton who bought into that kind of bunk.

Joseph wasn't a simpleton, and he wasn't superstitious.

So why had he hailed a cab to take him to Seoul Tower?

He should go back. He leaned forward, about to tap the driver's shoulder to get his attention but then stopped.

After all, this was only a place. Hadn't he just convinced himself that there was nothing mystical here? Visiting the spot of the accident wouldn't leave him any better off.

Which meant it couldn't leave him any worse off either.

With all his railings against superstitions, he'd been foolish to avoid this place so zealously. Hadn't he found his way to nearly every other major tourist attraction in Seoul? The Gyeongbokgung Palace, the war memorial... At some point or another, he'd seen them all. Not because there was anything impressive about the sites themselves, but because that's what tourists did when they traveled here.

Seoul Tower was the primary tourist trap in all of South Korea. What reason did he have to avoid it any longer?

"You say something?" asked the driver.

Joseph shook his head. "No."

"We're almost there."

Joseph took a deep breath. Repeated his newfound mantra that this location was no different than any other spot in Seoul.

A tourist trap.

Nothing else.

He crossed his arms. And waited.

The tower loomed into view.

CHAPTER 31

"Thank you so much for letting me share the cab with you. I have some won in my purse. You sure you don't want me to pitch in for the ride?"

The bald Australian drama teacher and his sun-tanned wife both smiled at her. "It's nothing," he replied. "We were glad for the company."

Jolene tried to return his smile. She'd gotten herself so lost in the subway system that the moment she found English speaking tourists she'd latched onto them. And when she found out they were on their way to the Seoul Tower, she'd made some ridiculous comment about how she'd never seen it before but heard it was lovely.

One Uber call later, and here they all were.

It beat staying lost in the bowels of Seoul.

Just barely.

"We're taking the lift up the rest of the way," the woman said. "Want to come with?"

Jolene couldn't even bring herself to look at the cable car above their heads. "No, I think I'll walk."

The teacher frowned. "The guidebook said it's really steep."

Jolene smiled. "I could use the exercise."

The Aussie couple waved and walked off.

What had she gotten herself into? At least now that she knew how to call an Uber car, she could find her way back to the B&B. Maybe she should turn around and head home now. The only problem with that was she'd most likely end up with the same driver who'd just dropped her off. Better to spend a few minutes at least pretending to look around. According to the Aussies' guidebook, it was a half hour walk to the base of the tower.

An endless path stretching far up the mountainside.

No wonder Chelsea had taken the sky lift.

Jolene stared at the trail before her. Did she have the energy for this? Did she even have a choice? The only other option was the cable car, which wasn't an option at all.

One foot in front of the other

One step at a time.

If she wanted to wax poetic, she could come up with a dozen metaphors, a dozen pithy sayings about how life and recovery and healing were all like this mountain trail.

But she wasn't in the mood for platitudes.

Maybe God wanted her to come here. Maybe it was part of his plan. She certainly had done a decent job ignoring him lately. Was this his way of getting her attention?

Well, God, I'm listening.

The only problem was heaven was silent.

And her thighs were burning.

And the trail continued to stretch higher and higher.

CHAPTER 32

Even though most of the tourists took the cable car up to the base of the tower, Joseph found the hike was a good way to clear his mind. Focus his attention on a whole lot of nothing.

Tomorrow would be an easy day at the Seattle office since he'd been scheduled to still be in Seoul. If he wanted to, he could even stay at home.

Not that there was anything or anyone waiting for him there.

It was silly to be thinking any extra about Chelsea just because he was near the spot where she died. It was the same reason he didn't visit his parents' graves or even his daughter's. Places were just places.

He'd heard some people talk about feeling close to their beloved departed, but it was all bunk. Psychological coping mechanisms at best. Grief-induced delusions or occult-related hallucinations at worst. Wherever Chelsea was right now, she wasn't some ghost stuck around Seoul. Joseph was no expert on Scripture, but he knew that much at least.

So why was it so hard for him to get her out of his head? Why did he still hear the fear in her voice when she'd called him before the cable snapped?

And why did the city of Seoul still run those stupid cable cars anyway? Did any of those tourists up there know, did they have any suspicion that five years ago, a major accident had claimed the lives of three visitors and injured scores more? That among the deceased was a girl so full of life and zest that she'd traveled to five different foreign countries as an undergrad and had plans to visit two more before she started grad school?

Did they suspect, did they have any hint that the girl who died here was a daughter so blinded by love she refused to acknowledge her father's shortcomings? Refused to hold a grudge for all the times he failed her?

It shouldn't have been Chelsea. She was full of energy, plans, excitement. She wanted so much out of life. Wanted to fix the American foster system, solve world hunger, singlehandedly put an end to the clean-water shortage across the globe, and expose every single corrupt politician in DC. She would have done all those things—and even more—if God had given her a chance to live.

A chance to rise to even a fraction of her full potential.

It wasn't fair.

It shouldn't have been her.

Why did the young ones, the bright ones, the ones with the most promising futures and most glorious smiles and most irritating stubborn streaks get taken while men like him were left behind? Men who managed to ruin their families, estrange themselves from everyone important to them, destroy their health and their self-esteem, and sabotage every single relationship that mattered? What kind of God would take a girl like Chelsea and leave a man like Joseph?

It would never make sense.

His heart was pounding in his chest, but he wasn't about to slow down. Wasn't about to admit defeat. He glared up at the tower still so far ahead in the distance, dared the path to get the best of him.

If he could survive losing his daughter, losing his wife, if he could stumble his way through the past three and a half years stone-cold sober, he could reach the top of this mountain.

There was simply no other option.

CHAPTER 33

S he shouldn't have come. Less than halfway up the trail, Jolene had to stop. It was too much. She was too close. She could feel Chelsea in every breath she took, every rustling of the leaves, every chattering tourist who shared the forest trail with her.

She'd spent the past five years missing her daughter, begging God to bring her back, trying to catch hold of a memory that would make it seem like Chelsea was still with her.

She'd gotten her wish, and she realized it was the last thing she needed. What was she thinking? Every breeze held the sound of Chelsea's voice. Every movement in the trees was like the rustling of her long brown hair.

Too much.

She could hardly breathe.

How was she supposed to go on like this? How did God expect her to survive this burden? It was enough for him to ask her to live in a world without Chelsea in it. Now he'd thrown her onto an impossibly steep mountain trail where every rock underfoot reminded her of her daughter's first steps on those chubby, wobbling legs. Every branch that scratched against her was like the tugging of that little preschooler's hands on her shirt. *Mommy, I'm thirsty. Mommy, I want a snack. Mommy, when I grow up, I want to be boo-tiful like you.*

She couldn't go on. Wouldn't go on. If she called the Uber now…

But of course, she'd need wifi for that. Wifi that wasn't available out here on this stupid trail.

Angry tears streaked down her cheeks, hot and scalding. Acidic, like the bitter sorrow in her heart, the gnawing emptiness that only grew each year in spite of everyone's pat promises that time would heal her wounds.

Sometimes Jolene felt like she was the only human being in the entire world who still remembered her daughter. Still felt as raw and shocked and wounded as the day Chelsea died. *Time heals all wounds?* Maybe for everyone else. For her ex-husband, who waited a full three weeks (if you were to believe his timeline to begin with) from his daughter's death to the start of his affair with the busty intern. For Mena, who was so outrageously in love with her super saint of a fiancé that there was no room for any sorrow. For all of Chelsea's old friends from high school and college, the ones who'd cried their eyes out at the funeral and hadn't spent a moment at Chelsea's grave, hadn't shed a tear in five straight years for that girl who was doomed to remain twenty-two perpetually in everyone's memory.

Everyone's memory but Jolene's. She still celebrated each and every birthday. Celebrated by locking herself in her room and throwing on music meant to drown out her bitter cries.

Each year served as a reminder of what Chelsea hadn't achieved. What her daughter would never accomplish.

This is the year you would have graduated from grad school.

This is the year you might have gotten married.

This is the year you might have become a mother.

Maybe that's why Jolene had distanced herself from some of the other women at church, women who were busy traveling across the country to visit grandchildren and new additions to their happy families. What reason did Jolene have to travel? What reason did she have to celebrate? This trip to Seoul was her first time out of Orchard Grove in two and a half years. She spent her life now in a little bubble with a fifteen-mile radius that encompassed her home, the grocery store, and church when she wasn't too tired to attend. No wonder she felt so overwhelmed here in a city this huge.

She'd been so stupid to come here.

A mistake she didn't intend to repeat.

She'd seen enough. Finding her way to the top of the mountain, making it all the way to the tower that was responsible for her daughter's death was nothing but salt in wounds that were supposed to have healed years ago.

Wounds that had no reason to be so gaping and raw and exposed.

Wounds that might kill her if she didn't find a way to pull herself out of her misery, find peace with what had happened to her daughter, and manage to move on with her life.

CHAPTER 34

Finally. **From the top of** the mountain, Joseph stared down at Seoul. Nothing much to speak of, to be honest. The city sprawled outward instead of upward. A mess of winding roads, congested traffic, and huge office complexes where men worked hundred-hour weeks to the detriment of their families and their mental health.

Joseph could readily admit that he was a workaholic. It was a label he wore with a hint of pride. But even his career ambition paled in comparison to most of the men in the South Korean offices. If Jolene thought he was a negligent husband, it was nothing like here, where workers weren't even allowed to stand up from their cubicles before their bosses left for the night. Where company dinners and drinking sessions kept them past midnight several times a week.

What was he doing? Even if he hadn't wanted to get to the airport early, now he'd have to backtrack all the way to his hotel, pick up his suitcase, then ride the bus for the hour ride to Incheon. At least he'd be home soon. He'd never been more ready to get to Seattle.

Around him, young couples walked hand in hand. He'd always known the tower was a tourist trap. He hadn't realized it was also where all the local couples flaunted their young love. He walked along a fence with colorfully engraved locks attached to each link. Most of the Sharpie scribbles were in Korean but were full of enough hearts that he could get the general gist.

Great. He'd come to the Korean equivalent of a high-school dance and was here with a bunch of teens and tweens who pretended to be a decade older.

Who pretended to have the slightest clue about true love.

Whatever dysfunction had seeped in and ruined his relationship with Jolene, he still loved her. Even when he was sleeping with Denise, sick as it might sound, he had never loved anyone but his wife.

At least not in the same way.

As he strolled aimlessly along, he indulged in one of his most masochistic mental pastimes. Wondering what life would be like if Chelsea hadn't died.

He wouldn't have had the affair. At least, that's what he told himself. He'd still be with his wife. They would have worked out whatever tensions or struggles had weighed down on their marriage. Without the drinking... No, who was he kidding?

It took Chelsea dying, Denise dumping him, and his wife divorcing him to bring Joseph to the point where he was ready to stay sober for good.

As much as he hated to face the truth, if Chelsea were still alive, he might very well still be caught in the clutches of his alcoholism. Maybe even dead by now, killed by a car accident or liver disease.

Why did God use tragedies to make people rely on him? Why couldn't he teach Christians what they needed to know before they were forced to learn all their lessons the hard way?

During his impromptu Bible study after that day's fundraising luncheon, Joseph had read a verse in Proverbs that still now pricked at his conscience. *A person's own folly leads to their ruin, yet their heart rages against the LORD.*

How much energy had Joseph spent over the past five years blaming God for Chelsea's death and everything that happened afterward? Even if the accident wasn't Joseph's fault, the affair certainly was. Same with the drinking that ruined his marriage.

And yet he was still so ready to blame God.

I will restore the years the locusts have eaten. The words of that speaker still replayed in his mind. He didn't know what that restoration would look like, but he wanted it.

Wanted that sense of hope and purpose and belonging he'd heard in the young man's speech.

What did he need to do? How could he ever find that peace?

God, I'm sorry for all the times I've blamed you for what happened to Chelsea. It wasn't your fault.

The words were hard to choke down. Hard because if it wasn't God's fault, then whose was it? In a world ruled by God's sovereignty, there wasn't such a thing as an accident, was there? But how else could he explain his daughter's death? How else could he explain why Chelsea was no longer with him, enjoying the life she'd been so excited to lead?

I will restore the years the locusts have eaten.

It was a bold promise. But maybe Joseph would find the faith one day to take God at his word.

Maybe he'd find the courage to trust again after all.

CHAPTER 35

N ope. She wasn't going up that mountain. Not just because she was dog tired. But because she didn't have to.

Trekking up to Seoul Tower, visiting the sites her daughter wanted to see the day she died—what good would that accomplish?

She was done. What time had Mena said they were meeting for dinner? Whatever it was, Jolene didn't want to be late. Unwilling to try her hand at the Seoul subways again, she decided to find a hotspot once she got off the trail and call an Uber.

She shook her head as she made her way back down the path. She'd been stupid to come here. Stupid to think that she had the emotional fortitude to visit the site of her daughter's death.

Then again…

What use was there in running away? What good had that ever done her?

She'd been so quick to run early on. Run from her grief.

In so many ways, she was still running. From her ex-husband who so inconveniently showed up in Seoul. From her ex-boyfriend who apparently still refused to take no for an answer.

Always running.

Maybe that's why she had all but stopped going to church. It's possible. Something had been stirring in her heart since she heard

Mena's fiancé and his impassioned speech. If Jin-Sun could overcome all the sorrows he'd experienced growing up in North Korea, if God could bring him comfort and peace after those tragedies, maybe it was possible for her too. But where to begin?

You may be a thousand steps away from God, but it's only one step back.

She couldn't remember where she'd heard the pithy saying. A church sermon maybe? Or something from one of the women's Bible studies she used to attend? Whatever it was, the words ran through her head relentlessly.

You may be a thousand steps away from God, but it's only one step back.

Here she was complaining that God felt so far away, but maybe she was the one who'd moved, not the other way around.

Maybe she was the one who turned her back on him when all this time it felt like he had deserted her.

Only one step back...

It sounded cute and inspiring if you were listening to a motivational speech. Not quite so helpful if you didn't even know how to get yourself back on the right path. Where should she even start?

Maybe some people were just better at living out the Christian life than others. Maybe Jolene's spirit was too riddled with sorrow and heartache and bitterness...

Bitterness. Why did the word turn her stomach sour like that? What was this sloshing unease in her gut? Guilt?

Why should she feel guilty? She wasn't the one who'd betrayed her spouse of twenty-five years when some perky intern came to town. She wasn't the one who went on a drinking binge every night of the week, lying through his teeth about trying to become sober. Joseph had ruined her life. He had ruined it long before she set her mind to finally divorce him. As if she was just supposed to roll over and forgive him...

Was that what all this was? Was this about how she was still bitter toward her ex? Seriously. How many times do you have to pray and tell God you forgive your husband when he cheats on you and ruins your daughter's life and breaks your heart every single time he drags that cursed bottle to his lips?

There comes a point when you have to stop enabling. Have to admit that the problem's never going to disappear. That's why Jolene finally left him. And now she was the one feeling guilty as if she were the one to blame?

She thought about her run-in last night with Joseph, about the way he barged into her room smelling like beer. That man would never change. And Jolene shouldn't feel guilty that she was trying to move on.

She charged down the path, ignoring the bursting in her lungs and the burning in her thighs. There was a little souvenir shop at the base of the trail. She'd check for wifi, call herself a car, and get herself far away from Seoul Tower and the torturous memories that haunted it.

CHAPTER 36

There was a lightness in Joseph's spirit he hadn't experienced in years. Or maybe in his entire life. He couldn't pinpoint the change, at least not exactly. If he were trying to walk a coworker through the steps he'd just taken to finally feel at peace, he wouldn't know where to start.

But here he was.

Able to accept the fact that the accident that had claimed his daughter's life was a tragedy, but that it was still possible to hold onto a belief in a powerful and loving God.

Able to somehow understand, even if he couldn't wrap his mind around it in any logical way, that even though God could have kept Chelsea from dying, he bore no guilt for his daughter's death.

In one way, it didn't change anything. Chelsea was still gone, destined to live in his memory now as a perpetual twenty-two-year-old. She would never give him grandkids, never see how far he'd worked to overcome his addictions.

This rebirth in his spirit wouldn't change the past.

But in another sense, it changed everything.

Maybe now Joseph could move on. Instead of living perpetually in his regrets, pining for a wife who'd given up on him years ago and a daughter he'd never see again, maybe he could start looking ahead to the future without the ghosts of his guilt tying him down like dead weight.

He turned around. Made his way toward the trail that would take him back to the city. He didn't need the view from the mountaintop anymore. This change, this reawakening in his tired and weary soul, wasn't dependent on his altitude or his position on the globe. He could carry it with him wherever he went. He just hoped that he could walk in such a way that he wouldn't lose this feeling.

He was already starting to make plans to solidify his commitment. Get more serious about attending Chuck's Thursday morning men's prayer breakfast. Buckling down and making Bible study a priority, whether he was at home or in his office or traveling the globe. If God could do this work in his heart, if he could teach Joseph to finally forgive himself after all that had happened, then he was worth carving out a little extra time for in spite of his busy schedule.

It wouldn't atone for all the mistakes of his past, but it was a start.

He hurried down the trail, rushing for no apparent reason other than the joy and energy that surged through his being.

And then he saw her.

"Jolene?" He called her name. She didn't hear. She was too far down the trail. "Jolene?"

Maybe he was mistaken. Maybe it wasn't her.

But wouldn't he recognize his wife anywhere?

"Jolene!" He didn't know why he was running toward a woman who probably didn't want to talk and certainly wouldn't be happy to see him. Didn't know what he'd say to her once he did catch up. But his legs propelled him forward as if they had a force and a gravity and a will of their own.

She was so far ahead. If he didn't know her that intimately, he would have never been able to recognize her. But there she was. The wife he'd loved, the wife he'd hurt so badly.

He burst forward with all his strength, praying to God that he could catch up before she disappeared from his life again, this time for good.

CHAPTER 37

The man behind the counter leaned toward Jolene. "You want to buy a lock?"

"A lock?" she asked, thinking perhaps his accent garbled whatever he was trying to say.

He nodded. "Yes. You buy it and write the name of the one you love then hang it on the tower fence."

"I'm single," she answered. "Do you have wifi here?"

He pointed to the password that was taped on the counter. "You sure you don't want the lock?"

"I'm sure."

She connected her phone, wondering how soon she could get an Uber up this way. She hated that she couldn't remember what time she was supposed to meet Mena, hated to think she might end up late.

"You want to buy a coffee at the café?" The man gestured toward the tiny cafeteria attached to the shop.

Jolene sighed. "Sure." She may as well get something while she waited. According to the app, it would take about ten minutes for her driver to arrive.

Once she sat, she noticed her piercing headache. She was too old to be running up and down mountain trails like that.

She ordered her coffee and checked her Uber app for the

seventh time in the past thirty seconds.

"Jolene?"

No. It couldn't be. Out of all the stupid souvenir shops plastered around Seoul...

"Joseph?"

He was out of breath. Had he been running? In the fluorescent lights from the café, his forehead shimmered with sweat.

"What are you doing here?" she asked.

He collapsed into the seat across from her. "I saw you on the trail. I thought we..." He stopped. What was he going to say?

She was too tired for any of this. With as caustic as she'd been feeling toward her ex just a few minutes ago, she didn't have the energy to tell him all the reasons why his presence here was so repulsive.

"Listen," he panted, "I don't know why you're here, and I'm guessing you don't want to waste a whole lot of time talking to me, and that's fine. I'm ready to give you space. But first..." He took a few more noisy breaths. How far up the trail had he been? And had he run all the way down here just to break her short period of calm and quiet before the Uber car came?

"I need to apologize to you."

His words caught her off guard. Maybe the jet lag was catching up to her. She must be hallucinating. It was the most logical explanation. In their twenty-five years of marriage, had he ever once initiated an apology?

"I was a terrible father and a terrible husband, and I made your life miserable. I made our marriage miserable. It's only by the grace of God and some huge miracle that Chelsea..." His voice caught. "That our daughter didn't despise me with every ounce of her being. The more I think about it, that's probably because you sheltered her from so many of my problems. I can only imagine what an impossibly hard predicament that was for you all those years."

Jolene stared. Did he seriously expect her to formulate some sort of coherent response? What was he thinking?

"I know I told you last night that I've changed, and maybe at first I was mad that you didn't believe me. Then I realized that I haven't given you any reason to trust me. None at all."

She was about to mention the fact that he'd broken into her room smelling like cheap beer last night while still proclaiming his sobriety, but he was rambling on without any sign of slowing down.

"I know one simple apology won't change the lifetime of hurt and heartache I've caused you. And believe me, I'm not trying to put you into a position where you'll ever get hurt again. I've caused you too much pain. I recognize that. I'm not asking you for anything except to hear me out. Hear me out, and then I'll be out of your life again. It's time for both of us to move on. I realize that."

Jolene glanced at her phone. How much longer was that driver going to take?

"I've been stuck in the past. Thinking that maybe one day I could prove to you that I'm a new man. That's why I was so upset last night when you thought I lied to you. You smelled beer on my breath because I'd gone into a bar, but I didn't take a drink. I guess I had this childish notion that if I just stayed sober long enough, I might erase all my other shortcomings. I was wrong. Now I want to move on. I really do. I know it's too late for us to make it work together, but that doesn't mean we should hang ourselves on past regrets. I made a ton of mistakes, I hurt you more than I could ever expect to be forgiven for, and I'm truly sorry. If Chelsea were here…"

He winced. Jolene buried her face behind her cup of coffee and took a large, scalding gulp.

"If Chelsea were here, I'd beg her to forgive me too, even though that girl was so loyal she could never bring herself to see me for what I really was. But you did, and you stayed by my side far longer than anyone would have expected you to. I'm sorry that I dragged you down with me. Like I said earlier, I don't expect anything from you anymore. You don't even have to tell me you forgive me. But I…" He cleared his throat.

"I saw you with those flowers last night, and I got jealous. But the more I thought about it, the more I realized how selfish that was of me. Since our earliest days, since college when we were young and crazy and in love with each other, I've wished you nothing but happiness. And since I obviously couldn't bring you the happiness you deserve, I came here to tell you that… Well, I want you to know that… What I'm trying to say is as long as he's good to you, I'm happy. I don't want you to go into any future relationship, no matter how serious it is, feeling guilty for moving on."

His stare was so intense she could feel her face heating up.

"That's what I came here to say."

"That's all?" Jolene raised her eyes to his. Remembered how at one point she could lose herself in his gaze, those eyes that held the promise of all the happiness and excitement the universe had to offer.

Eyes that now may as well have belonged to a stranger.

He nodded his head once. "That's all." He waited. "Are you going to say something?"

Her phone beeped at her. "My Uber's here."

She could hear his throat muscles work while he swallowed. "Oh. Ok. Well, then, I guess this is goodbye?"

What was she supposed to say? What did he expect?

"Or if you wanted, you could cancel the car and we could…"

Could what? Jolene waited.

He raised an eyebrow. "Share a snack? Let me buy you something?"

There was more behind his words than she wanted to admit. A hopefulness that made suspect the spiel he'd just given her of how he'd chased her down a mountain so they could have some sort of closure before pursuing separate lives.

Or was she reading too much into it?

At this point, she was so exhausted and confused she wouldn't have trusted herself to make any type of decision.

Her phone beeped again. "I have to go."

"Ok." Did his expression fall, or was that just her mind trying to make sense of this entire exchange? "I'm sorry," she stammered.

"Don't apologize." He stood up when she did. Gave a smile that for once didn't seem to demand anything in return. "I'm glad I ran into you before you left. You're sure you don't want to stay?"

This time, the earnestness in his gaze was unmistakable. This was Joseph, her ex-husband, who'd just apologized to her, taken responsibility for all the ways he'd messed up her life, and he was asking her to stay.

For a snack.

What could it hurt?

She took in a deep breath and stared out the window of the store. "My car's waiting."

"Your car. Right." He followed her to the door and held it open. "Looks like it's raining again. Do you have an umbrella?"

She shook her head.

"Want mine?"

She let out her breath. Why was he doing this to her? "No. Thank you," she added and reached for the door handle.

"Little rain never hurt nobody?" he offered weakly.

The words were so familiar, bringing back memories of happiness and love, memories that were now permanently tarnished by grief and pain.

She stepped outside, where it had started to drizzle, and got into the Uber before she could change her mind. Resisting the urge to look back, she buckled her seatbelt as the driver began his descent down the mountain.

CHAPTER 38

I f there had been any doubt left in Joseph's mind, the last five minutes had dispelled it all.

There was nothing left for him in Seoul.

The ride back to his hotel was long and belabored, just like his current wait in the rain for the bus that would take him to the Incheon airport. It was pouring, but that didn't matter.

A little rain never hurt nobody.

He had to get out of this city.

What had he been thinking back there? No matter what happened in the future, he'd look back on that pathetic little speech in that cheesy souvenir shop with a mix of embarrassment and disappointment. He'd bared his heart, bared his entire soul, only to get brushed off by the woman he'd loved for decades.

Not that he'd expected a big, sappy reunion with Jolene crying onto his shoulder and proclaiming her forgiveness. But a little something might have been nice. How about *I forgive you,* or *It means a lot to me that you took the time to say those things*? No. Not so much as a *Good to see you again, Joseph. Have a great life.*

Nothing.

He may as well have been pouring his heart out to a bowl of noodles.

Oh, well. What should he have expected? Maybe his

redemption wasn't as much about finding closure with Jolene. Maybe it was about the fact that he'd finally taken responsibility for his actions. What Jolene did with that was her problem, not his.

It was so easy to revert back to old habits, to bitterness. How many reasons would he find to be angry at her before the day was through? After running halfway down a mountainside just to talk to her, and she couldn't spare an extra five or ten minutes because she had a driver waiting?

It wasn't his problem anymore. That's what he had to keep on reminding himself. He'd done what he needed to do to move on. Isn't that what he'd set out for in the first place? If he'd expected any major cathartic healing to take place between the two of them, he'd been a fool.

A fool who would now have to accept the fact that he'd humiliated himself in front of a woman who couldn't care less about him. That's what he'd misjudged. For some blindly arrogant, foolish reason, he assumed that Jolene had spent the past five years pining away for him, wishing for that apology that felt like crumbles of cement in his mouth after he delivered it.

And she hadn't even cared. His words meant nothing to her. He may as well have been a pushy salesman trying to sell her cosmetics in a crowded Seoul marketplace.

Well, at least his conscience was free now. There was nothing left except get out of Seoul, nurse his bruised ego, and move on. Try to maintain some sense of the spiritual excitement and energy he'd experienced on top of that mountain.

And maybe now, maybe with that long overdue apology finally out of the way, he could move on with his life and try to maintain that true and lasting peace.

CHAPTER 39

"**M**ena told me to apologize to you that she's late. I'm here to pick you up and bring you to dinner."

Jin-Sun smiled comfortably at Jolene at the doorway of her *hanok*. If he noticed the puffy black outlines around her eyes, he was kind enough not to say anything.

She cleared her throat, trying to erase the last traces of her recent cry-fest. "Thanks. Let me grab my shoes, and I'll be ready."

"You might want to bring an umbrella too. It's been raining all afternoon."

As if she hadn't noticed.

The short walk to the subway tunnel gave Jolene time to compose herself. In a way, she was glad it was Jin-Sun here and not Mena. She still needed time before she could pretend to function like a normal adult.

Whatever Joseph had set out to do that afternoon at the Seoul Tower, he'd accomplished. If his purpose was to make her feel guilty for all the bitterness she'd harbored against him, he'd been far more successful than he could have ever imagined. Same thing if his goal was to send her into a spiral of chaotic emotions that tore her insides to shreds.

It wasn't right. How could you apologize to someone in a way that left them feeling even guiltier than they already did? Joseph had been a master at manipulation during their marriage, but this felt different.

As much as it confused her to admit, she suspected he was trying to be helpful. Trying to do what he thought was the right thing. As if a conversation like that crammed into the few minutes Jolene had left before she had to catch her car were somehow supposed to bring healing to such a broken relationship.

No, that wasn't it, either. He wasn't trying to get back together with her, thank God. So what was he trying to do? Absolve himself of guilt? Then why would he humble himself like that? It wasn't like him, and that's what she couldn't understand.

Maybe he really was a new man like he claimed.

But as often as the thought occurred to her, she had to shut it down. Remind herself that addicts don't change. Adulterers don't change. Sure, they might feel guilty. They might feel remorse when they get caught or even experience a twinge of compassion for the people they've hurt, but in the end, the root issues are still the root issues.

An addict doesn't recover overnight like that.

Then again, it had been over four years since the divorce. Maybe he really had...

No. She wasn't going to think about that. What good would it do? The second she thought that Joseph might have seriously turned his life around—a feat he'd claimed yet failed to achieve a thousand times since their wedding—she started to think about all the other *what ifs*.

What if he learned to finally keep his word?

What if he learned to finally take responsibility for his actions?

What if he learned to finally break his addiction?

Then how do you explain the beer on his breath last night? Sure, he denied drinking anything. His words hadn't been slurred, not yet. He hadn't acted drunk. But the moment she opened herself up to hope, she became vulnerable again.

And she had to protect herself.

It was pure and simple common sense.

Had she already forgotten the basics? After years trying to find healing and wholeness after Chelsea's death and Joseph's infidelity, was she so stupid that she'd consider giving him a second chance?

Except he hadn't asked for a second chance. So why did she feel so disappointed, as if that conversation should have ended differently? What else should she have done?

What else could she have done?

"You got your money pass?" Jin-Sun asked when they reached the bottom stairs.

"Yeah." After fumbling through her purse, Jolene swiped her subway card, thankful that this time someone who knew the underground system was leading her.

She was so tired of walking down dead ends, trying to reach some impossible destination.

She was so tired of feeling lost.

CHAPTER 40

"**I don't know what I'm** thinking," Joseph confessed.

Chuck sighed on the other end of the line. "These matters of the heart are always complicated. In fact, if my wife were here right now, I'd have you talk to her instead of me." Chuck laughed, and even though Joseph knew he was joking, he didn't see how his sponsor could find any humor in this situation.

"You made the right choice," he finally announced. "It wasn't easy, but it was the godly thing to do. I'm mighty proud of you." Chuck had perfected the paternal tone, but Joseph still wasn't sure he believed his words. If he'd had done the right thing, why did it feel like he'd just made the biggest mistake of his life?

"You can't hold onto her forever. At some point, you have to let her go." Chuck's words were filled with wisdom. Joseph knew that much, but it didn't mean he liked what he heard. If he'd done the godly thing like Chuck had claimed, wouldn't you expect God to reward him? Convinced Jolene to give him a second chance?

Or a thousandth chance, as the case may be.

"When you told her that you wanted her to be happy," Chuck asked, "did you mean it?"

Joseph should end the phone call right now. Why did this conversation sound like such a good idea a few minutes ago? "Of course I meant it."

"Even if what makes her happy is a relationship with another man? Even getting engaged to him? Marrying him?"

"I don't know." Joseph couldn't keep the explosive anger out of his voice. At least the sidewalk was crowded enough and the noise from the street loud enough that nobody would care if he lost his cool.

"God promises to reward us when we follow his Word. He doesn't promise to make all our troubles go away or to make things turn out the way we hope they will."

Joseph let out a sigh. "Yeah, I know." Yelling wasn't the answer. Apparently, nothing was the answer.

"I'm sorry you're going through this hurt, son."

"Thanks."

"I'd love to pray for you if you've got the time."

Joseph always felt silly listening to his sponsor pray over the phone, but he figured right now he could use all the extra encouragement from heaven he could get.

"All right. That sounds good."

"Dear God," Chuck began, and he covered Joseph's angry, disappointed soul with his prayers.

CHAPTER 41

J in-Sun seemed happy to carry the conversation as they made their way from the subway station to the restaurant. Jolene was grateful. She'd done her best to shove Joseph out of her conscious thoughts, but keeping him there in the abyss where he belonged was taking nearly all her mental energy.

The one thing she could do was listen, and so she did, occasionally asking questions to keep the discussion rolling. Jin-Sun told her about his school in North Korea, about his friends there, the games they'd played, the tricks they'd devised during the worst of the famine to steal from unsuspecting travelers.

"What about when you escaped?" she asked. "What's the underground railroad like?"

He sucked in his lips for a second. "Actually, Freedom Korea has to keep that information somewhat classified. I can't give a whole lot of details."

"Oh." She should have known. But how could she?

Before she could stammer a better reply, Jin-Sun continued, "But I can tell you our network stretches throughout Southeast Asia. It's very elaborate. We work with some of the most courageous men and women who are committed to bringing refugees to safety."

"That's really neat."

For the first time since they got off the subway, he went more than five seconds without speaking. She hurried to change the subject. "And you and Mena. She said you've been dating for about a year?"

His face lit, and she could almost feel the heaviness lift from his shoulders. "Yes, she's the one I mentioned who led me to Christ after I arrived here. We attended the same church too, but it wasn't until I started working at the Freedom Korea offices we got serious. I'm so happy the Lord brought us together."

The words sent pangs of remorse and regret shooting through her soul.

"Well, you and Mena, you're so happy together. You can tell you're perfect for one another."

"Thank you. It took me forever to get the nerve to ask her out, so I'm glad she waited for me."

"What took you so long?"

She expected Jin-Sun's smile to brighten like it always did when he talked about his bride-to-be, but instead, he frowned. "I'd been in love with a girl back home. Don't feel bad. Mena knows all about my past. I was in love with someone else, but she betrayed me when she learned about my mother's connection to the underground church." He held up his hand, which was missing two fingers. "That's how I lost these."

Jolene couldn't keep from staring. "How did… When were you…"

He shrugged and shoved his hands into his pockets. "It's ok. It was a long time ago, and the Lord has brought me so much healing. But it wasn't until I learned how to forgive this woman from my past that I found the freedom in my heart to ask Mena to be my girlfriend." The lovestruck smile lit his features once more. "And soon my bride."

Jolene couldn't help but return his grin, even though her heart was miles away, at a little gift shop near the base of Seoul Tower.

CHAPTER 42

Seoul had nothing for him anymore. That's what he kept telling himself as he dragged his suitcase onto the curb and wheeled it into the Incheon Airport.

So why did he feel like he was leaving everything behind?

He was stupid to think he could visit Seoul Tower and not be impacted, not be reminded of his daughter every single second. When he boarded that plane, it would be like saying goodbye to her again.

Losing her again.

But there was more to it than that. If God ever gave him and Jolene one more chance at reconciliation, today was it. And instead of begging her to give him another shot, he'd spouted off some drivel about wanting nothing more than for her to be happy.

He realized as he made his way to the counter that he'd been lying pathetically.

At least he hoped that marriage counselor would love her the way she deserved.

The way Joseph had tried to and failed.

He couldn't complain. She'd given him more than his fair share of chances, and he'd blown them all one by one. Like a walking midlife cliché with a drinking problem.

The kind thing now would be to release her. Pray for her

happiness. Wish her and this boyfriend of hers all the joy in the world.

Except the thought of Jolene with another man made his intestines knot up while he stood in line at the ticket counter.

He would always love her. May as well face it. There would always be some sort of spark there when he thought of her. The one who got away… thirty years later. It was too late for him and Jolene.

The ticket agent was ready for him. He grabbed his suitcase.

Time for him to move on.

Time to leave Seoul for good.

CHAPTER 43

This was a mistake. She shouldn't be here. She should hurry back down to the lobby and catch the Uber driver before he took off again.

She startled when the elevator opened and three men in business suits got out, staring at her quizzically. Straightening her spine, reminding herself that she had just as much right to use the elevator as they did, she stepped in through the doors before they closed.

Three floors up. Hardly enough time to plan what she was going to say or think about what she should do. The elevator dinged, the doors opened, and there she was.

Misty had given her the room number. It had been an awkward conversation, but Jolene and her ex-husband's secretary had always been on good terms. So often when she needed to get a hold of Joseph but couldn't, it had been Misty she called.

Room 311, Misty told her. Just a few steps down the hall, which was a good thing. Any longer, and she would have been tempted to run away. And then what? She'd walked out on Mena and Jin-Sun's celebration dinner for this. She wasn't going to make it all for nothing.

She still felt bad about ditching the party, but she'd find a way to explain to Mena later on. Tell her about her conversation with Jin-Sun on the way to the restaurant, about how his words about forgiveness sat festering in her gut until she got up and called Misty to track down her husband.

Her ex-husband, that is.

Hopefully, that wasn't a Freudian slip. Jolene wasn't here to make sparks fly or to feel butterflies start flopping around in the pit of her stomach. She was here because she realized that as long as she held on to this bitterness, she'd never be able to fully heal.

So why was her heart racing as if she were a teenager about to meet her date for the senior prom? Why did Joseph's face, that angular profile she'd always loved, loom larger than life in her memory, making her weak and clammy?

She should leave. She needed less confusion in her life. Not more.

It wasn't right for her to be here. She couldn't do this.

Yet there she was knocking, albeit ever so timidly, outside room 311. Praying to God she wasn't making the biggest mistake of her life. Hoping her brain would catch up to her emotions so she'd have at least something relatively coherent to say when Joseph opened the door.

Except he didn't.

Funny.

She knocked again, louder this time, while her mind raced through a dozen terrible scenarios. What if it was Joseph's mistress who opened the door, that annoyingly perky intern Denise wrapped up in nothing but a bathrobe? Or what if Joseph was drunk? Wouldn't that be the perfect way to end a day like this?

But he wasn't there at all.

She tried one last time, realizing how much she needed to see him again. *For closure*, she reminded herself. Closure and nothing else.

He'd poured out his heart to her. Expressed his sorrow and remorse over all the terrible things he'd done.

She needed to tell him she forgave him. Her life would feel like it was on perpetual hold until she said those words.

And it had to be now. Once she got home, life would take over again. She'd find excuses. She'd make herself too busy. Or she'd try to do by phone or email what had to be done in person.

Joseph had made the effort to talk to her face to face this afternoon when he offered his apology. The least she could do was return the favor.

If he was in, at least.

Which he obviously wasn't.

So what now?

She connected to the hotel wifi to call the Uber. This whole detour had been a huge waste of time. She sighed and straightened out her windbreaker. At least she had her umbrella. She'd need it while she waited out in the rain.

CHAPTER 44

R idiculous. Absolutely ridiculous. How could anyone make such a colossal mistake? He didn't know whether to blame the airlines or Misty's new assistant, but for whatever reason, the flight change had failed to update in the airport's system.

"We can put you on a flight out first thing in the morning," the far-too-chipper agent had told him.

"I don't need to go out in the morning. I need to go out now."

A frown that lacked any sincerity. "I do apologize for the inconvenience. Would you like me to book you on the 5:20 flight tomorrow morning?"

"No." What point was there in waking up that early? "I'll just keep my original plans and fly out tomorrow afternoon."

"If you're sure."

"Of course I'm sure." Echoes of the conversation ran through his head as he made his way up the elevator to his hotel room. At least they hadn't given his room to anybody. Good thing since the company had paid for it through checkout time tomorrow.

He rubbed his throbbing temples, opening his eyes reluctantly when the elevator door opened. He needed a shower. And a shave. And a new secretary...

He stopped. Was he in the wrong building?

"Jolene?"

She glanced at the floor. When had he ever seen her so sheepish? "Hi."

"What are you doing here?" His eyes scanned her. Was she hurt?

"I called Misty. Asked where you were staying."

That still didn't explain. "Why?" He hoped the word didn't come out too abruptly.

"I wanted to talk to you. About what you said earlier." He paused with his key in his hand. What now? Did he invite her into his room? Find some hotel lobby that wasn't crowded? Suggest they go for a walk in the rain and hunt for someplace to eat?

"I won't take long." She shifted from one leg to another. "I just... I've been thinking a lot about what you said, and I really appreciate your honesty."

For once. Her mouth didn't say the words, but her eyes did. She glanced down again.

"And after thinking about it, I have some things to say too."

He forced his heart to calm down. This wasn't some junior-high romance where she was going to confess she'd had a secret crush on him all the way since last week. They were two adults, two adults who'd taken a shot at love, counted their losses, and were trying their hardest to pick up the shattered pieces and move on.

"Go ahead." He tried to brace himself for whatever was coming next. Was this the part where she told him she and that therapist dude were getting married?

Or would she fling herself against his chest, crying about how much she missed him?

No, he had to stop thinking like that. This was about Jolene and what was best for her. That was all.

Her lip trembled. He fought the urge to reach out and stroke her cheek. Offer some comfort or reassurance. How many times had they run into each other in Seoul since last night? And he still hadn't touched her. Not even a simple handshake.

Some things couldn't be brought back from the grave. Their daughter, for one. Their relationship for another.

So why did his pulse surge with hope? He had to gain control of himself. He was such a fool, and if he couldn't master his emotions, he'd end up humiliating himself even more than he had in that souvenir shop when he might as well have been baring his soul to a paperweight.

A 150-pound paperweight with light, silky curls, a soft figure, and a body where he could still remember each and every contour, crease, and crinkle.

This wasn't working for him. He had to get her out of his head. Had to realize that whatever it was that she said, it wasn't going to be what he wanted so desperately to hear.

She took in a deep breath, as if the effort of what she was about to tell him was physically painful. Joseph braced himself, both mentally and physically. Whatever was coming, he could handle it.

She looked up at him. Met his eyes for the first time.

His pulse surged. Then stopped entirely. Then pounded violently in his ears.

"I came to tell you that I forgive you. For everything."

CHAPTER 45

S he hadn't known time could pass so quickly. When
Mena texted to make sure she was all right, Jolene was
surprised to discover just how long she and Joseph had been
standing in the downstairs lobby of his hotel. They had come here
to say good-bye nearly an hour ago.

"Everything ok?" Joseph asked.

Jolene leaned over her phone. "Yeah, just making sure Mena
knows I'm not crying in some subway station." She smiled. At
least when she told Joseph about her troubles earlier, he hadn't
laughed at her. Apparently, it was pretty common for tourists to get
just as lost as she had or even more so.

When she finished texting, Joseph was leaning toward her.
Hopeful. Expectant. "I don't know if now's the best time, but I was
planning to grab a bite to eat at the airport, and..."

"I'm starving," she interrupted.

"Really?" he asked. She had to laugh at the earnestness, the
relief in his expression.

"Yeah. Do you know any places around here?" She stopped.
The smiles melted off both their faces. "I mean, or we could just...
Maybe we should..." What was she saying? After an hour of
relatively easy conversation—if you could call it easy when you're
talking to your ex-husband and dissecting every single regret,
every single mistake both of you made, wondering what might

have happened if life had gone a different way—why did the subject of dinner out make them both stare at their feet and shift from one leg to another like a pair of preteens at a co-ed dance?

He cleared his throat. Smiled. His five o'clock shadow was deep and pronounced, and she vividly remembered the feel of his skin against hers so many, many years ago.

He reached out his hand. "Would you care to join me for dinner?"

"Me?" Of all the dumb things she could have said, her brain couldn't have picked a different word?

Thankfully, he didn't laugh at her. Maybe he recognized just how awkward this was for both of them. How huge of a learning curve they faced. There were no guidebooks to teach you how to date your ex-spouse.

No, this wasn't a date. As painfully strained as it had been, they'd even found a label for their relationship status.

Reacquaintance.

A fancy word for a convoluted concept, a concept in which neither party bore any preconceived ideas, any unspoken promises, or any false hopes.

Getting to know each other all over again. Because they'd both come to realize that even though they shared a past history, so much of it painful, they were different people now than they'd been when they separated.

Strangers compared to who they were over half a lifetime ago when they met.

Thus the deliberate step of reacquaintance.

No promises.

No false hopes.

Jolene repeated the words to herself like a mantra.

"Come on." Joseph smiled. Took her hand.

She tried to ignore the electric zing that shot through her body at his touch, but the look in his eyes told her that he had felt it, too.

He glanced out the window of the lobby and frowned. "Looks like it's raining pretty hard. You sure want to go out in this?"

She zipped up her windbreaker and gave him a smile. It wasn't as flirtatious or as confident as it had been when they went out on their first date over thirty years ago, but it was a start.

"I'm not worried. A little rain never hurt nobody."

THE END

DISCUSSION QUESTIONS

S uggested discussion group questions for *Seoul in Love* by Alana Terry.

1. What's the farthest you've traveled away from home?

2. What would you say is the most exotic or foreign place you've been to?

3. Where would you like to take your next dream vacation (assuming money and time were not issues)?

4. Have you known anybody struggling to overcome an addiction? What advice do you have (or have you heard) to help a loved one who is an addict?

In addition to their grief and his alocholism, Joseph's work schedule was also a big stress on his marriage.

5. How does work stress impact your relationships?

6. (For married people) What is the most difficult season in your marriage to date? (For singles) What do you anticipate will be one of the difficulties of marriage?

7. Are you sentimental about certain areas? Is there a certain spot that makes you feel closer to somebody you've lost?

MORE BOOKS
by Alana Terry

Find the latest information and connect with Alana at her website:
www.alanaterry.com

Request a free book when you join the Alana Terry Readers' Club!

Sweet Dreams Christian Romance

What Dreams May Come: She's got her heart set on becoming a missionary. He's determined to recruit her for the job.

Kennedy Stern Christian Suspense Novels

Unplanned (Book 1): Kennedy's pro-life worldview is shaken when she receives a mysterious phone call from a girl who's far too young to be pregnant.

Paralyzed (Book 2): It's hard to heal from the past when the past wants you dead.

Policed (Book 3): A rogue police officer can ruin a lot more than a perfect evening out.

Straightened (Book 4): Worldviews collide and body counts rise when a conservative politician finds out his son is gay.

Turbulence (Book 5): Kennedy's arctic adventure might come to a crashing halt before it even begins.

Infected (Book 6): Isolated in a hospital lockdown during a global epidemic, Kennedy can only guess who will survive.

Abridged (Book 7): When the fight for women's rights becomes a struggle for mere survival.

Orchard Grove Christian Women's Fiction

Beauty from Ashes: A baby was never part of Tiff's plans. Especially not a sick baby struggling for life on a ventilator.

Before the Dawn: When depression steals your identity and leaves you without a name …

North Korea Suspense Novels

The Beloved Daughter: Behind North Korea's closed borders, a young girl is dying for freedom.

Slave Again: She traded in her prison uniform for shackles of a different kind.

Torn Asunder: Hannah's secret mission could rip them apart and cost them both their lives.

Flower Swallow: Join Woong on his journey through flood, famine, and a shaman's curse to freedom and redemption.

ABOUT

www.alanaterry.com

Alana is a pastor's wife, a
homeschooling mom, a self-diagnosed
chicken lady, and a Christian suspense
author. Her novels have won awards from
Women of Faith, Book Club Network,
Grace Awards, Readers' Favorite, and
more. Alana's passion for social justice,
human rights, and religious freedom shines
through her writing, and her books are

known for raising tough questions without preaching. She and her
family live in rural Alaska where the northern lights in the winter
and midnight sun in the summer make hauling water, surviving the
annual mosquito apocalypse, and cleaning goat stalls in negative
forty degrees worth every second.

Author Site: www.alanaterry.com

Newsletter Sign Up: www.alanaterry.com/newsletter

Facebook: www.facebook.com/alanaterrywrites

INTRODUCING

I hope you enjoyed taking a journey to South Korea with Jolene and Joseph, and I just know God has good things in store for their future! If you'd like more inspirational romance that's meant to glorify God and illustrate the way he can work everyday miracles in each of our lives, I have a free, exclusive novel just for you.

Dare to Dream Again is the story of Gloria, who thinks that VBS is the perfect opportunity to set her daughter up with her childhood friend. What Gloria doesn't expect is that while she's playing matchmaker, she's about to get a surprise change at love herself. You can't get this novel anywhere else, so grab your free copy today!

Speaking of novels, if you like learning about new places, check out my North Korea Christian suspense series to read more about refugees like Jin-Sun. You might also be interested in *What Dreams May Come*, a US-based romance inspired by the true story of how my husband and I fell in love a full twelve months before we met face to face. Read *What Dreams May Come* today.

Now it's time to read *A Kærasti for Clari*, a story from Carol Moncado about yet another flowery mix-up. We're out of South Korea now and traveling to a palace in Ejyania. Enjoy the story. I'm sure you will!

ALANA TERRY
Author of *Seoul in Love*

Out of the Blue Bouquet

A Kærasti for *Clari*

a Novella

by

USA Today Bestselling Author

Library Cataloging Data

Moncado, Carol (Carol Moncado) 1975-

A Kærasti for Clari / Carol Moncado

Summary: Joel Christiansen delivered flowers to the palace and found his life turned upside down.

Clari Sørenson's job as social media manager for Eyjania's Queen Mother keeps her busy. An unexpected treasure hunt with a cute guy might be the vacation she needs.

Between clues and a snow storm, they're drawn to each other. Her grandparents, and even the Queen Mother, have been after her to find a boyfriend, but is Joel the Kærasti for Clari?

1. Christian fiction 2. man-woman relationships 3. Icelandic Grandmother 4. Mountain Lake Cabin 5. Treasure hunt 6. romantic relationships 7. Ice Skating 8. Royalty 9. Orphan

CONTENTS

CHAPTER 1

"**I have flowers for Katrín.**" Joel Christiansen double-checked the last name, but it was still illegible. He showed the security guard. "I can't read it."

The guard did a bit of typing on his computer. "There's only one. Katrín works in the second kitchen. I'll have her sent up." He nodded toward the chairs. "Have a seat."

Okay then. Not exactly what he'd been told to expect. As a Yfir Delivery driver, he normally just dropped off his package then left. This was his first time delivering for this florist, and he didn't take deliveries where he had to wait.

You couldn't make enough money that way, despite the generous tip promised - and his big plans to nap later.

But at the Eyjanian palace, you did as you were told.

No more palace deliveries for him - not unless the tip was always this fantastic.

A few minutes later, the door to the security office opened. Surely, the harried young woman wasn't Katrín. Her nearly black hair frizzed in a halo around her head, and her apron had more wet spots than dry.

"You wanted me?"

The guard nodded toward Joel. "He has flowers for you."

Katrín actually snorted. "Nope. Not for me." She turned to

Joel. "No clue who's playing a trick on you, but you need to double check your order."

He held out the card. "It says Katrín."

She took it from him. "But my last name doesn't start with a Z, so it's not mine. I've got to get back to work. You might try opening the card or calling the shop."

Joel closed his eyes and tried not to snap at her. It wasn't her fault the flowers were addressed wrong. When he opened them, she was gone, so it didn't matter what he might have said.

"What are you going to do?" the guard asked. "Your cell phone won't work down here. If you need to call the shop, you can do so from the phone on the table next to you."

"I can't get data?" he asked. If there was data, he could just text the guy who owned the shop.

"No."

Joel looked up the phone number in his list of recent calls. A minute later, he spoke with the owner. Ten minutes after that, the owner called back after finding the error. Two orders. Listed next to each other. One name. The other address. Both spelled wrong.

Clari Sørensen. Because that looked nearly the same as Katrín something-with-a-Z.

The guard looked her up. "She manages the Queen Mother's social media. I don't know if she'll be able to come down here to pick them up, and you can't leave them."

Never again.

The palace was a place he'd always wanted to tour, especially after delivering several times - including twice to actual offices - but he didn't think he'd deliver again.

This time it took nearly ten minutes for someone to arrive.

"You sent for me?" This woman didn't seem nearly as annoyed though she typed furiously with her thumbs as she propped herself up on crutches. A boot covered the lower half of her right leg. Straight, light brown hair hung forward, blocking his view of her face.

"You have a delivery." The guard nodded toward Joel again.

She turned, still looking at her phone. "What is it?"

Joel cocked an eyebrow. Really? Finally, she looked up. "You have some flowers, ma'am. However, there was a bit of confusion, so I'd appreciate it if you'd open the card before I leave so I can verify you're the intended recipient."

Clari didn't roll her eyes, but Joel knew she'd been tempted. Or maybe she wanted to hit him with a crutch.

After opening the small envelope, she read it aloud. "Clari, you have the day off, and a surprise awaits you at the end of your journey. Verify with your supervisor, grab your things, and drive to the place you got the scar on your knee when you were four." She held it out to him. "What's this supposed to mean?"

Joel shrugged. "Just what it says, I guess. Look, lady. I didn't send the flowers. I'm just the Yfir Delivery driver who dropped them off."

She hadn't been listening to him as she put the phone to her ear. "Kim? Do I have the day off?"

The office door opened, and a woman with an earbud walked in. "Yes. You do." She pressed the button on the side of it and held out a coat and bag. "Now get out of here. You have a surprise waiting for you."

The two women talked for a minute though Joel didn't hear what they were saying. He didn't try. He hadn't gotten the tip yet, and they were blocking his access to the outside. Finally, Clari turned, working on her phone again.

"Will you drive me? I'll pay your Yfir rate, but I clearly can't drive." She motioned to her right leg and its boot.

He stifled a sigh. "Sure." With nothing else lined up, he might as well.

A few minutes later, they were in his car. Clari chose to sit up front next to him. He handed her the colorful bouquet of Eyjanian wildflowers. After she put her seatbelt on, she held out her hand. "I'm Clari."

"I know." He didn't shake it.

"Why are you being rude?"

He gave her a side glare. "You started it."

"How?"

"You didn't have a conversation with *me* inside. You talked in the general direction of your phone and hoped I heard you too. And you didn't tip." He wouldn't have let her. Not with the tip the florist had already promised, but she didn't know that.

"Why would I tip?" she challenged. "I had no idea flowers were coming. How do you know I even have any cash on me?"

"The Yfir app will let you."

"Fine. I'll give you a tip when we're done, but at least tell me your name so I can request you as my Yfir driver."

In less than a minute, the app paired them up. "The Akushla Skating Rink?" That's what his app said. "You got a scar there?"

"I fell, and another kid hit my knee with his skate."

Whatever.

He put the car in drive and slowly left the palace grounds. Joel wanted to ask what it was like working for the Queen Mother, but he wasn't sure he wanted that much conversation with this woman.

The ten-minute drive passed in silence though Clari spent most of it on her phone.

"Can you come in with me?" she asked. "These crutches aren't easy to maneuver on." For the first time, he sensed uncertainty and hesitation. "I'd appreciate it."

Reluctantly, Joel nodded. "I'll let you off here and find a place to park." Once in a spot, he trotted toward the entrance where she waited. "Let's find this clue."

Clari struggled to hold back tears as she hopped along behind her Yfir driver. He held the door for her, but that and driving seemed to be all he was good for besides being cute with dark, curly, Josh Groban hair. Clearly, he had no clue what this was all about and didn't seem inclined to be overly helpful with the clues.

They went to the skate rental desk. She introduced herself, but the bored teenager didn't have a clue what Clari was talking about. He slouched his way to the office and talked to another man. Clari watched them through the window. Finally, the older one rummaged through the piles on his desk and handed over a full-sized envelope. The kid walked over and gave it to Clari.

She slid her finger under the flap and pried it open. The card had a stick drawing of a cat on it, but no words.

The inside was similarly without a verse, but a square piece of paper with words typed on it had been pasted in place.

Clari,

Head to the spot where you got your first kiss.

First kiss? Her real first kiss or her six-year-old first kiss?

Which one was closer? That mattered less than which one was easier to get to from the car.

"Where next?" Joel seemed resigned.

"Alfred the First Primary School." Start with the six-year-old kiss.

With a sigh, he pushed off the counter. "Let's go. I'll pick you up out front."

He hurried away, but at least there was a purpose, and that purpose would benefit her. She crutched her way out the door as Joel pulled his car to the curb. He got out to open the door so she could toss her crutches in the back.

"Thanks."

Joel mumbled something that may have been "you're welcome" but might have been "chew your gum."

Neither one of them said anything as he drove halfway across Akushla to her elementary school. She breathed a sigh of relief when she saw an envelope taped to the fence near the playground.

He put the car in park. "I'll grab it for you." Before she thanked him, he was out of the car and trotting toward the envelope. In less than thirty seconds, he was back in the car. "Where next?" he asked as he handed it to her.

"Do you really not have any idea who this is from?"

"No, ma'am."

Stifling another sigh, she opened the card.

Clari,

This place always gets your seal of approval. Remember when your class took a trip when you were seven?

"Where to?" Joel asked her.

"The Akushla Zoo." As a girl, she'd loved the seals and sea lions.

"Not too far. Are you going to need to go in though? Borrow one of those wheelchairs?"

"I'll be fine." She wouldn't be. The seals were on the far side of the park. Though not big by zoo standards, it would tax her already sore arms.

This time, when they arrived, Joel didn't pull up and wait for her to get out. Instead, he walked straight to the entrance and talked to the attendant. He returned with one of their loaner wheelchairs.

How would she maneuver it by herself though? Maybe one of those motorized scooters would be a better idea.

"I'll be right back."

So the guy had gone from grumpy and reluctant to grumpy and helpful? Whatever. She wouldn't complain. Not when he was going to wheel her to the seal exhibit.

She tried to arrange herself in the wheelchair so that it was remotely comfortable. About the time she got the feet platform things situated, Joel returned.

"The entry fee has already been taken care of," he told her as they headed for the gate.

"So whoever set this up thought of everything?" She pulled her coat a bit tighter around her as he pushed through the gate held open by the employee.

"Looks like it."

It only took about five minutes to get across the zoo. The handler was getting ready to do a feeding show with the seals.

Clari held up a hand before he got started. "Excuse me. I think you have something for me."

The guy grinned at her. "Are you Clari?"

"Yes."

He winked at her. "I do have something for you, but not yet. Come closer."

When her chair was as close as it would go, he handed her a bucket filled with partially thawed dead fish.

"Miss Clari is going to be my assistant today." A group of school children was gathered around. "Who wants to feed Benji?"

A chorus of "me" sounded around the area along with waving hands covered by mittens. He picked two who joined Clari near the rock wall enclosure.

For nearly ten minutes, he regaled the crowd with tales about King Benjamin the First Seal. Benji would do a trick then Clari would hand a fish to one of the kids who would toss it to the seal. In all, six of the children helped feed King Benji.

Finally, the presentation ended. The children who'd helped washed their hands in a nearby sink while Clari handed the bucket back to the caretaker.

"And as soon as you wash your hands, I have something for you," he told her.

Clari waited for the children to finish then Joel helped her over. Once her hands were dried by the powerful air dryer, she put her gloves back on and took the envelope from the caretaker.

"Thanks for your help." His grin widened. "Hope you have a great day."

She opened the card and read the words inside then groaned. "Do you know how to knit?"

CHAPTER 2

K nit?

"Can't say that I do." Joel pushed the wheelchair through the seating area toward the entrance. He'd enjoyed watching her with the kids. She looked like she was good with them.

His phone buzzed. Probably his sister again - and the reason why he made his attitude improve, at least outwardly. Her recent struggles with life in general reminded him that being a Yfir driver for a day with a nice lady wasn't anything to complain about.

He went on. "My sister does, though. I can call her if you need me to."

Clari held up the card though he couldn't read it. "I have to go to Rachel's Raveling Repository and complete a task she has for me."

Joel threw his head back and let loose with his biggest laugh. "Would you believe Rachel is my sister?"

"Not really, but why would you make something like that up?"

"I wouldn't. I will text her and tell her we're on our way in a minute, though." He left Clari in her wheelchair near the entrance and trotted off to get his car.

YOU WON'T BELIEVE THIS, he typed. I'M YFIR DRIVING YOUR

TREASURE HUNT PERSON. WE SHOULD BE THERE IN ABOUT TWENTY MINUTES.

A minute later he got an LOL back.

When he arrived at the curb, one of the zoo employees had helped Clari to it. She got situated, and he pulled out.

"I want to apologize for earlier." He looked for oncoming traffic then turned. "I didn't sleep well. I was told the flower delivery would take half an hour tops from the time I got to the florist shop. I'd planned to go home and go back to bed." He hesitated. "It's been a long week, but the friend who was supposed to deliver it wasn't able to, and since I've been cleared for palace deliveries before, he asked if I could. I shouldn't have taken it out on you."

Clari had turned to study him as he drove. "Thank you. I appreciate the explanation and the changed attitude. I have no idea who set this up, but they must not know I broke my ankle a few weeks ago."

"What exactly do you do at the palace, if you're allowed to tell me?"

"I handle all of the Queen Mother's social media presence. Facebook, Twitter, YouTube, and Instagram mostly, but as others pop up, I look into whether or not the queen needs an account. I usually make one immediately, then set it to private and don't use it unless it becomes a viable platform."

"So you write most of the posts, too?"

"A lot of them, but not all. Some come from other offices in the palace. She writes a few a week herself. They are always signed with QME."

"You actually work closely with her then?"

He sensed hesitation on her part. "Somewhat. We meet occasionally, but she wouldn't consider me part of her inner circle or anything like that."

"I'm just curious," he reassured her. "I would never presume to ask a favor or anything."

"You'd be the first," she muttered.

"You get asked stuff all the time?" he asked, hoping he wasn't right.

"Like you wouldn't believe."

He thought about placing a reassuring hand on her shoulder, but held back. "What about the rest of the family? Have you met them?"

"Most of them in passing, but that's it. I doubt any of them, but the Queen Mother and maybe Princess Genevieve, would recognize me if I ran into them on the street."

Joel wondered about that. Weren't some people really good at remembering names and faces? That seemed like it would be a good skill for members of the royal family to have.

He pulled into a spot near Rachel's store. "Maybe you won't actually have to knit. Maybe it'll be something easier than that."

Clari opened her door and turned to the side. "Not with my luck."

Joel rushed around the car to help her, but she was already on her feet and reaching for her crutches over the seat. "Wait for me next time. Let me help."

She didn't say anything but Joel was almost sure he saw tears in her eyes. Why? Was it that hard on her and her arms?

He made sure she got onto the sidewalk safely then hurried ahead to open the door.

His sister's only employee greeted them. "Hey, Joel! And you must be Clari." She held out her hand. "I'm Anabelle."

"Nice to meet you." Clari smiled at Anabelle. "Do you have something for me?"

"I will. But first, have a seat." Anabelle motioned toward the cozy area in the front corner.

Clari sat in the big green chair while Joel took her crutches to set them aside.

"Joel!" He turned to see Rachel coming out of the back. "It's been forever." She gave him a big hug. "We live ten minutes apart. I should see you more than once a month."

"You only see your sister once a month?" Clari asked from her seat.

"How often do you see your family?" Joel asked, leaving his arm around Rachel's shoulders.

"Every Sunday for dinner. We all go to my grandparents' house. Sometimes it's somewhere else, and not everyone makes it every week, but there's always at least two dozen of us there."

Joel tightened his grip on Rachel's shoulder as she stared at the ground. "That's great, Clari. How many kids does your grandmother have?"

Clari started talking about her grandmother's five kids, and their kids, and how she was the only biologically related female in the bunch.

Anabelle brought a basket out of the back. "That sounds a lot like one of our customers' family. Mrs. T has a ton of kids and grandkids, but only one granddaughter."

A grin crossed Clari's face. "Mrs. T is my grandmother. She loves your shop."

Joel felt Rachel straighten her shoulders and move away from him. "And we love her. But now you have a task to complete."

⁂

Clari watched Joel and his sister out of the corner of her eye while she tried to organize the mini-skeins of yarn in rainbow order.

What color should she start with? Red seemed like as good a point as any.

She tried to give them their space by not staring, even though they were on the other side of the shop.

"They'll be fine." Anabelle sat next to her. "It's been a rough year. They're pretty much the only family they have left, but they tend to work opposite schedules since Joel's finishing university. That makes it hard for them to get together as often as they'd like."

Clari wasn't sure what to say, so she just kept rearranging the mini-skeins until she thought she had them in the right order. "How's this?"

Anabelle smiled at her. "Close enough." She reached behind the counter and picked up a card. "Here's your next clue."

"Thanks." Clari opened the flap and pulled a single picture out. A smile crossed her face. "Of course." The big pond at the park near her grandparents' house. She'd spent many happy hours near there.

A glance at Joel and Rachel showed they were still engrossed in their conversation. She wouldn't interrupt. The lake would wait a few more minutes.

"So you know my *amma*?" Clari asked Anabelle who seemed to pick up on why she was stalling.

"We love Mrs. T, even though we can't say her last name. We've tried."

Clari laughed. "*Thorbjørnsdóttir*. It means daughter of *Thorbjørn* in Icelandic."

Anabelle grinned. "If you say so. She comes in a couple times a week to say hi and look around. I'm pretty sure she has far more yarn than she can use in a lifetime. Either that or she knits way faster than anyone else ever."

Clari thought about it. Had she ever seen Amma knitting? Before she said anything else, Joel walked over. "Ready for the next stop?"

She stood and reached for her crutches. "Let's go. But can we grab something to eat? I was going to have a late lunch today and never did."

"Sure." Joel held open the door to the shop. "What sounds good?"

After a few minutes of discussion, they settled on a drive through nearby. As she munched on her cheeseburger, Joel drove toward the park.

"Thank you for stopping." She took another bite and spoke

around it. "This really hit the spot."

He took a sip of his milkshake. "I already ate, but I won't ever turn down one of these."

"Only a crazy person would," she told him as she reached for her own milkshake.

"Where are we going next?"

Clari showed him the picture of the lake. "Except it's probably iced over by now."

"Isn't everything? I don't think I know that park. What part of town is it in?"

"It's not far." She stirred her shake with the straw. "I am really glad I didn't have to do some ice skating thing at the first stop. That would have been really hard."

Joel didn't say anything until she told him where to turn to get to the park. Finally, "I hope this treasure hunt doesn't last too much longer."

Of course, that's what he thought. "I can get another Yfir driver," she told him. "I'm sure you have other things to do."

"It's not that. I think it's supposed to storm tomorrow, and I need to go shopping first. I'm not a fan of driving in winter storms so I usually just stay home."

"Same here." Something they had in common. "Tell you what. We'll do a couple more, and if it's still not done, I'll let you off the hook. I can try to call the florist and get a hint about who sent the flowers and go straight to the source."

"It was an order placed somewhere else and sent here. From another country even maybe."

"I don't know anyone in any other countries." Did she? Not really. Her best friend, Gina, had been living in the States for a while, but she wasn't the kind to send flowers or set up this ridiculous treasure hunt.

"I'm not sure, but that's the impression I got when I called to get the right name."

"Right name?"

"It was originally addressed to the wrong person. They found someone with the same first name, but she insisted it wasn't hers, so I called to have the guy double check."

"If the clues weren't so specific, I'd wonder if there still wasn't an error somewhere."

"My sister knew it was you and who your grandmother is, so I think it's pretty safe to say they were meant for you." He turned into the parking lot near the lake. "Any particular part of the lake?"

"Hopefully the bench on this side, and hopefully there's no ridiculous requirement either."

"At least the one at my sister's shop was easy."

"I'm not even sure I did it right, but Anabelle said they'd take it anyway."

He put the car in park. "I'll check the bench for you."

Before she thanked him, he crunched through the thin layer of snow covering the grass. Was it supposed to snow overnight?

She pulled up a weather app on her phone. Five to six centimeters of snow expected overnight with another six to eight centimeters during the day tomorrow. Not too bad. It would triple what was already on the ground, plus a little more, but not enough to affect the city. People would need to be a bit more careful while driving, but generally, people drove pretty well in this kind of weather. It wasn't until there were a couple dozen centimeters that it started to get too worrisome.

Joel returned with a card in his hand. "I don't see anything that you might need to do, but open it and see."

Clari took a sip of her drink before she slid the flap open. She read the note inside.

Clari,

You always said you'd never forget your fifth birthday. Go to the place where you celebrated for your next clue.

Her fifth birthday? Where had she gone for her fifth birthday? Right. Of course.

She groaned as the other implications hit her.

"What is it?"

"I hope you've got a full tank of gas." Then she remembered his statement. "Actually, I can call someone else for this one. It's going to take a while. You need to get to the store, then home to get some rest."

He didn't hesitate. "No. I'll take you and stop at the store later. Even if I didn't, I should be fine. More that extra junk food you stock up on before sitting at home for a couple days. Where are we going?"

"I'll pay extra if you take me." She'd never get there on her own right now.

His eyes narrowed. "Why?"

"Because it's not close, and I'm keeping you from other things you'd rather be doing."

"It'll be fine. Now, where are we going?"

"A cabin off Lake Akushla." A lake with the same name as a city it was nowhere near.

He gave a resigned sigh. "Let's go."

At least the snow wouldn't start until overnight. By then Joel would have delivered Clari safely to her final destination, and he'd be in his flat with a fire blazing. Lake Akushla wasn't close, but he had enough time.

Didn't he?

In fifteen minutes, they'd left the more urban part of the not-very-urban Akushla and headed into the mountains.

"I appreciate you doing this for me," Clari told him as she stared out the other window.

"My pleasure." With his intentional shift in the presentation of his attitude toward Clari, he'd found his actual attitude shifting as well. And he wasn't going to charge her for any of this. He'd gotten a huge bonus for the last minute delivery to the palace, more than he normally made in a full day of driving, but his attitude had been pretty deplorable. "So what part of the lake are we going to?"

"The north side. My grandparents have a cabin there."

Good thing they were coming in from the southwest, even if he did hate this drive. It wouldn't take as long to get to the north side as if they'd been on the other end of town when they left. That direction was much longer to get around the lake.

Such were the vagaries of driving on an island nation with mountains in the middle.

"How much time did you spend up here as a kid?"

Clari adjusted the heating vent a bit. "We'd spend a week in the summer. If weather permitted, we'd spend several days at Christmas. Technically, there's about two-and-a-half hours of daylight during Christmas week, but the reality is that it's always in shadow. The way the mountains are, the little bit of sunlight is blocked for most of it."

"I bet it has a fantastic view of the aurora borealis, though."

"Oh, yeah. I wish I had my camera with me. There's almost always some lights around, it seems." She shrugged. "Not *always* of course, but it feels like it sometimes."

"I've never seen them outside of one of the parks in Akushla. Since they made the whole switch to 'no light pollution' street lights thing, it makes for some decent viewing."

"That is one good thing King Benjamin's done." Clari clapped her hand over her mouth then moved it slightly so he could hear her. "You didn't hear me say that."

Joel chuckled. "Not allowed to talk bad about the family."

"Not allowed to talk about the family at all, really, but definitely nothing that could be considered disparaging."

He reached over and rested his hand on her forearm. "I won't say anything to anyone about it, but you're not wrong. The king isn't very popular and isn't doing anything to make people like him more. The nationwide light initiative was a great move though. People do love having less light pollution when they get even a short distance away from town or in a park."

"I've met him a couple times," Clari admitted. "He's not the warmest person around, but everyone knows that. I think losing his father at such a young age affected him more than most people realize. That's me the Eyjanian citizen making the statement, not the palace employee."

"Losing a parent at thirteen affects anyone. It's traumatic at any age. To have the responsibility of running a country placed on your shoulders at the same time surely makes it worse, even if Princess Louise did most of it until he turned eighteen."

"I can't imagine life without my parents."

Joel didn't respond immediately, but after a few seconds decided to go a different route. "I'm not asking you to violate any confidences, but rumor has it that the Queen Mother became a recluse, from her family as well as the public, for a long time, too. In a sense, the king kind of lost both parents at least for a while. I wonder if that explains why he is the way he is."

"It might." She didn't actually confirm that the former queen had retreated from daily life inside the palace as well as out, but it was as close as she would come. Joel believed he could safely assume the accuracy of his statement.

"You're close to your family?" he asked. His sister and Anabelle had insinuated just that.

She nodded. "I talk to my parents almost every day and my brothers once a week or so. That's besides seeing all of them most Sundays at Amma's house."

The term startled him. "Is your family Icelandic?" Native Eyjanians didn't use that term for grandmother.

"Amma is. Afi is Eyjanian, but my *amma* insisted on keeping some Icelandic traditions. She didn't change her last name when they got married. She's still *Thorbjørnsdóttir*. My great grandparents apparently threw a fit, but she won them over. They loved her, just wanted her to take my *afi's* last name. When she reminded them the kids would all have their last name, they accepted it."

The kilometers sped by as they talked about their families and growing up. Joel carefully avoided anything about the last few years - or looking too closely at the accident scene they passed. He hoped Clari didn't notice.

Lake Akushla sort of came into view in the distance as a flake landed on the windshield. Joel glanced out at the sky. There weren't any stars, but what he could see of the clouds didn't look particularly ominous. Yet.

One downside of living this far north and being so far from anything that produced light except the moon - it was hard to tell what the sky looked like when it was cloudy. Or see the mountain lake vista as you drove through the pass.

"Now where?" He glanced a little nervously at his fuel gauge. Wasn't there a town not too far away?

"Just keep going. It's on the far end."

His odometer told him how far he'd gone since his last fill up. He should have plenty to get to the other end of the lake and back to the town he knew was nearby.

Hopefully.

Or should he mention it now?

No. Based on his usual consumption, he really should have enough to get to the cabin and back to town at least twice. No sense in stopping this excursion before then.

But the road hugged the winding coast of the lake, taking them almost twice as far as it would have been if the road was straight. The snowflakes had begun falling a bit more in earnest as well.

"How much farther?" Should they turn around? "I'm going to need to fill up in town and think maybe we should go back to do that."

She pointed to a street sign barely illuminated by his headlights. "That's the turn. We're basically there. Let's get the clue, and we'll head out."

He made the turn and crunched over gravel and snow until he saw the cabin.

Or what must pass for a cabin in Clari's family.

Because in his family, they couldn't have even dreamed about owning something like this. The house he grew up in would fit inside at least twice if not three times.

"Cabin?"

She shrugged. "Afi's parents were quite well-to-do, and he was an only child."

That explained the last name thing a little more.

"Why don't I run in for you?"

Clari winced. "It's nothing personal, but I can't give you the code."

He nodded. "Then let me help you."

Before he could turn off the engine, it sputtered.

And died.

CHAPTER 3

D read filled Clari. "Was that the engine dying?"

"I think so. Usually, I get another thirty or forty kilometers before I have to refill." Joel tried to turn the engine over, but nothing happened.

"Driving through the mountains changed your consumption?" Something Clari usually thought of.

"I guess." He sighed. "Any chance your *afi* keeps some extra around here?"

"I don't know." She opened her door. "But right now, let's get inside, and I'll see if I can call."

The snowfall had increased in intensity in the last few minutes. If Afi didn't have what they needed, she could call the station in town, and they would send someone out, but likely not until the storm ended.

Joel helped her up the stairs to the front door then carefully walked back to get some things from the car, including her wildflowers, while she punched the code in. When the whirring and click told her it was open, she turned the handle.

The first thing she noticed was warmth.

Not just in from the cold, but actual warmth.

"Someone has been here," she told Joel as she crutched her way in.

He stopped and put a hand on her arm. "Do we go in?"

It took strength not to roll her eyes. "Yes. No one is here, *now*, but the heater has been turned on." She pulled her phone out of her pocket and text Afi.

His reply came a moment later.

IT'S CALLED SMART TECHNOLOGY, *SONARDÓTTIR*. I TURNED THE HEATER UP A LITTLE WHILE AGO SO IT WOULD BE WARM WHEN YOU ARRIVED. UNFORTUNATELY, YOUR SURPRISE HAS BEEN DELAYED AND WILL NOT ARRIVE UNTIL AT LEAST MORNING. WILL YOU BE ALL RIGHT THERE UNTIL THEN?

Her surprise? She told him she'd manage and asked what the surprise was. He wouldn't tell her.

Joel asked what she'd found out, and she read the text to him. "*Sonardóttir?*"

"Granddaughter. Specifically, daughter of my son. Out of all the kids and grandkids, I'm the only girl not grafted in by marriage. They both call me that when they're not encouraging me to find a *kærasti*." At the look on his face, she explained. "Boyfriend."

"Ah." He didn't say anything else. Something bothered him?

"Listen, I'll call the garage in town. They'll send someone out, but not until the storm passes. Some parts of that road get slick pretty quickly. I really don't want Afi to know I'm stuck here with some guy I just met. I know your sister is Rachel, and Amma loves her, but still. Does that work for you, or do you *need* to be back tonight?"

He closed the door behind them and flipped the lock. "It's fine."

"Good." Clari turned and really looked at the room for the first time ever. It had always been part of their family traditions, and she'd never thought about what it must look like to an outsider.

The main room extended two full stories with windows facing the lake. To the right was the kitchen with its modern appliances and granite counters and enormous island. Also on the right, past the kitchen, was a table that seated at least a dozen.

In the center of the room and to the left was a spacious living area filled with comfortable couches and chairs arranged in several smaller groups to allow for conversation or gaze at the lake in the summer.

Clari set her purse on the island and started for the far side. "I need to use the bathroom." In the corner opposite the dining table, a half set of stairs led to the room she always used. "If you go upstairs, there's one you can use as well." The full staircase clung to the wall by the dining area.

"Thanks."

She flipped the light on in her room. Sometimes she felt a little guilty about being the only girl in the family, but not when she got this whole room to herself. Occasionally, when the boys had girlfriends, she'd be asked to share, but not often. Most significant others didn't get to come to the cabin until there was a ring and a date. That meant she didn't have to share often.

She hobbled to the bathroom on the far side of the room. The slate flooring led to the sunken garden tub that called her name, but she didn't have time to enjoy it. Even if she didn't have to keep a cast dry anymore and could remove the boot if she was careful, she wouldn't abandon Joel for that long.

A few minutes, later she passed her bed and returned to the living area to find Joel staring out the window.

"It's snowing pretty hard."

"We'll be fine. Afi has a generator if we need it, but we're not on the main power lines way out here. We shouldn't lose power, there's a tankless water heater and about eighty-three fireplaces with plenty of wood stacked outside. There's nothing to worry about."

He didn't answer but stood there with his hands shoved deep in his pockets.

Whatever. Maybe he was worried about food.

"And Afi always leaves provisions here. It's all canned food and stuff, so nothing mouthwatering, but it'll keep our bellies full. Every once in a while, a stranger needs to take shelter. There are instructions on the door for how they can get into the basement. The rest of the house is locked off, but there's plenty of food down there to last the royal family for the whole winter."

That made Joel chuckle. "Actual winter or Eyjanian winter?"

Clari laughed with him. Ancient Eyjanians, like the ancient peoples of other nations this far north, had only thought in two seasons - summer and winter. Eyjanian winter lasted about eight months. "Probably Eyjanian winter, even with the size of the royal family." There was eleven in King Benjamin's immediate family alone - his mother and nine younger siblings.

"I guess we won't starve, then." His shoulders relaxed a bit, but she still saw the tension in them.

"Why don't we play a board game or something? There's no television up here, but we do have some movies and a ton of games."

Joel turned from the window. In the dim emergency lighting that remained on most of the time, she could barely make out his face. "Sure. That sounds great, but first how about we make a fire? I know you said the heater won't go out, but just in case, we won't be starting from scratch."

She smiled, not understanding his comment, but sensing fear behind it. "Sure."

Joel loaded his arms with wood once more. There was already enough inside to last for days, but he wouldn't chance it.

As he walked back into the cabin, his phone vibrated in his pocket. Nothing he could do about it until he set the firewood down. Once he tossed another log onto the already blazing fire, he pulled it out.

Rachel? She rarely called him, especially since they'd just seen each other. He swiped to call her back, grateful for the increasingly ubiquitous cell phone service in the more rural areas of the country. King Benjamin had done that right, too.

"Joe?" The use of his old nickname and the tears in her voice caused Joel to grip the phone even tighter.

"What's wrong, Rach?"

"I'm fine," she told him between sobs. "It's Anabelle. And Gracie."

A feeling of dread filled the pit of his stomach. "What happened to them?"

"They're fine, too. Kind of. It's their parents."

His stomach clenched. "What about them?"

"They were heading back from Lake Akushla today and…"

He knew. As soon as she said it, he knew they were the ones they'd seen being pulled back over the side of the cliff. "Near the last switchback?" And the most dangerous one.

"How did you know?"

"I drove by it."

"You *drove* to Lake Akushla? And you didn't go the other way? What are you doing there? Please tell me you're not coming home tonight."

It wouldn't be any lighter come daytime though that part of the road did get the indirect sunlight Clari indicated the cabin missed out on. He'd keep that in mind on the drive home. "Clari's next clue sent her to her grandparents' cabin. I drove her up here. We can't leave until the storm lets up even if we wanted to. I ran out of fuel right as we arrived."

"Joel! How could you?" The fear and reprimand in his sister's voice served its purpose.

"I forgot to check. I know it was stupid, but we were going *up* the mountain, not down. I would have made it to the town, but we didn't stop there."

"At least you're not alone."

No. He wasn't alone. Not technically. But he suspected Clari would sleep in the room she claimed as her own and expect him to stay in one of the ones upstairs filled with bunk beds. It would be almost like being alone.

"If you need to, you should tell her." Rachel's soft words came through the phone. "It might help."

"We'll see." He wouldn't. Wouldn't burden an already stressed Clari with something from his childhood.

"You never told me how you ended up as Clari's Yfir driver. I thought you were taking the day off."

"I was going to." Joel sank onto one of the couches. "But a friend called me about a Yfir Delivery, and I couldn't ignore it. I'm cleared for deliveries to the palace, so I took the job. The tip made it completely worthwhile." It had finally shown up in his app.

"Was driving her around part of it?"

"No, but you saw her leg. She can't drive and wouldn't have been able to do most of this via public transportation. Well," he amended, "she might have been able to, but she'd just now be getting to your store."

"And we're closed."

"Exactly." A fresh wave of grief came over him. "How's Anabelle doing?"

"I don't know. She texted me, but didn't answer when I called."

Odd. His sister's best friend *always* answered the phone and texts, except while she was sleeping and with news like that, there was no way she'd have dozed off. "Did she know the cause?"

"If she does, she didn't say. Just that they were in an accident near the same switchback, and she'd just been notified they were gone. She won't be at work until further notice. Like that was my main concern."

"Sounds like Anabelle, though. I guess she'll be raising Gracie from here on out then?" The toddler won the heart of anyone she came in contact with.

"I guess. It wouldn't surprise me to find out her grandparents will try to take Gracie from her. She's really the only family Anabelle has left. She can't stand to be around her grandparents most of the time."

Joel had heard enough bits and pieces that he didn't blame Anabelle.

A door opening caused him to turn. "I've got to go, Rach. Tell Anabelle she's in my prayers."

"I will. Let me know before you leave for home. Love you. And you need to tell Clari why you're going to have nightmares tonight."

Before he could tell her that wasn't part of the plan, Rachel hung up.

"What was that about? Everything okay with Anabelle?"

Joel turned, but his breath caught when he saw Clari. She'd looked very professional and put together when he'd met her, but she'd been coming from her job in the Queen Mother's office.

Now, she'd changed into clothes she must have had stashed in the room she'd disappeared to. Black leggings were covered by an eggplant-colored shirt. Her hair hung in waves past her shoulders and practically begged for him to thread his fingers through it.

Whoa.

Where had that thought come from?

"Anabelle?" she asked again. "What happened?"

Joel sat on the chair. "That accident we saw?"

Clari sank to the couch near him. "She couldn't have been in it."

"No, but her parents were. She texted Rachel that they didn't make it. That's all Rachel knew."

Clari's gasp mirrored his own disbelief a few moments earlier.

"Anabelle has a two-year-old sister that she's probably going to have to raise by herself. Her grandparents may try to take the little girl which means Anabelle will have a fight on her hands while grieving her parents."

"Poor Anabelle."

He looked over to see Clari wiping her cheeks with her fingers. "Will you get in trouble for not being at work tomorrow?" he asked. "Because if it's all the same to you, I'd rather not head back to Akushla until the roads are completely clear."

CHAPTER 4

"**S** hoot!" **Clari jumped out of** her chair and used a crutch to help her get to her bag on the island in the kitchen. "I forgot to call my boss."

She rummaged around until she found her phone then held the button until she was able to give a voice command to call. Briefly, she explained the situation only to be told that she wasn't expected in for over a week. Apparently, the surprise included time off.

A minute later, she was back on her couch. The one she almost always claimed. "So whoever planned this planned to spend some time here." She turned to stare at the kitchen. "I wonder if that means there's decent food."

Joel hopped up. "You don't need to be hobbling around on that foot. I'll look." He opened the fridge. "Fresh milk and eggs."

"That's a good start."

"Fresh vegetables, too."

"Even better." She leaned against the side of the couch and stretched her legs out. "Did you pick a game?"

He held up two decks of cards. "How about Rummy?"

"I haven't played that in ages." She re-situated herself on the couch. "You can deal." Clari pointed toward the wall. "There's a bank of light switches over there. We'll need to see better."

Cards in hand, Joel stopped at the wall near the front door, flipping one switch after another until they settled on lighting that wasn't too glaring, but bright enough for the game.

"Tell me one of your favorite memories here?" Joel asked as he shuffled the cards.

"My fifth birthday."

"Ah, the one on the card."

"Yep. It was the weekend before my birthday." She blinked as the date registered. "My grandparents made sure everyone was here, including my best friend." She leaned the side of her head against the back of the couch. "I didn't understand it until much later." Before going on, she realized she'd only known Joel a few hours and wasn't quite ready to tell him the whole story.

It involved too many other people's pain.

"Anyway, the whole family was here. I got to pick everything, or my favorites were already picked for me. My favorite meals, games, all of that. Mostly, I just loved spending time with my family, though, because in those days we didn't get together very often. When I made my birthday wish, I wished we would have lunch at Amma and Afi's every week."

"And Sunday lunches were born?"

"Exactly. It's still my favorite day of the week. I love going to church, but I also love getting to see my family."

Joel dealt the cards. "I get the feeling there's a lot more to the story than that."

Clari picked up the cards in front of her. "Maybe. But I barely know you."

For ten minutes, they took turns drawing two cards and discarding one, each rearranging the cards in their hands until, finally, Clari had enough points to lay her melds down.

"Good start," Joel told her as he picked up the discard pile. "But watch this."

She groaned as he laid down set after set of cards, somehow ending up with just four left in his hand. "Impressive." After pulling two cards off the deck, she decided it was time to turn the tables a little bit. "What's your favorite childhood birthday memory?"

Joel didn't hesitate. "When I turned ten, Rachel and I got to go ice skating, which we rarely got to do. My parents were there, but they just watched. I guess my mom broke her wrist ice skating as a kid, so she didn't skate anymore. Dad stayed with her because he didn't want her to be alone on the sidelines. After we finished skating, they took us to the zoo where we fed the seals." He nodded toward her with a raised eyebrow. "When we got back to the house, all of my friends were there for a surprise party, including some of the extended family we rarely saw because they live in San Majoria. One of my cousins and I were best buds whenever we were together, so that was extra nice."

"That's awesome. There's nothing quite like family, is there?"

This time he didn't speak right away. "No. There's not."

"And there's more to that story?" Would he think she was prying? She didn't mean to.

"Like you said, we've only known each other a few hours."

Right. She didn't push, and the conversation for the rest of the game revolved around the innocuous.

Joel pulled the cards into a pile toward him. "Are you ready for something to eat?"

Clari shook her head. "No thanks. I'm still full from earlier. In fact, I think I'm going to turn in. Will you be okay? Help yourself to any of the food, and you can sleep in any of the rooms upstairs. The other room down here is my grandparents though." The double doors on the wall underneath the upstairs walkway weren't locked, but no one ever went through them without an invitation.

Joel didn't look up as he flipped a couple of red-backed cards into a pile before putting the next two blue-backed ones in a separate one. "I'll be fine. I may just sleep out here on a couch by the fire though. I don't like leaving it unattended."

She glanced over at it. Though it had been roaring enough that she'd turned the heater down a bit earlier, it had almost died out.

There wasn't really anything to leave unattended, especially if he closed the glass doors.

But something in his tone told her there was more to it than that. Maybe he knew someone who'd been in a house fire.

Without pushing him on it, Clari leveraged herself up from the couch and grasped one of her crutches. "Then good night. I'll see you in the morning." Such as it was in this part of the world in late November.

"And maybe by then, the snow will have stopped, and we can head back to Akushla, or your surprise will have shown up."

Clari had almost forgotten about that. If she hadn't heard what the surprise was by morning, she'd call Afi and convince him to tell her.

Meantime, a good night's sleep was just what she needed.

Joel fought the growing apprehension as Clari's door closed behind her. Should he tell her? Ask her to sleep on one of the other couches? Beg her to let him sleep on the floor in her room?

Anywhere but one of those bunk beds.

Alone.

Anywhere at the lake alone.

Incoherent prayers fled from the depths of his soul upward. Would this be the time God would hear his plea and no nightmares would plague him?

He didn't hold out much hope of that, but he prayed anyway.

After putting both decks of cards back in their respective boxes, he walked back into the kitchen and pulled out some veggies. He could eat them raw as a snack. No sense in actually trying to make something just for himself.

After munching for a few minutes, he washed it all down with a bottle of water. He turned out the lights then laid down on one of the couches. Pulling the blanket off the back, he rolled onto his side before plumping the throw pillow under his head.

Sleep wouldn't come easy, but he focused on breathing in and out slowly. He counted backward from a thousand, concentrating on not missing any or getting distracted by other thoughts, good or bad.

999

998

997

Focus. Don't get distracted.

More counting.

948

947

Keep going. You're getting sleepy.

Still more.

862

861

860

He felt himself drift and fought to let the sandman carry him away while praying for a dreamless sleep.

Darkness enveloped him.

Mom? Dad? Rach?

No one was there.

No one was anywhere.

Joel sat straight up, cold sweat pouring off him.

"What is it? Are you okay?"

He couldn't see who it was. Then he remembered. "Clari?"

"Yeah. I'm here. You were having a nightmare of some sort."

His breathing started to even out as he swung his legs over the side of the couch and braced his hands against his knees. "Most likely."

She sat on the on the other end. "Want to talk about it?"

Joel made himself take a deep breath then lean against the back of the couch. "Not really but I probably should."

Clari didn't say anything but just waited.

"We rented a cabin on the other side of the lake when I was about six." He closed his eyes and tried not to dwell on the feelings. "I was supposed to go fishing with my dad. We were going to leave early in the morning and be gone overnight and be back after dinner the second day. I wasn't feeling well, so I didn't go."

He ran his hands down his face. "My mom and Rachel decided to go grocery shopping in town. They didn't realize I was still asleep in the other room."

A small gasp came from the other end of the couch. "How long were you left alone?"

"Nearly three days. One of those horrific rainstorms came up, and my mom and sister decided to stay in town. My dad didn't make it back because of the rain and all. It wasn't until he made it to town and ran into them that they realized what must have happened."

With his eyes closed, he tried not to relive it. "They left Rachel in town with a friend and drove through the downpour until they got to the cabin. There were a couple of low water areas, but the truck was big enough to get through them. Barely. By the time they got there, I was a mess. There was enough food and water than I didn't go hungry or anything, but ever since, I haven't been able to be alone overnight outside the city. Here or at the beach or wherever, I can't sleep alone. Usually, my dad or a friend stays in the room with me. As long as I'm not alone, I'm okay."

Clari shifted on the other end of the couch. "Why didn't you say something? I would have stayed out here with you or in one of the rooms with the bunk beds."

"I don't do bunk beds anymore either. Not if I can avoid it."

She stood, and he heard her crutches thunking on the floor. "Then I'll sleep out here on one of the other couches. Try to get some rest."

Even though she didn't say anything else, he knew she was there, and that helped immensely.

Feeling much more at peace, Joel blew out a deep breath and stretched back out on the couch. This time he sunk into a deep sleep and didn't wake up until the smell of bacon woke him up.

"Did the light bother you?" Clari asked from the kitchen.

Joel sat back up and stretched his arms over his head as he yawned. "No. But the smell of bacon might have had something to do with it."

She chuckled. "I can't say I'm sorry about that."

"Never apologize for bacon."

"And eggs. They're almost ready. If you want to wash up, they should be done by the time you are."

When he came back downstairs, she had set two plates on the island with glasses of orange juice next to them.

He slid into the chair in the middle of the island so she could have the end one with her bad foot. "How did you sleep?"

"Fine. I nap on that couch all the time. It's one of my favorite places in the world."

Joel didn't know if he believed her or not, but he appreciated the sentiment. "Thanks."

She sat next to him and bumped her shoulder into his. "I do wish you would have told me last night. I would have stayed out here all night."

"I know, but I was hopeful. I prayed hard, did the relaxation breathing techniques I've learned, counted backwards. It surprised me how quickly I fell asleep. If only the nightmares had stayed away, I would have been fine."

"But they didn't," she pointed out gently. "And if we're here another night, we'll both sleep out here again."

Clari let her head flop back. "This is one time I wish Afi would let us have a television and DVDs in the cabin. Usually, there's a ton of us here, so there's always something to do and someone to do it with."

Joel raised an eyebrow.

She rolled her eyes. "I'm tired of board games for two people. You need at least three and really four or five to make most games worthwhile. Movies would give us something else to do."

"What about MyBingeFlix on your phone? Stream a movie that way."

Clari popped up as best she could. "That's brilliant." She grabbed her crutches. "I have my laptop in the car. I have some movies downloaded on it." She had a couple of the Happily Ever After TV movies on there. Would Joel go for HEA TV?

"Wait!"

She stopped and looked at Joel. "What?"

"I'll go. You've got those ridiculous crutches. You'll get hurt."

She sat back down and hoisted her leg up onto the couch. Stupid boot. She was so ready to be done with it. "Thank you!" she called as he walked out the door.

Her phone buzzed. The auto shop in town. The man told her what she'd expected to hear. As she hung up, Joel returned, her laptop bag in hand along with a backpack. He'd mentioned being a student, hadn't he? Was he missing classes? He closed the door, stomped his feet, and shuddered.

"So it's still snowing?" Despite the mid-afternoon hour, it was dark outside, and she couldn't really see.

"Yep. Still coming down hard, too, though I think it's slowing down. Did you ever get a call from the shop in town?"

"They called while you were outside. They'll let us know when they can send someone out, but that it'll probably be tomorrow."

Her phone buzzed again. She swiped across the screen. "Hi, Afi."

"Hello, *Sonardóttir*. Are you still at the cabin?"

"Of course."

He sighed. "I got a call from your surprise."

Clari blinked. "My surprise is a person?"

"Yes. Gina is on her way, but her flight has been delayed due to weather. She was supposed to meet you at the cabin yesterday. She was the treasure at the end of your hunt."

Clari's shoulders slumped. "And I've missed a full day with her."

"She hopes to be in tomorrow morning. She's in Auverignon just waiting for the storm to break and will be on the first flight over."

"Thanks, Afi. We'll be here waiting." Clari winced as she realized what she said.

"We?"

"Joel. He's the Yfir Delivery driver who delivered the flowers. I can't drive, so I hired him as my Yfir driver, but he didn't realize how much further the cabin was from town or how much extra fuel he'd used coming up the mountain. The shop in town will bring us more after the storm stops."

"I'm not sure I like this, *Sonardóttir*." She heard the frown in his voice.

"His sister is Rachel from the yarn store Amma loves so much."

"Amma loves Rachel and Anabelle," Afi admitted.

"See? Joel's a good guy. He's got approval to deliver to the palace. He could even deliver to some of the offices in the palace if he had an escort, not just the security office." The Queen Mother's office was not one of those locations, though. That's why she'd had to come down.

"Very well. But if he tries anything…"

Clari smiled. "I know, Afi. I can take care of myself. Or beat him with one of my crutches."

Joel's head snapped up. She rolled her eyes toward the

ceiling. He smiled and turned back to the text on his phone.

After a minute of exchanging "I love yous," and having him tell her an interesting tidbit of information, she hung up. "You won't believe this."

"What?"

"Afi said he and Amma have a television and DVD player in their room along with a ton of DVDs."

Joel chuckled. "Figures. Want me to move it out here? Would they be okay with that as long as we move it back?"

"He suggested it." She tried to get more comfortable. "If you wouldn't mind, I would appreciate it."

She laid her head back and tried not to let tears overwhelm her. Gina was just a few miles away. A few hundred miles, but so much closer than the thousands of miles away she usually was.

"You all right?" Joel's voice sounded strained. When she opened her eyes, Clari realized it was because he carried a television - much larger than she expected. He set it on one of the coffee tables. "What is it?"

"Afi told me what the surprise was." A tear leaked out of one eye. "My best friend was supposed to be here yesterday, but she's stuck in Auverignon until the weather clears in Akushla."

"I'm sorry. Is there any ETA yet?"

Another tear followed the first. "Hopefully, she'll make it to Akushla tomorrow morning then drive up."

"And then I will get out of your hair."

Clari sat up and stared at her reflection in the window. "You're not in my hair."

In the window-mirror, she watched Joel walk toward her. He took the spot next to her on the couch and wrapped an arm around her shoulders. As he pulled her closer to him, she felt warmth and safety surround her. How could she be so comfortable with Joel already?

"Thanks," she whispered.

His hand rubbed up and down her arm. "My pleasure." They sat in silence for another moment. "Now, what do you say we get this set up and watch a movie?"

"I think that sounds like a great idea. Why don't you get the DVD player and pick a movie? I'll get it all plugged in."

"Sounds great." He stood and walked back into her grandparents' room.

Clari hobbled over to the television using one of her crutches to hold her weight. It took a bit of maneuvering, but she managed to get a power strip plugged in, and the television plugged into it.

"Okay, here we go." Joel walked out of the room with the DVD player and a small stack of DVDs. "We're going to have a marathon."

"What kind of marathon?" She had no idea what kind of movies her grandparents would have stockpiled, except that it wouldn't be anything remotely inappropriate. Likely a bunch of things mostly suited for small-to-medium-sized children.

He set it all down, then held up one movie box with a giant grin on his face. "*Jurassic Park.*"

CHAPTER 5

J oel gaped at Clari as he pulled the bag of popcorn out of the microwave. "You've never seen any of the *Jurassic* movies?"

"Nope. Not a fan of the genre."

"What genre? Dinosaurs?" He dumped the popcorn into a bowl.

"Thriller. Isn't that what it is?"

Joel set the bowl down next to Clari. "I guess, but not really, I don't think. It's a zoo full of dinosaurs that escape, and people try to live through it. Plus there's dinosaurs."

She took a handful of popcorn. "I don't see the fascination."

He opened the box and popped the DVD out. "Give it a try. If you don't absolutely love it, we'll skip to *Jurassic World*. Even if you don't love the genre, it's got Chris Pratt in it." Every girl like Chris Pratt, didn't they? His sister and Anabelle sure did.

With a long-suffering sigh and a twinkle in her eye, she agreed. Joel finished getting it set up, made sure the remote was next to Clari, then turned most of the lights off.

He sat on the other end of the couch from her and tried not to remember what it was like when he had his arm around her half an hour earlier. The rush of emotion had caught him off-guard. She was nice, clearly good to her family and grandparents, pretty, but he hadn't thought himself overly attracted to her.

That changed when he saw the first tear fall.

A memory flashed through his mind. Rachel had been dating some guy the first time she'd seen this movie. They'd sat next to each other on the couch. Every time Rachel startled at a dinosaur coming out of nowhere, she'd grabbed onto that guy.

Maybe he should offer to sit closer to Clari.

"You know, if you're not used to thrillers," he started, "you might want a pillow to hold onto." *Chicken.*

"I may make you come sit over here so I can smack you every time I'm scared." She tossed her pillow at him. "In fact, I think I'm going to."

While the popcorn had popped, they'd rearranged the room a little some. There was no shortage of chairs and sofas to sit on, or low tables for the television. They'd moved Clair's favorite couch a couple meters from the television and put several ottomans in front of it to prop their feet on. By the time she settled back down, Clari was close enough their arms nearly brushed against each other.

The opening scene with the velociraptor in the cage killing the worker wasn't overly startling though Clari hugged the pillow to her chest.

"This isn't gory, is it? I don't do gore."

"Not really. You do see a guy kind of get eaten, but there's very little blood." He grimaced. "That sounds worse than it is. I wasn't even ten yet the first time I saw it."

"Okay." She didn't sound convinced.

"And you've got a while before anything else bad happens." Did she mind the spoilers?

She glanced at him, uncertainty all over her face, but she didn't say anything. About the time the cast headed back to the Jeeps from the sick Triceratops, Clari looked over at him. "I thought this movie had more dinosaurs and scariness."

"It will."

"And that's when I'll hit you with the pillow?"

He grinned and reached for popcorn. "Probably."

By the time the game warden drove the gas-powered Jeep away from the chasing T-Rex, Clari was curled up as close to him as she could get with her boot on, and his arm was wrapped around her shoulders.

"Can we be done now?" she whispered into his shoulder.

"What if I told you only one more person dies?" Right? "No. Two, but you only kind of see one of them. Sort of."

"You mean people actually get off this island alive?" Her skepticism was well-founded.

"Of course. How else could there be sequels?" He rubbed a hand up and down her arm. "And we've got a while before anything else bad happens."

"You said that last time."

"And I was right last time."

She finally looked back up at the screen as Dr. Grant climbed the tree with the kids to pass the night.

By the time the helicopter showed up, she'd laughed a few times, jumped a few more, and even grabbed his shirt once - and didn't let go.

As the music played, Joel took the remote and hit stop. "It wasn't so bad, was it?"

Clari slowly unfolded herself and moved away from him. "I guess not. It wasn't as bad as I thought it was going to be."

"We'll skip II and III then. They're worse. In II, they take a T-Rex from the backup island to San Diego, and he gets loose."

She raised an eyebrow. "That sounds like the smartest thing ever."

"Exactly. I think III is worse in terms of on-screen deaths and stuff. We can go straight to *Jurassic World* and Chris Pratt. There's probably more deaths, but they're mostly off-screen, and there's not much blood."

Clari stretched her arms over her head. "I can do that. Want more popcorn?"

He stood, needing a few minutes away from the sudden attraction he'd been feeling. "I'll make it."

But when he returned after putting the next movie in and sat back in his corner of the couch, she immediately curled up next to him.

"I don't want to watch this alone."

"You won't. I'm right here." His arm wrapped around her shoulders and tugged her closer. Before he realized what he was doing, Joel turned and pressed a kiss against the top of her head.

Clari looked up. "Did you really just do that?"

He had to look like a deer in the headlights. "Do what?"

"Kiss my head?"

His gaze flickered from her eyes to her lips. Did he dare? Was this really what he wanted to do?

Yes.

Without waiting for Clari to say anything else, Joel kissed her.

Clari found herself sitting next to Joel, but not paying any attention to *Jurassic World*. From what she could tell from staring at the screen but not really seeing what was happening, Joel had been right that it wasn't overly gory. She didn't do gory. Never had. To be honest, the first movie hadn't been as bad as she expected, but she had found herself rather enjoying being so close to Joel.

The movie ended with Claire and Owen walking off into the sunrise. She'd have to watch it again sometime when she was better able to focus.

"I think I'm ready to go to sleep." Clari moved away from Joel. That kiss had been replaying in her mind for the last two hours, and she still wasn't sure how she felt about it.

"If you want to sleep in your room, I'll be fine." Joel stood up and headed for the DVD player. "You don't need to sleep on the couch."

She didn't believe him for a minute. He needed someone to be in the room with him. She hadn't been lying when she told him this was her favorite couch. Without commenting to Joel, she grabbed one of her crutches and made her way to her room. Once she was ready for bed, she went back out into the living area and laid down on the couch.

"I mean it. You don't have to stay out here." Joel was getting his bed ready on another couch.

"I don't mind. Really. I'd rather sleep out here and you not have nightmares, than sleep in my room and have you have nightmares." Did that even make any sense?

"Well, thank you. I appreciate it."

As she settled into sleep, Clari heard Joel's even breathing from near the window. Would Gina get there in the morning? Or would it be another day or longer before she made it? At least they were supposed to get to spend a week and a half together. That meant even missing the first couple of days would leave them plenty of time.

The next morning they woke up to banging on the door. Clari wrapped a blanket around her shoulders as she used her crutch to help her across the room. Joel just looked groggy. She opened the door to find an employee of the auto shop in town standing there.

"I've been told you need fuel?" he asked.

"Yep. Let me get the keys so you can open the tank." Joel tossed them to her, and she handed them to the man. He thanked her and headed for the car she closed the door but watched out the window. Joel started a pot of coffee. When the man came back with the keys a few minutes later, she opened the door and invited him in.

"Would you like something warm to drink?" she asked. "What do we owe you?"

"Nothing. Your grandparents have always been great

customers. It's our pleasure to help you out. I do have an insulated mug in the car I wouldn't mind filling up with some coffee though."

He handed over the keys and left to get his cup. Clari tossed the keys back to Joel, who put them in his pocket. She hadn't considered that he had no extra clothes. He was still wearing the same thing he had been when he dropped off the flowers. At least she had clothes to change into in the cabin. "You can head back whenever you're ready," she told him.

"I'm not leaving you here by yourself."

"I'm a big girl. I can handle myself."

"How will you get home when the time comes?" he challenged.

"Gina will be here later today. She'll have a car. Or my *afi* will come get me."

"I'm not leaving you here by yourself," he reiterated. "No more questions about it."

Was he thinking about that kiss too? Or had he already forgotten about it? Was it really the best plan to stay here afterward? Alone together? The kiss had been intense, but not long. At the same time, it had hinted at so much more.

The auto shop employee came back with his coffee mug. She filled it up and handed it back to him. "Thank you so much for your help. We appreciate it." He saluted with his coffee cup. "My pleasure." As he started for the door, he continued. "Try to be a little more careful with how well you pay attention to your fuel consumption next time."

"I will," Joel told him.

And then they were alone again.

"So are we going to talk about what happened last night?" Joel asked her.

"I don't know. You tell me." She didn't look at him.

"I think we probably should. Don't you?"

"You kissed me. I kissed you back. End of discussion."

Wasn't it? Did there have to be something more? But if there was, at least Amma would get off her back about finding a *kærasti*.

"Maybe."

Clari took a seat on her couch. "It doesn't need to be more than that. Just a nice kiss between two people forced to spend a bunch of time together unexpectedly."

"Maybe," he said again. "Or maybe there's something more. You don't think there's an attraction between us that might turn into something?"

She shrugged. "I think I'm the first person you've told about being left alone since you were little. That means something to you."

He didn't reply, but sighed and turned toward the television. "I guess we're ready to put this back? Or do you want to leave it out here for when Gina gets here? Or I can take you to Akushla with me, and then you come back with Gina driving."

"Leave it." At least she and Gina could watch movies that didn't require Clari to peek out from between her fingers. Maybe Amma had HEA TV movies on DVD in the other room. That was more Clari's speed. Gina's too. "I'm going to hop in the shower and change before we head back to Akushla. I'm sure one of the dressers upstairs has clothes that would fit you if you'd like to take one, too."

Joel held out a hand to help her up.

"Thanks." She reached for the crutches leaning against the side of the couch, but before she could get them situated...

Joel kissed her again.

CHAPTER 6

The drive back toward Akushla was filled with silence. Maybe whatever Joel thought he felt for Clari was just his imagination. She clearly didn't seem to have any of the same feelings. She hadn't said much of anything after the second kiss, but hobbled off to take a shower. Then he found clothes in one of the dressers like she suggested and took one of his own.

As they reached the series of switchbacks, he gripped the wheel tighter. This was the area where his parents had died several years earlier, and where Anabelle's parents had crashed just a couple days before.

He hated this route. So why had he taken it?

He'd planned to go the other way.

But this one would get them to Akushla faster, and Clari's friend had finally gotten a flight out of Auverignon. She would be arriving about the time they made it to the airport.

"Are you okay?" Clari asked him as he slowed down further going into a corner.

"I hate this drive." He still hadn't told her about his parents. Just about the time he'd been left behind. Maybe he should. Maybe opening up to her a little more worried show her he believed there was potential for more to their relationship.

"My parents died about the same place Annabel's parents did."

Clari gasped. "Oh my! Why didn't you tell me? We could have gone the other way."

"I know. But it takes longer. And you need to get to the airport."

"Not that quickly. Afi and Amma will pick Gina up if I'm not there yet. It wouldn't have been a big deal."

"Still. I know you want to be there when she arrives. Her flight lands in an hour?"

"Something like that."

He tried to make himself relax, even a little bit. "Then you should be there by the time she makes it to baggage claim." He wouldn't push the speed on the switchbacks, no matter how badly she wanted to get there on time. Maybe in a genuine emergency, but no other reason.

She didn't say anything else, but he could almost hear her reassuring him the other way would have been acceptable.

Finally, they reached the last switchback. The one Joel dreaded most.

He felt sweat beading on his forehead as he gripped the wheel even tighter. He could do this.

God...

That was the only prayer he could get out. No other words came, but the tension between his shoulder blades began to ease even before they came out of the curve.

He glanced toward the cliff heading upward on one side and then down toward the river on the other.

But what he noticed was Clari's eyes closed and her lips moving.

She was praying for him.

"Thank you." The tension eased further as they passed the spot where both accidents happened.

"It seemed like the best thing to do."

"It worked. I haven't been that relaxed driving this road in years."

Clari gave a half-snort, half-chuckle. "That was relaxed?"

"Much more so than usual. I rarely take this route, but I have to sometimes for Yfir. I do fine driving up, but coming back..."

"It's hard. Thank you for going this way, even though you hate it." She reached over and put a hand on his forearm. "I appreciate it."

He gave her a half-smile but didn't say anything, though he wondered what she thought about that second kiss.

It was all in his head, wasn't it?

There was no mutual attraction.

"So what are you and Gina going to do while she's here?"

"I'm not sure. She'd planned for us to spend a few days at the cabin, catching up. I'm not sure what her plan was after that. Maybe spend the rest of the time in Akushla. I could probably get her a semi-private tour of the palace. She'd like that."

"Most people would like that. I would. So would Rachel and Anabelle."

She hesitated. "If I can arrange it, you guys can come, too. It won't be much more than the official public tour, but a little bit of behind-the-ropes. A couple of rooms that aren't being used. A glimpse at the Hall of Monarchs, but like no one is actually allowed in there. I'm not even sure King Benjamin is allowed in there without the palace curator with him."

That made Joel grin. "Really?"

"I have no idea. But let me see what I can do." She pulled her phone out of her pocket and tapped on it. "Hello, *frœndi*. It's Clari." She held the phone away from her mouth. "My father's brother. Could I arrange a tour of the palace for a few friends later today?"

She made a few noises of agreement then thanked him and hung up. "I know Rachel doesn't close the store until six. My *frœndi* will give us the tour himself at seven." Clari held out a hand. "I'll text Rachel for you."

They were on a straight stretch of road with no cliffs on either side and no traffic. He used his thumbprint to turn it on then handed it over. She maneuvered through the apps, but instead of typing, the speaker came on.

"Hello?"

"Hey, Rachel. It's Clari. Joel's fine," she hurried on.

"Hi!" he called loudly. "I'm driving!"

"Hi, guys. I guess you're finally on your way back from the lake?"

"Yes. We'll be in Akushla in less than an hour, but I've got an invitation for you. Anabelle and her sister, too, if they're up for it."

"What's that?" Rachel asked.

"A tour of the palace. My best friend is coming in, and I'm taking her. I'd like you, Anabelle, her sister, and Joel to come, too."

He could almost see Rachel blinking in surprise. "I'd love that. Let me check with Anabelle though. If she needs me tonight…"

"Of course. If tonight doesn't work, then anytime before Gina leaves would be good, too. And if it doesn't, then we'll find another time."

"Thank you."

"And if there's anything I can do for Anabelle, please let me know."

"I'll pass that on."

Clari and Rachel exchanged few more pleasantries and phone numbers, then hung up. Half an hour later, her phone pinged. "We're going to the palace the day before Gina leaves." It pinged again. "And her flight just landed."

A gnawing emptiness started to fill his inside. A week? Could he find a way to win her over before then? Or would he even have a chance?

Clari held onto Gina as though she'd never see her again. It had been years since they'd last been in the same place.

"It is so good to finally be here," Gina whispered as they clung to each other.

"I'm so glad you're here," Clari whispered back.

"But what's up with your leg?"

They finally pulled apart. Clari held out her booted foot. "I broke my leg a few weeks ago, but I haven't really talked to you since then. You were off on your trip through New Mexico and Arizona. I didn't want to bother you with it."

"And Afi didn't say anything either." Gina gave a mock glare toward the city. "Silly old man."

Clari laughed. "Don't let him hear you say that," she told her friend, knowing what the response would be.

"Oh, he's heard me." Giving each other a hard time was part of how Gina and Afi defined their relationship. "Now, we need to go to the cabin. Because I need some rest and relaxation."

Clari tucked her crutches under her arms. "You'll have to drive my car."

Gina stopped in her tracks. "You can't drive, can you?"

"Nope." She held out her boot. "This is my driving foot."

"Then how did you do the treasure hunt?"

Clari nodded toward Joel standing next to his car. "My Yfir driver, Joel. His sister owns Amma's favorite yarn store."

"Small world."

"And he's going to take us to my flat. We can chill there."

Gina hesitated then grinned. "Sounds perfect."

Joel helped load Gina's suitcase into the back of his car while Clari took her seat in the front. The two of them whispered furiously for a minute before getting in.

"I don't actually know where you live, Clari." He put the car in gear and looked over his shoulder before pulling into traffic.

She gave him directions to her flat not far from Rachel's yarn store. Gina chatted with Joel the whole twenty minutes it took to get there.

As they stood on the sidewalk, Clari sent Gina upstairs while she turned around. "Thank you, Joel. I appreciate all you've done the last few days."

He shoved his hands in his pockets. "It's not like I was able to go anywhere."

"I know, but you didn't have to do so much. The pasta for lunch yesterday was fabulous."

"My pleasure."

"And thank you for letting me hide next to you when the dinosaurs attacked."

That made him look up and smile. "I'm glad you've finally seen one of the best movies ever."

"I will have to watch the other one again sometime. I couldn't focus on it."

His eyes bored into hers. "That kiss affected me, too." He pushed off from the car. "Maybe someday we'll actually talk about it." He leaned closer. "Maybe someday you'll admit there's something between us, and we'll actually *do* something about it."

She felt her cheeks heat even as the cold seeped in. "It's possible. I'll see you next week for the tour."

He tipped an invisible hat at her. "Until then, if not before."

Clari turned and crunched her way into the building, making her way slowly up the stairs. Gina had flopped into the big chair and waited for her.

"I want to hear all about you and Joel and two days alone at the cabin."

"There's not much to tell." Clari collapsed onto the couch. "He delivered the flowers, which I forgot at the cabin, by the way, then drove me around to all the places. We got stuck up there. Watched a couple movies. Played a few games. That's it."

Gina's eyes twinkled. "He kissed you, didn't he?"

Clari felt color rush to her face again. "Maybe."

Gina squealed. "More than once?"

"Maybe."

"So? Are you going to tell Amma you finally have a *kærasti*?"

"No. Because I don't. He wanted to talk about it. I'm not convinced there's anything between us besides being stuck together at the cabin." She closed her eyes as she sighed. "I couldn't even tell him why I have my own room at the cabin in a family the size of mine."

"Why would you? It's a pretty personal story, and it's not really yours to tell."

"He told me about a couple of deep secrets, but I didn't share my own. Doesn't that mean I don't trust him enough to tell him why we had my birthday party at the cabin and my whole family granted my wish?"

For all her fun-loving sides, Gina knew how to be serious. "Do you trust him? Are you attracted to him?"

Clari wrinkled her nose. "He is pretty cute. And he did take good care of me, even when he really didn't want to be there."

"So should you call him?"

Using her hands to help, Clari swung her leg up onto the couch. "Maybe. Or I'll see him next week when we do the palace tour. See how that goes and if he actually asks me out."

"And if he does?"

"I'll say yes."

"And if he doesn't, you'll ask him?"

Clari rolled her eyes at her friend. "Probably not." For the next few hours, they caught up on almost everything. The next morning, Clari finally called Gina out. "Don't think I haven't noticed. It's your turn. Tell me all about this guy in your life."

Gina waved a hand her general direction. "Nothing to tell. It's over."

Not exactly what Clari expected to hear. She'd half expected to see an engagement ring.

"I did meet a cute guy at the hotel in Auverignon, though. He's supposed to call me when he's here next month."

"Next month?" Clari sat up. "Are you moving back?"

Gina grinned and held up jazz hands. "Surprise! Need a roomie?"

Clari hesitated. She loved Gina, but they'd been roommates at university once. It hadn't gone well.

"I'm kidding! But if you'd let me crash here until I find a place that would be fantastic. Afi already has a couple of leads for me."

Afi knew before she did?

"It's a long story, Clari," Gina told her softly. "Afi has been an invaluable shoulder to cry on. Almost like my own *afi* would have been."

"Then I'm glad you had him."

Gina sat down next to her and laid her head on Clari's shoulder. "Thank you for sharing your family with me."

Clari rested her head against Gina's. "They've always been your family, too."

"Not always, but close."

Clari's phone buzzed. A text from Joel.

I'M COMING UP. I HAVE SOMETHING FOR YOU.

CHAPTER 7

J oel held the flowers in front of him and waited for Clari to open the door. But instead, it was Gina that greeted him.

"Hi! Come on in." She stepped aside and let him pass. "Thank you for running back up to the cabin."

"You drove back to the cabin?" Clari asked from her seat on the couch.

"I took the long way." He held up the bouquet. "You left your flowers from Gina. She'd had your *afi* leave the last clue there when he dropped the food off. I brought the perishable stuff back with me so it wouldn't spoil." Crossing the room, he held out the flowers for her. Their fingers brushed as he handed them over. Electricity zapped through him.

From the blush on her cheeks, she noticed, too.

"Thank you. That was very considerate of you."

"I was happy to." He pulled a card out of his coat and handed it to Gina. "Is this what you wanted?"

She took it from him. "Yes, but I already told Clari what's in it. I'm moving back to Akushla from the States."

"That's great news, right?"

Gina nodded, though her expression seemed guarded at the same time.

Joel started for the door. "Now that I've made my deliveries,

328

I'll see you ladies next week for the tour."

After goodbyes, he went back to his car and drove to Rachel's shop. The food would be unloaded there. Clari's *afi* had told him to keep it. Instead, he'd pass it on to Anabelle. It was a rough time for her. She didn't need to add grocery shopping to her list of things to do.

From what Joel understood, she was having enough issues dealing with her grandparents.

The front door was already locked, so he rapped on the window until Rachel opened it.

"Come on in. Anabelle stopped by, but she already left. If you want to leave the food here, I can get it to her."

"Thanks." He left the door propped open slightly and grabbed several bags out of the back of his car. "What can I do to help while Anabelle is taking a few days off?"

"You want to come work for me?" Rachel was understandably skeptical. He'd always supported her venture but had little actual interest in it.

"I'll help you while you need it. Yarn really isn't my thing, but I love you, so I'll learn what I need to."

Rachel came over and gave him a hug. Joel wrapped his arms around his sister. At least they still had each other.

"Do you know how glad I am you weren't with Mom and Dad that day?" she asked, tears evident in her voice.

The one part he hadn't told Clari. He had planned to go with them, but at the last minute canceled because he had a blind date. The date hadn't gone well at all, but he'd regretted not spending that time with his parents.

Then Rachel reminded him that if he had gone, she would have been left without any family at all. She'd taken her half of the inheritance, finished her last year at university, and started her own business. Joel took his and invested part of it safely. After taking some time off, he paid for his own university and was finally almost done. He was going to use the rest of the money to set up his own business doing accounting for other small businesses like he did for his sister. She'd had such a hard time finding a good person that he'd taken over almost as soon as she opened.

"I'm glad I'm here with you," he told her. "Even if it means I need to learn about yarn."

She laughed and moved away. "Come on. You're about to get a lesson."

Worsted. Sport weight. Self-striping. Gradient. Bootheel.

He wouldn't be able to tell one yarn type from another by sight anytime soon, but at least he had some idea what the tags meant.

"I expect you here by nine every morning," Rachel told him as she pulled her keys out of her bag.

"Anabelle doesn't work every day," he reminded her.

"So? Unless you're in class, I need you. Please?"

He turned to see her looking at him with the big eyes he could never resist. "What is it?"

She pulled her coat on. "I just don't want to be alone."

Like he hated being alone at the cabin, she wouldn't want to spend much time on her own after the death of Anabelle's parents. He'd been away at a different university and, thanks to another storm, he hadn't made it home for a couple of days. She'd had to deal with everything on her own.

He took his keys out of his pocket and smiled at her. "I won't leave you alone, ever. You know that. Not really."

"I know, but since you're not working regular hours right now, I'd rather you be here in person."

"I will be, even though I generally have an aversion to nine in the morning."

"You have an aversion to any time that ends 'in the morning.'" She gave him a small but genuine smile. "I'll see you then."

He went out the front door, waited for her to lock it behind him then drove around so he could see the alley between the buildings then watched her get in her car and pull out. There had been a mugging a few blocks over the week before. Couldn't be too careful.

She waved as she drove past him. Joel returned to his flat, took a shower, and collapsed.

As he suspected it would, morning came too soon, but he was back in the shop at nine. They wouldn't open for an hour, so he was there to help Rachel do whatever she needed from him.

When he opened the door for customers, one walked in almost immediately. He greeted her warmly. "Mrs. T, how are you this morning?"

She glared at him. "You are Joel?"

He winced. "Yes, ma'am."

"You spent two days alone with my granddaughter at the cabin?"

He was about to get read the riot act from an elderly Icelandic woman. "Yes, ma'am."

A smile broke across her face. "Thank you for taking care of my *sonardóttir*."

Joel smiled back. "My pleasure."

She took his face in her hands and studied him more carefully. "You'll do."

"What is it, Amma?" Clari rushed into her grandmother's house to find her *amma* sitting in her favorite chair and grinning like the cat that ate the canary. "What's so urgent?"

Clari and Gina were on their way to a favorite restaurant when the text came in. Come over. Now.

"I wanted to see my *sonardóttir* and her bestie. Is that all right?"

Clari lifted a brow. "Bestie? Have you ever used that word, ever, Amma?"

"Yes. I said it to your *afi* earlier when I told him I wanted you to come over." Amma glared at her. "Now, come give me a hug."

When Amma says to give her a hug, you do as you're told. Clari gave her one followed by Gina, who held onto Amma for a longer period of time.

"Dinner will be ready in about twenty minutes. You will join us, won't you? Afi is making his specialty."

Clari glanced at Gina's whose eyes and smile could light up the most dismal 23-hour-long-night. "Of course we will, Amma."

They sat in the living room and talked until Afi announced dinner was ready, but before they could make it to the table, there was a knock on the door.

"Clari, will you answer that?" Amma asked, continuing toward the other room.

Clari exchanged a look with Gina. Amma was up to something. Clari opened the door to find Joel standing there.

"Hi," she said, feeling confused. "What are you doing here?"

He held up a bouquet of flowers. "Your grandmother invited me. These are for her."

She took a step back. "Come on in. I hope Afi knows and made enough for dinner."

The knowing twinkle in Afi's eye when they made it to the table, and the fifth place setting, told her all she needed to know. Her grandparents were playing matchmaker.

Lively conversation swirled about as they ate. When they finished, Amma put the next part of her plan into motion.

"Clari, would you and Joel please clean up? I'd like to talk with Gina for a few minutes, and I'm sure Afi would like to sit as well."

She smiled at her grandmother. "I'd be happy to. Joel is a guest though. He can join you in the other room. I'll be in presently." It would be awhile. Maybe long enough for Joel to go home. Afi wasn't known for cleaning up as he cooked.

"I'm happy to help," Joel told her, thwarting that plan. "We'll be done in no time."

He only said that because he hadn't seen the kitchen.

Amma, Afi, and Gina went back into the living room.

"Any particular way to do this?" Joel asked.

Clari surveyed the table. "I'll start in the kitchen. If you want to put the food away, then start bringing in the dishes that would be fantastic."

There was no automatic dishwasher in the house. Clari went into the kitchen and began setting it to rights. Soon the counters were cleaner and the dishes organized and ready to be washed.

"I'll wash so you can dry and put away. I don't know where anything goes." Joel brought the last of the dishes in from the other room.

She shot a grateful look his way. Clari hadn't been looking forward to washing all the dishes herself. Drying and putting away appealed much more even if she did have to hobble. "Thanks."

As they worked, they talked about the weather, family plans for Christmas, and not much of anything significant. It had been nearly an hour when they finished.

Clari wiped her hands on the towel then folded it over the rack as Joel did the same. Before she could move away, his arm wrapped around her waist and pulled her close.

"I have a question for you."

She rested a hand on his chest. "What's that?"

He leaned slightly closer. "Will you have dinner with me after your time with Gina is over?"

"A date?"

His lips quirked into a half-smile. "I'd rather not invite your grandparents if that's okay with you."

"That's fine with me, but Gina's moving back to Akushla. My time with her won't end next week like I thought."

"I know, but the next week is set aside for you and Gina to spend time together. After that, the night after the tour, will you have dinner with me?"

Clari stared at him for a moment, then nodded. "I think I would like that."

His shoulders sagged in relief. "I know I will." Joel leaned down and brushed a quick kiss against her lips. "Now, I'm sure your grandparents and Gina are waiting for us." He winked at her. "We don't want to give them any reason to come looking."

She didn't move away. "We wouldn't want them to find us in a compromising position, though I don't think this qualifies."

His chuckle had to be the nicest one she'd ever heard. How had she not noticed that at the cabin?

"I think you're right." Another quick kiss and he let go of her waist but took her hand.

She noticed he loosened his grip as they reached the living area, allowing her to slip her hand from his without having to pull.

"Sit, sit!" Amma waved toward the love seat, conveniently left open for them.

Clari shared an amused glance with Joel then Gina, who clearly tried to hide a smirk and failed.

They took their seats on the love seat, but not right next to each other - though they weren't hugging the armrests either.

Amma looked straight at Joel. "When we spoke earlier, you said you thought it was nice for Clari to have her own room at the cabin, but I know she didn't tell you why she does."

Clari stared at her hands. Amma was really going to tell him the story? Now? She could see if they were engaged, but Amma and Afi never talked about the reasoning why. With anyone.

"It's all right, Mrs. T. You don't need to tell me." Joel's gentle voice warmed Clari's heart. He wouldn't push.

"No. It is time you know. It is time *Clari* knows."

That made Clari look up, her eyes wide as she stared Amma. "Time that Clari knows what?"

CHAPTER 8

J oel shifted nervously in his seat. Clari didn't know the whole story? She'd seemed to indicate that she did when they talked about it at the cabin - she just hadn't known him well enough to confide in him.

"It's time you know the whole story, dear one."

"Your daughter, Clarice, died when I was five. I never met her. I'm the only girl in the family, so I get her old room."

Mrs. T shook her head. "Not exactly."

Joel could almost feel the tension radiating off Clari. "What do you mean, not exactly?"

Mr. Sørensen - Joel had to remind himself the couple didn't share a last name - reached across the opening between chairs to take his wife's hand. "Clarice married a wonderful young man shortly before you were born. His family lived in the northern part of Eyjania, and they moved there to be close to his ailing grandparents."

Seemed like good people, right? So where was the mystery coming from?

"We talked as often as we could, though not as much as we would like." Mrs. T took the tissue Mr. Sørensen offered and dabbed below her eyes. "A few years later, we got a visit from an investigator. Clarice, along with her husband and daughter, had disappeared, but no one knew what happened to them. Eventually, they were declared dead. Their car was found off one of the switchbacks coming from Lake Akushla, but there was no evidence they'd been inside."

"No proof they hadn't been, either," Mr. Sørensen added. "Some people survive those crashes. One theory was they had and tried to walk out, but got lost and never seen again. By the time the car was found, it had been long enough that any evidence they'd walked away was long gone."

Mrs. T took a deep breath. "We grieved, but accepted the reality that our beloved daughter and her family were gone." She smiled sadly toward Clari. "That was the year we threw the big birthday party and asked you what you wanted. You were her namesake, and it was a way to give one last thing to our girl. We knew you wouldn't choose anything frivolous, and I've loved every Sunday we've spent together as a family."

Joel pulled a couple of tissues out of a box on the table beside him and handed them to Clari. She needed them as badly as her *amma* did.

"I have, too," Clari whispered as she wiped at the tears. "Why didn't anyone tell me sooner?"

"There's more," Mr. Sørensen told them. He squeezed Mrs. T's hand then let go and leaned his forearms against his legs. "Do you remember a couple of years later, we were at the cabin, and you found a bouquet of wildflowers in your room? You loved them."

Gina piped up. "That's why I sent those. You've always loved Eyjanian wildflowers."

"So did Clarice," Mr. Sørensen said. "You don't remember the note. A single dot on one line. Four on the next. Then three."

"I love you?" Clari asked.

"It was Clarice's way of leaving us notes. She'd done it since she was little." Mrs. T used the tissue to wipe away more tears.

Clari looked at Joel, skepticism written on her face.

"Someone sent you a secret message from Clarice after she already died? That's creepy."

Mr. Sørensen shook his head. "No one could have gotten in there without knowing about the secret passage. The flowers were left near the entrance to it. Even the boys didn't know about it until later, so it had to be Clarice."

Clari's shoulders sagged. "Amma, Afi, I know you want to believe Clarice and her family are still alive, but that's a little far-fetched, don't you think?"

The elderly couple just shared a look. "Believe what you will, s*onardóttir*. Your *afi* and I know they didn't die in the woods after that accident."

Gina's phone shattered the silence. "Sorry." She reached into her purse and turned it off.

The spell, such as it was, had already been broken. Mrs. T struggled to stand, looking more like an elderly woman than Joel had seen her look thus far. Mr. Sørensen helped her to the stairs, then turned as she went up them.

"Don't break your *amma's* heart, dear Clari. We know the truth. Our Clarice and her family lived." He followed his wife up the stairs.

Once they were out of earshot, Gina broke the silence. "Wow. I've never thought your grandparents were remotely senile, Clari, but..."

Clari wiped at her tears again. "I haven't either, but this is pretty far out there." She leaned her head back against the couch. "I guess I'll ask my dad about it, see what he says."

Gina stood. "Nature's calling. I'll be right back."

"Thanks for sharing," Clari called after her. She turned to look at Joel. "Do you still want to go on that date?"

"Why wouldn't I? Even if your grandparents are wrong in this one sincerely held belief, they're right in many others, including that their *sonardóttir* is pretty fantastic." He reached over and brushed a tear away with his thumb. "In fact, I'd like to ask their *sonardóttir* if I could be her *kærasti.* You know. When she's ready to have that conversation."

Clari gave him a weak smile. "Maybe after that first date. There's too much to absorb tonight without tossing a new relationship into the mix."

"I understand." Joel stood. "Why don't you go look after your grandparents, and I'll see you soon? I'm at the yarn store when I'm not in class for at least the next week." He held out a hand for her to grasp and helped her up. "You could stop by." He leaned down and kissed her cheek. "I'll watch for you."

Clari patted his upper arm. "I'll try to stop by." She pointed toward a cabinet. "I'm pretty sure that's full of yarn Amma bought from Rachel. I've never seen her do anything with it, though."

"I'm sure she has her reasons."

Clari grabbed a crutch though she'd been hobbling along without one since dinner. She walked him to the door. "Thank you for coming tonight. I know it meant a lot to my grandparents."

He grabbed his coat and slipped it on before he reached out and brushed the hair off her temple. "I'm glad I came. If you want to talk after you ask your dad about all this, you know how to reach me."

She nodded. "I will."

Joel wanted to kiss her again but held off. There would be enough time for that later. "I'll text you soon." At least he could keep in contact with her that way.

She didn't respond, but smiled at him, then turned at a noise inside. "I'm going to check on Amma and Afi. I'll talk to you later."

Joel turned and went down the steps, pulling his coat further around him as he did. He needed another good night's sleep, but he knew this time he'd fall asleep praying for Clari's family.

Clari curled up in the chair in Rachel's shop and sipped the tea Joel's sister provided for customers. Clari hadn't bought anything, but Rachel waved that notion off.

"What did your father say?" Joel asked while Rachel helped a customer.

"He understands why they believe what they do, but thinks it was someone playing a practical joke or even one of his brothers. They did know about the secret passage before then - I still don't, by the way - and he wonders if one of them put them there as a way to kind of console my grandparents, and it turned into this whole thing. He thinks it's Thor, but whichever brother it is never wanted to confess because it would hurt their parents all over again."

"Thor? You have an uncle named Thor?" Joel shared the same amused disbelief most people did when she told them that.

"Yes. It's not an uncommon name in Iceland. Amma's last name is *Thorbjørnsdóttir*. Her father's name was *Thorbjørn*. They shortened it to Thor for my uncle. This was long before the movies, remember."

"Okay, then. I don't suppose he's the one who works in palace security?"

Clari couldn't help but grin. "Actually, he is. So Thor is one of King Benjamin's security personnel."

Joel just shook his head. "I didn't meet him, did I?"

"No, but my father thinks it was Thor who put the flowers there as a way to console them, but it got way out of hand. My uncle has always maintained his innocence, but Papa isn't convinced." She shrugged. "That's all I've got. Amma and Afi are convinced, so I think we're just all going to let it drop. There's no point in forcing them to believe my aunt and her family are really gone when there's no real harm in letting them continue as they have been."

She took another sip of her tea, watching Joel over the top of her cup. Holding it just far enough away that she could talk, she winked at him. "And Gina has plans tomorrow night that don't include me, so if that offer of dinner still stands…" Clari couldn't believe her own boldness.

Joel winced, and she tried to brace herself with another sip. "I would love to, but I have a big exam first thing the next morning. I'll be studying all night."

She knew he attended university, but that was all she knew. It was time she asked him about his studies. They talked for half an hour until Rachel needed his help with something. Clari decided it was time to leave.

But then an idea struck her. She'd have to call Rachel later to make sure it would work, but Clari had a feeling it was going to.

That's how she ended up on Joel's doorstep with a basket of food the next evening.

His face showed his surprise. "Hey! What are you doing here?"

She held up the basket with the hand that wasn't balancing the crutch. "Bringing you dinner. Your sister said it was a good idea because you probably wouldn't eat."

Joel's grin as he held the door open told her the guess had been right. He reached for the basket. "Come on in."

Clari half-hobbled into his apartment. Though it was nicer than she'd expected for a Yfir driver attending university, it wasn't ostentatious or even out of her price range should she ever decide to move.

After setting the basket on the table, he turned to her and pulled her into his arms. Clari could get used to the feeling of being in them. In fact, she rather liked it.

"Thank you." His voice was soft as was the look in his eyes. "I appreciate this."

Clari did something she'd never done before. She leaned up and initiated a kiss.

But Joel didn't let it stop there. His arms tightened around her as he kissed her back. Clari's hands slid up his chest and around the back of his neck until her fingers could play with the curly hair at his nape. She wondered if she could get away with running her fingers through the unruly mop.

But Joel's increasing intensity drove those thoughts from her mind. Time ceased to exist until he moved back.

"Wow," Clari whispered. "I've had boyfriends, but I'm pretty sure I've never been kissed like that before."

Joel gave her a soft kiss. "That's the kind of kiss I wanted to give you in the kitchen, but I definitely wouldn't want your grandparents walking in on that."

Her face had to be flushed already, but it heated further at the thought of Amma or Afi finding them in such an embrace. "I think it's best for that sort of thing to be reserved for when there is no chance of anyone seeing us."

He chuckled. "I agree." Then he moved away from her. "I trust you brought enough for both of us to eat?"

She couldn't hold back the snort. "I probably brought enough for an army."

"Then let's dig in."

Their meal was companionable. They talked about Joel's career aspirations, and she told him what she could about life in the palace. She didn't tell him the Queen Mother would be ecstatic that Clari had found someone she really liked. The Queen Mother had been after her for ages to find a "nice young man."

"Are you ready for your test?" she asked as they put the rest of the food away.

"I think I'll be fine, but I do need to study." She could hear the regret in his voice as he turned away from the refrigerator. "Will I see you tomorrow?"

Clari rested her hands on his abdomen and leaned up to give him a soft kiss. "I hope so. I'll try to stop by."

"I'll be there after eleven." He winked at her. "By the way, I'm pretty sure I know what your Christmas present is going to be."

Her eyes narrowed. "Really? I'm not sure I like the sound of this."

"You'll see." He rested his hand on her lower back as she

made her way to the door.

She was going to have to come up with something equally fantastic. Rachel would help.

Joel leaned in. "I'm pretty sure I've got the best end of this deal already. We haven't actually talked about it, but I think your *amma* has gotten her wish."

"What's that?"

"A *kærasti* for Clari."

She groaned. "Fine. Yes. Amma got her wish." After another quick kiss, she went out the door. "Now get to studying. No *kærasti* of mine is going to flunk a test."

His laughter followed her down the stairs to where her Yfir driver waited. This driver wouldn't worm his way into Clari's heart the way the most reluctant one had just over a week earlier.

A week Clari wouldn't trade for anything.

Because she finally found her *kærasti*.

EPILOGUE

J oel bowed deeply at the waist. "Your Majesties, it is a pleasure to meet you."

Queen Mother Eliana clapped her hands together. "Nonsense. It is our pleasure to meet you."

King Benjamin didn't look like he shared her sentiment but gave a tight-lipped smile.

Clari's uncle, Thor, also bowed. "Our apologies, Your Majesties. I was told no one would be in here. We will take our leave."

Joel glanced around the drawing room. In one corner, a red grand piano sat in front of mirrored doors. Artifacts glittered around the room. Swords, daggers, paintings. All telling the tale of Eyjanian history.

The Queen Mother smiled. Joel had seen that smile many times on television and in pictures, but her graciousness couldn't be fully portrayed in any other medium.

"Thank you for bringing Mr. Christiansen to see me, Clari. I look forward to having you back in the office on Monday."

Clari stammered something about looking forward to being back. Joel, Rachel, Thor, Gina, and Clari all scurried out of the room.

"Anabelle would have died," Rachel whispered once they were in the hall. Her friend had insisted they keep their tour appointment despite Gracie's cold that kept the two of them home.

Clari gave him a look, but wisely no one said anything else.

Anabelle wasn't a big fan of the king's. Everyone loved Queen Mother Eliana though.

The rest of the tour sped by as did the weeks leading up to Christmas.

Joel spent more time with Clari than he did apart - when they weren't working, or in school, or sleeping. All his free time was spent with his girlfriend.

The one he'd waited two whole weeks to tell her he loved her.

Christmas morning didn't dawn, not this far north, but several days were spent at the cabin just the same. Joel got to know the rest of Clari's extended family. Rachel shared Clari's room with her. Thor showed them the secret passage leading to the basement and to a path that led to the lake.

As he expected, Christmas morning with such a large family was rather boisterous, but still somehow controlled.

Amma and Afi, as they'd insisted he call them, seemed to have aged in the last few weeks. Something more might be going on with them, but they wouldn't share. Clari chalked it up to the conflict over Clarice.

The younger children, all boys, did surprisingly well at taking turns opening presents. All of those over twenty no longer received a gift from each family as they did when they were younger. Instead, they participated in drawing names. Clari had drawn her uncle and decided it was time someone presented him with a replica of Thor's hammer from the movies.

He loved it.

So did the kids. In fact, one of them took off with it. Thor bellowed, and his namesake son sheepishly handed the hammer back to his father.

"Are there any others?" Afi asked the group.

Clari seemed to be purposely avoiding looking at him. Joel knew why. There hadn't been a gift under the very large tree for her from him.

"I have one," Joel told the family, then turned to Clari. He took a deep breath and slid down onto one knee.

The family gasped. Clari covered her gaping mouth with her hands. "What are you doing?" she whispered.

"I've talked with your *amma* at length, Clari. Sometimes, when you meet the right person, you just know. That's how it was for them. Amma and Afi married less than six weeks after they met and look what they've created together. I don't want to do anything quite that crazy, but I do know I love you. I want to spend my life with you."

He pulled the box out of his pocket and opened it. "Clari Sørensen, will you do me the honor of being my wife?" Joel leaned a little closer. "And in case you were wondering, Queen Mother Eliana gave her blessing, too."

That broke the ice a little bit as laughter sounded around the room.

Tears streaked down Clari's cheeks. "Of course!" She flung her arms around Joel's neck, nearly knocking him off balance. "I love you."

After a kiss suitable for the crowd they were in, Joel moved back and slid the ring onto Clari's outstretched finger.

"Guess I should call that florist in the States and thank them for messing up that order." He gave her another kiss.

"I don't know about that. If the order had been right, we still would have ended up here."

Joel shrugged. "I don't know. If it had been right, I don't know that I would have stayed long enough to find out you needed a Yfir driver."

Clari giggled. "Now I have my own Yfir driver forever." She kissed him again. "I'll always be thankful for that bouquet that came out of the blue."

THE END

DISCUSSION QUESTIONS

S uggested discussion group questions for *A Kærasti for Clari* by Carol Moncado.

When Clari and Joel first meet they do not have the best first impression of each other.

1. Have you ever had an opportunity to meet someone and had a poor first impression, only to find out later that your impression was wrong?

2. How has that changed the relationships with other people?

Clari has to rely on Joel quite a bit and seems to have trouble with it at first.

3. Have you had a time when you have had to rely on someone?

4. Do you find it difficult to rely on people?

Joel and Clari live fairly far north and have limited daylight in the winter.

5. Do you think you could live in a place like that?

6. Why or why not?

While at the cabin, Joel got the call about Annabelle and Gracie's parents being killed in a car accident.

7. Have you had a friend that lost a loved one before?

8. How have you comforted them?

9. If you lost someone, what has been the thing that has best comforted you?

Joel struggled with nightmares while at the cabin with Clari.

10. If you knew him what verses would you recommend for him to read or memorize to help him with the nightmares?

Joel had a traumatic experience as a child that was affecting his adult life.

11. Have you had anything happen to you that you still experience the after effects of as an adult?

Clari and Joel decide to watch a movie while stranded at the lake house.

12. What would be your ideal movie to watch while stranded somewhere?

Gina and Clari have a conversation about family and Gina thanks Clari for sharing her family.

13. How does your family relate to others outside of the family lines?

14. Are they more accepting and have an open door to friends or are they more "blood is thicker than water" and don't like to include outsiders?

Rachel and Joel have a fairly close relationship as siblings due to the death of their parents.

15. Do you have any siblings and if you do, how is your relationship with them?

16. Are you close like Joel and Rachel? Or is it a more distant relationship?

Clari found out a secret that her family had been keeping from her.

17. How would you have felt if your family had kept a secret like that from you?

18. Do you think Clari handled it well ?

MORE BOOKS
by Carol Moncado

Find the latest information and connect with Carol at her website:
www.carolmoncado.com

Candid Romance

Finding Mr. Write
Finally Mr. Write
Falling for Mr. Write

The Monarchies of Belles Montagnes

Good Enough for a Princess
Along Came a Prince
More than a Princess
Hand-Me-Down Princess
Winning the Queen's Heart
Protecting the Prince
Prince from her Past

Serenity Landing Second Chances

Discovering Home
Glimpsing Hope
Reclaiming Hearts

Crowns & Courtships

Dare You
Heart of a Prince

Serenity Landing Tuesdays of Grace

Grace to Save

Serenity Landing Lifeguards (Summer)

The Lifeguard, the New Guy, & Frozen Custard
The Lifeguard, the Abandoned Heiress, & Frozen Custard

Serenity Landing Teachers (Christmas)

Gifts of Love
Manuscripts & Mistletoe
Premieres & Paparazzi

Mallard Lake Township

Bargains, Ballots, & the Bakery

ABOUT

www.carolmoncado.com

When she's not writing about her imaginary friends, USA Today Bestselling Author Carol Moncado prefers binge watching pretty much anything to working out. She believes peanut butter M&Ms are the perfect food and Dr. Pepper should come in an IV. When not hanging out with her hubby, four kids, and two dogs who weigh less than most hard cover books, she's probably reading in her Southwest Missouri home.

Summers find her at the local aquatic center with her four fish, er, kids. Fall finds her doing the band mom thing. Winters find her snuggled into a blanket in front of a fire with the dogs. Spring finds her sneezing and recovering from the rest of the year.

She used to teach American Government at a community college, but her indie career, with nearly two dozen titles released in the first 2.5 years, has allowed her to write full time. She's a founding member and former President of MozArks ACFW, blogger at InspyRomance, and is represented by Tamela Hancock Murray of the Steve Laube Agency.

Author Site: www.carolmoncado.com
Facebook page: www.facebook.com/CarolMoncadoBooks
Reader Group: bit.ly/MoncadoReaderGroup

Out of the Blue Bouquet

INTRODUCING

I t is my sincere hope that you enjoyed reading my story of royalty and mis-delivered flowers, *A Kærasti for Clari*.

Now it is my very real pleasure to introduce the fourth book in this collection, *Premeditated Serendipity* by Chautona Havig. Chautona writes books that are sure to touch your heart and *Premeditated Serendipity* is no exception.

Whether you are reading this collection for the first time or the dozenth time, I know you will enjoy reading the story of Reid and Kelsey. I think we can all agree, sometimes romance needs a little… shove.

USA Today Bestselling Author

Author of *A Kærasti for Clari*

Out of the Blue Bouquet

Premeditated *Serendipity*

a Novella
by

Chautona  *Havig*

Published by

Havilah Press

Summary: When Wayne Farrell hears about his niece's floral fiasco, it sparks a plan to mix up his own orders in an attempt to play matchmaker. Reid has his reasons for not pursuing Kelsey… yet, and Wayne's interference only makes an already difficult situation even more awkward. Premeditated Serendipity—because romance sometimes needs a little shove.

1. Christian fiction 2. man-woman relationships

CONTENTS

CHAPTER 1

A leaf performed a lazy pirouette as it spun from a low-hanging branch in the brisk November air. It rested a moment at its curled tip, before taking a bow and dropping to the ground. Reid Keller paused in his quick stride across town to watch the performance before stepping around the leaf to hurry to his appointment.

"Who knew you were a softy, Reid?"

The voice? Wayne—his landlord and the town florist. *Speaking of softies...* Reid turned and tried to stifle his impatience. But at the sight of Wayne holding out a daisy to him, all impatience vanished. "Wayne..."

"Take it to her. Tell her how you feel."

"Not telling her anything, Wayne, but I'll take it to her. Tell her you were thinking of her."

The minute Reid's fingers grasped the stem, Wayne turned to go. "Leave me out of it. I'm not the fool in love but hiding it from a girl who obviously cares about him, too."

Really? I hadn't seen that yet. Cool. Just a few months more until a year is up. If she hasn't given up on me by then, done. A glance back showed the mostly empty daisy barrel. *And look who's talkin', old man. Isn't there some kind of saying about calling someone something when you're it yourself?*

At the corner of Second and Center Streets, with a wide bank of windows welcoming him as twilight descended over Fairbury, a small, narrow, brick building stood with a cross on the glass door. Beneath that cross: three simple words. The Prayer Room.

Reid paused just out of sight and watched for a moment as Kelsey Jackson sat alone in the darkest corner of the room. A lone pot light shone just enough light on her to show off the reddish glints in her brown bob. A guitar on her lap, her graceful fingers plucked at strings, slowly... faster... slowly again.

How can she pray in song like that? I can't make my prayers make sense at all with just plain words. But hers come out in rhymes and everything. A new thought struck him as Reid reached for the push bar on the door. *Is that what David did when he wrote all those Psalms?*

Sometimes opening the door stopped the song. He prayed this wasn't one of them as he slipped inside Fairbury's newest addition.

The Prayer Room. Alexa Hartfield, a local author and celebrity, had brought back the idea after a visit to her hometown in California. *"It's just a building—now where the old Christian bookstore used to be. People go in and pray at all hours of the day* and *night. There's always someone there to pray* with *them if they want."*

The more the singles class at First Church had heard about it, the more determined all of them had become to make it happen in Fairbury. And Reid, fresh out of prison, a recent graduate of culinary school, and newest resident of Fairbury had been in on the project almost from the beginning. His "watchman" hours over the room? Five-thirty to seven-thirty, Monday through Friday and on call during weekend hours. The shift directly following Kelsey Jackson's. Could anything have been more perfect?

Gentle notes reached him, but no words. A note here... one there. Just close enough together to create a melody, far enough to create longing. Tapping the recorder button on his phone, Reid stood there, just listening.

In time, Kelsey's voice reached his heart, and as he listened,

Reid forgot about his feelings for her, lost in his wonder for the Lord.

Only You can stand when I am weary,

Holding me when as lonely here I pray.

Only You can keep my feet from stumbling.

Only You can wash these tears away.

By Your side, my heart it never wavers,

Keeping me from other loves untrue.

By Your side, I never know true heartache.

By Your side, forgiveness comes anew.

Take the mess I make of each action

And make it pure once more for only You...

Only You...

By Your side...

Day by day...

Help keep me true to You.

The hush surrounded him—that beautiful hush that only came during Kelsey's hours as watchman. The others all played worship music, but Kelsey chose silence and prayerful song.

Reid missed the sound of her settling the guitar in its case and snapping the latches shut. He didn't hear the swishing of her scrubs as she crossed the room. But he did feel her hand slipping into his and the gentle squeeze she gave it. "You okay today?"

How does she do that? Anyone, no matter who it is—she can show affection to anyone. I just sit there silent and make them feel all awkward.

"Reid?"

"I'm good. Just letting that one sink into my soul." Against his will, his eyes opened and fixated on hers. "You really have a gift, Kelsey."

To his relief, and utter disgust with himself for noticing, Kelsey kept hold of his hand as she tugged him toward "her" corner. Did she pause before she dropped it to retrieve the guitar again? He didn't know, but it seemed like it. *Maybe Wayne's not crazy. Wouldn't that be great?*

"Listen. This tune just keeps playing in my heart. I can't get away from it. I probably heard it somewhere, but I don't care. It's been a bad week at the clinic, and this just feels so *healing* after it all."

Again, she played the slow, haunting notes that somehow soothed instead of ached. "I love that. Got it recorded, too."

"I'll check Dropbox later, then." After a few more notes, Kelsey put away her guitar again, this time with evident reluctance.

Because she loves that song so much, or because she has to leave? He swallowed hope and didn't allow himself to add, *me.*

"Did you have a good day today?"

Reid picked up the guitar case, ready to follow her out to her car. "Yeah. The boss says I'm getting a six-month raise at the first of December. Says I'm doing great." The moment he spoke, Reid wished back the words. "Ouch. That sounds full of myself, doesn't it?"

"Sounds honest to me. He said it, not you."

"I repeated it?" Again, he wished the words back. *Now I just sound like I'm fishing for... something.*

"Nope."

The little, banana yellow VW Beetle meant the end of that day's chat. Reid pulled the little flower from his shirt pocket and offered it before stowing her case in the passenger's seat. "Compliments of Wayne, of course."

"Yeah... but you brought it."

Another squeeze of his hand—had she been holding it all the time? The memory of following her out the door told him no. *Still... she didn't hesitate.*

"Thanks, Reid. See you tomorrow."

He stood there, hands in his pockets, watching as Kelsey pulled out of the parking space and zipped down Second Street toward the highway. When the red of her taillights disappeared around a corner, he turned to go back inside and saw Sister Arlene waiting for him to open the door for her.

"Hey there, Sister Arlene. Sorry about that. Kelsey had another one of her inspiring prayers today. Want to hear it?"

And that's all it took to wipe out the matchmaking glint in the elderly woman's eyes and spark a less personal one—for him, anyway.

Kelsey entered her Brant's Corners duplex on a mission to change out of her soiled scrubs *immediately.* Guitar on the couch—she grabbed it and wedged it between the mountains of blankets threatening to topple it off. Purse in the chair. By the time she reached the washing machine in the closet behind the kitchen, she'd stripped down to her underwear and bra.

As she dashed for the shower, she ordered Siri to call her uncle. His voice broke through the shower spray as Kelsey stepped inside. "Did you do it?"

"Half of it." Try as she might, Kelsey couldn't keep the defeat from her tone. "I asked about his day—even held his hand for a minute. But I couldn't make myself ask."

"I have to meet this guy."

She stood there, water forcing soapy drizzles over her face and listened, waiting for more. It didn't come. "All right, Uncle Mel. Tell me. Why?"

"C'mon, Kelsey! You were the first girl at Brunswick High to ask a guy to prom. You've asked out more guys than all the women I've ever heard of—combined! But this one…"

Kelsey swallowed a few times, rinsed the rest of her hair, and fumbled to ask the one question that had burdened her for weeks. "You don't think it's the Lord, do you? Do you think He's preventing me because it's not right for me?"

Uncle Mel's cough spoke more than a month-long sermon series. "Do I have to answer that?"

"No. You're right. I'm imposing this on me, not the Lord. Am I nuts to do it?"

"Well, if it were any other woman, I'd say yes. If you like a guy and want to get to know him better, I don't see why you have to wait around for him to figure it out. And, as a guy myself, it's kind of nice to know that at least sometimes a guy doesn't have to be the one to put himself out there."

"Projecting, are we?"

Uncle Mel's laughter took the sting from the entire conversation. "Perhaps a bit. *But,* since *you* have a history of asking out all the wrong men, waiting to say yes to one who you are interested in instead of pursuing him this time... yeah. It makes sense to me!"

After shutting off the water, Kelsey stepped from the shower, grabbed a towel, and wrapped it around her. "That paramedic... Daniel something. He asked me out today."

"What'd you say?"

Phone in hand, Kelsey went to find yoga pants and a t-shirt. "I told him to ask me next time he saw me. I didn't want to say no, but I wanted to think about it."

"And you're not going."

At that moment, Kelsey realized she never would have. "No. I thought maybe if Reid heard me say I needed to get ready for a date, it might get him moving, but that just made me feel icky. I mean, using one guy and manipulating another. Who is this person I've become?"

"But you didn't, Kels... you didn't. Temptation isn't equal to commission of sin. Remember?"

"Yeah. You're right." But even as Kelsey wrestled into her clothes and combed through her wet hair, the reflection she saw had nothing to do with her physical appearance. She saw a young woman half in love with a guy who might not be interested in anything else. "Am I as pathetic as I feel?"

Uncle Mel murmured loving reassurances and reminded

Kelsey of half a dozen botched relationships with guys she'd been sure were "the one." "Oh! Hey! I almost forgot to share my new theory!"

"What's this one? I swear, you've gone from one every other week to one a day. Is Reid secretly married this time or is he heir to a fortune as long as he doesn't marry before he's thirty?"

This time Kelsey giggled, but with only a few miles separating them, Kelsey and the most important man in her life collapsed into fits of mirth. "You've..." Uncle Mel wheezed as his laughter turned to guffaws. "You've got to stop reading those Regency and Victorian romances."

"They're fun! And besides, if those women had to wait back then, I can, too." Phone in hand, Kelsey sprinted for the kitchen and began assembling a salad. "So... theory, my uncle-papa."

"Well, I was talking to Joan Oberton. She works in that prison ministry."

"The one Reid was in?"

Uncle Mel's shrug—oh, there'd been one, and Kelsey could have *sworn* she could hear it. "Don't know. She just works with one. Anyway, she says she always counsels new believers not to date for a year after conversion. She uses that Old Testament thing about not working or going to war for a year after marriage as proof that they need to concentrate on the Lord for a year before mixing other serious relationships into it. Maybe he heard her telling someone—or maybe she told him."

February. Valentine's Day. He was so embarrassed to admit that his re-birthday was on Valentine's Day. Three months.

"Kels?"

"Could be," she finally admitted. "And really, what's three more months? With Thanksgiving, Christmas, and the flu season ahead of us—"

"Only you would lump flu season in with holidays."

"As I was saying before the man who taught me never to interrupt interrupted me..." Kelsey did a happy dance at the chagrin she knew her uncle now wore. "…I'll be busy with fun and flu, so maybe it'll keep my mind off him."

The fits of laughter returned. Uncle Mel found his voice first. "Yeah. I'll keep trolling the pawn shops for a cheap guitar. You keep seeing him *every day* and pretending you *don't* care. Yeah. I bet I succeed before you do."

Panic hit her at those words. She stared at a tomato in her hand, wondering when she'd picked it up and how she'd managed not to divest her hand of a finger or two in the process. "You don't think he knows, do you?"

"If he does, and if he's letting you go on without any idea that he is or isn't interested, then you don't want him anyway."

The first slice of the knife took off the very tip of her nail. "I gotta go. Nearly cut my hand. And you're nuts if you think he's that kind of guy. He's not. I just know it."

With silence filling around her, Kelsey sighed, flicked the piece of nail aside, and tried the tomato again. "I just know it, Lord. I just know it."

CHAPTER 2

R eid appeared as Wayne pulled two buckets of white daisies from the back of his minivan. "Mornin'. You're up early."

The younger man started to scratch his head and jerked his hand down. Just like every time. "Couldn't sleep. Heard those squeaky brakes of yours and thought I'd come help while I wait for The Coventry to open."

Setting the buckets down with a huff, Wayne pointed. "Can you take those up by the front door? I'll get 'em in the barrel as soon as I can."

But instead of retrieving the next buckets of fresh flowers from Rockland's flower mart, Wayne went to pour a couple cups of coffee. He met Reid at the entrance to his workroom and suggested they sit for a bit. "Tell me when you're going to ask Kelsey out."

He saw it. The darkening of Reid's eyes from amber to umber, the wall slowly rising. Then it shifted almost as if nothing had changed. "February—the fourteenth, if you must know, but not why you think."

"Three months? It better not be for romantic reasons, because waiting like that just... *isn't.*"

Reid sipped at coffee that probably didn't meet some culinary standard or another but said nothing. Just as Wayne was about to press again, Reid set the cup down at his feet, rubbed his hands on his pant legs, and inhaled like one about to jump off the high dive. "It's just that I kind of made a commitment to myself."

"To yourself." Wayne gave his best imitation of his father when he'd done something stupid.

"Yeah. No dating for a year."

Oh, for cryin' out the wazoo. Great. How do I work with that? When Reid proved less than forthcoming as to what would make him do something so obviously idiotic, Wayne asked. "Okay, why?"

"There's this lady who worked the prison ministry—helped those of us going through the anti-recidivism program. Anyway, when I moved here, she's the one who brought me food and stuff that day."

"Joan Oberton? From Brunswick?"

Reid nodded. She stood up there in my living room and prayed for me. It was nice, you know? Some lady who probably was afraid I'd tie her down and force her to take drugs or something just stood there and prayed for me. Then when she got done, she looked up at me with this weird expression on her face..."

At this, Wayne laughed. "Joan's face *is* a weird expression."

Again, with the hands rubbing against his legs. Reid fumbled and fought until Wayne nearly shook the words out of him. "Well, she said something. She said, 'The Lord has given me a prophecy for you.'" Reid reached for coffee he obviously didn't want to drink and took a swig anyway. "I'll be honest. I thought I'd gotten duped about this Jesus thing when I heard that."

"I would'a run, so kudos to you for not burning your Bible right there."

"Well, she kept going. Said, 'I know the plans I have for you,' declares the Lord, 'plans for welfare and not calamity to give you a future and a hope. Make it your ambition to lead a quiet life and work with your hands. Treat younger women as sisters in absolute purity.' As the Israelites spent their first year of marriage free of duty, let your first year as the Bride of Christ be committed only to the Lord.'"

Silence, broken only by the constant hum of the floral coolers, descended over the room as Wayne worked through his emotions. When all attempts at diplomacy failed, Wayne went for his true opinion. "Excrement."

"As in…"

"You heard me." He fought to extricate himself from a couch too comfortable for his own good and began separating flowers. "Listen, Reid. That prophecy stuff…" Wayne shook his head. "Just not cool to do that to someone. You don't have to follow that."

Reid began explaining as he got up to carry in the rest of the buckets. "I know. But when I found out most of those words were straight from the Bible, I thought about it. I mean, it makes sense, don't you think? Take time to focus on learning what the Lord wants of His people. I mean, I'm one of those now, you know?"

It galled not to blast out every objection he had up front, but Wayne knew enough about human nature to know he needed to tread as lightly as his lead feet would allow. "Look, my objection isn't that Joan spoke Scripture to you. That's good. If she'd said, 'In my opinion, based on these verses, and in light of your recent circumstances, you should consider…' That would have been good—smart. I couldn't argue with it. But she didn't! She called it a prophecy—that *God* took those verses, out of context, and told just you to 'live them this way.'"

"Well, yeah, but—"

"You can't just do that! You can't go around telling people that 'God said this and that.' Just because you use Bible words, doesn't make your ideas from the Bible. It's a serious thing to claim that *God* spoke to you, outside the whole counsel of the Bible, *and gave you extra revelation about it!*" He cleared his throat. "Sorry."

"Soapbox?"

"Yep." Wayne stared down at a pile of daisies and calmed his racing heart. "Stirs my blood in all the wrong ways." He picked a perfect daisy and held it out to Reid. "People do this too often. They take their own agendas, wrap it in a few Bible verses and some Christianese, and the next thing you know, someone's in *sin* because they didn't obey someone's so-called 'prophecy.' Well, I'm telling you now. Those verses are out of context. And out of context isn't something *God* does."

Reid's fingers closed around the stem, and he gazed at it as if transfixed. "Yeah... that's what Tom Allen said."

"Tom's a good guy." Wayne choked down what he really wanted to say and went for the sanitized truth. "If the rest of his church were like him, I'd be a part of it."

"They're mostly people who—"

The words flowed... the pain, the heartache, the double-standards imposed on him by people wielding Bibles with the grace of a blind man on a mass shooting spree. When he finished, Wayne dropped his head into his hands and forced himself not to weep. "Just because they are a 'card-carrying Christian' or sit in a pew on Sunday, doesn't mean what they say is right." His head shot up again. "Just remember that."

Reid stood there, hands shoved in his pockets, looking as miserable as Wayne felt. "Wayne, I'm sorry. If I do that, you'll tell me, right? You'll tell me I'm out of line. 'Cause even if what I say is true, doing that to someone isn't ever right. It can't be."

He needed Reid out of there before he lost his self-control. With a nod to the flower, he sent Reid on his way. "Get her a fresh one before you go in today. Tell her about the daisy—all of it. Tell her how you feel. And if God doesn't want you having a relationship, He knows how to put a stop to it before it's too late."

With a glance back at him, twice, Reid left. Wayne, on the other hand, stood rooted in place and wept until the pain disappeared. The only proof that he'd even bared his hurt to anyone was a lone coffee cup abandoned by the corner of the couch.

Give him the courage, Lord. I think he needs it.

Daisy in hand, Reid reached The Prayer Room that evening still uncertain if he'd give it to her or not. Two days in a row might say more than he was ready for. Wayne had insisted that a date after nine months of focus only on the Lord wouldn't be the destruction of his faith. *As if I hadn't already been thinking about her every day.* His mother's saying came to mind. *And definitely twice... or more... on Sundays.*

Then a sense of the ridiculous came over him. *I'm making too much of a stupid flower. She knows they're from Wayne, anyhow.* And with that, he peered through the window to watch for just a moment. Did she wait for him to arrive? He'd never allowed himself to look, but this time he did. He stood there, watching, waiting.

But Kelsey only plucked at strings and sang. Just as he started to push open the door, a hand rose from the strings and wiped at her eyes. *Oh, no...*

All hesitation vanished. Reid pushed open the door and crossed the room. The broken, fractured words tore at his heart....*comfort to the broken... strength to the weak... love to the lonely... hope for even me...*

Again, her voice cracked, this time on "me."

Kelsey nestled the bottom of the guitar in the case and leaned on it, her forehead resting on the headstock. Reid just sat beside her, waiting. When she lowered the rest of the guitar into the case, he reached for her hand and prayed.

"I don't know what happened, Lord, but Kelsey is hurting. If I know her like I think I do, it's more than just her. She hurts for others. So, whoever else is hurting, please comfort them, too. Her prayer-song is right. Help us remember that. Help us remember that only You can really comfort the broken, strengthen the weak, and love the lonely." He swallowed a rising lump in his throat and choked out. "And yes, help her know just how much hope You have for her."

Tears splashed onto their hands. A hiccough filled the room. Kelsey's shoulders shook. Unable to do anything else, Reid reached across her for a box of Kleenex and squeezed her hand as a hint to take them. "Sorry."

"Don't be." He tried again, this time remembering the verses he'd learned to pray when nothing seemed to go well. "Lord, I pray with the Psalmist. 'The righteous cry, and the LORD hears and delivers them out of all their troubles. The LORD is near to the brokenhearted and saves those who are crushed in spirit. Many are the afflictions of the righteous, but the LORD delivers him out of them all.' So please deliver us from the afflictions hurting Kelsey and those she cares about. Stay near to their broken hearts and relieve their crushed spirits. We cry out to You and know You will hear us...'"

The hush of The Prayer Room, the Scriptures spoken with confidence and faith, and that wonderful connection that happens when two people pray together worked the Lord's magic in Kelsey's heart. Her eyes glistened with unshed tears. A smile hinted they might be happier ones. "I love how you've memorized so much already. It shames and encourages me at the same time."

"When you don't have much else to do..." He squeezed her hand again. "Are you going to be okay?"

"I will. But Lily Allen... probably not."

She led him to the small, semi-private room at the back of the building. There, stuck to the wall, hung hundreds of sticky notes, each with a prayer request. One asked for favor with a job opportunity. Another requested restored relationships in the family. Children had written a row of beautiful, simple prayers—health for a sick puppy, Daddy to say it's okay to a new kitten, that a bully at school would be nicer. Above them all, Romans 12:12 had been painted in a lovely, flowing script. "...rejoicing in hope, persevering in tribulation, devoted to prayer."

But there, off to the right and rather low Reid spied Kelsey's bubble writing before she had a chance to point it out to him. The words... simple. *Please pray for Lily Allen—health.*

"Tests came back?"

A fresh tear fell on her cheek. Reid ordered himself *not* to wipe it away, even as his thumb caught it and flung it aside. That's all it took. Kelsey dropped her forehead to his chest and wept. "They can't do any more for her, Reid. Six months at the most. That's all we have with her."

All caution fled. Reid pulled Kelsey close and held her. "I always feel like I should be happy for someone going home to Jesus. My head says that's the right attitude, but…" He swallowed hard. "I just can't. Their girl isn't old enough to be without a mom."

How long they stood there, he didn't know. No one came in, no calls interrupted them, nothing. All at once, Kelsey stepped back, obviously embarrassed. "I'm sorry. I just blubbered all over you. I—"

"I thought that's what Christians did. Something about bearing the unbearable?"

She grinned and brushed away fresh tears. "Bearing one another's *burdens.* Yes. You're right."

And then Reid saw it—her eyes catching sight of the daisy in his pocket. Without a second thought, he pulled it free and tucked it behind her ear. "There. It looks better on you than me."

Inadequate as a declaration of his feelings? Definitely. But I'm not exactly the declaring type. That's more for those old movies Mom likes. The smile on her face—in her eyes. *Does she know what I want to say and can't?*

"I love Wayne's daisies." Reid's heart sank at the words and rose again as Kelsey added, "Thanks for bringing it. It can't be fun walking around with a daisy in your pocket."

Don't say it—don't say it—don't—He said it. "Some people are worth the utter humiliation."

The small smile, the way she touched the petals half-covering her ear… it all meant one thing. Appreciation.

Kelsey didn't look at him again, but she did speak. "I've always wondered why he does it—buys all those daisies. It's got to be expensive giving away so many."

He nudged her from the close quarters of the "prayer closet" and back to their usual spots in the corner. "He told me about it when I first moved in. I guess the whole shamrock thing for St. Patrick's Day? It's a thing. Supposed to remind you of the Trinity—three leaves in one little leaf."

"Yeah, I heard about that in school—back before telling kids stuff like that was 'teaching religion' and forbidden." Her face drained of color. "Did I just do a 'back in my day' thing? I'm not *old* enough for that!"

Reid gave her the blankest look he could manufacture and shook his head as if to clear it. "Don't know what you're talking about. Anyway, for Wayne, it's a reminder of God—who He is."

That caught Kelsey's attention. She stared at him, gape-jawed, confused. "What? I didn't know Wayne Farrell is a Christian!"

"Well, calling himself one isn't easy. The way he put it was, 'I've been burned by the church. I'm done with them for now. I'm barely holding onto God.'"

"Oh! Did he say what happened?"

The old Reid wouldn't have hesitated to tell the whole story, but Christian Reid couldn't do it. "I want to tell you, but he didn't say I could. Bet he'd tell you if you asked him, though. But those flowers... Those are how he *is* the church right now."

A click sounded, and the furnace kicked on. Hot air whooshed up behind their chairs as Kelsey wrestled with that idea. "I should pray for him more. I never really think of it, but man..."

Reid retrieved the flower from behind her ear again and handed it to her. "Wayne says the sunny golden yellow is the Light—Jesus, the 'S-U-N'—of God. He says that we need the sun to grow from little seeds to strong plants. So, it's new life in Jesus—a strong life." He pointed to the ring of white around that sun. "Those white petals are the purity He creates in us. Wayne says Jesus took away the ugliness and created a pure me. He dumped red blood all over me and now only sees white. I'm pure in His eyes."

A giggle—the last thing he'd expected. Kelsey gave him a sidelong glance and a wisp of hair slid along her cheek. Reid ached to brush it away again. His finger twitched, but he resisted... barely. "I thought you were going to say something about plucking the petals."

"I always thought that was kind of awful. I mean, one second you have a nice flower, and the next you have a broken heart and half a flower."

"Leave it to a guy to kill all the romance from the thing."

If he hadn't seen a smirk try to form before she managed to hide it, Reid's awkwardness might have shifted into panic. Instead, he tried to remember what else Wayne had said. "Wayne calls daisies 'nature's sap-o-meters,' you know. He says people say it wrong. They look at the daisy and start pulling them off with the whole..."

Reid paused, snatched up one of many sticky note pads lying about the room and a pen.

he loves me

he loves me not

he loves me

he loves me not

he loves me

"Yeah. I mean, you get a fifty-fifty chance." Kelsey's voice dropped to a whisper. "Just like in real life. He either does, or he doesn't."

Pulse pounding, heart racing, Reid fought to maintain his cool. "Well, according to Wayne, because of Jesus, it's really like this." And one by one, he crossed out the nots and turned each of the lowercase Hs into capitals. "With Jesus, it's always, 'He loves me.' Period."

"Wow..."

Every instinct screamed for him to cup her jaw, turn her face toward him, tell her how he felt—better yet, *show* her. Only the Lord's assistance could have kept him talking at that moment.

"Wayne said, 'When I give people those flowers, the people don't know all that. But I pray over that barrel when I fill it every morning. I pray over every one I personally hand someone. I pray for the ones I know are missing every night. I ask God to show those people just how much He loves them.'"

Tears flowed again. Reid held her hand and waited, praying that they were good tears this time. Praying that she wouldn't know he'd gone upstairs that day and cried, too. And then, before he knew it, he'd told her. "If I'd known that God's love was real, maybe I wouldn't have made some of the stupid choices I did." It felt a little fanciful, but Reid found himself adding, "I wouldn't have gotten all those petals so dirty."

"But they're all clean now." Kelsey brushed her thumb against the white petal. "I've never seen a daisy as special before— except that Wayne gave them out. I always kind of thought they were 'filler flowers'—like carnations, but happier-looking ones. Carnations always look overdressed for the party, you know?" A blush filled her cheeks as she added, "Silly, huh."

"Nope. I'll have to tell Wayne that. He doesn't like carnations, either."

A faint whisper reached Reid's ear as she stroked a petal once more. *"He loves me..."* Her other hand gave his a squeeze. "You know, I never did that 'he loves me—he loves me not' thing. It felt like a recipe for disappointment."

As she spoke, an idea bloomed in his heart. Reid extricated his hand from hers and folded the sticky note in half. He stared at it for a moment before tucking it into her now-empty hand. *Lord... three months. I'm trusting that if it's right, in three months...*

"Thanks."

The word might have been underwhelming or disappointing had he not seen her tuck it into her wallet as she climbed into her Beetle a few minutes later.

As always, Reid stood, watching until the taillights disappeared around the corner and out of sight. *Okay, Lord... okay...*

CHAPTER 3

The apartment above **Wayne's florist** shop boasted one room, a bathroom, and a combination kitchenette-living room. But windows looked out over the Fairbury square and the back alley. "Just in case I ever have to get out in a hurry," Reid had joked when Wayne showed him around. Finding out one guy had nearly been iced in that very apartment—by his ex-gang, no less—hadn't inspired much confidence. Still, Reid's license had been suspended until the following June, and his job was in Fairbury. That meant needing the cheapest apartment possible.

The clock read seven-thirty as he grabbed his chef's jacket off the ironing board and pulled it on. If he hurried, there'd be time to stop downstairs and order flowers for his mother's birthday. Sunflowers—her favorite. He checked his wallet, double-checked that he still had the fifty-dollar bill stuffed behind his ID, and with jacket in hand, jogged down the steps to the back door. Wayne had it propped open as he carried bucket after bucket of fresh flowers into the shop.

"Hey, Reid."

"Need a hand?"

"Nope!" Wayne winked and held up beefy arms that were probably rock-solid muscle wrapped in a protective coating of "insulation" as he called it. "Gotta get in my workout. You need something?"

Reid inched toward the door. "I just wanted to write a card out for Mom's flowers. You said you'd get her some—" He broke off as Wayne hauled out a bucket of rich, autumn sunflowers. "You got 'em."

"Can't let your mama down on her special day. You go in and write your note. Leave it on the ticket wheel. I'll get it delivered before you're off work. Mandy's not going to make it today, but if I have to, I'll get Señora Rojas to drive it over. She picking you up after your stint at The Prayer Room?"

"Yeah. Couldn't get anyone to take my slot, so…"

"I could come down after six if I get done—would probably know by five-forty or so if it'll work for me."

In other words, you want to make sure I have plenty of time with Kelsey before you take over. Gotcha.

"Reid?"

"Thanks. That'd be great. I'll just go in and write that card. Don't want to be late. Not after yesterday's performance eval."

Wayne followed him inside. "Good one?"

"Great. I'm getting a raise."

Reid considered half a dozen of the birthday card offerings, but none suited his mother *or* the arrangement. Instead, he grabbed one with a creamy background and the words, *For You* in an elaborate script at the top. It would take some tiny print to write out what he wanted to say, but his penmanship had always been on the microscopic side. After a moment's thought, trying to recall the message he'd worked on for days, Reid wrote.

I never know how to tell you how I feel about you, so I don't. But you mean everything to me. I love you. Reid.

A second read told him he'd done his best. With a heart light and an even lighter wallet, he left it and the money on the ticket wheel and took off for The Coventry at a half-jog. *She'll love them.*

At the corner, Officer Crane waved at him and told him she'd be in for lunch. A group of teenagers raced up the road, backpacks bouncing as they rushed to meet the first bell—and wouldn't make it. And Mike, the general manager, pulled into the parking lot just as Reid reached the back door. He climbed from his car and called out, "I almost beat you today!"

"Got hung up with Wayne." A glance at his phone told him he still had three minutes to spare. "Good thing I jogged it!"

"It's not going to hurt anyone if you're five minutes late now and then. As long as we're ready to go for lunch, you're good."

Do the other guys have it this good? I doubt it. His gaze rose heavenward as he waited for Mike to unlock the door. *Yeah. Didn't read this morning, either. Didn't pray. Well, I'm praying now. Thanks for this place. I still can't believe You did this for me.*

In the humid coolness of his workroom, Wayne Farrell eyed the bucket of sunflowers in much the same fashion as a sculptor might regard a block of marble. Mason jars and sunflowers—there couldn't be a more harmonious mix. But his sense of aesthetics protested against an easy or clichéd choice. If time were of no issue, he would have spray painted a miniature milk can a milky white to set off the fiery golden yellow of the petals to perfection.

But every clip on his order wheel, something he'd bought on a whim from a closing diner, held at least two pending orders. "There's no time for that."

Although muttered under his breath, the words didn't escape the Vulcan-like hearing of his assistant in the main shop. "No time for what?"

Before he could answer, the phone rang, and Wayne snatched it up and punched the button before Señora Rojas, otherwise known as Mrs. Efficiency, could move a hand. The name on the screen registered half a second too late. "Mom!"

"Oh, Wayne. It's terrible. Brooke made some awful mess at work. You should call her. I think she'd appreciate sympathy from someone who understands the business."

Just like you to expect me to read between your blank lines and decipher your meaning. Saying it, while cathartic, would produce the loudest silent treatment known to man. So, Wayne settled for a simple question. "What did Brooke do?"

"Oh, it's awful!"

So you said.

"—had all these orders, and I don't know how she did it, but she sent them out all mixed up."

"How do you mix up orders? It's on the printout. You don't just mix them up. I think Brooke is pulling your leg."

No matter how carefully he tried to explain the process, his mother insisted that his niece's job was now on the line. "They're making her call everyone involved and issue an apology as well as do whatever it'll take to leave all parties satisfied, but Lydia is convinced that Brooke will lose her job over it."

"If she did this—if she sent a bereavement bouquet to someone instead of a dozen proposal roses or something, yeah, she'll lose her job. There's no way she won't. But it's probably not going to be that bad. Surely, a florist with any sense is going to go, "I don't think this bunch of black roses is supposed to go on a congratulations on the new baby bouquet," and make a call."

"But it's already done! And she's just picking up the pieces. Call her, Wayne. She needs to hear that it could happen to anyone."

Refusing? Not an option. But he could delay. "Look, Ma. I can't do it this minute. I have twenty orders to fill myself—fill, not process. But when I'm done, or maybe after I close, I'll call. She's a gifted floral designer. Even if she loses her job, someone will snatch her up. I'll tell her to get references from the people she made it right with. People respect that. It'll be okay. Tell Lyddie not to worry."

If he disconnected a little too quickly, well, could anyone blame him? His gaze shifted to the sunflowers once more and then to the receipt with the hand-scrawled enclosure card. A mix-up like that could destroy relationships. *Or spark them.* His dedication to excellent customer service protested. *You can't do it. No way.*

But the idea, once planted, sprouted and bloomed before his mind's eye. It would work. Just deliver the flowers to Kelsey and then "fix" his "mistake." And he could confess. *After* the planned mishap. "Sometimes serendipity changes the entire direction of a person's life." The fact that serendipity required no interference to *be* serendipity interrupted his burgeoning plans for only a moment. "And at other times, we have to arrange for a little premeditated serendipity."

"What are you talking about in there?" Señora Rojas swept aside the curtain that divided workroom from shop. Hands on hips and looking more like a flamenco dancer than the efficient shop manager that she was, she eyed him with suspicion. "Look at you." Her thick, Spanish accent always added just a hint of spice to the air. "You have twenty-one orders, and you stand there looking e-stupid. Get to work." And with a hand flung over her head as if to finish an act, she turned and swung the curtain shut in one fluid, graceful movement.

Who's the boss here?

The enclosure card beckoned, taunted. In cramped, minuscule print, the words couldn't be more perfect. *I never know how to tell you how I feel about you, so I don't. But you mean everything to me. I love you. Reid.*

Had it been any other card, there might have been room for a salutation—Mom. But there wasn't, and that made everything just a little too perfect. The shop bell jingled. Señora Rojas's voice reached him as she assured a customer that, of course, they could do a *rush order* before noon. "Wayne is the *finest* and most *dedicated* florist around. He would never leave *a customer waiting for an order.*"

Perhaps he wouldn't have done it—before. His sense of pride might have prevented a lapse into the risky world of... matchmaking? Wayne winced. But, that's what it was. If he did this, he'd be a *matchmaker*. A strange mixture of tingling excitement and churning gut left him still undecided.

However, as Señora Rojas continued to send overly-loud digs

at him as she wrote up an order for a cheerful bouquet of hydrangeas and daisies, he made up his mind. Wayne strode to the front, plucked a duplicate enclosure card from the rack, grabbed an envelope, and gave the customer an absent-minded, or so he hoped, wave as he disappeared into the workroom again. As the curtain swooshed behind him, he heard Señora Rojas make a comment about his mind when fixated on his work.

That's what you think.

It didn't take long to copy the card, though writing with such tiny print proved more difficult than he thought. Two identical arrangements—one in the expected mason jar, one in a contemporary cobalt blue vase. And hours later, when his phone alarm went off at two-thirty, Wayne left the remaining orders abandoned on the ticket wheel, grabbed the two arrangements, and bolted out the back door. *Gotta deliver these while I've got the guts.*

CHAPTER 4

Kate Whyte bolted from the door the moment Kelsey came into view. "I'm late. And so are you."

Happy day to you, too.

Kelsey called out an apology, though, and pushed inside. The floral display on the table by the door—you could tell the season just by looking as you came into The Prayer Room. They'd changed from chrysanthemums to dried flowers and wheat. In a couple of weeks, there's probably be holly or poinsettias or something.

I wonder if Wayne does it. Never thought of that.

A sniffle in the prayer closet told her she wasn't alone. She unbuckled the case and pulled out her guitar before moving to the closet. But a teenager met her at the doorway. Kelsey offered the brightest grin she could and asked if she could help. "Kate had to leave."

"Good."

Oh, great. What horrible sin have you committed?

As if the girl heard the silent question, she muttered. "I swear she sees me as a walking sin. Like my mere existence is, like, proof of God's wrath on America or something."

Why is it that something that would sound overly dramatic for anyone else seems understated for Kate?

Before she could offer to pray, the girl scooted toward the back door. "Thanks for being cool. I'll come in later next time."

And with the backdoor chime sounding, the girl was gone. Silence. Kelsey scanned the prayer walls, looking for any new sticky notes. A possible divorce, a wayward teen, gratitude for provision. All in a day's prayer.

She hadn't even had a chance to sit down and tune her guitar when the front door opened. Kelly peered around the wall and saw Wayne from The Pettler, standing there with a vase full of sunflowers. "Hi, Wayne!" She plopped her guitar down in a wingback chair and hurried to his side. *Uncle Mel. He probably thought I needed cheering up—so sweet.*

"Got a delivery for you." The man's expression closely resembled that of a constipated baby as he stood there holding it out to her.

"You okay?"

"I'm good." He shuffled his feet as she took the flowers, and that's when she saw it—excitement. The man nearly exploded with excitement.

Over flowers?

One step at a time, he backed toward the door. One *slow* step at a time. "You have a good day now."

A tip! Kelsey held up one hand and asked him to wait as she raced for her purse. "Just a second…"

"No, no. You enjoy your flowers. I just love seeing people's faces when they get 'em. It's why I do this."

"Yeah, right. You just love flowers. I know you." She stroked a petal, remembering Reid's description of Jesus and the flower. "Reid told me about the daisies—beautiful."

Still, he inched back once more, each step slower than the last. And that's when it hit her. *He wants to see me read the card.* So, with a wave and another hearty thanks, Kelsey set the bouquet on an end table and pulled the card from the fork. The tiny envelopes—as a child, she'd thought they were the most wonderful things in the world.

A whoosh of cold air entered as Wayne backed through the door. She could still feel his eyes on her. But all thoughts of Wayne dissolved as she saw the writing on the card. *Reid's!*

She blinked, twice, trying to focus but too excited to be successful. Then the words appeared. *I never know how to tell you how I feel about you, so I don't. But you mean everything to me. I love you. Reid.*

"No… no way. Lord, really?" Wayne forgotten, Kelsey spun in a circle in a happy hallelujah dance. "You know I'd begun to doubt this waiting thing. You know it! And look!" She waved the card, print facing heavenward, as if the Lord needed just a little assistance to see the wonderfulness that *was* that card.

A fumble for her phone, a glance at the time, the sigh of her heart. *Two and a half hours until he comes…*

"Hey, Reid? That guy from the flower shop is out there. Says he needs to talk to you?"

Reid looked up from plating a salmon and wild rice and nodded. "Be right there." Steamed broccoli, garlic, butter, and dill drizzled over both broccoli and salmon—done. He slid it under the heat lights and nodded at the server who whisked it away again.

The door slammed shut behind him before Reid could catch it. "Does it to me every time." He gave Wayne a shrug and a wry smile. "What's up?"

"Um…" Red-faced, feet shuffling, hardly able to glance in even the direction of Reid's eyes, Wayne looked like a little kid who'd broken the front window—again.

"What? I've got prep work before I'm off."

"So…" Wayne shoved his hands in his pockets. "Okay, you know how I told you about my niece?"

"The floral designer?"

A nod, another shuffle. Wayne cleared his throat. "Well, so Brooke had this big mishap at work—somehow got orders all mixed up. Sent stuff to all the wrong people. Mom's convinced she's gonna get fired."

"Yeah... that's tough. I'll add her to the prayer board the minute I get—"

But as Reid turned to go, Wayne interrupted him. "Your mother's flowers—that card? Yeah. It went to Kelsey just a while ago."

Each word reverberated in his mind until he ached to crush it out again. He could only manage an abrupt reply. "What?!"

"I'm sorry—well, I want to be sorry, but I can't be. If you saw her face when she read that card."

"The card I wrote for *Mom*?" Reid's brain scrambled to recall the words he'd written, but only one stood out. Love. "The one where I said I never tell her how much I love her? You gave that to *Kelsey*?!"

There, Wayne had the decency to blush and stammer a bit. "I—I—yep. And if you could have seen her face. She danced. If you'd seen—"

"Well, I didn't." Something niggled at him. What about the situation didn't fit? Before he could work out that problem, the reminder that Kelsey sat in The Prayer Room with his mother's sunflowers, thinking he'd admitted how much he loved her. A groan roared from the depths of his heart. "What I am I supposed to do? I can't tell her it was a mistake. It'd hurt her—"

"Then don't!" Wayne stepped forward. "Look, it's my fault. I did this. But you don't have to tell her that. You'da sent 'em eventually. So just take the... mix-up as a... blessing and..." With each word, his argument petered into worthlessness. "Reid, really. I want to say I'm sorry, but I can't. She was so happy. So, I'm not sorry." Wayne's repeated apology rang true, annoying as it was. "But I will ask your forgiveness."

A lifetime habit of raking his hands through his hair when frustrated reemerged, despite his fight against it. *"Chefs never touch their hands to their face or their hair. Don't forget that."* His culinary arts teacher had been adamant, and yet he'd blown it.

Again.

"Wayne, of course, I forgive you, but I won't pretend I'm not ticked."

The man's shoulders slumped as he turned to go. "I hope you'll just let her have them…and everything that goes with it. You're both so in love it hurts to watch. So, take my mix-up as a gift, would you?"

"And Mom's flowers? How much do I owe you for those? Can you still get them to her, or should we stop by the store?" Reid mentally berated himself for not demanding a redo—free. It was the least—

"—took 'em already. It was the least I could do. I'll slip a refund under your door. I really do hope it works out for you, though. I do."

For the next two hours, he prepped the night chef's work and wrangled the question in his mind. *I have to tell her. I can't have a lie like that out there. Three months. It's just three more. By then, the awkwardness would go away. And if I tell her right away, she won't have time to say or do anything to be embarrassed about. That would help.*

Marco, the night chef, checked the kitchen as he swept in and nodded. "You're good to go. Thank you."

Reid hadn't made it to his apartment before his phone rang and his mother's face flashed on the screen. "Hi, Reid! I just had to call and thank you for the flowers. Silly, when I'll be there so soon, but they are gorgeous. That card is the sweetest thing I've ever gotten. I'll probably—"

"Frame it." They laughed as he added, "You've framed everything else I ever gave you—including that popsicle stick frame in kindygarden."

"Well, I've got to go get ready. I have a hot date with a cool dude tonight."

His groan earned him a couple of curious expressions as he hurried toward the alley behind The Pettler. "Mom, just don't.

Trust me. Don't."

"Whatever. I'll see you, soon. Love you, Reid."

It took effort, but he made himself voice it. "Love you, too, Mom."

The stairs—two at a time. He had his jacket and t-shirt off before he made it to his bedroom. A clean shirt—buttoned down for dinner, of course—waited for him. Deodorant, a fresh sweep of the comb through unruly locks. And as if penance for his earlier mistake, he scrubbed his hands again, too.

Yeah. Just procrastinating. Time to get this over with.

Wayne stepped out the back door as Reid reached the bottom of the stairs. "We okay?"

"Not going to pretend I'm not still ticked, but we're good. Mistakes happen to anyone, I guess." He turned to go, and spun back again. "Wait. How'd Mom get the card if you gave it to Kelsey?"

"Copied it down on the receipt when I wrote it out. So, I just copied that onto a card. I'm just sorry your Mom didn't get it in your writing." He held the door open wide. "Want to come in and rewrite it for her?"

Reid would have refused—started to. But Wayne added, "It took up both sides of the card in my big writing."

She'll want to frame it. I'd better. "Still got that receipt?"

Señora Rojas eyed him as he and Wayne entered the front. "We need the receipt for the sunflower delivery to Ferndale."

How she did it, she probably didn't even know. But Señora Rojas reached into the middle of a stack of invoices and pulled one out. The right one, of course. Reid groaned again as he reread the words. *I never know how to tell you how I feel about you, so I don't. But you mean everything to me. I love you. Reid.*

"If she never speaks to me again, I'm blaming you."

Reid expected Wayne's demand that he keep quiet about the mix-up, but Señora Rojas stepped forward. Cupping his face in both of her hands as if he were a little kid again, she locked her gaze with his and said, "This girl loves you. Do you hear that? Whatever you do, don't break her heart. You're not that man."

And with that, she disappeared out the door with orders for Wayne to give Reid a refund. "You don't have to do that, Wayne. Mom got her flowers. You made it right."

But Wayne pulled an envelope from his shirt pocket and tucked it into Reid's. "Let me do the right thing, okay? Wait'll Brooke hears. She'll get a laugh at her old uncle."

"Don't tell her. There's no reason to make her feel worse."

"Wor—" Wayne coughed. "Yeah. You're probably right."

As he pocketed the card next to the envelope, Reid backed away. "Pray for me, man. I can't botch this. Not now that I know she might be okay with an 'us' someday."

He'd expected another protest. He didn't get it. Wayne just nodded. Reid dashed out the front door and half-jogged down to The Prayer Room.

The wind blew a swirl of lazy leaves around his ankles as he reached for the push bar and held on. *Okay, Lord. You got this? Because I know I don't have a clue what to say or do. So, um, help here? Yeah. Help.* He tried not to add it, but the thought forced its way past his emotional defenses. *Please don't let me lose my chance.*

For the first time that week, Kelsey looked up as he entered. Reid tried to smile. Kelsey beamed. In one fluid movement, she hopped up, set her guitar in its case, and strode to his side. Without even the slightest hesitation, she wrapped her arms around him and held him close. "Thank you for the flowers. You can't—I can't—"

Reid listened, his heart breaking as she inhaled, exhaled, and tried again. "Just thanks."

He had to do something—fast. One minute he pulled her toward her usual spot, the next he had her in the back corner of the prayer closet, hoping no one would come in before he managed to make her hate him. "Every word on that card is true. I've been waiting six months to ask you out, and every day, I—" *Why couldn't I be good with words—just this time, God? Really?* Reid tried again. "It's not easy for me to tell people how I feel. But..."

"I know. You said it—in the card. Maybe you're better at writing."

Oh, Lord, help!

Once more, he tried to confess the whole mix-up without destroying any chances they might have. Complete honesty. So, he began with the prophecy, Wayne egging him on, even his mother telling him she wanted to meet this girl he wouldn't stop talking about. And Kelsey glowed with each word. That bubbly, vivacious side of her that only showed outside The Prayer Room nearly exploded with the happiness he increased by the second. *And I'll kill it in four words flat.*

"I've been *waiting* for February so I could ask you out."

"Ha! My uncle was telling me about Joan Oberton's thing about how new Christians shouldn't date for a year! I told him if that was it, you'd be mortified to do it on Valentine's Day!" And with that, her hands clapped over her mouth. A muffled, "I can't believe I just told you that."

He tried not to react, truly. But a smile formed and, before he knew it, the question followed. "So, you talked to your uncle about me?"

"Yeah. I mean, he's the closest thing I have to a dad, you know."

Might need to buy a shotgun proof... suit of armor for when he hears this. Ugh. Another glance at her showed Kelsey just beaming. *Better get it over with before she expects a proposal or something.* "Um, coming here, every day, seeing you? It's what keeps me going when I don't want to chop another carrot or fillet another fish. But..."

"That prophecy thing. What do you think about that? It sounds..."

Only then as her voice trailed off did Reid notice their hands wrapped together. He fought back the urge to hold her again and concentrated on the picture of intertwined fingers that looked oddly like a beating heart. "I don't know. At the time, I talked to a couple of people. They both said they didn't think I was obligated to 'obey' Scripture used out of context to support an idea like that. But I decided it wouldn't hurt." He gave her what he hoped wasn't too pathetic of a smile. "Lately, it's been really hard."

"I'm glad you didn't wait another three months. I thought I saw things that might mean... something. But..." Kelsey shrugged. "You don't want to assume."

"Yeah. Well, I was going to stick to it. I figured if we were what the Lord had in mind, then you'd understand come February. But..."

Her head dropped to his shoulder. "Yeah."

Reid didn't allow the warmth of her cheek on him to derail his confession, but temptation didn't make it easy. "Today something awkward happened. Telling you kind of got taken out of my hands."

Kelsey stiffened. "Huh?"

"The flowers? That note?"

How anyone could go more rigid, Reid didn't know, but she did. "What are you talking about?"

"They were for my mom." His mind corrected his earlier calculations. *Make that five words flat.* "Wayne's niece did some order mix-up thing, and you got Mom's birthday flowers... her note."

Shocked eyes, red face. Kelsey jumped to her feet. "Wha— oh, no, no, no. I did not—" She fled the prayer closet. Reid followed on her heels.

"Kelsey, wait." She didn't. "I'm not sorry it happened. Who knows how long it would have taken me to tell you?" Still, she kept going, packing the guitar with speed that he'd never seen in her. "That card said everything—well, no. But *some* of the things I've wanted to say for months."

"Yeah, right. Don't bother, Reid. I'm so—"

He caught her hands and as she tried to leave. "Kelsey, please. Listen." She paused and attempted a red-faced glance in his general direction, but the sight of tears prompted him not to force it again. "I just wonder if maybe the Lord did this. Maybe this was His way of telling me I didn't have to keep waiting for this year to be over."

"Oh, come on..."

"No, really. I was panicking all afternoon. But it worked out so right. I don't know how I would have tried to tell you anything. So..."

This time, she looked at him—really looked. "Yeah. Okay." A sigh, ragged and pain-filled. Reid ached to hold her again, but his brighter-self told him to take it easy.

One at a time, Kelsey took back her hands and reached for her guitar. Reid wrapped his fingers around the handle and gave her his best excuse for a smile. *Is this it? Awkwardness? Okay. Maybe three months after all. Just don't let her hate me. Or Wayne. It's not his fault, I guess.*

They walked to her car without a word. As usual, he settled her case in the front seat and shut the door. This time, she had the driver's door open, ready to go. Reid scrambled for something to say, but nothing seemed right. Instead, he just asked, "See you tomorrow?"

"Yeah."

Reid stepped away from the car, hands shoved in his pockets, glad he hadn't taken off his coat. Kelsey started to climb in but backed out and peered over the top of the car. "Reid?"

"Yeah?"

"Why do you carry my guitar out here every day?" She waggled a finger at him before adding, "And don't tell me because it's dark. We both know it's safe. This is Fairbury! A cop could be here in less than a minute—on foot."

Reid pressed himself against the passenger side of the car, only the vehicle separating them. "It's a few minutes with you—

outside The Prayer Room. I don't have to be quiet out here. I can just be… me." He dropped his forehead to the top of the car. "Yeah, I know. It's not the whole treating you like a sister like I said I would, but it was as close as I could get and still try to show that someday I hoped…" Oh, the words sounded so cheesy. Still, he couldn't think of anything better. "Well, I hoped you'd be more than just a sister."

"I see."

"Kelsey…"

She climbed up on the edge of the door opening and reached one hand across the top of the car. Reid caught it in his. Embarrassment still hovered in her features, laced her words, made her hand tremble. But Kelsey finally met his gaze and sighed. "Well, three months isn't *that* long if you decide you still need to wait."

And as on every day, Reid stood there watching as her taillights disappeared around the corner and into the night. *You'll wait. Wow.*

Not until he'd been inside for a good twenty minutes did Reid realize he'd forgotten to thank the Lord.

And that Kelsey had forgotten her flowers.

CHAPTER 5

A s his mother negotiated around a tractor just a couple of miles from the Brant's Corners turnoff, she gave him another curious glance, and again, said nothing. This time, Reid couldn't stand it. "What?"

"Reid, you haven't said more than a word or two since you got in the car. Just because you wrote me a nice note today, doesn't mean you're off the hook. Talk. What's bothering you?"

The reminder of the note sent him digging for the replacement. And as he handed it to her, he told the story—all of it. "Mom... I thought..."

"But she intimated that she'd wait?"

A grin formed before he could hope to repress it—just as it had *every* time he'd remembered her saying, *"Well, three months isn't that long."*

"And that's why you're taking her the flowers? Did she leave them behind on purpose?"

He shrugged. "Maybe, but I think she was just so embarrassed that she wanted out of there. Forgot them."

She didn't say it, but Reid could hear her thoughts as loudly as if she'd shouted them. "You keep thinking that."

The turn at Brant's Corners meant he'd have to direct her to a house she knew he'd only been to once. *And I could do it blindfolded.*

His mother only looked at him.

"Turn right at the first street after the market. Left at the first street after that. Third duplex on the right."

"And you've been here once?"

"Yep." *Physically. A hundred times in my head.*

As she pulled up to the house, his mother caught his arm and stopped him from bolting from the car. "Reid?"

"Yeah?"

"Ask her out. I think waiting now would just be stubborn. You've fought it this long. Fighting it when she *knows* is only going to hurt you both."

"But—"

His mother cut him off again. "No, Reid. Listen to me. The point was to concentrate on your faith for a year, right?"

"Yeah."

"Well, now you're concentrating on her already. At least you can work on your religious stuff together. That's good for relationships. Look at Uncle Mark and Emily. They've got the best marriage I've ever seen, and she always says its 'the Lord.'"

His mother might not believe... not yet. But she seemed to have a better grasp on the idea than he did. Besides, she was right. Kelsey had been a believer a lot longer than he had. Why shouldn't he learn with and from her? "Okay, Mom. Be right back."

"I'm timing you. If you're in there for less than five minutes, I'm going to march you right back."

You'd do it, too.

Still, he found himself dragging his feet all the way to the door. As he waited for her to answer his knock, he stared at the folded sticky note in the card fork. *Take it out? Leave it in?*

Too late to decide. The door opened with Kelsey standing there looking more adorable than ever. Her face flushed as she glanced down at fuzzy sleep pants and a baggy long-sleeved T-shirt. The sleeping bear on the front was encircled by the words, "Don't mess with me. I'm hibernating."

"Not a morning person?"

She grinned. "I can't believe you brought those. Come in! How'd you get here?"

A pile of unfolded laundry taunted her, but Kelsey had a hot date with a cold pint of Ben & Jerry's at the other end of the couch. "I just wish I knew if he meant it—I mean, *really* meant it."

"Um, from what you've said..." Uncle Mel's voice teetered on the edge of amusement. "He kind of said it, over and over. Guys don't do that. Especially guys like Reid. You said he doesn't talk much."

Kelsey snorted ice cream out her nose. "Ew! Ow! I blame you for nostril frostbite syndrome! Ow!!"

"I studied every single page of your coursework with you. There's no such thing. Snorting ice cream isn't illegal, but it's still stupid. Don't make a habit of it."

"Apparently..." Kelsey giggled as she wiped ice cream on her sleeve. "I already have if you knew what I did so quickly. And Reid talks like anyone if he's outside The Prayer Room. I just don't get to see him out there much, and it sounds like it'll be another three months before I do."

This earned her a resounding, "No, Kelsey. No. You ask him out. He sounds like he could use the encouragement now. Just ask him."

"But if it's a commitment to the Lord, is it right for me to do that?"

"He's already thinking about you anyway, so you guys think about the Lord together."

Before Kelsey could formulate a protest, a knock at the door saved her. "Someone's here. Landlord, maybe?"

"I'll stay on until you tell me you're good."

"Ever the over-protective uncle." But as she stood on tip-toe and peered through the little window, a burst of sunflowers shone in her porch light. "It's Reid!"

Uncle Mel laughed as he said, "And I'm out. Bye!"

Kelsey dropped her phone on the rickety old stool that served as her entry table and jerked open the door. He swept his eyes over her before grinning. "Not a morning person?"

Mortification hit hard and fast. Kelsey suspected she stood there grinning like a fool, but tried to cover it. "I can't believe you brought those. Come in! How'd you get here?"

"Mom and I are going out to dinner in Brunswick, so she—"

"Is she out...?" Kelsey saw a silhouette in a running Mazda and shoved her feet in her "outside slippers." "Be right back."

"Kelsey, she—"

But she didn't wait. Shivering in the cold, night air, she hurried to the driver's side and pleaded, cajoled, and ultimately bullied his mother out of the car and into her duplex. As she hauled her pile of laundry from the living room to her bed, Kelsey insisted they take a seat. "I won't keep you long, but I never get company, and when else will I get to meet your mom?"

Her bedroom mirror mocked her. Sleep shirt—no wonder he'd joked about not being a morning person. Ice cream on the sleeve... *And probably a bit of snot, too. Ew!*

She ripped off that shirt and grabbed for one out of the laundry pile—sweater and fuzzy sleep pants. *Great. What a way to ensure I look as* thick *as possible. Ugh.*

Still, it was better than ice cream snot. She hustled down the mini-hall again, chattering as she went. "Can I get you drinks or something?"

Reid's mom stood and held out her hand. "I'm Pat. It's so nice to meet you after all this time."

To her disgust, Kelsey blushed. A glance at Reid showed him glowing brighter than a cartoon thumb after contact with a hammer. A few stammers, another flush of red—just in case hers had faded or something—and she gave up. Reid came to her rescue. "Mom, do you have to make her convinced I'm nothing more than some obsessed guy? I'm trying to convince her that she should give me a chance, remember?"

That's all it took. Just as Kelsey dropped into one of her cute but oh-so-uncomfortable chairs Pat popped up. "Great. You do that. I'll be in the car. Don't hurry." She whispered something to Reid, gave Kelsey a great big smile, and moved toward the door. "It really is great to meet you. I hope... well, I hope to see you *very* soon."

And with that, before Kelsey could even hope to remember to stand again out of basic courtesy, Pat slipped outside and into the night. She stared at Reid. "What just happened?"

"My mother hinted, not too subtly, either, that she wants you to say yes to our invitation to join us for dinner."

"No!" The way Reid's face fell told Kelsey all she needed to know about his sincerity regarding his feelings. "I don't mean that I wouldn't like to. I would. But it's her birthday, and we'd spend the whole time with "get to know you" kind of conversation. This should be for just the two of you." A smile formed in her heart and Kelsey let it show. "Besides, call me selfish, but I'd like our first date just to be us. Is that awful?"

He shook his head. The seconds passed. Reid glanced at the door, at her, and back at the door again. "I should go."

As she followed him outside, her heart ordered him to ask him out—even if just for a coffee when he got done at The Prayer Room the next day. "I—"

"Would—" Reid shook his head. "Sorry, what were you going to say?"

All courage fled. "I just hope you have a nice time with her. Your mom seems nice—fun."

"She is. I just didn't see it until I'd done my best to ruin my life."

"Sounds like a typical teenager to me." Kelsey gave him a

quick hug. "I'm freezing. Thanks for bringing the flowers…"

His next words came out in a rush. "That 'get to know us' thing at The Prayer Room on Saturday. Want to have dinner together first?"

All shivers stopped as a warm glow filled her to her fingertips. "Definitely want that."

CHAPTER 6

K elsey met him outside **The Coventry** at five-thirty, her smile and the banana Beetle the only bright spot in an otherwise dreary, miserable day. Headlights flashed him, one after the other as cars poured into the restaurant's parking lot. Reid hopped inside and pulled the door shut tight behind him. "Whew. I think the whole town is out tonight. Glad I made reservations."

"I am under orders from Uncle Mel to make sure Marcello's isn't going to put you in trouble with your boss..." She winced. "Or your wallet."

"Ramon loves Marcello's He eats there now and then. And even if it would have been tough, I got a refund on Mom's flowers for the mix-up, so it's almost free—sort of." Reid waffled over telling her about his secret stash, but at her second glance at him under the streetlight, he decided he'd better. "Really. And besides... I've been saving date money almost since I met you."

The two-minute drive between restaurants passed before she responded. In fact, they made it inside, to their table, and ordered drinks before Kelsey asked what he meant. "Saving date money?"

Low lighting, a small bowl of full rose blooms, and soft, acoustic music set an ambiance he couldn't have dreamed of even in his dreams. *Pizza and beer—that was my idea of a nice date. No wonder Mom insisted we come here. Gotta redefine my idea of dates. Just need some less expensive ones, too.*

"—can't always be doing something expensive. Sometimes we just need to *be,* you know?"

Reid shot her a curious look before grinning. "I was just thinking that this is nice for special, but we'll need less expensive things for regular, and you say that. Glad you understand. I've gotta pay off my school bills."

"Right. But you still didn't answer about saving date money."

Well, here goes. "It probably sounds pathetic to you, but just because I decided to do the year thing, doesn't mean I remembered all the time. So many times, I'd start to ask you if you wanted to get coffee or an ice cream." He fiddled with the corner of a menu he hadn't even opened as he searched for words that didn't sound quite as pathetic as the ones forming in his mind. "So, to keep myself from going crazy, I'd take the money it would have cost and stuck it in an envelope. If you found someone before I could ask, I figured I'd have a decent savings in there. If not..."

From behind the menu, Kelsey's low murmur told him all anxiety over the flower mishap was gone. "I owe Uncle Mel an apology. He told me a guy wouldn't keep saying how glad he was that everything worked out the way it did unless he meant it." Her eyes peered at him over the top of the menu. "So, if I get a big bowl of their French onion soup and a salad, will you believe me that it's what I really want?"

"Seriously?"

Kelsey shrugged. "I... well, we're giving those testimonies and things. I just got really nervous. I don't think I should eat anything too heavy." As she lowered the menu, he saw flushing cheeks and her chewing the corner of her lip. "Forgive me?"

"As long as you don't hate me for getting a steak. Mom changed her mind last minute last night and wanted Olive Garden. I'd planned on a Santa Fe steak."

The server brought bread and took their orders. The music switched to a harp playing some song he'd heard somewhere—at Christmas, maybe. "What's this song?"

"'Greensleeves,' I think,"

The name didn't sound familiar. "Guess I was wrong." She buttered slices of bread with one eye on him, waiting. Asking. Reid accepted a proffered piece and tried to explain. "It's just that it sounds familiar—almost like Christmas, but I can't place it."

"It's the tune from 'What Child Is This?'"

"Doesn't help."

Kelsey sang a few lines until Reid caught on. "Oh! Yeah! From the pageant my mom took me to every Christmas. A shepherd always sang it." Complimenting anyone—akin to torture. Trying to compliment Kelsey—definite torture. Not doing it— inconceivable. "I love your voice."

Apparently, he'd said the right thing if the smile and the glow in her eyes meant anything. "Thanks. So," she began as if in a rush to change the subject. "Tell me how you decided to become a chef."

"You'll hear about that during my testimony. Tell me why you became a nurse."

Reid expected her not to want to talk about herself like that, but she did. Eyes sparkling, even in the dim lighting, hands waving, she told of her childhood dream of becoming a wedding planner. "I saw that movie as a kid, you know. But then in my tenth-grade biology class, this girl just dropped from her chair onto the floor. I'd taken all kinds of CPR classes and first-aid things. So, I'd be ready for any wedding emergency, of course."

"Of course."

A tap on his leg—not much of a kick but the message was clear. *Don't mess with me, bub.* Her wink told him he was already forgiven. "Everyone freaked out, of course. One girl tried swinging her arms around, but I saw this flutter of her eyelid and rolled her onto her side. I was sure it was a seizure, but she never seized. Just lay there with that eye twitch and a bit of drool. The paramedics said I did the right thing."

"What was it?"

"A seizure—absence seizure they're called. Typical can happen so quickly no one notices. But atypical are longer, so she fell." Kelsey stared off for a moment before shaking herself. "Sorry. I just never forgot what Mr. Matheson said. He said, 'You'd be a good nurse, Kelsey. You kept your cool and knew what to do. And you just did it.' Made me feel so good."

That, Reid could relate to. "I get it. That is a good feeling."

"When I told Uncle Mel, he said, 'Sounds to me like wedding planning has a rival.' And when I asked why, he said, 'Because that good feeling? You'd feel that every time you helped save a life—every time you made a scared patient or loved one feel better about what was happening.'"

Before he could formulate any kind of response, their eyes met and held. Her hand squeezed his. When had they joined hands? *When have I ever been so comfortable with a girl that I can stop thinking about her even when I don't?*

The Prayer Room nearly burst its seams with the number of people crowded into the room. Had Terry, the captain of the fire department, been available, they'd have been ordered outside. Of that, Kelsey had no doubt. The director of the ministry, Michelle Tackett, stood before the room, sharing the goal, the purpose, and the short history of just how The Prayer Room came into being.

"We have people here almost twenty-four hours a day. Even the tourists come in and visit—leave their own prayer requests on the walls." She pointed at the various clay jars around the room. "Those all have prayer requests, and we never stop praying for them."

I forget, though, Lord. Help me remember that yesterday's prayers are just as important as today's or tomorrow's. Music filled Kelsey's mind, drowning out Michelle's words. A line... two.

Lost in a prayer she couldn't have vocalized if she tried—not without her guitar, she almost missed the squeeze of Reid's hand as he was called to the front.

"—is Reid Keller. Reid came to us as a brand-new Christ-follower. His desire to learn and serve humbled me. Outside The Prayer Room, he's a driven, fun-loving guy. He'll hold his own in any argument, and asks a million questions if he thinks you're wrong." Michelle winked at him. "Yeah, you thought I didn't know that about you."

Reid shrugged. "My culinary arts teacher taught me to do that."

"But here... in this place..." She put an arm around his shoulder. "Reid becomes another man. He's quiet, reserved. People come in to pray, and he comes to sit with them—listen if they're praying aloud. He'll pray *for* them if they ask, and if he thinks they want him to but don't ask, he'll offer. Just an amazing guy."

Embarrassed, Reid tried to brush it off. "And here I thought I was just a guy." He glanced her way. "I think you should listen to her..." He gave a ruddy grin and added, "She makes me sound good."

The way the entire room laughed, Kelsey decided the town must have been gossiping about their date already.

But before Kelsey could think up a retort worthy of his reply, Michelle continued. "But folks, you've got to hear this guy's story. Too often we expect a 'Prodigal' type story when a young man comes to Jesus, but this guy... Well, I'll let him tell it."

For months, she'd wanted to know more about Reid's past—what had sent him to prison, how he'd found Jesus, how he'd become a chef—but the purpose of The Prayer Room was prayer rather than fellowship. Their few minutes chatting by her car each evening, interacting at other events, or texting on a weekend hadn't been conducive to asking a rather personal question. Now she'd finally learn his story.

Reid stood behind the mic, his eyes roaming the room in what appeared to be an unexpected case of stage fright. But at the sight of her, he smiled. A few chuckles rippled around the room, and he shrugged. "I defy anyone to look at her and not smile. Okay. I had a moment there. I got up here and tried to figure out how to talk about *me* and froze. But it's not about me, is it?"

Oh, man. If I weren't half in love with him already, I would be now.

"This is about *Jesus* and what *He* did in me. Here goes. So, I had a pretty typical American childhood. Little league, campouts in the backyard, and teenage angst." A shake of the head—of his voice. Reid shrugged. "I made a lot of stupid choices in high school, but doing drugs wasn't one of them. Got drunk a few times, but I didn't like the way I felt afterwards. Just figured drugs would be ten times worse. But then I found out just how much a desperate kid would pay for the smallest bit of meth."

At those words, Kelsey froze. *Don't... no... no... no...*

"—started dealing in tenth grade. By halfway through my junior year, I was making more money each month than my mom was." He tossed her a sheepish look and shrugged. "I was one of the few successful ones. I dropped out, convinced I'd have a drug empire before I hit thirty. I dreamed of mansions, a nice home for my mom, cars... the works. And I was on my way, too."

She couldn't listen anymore. But despite ordering her feet to flee, Kelsey sat rooted to the chair, trapped by words she didn't want to hear. *Why? Just... why?*

"Six days after my twenty-first birthday, I found out the cops knew all about me. They waited until they had enough proof to nail the case and I went to prison. Five-year sentence.

"Look, when you're a scrawny kid who looks more like fifteen than twenty-one, prison is..." He gave Michelle an apologetic look. "Sorry, I don't know what else to call it. It was my idea of hell. I didn't think anything could be worse."

Well, it could. You could have been your customer. You could have been lying on a slab in a morgue. In her mind, she'd screamed the words. But Reid kept talking as if he hadn't heard a thing. *Why don't you listen? You sold drugs to innocent kids! How could you do that?*

"—met a guy inside. He'd been there for a long time—repeat

offender. He became kind of a mentor to me. Told me to get my GED. So, I did. He protected me when I would have become bate."

From the crowd, someone called, "What's that?"

"Recruited to a prison gang. It's spelled b-a-t-e... like on probate for the gang." A shudder—Kelsey watched one ripple over him. "Guys, look. I don't know how to explain it, but inside, you don't get to make that choice. And it was coming. But Harv—the guy I told you about. He protected me. It got me bumped into an anti-recidivism program. And as part of that program, we had to attend group sessions. We had choices, but I took the religious one because I figured if I said a few things about wanting God and to change, I'd get a pass."

No longer did Kelsey regret not eating more at dinner. By that point, she only wished she hadn't eaten at all. Her stomach churned as two sides of herself began to war against each other. *You'd forgive him if he'd murdered someone.*

No... that's the problem. Drug dealers are murderers!

Now you're just being judgmental. Jesus died for those sins. He's paid his debt to society, and the Lord paid his debt for sin. It's done.

Doesn't mean I have to like it.

So what? Now he's not good enough for you?

That thought snapped her out of the spiraling swirl of doom. *Okay, Lord. Help me be honest with him, though. He needs to know it's a problem I'll struggle with.*

Reid's voice broke through her thoughts. "Who knew my trying to cheat the system would change my life for the better?" He swept the room with a rueful look, and when his eyes met hers, he faltered. Confusion replaced the eager expression he'd worn.

"Even Harv told me to watch out for those 'religious nuts.' He said once they 'reeled me in' that I'd never really be 'one of *them.*' They just wanted numbers and more money from their people."

A few murmurs of protest rippled around her. A couple of men growled, "Not true." A woman wept. "I'd be the biggest outcast of them all, then, but no one ever makes me feel less-than." She choked back the words when her eyes landed on Kate Whyte. "Almost no one, anyway. There's always someone who feels they were born saved."

Reid nodded as they spoke. "Yeah. That's what I tell him. See, I still write him. And so far, I can still say no one in the church has ever asked me for or made me feel pressured to give anything. It'll happen someday—either out of need or because the church is full of messed up people like me. I mean, aren't we all in some ways? That's what my Bible says anyway. It's what keeps me from feeling like I don't belong when I meet people who have probably never deliberately broken a law in their lives."

He's talking to you. Now how do you feel? Is he right? Do you judge him and feel better than him because your sins are all nice and neatly hidden where only the Lord knows about them or what?

When the testimony ended, she didn't know. Kelsey sat there, tears streaming down her face faster than she could mop up the mess. By the time Reid reached her and put an arm around her shoulder, she didn't even know if she cried for repentance over her own hypocrisy or because a fresh wave of loss hit her at the incessant reminder that Reid had been one of *those* guys. He'd sold drugs to inexperienced, unsuspecting kids who just wanted to know what it was like. He could have killed people with them.

Just like that creep who killed Kenny.

CHAPTER 7

With the doors of The Prayer Room locked, and a burger feast spread out on chairs between them, Reid waited for Kelsey to finish food he'd nearly had to force her to order. As he waited, he prayed. *Don't know what happened, but it's not good. Michelle said once that everyone has some "unpardonable sin," as if God blew it when He said He'd wash them* all *away. Maybe drugs are hers.* Protest welled up in him. *But I never actually* did *drugs.*

Kelsey wiped her mouth, the burger only half-eaten, and sank back against the chair. "We have to talk."

A crass saying he hadn't used since junior high tried to surface, but Reid stuffed it back down and simply said, "I figured."

A word—two—five? He couldn't tell just how many she'd actually attempted to speak. One second she'd taken a deep breath and rattled off a few incoherent words and the next, tears poured again. She might hate him now for all he knew, but Reid couldn't stand to see raw pain without at least attempting comfort—even if it did mean she pushed him away.

But she didn't. As he moved to the chair on the other side of her, Kelsey clung to him and sobbed. Between snorts, sniffles, and guttural wails that broke his heart, words emerged. "—Kenny.— little brother.—first time.—OD'd.—organ failure."

It's all he needed to know drugs most definitely were the

issue. "I'm so sorry."

"How could you do it?" She sat up, almost glaring at him through the still-watery eyes. Accusation etched every feature. "You gave drugs to kids like Kenny! How?"

For the first time, the answer he'd always used to justify didn't comfort him anymore. "They were going to get them somewhere. I figured, why not from me?"

"And some jerk like you gave a kid, one who didn't know how to even use the stuff right, over a hundred fifty milligrams of methamphetamine."

I'm a jerk now because I used... Something deep in his spirit ordered him not to become defensive. Then he heard the real pain behind her words. "How old was he?"

"Sixteen." Streaks of blackish brown smeared across her cheeks like war paint. "We still don't know where he got the syringes—"

"Wait, he *injected* a point and a half of meth? The first time?"

Kelsey nodded, her eyes fixated on the floor in front of her or possibly her shoe. "He was a scrawny kid—short. Too much. And that stupid dealer *knew* it was his first time. He could have *told* him, but he didn't."

The hims jumbled in Reid's mind, but the meaning—clear. "Well, a smart dealer would have."

Her head shot up. "What? Like dealers care."

"A lot don't. You're right. But a smart dealer tells you to find someone who knows what they're doing." The incredulous look she shot at him prompted a reply before she could challenge him. "Kelsey, dealers want repeat customers. Frankly, they want people addicted. It's good business. Dead customers don't buy more."

But Kelsey shook her head. "That's not what this guy said when I found him. He said there was always someone else to buy."

Stomach churning, Reid nodded. "He's right. There is. But that doesn't make it good business. I bet he used. Can't believe he talked to you, though."

Her face flushed. "He didn't know who I was—not until his trial. I found him, talked to him, made him think I wanted some, bought it—fifty bucks for that point whatever!" She must have seen his admiration because she ducked her head. "Then I took it to the police, gave it to them, and told them where I found him. I thought they could match the batch and prove it was him."

Even as she spoke, Reid shook his head. "How long after?"

"Yeah. That was the problem. It was two months—new batch. Still, they got him with my testimony."

He'd never heard such venom from her—didn't know she had it in her.

The furnace kicked on. A metallic *ting* followed by a muffled *bang* somewhere below as metal expanded marked another round of silence between them. Reid rubbed her back, waiting. Kelsey wrung her hands together as she worked through emotions he couldn't even imagine. A whispered question finally broke the muffled whoosh of hot air through the vents. "Did any of your customers die?"

Denial rose up in him—defensive, adamant denial. But Reid chose frank honesty. "I don't know. I never heard of anyone." When she gazed at him as if to determine if he spoke truth or a lie, he added. "They didn't even try to pin anything like that on me."

"Why didn't he just tell Kenny how to use it? It's basic protocol. You never give people any kind of drug without basic dosage—"

Reid couldn't help a smile. "Kelsey." She glared at him. "No, really. Listen to yourself. You're thinking like a nurse. That dealer wanted a buck. He only cared about that buck right then. Probably to justify using himself. He sounds like a real loser."

"You would have told him? You would—?"

"I would have told him to have an experienced friend there."

Her shoulders slumped. "Kenny was a good kid. He didn't have any experienced friends."

She'd hate his next response, but Reid chose to stick to truth.

Just don't let her hate me more than she does already. With that prayer shooting heavenward, Reid blurted it out. "Then I'd have introduced him to someone if I could. But if he insisted on buying without it, well…"

"You'd have sold it to him."

He nodded. "I would have. At least he'd have good stuff from me. I didn't sell bad ice. But he'd buy it from anyone if he was that determined, so I'd have sold it."

Jumping up from the chair, Kelsey ranted as she began pacing. "Why did he have to be so curious about everything? He'd be alive if he hadn't gotten curious about what the big deal was." Mid-stride, she whirled to face him and almost lost her balance. Reid jumped up to catch her and found himself gazing into her eyes, lost and aching in the pain he found there.

"Would you today—if you had it? Would you sell it again?"

"Never." With his thumb, Reid wiped away a tear. "Yesterday, I would have said because it's illegal. And that would have been enough for me now. Today…"

She searched his face for some answer, inching a little closer with each second. Kelsey dropped her head to his chest and shuddered as she whispered, "And today…?"

Reid cradled her face in both hands and waited until she found the strength, courage—he hoped *love*—to meet his gaze. "Today I couldn't after seeing how much it hurts you. I guess I see why it's illegal, finally." He shook his head. "No… that's not right. I *knew* why. Now I *feel* it."

Her hands slipped around his neck, and she would have kissed his cheek, but Reid chose to alter the target. Over six months of waiting. He'd never shown that kind of self-control. *Worth every second of it*, his heart shouted as Kesley rocked back on her heels before curling in a ball against his chest. *Does life get any better?*

A muffled murmur dashed cold water against his overconfidence. "This is still going to be hard for me. My head says sin is sin. The hole Kenny left in my heart says there's a special place in hell for drug dealers."

It might drive her from him again, but Reid found himself unable *not* to say the words burning in his heart. "Even those washed by the blood of Jesus?"

The scent of wood smoke and cinnamon candy wrapped comforting, nostalgic arms around her as Kelsey burst into Uncle Mel's living room, calling for him. The little man with his plaid flannel sleep pants and Rockland Warriors t-shirt appeared with a cup of hot chocolate—it couldn't be anything else—sloshing over his feet. He yelped and asked, "What's wrong?" at the same time.

"Your feet!"

But Uncle Mel had already begun to pull off his socks one-handed. "Never mind them. Nothing a little aloe can't fix."

Kelsey attempted another protest, but the man had a bottle of aloe in hand and had led her to the couch before she could finish it. "I didn't mean to startle you," she ended with a lame attempt at an apology."

"Yes, yes. You are just the foulest thing ever to live and should be tortured for your crimes." He winked as he squeezed another dollop of the greenish gel on his foot. "There, do you feel better?"

"Do you?"

Uncle Mel's *look*. No parent on the planet had ever perfected it better than her stand-in for a father and mother all rolled into one. They sat, staring at one another in a silent impasse. Kelsey capitulated first. "Reid... his prison record?"

"Yes. You knew about that."

"Yeah. He went to prison for dealing drugs!"

With feet propped on the coffee table and a twinkle in his eye, Uncle Mel nodded. "I know. Would you mind wiping up the chocolate and bringing me what's left?"

She'd made it as far as the paper towels before his words, "I know," registered. "Wait! How did you know?"

"I looked it up when you first mentioned it." As she handed

him his cup, Uncle Mel added, "Didn't you ever think to do an internet search?"

She hadn't. Kelsey dropped into the chair she'd done her homework in, sat in with the letter from Rockland University welcoming her as the newest "Warrior," wept in as the officers came to tell them about Kenny. "I guess I knew stuff like that was public record, but I never even thought..." She scowled at him as a second revelation dawned. "Why didn't you tell me?"

"I figured maybe the Lord kept you ignorant of that particular fact for a reason. Who was I to interfere?"

"You've interfered in enough things over the years," Kelsey snapped.

"Kels..."

"Why did it have to be drugs?"

And at those words, Uncle Mel held out his arms and pulled her close as she leaped through the air separating them. "I have a theory about that..."

"You and your theories." But despite the asperity in her tone, Kelsey snuggled close and allowed the familiar warmth and comfort that only Uncle Mel could offer to work its wonders in her attitude. "What's this one?"

"I think the Lord allowed you to remain blind to the one area that you couldn't be objective about until your heart was knit too closely with Reid's to sever easily. In the beginning, you might not have given him a chance, but I know how much you care about him."

"I think I love him," she whispered. "I don't think it would hurt so much if I didn't."

Something that sounded like, "You're probably right," or "I was totally right" rumbled into her ear as she pressed her cheek against his chest and inhaled the faintest traces of his Irish Spring soap.

"Kelsey?"

"Hmmm?"

Uncle Mel cleared his throat in that way he always did before giving her a bit of a reprimand. "Remember how that counselor said that the first true step to healing would be to forgive the dealer who gave Kenny the drugs?"

Heart sinking, Kelsey sighed. "Yeah. I know."

"I didn't push. I thought it was best left between you and the Lord. Then you stopped talking about it, so I allowed myself to believe you'd finally managed." Gentle hands stroked her hair and soothed an ache she sometimes forgot she carried—for a while, anyway. "Well, now's the time to do it. If you don't, you'll eventually drive Reid away. I don't think you want to do that."

"Do you really think—?"

But Uncle Mel didn't let her finish. "You know it, girlie. Just be *willing* to let the Lord work the change in you. He can handle the rest without your help. Give Him this broken piece of your heart and watch the miracles He can do with it."

"I know, but—"

"Willing, sweetheart. You just need to be willing."

And the more he talked, the more her heart softened until words formed. Uncle Mel stopped mid-sentence, stood, and retrieved a guitar from the closet. "Let's hear it."

A few sour notes followed as she worked to get the instrument back in tune, but as she finished, the words tumbled forth, awkward, jumbled, discordant, but after a couple of rounds, she found a rhythm.

Teach me to trust and be willing,
The son who obeys.
Even when I've failed You
May I turn back to Your ways.
A heart yielded is all I must give.
So today I'm confessing.
For You alone, I live
And give thanks for this blessing...

Of You... only You...
Make me be willing...
And yielded to You...

The crackling of the wood in the fireplace, the ragged breath of the man she loved most in the world beside her, an occasional note plucked as she sat patient, waiting for the Lord to whisper His Word into her heart.

And then it came. A verse she'd never understood as a girl. *"For this reason I say to you, her sins, which are many, have been forgiven, for she loved much, but he who is forgiven little, loves little."*

"I bet Reid thinks he's been forgiven of a lot more sins than I have."

Uncle Mel nodded. "Probably. We get that way about things."

A sigh... first of discouragement and then of gratitude. "He's wrong."

CHAPTER 8

The last two hours before leaving work had been difficult for months, but during the week after the floral fiasco it escalated to torture. Reid's usual tricks of working slower to drag out every second—failed. He had all his work and part of Marco's done before the night chef even arrived. And still, he waited. The scent of the Friday night prime rib roasting usually drove him crazy, but not that day. He stood there, wiping the prep table…*again,* just for something to do.

Movement in the corner of his eye caught his attention. Reid stared at his boss, confused. "Ramon?"

"Can you come with me, please?"

Nothing about Ramon's stance, his manner, his tone—nothing should have prompted the dread that washed over him. But as he stepped into Ramon's office and saw Officers Crane and Tesdall standing there, he knew. Something had happened. *And now I have to prove I didn't do it.*

The injustice of that idea tried to stir anger and defiance in him, but something Harv had said once fought back. *"You'll be the guilty one whenever anything happens. Don't let that make you stupid. When you've done stupid things, that's a consequence. Doing your time doesn't take away consequences. It just means you've paid one of the debts. Just one. When you let yourself get worked up over suspicions, you make dumb mistakes. Don't do it, or you'll be back here with a longer sentence. Don't ever want to see you on this side of the bars again."*

"Reid?"

He jerked his head up and met Ramon's eyes. "Yeah?"

"Did you hear us? You zoned out there."

A gesture told him to be seated. The desk that separated him and the officers from Ramon held nothing at all but a piece of paper and a plastic-wrapped packet. Reid's heart sank with him as he dropped into the chair. "Where'd you get that?"

"Interesting question."

Reid whipped his head around to look up at Officer Tesdall. "Why?"

"They found it in your locker, Reid."

Cold, nauseating sweat soaked him in an instant. Unable to take his eyes off the packet, Reid shook his head like a dog out of water. "It's gonna sound lame and all that, but it's not mine. I've never seen it before." There, he found the self-control to stop shaking and meet Ramon's gaze. "I don't know where that came from. I'd never disrespect you by bringing drugs in here. I'd never risk my program by going near the stuff again." He ached to mention the Lord, Kelsey—how he wouldn't ever risk his relationship with either of them for drugs. Ever. But Reid knew better.

"I know you wouldn't, but they have to talk to you. As for me, I have to suspend you until the investigation is over. It's in the contract with the program, or I wouldn't." The man looked ready to vomit. "I hope you understand."

"Yeah. You gotta do it, or we're both..." Reid closed his eyes and fought for control. "Yeah. Thanks."

Ramon didn't stop there. "You'll get your salary, but if you are prosecuted for this, I have to demand that back. If you agree, read and then sign this."

The paper slid across the desk before Reid could process Ramon's words. A pen appeared. He read the words in a daze.

Suspended with pay pending criminal charges. Fired and money to be returned in ninety days if prosecuted for the charge of possession of an illegal substance with intent to distribute. His head snapped up. "Are—?"

"If you agree to the terms, I suggest you sign it now. They need to take you in for questioning."

But if I got it plead down to possession only, I wouldn't lose my job. Wouldn't have to pay it back. You could be out a lot... Understanding hit hard and fast. It ripped through his emotions until only the tiniest thread of self-control kept him from sobbing.

Reid stuck out his hand and met Ramon's pointed stare. "Thanks for this—for *all* of this."

"You didn't do this. I know it. Now let them prove it." Reid's lack of confidence in the police's commitment to proving him innocent must have shown because Ramon stood and came around the desk to give him a rather awkward hug. "These aren't Rockland cops, Reid. They care about everyone in Fairbury—even you."

They didn't cuff him or flank him on either side as they escorted him outside. Tesdall gave Crane a questioning look, and she scanned the area. "Yeah. Let's do it."

"Do what?" Reid did a visual sweep himself but saw nothing but a bunch of curious onlookers as they drove past. "What?"

"Why don't you walk down to the station. We'll see you in about five, okay?"

"What?" He stared, confused. "Why aren't you taking me in?"

Officer Tesdall stepped a bit closer and dropped his voice a little. "Look. Right now, you're just a person of interest we need to question. So, if you walk away from here without our escort, no one knows about it until necessary."

"Can I take ten, then?" That he asked surprised even him, but Reid knew that if he passed The Prayer Room and Kelsey saw him, he'd have to explain.

This time, Officer Crane spoke up. "Go tell Kelsey about it. Sure." Both Reid and Tesdall gave her quick looks. With an exasperated huff, she threw up her hands. "This is Fairbury, guys. Everyone knows."

The cruiser rolled out of the parking lot, but Reid stood there at the side, praying. Well, he *thought* it counted as praying, despite the words that refused to come. As he turned to head to the police station, a verse he'd read that morning in Jeremiah sprung to mind—a promise that the Lord would defend Israel. *Will you defend me, too? Will you plead my cause? I don't ask for revenge, just proof of my innocence.*

Old movies with their scenes of men marching through dusty streets to be hanged played out in his mind to the tune from *The Good, the Bad, and the Ugly.* Reid crossed the street and paused at The Pettler's door. A step inside would only take a moment, and maybe Wayne should know.

Señora Rojas greeted him. "Oh! Reid. You are a good boy—stopping to get your *querida* a rose, maybe?"

He couldn't have said no if he wanted to. Craning his neck to see through the narrow crack in the curtain that separated the shop from the workroom, Reid waited for the woman to choose the perfect rose. After all, it wasn't like she'd let him make such a momentous decision himself! But Wayne's back was to him. "I'll just say hi to Wayne while you ring that up, okay?"

She whirled in a movement more expected of a dancer than a shop manager. "Is everything okay, Reid?"

"It will be. Just let me know—"

"You pay with your rent. I'll have Wayne bring you a bill. Here. Take it." She handed him one, long-stemmed rose. Too dark to be pink, too light to be red.

Aren't there rules about colors? Red's for true love or something? What's pink? And is this like somewhere in between?

"Reid?" Wayne stood in the doorway, staring at him. "You're off early…" The man's face softened at the sight of the rose. "Good choice."

No, Wayne. I didn't get fired.

"Thank you. Now let him go—"

But Reid cut off Señora Rojas. "I'm on my way to the police station, Wayne. They found stuff in my locker."

"What?" Wayne and Señora Rojas gave each other sharp glances before turning back to him. Wayne found is voice again first. "Yours?"

"No. But it looks bad—being in my locker, my record." To his disgust, his voice cracked as Reid added, "And now I have to go tell Kelsey…"

But Wayne moved to his side, clapped a hand on his shoulder, and led him from the building. "Give the girl a chance. She cares about you. She's not going to dump you over circumstantial evidence."

If I was only that confident…

Still, Wayne's reassurances did buoy his spirits as he hurried down to The Prayer Room. The gentle sounds of plucked strings greeted him as he entered, but Kelsey didn't sing. She just sat there, eyes closed as random chords played as if of their own accord. Her eyes opened—a smile.

"Hey… you're early." Kelsey glanced down at his hand and back up at him. "Is that for me?"

The rose! Reid stepped forward and offered it. "I—"

"Thanks. It's beautiful." A kiss to his cheek—it stabbed like a dagger in his heart.

I'm going to break yours. He stood there, aching to take her hand, hold her, anything. But it seemed like a cheap shot to soften any defenses she might have before he ruined her day. "Um, there's a problem."

"If you're breaking up with me already, my Uncle Mel's going to have something not-very-nice to say to you."

Teasing. She was so confident in him—trusted him enough that she didn't think for a moment that he'd hurt her. And now he had to. "I can't imagine ever breaking up with you, but you might…" He closed his eyes and swallowed the lump of pain that threatened to choke him. "They found stuff in my locker today—at work. It's not mine, Kelsey. Even Ramon knows that. But he had to suspend me with pay until I'm cleared. I'm on my way to talk to the cops now."

Her expression shifted from teasing to disbelieving. "Stuff?" Understanding dawned. "What? How—?" Kelsey clamped her mouth shut. "You're innocent, but the police want to talk to you?"

"They have to, Kelsey. It was found in *my* locker."

"And you're suspended. Doesn't that kill your place in the program?"

Reid shook his head. "No. Only if I get fired. I can get laid off without penalty, but not fired." This time, he reached for her hand—took it. She didn't squeeze back, but she didn't pull away, either. "Ramon's still paying me. He knows I'm innocent. Do you have any idea how good that makes me feel?" *Do you have any idea how much I need you to be as confident?*

But she only sighed. "I bet. Okay, well, come by when you're done. I'll stay through your time for you."

So many words ached to be set free, but Reid just nodded and choked out a thanks. At the door, he turned and saw her staring at the rose. "I didn't do this, Kelsey."

She didn't reply.

CHAPTER 9

The interrogation room—small, but less institutional than the one he'd sat in eight years earlier. The faces of the officers—infinitely less intimidating. Officer Tesdall had disappeared, but an even younger man, Officer Granger, sat beside Officer Crane and eyed him with curiosity. Chief Varney stuck his head in the door. "Judith, I've got a lawyer on the way for him. Ramon called and said to make it happen."

Officer Crane nodded. "Sure thing, Chief." She turned to him. "Well, this could take a bit. Would you like something to drink? Water? I've got change for the machine if you'd rather have soda."

"Can't afford soda. Water would be nice."

"I've got change—"

But Reid shook his head and tried to explain. "Can't afford a dentist. So, I'm careful what I eat or drink until my six-month mark. Then I get dental and vision added to my benefits." He didn't add his next thought. *But if you guys arrest me, I'll get fired, and all the matching funding for my loan repayments disappears. I'll be worse off than ever.*

A pricking in his spirit shifted that idea. *Okay, financially, I will be. I'm still better off, Lord. I know that. Thank you.*

"Do you mind if we get some of the preliminary stuff down for the record to save time?" Officer Crane gave him a rather understanding smile. "Just name, age, address, workplace—stuff

421

like that? We won't ask any questions related to the case."

"Sure."

And it began. Name, date of birth, address, next of kin, employer, terms of his program. Reid felt an odd sense of déjà vu as he rehashed the same conversation he'd had with Kelsey a couple of nights prior. "I'm one of the pilot cases in the Freedom in Education program." His heart sank at what his caseworker would think when she heard about it.

"And what does this program do?" Judith Crane nodded at a recorder on the table. "For the record."

"Well, they take prisoners who demonstrate initiative and a desire to make a permanent change in their lives and guide them in career training. We even got a field trip to check out different types of businesses and career tracks to get a feel for what we wanted. When I watched a chef make this amazing sauce out of just a few ingredients, I knew. I wanted that."

"So, they trained you to be a chef?" Officer Granger apologized for the interruption but asked one more question. "Did you get a certificate or…?"

Reid told about the online classes he took to fill the general education requirements for his AA degree. "Once I finished my sentence—that's part of the program. No parole. They want you to be able to go where you need to for school and everything. Once I finished, I went to the Illinois Institute of Art in Chicago."

"And how did you pay for that?"

Again, he launched into how the Freedom in Education program worked. From the sponsors who provide the money at low-interest rates, to the free housing provided by volunteers, to the other sponsors who match all repayments. "I graduated from there, two years after I got out of prison, with my AAS and thirty-thousand dollars in debt. If I am not fired from my job, they'll match dollar for dollar. If I am, I have to pay back all of it myself." He met Officer Crane's gaze and held it. "As you can imagine, this is not a good scenario for me on that score, either."

"So, you can become a chef for thirty thousand dollars?"

Officer Granger whistled. "Seems cheap."

"I got about fifteen thousand in grants, so more like forty-five if you don't have to pay room and board. Still, it cost the state more for me to be in prison for three years than this cost me. They're trying to get it so people can have early releases if they get in this program. Put the cost of their final year or two toward education instead of upkeep and free up prison space."

He could see it—by the way they exchanged glances and the relaxing of their features, these cops were impressed. *Good. Maybe I'll get a chance.*

The lawyer appeared, asked for a private consultation, spent ten minutes trying to convince Reid to confess now, and left when Reid fired him. He stuck his head out the door and called for Officer Crane. "Might as well come in. I trust you more than that guy."

"Decided you were guilty?" She grabbed a fresh bottle of water as she passed a mini fridge and headed his way. "Yeah. It happens. Sorry."

"When you blow it, you have to be ready for the consequences." It hurt to say it, but Reid had found that it helped, too. "I blew it. Most people who do time go back. I have to prove myself again."

And with that, the tone shifted. Officer Crane became focused—direct. "Okay, how did two grams of high-grade, supposedly, meth end up in your locker at The Coventry?"

"Wish I knew."

Officer Granger eyed him. "Oh?"

"Figure of speech, Granger. Cut it out." She turned back to Reid with her next question. "So, you deny that you purchased the meth and stored it in your locker at work?"

"I do. Any idiot who did that deserves what he gets. That's probably five hundred in street value—at least. Bet it's higher than it was eight years ago. Anyway, would you put a stack of twenties in your locker and leave it unlocked?"

The officer added a couple of lines to her notes as she added, "Yeah, we were wondering about it being unlocked. Why is that?"

"This is Fairbury. Who's going to steal anything? I mean, c'mon. Someone *put* something in there. And also, this is me. I don't have anything anyone could want. I don't have anything valuable, and I leave my money in the bank where we hope it's safe." Reid considered the wisdom of asking and decided he needed to. "How'd you know it was there, anyway? Seems like a weird place to search for drugs?"

"Well…"

Then it hit him. "Oh. Wait. You heard there was a packet in town, and who else has a record for dealing?"

"Nope." Crane eyed him for a moment, consulted a file, and leaned back in her chair, dropping the pen as she did. "We nailed a guy with another packet. He cooperated for a reduced charge."

"And he said I had some?"

She flipped open the file, searched for a moment, and found the line she wanted. "His words were, 'the guy at The Coventry— average height, brown hair, curly.' So, we go to The Coventry, get permission to search, open your locker, you fit that description…"

"Yeah, and so does the manager, Mike, and one of the bus boys."

Granger leaned forward and locked eyes with him. "But they don't have all that meth in *their* lockers."

Each quarter hour that passed increased her panic by a factor of ten. She'd listened to his news with, what she hoped, was dispassionate objectivity. Well, she hoped it *looked* like it. But as he'd disappeared from view, her nerves calmed a little. *In his locker, Lord. He's not that stupid, right?*

But an hour passed. Two. And during that time, Kelsey's confidence wavered. With trembling fingers, she pulled out her guitar, tuned it, and began to pray. Line after non-or-half-rhyming lines that made little sense wobbled out into the room. A woman came in to pray. Kelsey stopped her futile attempts to sing and just played with quiet, soft notes until the woman left again. An hour and a half.

She composed a text. JUST CHECKING IN ON YOU. EVERYTHING OKAY? NEED A LAWYER? A second read prompted a bit more confidence. *There. That's supportive, isn't it?*

She zipped another one to Uncle Mel. REID NEEDS PRAYER. LAW TROUBLE.

Half an hour after the first text, she called. It went to voicemail. "Getting concerned. Okay, I'm worried. Praying. Do I need to send a lawyer? Uncle Mel might know someone…"

Another half hour. Half an hour of switching from slow to even slower, and back to slow again as her fingers tried to pray for him. But as the silence from him and from Uncle Mel grew longer, stronger, her mind began to doubt, to question. *Maybe he's guilty. Maybe they arrested him. Maybe…*

Prayer failed. She tried, but her fingers wouldn't move, her heart couldn't sing. So, with a vacuum cleaner in one hand, a trash bag in the other, and a dust cloth dangling from her scrub pocket, she worked from the left of the door, counterclockwise around the room, picking up crumpled sticky notes, candy wrappers, and tissues. She dusted, vacuumed, and made the room shine.

Still no word from Reid.

Uncle Mel called first. "What's wrong, sweetheart? You said Reid's in trouble with the law? What'd he do?"

"They found something in his locker at work—the police. Drugs, obviously. How did the police know there was anything there?"

And with his characteristic calm, Uncle Mel flung out half a dozen scenarios where an innocent person with a prior record would be the first choice for questioning. "But Kels, listen. He has to be innocent. No one would hide drugs in a work locker. You have no true privacy. Your employer holds that power."

"I know. In my head, I know. But it's been almost three—no,

over three hours. Why would they keep him that long?"

"They have to be thorough, Kelsey." Uncle Mel started to say something else and stopped mid-sentence. "No, no. Backup." A huff of a sigh filled the phone. "Lord, we have a situation. Reid is in trouble, and Kelsey needs a reminder of how You change people from the inside out. Please help them both and help us all know what we need to do to support them. This we ask you, Jesus. Amen."

It took a second… five. But Kelsey managed to add, "Amen."

She promised to call when she heard. But as she disconnected, the fears that had taken root during their prayer grew into an image—that of her brother lying, *dying* in the hospital bed, begging her never to take drugs. *"It was so stupid. Don't do it, Kels."*

That image held her captive until she couldn't breathe. Scribbling a prayer request for Reid, she slapped it on the wall of the prayer closet, stowed away her guitar, and locked the building. She dashed to her car, a sob in her heart as she realized she couldn't remember the last time she'd had to load up her guitar herself.

I can't do it, Lord. Not now. A silent whisper in her heart added, *Maybe not ever.*

CHAPTER 10

The Prayer Room—locked again. For the third day in a row, he'd shown up just past two-thirty, and the previous watchman had given up, locked the door, and left. Without evidence of a more substantial nature, the police hadn't charged him. No fingerprints, although they claimed he could have used the plastic kitchen gloves, no witnesses who saw him putting the drugs in there, and only the vague description from a man who now refused to identify Reid as the one who had purchased the drugs.

As Reid unlocked the door, Wayne drove past. He lifted a half-hearted wave and slipped inside. The silence tore at his heart. *Remind me what the minister said, Lord. About how pain makes it hard to trust. This isn't her fault, but it still hurts.*

The silence tore a deeper hole. In seconds, with the help of the sound system and a tablet, Anthem Lights filled the room with soft, harmonious strains of "In Christ Alone." Reid stood there, allowing the words to soothe and comfort before heading to the closet.

He read each sticky note, each heartfelt plea to the Lord. Read and prayed. Sometimes, asking the Lord to answer each one seemed an exercise in futility. *Why did God need us to agree with one another in our requests?* But since the interrogation, since the police still hadn't found the owner of the drugs, a need—a *craving*—for the prayers of his brothers and sisters consumed him.

And then he saw it. Surrounded by half a dozen other yellow sticky notes, familiar writing. Large, bubbly letters—a request for him. *She cared enough to try. I guess I just need to keep waiting.*

A teen came in—discouraged and uncertain. Reid just sat there, waiting. "Aren't you going to tell me how God makes everything great and stuff?"

"I think He does, yes. I just think we expect great now instead of later."

"Later?" If Reid hadn't seen the boy's lip quiver, he might not have heard the fear in the bitten-out words. "Like we have to wait until we *die* for it to get better?"

How to explain the confused jumbles of his thoughts? Reid didn't know. But he had to try. "Well, yeah. We do have to die for it to get better. That's what being a Christian is, isn't it? The stuff that isn't right and pure dies, and Jesus makes us alive again?"

"You bought the whole package, didn't you? Just say a prayer, sing some I-love-Jesus songs, and everything'll work out right."

Again, Reid heard pain behind the derision. "I wish that were true, but it doesn't seem to be the way things worked for the guys who wrote the Bible. I mean, they prayed. Sure. They sang some I-love-Jesus songs in prison, once. Yeah, that worked out all right. But later, not so much. They all suffered from what I hear."

"So, suffer here, die, and then it gets better?" The kid jumped up as if to go. "No wonder some churches teach that suicide is a ticket to hell. Otherwise, their members would just off themselves to get it over with."

A clenching in his gut told Reid to keep trying. "I'm Reid, by the way."

The kid whipped his head around and pierced Reid with his gaze. "The guy with the drugs? We heard about how you got arrested."

"Yeah… but that was eight years ago and before I cared what

God thinks about things."

"You think God cares—wait." The boy's eyes shifted to suspicion. "Eight years ago? I thought Friday…"

The one problem with Fairbury—no privacy or even any hope of it. So, knowing anything he said would likely be repeated with embellishment and enough censure that it probably wouldn't even resemble the original statement, Reid tried for a simple explanation. "Drugs were found in my unlocked locker at The Coventry—a big haul of it. The police did not arrest or charge me with anything because there's no evidence that I am connected to them. And I'm not."

"But they questioned you?"

"They'd have been lousy cops if they didn't. Just because it was in my locker, doesn't mean it's mine. Any fool knows better than to do something like that. *But* not even to question me? Crazy stupid." He tried again to make a friend of the kid. "Hey… oh. Didn't get your name. Sorry."

"Dylan."

"Well, Dylan. I'd be a jerk if I didn't throw this out there just once." Reid waited for Dylan to show some sign of attentiveness before he continued. "Drugs aren't worth it. Even if they weren't illegal, they're not worth it. And I made a lot of money—still not worth it. If you'd seen the things I have, you'd know what I mean. Just trust me."

Despite the boy's reassurances that he had no interest in drugs for any reason, Reid wasn't confident that he'd really made an impact. But as he walked to The Diner after his now *double* shift at The Prayer Room, he overheard Dylan talking with a couple of girls. "—said he didn't do it. The police didn't arrest him or anything. And c'mon. What fool puts a ton of drugs in a locker and leaves it unlocked?! Not an ex-con!"

Well, maybe they do listen. Wish I would have had someone just be real with me.

Ten days. Ten days of a paid vacation he didn't want—

couldn't enjoy if he wanted to. Ten days of fear, wondering, waiting. Ten days of only seeing Kelsey in passing.

A text on Thanksgiving Day. A prayer that all would be well. Gratitude for having met him. It shredded a corner of his heart. *If she is so glad she met me, why's she avoiding me? Why can't we work this out?*

But another text came—a number he didn't recognize. The name flashed. Mel Jackson. Uncle Mel?

The text had been brief but encouraging. HAPPY THANKSGIVING. SO THANKFUL FOR YOU IN KELSEY'S LIFE. GIVE HER TIME. SHE LOVES YOU.

But while the world shopped for deals on Cyber Monday, Reid got a call from Ramon. A minute later, he tore down the stairs and burst into Wayne's workroom. "I'm back on the job! Ramon says he can't afford to keep paying a good chef to do nothing. The police have cleared me!"

Wayne stabbed a rose into a mini Christmas tree and turned to him, a smile splitting his face. "Knew you would be. What'd Kelsey say?"

"Haven't told her yet."

Picking up a white rose, Wayne turned back to the little tree and found a place to insert it. "I think you should. She's scared, but she's not unfair."

"I will." A floral pick with a red and gold wrapped present at the top appeared on the tree, but Wayne removed it almost immediately. Reid chose to change the subject with a joke. "So, you're not going to deliver this to the Ephron family for Hanukkah, are you?"

The answer came swift—too swift, actually. "Brooke didn't do that as far as I know."

And something in that statement struck home. Reid watched as Wayne positioned a white flower he didn't recognize next to a small red rose. "Hey, Wayne? What is that?"

"Amaryllis."

"And you gave Kelsey Mom's flowers on purpose, didn't you?"

Wayne's hand froze on another amaryllis in the bucket before him. "What?"

"Why, Wayne? How could you do that to me—to us?" Reid skirted the table to face him. "Wayne?"

As anger welled up in him, Reid fought back the frustration that comes with interference—especially when that interference now included a certain measure of estrangement. But Wayne didn't look sorry at all when he finally looked up and faced Reid's growing anger.

"Why? Because you were hurting. I watched it every week. You didn't see it. Maybe you didn't even feel it, but when I found out it wasn't shyness or even that you weren't sure, but it was someone playing Holy Spirit in your life, I couldn't stand it." The man wiped at... were they tears?

"I—"

"No, Reid. You listen. When I heard what Brooke did, my first thought was, "I wish she'd have messed up your flowers— sent them to Kelsey instead. And the more I thought about it, the better idea it became."

"Because it's right to lie about something like that."

Defensiveness. Wayne's face became a mask of pure defensiveness. "I never lied, Reid. I deceived, you, sure. I always meant to confess—like at your wedding or something. But I never said what wasn't true." Here, he had the decency to look away. "If you thought it was Brooke, well, I wasn't going to correct you until the little mix-up had a chance to work some magic."

Where the words came from, Reid could only imagine. He heard himself make an argument he couldn't have planned if he tried. "So instead of playing Holy Spirit in our lives, you did what? Played Santa Claus? Cupid? That's somehow better? At least Mrs. Oberton really tried to help me grow spiritually. You just forced something. Now look where we are!"

And with that, Reid stormed from the building. He'd made it to the back of The Coventry when a guy called out. "Hey! Been waiting for you. I need a point—bad."

Reid turned around and stared a guy in obvious need of a fix. "Sorry. Got nothing—"

"Oh! I thought…" He leaned closer to get a better look, putrid breath nearly knocking Reid over. "You're not—thought…"

A car pulled into the lot—Mike's. The guy took one look at it and moved forward, but when Mike got out, scowling, he bolted in the other direction. "Hey! Good to see you back, Reid." As he neared, Mike jerked his head in the direction of the guy's retreating back. "Who's that?"

"Someone who thought I was someone else—and that I had meth, I suspect."

"I was glad to hear you were cleared. The temp we got…" A low whistle filled the back room as Mike let them in. "Man, it's good to have you back. Right now, I'd take you with a load of drugs as long as it didn't affect your work." At Reid's stunned silence, Mike clapped him on the back. "It's a joke, man. Just my way of saying welcome back."

"Thanks." As Reid rounded the corner and saw the kitchen gleaming, everything laid out for him, ready for the new day, he sighed with satisfaction. "Yeah. Thanks, Mike. It's good to be here."

Reid's text came at ten o'clock. BACK AT WORK. COPS CLEARED ME. WOULD YOU TAKE YOUR SHIFT TODAY?

Another one came on its heels. MISS YOU.

On her lunch break, sitting in the clinic breakroom with a wilted salad on the institutional table before her, Kelsey called Uncle Mel. "The police cleared Reid."

"Why don't you sound as ecstatic as I think you should."

"What if they're wrong? What if all he learned was how to

work this better?"

Rarely did her uncle even hint at displeasure, but his silence screamed his for all the world to hear—if they could have seen him, that is.

"Uncle Mel..."

"Why would you say that about someone you claim to love?"

She'd asked herself the same question for almost two weeks. Kelsey just didn't like the answer. Still, he'd never let her get out of admitting it. "I'm afraid."

"Aaah... now that we can work with." Uncle Mel began his Socratic approach to correcting unBiblical thinking. "So, Who is Love?"

"God."

Again, he asked, "And what kind of love is God?"

It took a good minute to figure out where he'd gone with his questions. "Oh..." Kelsey stared down at that unappetizing salad, promptly recovered it, and lobbed it at the trashcan. A perfect shot. "Perfect Love."

"That's right. So... what does the Bible say about Perfect Love?"

"Thanks, Uncle Mel. I'll go."

"Go where?"

And at that moment, she realized what she'd done. Desperate for an excuse to get off quickly, she cleaned up her space at the table and left the break room. "The Prayer Room. I've been AWOL since this whole thing. I just wasn't ready to talk to him yet. I was afraid I'd let my emotions cloud my judgment."

Quiet, calm, firm—truth spoken but with no condemnation— Uncle Mel's reply tore at her heart as the door to the clinic opened and a whoosh of air signaled the arrival of their next emergency. "I'd say you already have."

CHAPTER 11

The curtain to the workroom flung open with the dramatic flair that only Señora Rojas could wield. "What is wrong with you? You snap at me for not getting the orders fast enough. You snap at me for bringing them too fast. You want quiet. Where's the music?" She stepped close and swept him with the experienced eye of a woman who knows how to read a man. "Are you—no. No, you are not. So, what is it? What gives?"

Wayne fumbled with a rose and nearly took off the tip of his finger at the same time. *And with that question, I can tell what decade you learned English in.*

"Wayne! Do not make the fun of me. What is wrong with you?"

And the use of "the" where no native speaker would have, told him just how upset she was—and that he'd spoken aloud. The only person who had ever made him dread confessing more had been his second-grade teacher. Mr. Ellison. Wayne shuddered at the memory. But when Señora Rojas threatened to slap him, he decided he must have zoned out more than he realized.

"Sorry. Reid's mad at me."

"Why should he be mad at you? You help him with his girl. He forgives you. It isn't your fault this drugs were found."

I'd better not correct that one. A quick look in her direction showed eyes flashing, red lips pursed as if waiting for her next biting comment, but she didn't seem upset at *him* at present. "Yeah. About those flowers." Deep breath. A deeper one. Exhale. Wayne tried for a jocular approach, fumbled, and blurted out, "I just... sent them, but Reid thought it was part of Brooke's mix-up."

"He thought..." She shook her head, cocking it much like a confused puppy.

How did I never realize how beautiful you are?

"He thought it was the accident—that you did it?"

Again, with the extraneous "the." Interesting.

Another step closer, her hand rested on his sleeve. "Wayne, what is it? I see the pain in your eyes. What is so bad? They confess their love. They have a fight. This is what people do. It will be fix when everything is over. You'll see."

"But Reid is mad. He thinks I lied." Hours of conviction nearly exploded in him as he gazed down into her dark eyes. "I guess I did—by letting him believe one."

"Does Kelsey know?"

Wayne shook his head. And with that, the moment... had it been one? It was gone. Señora Rojas stepped away, flung a hand in the air, and marched out of the room, calling back, "So, go tell her. I see her go past just a few minutes ago. I can finish that. Go."

He'd made it as far as the sidewalk before Wayne backtracked and grabbed a sunflower from the cooler. "Peace offering."

"She'll slap you with it if you're not careful. Go."

All the way down the street, Wayne rehearsed what he'd say, but as he stepped up to the door and saw her sitting beneath a lone pot light, picking her guitar, his mouth went dry. *If she wasn't a kid, and I saw that every day, I might have fallen for her myself. Okay, God. Help.*

Her short hair swept along her jaw as she played, eyes closed. But when it registered that someone had stepped into the room, Kelsey popped her head up. Disappointment, surprise, happiness— they rippled across her features, one after another. "Wayne!" Fear followed. "What is it? What happened?"

"Huh?"

Relief—that was good, wasn't it? She held her hand against the strings and tried to explain. "I thought maybe you came with bad news about Reid."

"Good news, actually. The police cleared him."

"Yeah. He sent me a text."

Well, that's better than I expected. Maybe... He'd just about decided to go back when he realized he'd have to face his shop manager, and Señora Rojas would march him down by his ear if she felt it necessary. *Why do I put up with her?*

"Wayne?"

He crossed the space between them and thrust the sunflower into her face. "I owe you an apology."

"For what?"

"Butting in."

Kelsey gave him a confused look but took the stem and smiled. "I used to love roses best. Now I can't decide between daisies and sunflowers."

Once more, she gazed up at him, questioning. Wayne tried yet again. "Butting in. With you and Reid. The sunflowers."

"I understand. Accidents—"

"Deliberate accident," he corrected. "I did it deliberately. I saw him hurting, every day. He wanted to say how he felt so many times, but when I found out he didn't because some woman tried to guilt him into a year of singleness..."

Her head snapped up. "I thought he chose to do it."

With his conscience protesting that he'd gone too far, Wayne backed up. "Yeah. You can look at it that way. But hearing about how she handpicked Scriptures to support her ideas and called it a prophecy—it set off every warning bell I have." He turned to go, but at the door, he glanced back and watched her as she stroked a golden petal. "I hope you'll forgive me. If this problem between you guys is my fault, I'll never forgive myself.

"I forgive you, Wayne. And you weren't the problem with us. I am. I know it, but it's not so easy to ignore those 'warning bells' as you put it."

"Try, will you? Don't let your personal issues isolate you from people. It just becomes worse. Ask me how I know." And before she could take him up on the challenge, Wayne jerked open the door and strode back down the street to his shop... and Señora Rojas.

Nerves made playing impossible. The walls of The Prayer Room became less of a comfort and more prison-like... stifling. Still, Kelsey sat there, hands resting on the strings, occasionally fumbling for a note here, a chord there. Always prayerful in spirit but unable to pray.

Five o'clock came, and much to her disgust, she found herself in the restroom, checking her hair, bemoaning not having brought something less... *medicinal* to wear, and vowing to create a mini makeup touch-up for her purse. A brush through her hair—the short bob didn't need or really allow for much more. *I wonder if he'd like it better longer. Growing out would be awful, but I could put it up for work after that...*

A prayer exercise a Sunday school teacher had taught them to help develop the habit of daily prayer came back to her, and Kelsey found herself following the little routine without trouble. *You know every hair on my head—help* me *to know You even a fraction so well.* The little wrinkles on her forehead reminded her of the many prayers for help through grammar quizzes. *Help me keep my mind trained only on You—not me, not my fears, not my desires. You.*

Her eyes—did they look that sad to others? Kelsey prayed for the ability to see others as Jesus did. *Especially Reid. Please. Don't let me bring up the mistakes of his past—mistakes You have covered. Who am I to hold against him what You don't.*

A smile formed as she remembered daily praying to "sniff out everything nasty in her life and eradicate it." *And truth—help me only to hear and speak truth.*

Hands shaking as she regarded them, Kelsey prayed for opportunities to use them to serve others—to show love. *Please keep me from being that "talk to the hand" person. That's not who Your Word teaches me to be.*

As she finished, her prayer for feet that run to kindness and love and flee from selfishness and fear still filling her soul, the backdoor chime rang. Disappointment flooded her until she remembered asking for help in serving, in being kind. *No time like the present, eh, Lord?*

She missed him at first. After a glance around the room, Kelsey decided whoever had started to come in had gone away again. Guitar in hand, the notes came. The words followed. Lost in worship and prayer, she wouldn't have noticed if anyone entered or not, but as the last note died, Reid's soft murmur reached her.

"I missed that."

In her heart, Kelsey leaped from the chair and flung herself across the space separating them. Apologies poured from her. In her heart. But in actuality, she sat rooted to her chair, only her gaze rising to meet his. Emotion choked her at the sight of him leaning against the same pillar he so often had, hands stuffed into his pocket and eyes on her. So many things she wanted to say—so many. But only one word deigned to obey her pleas.

"Sorry."

He nodded. "I get it. I do."

The words—everything—it flowed. Kelsey didn't remember putting down her guitar, standing, none of it. But she found herself in the middle of the room, arms around Reid, apologizing. Listening as he prayed for them. Praying with him.

A voice near the door snapped them out of their little world. "Well, it's about time."

Reid turned, his arm around Kelsey's waist as if not willing to be *too* separated yet. "Good evening, Sister Arlene."

"You taking over for her?"

Kelsey nodded. "Except, I think I'll stay until he's done." Beneath her breath, she whispered, "Do you want to do something afterward? Maybe get coffee and meet Uncle Mel?"

"Get out of here. Both of you. He's been here all day every day for the last couple of weeks. Go. I've got this."

She might have squealed if Reid hadn't demurred. "Are you sure? I thought you didn't like weeknights."

"My boy got me one of those Hopper things. I can record my shows and watch them later—without commercials, too. Best thing ever. Now get out of here." She stepped forward to hug them. "Our first Prayer Room romance. Better than TV any day."

Again, Reid hesitated, but when Kelsey teased that he was looking for another out, he had the guitar packed and in hand before she knew what hit her. "Can we stop by my place first? I didn't change before coming, and if I have to meet this uncle of yours, I shouldn't smell like stale food."

"Mel's good people," Sister Arlene informed them. "Of course, you know that, Kelsey. You tell Mel that there isn't a better boy for you out there. He'll listen to me."

As they stepped into the night, a giddy feeling washed over her. "I feel like we're skipping school after second period. And I wonder what Sister Arlene would think if she knew Uncle Mel's been rooting for you through this whole mess—the one I made."

Reid didn't respond, but she hadn't expected that he would. But a smile formed, and it spread from him to her heart. *There. If that wasn't an easy way to make "meeting the family" easier, then I don't know what was. Thanks for that, Lord.*

CHAPTER 12

As they stood in line to order coffee at a shop in Brunswick, Reid scrambled for some idea to make the evening more "date-like." They'd need to eat at some point—definitely. But there had to be something they could do to just *be* together and make a memory or two. *Isn't that what Mom said made the best dates? Ones that just create a neat memory? So, what do I do?*

It hadn't been a *real* date, but his mother had often spoken of a night window shopping with her father after dinner at a nice restaurant. *That might work. Make a game of it.*

Their turn at the counter came, and every scent in the place assaulted and overwhelmed his senses. "Just odor me anything."

"Odor? You mean order?"

"That, too. I can't think." His heart demanded he make a cheesy comment about being too close to her to think, but his brain stopped him in time. *Don't be stupid.* Something in her expression told him she guessed his thoughts. With a shrug, Reid tried to deflect. "Well, it's true."

"Cute, too. Cheesy…"

Another shrug. "That's why I didn't let myself say it."

As they waited for their cups of hot, caffeinated deliciousness, he offered his idea. "Why don't we go down on Stinton and walk around down there—window shop. You can 'buy' anything you want with one condition."

"It's all in your head?"

"That, too," he agreed. "But no. That's part of window shopping. The rules for this is you can pick out anything for anyone but yourself." The moment he vocalized it the idea sounded a lot less interesting than it had in his imagination. "Unless that's just stupid."

The barista handed over their cups as Kelsey gave hearty agreement. "I think it sounds fun. Let's walk over—just two blocks."

If he prayed that she'd forgotten her gloves, well, he hoped the Lord would understand.

The first interesting window came half a block from Stinton Street. An antique store was lit up with Christmas lights and decorated like an old-fashioned living room—tree, settee, end table, old toys all around the base of the tree, the works. Kelsey froze and pointed to an ornament almost touching the window on a low-hanging branch. "Look at that! Hand-painted. Wouldn't that be perfect for Wayne? I mean, who else would truly treasure a hand-painted poinsettia?" She bent in contortions he'd never have attempted, trying to see the price on the tag. "Can you shine your phone on that? I think…"

Reid found the flashlight app and positioned his phone at all angles until she stood up. "I'm coming in for that on Saturday. Wayne needs it. And I want to show him I forgive him. I don't think I actually told him."

He stiffened. "Forgive him for what?"

"Didn't he tell you?" She turned to face him, and if she hadn't been explaining Wayne's visit, Reid might not have been able to resist a kiss right there. "It's kind of cute when you think of it."

"Cute?" Reid sighed. "I guess. I'm not sorry he did it—not now. But at the time, I felt like my choice had been taken from me." He nudged her forward. "Of course, the minute I saw you with them, I was glad. Still…"

A blast of wind hit them from behind as they rounded the corner. Each gust pushed, shoved, drove them onward as if striving to prevent the mental destruction of their budgets. Reid stopped first. In a clothing boutique window, a fuzzy sweater hung from an impossibly skinny mannequin. He'd seen Kelsey in a gauzy summer top of that ultra-pale pink, and nothing had set off her skin better. "That. Right there. For you. If they were open, I'd break the rules, go in, and buy it."

She stepped into the doorway and held out her hand for his phone again. App on, he handed it to her. By the low whistle and emphatic shake of her head, Reid surmised the price to be far from reasonable. "At a hundred fifty bucks, you'd better not."

"For a sweater?"

"Yeah. I thought you'd see sense. I'd be afraid to wear it." In a move he doubted she noticed, Kelsey wiped at her coat front and muttered, "I'm too clumsy with spills and drops to be trusted with pricey clothes."

Self-preservation demanded he say nothing. Kelsey eyed him with curiosity before busting out in laughter. "Wise move. Don't lie but don't agree. Just keep mu—oh! Wow."

They'd reached a gift shop with a display of delicate music boxes in the window. "Oh, one of these—if I could give my mom a gift, it would be…" Her finger swung back and forth between boxes he couldn't be sure of until it landed on a ballet dancer that appeared to move across a floor, if the track in the box meant what he thought it did. "That one. Mom loved music boxes. I have five of hers."

He'd never wanted to ask, but the time seemed perfect for it. "What happened to her—and your dad."

They passed two more stores before she answered. "We were missionaries in North Thailand. Uncle Mel came to visit, so when news came of missionaries needing medical help in the northeastern corner, Mom and Dad left us with him and drove over to bring more supplies." A catch in her throat showed the pain it still caused. "They never made it. Tire blew out, Dad lost control of the van they were driving, and no one found them for days. So, we came back to America with Uncle Mel."

"I'm sorry."

"Thanks. You know, Kenny was only two. He didn't remember any of it. That always hurt the most. But one of the first things Uncle Mel did when we got back was take me into a room at his house and show me Mom's music box collection. He said, 'She has friends who would like one as a keepsake, but you pick out five. Those will be yours.' Then he pointed to an egg that opens when you wind it. 'That was her favorite.' Of course," Kelsey stopped in her tracks, leaned her head against his arm, and sighed. "I picked that one."

"Of course. I'm still sorry." Reid might have said more, but a specialty sporting goods store display showed a selection of fishing rods. "Oh, that. Right there in the middle with the red striping. I'd get that for my mom, but I bet it's three hundred bucks. Wow, that's a beauty."

"You fish?" Kelsey gave him the oddest expression. "I'd never have guessed that. Ever."

"That's because I don't. But Mom does. Loves it."

And without him even having to try to create a reason to do it himself, she slipped her hand into his and sighed. "We'd better introduce her to Uncle Mel. Maybe then we'll get a break from hours of explanations about why this fly is better, and that tie is best."

"Wait. Your uncle does that, too?"

Kelsey laughed and dragged him across the street. "He's part of a fishing club. It's *all* they talk about. But meetings are only once a month. He doesn't enjoy a lot of them one-on-one because they get kind of crass." She eyed him with a suspicious look. "Your mom isn't crass, is she?"

"Not usually, no."

With an exaggerated sweep of her hand over her forehead, she whistled. "Whew! That's it. We're introducing them. And that…"

She pointed to a lacy scarf. "I wish for Michelle. She collects scarves. And I've never seen a more beautiful one."

"I've never seen you in a scarf." The moment he spoke the words, Reid wished them back again. In an effort to deflect from his obvious notice of her wardrobe, he remarked on the color. "That gold is really nice. It would look great on you."

As she tried to find a price tag on the thing, Kelsey didn't attempt to hide her snort. "Yeah. Not hardly. All yellows make me look sickly. Most greens, too. And I don't have the neck for a scarf."

"I like your neck." Reid cringed as he heard the words spoken. "Well, that didn't come out well. I now sound like a vampire." Desperate to redeem himself, he pointed at it again. "When you come back for that ornament, get the scarf. I'll pay you back. Michelle took a chance on me."

Though she nodded, Kelsey didn't speak until her next stop before a tea room. "I should take Aunt Grace out for tea soon. It's been a long time."

"Who's Aunt Grace? You've never mentioned an aunt."

But Kelsey didn't answer. She stood there, typing note after note into her phone. Only when she pocketed it and took his hand again did she try to explain. "That's because she's not really my aunt. I just always called her that because she did stuff with me even though I was just a kid, you know?" She paused under a streetlight and peered up at him. "Reid?"

"My dad?"

"Yeah."

He led her across a side street to the next block as he prayed for a lack of judgment on his mother. "Never had one. I used to ask Mom all the time, and at first, she'd just say, 'Sometimes guys don't stick around to raise the babies they make,' but one day I must have pushed too hard, or it was a bad day or something." He swallowed hard. "She got all upset and screamed at me. Mom never was much of a yeller, but that day..." Again, the same lump formed and he forced it down again.

"You don't have to talk about it. I was curious, but it's none—"

"No... really." They stood there on a street corner decorated with Christmas lights, giant ornaments, and every bit of Midwestern winter festivity surrounding them. It almost felt wrong to desecrate the moment with the only time his mother had ever been ugly to him. "She screamed that day, though. She told me every fault I had and which guy I could have gotten it from." His voice dropped to a whisper that even he could hear the pain in. "There were several. It had been a bad time in her life, but getting pregnant with me kind of snapped her out of it."

This time, as Kelsey squeezed his hand, she wrapped her other hand around his arm and leaned against him as they walked. "Your poor mom. That must have been hard to admit. Sounds to me like she was yelling at herself instead of you."

He hadn't planned it—couldn't have if he'd tried. But in front of a pet store with a display of cages of every kind, Reid pulled her close and kissed her until he forgot where they were and what they were doing. Only when a few snowflakes turned into a shower of half-dollar sized ones did he step back and take a steadying breath. "Maybe we should go meet this uncle of yours—ask him to join us for dinner. I think we need to have him join us."

When her hand slipped back into his as they turned to face the wind on the way back up the street, Reid could have sworn she said, "And maybe your mom."

The Diner bustled with shoppers stopping in for hot chocolate and pie. But in a coveted corner booth near the window, the men sat across from the women. Kelsey listened to Reid's mom tell Uncle Mel about her latest fishing escapade, while she tried *not* to laugh at the tiny jabs he gave her shins under the table at each effusive exclamation over Uncle Mel's equipment or trips.

Stop that before I bust out laughing!

She may not have spoken the words, but Reid read them loud and clear. He winked and assured her in equally silent words that he had no intention of stopping. As Pat and her uncle debated the use of strike indicators and things Kelsey only had the slightest knowledge about, and Reid kept tapping her with every exclamation, she opted for a new approach.

So, when her "chili size" arrived, Kelsey waited for Uncle Mel to offer thanks and about choked as he reached out to take Reid's and Pat's hands. *Since when do we hold hands for grace? Is that my benefit or* yours, *Uncle Mel?*

Another tap followed Pat's murmured, "Amen?"

"Will you and Reid come to church with us on Sunday?"

At the sight of Reid's face, Kelsey deduced that the growing flirtation between Uncle Mel and Pat would end with that question. But Pat just beamed. "Well, *I'd* love to, but Reid has his own church, you know. I wouldn't want him to—"

"Mom!" Reid stared at Pat until she dragged her eyes away from Uncle Mel. "If you're going to church, I'm going with you. Period."

"Then it looks like we'll be joining you. When and where?"

Reid gave Kelsey a, "Can you believe this" look and eyed his mother. Her time had come. This time, she jabbed his leg. Reid gave a yelp.

"Oh, for Pete's sake, it's just church. You'd think I've never been or something. We used to go for the pageant when you were a kid, remember?"

As Reid stammered an apology and tried to deflect the conversation, Uncle Mel gave her a sharp look. Kelsey tossed him an impish grin and waited. Uncle Mel didn't disappoint. "I think you can blame Kelsey for that one. I taught her better, but kids these days…"

This time a different kind of friendly debate began. Pat insisted that kids are always looked down on as not as good as *their* parents' generation. Uncle Mel argued that the truth of that didn't negate the fact that each generation did degrade into less and less desirable behavior. "Manners—there aren't any anymore, or so it seems."

Bite after bite, fry after fry, sip after sip. Reid and Kelsey fought not to look at one another for fear of losing all self-control, and Pat argued that kids these days had a better grasp of the state of the world around them than hers had. And by the time they finished, Uncle Mel suggested a short walk around the square to "cool off tempers."

Reid and Kelsey found themselves standing out in front of The Diner. Alone. Staring as their respective parental influences took off together, deep in discussion and apparently oblivious to them. Reid found his voice first. "Did that just happen?"

"Yes and no."

"Huh?" He took her hand and tugged her toward his apartment. "We can talk in the entry to The Pettler until they get there."

"Uncle Mel is interested. That's for sure. But I saw him give us that *look*. He's giving us a bit of privacy, and if it happens to give him more time with a pretty and interesting woman, he's not going to complain."

They'd only made it half a block when a girl stepped out between two buildings. "Hey, got any…" An unsavory euphemism for drugs dropped into the night air. "Mmm… sorry. Wrong guy."

Reid stared after her, oblivious to her questions. When he did snap out of his reverie, he gave Kelsey an odd look. "She's looking for a fix. That's the second person who started to approach me and took off."

"Fairbury has its first dealer?"

"Fairbury has dealers, Kelsey. Just not as many as some places, and from what I've seen, they're not very successful… yet."

"Why do you think people are coming to you? Reputation?" Even as she spoke the words, Kelsey winced. "Sorry, that didn't come out right."

"I don't think so." Reid led her to The Pettler and pulled her into the covered little alcove that held the entrance to Wayne's shop. There he pulled her into a hug and just held her. "I had fun tonight."

"Me, too." She didn't want to ask, but needed to. "Reid?"

"Hmm…?"

"Do you mind Uncle Mel and your mom?" Kelsey stepped back to try to see his expression in the semi-dark nook, but he pulled her close again.

"Nope. Hope you don't, because I haven't seen my mom flirt like that—ever."

This time, she stood back and crossed her arms over her chest. "Admit it, Reid. You *liked* her flirting! I was sitting there mortified at Uncle Mel doing everything he could to encourage her, and you were over there *enjoying* it, weren't you?"

One soft brush of his knuckles across her cheek, a kiss that could have lasted a second or an hour—she never knew—a murmured whisper that she only understood because she recognized the love in the tone… Kelsey thought he'd forgotten the question, but Reid finally shoved his hands in his pockets, gazing down at her.

She couldn't see his eyes, but she felt the intensity of his gaze. "Kelsey, any guy loves a little flirting.

CHAPTER 13

The bay window overlooked Fairbury's ice rink, and Kelsey and Michelle from The Prayer Room sat there across from each other, chatting over plates of scampi. But after a good hour, Michelle glanced at her phone, for what seemed like the hundredth time, and excused herself. "Sorry, but I promised Kelly Cox I'd take her watchman shift tonight. She has kids in the pageant."

"This has to let up soon enough. I have a full battery and a new book I can read on my phone. I'll be fine."

Even as Michelle counted out bills to cover her part of the check, she asked again, "Are you sure?"

"Totally. Thanks for coming." Guilt almost prompted her to confess that she'd like a bit of time alone. Almost. *Then again, she doesn't need to know why. I'll just enjoy teasing him a bit. I sure hope his phone doesn't chime or buzz while he's working.*

Kelsey gave one last wave as her friend rounded the corner to the entrance and whipped out her phone. First, she zipped him a message asking about tickets to the pageant Michelle had mentioned as she worked to compose her first message. With that sent, all efforts went to a little fun. And her creative juices failed. Text two: I MISS YOU.

Two minutes later, she thought of another one. DID YOU KNOW YOU GET ADORABLE CRINKLES AROUND YOUR EYES WHEN

YOU SMILE?

Her nerves gave out on the next one, but they rallied when she imagined that smile, those crinkles, and the joy he'd feel hearing about her love of them. Kelsey typed fast and hit send before she could chicken out. THEY MAKE ME SWOON & I'M NOT EVEN SOUTHERN.

Giggles—they prompted several curious looks, but no matter how she tried, she couldn't prevent them. Her sense of proportion got the better of her, and Kelsey decided she should add something a little less frivolous... not quite so shallow. *What do I love most about him? What made me love him in the first place?* She tried to think of as many things as possible, but one jumped out as preeminent.

PSST. NOTHING MAKES MY HEART FLUTTER LIKE YOU WHEN YOU'RE PRAYING WITH ME.

Would he be disappointed? Did guys feel like stuff like that was the spiritual equivalent of saying, "She seems... interesting"?

Just in case, she zipped off one more. AND DID YOU KNOW YOUR EYES GO FROM AMBER TO UMBER WHEN YOU'RE MOVED BY SOMETHING? TALK ABOUT DREAMY.

And with that, she couldn't—not another one until she saw how he responded to them. *If I went overboard, Lord. If it's too much too soon. If six months of knowing him and seeing him daily, praying with him almost daily, dreaming of him... daily. If all that is still too soon because it's just been a couple of weeks since those flowers accidentally ended up in my hands... on purpose, of course. If that's the way it is, can You just kind of delete the ones that are too much? Please? Thanks. I knew I could count on You.*

Page after page of her novel flipped past with a swipe of her finger on her phone screen. Only when she'd made it through ten percent of the novel did she remember it was supposed to be a comedy... and she hadn't laughed once.

Better start over.

But she didn't. Before she could slide the progress bar back to the beginning, Reid paused by a table across the room to speak to someone. Kelsey's mind ordered her to settle itself—behave rationally. Her heart responded with cartwheels and handsprings. *Aren't you pathetic. You told Uncle Mel not three hours ago that you still weren't sure a relationship with him was a good idea... yet. Do you remember that? Do you remember saying maybe that was the point of Oberton's prophecy? Maybe it was God? And look at you. Fickle. Wishy-washy. Double-minded and unst—*

There the self-recriminations ceased because she saw it. Clear as day, easy as you please, and another dozen or two of obnoxious clichés—Reid shaking the man's hand as he tucked something into the man's shirt pocket. Reid shoving his own hand in his own pocket as he turned to go.

Heart sinking, aching, crying, she fought back tears and stood to go. As Reid moved her way, she flopped back down in the chair and stared... gape-jawed. It wasn't Reid.

The kitchen bustled at twice the speed as usual. With half the staff out with a virus, Reid watched order after order pile up without any hope of staying on top of it. The next time their top server stopped to ask about an order, he pounced. "Can you get Mike in here? We need the help."

She took one look at the row of tickets and bolted. Mike appeared just as Reid finished plating a pot pie and roasted Brussels sprouts. "Anya said you needed hel...llo! Whoa. Let me grab a coat. Where do I start?"

"I'll get everything down, concentrating on main dish and appetizers. You plate and deal with appetizers and dessert if I get further behind?"

"Done." A moment later, still buttoning up the black chef's coat, Mike said, "By the way, your girlfriend is out there."

The words hardly registered. Reid pulled two more tickets from the lineup and began prepping them. "Is she?"

"When she saw the crowd, she started to go, but Anya put her and some other girl at the table overlooking the ice rink. I think

Anya's trying to keep the place packed with loungers so we can't get any more orders."

"Who's covering the front?"

Mike took an order for an onion loaf and began dredging the spiral-cut onions through the batter before dropping them in the fryer. "Ramon's out there."

The first time or two, Reid didn't know if he'd noticed or imagined things or if Mike's distraction was real, but after five minutes—minutes in which they received as many orders as they filled—Reid decided to ask. "Something wrong?"

"Huh?"

"You just look... well, ready to bolt."

That seemed to snap Mike out of it. "Sorry. My brain tells me we're ignoring the diners."

"Ramon's got 'em." Reid passed three plates in close succession and began an order of sautéed mushrooms.

For two more hours, the orders arrived almost faster than they could stay on top of them, and then everything fizzled. Exhausted, they collapsed against the prep table. In near perfect synchronization, each man pulled out his phone. Mike read his and bolted from the kitchen. Reid glanced up just for a moment and went back to reading a text from Kelsey.

The simple, "miss you" prompted a smile. *And last week, I thought this was over—done.*

A moment later, his ears burned at her "crinkly comment." At swoon, his face burned as well. *Swoon. That's a word you don't see or hear every day. A good one, though, I think.*

An order for two cheesecake slices interrupted his chance to devour the next text, but when he'd drizzled cranberry-orange sauce over them and sent them out again, he tapped one that began with "Psst."

She likes it when I pray, huh? I guess that answers the whole question of whether it's a lame way to get to know someone. Cool.

His fingers itched to reply, but another text popped up. *Wow.*

You were busy. Love it.

Any doubts he'd entertained about her ability to forgive, her sincerity regarding her feelings, or the chances of a long-standing relationship forming died at "dreamy."

Scrolling back to the first message, Reid read it once more. BOUGHT TICKETS FOR THE FUNDRAISER PAGEANT-PLAY THING FOR UNCLE MEL AND YOUR MOM. IF I BUY 2 MORE, WILL YOU GO WITH ME?

Reid zipped back a one-word reply. NO. He called Bookends and asked them to reserve two tickets for him. As soon as he confirmed they were his, he zipped back a second reply. JUST KIDDING. SORT OF. I'LL GO IF YOU WILL, BUT WE HAVE TO USE MY TICKETS, OR THEY'LL GO TO WASTE.

Now, let's get back to missing each other. Great place to start.

As he typed, another one came through. SO, I HAVE A DATE WITH THE CUTEST GUY IN TOWN. COOL. And before he could finish his text and reply to the latest, another one popped up. REID. GET OUT HERE. I'M IN THE DINING ROOM.

※❀❀ ※

Diners turned to greet him as Reid wove around table after table. He paused, shook a hand, smiled, nodded, offered thanks for compliments. And across the room, Kelsey appeared to be recording every movement. Then, as he turned away from the police chief's table, he watched her swing the phone to the other side of the room. *What are you doing? That's… that's just weird.*

A text buzzed his phone. It took only one glance to confuse and alarm him. CALL THE COPS ON YOUR CASE. FAST.

Reid stood in the center of the restaurant, his gaze darting back and forth between Kelsey and his phone. He tapped the screen and put the call through as he worked his way across to the most coveted table in the restaurant. "Wha—"

Kelsey jerked him down into a chair beside her. Finger swiping, tapping swiping again She groaned, looked closer, and nodded. "Watch." And with that, she shoved the phone in his hand.

In a rather odd, out-of-body experience, he watched himself shake hands with a woman he hadn't actually seen. Laughing, nodding, and then he turned. "Wow. Never realized how much we look alike from the back and the side."

"Did you hear yourself?" She leaned closer, her lips brushing his ear as she whispered, "Those people who thought it was you? The one who thought he could get drugs from the..." Kelsey hung air quotes as she continued her whispered rant. "'...chef' at The Coventry. That's who it is. It's Mike. He's selling drugs right here in the restaurant!"

Her phone glued itself to his hand as Reid stared at the screen. "No... Mike wouldn't. Man, I can see how someone would confuse us, though." Reid froze. "Wait! Is this why I called Crane? The police chief is over there, Kelsey. And he'd say this isn't even circumstantial evidence. It's just coincidence." At the disappointment that formed around her mouth, Reid forced himself to add again, "But yeah. I see how it would look like it."

Mike neared the table, and Kelsey stiffened. Heat streaked up Reid's neck as she turned to him, one hand sliding around his head and her fingers twirling in his hair. Again, her lips brushed his ear. "Try to keep him here... talking. Trust me. I saw him put something in someone's pocket. And that person gave him something, too. I bet it's cash."

A little far-fetched, Kelsey, but it's cute that you want to clear me.

"Reid, *please.*"

Mike paused as he passed, a smile on his lips. "Looks like you found her." He gave Kelsey a searching look before adding, "He's a good guy. Happy for you—both of you."

Another patron two tables over called out to Mike, but Reid, feeling Kelsey's near panic, acted on impulse... instinct. "Hey, Mike. Thanks. Have you guys actually met yet?" His mother had once mentioned who should be introduced to whom, but in the moment, he could hardly remember her name.

"I haven't, actually." Mike stuck out his hand. "Mike Lapora. Nice to meet you, finally. Reid never stops talking about you."

He froze, confusion and embarrassment mingling into an uncomfortable mixture in his gut. *But I don't talk about her at work. Not to you. Why would you say that?*

Kelsey, however, didn't miss a beat. "Wow. It seems like you know everyone in here. I guess that's probably your job, isn't it? I mean, I know a lot of people in here, but that's because I've squeezed their arms to death in an attempt to keep them alive."

The words—they made no sense. However, Reid suspected she'd planned it that way. She paused for just the right amount of time before leaning forward with a conspiratorial flair and murmured, "Blood pressure cuffs. If I die under suspicious circumstances, check my recent patients. I think testing the blood pressure sometimes sends people over the edge."

Laughter rang out through the restaurant. Several people glanced their way, curious. One set of eyes attached to a man halfway across the room, however, locked on Reid's in confused alarm. *Wait... aren't you that guy outside the restaurant that day Mike was late...?* The way the man fumbled for his wallet screamed guilt. *Maybe she's right. Where is Officer Crane anyway?*

On silent cue, Judith Crane stepped into the dining room, sweeping it with her gaze. The moment she saw him, she started his way, but Reid shifted his attention to the man who'd dropped back into the booth, attention fixed on a half-eaten plate. The officer froze, swept the room for the object of Reid's interest, and at that moment, chaos erupted.

Chief Varney stood, strode to Crane's side, and evidently asked just what she was doing there. The man began to mop perspiration from his face, and Mike's expression shifted from amiable to suspicious. He turned at the sight of Crane and Varney talking, jerked his head back to where the man tried to blend into the background and only made himself even more conspicuous, and then snapped back to Reid and Kelsey.

"Get them out of here, Reid. I can make things even worse for you. I've made sure of it. So, fix this unless you want to go back to prison in some serious debt."

If he hadn't known her to be reasonably astute about human nature, Reid would have believed Kelsey had dropped a dozen or two IQ points and actually needed enlightenment when she asked, "What's wrong, Mike? Why would you want Reid to go to prison? I thought the police said those drugs weren't his. And you just told me he's a good guy..."

She feigned understanding—or did she? Reid watched the scene play out even more confused than ever. *Don't overdo it, Kelsey. If he is responsible for drugs in this town, he's not above doing something desperate.*

"Police can be wrong. All they need is evidence that proves otherwise, and he's back in prison."

"Like what kind of evidence?"

Are you crazy? Stop baiting him! Reid tried to reassure her, in excessively strong tones, that he was *certain* Mike wouldn't have to supply evidence like that. "He's just concerned about me."

She gazed up at him, incredulity almost masking the anger building. "You're kidding, right? I distinctly heard a threat in there. But we both know you didn't put those drugs in your locker. I guess we know who did now, don't we?" She turned to glare at Mike, and Reid considered dragging her from the room before she could speak again. Kelsey, however, was too quick for him.

She folded her arms over her chest and continued a glare that would have quelled a wiser man. Mike, apparently, didn't fit into that category. "So, I have to ask again just *how* you plan to prove he did what we know he didn't do."

Behind Mike, a near-silent commotion began. And that's when Reid suspected that Kelsey's assiduity had more to do with keeping Mike there and distracted than trying to extricate information. Red-faced and seething, Mike leaned close and dropped his voice to a low growl. "You'll find that the police use what evidence they find to make arrests. Once he's arrested, he loses his job, even if the D.A. doesn't file charges. You guys wouldn't want that."

A voice startled all three of them—Officer Crane's. "I'm sure they wouldn't, Mr. Lapora. Why don't you come down to the station and tell us all about this... evidence?"

Mike turned and nodded. "I hate to do it, but when I found a few things, I knew I'd have to say something eventually." If Reid didn't know the man had to be half-panicked, he'd have believed every word.

But Kelsey wasn't done. She pulled her phone forward and passed it to Officer Crane. "You'll need this. As one party to the conversation, I definitely give consent to the recording."

Reid stumbled over his words as he tried to remember what exactly Mike had said. But when Kelsey kicked him under the table, he managed to choke out, "And I do, too, of course."

A voice at the table next to them jerked Reid from his confused stupor. "Did you hear that? Mike's the one with the drugs. Reid just proved it somehow. I knew he wasn't guilty."

What? Is that what we just said? But a second of reflection, a glance at Kelsey's triumphant face, and Mike shaking with fury told him it was. Then the inexplicable happened. Applause began at that table and spread through the room as people shared what had conspired. While it didn't completely drown out Mike's string of foul words, it did muffle them considerably. Kelsey squealed and sank back against her chair. "Whew! I was so afraid that wouldn't work!"

"Did you... *plan* this?"

She cocked her head and gave a one-shouldered shrug. "Well, when I saw you coming, I figured we'd have to try. And we did it! You're not just cleared. You're *cleared.*" A wink followed. "And you're welcome. Whew! That was fun!"

CHAPTER 14

U nder streetlights and Christmas lights, the snow blanketing Fairbury glistened, despite the intermittent moonlight that worked to plunge the town into darkness. Cars lined the streets hours before the fundraising pageant began. And in the "closet" of The Prayer Room, four women sat in a row, holding hands and praying that this time the funds would be enough to pay off the diabetic alert dog that a local boy so desperately needed.

Kelsey sat near the door, her fingers picking out a tune she couldn't have identified and trying to pray. A peppermint candle burned in the center of an evergreen wreath on the table by the front door, infusing the room with a faint scent of Christmas. Long sweater sleeves slipped over her hands, but still she fumbled. Her jean skirt and funky leggings—a frivolous purchase she'd just *had* to have when Reid had asked about a dinner before their date before the pageant.

All hope of sincere, prayerful thoughts abandoned at the memory, Kelsey set her guitar on the chair beside her and pulled out her phone. Reid's message popped up the moment she tapped his name. MOM GAVE ME A GIFT CARD TO ROSITA'S AND 20 QUESTIONS FOR US TO GO OVER. IT'S HER THANKS FOR INTRODUCING HER TO YOUR UNCLE. WILL YOU GO?

A glance at the phone clock said he'd be there any minute.

And then it buzzed. Uncle Mel. Kelsey snatched up her coat and slipped out the door. "Hey, Uncle Mel!"

"How would you feel if I started dating again?"

"Considering you've gone out with her twice, why ask now? You're already doing it."

"Kelsey..." Despite his attempt to sound stern and foreboding, she heard the grin in his tone. "I know, I know. But..."

"Yeah. We saw it that night. You guys hit it off faster than we did."

A cough—a snort. "Um, almost everyone has hit it off faster than you two—except that librarian in your town. Didn't she wait ten years for her guy?"

Nice subject avoidance, but it won't work. "Ruth. Yeah." Kelsey cleared her throat. "But seriously, I wish you could have seen what we saw."

"I hear a but coming. If it's the one I've got poking at me, I get it. I do. Already called Gerry. Made him promise to exercise church discipline if I get engaged to someone who isn't a Christian."

Her heart sank as she listened, but Kelsey chose truth over ease. "You're asking for a broken heart. What would you tell me in the same situation?" Before he could answer, she sighed. "Never mind. You know what? You have the Holy Spirit and the Bible to direct you. You don't need a niece who was just cheering the idea a couple of days ago trying to take over His job."

"What's wrong, Kelsey? This isn't just about what's right."

Her heart constricted into a ball that jumped up to her throat and choked her. "Just don't break your heart. Please. I can't stand it. Selfish, sure. But I can't."

"Will do. I love you, sweetheart. I'm also scary happy for you. Pat and I were talking about it last night. She was saying how she'd been afraid Reid might get tired of working so hard and having to give most of his money away again, but now that he has you, she thinks he'll stick to things."

"What!" Frustration hit her at the same time her body demanded warmth. Her teeth chattered as she tucked herself as close to the door as possible. "But he's—"

"I know. I told her. I said, 'Kelsey's a good influence, sure. She can affect his heart, definitely. But she can't regenerate it. Jesus did, though. That's where Reid's true change comes from.'"

This time, the shivers up and down her spine weren't caused by freezing temperatures and a sky spitting random snowflakes all over the town. "Wow. Total goosebumps. What'd she say?"

His voice shifted to the tone he used when most moved. "Oh, Kels... she said, 'I've been afraid to hope for that—that this Jesus stuff is real. I want it to be, but....'"

"No wonder you're willing to risk it. I get it, Uncle Mel. I do. Just be careful until you know. Please."

"Will do—"

Her squeal cut off whatever else he might have said. "What—?" Reid stood there, two flowers in hand. "Gotta go, Uncle Mel. Reid's here."

"Kiss him while you're outside. It's safer."

Kelsey agreed, but confusion stopped her sign off. "Wait. How'd you know I was outside?"

"Your teeth—the ones that cost me a fortune, by the way— probably have jagged chips from the way you've been chattering. So, kiss him, get inside, and get warm. Just keep it appropriate."

She couldn't resist. "You, too, Uncle Mel. Bye."

Without a word, Reid pulled her inside, took her phone from her, and began rubbing her free hand. "You're half-frozen."

In just above a whisper, Kelsey tried to explain. "The quartet is in there, praying. So, I went outside, and then Uncle Mel asked what I thought of him dating your mom, and...."

"Isn't it great? She might finally listen now."

"He thinks she will..."

Reid stopped mid-sentence about how she'd never dated

much because she didn't trust men with him. "What's wrong? You don't think Mom's right for him?"

The room swam around her until she leaned her forehead against his shoulder and sighed. "I know just the other day I was so excited about the idea, but my head knows what my heart didn't want to consider. Anyone who doesn't belong to Jesus isn't right for any Christian."

He stiffened for a moment, and dread smothered her until breathing became impossible. But when he spoke, her knees buckled with relief. As he said, "Mrs. Oberton said something about that, too. I just thought it was her. I didn't know it was in the Bible. I missed that," he grabbed for her, holding her close. "I could get used to this."

"Me, too."

Emotions swirled, danced, twirled. *Grand jetés* of hope leaped between their hearts until a sneeze in the prayer closet sent them jerking apart again. Reid nodded at the flowers in her hand. "That daisy? That one's from me this time." He winked as he added, "I got tired of bringing you another guy's flowers. And…" Reid's throat bobbed as he wrestled with emotions she only hoped she understood. "Don't forget that there's no 'not' in those daisies. He loves you."

Kelsey's heart raced when Reid continued to gaze down at her. A moment later, he added, "And so do I."

Fairbury bustled in anticipation of the pageant, leaving Reid and Kelsey seated smack dab in the middle of Rosita's. All around them people chatted, scolded children, and inhaled the spicy goodness of Rosita's carnitas, enchiladas, and chips with *pico de gallo.* "It's not as good as Mama Vega's in Rockland, but almost."

Kelsey giggled and shushed him. "Even hinting that anyone could be better than Rosita is asking for a lynching around here."

Their eyes met and held until the intensity became too much.

Reid saw her glance down at her plate just half a second before he would have. He cleared his throat and fumbled in his jacket pocket. "So, Mom's been reading everything out there on dating the past two weeks. I thought it was to make sure I didn't blow things with you, but now..."

A blush—so faint it took a pretty face and made it lovelier rather than giving her the appearance of a sun-kissed lobster—appeared on her cheeks. "Uncle Mel is... oh, I don't know. Maybe the word is smitten. It's kind of old-fashioned, but I don't know what else to call it. I've never seen him like this."

"Yeah. Mom, too." He unfolded the paper. "I could tear it into twenty pieces, and we could draw blind, but I thought maybe we'd just take turns answering the next?"

She eyed him. Concern... amusement... Reid couldn't tell which dominated the expression on her face. "You don't want to do this, do you?"

Reid shoved his mostly finished plate aside and gripped the paper. "I don't want to make you feel awkward. I agreed before I read the questions. They're kind of personal."

In one unexpected movement, she snatched the paper from him and began reading. One eyebrow rose. The other followed. Over the top of the paper, she regarded him once more. "You don't want *me* to feel awkward, or you think *you* are going to feel awkward?"

"Both?"

She scanned the list, hesitated, started to hand it back, and then began reading. "So, I'm supposed to ask you this question, right?"

"Okay. That works."

Kelsey eyed her chips, his face, and the chips again. Picking up one she tossed it at him and read aloud. "What are you looking for most in a relationship?"

Ugh. Forgot that one. Why does it feel like some weird interview? Reid's thoughts consumed him as he tried to explain without complicating things.

"Reid? If you don't want—"

He broke in while he still had the chance to prevent further awkwardness. "It's not me, it's you." *So much for no more awkward.* Reid tried again even as Kelsey stifled a snicker. "Okay, so that didn't work." He reached for her hand and squeezed. "I just don't want you to feel pressured or rushed by this kind of thing."

"Answer the dumb question."

"The problem is that I wasn't looking for a relationship. I just found you. And then all I cared about was making you smile when you'd had a bad day or just *being* with you."

"That's not the question, sweet as it is." Kelsey withdrew her hand, folded her hands over her chest, and let the paper crinkle in the process. "Today, right now. What are you looking for in *this* relationship?"

"You." Reid shrugged at her indignant huff and added, "It's the truth. I want to be able to spend time with you. I want to serve the Lord... *with you.*"

At that, she handed over the paper and grinned. "I can handle that just fine."

Reid skimmed the next question, reread it, and managed to hide the beatific smile that tried to form. She had to have read it and still chose to go first. "What makes you think we have a chance for a future together?"

She answered the question without even a second of thought. "You love the Lord. Anyone can see it." Her gaze dropped to her lap." And you're forgiving. I mean, I knew you weren't going to go back to dealing drugs, and I still freaked out on that as part of your past. It still freaks me out, but you just forgive and deal with it. If that isn't proof of a guy a girl should never let go of, I don't know what is."

"Anger is scary. Trust me, I know."

But Kelsey dropped the paper and gripped the table edges. "I wasn't angry, Reid. I was scared—terrified, really. I'd fallen for a guy who could have been Kenny's dealer. Then I found myself wishing you *had* been. Maybe he'd still be alive."

"I thought the Lord was in control of that one." When she didn't reply, he nudged the paper. "Go ahead. I dare you."

She asked if he thought opposites made difficult relationships. He asked how important family's approval affected a relationship. Back. Forth. The restaurant slowly emptied around them as time raced forward to the opening of the play. But, as the staff cleaned around them, they finally reached the last two questions. Kelsey read hers and flushed—dark, mottled, redness splattered across her face. "Um... well, um..."

Reid took the paper, read it, laughed, and winked. "I got this one. Totally have it. So, have you ever seriously considered marriage?"

"No." The single word hung between them. Reid waited for her to add... *something* to it. She didn't. She just waited. Only when he handed over the list of questions did he think he heard her murmur, "Not until I met you."

Their server paused by the table and informed them that the play would be starting in fifteen minutes. "We're encouraging everyone to go. You can get tickets at the door, and it's for a good cause, so..."

Reid pulled out his wallet, dropped a tip on the table, and waved the tickets he had at the same time. "We'd better hurry. You can ask me the last one on the way." A smile turned into a grin as he saw her read it, nod, and pocket the list. *Walking while I answer that—genius.*

The air bit into them with icicle teeth. Reid took her hand and led her away from Rosita's. Wind blasted, shoved, pushed them down the street toward the USO building. Cars streamed into the parking lot, out again, and parked up and down the street. Still, Kelsey didn't ask. Not until they reached the corner did Kelsey finally speak.

"Well, there's one more question before we can say we're done. Is there anything about me that you would change if you could?"

A snowflake fell—a real, beautiful, perfectly-timed snowflake. And beneath the decorative lights overhead and the falling flakes, Reid gathered the rest of his courage, held it close, and took her other hand in his. "Just one."

As he'd hoped, her face fell. For just a moment, he wished it were late summer in a field of sunflowers or spring surrounded by daisies instead of shivering in the cold wind and mantled with falling snowflakes. But one hand cupped her face—the other. The kiss he hadn't exactly planned but neither did he regret it. The better part of a minute raced past, but Reid allowed themselves the luxury of savoring what he hoped would become a treasured memory.

"Um, what was the question again?"

"What you'd change about me." Kelsey licked her lip before chewing on the corner. "You said there was just one thing. What is it?"

"Your last name. I think you need something more..." The word failed to produce itself at the needed moment. "You know what I mean. Where all the words start with the same letter?"

A hint of a smile formed before she ducked her head into his chest. "You mean alliterative?"

"Yeah. You'd be great as a double K."

Kelsey's protest came back half-hearted at best. "You make me sound like I'm a dude ranch!"

"Well, whatever. If I could change anything, I'd change your name to Kelsey Keller. That's my answer."

They walked again—each step making him more nervous and less confident than the last. *It's too soon. I knew it but so perfect. When else would I have such an opportunity?*

But at the steps of the USO, Kelsey tugged him close again. "I've always liked my name, but I think you're right. Sometimes you need a change of pace or just some new initials to spark up your life a bit."

Relief, joy, excitement—emotions bombarded him one after another. But instead of saying all the things he ached to, Reid heard himself say, "I think we can definitely make that happen whenever you think you're ready."

CHAPTER 15

A lone in the workroom, **Wayne** picked up stray bits of greenery, a semi-wilted amaryllis, and a tattered fern leaf. Beneath that, lay a perfect rose. Crimson—almost burgundy. Fragrant.

It would have to be tossed, but Wayne resisted. In the other room, he heard a spray bottle—proof that Señora Rojas was ready to leave. She'd clean the case and the door before gathering her coat and purse and informing him she'd return on Thursday. Four days. When had it gone from sounding like a dream vacation to an eternity?

Another glance at the rose. *She probably won't think anything of the color, but I'd know. And for reasons I am not ready to explore, it means something to me.*

With that thought in mind, he stepped through the curtain just as she turned toward him. Her eyes narrowed. "Did you clean up that pigsty you call a workroom?"

"All done." Heart pounding, feeling like a bigger fool than he ever had, Wayne offered the rose. His neck flamed hot enough that he suspected it matched the exact shade of the petals. "Merry Christmas, Lena."

Her name fell off his lips as if he spoke it every day, but he'd only said it once—the day he hired her. An awkward silence grew between them as Señora Rojas stared at the rose, glanced up at him, and returned her gaze to the flower. Just as he would have turned away with an order to leave, she plucked it from his fingers, lowered her lashes, and inhaled the fragrance.

"Merry Christmas, Wayne. Thank you."

"I—" He didn't know what he'd say, but *something* needed to happen and fast—before she left.

The bells on the door jangled, startling them and killing the hope of a... *moment.* A man rushed in. "My phone died. I missed the wife's message to pick up a centerpiece for tomorrow." His eyes darted to the empty case. "Is there *anything* in the back? She already thinks I don't—well. That doesn't matter. I need *something.* Fast."

Funny. I just thought the same thing a minute ago, but it was after giving a flower.

Señora Rojas took the situation in hand. "Wayne. What do you have back there?"

"Some greenery..." One by one, he ticked off his meager inventory. "And a dozen or so daisies—not exactly Christmassy."

"Can you spray them red? Do you have a large candle maybe? Or the mistletoe. Is there any of that left?" Even as she spoke, Señora Rojas pulled out the order book. "What is your budget?" When Wayne didn't move, she added, "Go! Make something amazing." And as he passed, she paused, rose in hand, sniffed it again, and offered it to him with a smile. Again, she said, "Thank you, Wayne."

A large vase, a candle inside, mistletoe, ferns, a few pine cones, and rose-gold ribbons. He dug through the top of the garbage can to ensure he hadn't tossed anything significant and came up empty. As much as he tried to avoid it, Wayne realized the arrangement *needed* that rose. So, encircling it with daisies, he stood back to admire it and nodded. "There."

Señora Rojas swept open the curtain. "Is it almost ready? He'll be late to dinner."

"Done."

She came to take it away, but at sight of the rose—*her* rose—she paused. "It's perfect."

"Wish I had one for you, still."

Her eyes met his and held for a moment before she whirled away with the centerpiece. Wayne wiped the counter again, a lonely daisy with two missing petals dropping into the garbage can as he finished up. He shut off the light and locked the back door. In the front, Señora Rojas had turned off the sign, turned out all but the front window light, and waited for him by the door.

His heart soared. *She waited. She never waits.*

"Wayne?"

"Coming." They stood there, the street lamps providing almost the only light. *Why do I keep feeling like a kid in school with a crush on my teacher?*

"The rose, Wayne?"

"Yeah. You were right, but I'm still sorry about that."

"I have it." Her hand clutched at her top over her heart. "It's here. The blossom would die, but this can't."

Buzzing filled his ears. Two of her appeared in his blurring vision. His breath whooshed from him followed by a great gulp of air. And everything cleared. Not knowing what else to do, he took her coat from her arm and held it out for her. Hands resting on her shoulders, Wayne murmured another wish for a wonderful Christmas and allowed himself just one more hint of the direction his heart demanded he go. "Thursday. It'll seem like forever."

"What are you talking about, Thursday? I will see you Tuesday. We have to get ready for the Valentine's Day that day."

The Valentine's Day. You used "the" out of place again. Hmmm...

Her hand on his cheek. Again, Wayne forgot to breathe. "Have a good Christmas. Call me if Reid proposes. I want to know."

"I will. I bet Brooke never imagined that this would happen when she made that goof."

"You must call her again—tell her the story. It will feel good after losing her job."

Mesmerized by Lena's eyes as she spoke, Wayne admitted he'd forgotten to call. "I just got busy with that little bit of premeditated serendipity and forgot."

"Then you call her. You tell her. This she will want to know." And before he could process it, she'd kissed his cheek and swept from the building with flair no one else in his life possessed.

Yeah... I'll call her on Christmas and let her know. And maybe I'll even tell her that I may have inadvertently set myself up to fall in love, too.

THE END

DISCUSSION QUESTIONS

S uggested discussion group questions for *Premeditated Serendipity* by Chautona Havig.

Premeditated Serendipity is a story about second chances both with others in our personal lives and with Jesus.

1. Are second chances really possible, or are we forever doomed to trying to live down the mistakes of our past?

2. As Christians who have received the ultimate second chance, how should we treat others as they attempt to live differently than they did in the past?

Despite the effectiveness of Wayne's meddling, he did ignore Scriptural principles in favor of his own desires for Reid—in particular, honesty. Read **Ephesians 4:25**.

3. Is there a more biblical way he could have addressed the issue?

Prayer plays a pivotal role in this book. As Christians, we have the honor and privilege to participate in at least three forms of prayer—personal prayer, intimate prayer with just a few people, and finally corporate prayer when the local body of Christ united in petition.

4. How do those differ from one another? What spiritual benefits do we give and receive with communication with our Lord?

Everyone has different communication methods. Some speak, some think, others write. The same is true of prayer. Reid was a quiet, conversationalist when praying. Kelsey prayed through song.

5. Why do we think we have to pray like the person behind the pulpit on Sunday mornings to communicate with God?

The Prayer Room exists as a place for people to come and have a quiet place to pray and/or have others pray for them. In a world where churches must keep doors locked, one central location for all Christians in a town can be a blessing.

6. Do you have a place you can go to pray away from the distractions of home and life? Is a place like that beneficial?

Michelle once said that each person had their own "unpardonable sin." Kelsey's, obviously, was about dealing drugs. She put those who peddle illegal narcotics on a fast-track to hell.

7. As Christians, why do we do that? Why do we create unforgivable sins that God hasn't?

Wayne had been wounded deeply by the church, and as a result, he alienated himself from the Body of Christ.

8. What should Christians do when they find one another actively avoiding fellowship?

9. How could Reid have attempted to facilitate reconciliation between Wayne and the local church?

Mrs. Oberton's "prophecy" was lifted straight from the Bible.

10. Why do you think so many people have trouble with it?

11. Was she wrong to encourage Reid to focus on the Lord alone for one year?

12. What might have been a better way to handle it?

After Kelsie and her brother lost their parents in Thailand, Uncle Mel stepped in as both parent and uncle. Often, we, or people in our lives, need someone to step in and serve us in this way.

13. What Scriptures can we use to guide us in relationships like that?

In several of my books, Kate Whyte or her daughter, Cadence, try to impose self-righteous rules on others. As a result, they run roughshod over the hearts and souls of many in Fairbury. But no one seems to do more than counter opinion with truth now and then.

14. Why do many churches overlook unloving responses to one another?

15. How can we behave biblically in this area?

PERSONAL NOTE

Many of my books take place in or near the fictional town of Fairbury. The characters in *Premeditated Serendipity* have either shown up in these other books or will soon. For example, the fundraising drive for the Diabetic Alert Dog (DAD) is in a "noella" (my word for Christmas novellas), *The Second Noel,* in the *Wonderland Wishes Collection.* In that story, I write about the little boy who needs the DAD and shine a light on another side of Fairbury—the one with people going all out to do what it takes to help a struggling family. The officers you met in this novella are featured in another Christmas noella, *Silenced Knight,* part of the *Mystery of Christmas 2* collection.

A place in Alexa Hartfield's hometown, where I happen to live and write, inspired The Prayer Room. Each night around nine o'clock, I arrive at The Lighthouse and write until about five in the morning. Sometimes people come in to pray or ask for prayer, but usually, it's just me, the Lord, and my fictional characters. But the prayer walls are real. The clay jars half full of prayers really do exist, and they really are prayed for almost indefinitely. It's a beautiful ministry for our city, and I am honored to be a part of it.

To celebrate the beautiful people who make this place possible, I put bits of different peoples' personalities into my characters. In Michelle, you find our director, Tara, and her passion for The Lighthouse. In Kelsey, you find Tara's bubbly personality. Dan, the man who relieves me at five o'clock, carries my backpack out to the car every day—because he's just a nice guy that way, and I thought it fit well with how I'd created Reid. And in Reid, you find much of the other director, Dakota. Dakota has that quiet, steadfastness that is just beautiful to watch.

To see The Lighthouse and how it functions, visit my YouTube channel.

MORE BOOKS

by Chautona Havig

Find the latest information and connect with Chautona at her
website: www.chautona.com

The Rockland Chronicles

Aggie's Inheritance Series
Ready or Not
For Keeps
Here We Come
Ante Up!

Past Forward: A Serial Novel (Six Volumes)
Volumes One through Six

HearthLand Series: A Serial Novel (Six Volumes)
Volumes One through Six

The Hartfield Mysteries
Manuscript for Murder
Crime of Fashion
Two o'Clock Slump
Front Window

The Agency Files
Justified Means
Mismatched
Effective Immediately
A Forgotten Truth

The Vintage Wren (A serial novel)
January (Vol 1.)

Sight Unseen Series
None So Blind
Will Not See
Ties That Blind (Coming 2018)

Christmas Fiction
Advent
31 Kisses
Tarnished Silver
The Matchmakers of Holly Circle
Carol and the Belles
Christmas Stalkings
Christmas Embers
The Second Noel
Silenced Knight
Merri's Christmas Mission

Standalone Novels
Noble Pursuits
Argosy Junction

Discovering Hope
Not a Word
Speak Now
A Bird Died
Thirty Days Hath…
Confessions of a De-cluttering Junkie
Corner Booth
New Year's Revolutions

Meddlin' Madeline Mysteries

Sweet on You (Book1)
Such a Tease (Book2)
Fine Print (Book 3)

Ballads from the Hearth

Jack

Legacy of the Vines

Deepest Roots of the Heart

Journey of Dreams Series

Prairie
Highlands

The Annals of Wynnewood

Shadows & Secrets
Cloaked in Secrets
Beneath the Cloak

Heart of Warwickshire Series
Allerednic

Not-So-Fairy Tales
Princess Paisley
Everard

Legends of the Vengeance
The First Adventure

ABOUT

www.chautona.com

Chautona Havig lives and writes in California's Mojave Desert. This book, like most of hers, fits into the Rockland Chronicles, a metropolis surrounded by towns and stories of the people who live there. In each book, you'll find connections to others by way of settings and characters. In all her work, Chautona strives to use story to nudge people to the feet of the Master Storyteller.

Sign up for her newsletter and receive weekly installments of the serial novel, *The Vintage Wren.*

Connect with Chautona Online:

Newsletter:	chautona.com/newsletter
Website:	chautona.com
Facebook:	facebook.com/pages/justhewriteescape
Instagram:	instagram.com/ChautonaHavig
YouTube:	youtube.com/user/chautona/videos
Twitter:	twitter.com/chautona
Goodreads:	goodreads.com/Chautona
BookBub:	bookbub.com/authors/chautona-havig

Out of the Blue Bouquet

INTRODUCING

When I heard Amanda's idea about a florist who botched a veritable bouquet of orders, I begged to be a part of it. I mean, who wouldn't love to dive into a project like that? And since Wayne had made cameo appearances in many of my stories, I thought it was about time that people got to know just a little more about him. So, I asked Amanda if I could make him her character's uncle, and the rest… well, you know what happened.

So, here we are with *Out of the Blue Bouquet*! After reading all the stories in this floral fiasco, it's time to get to know Brooke Hutchins and see just what happens to the poor girl who started it all. I've only read bits of it myself yet-Amanda has kept it rather close to her chest until now-but I'll be diving in and reading all the books in order, just as soon as I get my copy! From those bits she did share, I can tell this is going to be a wonderful book. So, grab a cup or glass of your favorite beverage, get comfortable, and enjoy! I know I'm going to have a nice bouquet of sunflowers beside me when I get started!

May the florists never send your "I'm sorry" bouquet meant for a friend whose feelings you hurt to your child after she announces her engagement!

Chautona *Havig*

Author of *Premeditated Serendipity*

Out of the Blue Bouquet

Out of the Blue *Bouquet*

a Novella

by

Amanda Tru

Published by

Walker Hammond Publishers

Walker Hammond

Publishers

Out of the Blue Bouquet by Amanda Tru

Copyright © 2017. All rights reserved.

PUBLISHED BY: Walker Hammond Publishers

All scripture quotes or references are from the English Standard Version of the Bible.

Library Cataloging Data

Tru, Amanda (Amanda Tru) 1978-

Bride of Regret / Amanda Tru

Summary: When Brooke is left in charge of Crossroads Floral, she accidentally sends the flower deliveries to the wrong people. Unfortunately, some of those wrong people include all of the ex-girlfriends of the most eligible bachelor in town. Are Brooke's mistakes a complete disaster, or can there be something beautiful in an out-of-the-blue bouquet?

Identifiers: ISBN-13: 978-1-68190-042-1 (trade) | ISBN-13: 978-1-68190-041-4 (Print on Demand) | ISBN-13: 978-1-68190-040-7 9 (ebook)

1. Western 2. Mail Order Bride 3. Traditional Romance 4. male and female relationships 5. Christian Inspiration

CONTENTS

CHAPTER 1

"I don't think this is a good idea!" Brooke spoke emphatically into the phone. Giving a little too much oomph to her car door, it slammed shut, as if to punctuate her words. "I just arrange the flowers. Making sure the orders are delivered is not part of my job description!"

"You are my employee," Brooke's boss insisted on the other end of the call. "As such, your job is what I say it is. It isn't that hard. Tylee has all the information you need."

Brooke sighed and nervously twirled a lock of blonde hair around her finger as she paced in front of her older model Volkswagon Jetta. "Isn't there another way, Helen? I don't mean to be disagreeable, but I'm really not comfortable with this. You just started the online business, and you expect me to take care of all of those orders as well as the local ones? I don't know the computer passwords or how to manage the site. In fact, you've expressly *not* taught me or given me any kind of access to anything other than the flowers. I don't know the first thing about what to do!"

Helen's voice was icy. "Brooke Hutchins, would you please think of someone other than yourself? I am at a funeral for a family member! I am grieving, and you can't manage Crossroads Floral for one day?" Loud sniffing came through the line, suggesting that a generous display of tears was forthcoming.

Guilt started to creep up, but Brooke pushed it away. This was Helen Garrison. There was none tougher than the sixty-six-year-old woman. While most her age were retiring, Helen had just expanded her company into the world of online business. She was stubborn, resilient, and only had feelings if they were convenient for getting her what she wanted.

Brooke put her hand to her already aching head, trying to think of a way to placate the woman who filled out her paychecks. "I didn't realize you were so upset about the funeral," she finally managed. "I thought he was someone you weren't especially close to, a distant relation. Didn't you say he was your cousin's husband?"

"He's actually my cousin's first husband," Helen clarified. "But her second and third husband won't attend the funeral, so I'm all she has. We were all so close at one time, and now we'll never get a chance to say goodbye." More sniffles.

Brooke shook her head in confusion. She wasn't sure how to respond, but she was pretty sure she didn't want any more details. "And there is no way to delay the orders a day?" she asked instead, flinging the question out in one last-ditch effort.

"No, there is not," Helen said, the steel in her voice now replacing the tears. "It isn't that difficult, Brooke. Like I said, Tylee has all the information, and I gave her instructions, like a substitute plan for just one day."

Brooke slowly let out her breath, trying to calm her frayed nerves. Normally a substitute plan would be adequate, but knowing that all the information resided with Helen's granddaughter, Tylee, was more than a little unnerving. Tylee was young, forgetful, and altogether silly. Brooke really figured she had a better chance of handling the day's duties without Tylee's assistance.

"I guess I can call you if I run into difficulties," Brooke said, finally resigning herself to her fate. Opening the car door once again, she reached back in to grab her purse. Now that there was obviously no way out of the day's duties, Brooke wanted to hurry and get the mess figured out and over with as soon as possible.

"No, you cannot," Helen shot back. "I am turning my phone off. I need the time to grieve and not be bothered."

"But what if there's a problem with the orders?" Brooke protested.

"For heaven's sake, Brooke! Just deal with it!"

Suddenly, there was no sound. "Helen?"

But the line was dead. Helen had hung up on her!

Fuming, Brooke gripped her phone so tightly her fingers turned white. It was that or throw the thing, and she couldn't afford to replace it. What really made her mad was that she wasn't given the chance to hang up on Helen first!

Slamming the car door a second time, Brooke grumbled a furious monologue at Helen, at the lousy November weather that had already turned the beautiful autumn colors drab, and at the stupid reality that meant she was barely making ends meet working at a small-town florist shop. Brooke felt like a complete failure, which was a feeling she'd rather grown accustomed to in her twenty-five years.

She marched to the front door of Crossroads Floral Co. and pushed it open. She immediately took offense at the bright tingling of the happy bell above her and vowed that first chance she got, she would take the thing down, at least while Helen was away.

"Oh good!" Tylee greeted, instantly rushing forward to give Brooke a quick, impulsive hug. "I was so worried you wouldn't come!"

"I'm here," Brooke said dryly. "But not by choice."

Tylee nodded. "Grammie gave me all of the lists and told me what to do, but I figured you'd still be worried about it since she's never had us do any of the work with orders before."

Brooke wasn't opposed to learning the business side of the floral shop, but Helen was controlling and unorganized, which was not a good combination. She never trusted anyone, not even her granddaughter, to use the accounts, and had therefore never taught any of them how to access the orders or any kind of records.

Brooke was the floral designer. Tylee was the delivery person. And their tasks never diverged. It was ridiculous to the point that, even if they happened to take an order, they had to write the information on paper so Helen could later input it into the computer. Then, all of the order instructions were printed off for Brooke each day.

With that being their background, they were now supposed to run the shop themselves? And Brooke had a bad feeling that all of Helen's "substitute plans" might be sorely lacking in organization. Possibly a worse feeling was knowing that, no matter what happened or what information they might find missing, they were completely on their own.

"Ok, show me what we need to do," Brooke said, determined to make the most of her fate. If they could get Helen's list of orders out of the way, then they would only have to babysit the shop to assist with any orders that were placed today.

Heading toward the front counter, Brooke tripped over a tall, plastic vase with a gaudy bunch of multicolored flowers. Catching her balance, she took deep breaths, waiting for both the pain and her anger to subside. Her shin would surely carry a bruise now, and all because of the horrid decorations Helen insisted on filling her shop with. Ugly fountains, flamboyant silk flower arrangements, and a few nightmarish statues all littered the front of the shop in a seemingly haphazard manner. Brooke had no idea why Helen kept the "merchandise." To her knowledge, not a single item from the resident collection had ever sold. The baskets, vases, and containers that were popular were located back in the store where Brooke worked and were items that she picked out and purchased as part of her supplies.

Brooke took the time to move an ugly, brown ceramic toad from near her foot, and then stood up to see Tylee's papers spread on the counter.

"By the way," Brooke said to the younger woman, "thank you for staying here to help me today. I know the funeral is for a member of your family as well. I'm not sure why you didn't go with Helen, but I really appreciate you not abandoning me and leaving me all of this work to do myself.

Tylee blinked her big, brown eyes in surprise, and then shrugged. "We weren't close at all to Uncle Art. He wasn't even really an uncle. He was married to one of Grammie's cousins, but then they got divorced a long time ago. I didn't even know who he was when Grammie told me that Uncle Art passed away. Then I remembered that he was the guy Grammie threw out of the house at Christmas dinner when I was about five. I don't think she's spoken to him since then."

Brooke raised her eyebrows. "Helen seemed pretty upset when I talked with her. Maybe Art meant more to her than she realized."

Tylee shook her head seriously. "I guess, but if she's this upset, then we'd better get used to running the shop ourselves. Grammie's cousins have a whole lot of exes, which means that's a whole lot of funerals she'll have to go to."

Brooke stifled an outright guffaw, barely managing a mere smile instead. Tylee may not be the hardest worker, the quickest learner, or even the most adept socially, but Brooke really did adore her. She was a ray of sunshine, and seeing the world through her unique perspective never ceased to cheer Brooke up. Most of the things she said weren't intentionally funny, but were said in a completely innocent and serious manner, which made them even more hilarious.

Brooke knew that the only reason Tylee worked at the shop was because of her grandma. When the cute brunette had graduated high school last year, college hadn't been an option. She'd had zero qualifications or work experience, and was rather adrift about what she wanted to do with her life. Helen had said she could work at the shop, and although she lacked skill in almost every area, Brooke was happy to have her.

"So this is the list of local orders," Brooke said, picking up one of the papers with way more enthusiasm than she felt.

"Yes," Tylee nodded. "The only order that isn't on the list is one that came in early this morning after Grammie printed this off.

She imputed it into the computer and clicked print right before she ran out the door, but I checked, and it didn't print because the printer was out of paper."

"Great," Brooke groaned. "Helen already turned her phone off. How are we going to get that order?"

"Oh, that's easy!" Tylee replied, a shrewd light in her eyes. "It was a Dylan Masters' order."

Brooke brightened. "Is it the same order as last week? Do you remember who you delivered it to?"

Tylee shook her head, "No, I think he has a new girlfriend."

"Isn't that the third one this month?" Brooke said, shaking her head.

Dylan Masters was one of their regular customers, but the recipient of his flowers was definitely not regular. The man was a Casanova.

Brooke wiggled her eyebrows and teased, "Did you manage to slip him your number so you can be next on his list of Crossroads women?"

"No," Tylee sighed dramatically. "He phoned the order in so I never got a chance. I'll have to try next time."

Tylee was already half in love with the man, and it was understandable. He was gorgeous, and it was easy to see why he had a never-ending line of girlfriends. Brooke had never actually spoken to him, but she enjoyed watching from afar as Helen and Tylee fawned all over him. Brooke had no qualm with teasing Tylee about her infatuation, though, because she doubted that the young woman would ever manage to give him her number. She was a little young for Dylan, who Brooke guessed to be in his early thirties, and it was awfully difficult to have an intelligible conversation with a man if you practically melted to the floor in a babbling mess every time he showed up.

"Wait, so if it isn't the same order as last week, how will we get the information?" Brooke asked, realizing that the crafty light in Tylee's eyes hadn't dimmed.

"I know Grammie's password to the computer!" she whispered conspiratorially.

"Really?" Brooke whispered back, surprised. Though they were alone in the store, a whisper seemed the appropriate voice level for such a topic. "How did you come by that?

Not only was Brooke impressed that Tylee had found the password, but she was also impressed that she would remember it!

Tylee opened her mouth to answer, but then, confusion suddenly clouded her brow, and she stopped. Instead, she walked over to Helen's desk and retrieved her grandmother's favorite coffee mug, the one shaped like a frog.

Returning to Brooke, she flipped it over and held it out.

Brooke accepted the mug, peering at the writing on the bottom. "Helen wrote her password on the bottom of her coffee mug?" she asked, incredulous.

Tylee giggled. "Yes! I've seen her looking at it when she's trying to log on and can't remember it!"

Brooke looked at the letters and numbers. "But it's just her initials and the year she was born!"

Tylee shrugged. "I've tried it, and it works for the computer, but nothing else. There is a different password for the online program and for different accounts, but the local orders are in a program that doesn't have a password lock. We can just type in Dylan Master's name and print out his missing order!"

"Tylee, you're brilliant!" Brooke said enthusiastically.

The young woman flushed, and Brooke realized that she had probably never had the word "smart" applied to her, let alone, "brilliant."

"Now, what are these other papers?" Brooke asked, picking up one of the other lists on the counter.

"Those are the orders that were placed online with Grammie's new website."

"But, Tylee, these are all orders for out of town, and some are… out of the country? What am I supposed to do with these?" It felt like she had swallowed a rock that was expanding in her stomach like a balloon.

"Grammie said you'd have to call the individual florists in each city." She pointed to one of the columns on the list. "See, right here."

"But with these being online, shouldn't the information be automatically sent to the florist local to where the delivery is?"

Tylee shook her head. "Grammie hasn't quite figured out how to make that automatic yet. This is a new company she's working with. So far she really likes it better than some of the others. Individual florists can set up their own website to draw in customers, then they get commissions on orders placed through them, even if they are fulfilled across the world. She offered a coupon code for customers yesterday, and it worked! She got orders placed from people around the world, to be delivered around the world!"

"She did that before she had everything figured out?" Brooke said, exasperated. This was typical Helen behavior. She would get excited about a new scheme and go all-in before taking the time to figure it out. Such things usually fizzled before she had learned everything, and then she was quickly onto the next "make-you-rich-quick" plan.

"Well, she said it would be easy," Tylee said, suddenly looking uncertain. "All you have to do is call the other florists, and their names and numbers are right on this paper."

"But some of these orders are overseas! What if no one speaks English? I'm sorry, I just don't know if my *Korean* is up to the challenge!" Brooke pointed to the order purposed for South Korea.

"Grammie didn't think it'd be a problem," Tylee reassured. "I heard her call in internet orders earlier this week. Of course, I think she's only had to do two so far. That promotion code really worked! How many do we have? Ten?"

"Something like that," Brooke grumbled forlornly. "I guess I'd better get at it."

"Oh! I have something that might help!" Tylee reached over and grabbed a white cup from the local coffee shop. "Coffee! I knew it was going to be a rough day, so I got you the largest size they have. I wasn't sure what you liked, but you seem like a straight-up black coffee kind of girl to me, so I went with it."

"Thank you," Brooke said, forcing a smile to the kind-hearted girl. The reason Tylee didn't know how Brooke took her coffee is because Brooke never took coffee. She hated it.

But now, looking at Tylee's eager-to-please face, she took a sip, thinking that if any day was a day to start drinking coffee, this was it.

Barely managing not to gag at the hot, bitter brew lurching down her throat, Brooke picked up one of the lists. She may as well start at the top, which as luck would have it, appeared to be a foreign country—some place called Eyjania.

Lord, I don't want to do this! Brooke prayed silently as she looked at the list in trepidation. *Please help me to get through this day and not mess things up too badly! Oh, and please let someone in Eyjania speak English!*

"Oh, let me get Dylan's order printed out for you," Tylee said suddenly, ending Brooke's impromptu prayer.

Taking a step to head to the computer around the counter, Tylee's foot found the ceramic toad Brooke had moved earlier.

She tripped.

Her arms flung out to catch her balance and keep her from crashing into a pile of Helen's decorations. However, before the hand found the counter, it found Brooke's cup of coffee.

Brooke screeched as the cup flew out of her hand. As if in slow motion, she made a grab for it with her right hand, then her left. Each impact only sent the cup in another cartwheel that spewed the coffee out like the blades of a fan. It finally crashed into the counter with such force that the lid flew off.

Brooke jumped back and put her hands up to shield her face as warm, dark liquid launched into the air in a fantastic splatter pattern.

"Oh no! Oh no!" Tylee yelped, hopping up and down from one foot to the other. But since the coffee had sat awhile, it was not very hot, and Brooke was pretty sure Tylee had managed to jump far enough away that the shoes hopping up and down were likely the young woman's only casualty.

Brooke, however, had not been so lucky. Coffee dripped from where it landed as the rich, brown brew now coated her hair, arms, clothes, shoes, the floor, Helen's decorations, the ugly ceramic toad that caused the whole problem...

And the order lists.

CHAPTER 2

B rooke grabbed at the lists, adding her "Oh, no! Oh, no! Oh, no!" to Tylee's.

She snatched them off the soaked counter. Part of her desperately denying that the papers were dripping with coffee, she shrugged out of her gray cardigan, placed the papers on a clean spot on the tile floor, and used her sweater to frantically blot at the brown mess.

Seeing what had happened Tylee rushed to the restroom and returned with a handful of wadded up paper towels. "I'm so sorry!" she fretted.

Accepting the paper towels, Brooke began blotting with those as well. But when she lifted a paper towel to discover that part of the printed list had stuck, torn off, and come along with the paper towel, she felt burning behind her eyes and a sob catch in her throat.

It was no use. As much as she wanted to rewind time and pretend that the scene in front of her eyes was just a nightmare that hadn't actually happened, the order lists were ruined, and there was nothing she could do to fix them.

"What can I do to help?" Tylee asked, wringing her hands. "I'm so, so sorry!"

"It's not your fault," Brooke said, closing her eyes on the unfortunate reality in front of her. "It was an accident." While sheer panic was her overriding emotion, what anger she did have was entirely directed at Helen's ugly toad. While she bore no ill will toward Tylee, she thought the toad might meet with an unfortunate accident of his own before Helen returned.

Lord, help me know what to do here! she prayed while forcing herself to take deep breaths.

Slowly, she opened her eyes and looked at the brown-streaked mess before her.

"You said you could access the order program on the computer?" She asked Tylee.

"Yes," she nodded eagerly. "But I can't access any orders from the website. That's a separate program with a different password."

Brooke studied the papers. "I think we might be okay," she said hesitantly. "The order sheets for today's deliveries are ruined. But this one for the online deliveries isn't bad."

She bent over the paper, not wanting to move it for fear of it tearing. It had been the furthest away from the coffee, and while the others had been soaked, there were only streaks of coffee marring this one, and most of the damage was around the edges.

Pointing at the list, she showed Tylee. "See, I can still read all of the floral shop names and most of the phone numbers. Some of the phone numbers are gone, but I should be able to just look those up since I have the shop names. The column for last names is fine, and even the instructions just have a few splotches. Theses streaks here are covering up a few first names, but most of the letters are still there. I think we can figure them out."

"I see what you mean!" Tylee said, relief filling her voice.

Brooke pointed to a row, "Look at this one. It says Sam Jones. But see the streak? It looks like it may be blotting out some other letters, but I can't be sure. I think it actually might be Samuel Jones. The 'J' is a little cut off too, so maybe not." Brooke sighed. "If we play it safe and send it to Sam Jones, it should still make it to the correct person, even if the name was originally 'Samuel.'"

"It's like a puzzle!" Tylee exclaimed.

"I'll start making the calls and marking things off the list, while you find the local orders on the computer," Brooke instructed swiftly.

Tylee headed off for her task, and Brooke quickly got a phone and dialed before she could doubt herself. In the next few minutes, she got Samuel Jones connected with his Thanksgiving bouquet.

Taking a deep breath, she next dialed Seoul, South Korea.

The phone rang several times, and Brooke mentally prepared herself to leave a message. Then the line clicked as it was picked up. A muddled voice mumbled something she didn't understand.

"Hello?" Brooke said. "This is Brooke from Crossroads Floral in the US. I'm calling to place an order via NetFloral."

"Yes, yes," the man responded. "No orders at night."

"Oh, I'm sorry!" Brooke said, feeling like an idiot. She hadn't done the math to realize that it was currently the middle of the night in South Korea. This poor man likely had his business and home in the same building, and she had just awakened him.

"I can call back in the morning!" she said swiftly, thinking she'd need to check a time zone map and do the math in order to know what time to call back.

"No, no," the man assured quickly. "I take order now."

The man was very nice, but it was obvious English was not his first language. His words were choppy, and Brooke was nervous that he wasn't understanding what she was saying. She so wished that she could either send the order via the Internet, as it was originally intended, or speak Korean. Since neither was a current option, she pushed forward.

She read aloud the information for the order and the address. After each bit, the man would say, "Yes, yes," and Brooke could tell he was writing it down. She then asked him to repeat the information, and he did so perfectly. She even read off the message for the card, after which, the man said "Yes, yes," and again recited it back correctly

Feeling relieved that she was obviously wrong in her initial concern, Brooke finally gave the name of the recipient.

"Jolene Gregory," Brooke said, careful to give slow and clear pronunciation. Thankfully, this was one name that wasn't badly damaged by coffee, and Brooke painstakingly spelled, "J-O-L-E-N-E."

"Yes, yes," the man said, and Brooke heard the scratching of a pencil. Then he repeated, "J-O-E."

"No," Brooke said quickly. "Jolene Gregory. The name is Jolene. J-O-L-E-N-E."

"Yes, yes. J-O-E—," and he held the sound of the "E" for a very long time, before finishing with a quick, "Gregory."

Brooke was at a loss for words in any language. She very much admired anyone who spoke more than one language, and at the moment, she desperately wished she was one of them! Her parents had insisted she take French and German classes as a child. While she didn't do half as well speaking either of those languages as her Korean friend spoke English, she really wished those German classes had been Korean instead. How was she supposed to communicate when the language barrier appeared insurmountable?

"Can you please write down the exact letters I say?" Brooke said, trying yet again.

"Yes, yes," the man confirmed.

"J-O-L-E-N-E, then put a space and write these letters, G-R-E-G-O-R-Y. Do you have it?"

"Yes, yes. Jolene Gregory."

Brooke felt a wave of relief. This was the first time he'd pronounced it correctly. "Yes, that's right," she said.

"Good, good," the man said. "Now I go to bed."

"No!" Brooke said quickly. "Can you please spell me the letters one more—"

But he had already hung up.

Brooke sighed, momentarily resting her head in her hands.

Lord, please help that order to get to the right person! With the right last name and the right address, she really hoped it would make it, even if the first name was spelled wrong.

Hoping that the South Korea order would be the most difficult of the day, Brooke looked at her list, telling herself she couldn't fall apart until she was done. But anticipating the next few orders on the list did nothing to boost her confidence.

"Hey, Tylee," she called, her brow furrowing in confusion. "I have two orders for the same town—Tracey, Oregon. But one of the addresses is too 'coffeed' to read. Do you think both orders go to the same address?"

"Oh, I remember looking at those orders! I think they are having a bachelorette party or something. Did you look at the description for what they want for the order?" Tylee laughed.

Brooke looked at the instructions. Even though no one could see her, she blushed, thankful that she wasn't the florist needing to fulfill that specific bouquet request!

Tylee was right. It was obviously a joke bouquet for a bachelorette party, which meant the order placed right after that one was probably the real bouquet to make up for the joke! The time stamp showed the orders placed about two minutes apart, and since Brooke had never heard of Tracey, Oregon, it must be a small town. While the street address on the first order was unreadable, but the one for the second order was thankfully very clear.

Brooke smiled in relief and marked a little line on the list, indicating that the two orders went together. "Well, we'll be sure both bouquets make it to the bride in Tracey. They'll definitely need the second one to make up for the first. And I'm glad I don't have to make either one! I just don't know that I can actually read off these instructions and not die of embarrassment. If we ever get one of those orders, Helen will have to put that one together without me!"

"You know you wouldn't have to ask Grammie," Tylee shot back. "She'd insist on doing it herself anyway!"

"You're probably right." Brooke sighed and looked down at the phone number. Then she noticed a number beside it. "There is a fax number on this one! I'll just type out the order information and fax it over. That way, there's no chance of mistakes, the florist will see exactly what the instructions are, and I won't have to give them!"

Brooke hurried over to the computer and scooted Tylee off. Two minutes later, she was printing out the information. She hurried over to the fax machine and sent the order. In another two minutes, she received confirmation that it had been received.

"Whew! That one was easy!" Returning to the lists, she sat back down on the floor and studied what she still had left to do. A few of the remaining orders had fax numbers as well, and Brooke made quick work of those.

The last order was the first one she had intended to do before the coffee catastrophe. With determination, she pressed the numbers to dial a country she had never heard of before.

"Hi! I'm calling from Crossroads Floral. We are a part of the NetFloral co-op, and I have an order that was placed on our site for your area. We don't have the automated settings right yet, so I need to phone the order in directly."

"Oh, yes!" said the woman on the other end of the line. "We've received several of those orders. And the automated system doesn't seem to be working right for anyone yet. Lots of florists are having to make calls. Let me get the order information, and we'll get it right out."

Brooke's relief was so great that she actually started shaking. Not only did this overseas florist speak perfect English, but this was Brooke's last online order, and she'd just found out that placing all the orders by phone was relatively normal!

"I'm glad you caught me," the florist said. "We're just about to close for the day."

Brooke looked at the clock, thankful that it was only nearing lunchtime in her time zone. She had too much work to do for it to be any later.

"I'm ready whenever you are," the woman announced cheerfully.

"The order is for a 'bouquet of flowers native to Eyjania,'" Brooke quoted carefully.

"We can do that!" the florist chirped.

Then Brooke read the info for the accompanying card, followed by the address for the delivery.

The woman read the correct address back to Brooke, and then asked, "And the name on the order?

Brooke bit her lip nervously. This was the tricky part. While she was reasonably certain about all the other info, the name was almost totally obscured with coffee stain. Plus, it looked to be a name she wasn't at all familiar with. "I'm not sure of the pronunciation," she said honestly. Maybe Catri? Or Calrin? It's C-A—"

Brooke paused, was the next letter an L or a T?

"T-R-I," she said, finishing quickly.

"Got it!" the woman said confidently. "And the last name?"

"I'll be honest," Brooke said self-consciously. "We had a bit of an accident. The last name is mostly obscured on my order list, and I'm unable to print out another. The most I can be absolutely sure of is that it starts with an 'S.'"

"Then 'S' is what we will go with," the woman said, not missing a beat. "It looks like the address is an apartment building. It shouldn't be difficult to find the correct person with the first name and the first letter of the last name."

"Thank you so much!" Brooke said, relief flooding through her.

"Thanks for calling!" the friendly woman replied. "I actually called NetFloral technical support yesterday, and they said they should have all the bugs worked out soon. I certainly hope so! I personally like this co-op a lot! We've had a lot of orders on our site for around the world, and I think it's pretty fun! And we get commissions on all those orders!"

"Yes, I hope things work out," Brooke replied. "It would be awfully nice to not have to make phone calls for each order." *Not to mention a whole lot less stressful if coffee is involved.*

Brooke hung up the phone and would have put her head in her hands to weep in pure relief if she didn't still have a mountain of work to do with the local orders.

The phone hadn't been down two seconds before Tylee called from where she sat at the computer. "Ummm, Brooke? Can you come look at this? I'm in the program, but want to make sure everything is right before I print."

"We need to hurry," Brooke glanced at her watch as she headed for the computer. "We are already behind. I need to get the flowers arranged and ready for you to deliver."

"I have today's date in the search box, which brings up this list," Tylee explained.

"Looks good," Brooke said quickly. "Click print."

"The weird thing is that it still isn't pulling up the Dylan Masters order."

"Maybe since Helen just added it this morning, it isn't showing up as an order for today. Usually, we take same day orders on paper and Helen logs it later. It should come up if you do a search for just his name."

The phone rang. "I'll get it," Brooke said. "Click print! We're running out of time."

By the time Brooke finished with taking down the info for a same day order on the phone, Tylee was proudly waving four sheets of paper. "These two are for you, and these are for me," she said, handing Brooke the lists. "I got the Dylan Masters order added and made two copies. You can work on the arrangements while I get the cards ready. Then I'll match them up and be off."

Brooke grabbed the sheets and headed to the back of the store. Breathing deeply, she let the smell of the flowers and plants reach all the way to her toes and calm her frayed nerves. For Brooke, there was nothing like the smell of a flower shop!

Thankfully, Tylee had managed to print off the instructions separate from all the address and other order info. That always made things so much easier. Taking a deep breath, she looked at the first order and began assembling a dozen red roses into a large vase.

"Ugh!" she called to Tylee. "We have a lot of orders today! It looks like close to twenty. After I get the first ten done, you should go deliver and come back for the last ones. Whenever I finish, I can help you with the deliveries."

"Sounds like a good plan," Tylee said. "I'm getting all the cards ready. Love must be in the air! I have a lot of, 'Had a wonderful time last night,' and 'You're beautiful.' Even a few, 'Can't stop thinking of you.' There's a couple 'Happy Anniversary,' and 'Happy Birthday,' but those aren't nearly so fun."

"You're such a romantic, Tylee," Brooke shook her head. "To me, those just sound like we have way too many Dylan Masters-types in town."

"That's because you're bitter and unhappy," Tylee said brightly. "If someone did something romantic for you, you would assume they were hiding something."

"Ouch!" Brooke said dramatically. Then, "But isn't there always an ulterior motive?"

"No!" Tylee shot back. "But how would you know that? You haven't been on a date in forever."

"Well, that's true," Brooke admitted. "And while I may not be completely happy, I'm perfectly content to watch romance from behind a bouquet of flowers."

She didn't mind making small talk with Tylee, but she wasn't going to bare her heart and explain why she wasn't interested in dating. Tylee was too young, idealistic, and romantic to understand.

Brooke hadn't ever been one to date a lot. The few she'd dared to call boyfriends had quickly lost the title and done enough damage to her heart that she was reluctant to let any other man make an application.

Several dozen roses, a live plant, and five mixed bouquets later, Brooke sent Tylee on her way while she worked on finishing the orders. By the time the last rose was in place, Brooke's back was hurting from standing so much, and she was exhausted. Tylee arrived back just in time to match the cards with the flowers, and then they divided up the remaining orders. Brooke loaded her share into her car and locked up the flower shop. She really hoped reports didn't get back to Helen that they had closed early, but that was the only way they'd get the orders delivered at a decent hour. Besides, Brooke was so tired and out of sorts that if the phone rang with one more last minute order, she thought she would scream!

Fortunately, the orders that had come in for tomorrow didn't look to be nearly as much, and as long as Helen was back, she should be able to get caught up on some purchase orders for supplies and hopefully recover from today. However, if Tylee brought her coffee again, she would immediately pour it down the drain!

CHAPTER 3

B rooke made quick work of the deliveries, and she really didn't mind it. She always enjoyed seeing the looks of happiness when someone received flowers. Pulling up in front of an office building, she glanced at the clock in her car. This was the last order, and it was five minutes before 5:00. She grabbed the large bouquet of roses and hurried into the building as fast as she could. The delivery was for a Kiffany Terrel. If the office where Miss Terrel worked closed at 5:00, Brooke could be in trouble for not making the delivery in time.

It was one of only a few multi-leveled buildings in town, and this one happened to be mostly comprised of medical offices. Looking at the envelope, Brooke saw that she was supposed to make it to suite 201, which meant the second floor. Upon entering the building, Brooke headed immediately to the elevator. But after pushing the button and waiting thirty seconds with the light above the button not even blinking, the sign advertising stairs was too tempting, and she abandoned the elevator. She held the flowers away from her body, trying to keep them balanced as her feet quickly climbed the cement stairs. Reaching the second story, she pushed the bar with her hip and made it through the door. She found Suite 201, which was the office belonging to an eye doctor, and reached the counter only slightly out of breath.

"I have a flower delivery for a Kiffany Terrel," she said,

peeking from behind the roses to the woman behind the desk."

"I'm Kiffany!" the stunning blonde said with a bright smile.

"Then these are for you," Brooke said, extending the flowers and setting them on the counter between them.

"Thank you!" she squealed, accepting the flowers and reaching for the attached card.

Her duty complete, Brooke turned around to exit the office empty-handed. At the door, though, she couldn't resist turning to watch. She loved this moment. The one where someone realizes that they are loved and cared for. The instant when a special message of love is communicated through the unique, beautiful language of flowers.

Kiffany opened the card and immediately squealed again. The card dropped from her excited fingers, and she looked at in on the desk, as if in awe. "I knew it! He loves me! He really does love me!"

Brooke didn't know what the card said. Tylee had taken care of the card. But it made her heart happy to know that her work had delivered such a special message. It almost made the trouble from today seem worth it.

Others in the office were now curiously gathering around the excited receptionist, including a not-so-happy woman in a white doctor's lab coat. Brooke let the door fall firmly behind her, happy to walk away with the one moment and leave before any other subsequent moments had a chance to mar the memory.

Once back to her car, Brooke called Tylee to make sure all of her orders had been delivered. After getting confirmation that the work for the day was officially complete, Brooke sat for just a minute, breathing out all the stress in great relaxing breaths that would make any yoga instructor proud. Finally, she pulled out and headed home.

Typically, Brooke might feel somewhat lonely on a night when she had nothing scheduled and no one to talk to. She lived alone in a one-bedroom apartment, and her list of friends who liked to do things socially was rapidly dwindling as most were now married or in serious relationships. Since Brooke wasn't interested in her own serious relationship or being a third wheel with her friends, loneliness was now becoming a familiar companion.

But tonight, she very happily spent the evening alone in comfy pants with a bowl of soup and a good book. A little time in a world of fiction gave her a much-needed respite from the reality of today and the gloom that waited tomorrow. Some days were harder than others for Brooke, and this had been a very hard day. The troubles only served to remind her that she was really going nowhere. A world without the hope that something would change was a difficult one to live in. But for Brooke, it felt as if she would forever be the florist in the back of Helen's flower shop. She longed for something different, but at this point, she didn't even know what different looked like.

It wasn't that Brooke disliked her job. She loved being a florist. Working with flowers and making beautiful art with them made her heart happy, as long as Helen left her alone. But she felt stuck, as if she was going nowhere very fast. Her older siblings were all highly successful in their careers, while Brooke didn't feel like working a small floral shop actually qualified as a career by comparison.

Brooke actually had a bachelor's degree in interior design. Right out of college, she had applied for all her dream jobs and was turned down. Then she applied for all those jobs that weren't quite her dream, but she could work her way up. And she wasn't hired. Then she applied for every job she could, just to have money enough to pay rent on a one-bedroom apartment. And she ended up at Crossroad Floral Co., owned by Helen Garrison.

After that, her confidence was so low that she could never manage to make herself apply for another job. At this point, she had no dreams or plans for the future. She was adrift without any ambition to even attempt to find her way to shore.

Her siblings had offered to use their connections to help her get a job in the city, but she had steadfastly refused. If she couldn't get there on her own, it wasn't worth doing. She'd always felt like the runt of the litter where her family was concerned. She desperately wanted to prove herself, by herself. Most of the time, she felt like she failed miserably.

The next morning Brooke got up early and ran a couple miles on the treadmill before breakfast. The stupid treadmill seemed almost an allegory for her life, and yet, as with everything else, she religiously made herself run nowhere at least four days a week.

By the time she showered, ate some cereal, brushed her teeth, and headed out the door, she was feeling pretty good. Hopefully, her boss was back from the funeral and today would be a normal day.

As usual, Brooke arrived at the shop early, much earlier than Helen and Tylee came to work. Though she didn't get to count all of her early hours for pay, the early arrival allowed her to do her morning devotions, unload and arrange her supplies, and look at some interior design magazines. It was her quiet time that allowed her to be fully prepared for when her boss walked through the door and the time clock started.

The phone was ringing as Brooke stepped through the door. She would normally have just let the answering machine get it, but it seemed strange to be getting a call at a floral shop at 7:00 in the morning. With a vague premonition that something wasn't quite right, Brooke hurried to the desk and dove for the phone, picking it up right before the call went to the answering machine.

"Hello! Crossroads Floral!" Brooke answered with far too much breathless energy for so early.

"I'm calling from Eyjania. There was an order that was placed for today's delivery, and we've run into a problem."

Dread settled like a large rock in the pit of Brooke's stomach. "Yes, I remember the order." Only this wasn't the friendly woman Brooke had spoken to yesterday. This was a man who was already sounding quite gruff. "What is the problem?"

"We sent the order out for delivery. It was a bouquet of flowers native Eyjania,' as requested. But the name we have doesn't appear correct, so my delivery man doesn't know who to deliver them to!"

"I'm so sorry!" This wasn't an employee she was talking to; this was the owner!

Brooke hurried to her work area and, with fingers shaking, scrambled through all the papers she could find. Pulling out the coffee-smeared list of online orders, she worked to keep her voice cool and professional, instead of revealing the complete panic she actually felt. "Let me see. I have the order right here. Let's see if we can figure out what the problem is."

Brooke bit her lip. This was one of those orders where she had guessed on a few of the letters in the first name. And with it being an overseas country, it was very possible that she had guessed wrong for the unfamiliar name.

She heard a noise that sounded distinctly like the impatient drumming of fingers. "Now, this may not be your mistake at all. In fact, I rather doubt it. The employee you spoke to yesterday wrote the information with a defective pen that she happened to think had pretty ink. Then she used the same pen to address the envelope for delivery. Both smeared terribly, and now the person delivering the flowers can't read the name. My employee thought she remembered the name you gave her, but she was apparently wrong."

The man literally growled his frustration. "I should have taken matters into my own hands and called to clarify the name from the beginning."

He muttered something else under his breath, but the only word Brooke understood was "incompetence." She could hear the stress in his voice and pictured some guy standing with a bouquet of flowers in his hand, waiting to find out who to deliver them to. Worse, Brooke had the awful feeling that the shop owner was wrong—it wasn't his employee's mistake at all. It was Brooke's.

Finding the order on her list, Brooke ran her finger across to find the recipient's name. "What is the name you have for the order?" she asked.

"I have Katrin for the first name." And he gave the spelling.

Brooke swallowed with difficulty. "No, that's not correct." Brooke squinted, trying to decode the letters. "The name I have is C-a-l-r-i."

"You mean Clari?"

Brooke paused, looking at the brown spots amidst the black spots that she was trying to decipher. "Yes. It could be that," she said pathetically.

"What's the last name?"

Brooke swallowed. If she was creative, she might be able to come up with an answer that would lay the blame on the owner's employee. Maybe she could say that the last name on the order had just this minute become damaged. But she couldn't. She couldn't sugarcoat the truth or let anyone else take the blame for something that may not have been her fault.

"All I have is 'S,'" Brooke confessed.

Then, with a voice as strong as she could muster, she explained, "We had an accident yesterday, and the information from the original order was damaged. It likely wasn't your employee's mistake at all. I just hoped that the first name and the first letter of the last name would be enough to get it to the correct person at the apartment building."

"It isn't an apartment building! It's the palace!"

"Did you say *palace*?" Brooke coughed.

"Yes!" the man thundered. "I have a man at the palace right now, and he doesn't know who gets the bouquet! Are you telling me that you don't know the last name? How do you think that makes my business look?"

Brooke gasped, "I'm so sorry!" Desperately, Brooke strained her eyes at the coffee stains. She could see a tiny bit of a figure beneath the brown tinge, but it didn't even look like a letter. "I think I see a funny looking 'o' after the 'S,'" she admitted, trying to give him at least one more clue. "But it doesn't quite look right. It almost looks like there's a line going through the 'o.' And there might be an 'n' at the very end, but it's so faint, I can't be sure.

"'S,' funny looking 'o,' and 'n.'" the man muttered. "Do you mean Sørensen? Could the name be Sørensen?

Brooke studied at the name, the letters falling into place like the pieces of a puzzle. "Yes! That's it!"

"I've got to go," the man growled. "You'd better hope Clari Sørensen is the right name. Otherwise, my employee's pretty ink pen and your Clari S. will be no excuse for either one of you!"

The line went dead.

Brooke weakly walked back to the front desk and dropped the phone on its cradle. She had messed up an order to a palace in a foreign country. She tried to tell herself that it wasn't entirely her fault. The shop owner had volunteered the fact that the name his employee had written down was smudged and illegible. But if Brooke hadn't provided the wrong name at the beginning, maybe it would have been easier to figure out.

She wandered back to her work counter and looked nervously at the clock. If she didn't hear within the next couple minutes, then that should mean that the flowers were successfully delivered, right? She tried to tell herself that she was sure Clari Sørensen was the correct name. It would work out, the flowers would be delivered to the correct person, and there would be no lasting harm done. But just the knowledge that she had messed up in such a grandiose way, completely unnerved her.

Brooke hadn't yet finished agonizing over what had happened when the bell rang above the door, announcing the arrival of Helen and Tylee.

The first red flag was that they were early. In all the time that Brooke had worked for Helen, the woman had never arrived before 8:30.

Then, the look on Tylee's face when she pushed the door open should have caused Brooke to immediately retreat. It was a clear, "run for your life" expression, which not even the happy jingle of the bells on the door could mask.

"Do you have any idea what you have done?" Helen hissed, rushing up to Brooke. The older woman's head didn't quite make it to Brooke's shoulder, but that didn't stop her from thrusting her face up as close to Brooke's as possible.

Startled, Brooke automatically stepped back, trying to recover her personal space. But her back bumped against the counter. She looked to Tylee for a little help, but the other woman was obviously too upset. She had stepped back from Helen as well, bumping against the front door and giving the bells a perturbed little ring.

"I'm not sure what you mean," Brooke said hesitantly. "What have I done?"

"Everything!" Helen squawked, arms flapping dramatically. "You did everything wrong! Every order from yesterday was messed up. And it's all your fault!"

Brooke's heart leaped painfully, and her stomach felt ill at the intensity of Helen's anger.

Brooke shook her head. "But I didn't... I don't understand. I know about the overseas order. But I just fixed that one."

Tylee, her voice small and miserable, spoke up. "Brooke, we sent flowers to the wrong people!"

CHAPTER 4

H elen had to be wrong. She had been so careful with those orders. There couldn't be more mistakes. She was sure.

Shaking her head again, Brooke insisted, "There must be some mistake. I followed the lists you gave me. I know they went to the people on the list." Frantically trying to prove her innocence, Brooke went around the counter to where the papers were still spread out haphazardly where she had left them.

"You mean these lists?" Helen said, grabbing the brown, crumbly papers off the counter and waving them under Brooke's nose. "The ones that you doused with coffee? The ones that you can't actually read?"

Brooke's gaze shot to Tylee, but her friend's eyes were downcast. It didn't seem that Tylee had mentioned any of her involvement in the coffee disaster, and it also didn't seem like she would receive any support from that direction. The poor woman was pale and literally shaking. If a fraction of Helen's anger turned her granddaughter's way, Brooke feared Tylee would collapse.

Brooke swallowed. Helen was too upset to see reason. If there was an actual problem with some of the orders from yesterday, Brooke needed to know the details so she could fix it. "Helen, if I messed something up, I'm sorry. It wasn't intentional. The lists we needed were illegible, and we printed out new copies of the ones we could. You've never shared the passwords for us to print out all of the lists. The coffee was a complete accident, and we did the best we could. Please tell me what the mistakes are so I can try to remedy them."

"So you admit that you hacked my computer without my permission," Helen spat.

"No. I logged onto the store computer to print out order lists," Brooke stated calmly. "If there were mistakes in the order it's likely because I did not have access to what was necessary to get them right."

"How dare you insinuate that this is my fault!" Helen huffed. "I wasn't even here!"

Brooke didn't back down. "If you had been here, it would have been nobody's fault! It wouldn't have happened! It should have been a quick fix to print the lists after there was an accident with the coffee."

"Since you so easily hacked the computer login password, I would have thought the other passwords wouldn't have been a problem," Helen snapped.

Brooke immediately shot back, "They wouldn't have been if you conveniently left them all on the bottom of frog cups. But I was a little busy and didn't have time to look!"

Helen's eyes narrowed. "I don't think you understand what serious trouble you are in, Miss Hutchins. You admit you accessed my computer without permission. You admit that you ruined the lists. And you admit that you used the ruined lists and placed the orders incorrectly. The blame rests squarely on your shoulders. Do you realize that I could sue you for the damage you did to my business, and have you arrested for hacking my computer?"

Helen's word sent a shot of fear through Brooke, not because Helen's threat wasn't ridiculous, but because the older woman rather specialized in the ridiculous.

Hoping to at least insert a thread of rational truth to her tirade, Brooke explained, "In order to arrest me for hacking, I believe you would need to prove I was accessing the computer for some illicit purpose. Since I got on it with your password, which was written in an open place, and I used it to do the job you assigned to me, there was no crime committed."

With a glance at Tylee, she continued firmly, "As for the rest of your accusations, yes, I admit to all of those. Now, if you would be so kind as to *tell me what mistakes I am admitting to*, I would really appreciate it!"

No, she was not going to rat out Tylee. While it was very true that Tylee was the one who knocked over the coffee and figured out the passwords to access the computer, Brooke wasn't going to admit any of that to Helen. With her boss so angry and set on Brooke being wrong, the truth wouldn't help anyway. It would just serve to make her furious at both Brooke and Tylee. Brooke would fully take the blame, and do it without complaint if it spared Tylee the wrath of her grandmother.

Helen glared at Brooke. "I already told you what you did. You sent all of the orders to the wrong people!"

Brooke felt her lips form a thin line as she struggled with her irritation. "Helen, I need to know what actually happened, with no exaggeration. We handled between 30 and 40 orders yesterday. I'm sure it wasn't *all* of yesterday's orders that were delivered to the wrong people."

"It wasn't all the orders," Tylee spoke up, with a quivering voice. "Just a few that we know of so far. A few of the names were messed up, and the flowers ended up being delivered to the wrong people. I think some of the instructions were missing for one order, and the bouquet sent didn't completely match what was requested. That's all we know of so far."

"So, how many orders are we talking?" Brooke asked, hoping that maybe things weren't quite as bad as Helen made it sound. "Maybe five orders?"

"Three so far," Tylee replied.

Brooke barely stopped her breath from releasing in a huge sigh of relief. Three orders. That didn't sound so bad after all. Nodding firmly, she spoke, ready to fix things the best she could.

"If you give me the numbers of those who have called in about the order mistakes, then I will call, make an apology, and see what can be done to make things right."

"That will not be necessary," Helen said coolly. "I have already made the apologies and refunded the money. All of the lost proceeds from those orders will be deducted from your pay."

Brooke kept her face stoic, but it was difficult. She didn't want to show emotion in front of Helen, and she especially didn't want to show the fear that Helen's words caused. She knew that it was probably right that she pay for the mistakes made, but those orders wouldn't come cheap. She was on a tight budget. The cost of three orders, she may be able to handle, but if any more order mistakes showed up, she might not be able to afford her bills with the dock in pay. How could she pay her rent without a paycheck?

"I would still like to see the orders that were wrong," Brooke insisted. It wasn't that she didn't believe Helen. There didn't seem to be any way around the fact that she'd messed up, but she had a driving need to know the details. "If I know what mistakes I made, maybe I can figure out if there were any other mistakes made, and I can prevent them happening in the future."

Helen sniffed in disdain. "Your job is to arrange the flowers. You will never handle another order again. We don't have time to waste. I found out about yesterday's catastrophe when I checked my email this morning. I then responded to the emails and sent refunds. I haven't done anything else yet, as taking care of your mess has already put us behind schedule. The orders for today need to be sent out, and I can't afford to have anything go wrong with them. My only consolation in all of this is that the mistakes were on the online orders. If you screwed up the local orders, it would have ruined me! It would have been all over town before breakfast!"

There was no point in defending herself or getting Helen to change her attitude on anything. "I'll go get prepped for today's flower arrangements," Brooke said dully as she side-stepped Helen to busy herself readying her supplies.

Finally releasing Brooke from her glare, Helen bustled over to the computer. "I'll print out today's orders. I want them done by noon for Tylee to deliver. Any other orders that come in will have to be completed for Tylee to do a second delivery this afternoon. I need to handle the online orders, so you and Tylee will have to handle the calls."

Eager to please, Tylee hurried over to the phone and pressed the blinking light on the answering machine.

A strained voice filled the shop. "Hi, ummm… this is Aimee Maxwell on Crescent Drive. I think there's been a mistake."

Brooke froze mid-stride.

"I just had some beautiful flowers delivered. But the card said they were from my mother for my birthday. Well, it is my birthday, but the problem is, my mother passed away from a sudden heart attack seven months ago. So if you could please give me a call back and let me know how I got flowers from my mother, I'd appreciate it." The voice cracked in a sob. "I'm just really confused." The phone number she mumbled was barely audible before the call ended.

Beep.

Brooke was going to be sick.

A new voice spoke up. "Hi! This is Michelle Thomas. There were some flowers delivered to me, but I think there's a mistake. The delivery girl just handed me the bouquet and said, 'These are for you.' I didn't realize that there was a problem until after she left. The address is correct, but the card says Tara. There's no Tara who lives here. I don't know if you want to come back to get the flowers. I feel bad that Tara might not get them. Anyway, call me."

Her phone number was followed by another beep.

"Hi! There were some flowers delivered—"

"How many messages are on the machine?" Brooke interrupted.

Tylee pressed the stop button and looked up at Brooke, pure panic in her eyes. "Fourteen," she whispered hoarsely.

That's when Brooke realized that Helen had been correct. Brooke had messed up *all* of yesterday's orders.

"This can't be happening!" Brooke moaned. "I followed the lists!"

Not able to bring herself to look at Helen, Brooke once again grabbed at the papers on her work counter. Her hands lit on the only white paper in the mess of brown coffee-stained ones. The list of local orders had been ruined, so they had printed out a new one, which Brooke had followed to every last detail. There was no way she could have made that many mistakes.

Her eyes scanned the names on the list, seeing nothing unusual. Then her gaze moved up to the heading area and caught on the date.

The month was right. The day was right. The year was not.

Tylee appeared at her elbow, looking over her shoulder.

"It's the date, Tylee!" Brooke whispered.

Behind them, Helen had once again pressed the play button. The litany of confused customers made for a nightmarish background to their conversation.

Tylee shook her head. "That was yesterday's date," she insisted. "I looked at the calendar before I printed."

"The year." Brooke pointed to the small set of numbers in the corner. "You used the correct date and month, but for last year. We sent flowers to a list of people from that date a year ago!"

Brooke watched the look of horror replace confusion, as Tylee finally understood that this was not actually the year written on the paper.

Tylee's breath rapidly pushed in and out, promising that a full bout of hyperventilating wasn't far off. "It's all my fault!" she gasped.

"No, it isn't," Brooke said firmly, reaching a gentle hand up to Tylee's shoulder. "I looked things over before you printed. I didn't see that the date was wrong."

"But I—"

Tylee was interrupted by the cheery jingle of the bells above the door.

Helen hurriedly pressed the pause button on the machine and turned to the man who entered the store. Her face lit up as if everything was right in the world. "Why, it's our favorite customer!" she said eagerly, rushing forward in greeting. "What can I help you with? Do you have an order for today?"

Even before he said a world, Brooke was overcome by a horrible premonition: Dylan Masters was not here to place an order.

Brooke's fingers once again scrambled through the papers. If the list Tylee printed was last year's orders, then it would make complete sense that the Dylan Masters order hadn't been included. Tylee had gone back in and reprinted that order. The question was, which order had she printed? One from last year, or the correct one from this year?

Dear, Lord, please…

Her fingers found the paper before she could finish the prayer. It shook in her hand as she brought it up. But the paper labeled with Dylan Masters name in tiny letters at the top did not list just one order. Instead, there were about ten separate orders with individual instructions for each. Completely confused, Brooke scanned each line, tuning out Tylee's whimpers and the conversation between Helen and Mr. Masters. Brooke had sent out each order on this list, but if Tylee had printed out Dylan's order separately, why would there be more than one on the page?

Still confused, Brooke's gaze returned to the top. Her eyes widened and her breath caught. There were too many tiny numbers at the top. There wasn't just a single date. There was a range. The first date was the same wrong one from the other orders, the date that was a year old. But the second date was the correct one. Yesterday's date. Tylee had apparently typed in Dylan's name and the date to bring up the order, but the previous date she'd used had still been selected. The result was that the page in Brooke's hand contained all of Dylan's orders from the past year.

Brooke shut her eyes, trying to breathe deeply, but Helen and Dylan's words found their way through her attempt at calm.

"Some women I know received flowers that I didn't order. From me." From the tone of his voice, Brooke knew this wasn't the first time he had tried to explain the problem to Helen.

Unfortunately, Brooke understood exactly what the problem was.

"What is it?" Tylee asked urgently.

"These are all Dylan Masters' orders," Brooke explained quietly. "Every order he made from the past year is on this page. Since this list doesn't contain any personal information, just the order numbers and instructions, I didn't know these were all from the same sender. When you filled out the cards, didn't you notice they were all from Dylan?"

"No," Tylee moaned. "He never includes his name on the card! It's like he just assumes the women know it's him. My paper didn't include the sender either. Just the order number, message, and recipient info. Grammie prefers it that way. She insists it is proper privacy procedures."

Brooke swallowed and turned to Helen and Dylan. Both were already visibly flustered. Helen couldn't conceive of what order mistakes Dylan was attempting to report. And neither realized that the scope wasn't just on the level of simple errors, but more on the level of debacle.

With a vise-like grip on the evidence that would condemn her, Brooke strode forward, knowing she was headed for the gallows.

Five feet before she reached Helen, Dylan's gaze swung up and met her own. Gray eyes flashed.

Brooke's heart leaped. She held his gaze steady, but only with great effort. She knew that in minutes, this man would hate her.

It wasn't just "some women." All of his many ex-girlfriends from the past year had just received flowers, and they thought they were from him.

Brooke knew the truth, and before she even said a word, she

knew the anger she would face from both Helen and Dylan.

There was no way out of it, and nothing Brooke could do to make it better.

The simple facts were that Dylan hadn't sent the flowers. Brooke had.

CHAPTER 5

"You're sure I can't just call these women up and apologize?" Brooke asked in desperation.

"No," Dylan said flatly, his eyes never leaving the road. "I already told you. When we broke up, I blocked and deleted their numbers. I have no way of contacting them."

"Plus, there's the added bonus of making me miserable," Brooke grumbled.

"Well, there is that," Dylan said seriously. "If you make a mistake like sending every woman a man has dated flowers supposedly from him, then you should have a little responsibility for trying to make it right."

Brooke's lips tightened into a thin line as she did all she could to bite back a retort. It wasn't enough that Helen was going to dock her pay for every order that was sent. Brooke probably would not receive a paycheck at all this month. It also wasn't enough that Brooke offered to call each woman up and apologize. Dylan instead insisted that she go to each delivery address in person to make the explanation. Even more humiliating, he insisted on accompanying her to make sure she completed the task.

So now they were on their way to girlfriend number 1 in Dylan's Porsche.

Brooke shot a sideways glare at the man beside her. He really was freakishly handsome. With his dark hair that waved perfectly away from his forehead and the hint of a 5 o'clock shadow, Brooke understood why he had a never-ending line of girlfriends. Any woman would probably be giddy to be sitting in the passenger seat of Dylan's Porsche. That is, any woman but Brooke.

"I have a list of ten women. That means you've had ten girlfriends in the past year."

Dylan shrugged. "I don't send flowers to every woman I date."

Brooke struggled to control her laughter. "And none of your relationships ended well enough to not block and delete them from your contact list?"

Again, Dylan shrugged. "Consequence of the game, I guess. Besides, it's easier that way."

"You know, we wouldn't have been in this mess if you would have bothered signing your name to your flower deliveries. If it had been included in the instructions, then Ty—, I mean, we would have realized there was more than one order being sent from 'Dylan.'" Brooke refused to cast blame on Tylee. She had so far kept her friend's part out of all her reports. After all, Brooke had been in charge. She had approved the lists before Tylee printed them, and she'd been in such a hurry that she hadn't thought about the orders beyond yet another bouquet of roses.

Only too eager to lay all the fault at Brooke's feet, it didn't seem to occur to them that she might be protecting someone.

Even now, Dylan didn't notice her slip-up and eagerly retorted, "It's never been a problem before. I shouldn't need to clarify which of my girlfriend's boyfriends is sending her roses. Besides, I'm not the one who sent last year's orders, or the one who gave the wrong information to people in other countries, or the one who had flowers delivered to the wrong people, or the one who repeated a customer's every order from the past year. I believe the blame lies solely with you, Miss Hutchins, and I don't think you should try to share."

It was pointless. The man had no mercy for what had happened and no shame in his robust dating history.

"Fine. I admit it. It's completely my fault." Right now, she just wanted to finish her sentence and go home. Unfortunately, even after she completed Dylan's tasks, she still had a long list of local calls to make. Helen had insisted Brooke take as long as necessary to solve Dylan's situation first, since that one was obviously the biggest fiasco. While Helen was going to call the list of the other local order mistakes, Brooke was supposed to call to make personal apologies after Dylan released her.

Brooke had no doubt that in a small town like Crossroads, she would be infamous by morning.

She hadn't cried yet, and wasn't about to start now. She would in no way give Dylan the satisfaction of detecting any weakness. If she could make it through the day, she would have a good, long cry when no one had a chance to see her.

She looked down at the list of Dylan's ex-girlfriends, and the same one she had delivered flowers to yesterday. She put her finger on the first name on the list "So is this Shauna Waterson the one we are headed to now?"

"No, we're going to Janice Thornton first."

"But she's the middle of the list. And the address is in the city!" The town of Crossroads was about forty-five minutes from a larger city called Brighton Falls. Crossroads Floral did deliver there, sometimes for an extra charge, but it seemed like it would be a better idea to take care of the closer orders first.

"Yes, but Janice is the craziest," Dylan said simply, as if that answered everything.

Great. She had to explain to Dylan's crazy ex why she received roses from Dylan.

And with that, Brooke stopped talking. She stopped asking questions. She stopped protesting. It was obvious at this point that every little bit of information she gained made things so much worse. She would go where Dylan told her and say what he wanted her to say, but she just didn't want to know anymore.

Twenty minutes later, Brooke realized she should have been watching Dylan's speed. He was pulling into a parking lot across from the Brighton Falls courthouse, and she was not at all ready to be at their destination so soon.

Dylan turned off the car and nodded at the courthouse. "Janice is in there. Just ask for Janice Thornton. She'll be hard to miss." Dylan glanced at his watch. "You may have to wait a while, but hopefully she'll have a break soon."

Brooke waited for Dylan to step out of the car first, but he remained seated, took out his phone, and began checking his email as if she was dismissed.

"Aren't you coming with me?" Brooke asked, the irritation clear in his voice.

Dylan blinked up at her. "I'd rather not. Janice and I didn't end things on the most pleasant of terms. I doubt she'll be happy to see me. And like I already told you, she's crazy."

Brooke leaned her head back and folded her arms across her chest. "If we know she works at the courthouse, I can easily call and ask for her. I thought you were my bailiff and were going to follow me to make sure I got the job done. If you don't care, I see no reason to embarrass myself at her workplace when I shall get adequate embarrassment over the phone."

Dylan sighed. "Fine, I'll go with you. But I'll just point her out and then stay out of sight while you handle it. You have to do it in person. There's no way she'll take your call."

Dylan hopped out and hurried around to open Brooke's door, but Brooke exited before he had a chance. She didn't like this man; she didn't intend to give him any opportunity to redeem himself by acting the gentleman.

Dylan strode swiftly to the front steps of the courthouse, with Brooke a half-stride behind him. Once through the front doors, Brooke slowed, taking in the high ceilings and impressive architecture, but Dylan, acting like he knew exactly where he was going, marched up to the front desk.

"Can you direct me to Janice Thornton please?" Dylan asked, flashing the woman on duty a smile.

"She is in the courtroom on the second floor," the woman answered, flashing him a flirtatious smile in return. "They are in session now, but you can speak with one of the security guards about where to meet her if you have an appointment."

"Thanks!" Dylan said.

Brooke was sure Dylan added a quick wink the brunette's direction.

Dylan headed up the stairs. Brooke tried to keep up, but couldn't resist flinging out, "Don't you want me to get her name?" she asked, pointing back at the front desk with feigned innocence. "Just in case you want to send her flowers too?"

Dylan shook his head, "Nah, I don't really need her name. If I use Crossroads Floral, actual names and info don't matter. They don't pay attention to those things anyway."

Brooke rolled her eyes. Why did the man have to be so infuriating! Just once she'd like to get the best of him!

They crested the stairs and entered a huge hallway lined with massive marble pillars. In the middle of the hallway was a set of large double doors. They headed toward the doors, but when they were still about ten feet away, the door suddenly opened.

Dylan immediately dove behind one of the pillars.

If he hadn't been so very serious, it would have been hilarious to see him. Well, truth be told, Brooke still found it hilarious. He looked almost like a child afraid of being caught.

Brooke calmly walked over to where he stood hiding.

"Go ask one of the security guards," Dylan instructed. "I'll wait here.

Brooke noted the sheen of sweat on his forehead and the ever-flickering lights in his eyes. He was scared!

Suddenly feeling that she really did need to meet the woman who could instill this much fear into Dylan Masters, Brooke walked over to one of the police security who was ushering people out of the courtroom.

"Excuse me," she said politely. "I need to speak with Janice

Thornton, and I was told you might be able to help me with that."

The guard nodded back toward the door. "Well, you could check with her, but I don't know if she'll see you without an appointment. She's on recess right now, but Judge Thornton can be particular about those appointments."

Brooke froze as a woman in a black robe emerged from the courtroom. Dylan's crazy ex was a *judge*?

Still not actually breathing, Brooke's feet propelled her forward of their own accord until she stood in front of a woman who looked like she belonged on the cover of a magazine rather than the center of a courtroom. Her lively brown eyes took Brooke in quickly and were framed by a beautiful mass of curly russet-colored hair. The black judge's robe she wore served to emphasize the color in her hair and eyes. Though she was a couple of inches shorter than Brooke, she had a commanding presence about her that grabbed immediate attention and respect. In short, there was nothing about this woman that seemed the least bit crazy.

Having a sudden ornery idea, Brooke deliberately turned and gave a ridiculous smile and wave at Dylan's head peeking around the column. He popped his head back under cover, leaving Brooke completely satisfied that she had got Dylan's goat, even a little. Unfortunately, that didn't change at all what she had to do.

Brooke turned back around as the black-clad woman emerged into the hall. Not sure what to do or what to say, Brooke, stepped directly in the judge's path. When the other woman stepped to go around her, Brooke matched her movements, staying in front of her so she couldn't get around.

"Can I help you?" Judge Thornton asked, the annoyance in her voice clear.

"I would like a few moments of your time," Brooke said, managing to find her voice. "I'm from Crossroads Floral. I'd like to speak to you about a delivery—"

"I'm sorry, I don't have time," the judge interrupted brusquely. "I am on a short recess. I'm sure you can leave a message with my assistant."

Successfully stepping around Brooke, she hurriedly strode down the hall.

Feeling desperate, Brooke followed on her heels. "But Judge Thornton, you need to know that Dylan Masters did not send—"

The judge whipped back around. "Did you say Dylan Masters?" As if she sensed his presence, her eyes scanned the area. "Is he here?"

"Well, yes," Brooke answered automatically. "He's right over there behind that pillar." The instant the words came from her mouth, Brooke realized what she'd done, but she didn't really care much. If mentioning his name would allow her to complete her assignment, then so be it. It didn't matter that she had just revealed his hiding place. A grown man shouldn't need to hide from his ex-girlfriend. It would serve him right if he tasted a little embarrassment and had to talk to her.

Sparks flew in Judge Thornton's eyes. She turned on her spiky heels and whispered something out of Brooke's hearing to one of the security guards. The guard then grabbed his buddy, and they both marched directly over to Dylan's hiding place.

To Brooke's horror, they demanded he turn around, and then slipped a pair of handcuffs over his wrists!

With a satisfied smile of pure glee, Janice Thornton led the way down the hall with Dylan and his escorts in tow.

"Wait!" Brooke called, hurrying to catch up. Now Dylan had been arrested, and it was all her fault!

CHAPTER 6

"Thank you for your assistance," the judge said formally as she walked swiftly down the hall. "This really doesn't concern you. I will take things from here."

"But it does!" Brooke tried to explain, practically jogging to keep up with the judge's quick steps. "I'm with him. I mean, he's with me. I mean... I'm the reason he's here! It was my mistake."

The judge's feet slowed as she looked Brooke up and down as if assessing her for the first time. Stopping at athe door marked with her name, she unlocked it and gestured for the guards to take Dylan inside. "You're with him?" she asked Brooke.

Brooke nodded eagerly. She couldn't let them take Dylan away. If that door shut without her, she had no idea what to do. Should she call a lawyer for Dylan or just camp out until someone gave her more information?

"Fine," the other woman said, her mouth puckering in a grimace. "You can come. But if you can't keep quiet while I interrogate Mr. Masters, then I'll have you taken down to lock-up until we are done."

Brooke nodded and followed the smaller woman into her chambers. The guards, obviously taking huge enjoyment from the fact that they'd just handcuffed Dylan and towed him into the judge's chambers, quickly left, but not without sending a few exaggerated winks the judge's direction.

Confused, Brooke's gaze swerved from the judge, to Dylan, and back again. Had Dylan really been arrested or not? The guards acted as if it was all one big joke, but both Dylan and the judge seemed so very serious. What was going on?

A large desk dominated the center of the room with a backdrop of heavily laden bookcases on the wall behind. The only thing not typical about Judge Thornton's chambers was the large arrangement of a dozen red roses in the center of the desk.

The judge calmly walked around her desk and sat. "Have a seat, Dylan," she said, almost pleasantly.

"No, thank you, Janice. I'd rather stand," he said calmly from his position standing at the wall beside the door.

Janice. As soon as Dylan spoke her name, Brooke could no longer think of her as Judge Thornton. She was Janice, Dylan's ex-girlfriend, and no black robe or judge's chambers could change that.

"I'd like to ask you a few questions," Janice said, steepling her hands on the desk in front of her. "You see, I'm confused. You haven't talked to me in months, then I get roses, and then the next day, you show up at the courthouse with your girlfriend."

"I'm not his girlfriend," Brooke jumped in. "If you'll just allow me to explain—"

Janice silenced her with an uplifted palm. The glare she sent her direction clearly reiterated the threat she had made earlier. Brooke was to keep silent.

"And your questions are?" Dylan asked, his tone bored.

"Why didn't you return my calls?" she asked

"I wasn't aware that you had called me," Dylan answered simply.

Janice's eyes narrowed. "Did you block my number?"

"Yes, I did."

Silence wrapped around the room for the beat of several seconds. Then, Janice asked, "Why?"

Dylan sighed. "Janice, we only dated for two weeks. I spent

the next two weeks trying to break up with you. The last time we spoke, we ended on good terms, but I told you I wouldn't be calling you anymore. That one good break-up was only after several bad ones. After that, I blocked and deleted your number. After breaking up with you repeatedly, I really didn't want to have to do it all over again."

Brooke held her breath, waiting to see how Janice would respond. Part of Brooke felt awkward being here for this personal conversation, but another part was thoroughly captivated by the drama. It was like a soap opera, and though she felt it almost wrong to be avidly watching such a personal scene, she couldn't bring herself to look away.

Janice stood, and as if too warm, she shrugged out of her black robe and hung it on a hook behind her. The blue pantsuit she wore was stylish and not much less intimidating than the robe. But somehow, the way she spoke made her appearance seem a façade.

Finally, she looked back up at Dylan, her tone soft and almost vulnerable. "Is that a good enough reason to sever the relationship entirely? Even without the romance, Dylan, we still had fun together."

"Janice, we can't be friends. You always want more." Dylan leaned his head back against the wall and shut his eyes, the frustration running off him like water. "This isn't anything new, which is why I blocked your number. We already covered this in our last breakup. We've already said everything there is to say."

"Have we?" Janice said, keeping her manner vulnerable as she traced an invisible line on her desk.

"Yes!" Dylan flung back. "You have repeatedly told me to get out of your life, which always seems to be about a day after you beg me to give us one more shot. Remember the time I refused to go out with you again, but then you showed up when I was eating lunch at the sandwich shop near my work as if you just happened to be in the neighborhood?"

"Come on, Dylan. That's how we are," Janice said, her arms taking off in dramatic flights of expression as she paced around her desk. "Fire and ice. I never knew if your 'no' meant no, or if it was a prelude to something even better. We were good together. Why end it?"

"My 'no' always meant no," Dylan's growled. "I stopped talking to you because we ended things well, and I wasn't up for another round. I was tired of not knowing which Janice I was going to get."

Dylan's manner of speaking left no glimmer of a doubt as to his feelings, at least in Brooke's estimation. But the words that would devastate a rational woman didn't even seem to faze Janice in the least.

"Really?" Janice asked, raising her eyebrows as if in amusement. "I'm not sure you have enough evidence to back that statement up!" Casually, she sat on the corner of her desk and waved her hand in a welcoming gesture, as if he was free to present what she expected to be an amusing case.

Dylan turned around and waved his fingers that were still firmly anchored in the handcuffs. "Exhibit A. The first time you see me in months, you have me handcuffed and taken to your chambers, where you proceed to question me and tell me how good we were together."

"What was I supposed to do when you wouldn't talk to me?" Janice bit out fiercely, any trace of vulnerability gone. "If you hadn't blocked my calls, then I wouldn't have needed to handcuff you!"

Suddenly stopping, she shut her eyes, took a deep cleansing breath in, then out. It very much looked like a rehearsed coping technique recommended by a therapist. Then, finally, she opened her eyes and spoke again, this time in a serene, almost sing-song voice "Dylan, looking at the evidence I have, you are the one who is unstable. If you don't want me back, why send me roses with the same card you always sent, 'You amaze me?' But then, the very next day, you show up with your girlfriend?"

"I'm not his girlfriend!" Brooke repeated emphatically. She could keep her mouth shut for all the drama, but drew the line at this. "In fact, I'm kinda the opposite. I'm like the president of the un-fan club for Dylan Masters."

With her eyes still locked on Dylan, Janice spoke. "I'm sorry. That title is already taken. By me. And it's a lifetime appointment. We really are a small club, but with Dylan's record, we're growing very rapidly."

Dylan shook his head, letting out a sound that sounded like a mixture between a groan and a humorless laugh. "As Miss Hutchins over there has been trying to explain, the flowers were sent to you by accident. The florist mistakenly repeated some old orders, and yours was one of them."

"I can't believe that," Janice bit back, standing back up. Stepping toward Dylan, her tone softened. "Maybe it was technically an accident, but I don't believe there is such a thing. Maybe this was meant to bring us together again. To talk." She closed the distance between them, her face only stopping a few mere inches from his.

Brooke's eyes widened as Janice's finger's trailed a long caress down his face. In a soft, melodic voice that would make the Greek Sirens proud, she whispered, "And maybe something more."

With his back against the wall and his head straining away from her caress, he growled, "Janice, we've been over this. I am not interested in a relationship with you now or ever!"

"Stop lying, Dylan!" Janice jerked back and literally stamped her foot in her sudden burst of anger. "I read the card. You don't tell a woman she's amazing and then turn your back on her the next day!"

Dylan's eyebrows raised as if he was considering her point. "Well, the card is still completely true. You amaze me. But not in a romantic way. You are an incredible judge and have achieved so much, but the person out of the courtroom is not the same as when you wear the robe for an audience." Pausing, he looked directly at her. With slow, emphatic words, he said, "Janice, we aren't meant to be together. You need to figure out who you are, and I can't help you with that."

Once again returning to vulnerable Janice, she ventured almost shyly, "What if who I want to be includes you?"

Pausing, she sidled up close to him again, this time reaching her arms around him to the handcuffs. With her arms embracing him, leaving no space between his body and hers, she fit the key in the lock of the cuffs, never taking her eyes off Dylan's face. "I'm better with you than I am without. I know you care about me."

Brooke watched closely, expecting to see Dylan melt under the physical contact. After all, Janice was a beautiful woman.

But the only muscle that moved was the one in his jaw, flexing with tension.

"No, I don't," he said stoically, "I don't care in the way you want me to. And I refuse to lead you on or pretend otherwise. Janice, find someone else."

Silence gripped the room. Janice's face colored to about the same hue as the red roses on the desk behind her. Ripping the cuffs off Dylan, she threw them to the floor in a startling clang of metal. "How dare—"

A knock sounded at the door.

The transformation was immediate. Like a blanket had been thrown over her, the anger lines on Janice's face vanished, and a calm light dawned in her eyes. With her face now perfectly pale and composed, she strode over and opened the door.

"Judge Thornton, the court is just about ready for you."

"Thank you," she replied serenely. "I'll be right there."

Shutting the door and turning back around, she paused, her gaze moving from the bouquet of roses at the center of her desk, to where Dylan stood, massaging his wrists.

"You didn't send the flowers?" she asked.

For the first time, Brooke detected a hint of pain in the question.

"No, I did not," Dylan replied, his voice completely devoid of emotion.

Janice nodded her head. Averting her eyes, she walked over to where her robe was hanging behind her desk. Without another word, she slipped it on.

While the drama had been difficult to watch, the silence was worse. For the moment, there was no anger, confusion, or manipulation, there was only hurt.

Brooke couldn't take it. Dylan was rather comfortably unapologetic, but Brooke was not. While she considered Janice's anger to be Dylan's responsibility and the fault of their previous relationship, she considered Janice's pain to be hers. If she hadn't sent the roses by mistake, then Janice would have never felt the sting of knowing that they weren't actually from Dylan.

"Judge, Thornton, I am responsible for this situation, and I do apologize," Brooke said into the silence. "I would really like to do something to make things up to you."

"What's done is done," Janice said, moving back toward the door. "There isn't much you can do about it. You can't rewind and make sure the flowers never came, and you can't make Dylan Masters care. I'm not sure what else there is."

"Well, there's revenge."

Brooke's words instantly gained both Janice and Dylan's attention. Janice paused, her hand on the doorknob.

The judge's mouth opened in a question, but stepping forward, Brooke hurried to explain, "This is my card for Crossroads Floral. My personal number is on the back. Maybe you were right when you said that the flowers didn't come to you by accident. Because of all of this, you now know how Dylan feels and can get the closure you need to move on. You do need to forgive him, but when you recover and find that special someone, give me a call. We'll send Dylan Masters a nice bouquet with a card that includes a picture of you with your new boyfriend and a message that says, 'Look what you lost.' It will be on the house, of course."

"An 'in-your-face' bouquet?" Janice said, accepting the card.

"Precisely," Brooke answered.

Janice was quiet as she seemed to inspect every detail of Brooke's business card. "I like it," she said finally, tucking the card into a pocket in the folds of her robe. She then turned back to Dylan, as if measuring his reaction to their plan. But he wasn't looking at her. Tracing his gaze, she found that, instead, he was looking at Brooke with an amused expression.

"She's never been your girlfriend?" Janice asked Dylan, indicating Brooke with a tilt of her head.

Dylan blinked in surprise. "No, of course not."

"And you're sure she's not your current girlfriend?" she pressed again.

"Yes, I'm sure," Dylan scoffed. "I think that would be obvious from the sheer degree with which she dislikes me."

Janice shrugged and turned the knob on the door. "Well, I believe the part about you not sending the roses."

And with that, Janice left for court.

CHAPTER 7

After driving for a solid five minutes in complete silence, Brooke couldn't take it anymore. They had just left the courthouse, and Dylan apparently wasn't intending to speak a single word about what had just happened.

"So, Janice...?" Brooke said finally slanting a look Dylan's direction.

That telltale muscle in his jaw flexed, but otherwise, his face remained expressionless.

After another two minutes of silence, Brooke tried again. "So, Janice...?"

"Is crazy." Dylan finally finished. "But I already told you that. That's why we saw her first."

"But you didn't tell me she was a judge," Brooke pointed out.

Dylan shrugged. "I thought 'crazy' was the more important fact at the time." With a deep sigh of resignation, he relented and began speaking. "Janice is a phenomenal judge. She is a few years older than I am, but she's still one of the youngest judges in the country. I had the misfortune of seeing her in the courtroom before I actually met her. I was so impressed with her conduct in the courtroom that I asked her out. However, at the time, I didn't realize that while Janice plays the character of a judge to perfection, that isn't who she is."

"Well, I didn't see her in the courtroom, I only saw the different-mood-a-minute version."

"Now you see why I needed you to explain things to her first. Although she is generally good about keeping her personal life separate from work, she has the most influence to make my life difficult."

"Are you kidding?" Brooke asked, incredulous. "I thought you were being arrested when you were handcuffed! How is that keeping things separate?"

Dylan laughed, but it sounded almost sarcastic, with no humor in it at all. "Janice wasn't serious. The guards knew I was her ex and got a kick out of it. I knew at the time that it was just Janice being dramatic and trying to punish me with a little embarrassment."

"Well, it certainly wasn't a pleasant experience," Brooke said, shaking her head. "But I do feel bad for her. Sometimes people who are extremely gifted have more trouble socially. And you did seem rather harsh at times."

"I certainly tried to be!" Dylan said seriously. "I've tried nice before. I've tried 'it's not you, it's me.' I've tried getting another girlfriend. I've tried every way known to man of breaking up with her, and nothing worked. After the last breakup, I finally felt like I somewhat succeeded and cut her off. But then, when I found out roses had been sent to her in my name, I feared it would start the breakup process all over again."

Brooke winced. "I don't suppose it would do any good to tell you again how sorry I am? I'm also sorry I outed your hiding place in the courthouse hallway. I didn't quite realize the level of drama you were trying to avoid. And I'm kind of sorry for offering her a revenge bouquet. For both your sakes, I hope Janice doesn't bother you again."

"Don't be sorry for that last one. It was brilliant! I'm in favor of anything that gets her moving on. In fact, if she does send me a revenge bouquet, I would like to personally refund you the costs!"

While they had been traveling back toward Crossroads, Dylan

suddenly made a left, turning off the main highway, onto a road that obviously saw much less use.

"Who are we going to see now?" Brooke asked, scanning her list to find an address that might match.

"Celeste Davenport," Dylan replied.

"Bouquet of daisies and sunflowers," Brooke said, finding the order on her list.

Dylan made another turn onto a tree-lined country road, but when he didn't say anything further about their destination, Brooke pressed, "Is that all you're going to tell me? That plan didn't work so well the last time."

Turning into a long lane, they headed toward a cluster of buildings, the most notable being a large red barn. "Celeste owns this farm. It has been in her family for generations."

Dylan stopped the car beside the barn and stepped out. Brooke stepped out as well. It was a beautiful farm, worthy of a calendar shot. Ahead of them was a classic white farmhouse with a wrap-around porch.

"So why Miss Davenport?" Brooke asked, meeting him where he gazed warily around the farm. "Is she next in the spectrum of crazy?"

"No," Dylan answered quickly. "Celeste isn't crazy. She just—"

They froze at the sound of a shotgun being cocked.

"Has a gun," Dylan finished.

"Celeste, it's just me, Dylan Masters," he called, putting his hands up as he slowly turned around. "We just came to talk about some flowers that were delivered yesterday."

"Well, in that case, I guess I can wait to shoot you," a pleasant voice sounded.

Slowly, Brooke turned to see a willowy blonde in boots and a cowboy hat.

"Hi, I'm Celeste Davenport," she said to Brooke, walking up and offering her hand—the hand not holding the shotgun. "I assume you're Dylan's new girlfriend."

"Hardly," Brooke answered. "I'm the one who sent you flowers by mistake. My name is Brooke Hutchins. Dylan is just making me come and apologize in person."

"Nice guy, isn't he?" Celeste said with a grin. "Well, this sounds like a story I'd like to hear if you don't mind following me to the barn. I have a few more animals to feed, and then we'll go inside for some coffee."

"Oh, I don't think—" Brooke started, but then she caught the look of urgency in Dylan's eyes and the slight shake of his head. Apparently, one didn't turn down Celeste's hospitality. "That sounds lovely," Brooke said instead.

"Sorry about the greeting," Celeste said, leading the way into the barn. "We've had reports of some shady activity in the area. One of my dogs turned up missing, and I've heard drugs may be coming through one of the outlying farms. Then, when I saw Dylan's suit, I thought 'salesman,' which of course, may have required a shotgun as well. I don't usually pull a gun on Dylan Masters, but I do like to have the option." Turning around, Celeste winked at Brooke.

About thirty seconds after Brooke met Celeste, she decided she liked her very much. She was like sunshine, and one couldn't help but feel happy and at ease in her presence. But there also seemed to be something tough underneath the surface, and Brooke didn't doubt that though she liked to tease, she really did intend to keep Dylan on his toes.

Celeste pulled open a barn door, and Brooke and Dylan followed. Brooke blinked in the sudden dimness and breathed deeply of the rich smells of hay and animals. It wasn't at all unpleasant to Brooke. Instead, it was rather calming.

She sneezed, perhaps having breathed a little too deeply.

"Bless you," Dylan's voice said in her ear.

She jumped, startled to have him so close.

Dylan smirked. "Sheesh, Brooke, I don't bite."

"Oh, I think you do," she replied seriously. Without waiting to hear his denial, she hurried after Celeste.

The other woman hefted a bale of hay into a stall. "So how did you send me flowers by accident?" she asked.

Brooke dutifully gave her official report of how she had spilled coffee on the order papers, forcing her to reprint. But she hadn't noticed the date range on the new print job and sent out old orders from the past year, instead of the new ones.

At no point did she try to make excuses or shift the blame to Tylee, Helen, or anyone but herself. "So I'm going around to the floral recipients to try to make things right. I am really sorry for any confusion the accidental order caused, Miss Davenport."

Celeste's rake paused in mucking out a stall. "So do you mean that all of Dylan's orders from the past year were sent out again yesterday? As in, all of his *many* girlfriends received flowers?"

Brooke shifted uncomfortably. She really didn't want to reveal Dylan's personal information. "Well, Dylan's weren't the only orders that were messed up," she said evasively. "In fact, all of the Crossroads orders were incorrect."

"I don't send flowers to every woman I date," Dylan grumbled from somewhere behind Brooke.

"Wow, that's rough," Celeste said sympathetically. "Don't feel bad about me. I have no illusions about Dylan. I had no idea why he sent me flowers, but I in no way thought he wanted to date me again."

"Well, it's good to know I managed to successfully break up with someone," Dylan said tiredly.

"I would think that, with all of your practice, you should be very good at it by now," Celeste said innocently.

"I suppose it's a lot like mucking out a stall," Dylan mused, nodding at her rake. "It doesn't take a whole lot of skill to clean up a bunch of manure. You just have to get the job done."

Celeste laughed. "Well, since you claim it is a skill-less job, why don't you and Brooke finish this stall while I get the other chores done. The more people working, the sooner we get to coffee!"

Brooke didn't have a lot of experience with farm work, and the promise of coffee definitely didn't inspire her. But she was happy to help. Accepting the rake, she eagerly began raking the soiled straw into a corner.

"Well, if it gets us done sooner," Dylan said under his breath. He shrugged out of his suit jacket and grabbed the pitchfork. Quickly, he began launching Brooke's pile of dirty straw out of the stall. Obviously, this was not his first time at this task. And, by the way his muscles stretched his dress shirt taut, Brooke guessed he wasn't entirely unfamiliar with manual labor and exercise.

Brooke tried to focus on Celeste's voice as the other woman went around the barn, speaking softly to the animals as she worked, checking on feed troughs and water, and giving her subjects a good pat when needed.

Raking a bunch of straw back to the corner, she accidentally elbowed Dylan. "Oh, I'm sorry!" she said, hurrying to get out of his way, but her feet got moving too fast and became caught in the straw. She felt herself falling and knew she was going to land right in the manure-drenched mess on the barn floor.

Strong arms came around her, pulling her back up against Dylan's solid chest. A strong jolt ran through her, like built up static electricity.

Her breath caught.

The instant she was upright, Dylan released her, as if only too eager to do so. Had he felt that strange current, too?

"Are you okay?" he asked gruffly.

"I'm fine," Brooke was swift to respond. "Thank you. That would have been an unhappy landing."

She didn't look at him. She didn't want to read his eyes and see his reaction. She just wanted to get away. Grabbing up her rake, she headed toward the opposite end of the stall and furiously began raking at the clean strands of yellow.

After a solid minute of her rake working at nothing and her thoughts working at everything, she was interrupted by the sound of Dylan clearing his throat.

"I'm feeling a little warm with all this work," he said. "You wouldn't mind if I just take off my shirt for a while? You know, just to get a little cooler?"

Brooke's gaze shot up to him in panic. Reaching up, he was loosening his tie. Then his fingers moved to the top button.

Then she saw his eyes.

He knew!

His gaze was full of mirth as he watched her, watching him. He knew he made her uncomfortable and was fully enjoying finding a way to increase that discomfort.

"Go ahead!" Brooke said with an amazing calm that contradicted her blazing red face. "I'm sure the animals will enjoy the view." With that, she leaned her rake up against the stall and retreated to find Celeste.

Walking down the length of the barn, a soft nicker drew her to a stop. A horse stuck his head out of a stall and looked at her as if trying to start a conversation.

"Well, hello there," Brooke said softly, approaching with an outstretched hand. She was a beautiful gray horse with a white blaze that ran from her forehead to her soft nose. Brooke let the horse smell her fingers, then she reached up and gently ran her hand down along the white blaze before reaching over to scratch the animal's neck. The horse leaned into her touch, seeming to enjoy it.

Horses fascinated Brooke, and she would have loved to have been around them more. However, her family had different priorities. Brooke's experience with horses involved a few times riding in exotic places, like along a beach in Hawaii. While she loved the memories and the experiences her parents had provided, sometimes she saw the value of simply getting to pet a horse in a barn in her hometown of Crossroads.

"I see you've found Jezebel," Celeste said, coming up beside Brooke.

"Oh, yes!" Brooke said, still enjoying the horse snuggles. "Is that her name? She's a sweetheart."

"Yes, she is," Celeste said. "Do you ride?"

"Oh, no!" Brooke said quickly. "I mean, I'd like to. I have before, once upon a time. But I've never had lessons or anything."

"Do you want to?" Celeste said, her eyebrows quirking up in question.

Brooke blinked. "Ride Jezebel?"

"Yes. She's a very gentle horse."

"Oh, no. I couldn't. I mean, we can't stay long. I'm sure Dylan—"

"Go ahead, Brooke," came Dylan's voice. "We have time."

Brooke shot a glare to where Dylan stood leaning against a post. Thankfully, he was still fully clothed.

"Oh, good!" Celeste said enthusiastically, opening the stall and hooking a rope to Jezebel's bridle. "Follow me. Just a few minutes on Jezebel will do you a world of good! Riding always makes me happy. You can't carry a load of worries when you are on a horse!"

Brooke reluctantly followed Celeste out one of the barn doors into a large, fenced riding area. It wasn't that she didn't want to ride a horse. The little girl in Brooke very much did want to ride. But she was also nervous that she'd completely humiliate herself with her inexperience.

"Ok," Celeste instructed. "Dylan, you mount first, and then Brooke can sit in front of you."

"Excuse me?" Brooke sputtered. "Dylan is riding with me?"

"I thought you'd prefer it that way," Celeste said innocently. "Jezebel adores Dylan, which isn't surprising at all since she's a female. She was Dylan's horse in the short time we were together. If Dylan is with you, Jezebel will be extra careful. But I suppose if you don't want Dylan, I can run and get a saddle for you to ride by yourself. Jezebel doesn't like the saddle much, though. She actually seems to prefer being ridden bareback. But if you'd rather…"

Brooke held up her hand in surrender. "Fine. I'll ride with Dylan."

Not daring to make eye contact with Dylan, she watched out of the corner of her eye as he gave Jezebel a quick, loving pat. Then he used a rail of the fence to stand on while he hoisted his leg over her back, mounting with a surprisingly fluid motion for a man in dress pants and a shirt and tie.

Dylan reached his hand down, offering Brooke assistance.

Taking a deep breath, Brooke followed Dylan's example and used the fence to aid in her mount. Thankfully, she'd worn leggings, a long tunic, and boots today, and the stretching of her leg was not accompanied by a rip. Her mount, however, was not nearly as graceful as Dylan's. She practically knocked him over with her little lunge onto Jezebel's back, and she would have slid off the other side if he hadn't kept his seat and grabbed her waist, balancing her upright.

Before she had caught her breath again, Dylan's arms were around her holding the reins, and Jezebel was moving forward.

Celeste, not seeming to notice Brooke's discomfort at all, kept up a rousing monologue as Dylan directed the horse around the perimeter of the corral. "After we broke up, I rather wished Jezebel had lived up to her name where Dylan was concerned. But she was never anything but sweet and obedient. Dylan, you know you're welcome to come ride anytime, right?" she asked. "I have no hard feelings and no expectations, but I do believe Jezebel might! She needs you to come visit!"

Not bothering to wait for a response from Dylan, Celeste busied herself picking up some twine near the gate of the corral.

"Are you comfortable?" came Dylan's soft voice in Brooke's ear.

"I'm fine," Brooke responded swiftly.

"Do you want—"

"Can you just please not talk?" Brooke said irritably. If he remained silent, she would have a lot easier time pretending that she couldn't feel the heat of his body behind hers or smell a masculine scent that, while reminiscent of hard work mixed with something rather spicy, was not unpleasant at all.

"Sure," Dylan said easily. "I was just going to offer to take my shirt off if that would make you more comfortable."

Instant laughter bubbled up before Brooke could contain it. He was teasing her yet again! The rascal!

What a ridiculous day! And now, in perhaps the most ridiculous part of all, she was riding a horse in Dylan Masters' arms while he teased and made her laugh.

She still couldn't stand the man, but she was beginning to tolerate him on occasion. Now, if she could just make it through the rest of the day apologizing to his ex-girlfriends.

CHAPTER 8

D ylan placed the reins in Brooke's hands. She took them hesitantly and felt every slight shift of his body behind her as he placed his hands in a relaxed position at her hips. Strangely, however, Brooke felt more relaxed than she had been all day. Maybe Celeste was right in that it was impossible to worry when riding a horse.

"Why don't you just ride Jezebel to the house?" Celeste called, opening the gate to the corral.

Jezebel seemed to know what to do without Brooke's guidance, which allowed Brooke to be almost lulled by the swaying movements of the large animal. Without intentionally doing so, her ramrod-straight back gradually relaxed against Dylan's chest as their bodies swayed as one unit to the rhythm of the horse's gait. His warm puffs of breath against her neck sent goosebumps all the way down to Brooke's ankles. She could feel the solid strength of muscles at her back, and the way she fit with him gave her an odd sense of belonging. She felt safe somehow, and yet every nerve in her body seemed electrified, and she liked both of those feelings way too much.

Approaching the front porch, Dylan took the reins back from Brooke's hands. "Hold on tight," Dylan whispered in her ear. "And remember I've got you."

Before she could ask what he meant, Dylan pumped the reins

swiftly, saying, "Come on, Jezebel!"

The horse took off.

Brooke let out a strangled shriek and gripped Jezebel's mane tightly. Dylan's arms stayed securely at Brooke's waist, and after the first burst of speed, Jezebel settled down into a brisk trot. They circled wide around the house and came back to a stop right at the front porch.

Dylan immediately slid off the horse and then offered his hands to help Brooke down. Thoroughly reminded of how much she disliked him, she pushed his hands away. He'd made the horse run on purpose, just to aggravate her. With all the warm, fuzzy feelings complete chased away, Brooke made no attempt to hide her dislike.

"Don't be too hard on him, Brooke," Celeste said cheerily. "You can't ride a horse without running her through some paces a bit!"

Still not mollified in the least bit, Brooke brought her leg over and tried to slip off the horse slowly, her toes reaching for the ground. All of the sudden, she lost her grip, and her slow dismount turned into a fast slide. For the second time in an hour, Dylan caught her before she hit the ground.

Now, even more upset by her own clumsiness, Brooke scrambled to her feet and hurriedly shrugged Dylan off, landing an elbow to Dylan's torso in her haste.

"Next time I'll be sure to let you fall!" Dylan said in protest.

"Please do!" Brooke shot back.

Celeste looked from Brooke to Dylan and then laughed. Shaking her head, she led the way up the porch to the front door. "Come on in!"

"Is the coast clear?" Dylan asked warily stepping through the front door.

"Yes, I believe so," Celeste replied brightly. "Nana was out raking up her garden last I checked."

"Celeste's grandmother lives with her," Dylan explained,

turning to hold open the door for Brooke to enter. "Her parents retired to Florida and still come back for the growing season, but Ruby stays all year long."

"What he isn't saying is that my Nana wasn't too happy with Dylan after we broke up. We ran into each other at the store a couple months back, and it was not pretty."

"She made it clear that I was an idiot for not doing everything I could to keep her granddaughter, which I probably was. And I think she said some worse things too, which I've tried to forget."

Brooke shook her head. "Dylan Masters, making friends, one breakup at a time."

Dylan flashed her a wilted half-smile as he methodically looked through all the windows and doors on the way to the kitchen area. It really did seem like he was terrified of Celeste's nana and was checking to make sure she really wasn't around!

Brooke followed them into the kitchen, pausing at the sight of the beautiful bouquet of daisies and sunflowers gracing the center of the table. She really had done a nice job with that arrangement. Too bad it should have never been created.

Celeste paused in gathering mugs for coffee and looked at Brooke intently. "You should definitely keep this one around, Dylan," she said finally, as if delivering a vitally important verdict. "Every other woman I know falls at your feet, but this one gives as good as she gets!"

Dylan shook his head. "I think she's definitely way ahead of me in overall points. After all, she did send flowers to all of my exes."

Celeste's laughter tinkled like little bells. After setting a mug of coffee on the table for each of them, Brooke sat down, gesturing for them to do the same.

Brooke took her seat, but stared at the coffee in front of her with great trepidation.

"Oh, my!" Celeste cried, jumping up. "Didn't you say that coffee started your whole mess? You poor thing! You probably want nothing to do with coffee. Can I get you some tea or hot apple cider instead?"

"I'd love some cider," Brooke said, even saying a quick prayer of thanks in her great relief.

A steaming mug of cider soon replaced the coffee in front of Brooke, and Celeste once again took her seat. Dylan, apparently satisfied with no sightings of Celeste's nana, also took his seat. But before he brought the mug to his lips, his phone rang.

"It's work," he said, looking at the number on his screen. "I'm sorry, I need to take this."

Dylan grabbed his mug of coffee and went out the door. But he didn't go far, and Brooke could still see him through the large front windows, standing on the front porch and talking into his phone. Taking a sip of her cider, Brooke turned her attention back to Celeste.

The woman across from her was, by all appearances a great catch. Even with her long, blonde hair pulled into cute twin braids, it was obvious that she was beautiful. And her light blue, forget-me-not eyes projected kindness, intelligence, and a bright, good-humored outlook on life. It was easy to understand why Dylan had broken up with Janice Thornton. But Celeste was a mystery. It seemed like any man who had Celeste for a girlfriend should bend over backward to keep her.

"I really am sorry about sending you flowers by mistake," Brooke said softly. "I know you acted like it didn't bother you, but it was still a pretty awful thing to do."

Celeste smiled sadly. "Dylan and I didn't have a terrible breakup, but it was quite clear that it was over. I had no dreams of him coming back to me or finding me suddenly irresistible. I knew the flowers had to be just a friendly gesture, for old time's sake, or a mistake. He didn't love me then, and I had no reason to believe he'd change his mind."

Celeste brightened, the brief cloud of introspection now parting. "You don't have any reason to apologize to me, Brooke. In fact, I really should be thanking you. The bright spot in all of this is that I get to have a good laugh at the thought of him trying to make explanations to half of the Crossroads' women who love him and the other half who hate him!"

"And where do you fall in that spectrum?" Brooke ventured. For some reason, the nature of Celeste and Dylan's relationship was far more interesting than perhaps it should be.

Celeste's blue eyes blinked as if she was slightly caught off guard by the question. "Well, sometimes I love him, and sometimes I hate him. But most of the time, it's a little of both."

But Celeste's answer wasn't quite good enough, seeming to raise more questions than offer answers. So Brooke pushed further. "I hope you don't mind me asking, but I'm a little confused. You seem like a woman any man would be thrilled to have as a girlfriend, and your feelings for Dylan were obviously strong enough that they still exist. So why did you and he break up?"

Celeste shrugged. "I suppose it's the same reason everyone breaks up with him."

"You mean you were the one who broke up with him?" Brooke asked, taken off guard. "With the way you talked about Dylan, I just assumed..."

"Yes, I officially called it off, but let's just say he wasn't upset."

Brooke shook her head, trying to clear it. "So what is the reason for all the breakups?"

Celeste sighed. "Dylan Masters is the prize every single woman in about a hundred square miles wants. The relationship falls apart when the girlfriend realizes that he's not serious, and she wants him to be. He's Dylan Masters—which means they aren't content to be another bead on his chain. Maybe he has commitment issues, or maybe he really just isn't interested in anything serious. But, you don't date Dylan hoping to have a good time. You date him hoping to be the one."

"But it's awful that he's lead so many women on!" Brooke protested.

Celeste shook her head. "He doesn't lead them on. Unfortunately, with a few months, I've gained a little perspective. At no point is Dylan ever serious. He never says 'I love you.' To my knowledge, he doesn't sleep with his girlfriends. In fact, he is a perfect gentleman, which, in itself, I think ticks some of the women off! Any hurt feelings are the result of the girlfriend assuming, or wanting too much."

"So in your case?"

Taking a sip of coffee, Celeste answered slowly, "Dylan and I dated for about a month, which is pretty long-term for a Dylan Masters relationship. We had a lot of fun, and I thought we were good for each other. But after that month, I realized that I wasn't the one. I could see it in his eyes. And I knew that time wouldn't change that fact, so I broke up with him. I liked him way too much, but I was smart enough to realize it was mostly one-sided. I got out before I could get in any deeper. I had my audition to be special, and it didn't work out. But I think that's how all his girlfriends feel. I guess that makes me just another bead in his chain."

"I'm sorry," Brooke said sympathetically. "You seem to be saying that it's not his fault, but the man leaves lots of broken hearts in his wake. How is that okay?"

"It's not intentional on his part," Celeste was quick to defend. "And for my part, I knew his reputation going in, as does probably every other woman he dates. He doesn't talk about his feelings or make any kind of promises that he doesn't keep. I think, if you really want to define it, ours was a really good friendship. That's probably the case of most of his relationships. But with a man as nice to look at, smart, and kind as Dylan, most women aren't satisfied with just friendship. I wanted a romance, which I most definitely did not get."

"Do you think that he'll ever settle down and stick with one woman?" Brooke asked, her eyes drifting back to where Dylan still stood on the porch.

"Everyone else seems to think he will," Celeste said with a shrug. "At least, that's the hope that keeps sending women to fawn over him and present their application to date him."

Her eyes drifted out to Dylan as well, and she continued thoughtfully, "But I don't know. With the number of women he's dated, I think he should have found at least one he wanted a romance with by now, so I'm more skeptical. I don't know a single woman he's ever dated longer than a month or had any serious romance with. Maybe he's just not the marrying and relationship type. I never quite figured him out enough to know what makes him tick."

Her coffee empty, Celeste stood and took her mug to the sink to wash it out. Over her shoulder, she added. "However, I'm fairly certain if he ever does find 'the one,' that all of woman-kind, including all his exes, will applaud and consider that a win. The woman who gets Dylan Masters to fall in love with her will not be resented at all. She will be admired and thanked for lassoing the uncatchable."

Brooke's laughter was interrupted by the squeak of the front door.

Dylan came walking in with his suit jacket slung over his shoulder, having apparently retrieved it from where he'd left it in the barn. "Are you ready to go, Brooke?" he asked. "Sorry to leave, Celeste, but there are quite a few other names to visit and cross off the list."

Dylan walked over to the sink and ran water to wash his empty mug out. Brooke stood as well, intending to follow Dylan to the sink with hers. But before she got there, a small figure rushed up and smacked Dylan in the back of the head with a rolled-up newspaper.

"Hey!" Dylan protested flinching and reaching up to rub his head. Turning around, he raised his hands to protect his face against the newspaper's continued onslaught while squawking, "Stop that, Nana!"

"I'm not your Nana!" the small woman shot back, waving the newspaper even more fiercely. "I could have been, but instead, you decided to break my Celeste's heart!"

"Nana, stop!" Celeste said, making a grab for the newspaper. "I already told you that I was the one who broke up with Dylan, not the other way around!"

"Yes, but you wouldn't have needed to break up with him if he hadn't broken your heart!"

Finally snatching hold of the newspaper, Celeste wrenched it from her nana's hand. "Obviously, Nana didn't take the breakup nearly as well as I did," Celeste said to Brooke while sending a look of reprimand the older woman's direction.

"And I see that she still sees me as the villain," Dylan said with a wince.

Celeste threw her hands up in frustration. "I've tried to explain to her, but she—"

"Is fully capable of forming her own opinions," the tiny woman interrupted. "And I sincerely think that only a cad of a man would throw a woman away only to send her a beautiful bouquet of flowers a few months later!"

"But, Nana, there was a mistake with the order. It wasn't Dylan's fault."

Celeste's efforts didn't seem to calm her nana in the least. The little silver-haired woman reminded Brooke of a small dog, like a Shih Tzu, who was eager to take on a German Shepherd.

"You are always making excuses for him, Celeste. But no excuse can change who a man is."

"That's very true," Brooke said, stepping toward the older woman. "But I'm really the one to blame for the flowers."

Nana turned and looked at Brooke, as if realizing, for the first time, that Dylan wasn't their only visitor.

Seizing the opportunity of her attention, Brooke hurried to explain. "I am a florist. In fact, I'm the one who arranged that bouquet on the table. And I'm the one who mistakenly sent it to Celeste."

Brooke's words seemed to give Nana pause. "I've never heard of such a thing."

Encouraged, Brooke pressed forward, a small kernel of an idea forming even as she spoke. "I'm trying to find all of the orders I messed up and explain what happened. In the case of this particular bouquet, I think the mistake was really that it ended up with the wrong person. I don't think the bouquet was meant for Celeste at all. It was meant for you."

"For me?" Nana asked, putting her hand to her heart.

"Yes," Brooke nodded with confidence. "I think that if Dylan had a chance to rewrite the card, he would talk about how, even though it didn't work out with him and Celeste, he still respects and likes both you and your granddaughter very much."

Nana turned to Dylan, her lips trembling. "Is that how you really feel, Dylan?"

Dylan nodded. "Very much so. I felt the loss very deeply when Celeste and I broke up. I hate that you have hard feelings toward me, especially because I only have the best feelings toward you and truly wish you were still a part of my life."

Brooke watched the older woman's eyes soften. Then she glided over and gently caressed the centerpiece of flowers. "I do so like daisies," she said with a smile. Then she looked back up to Dylan and reached out her wrinkled hand to his, her smile now turning rather shy. "Thank you for the flowers, Dylan."

"You're very welcome, Nana," Dylan answered. But his eyes weren't on Nana; they were set on Brooke.

Nana cleared her throat delicately. Turning to Brooke, she said sweetly, "You, my dear, may call me Nana." Turning back to Dylan, she patted his hand again and said firmly. "And you, my dear, may not."

The humor of the situation was completely lost on Brooke, for Dylan's eyes were still locked with Brooke's, and she couldn't read his expression. Maybe he was just thankful. There may have even been a trace of admiration in his gaze. But there was something else she couldn't identify. The only thing she knew was that the look made her mouth go dry, and she wasn't sure she could still feel her feet.

With great effort, Brooke tore her gaze away. "I guess we need to be going. I have many more apologies to make for all of the accidental orders. Celeste, thank you so much for your hospitality. I'm so glad I got to meet you, and I hope we get to see each other again."

"I'm sure we will," Celeste said, a strange sparkle in her eye. "I'm excited to see what the future holds, especially for you!"

"What do you mean?" Brooke asked, confused. "I can tell you that my immediate future isn't looking so rosy since I have to clean up all of yesterday's mistakes."

Celeste impulsively threw her arms around Brooke in a hug and whispered, "No, I'm talking about a future that includes me needing to revise some of my earlier theories on Dylan Masters!"

Brooke smiled, even though she didn't really follow what Celeste was meaning. Following Dylan out the door, they eagerly made their exit before Celeste could rope them into doing more work or Nana could locate the newspaper again and decided she really did want to attack Dylan.

The important thing now was that she had just marked another one of Dylan's exes off the apology list. For just a minute, she tried to savor that accomplishment and tried not to think of how many she still had left.

CHAPTER 9

"**Let's get some lunch,**" **Dylan** said, pulling into a parking space. "I'm hungry."

"Ok," Brooke agreed, mostly because she was hungry as well.

They got out of the car, and Dylan pointed to a building not far away. "There's a sandwich shop over there, and it's right across from our next stop."

"And where is our next stop?" Brooke said, hurrying to keep up with Dylan's fast pace. "With one ex-girlfriend a judge and another one a cowgirl, I'm curious as to who the next one will be!"

Dylan didn't answer, but pulled open the door of the restaurant for her to pass through. A few minutes later, they were sitting at a table with their sandwiches, which they had paid for individually, of course.

Glancing at her phone, Brooke realized it was already well past lunchtime. "Don't you need to get to work?" Brooke said, thinking of his phone call back at Celeste's farm. "Are they ok with you being gone this long?"

"I took the day off," Dylan said in between bites of his sandwich.

"That must be nice," Brooke said, without thinking.

"Not really," Dylan replied. "I'm swamped with work, but

after my third ex-girlfriend showed up at work, I figured I wasn't going to get anything done anyway, so I took the entire day off to solve the problem."

"Oh," Brooke said with a wince. "I'm sorry."

"Where do you work?" Brooke asked, suddenly realizing that she didn't know. She'd always seen him wearing a suit, but didn't know what his profession was.

"I manage investments at a bank," Dylan replied.

Brooke bit her bottom lip nervously. "Well, I can see why you didn't want ex-girlfriends in the bank making a scene."

"Yes, that sort of thing is usually frowned upon," Dylan said, a hint of humor in his eyes. "It may have been okay, however, if you had been around to rescue me."

Brooke froze, her mouth full of sandwich.

Before she could manage to swallow and ask him what he meant, he continued. "Thank you for stepping up and helping with Celeste's nana," his gray eyes were almost warm, yet they sparkled with something like admiration. "You didn't lie to her, but it's like you completely rewrote what happened in her mind. You told her a different story of what should have happened if I'd been given a second chance to send the flowers. You smoothed things over better than I ever could have. Thank you."

"You're very welcome," Brooke said, unable to stop the thrill of pleasure at his praise. "But I don't know that your thanks are deserved. After all, my mistake is what put you in that uncomfortable position to begin with."

"That may have been true initially, but with the way you worked your magic, the situation is much better than if Celeste had never received that accidental bouquet. If those flowers hadn't been sent, I would have never sought Celeste or her nana out, and Nana would have continued to resent me."

"That's a rough way to get a little closure," Brooke said with a smile.

"Yes, it is, but so far, you've managed to leave the situation better than you found it for two of my exes."

"Don't get ahead of yourself," Brooke cautioned. "I think you still have quite a list for me. You may still need to retract all thanks before this is over."

Dylan smiled, and Brooke's heart skipped a beat. With the way his eyes sparkled as they crinkled just a bit and his teeth flashed a quick hello to a set of deep dimples, all Brooke could think about was wanting him to smile again.

"I don't think I'll have to do that," Dylan said easily, "but I won't pretend my covey of girlfriends isn't a colorful lot."

"So who is next on the list?" Brooke asked, taking out the paper from her purse. Getting back on task was a good thing. Dylan saying nice things to her did such strange things to the rhythm of her heart that she much preferred putting those little checkmarks by the names on her list and maintaining a comfortable dislike for the man.

"Well, across the street—"

"Dylan, sweetums, it is you!" a voice gushed about a half second before a blonde form with long, bare legs threw herself at Dylan and planted her lips on his.

Brooke was startled at first, but seeing the shocked look on Dylan's face as he was very thoroughly kissed made her suddenly find the whole thing funny. She even tucked her list back into her purse, figuring that she could spare a few moments to just enjoy the show.

"I knew you'd come," the woman said, finally coming up for air and settling into his lap. "Thank you for the flowers. I knew you never meant it when we broke up. And then your flowers came, and I knew for sure that we are meant to be together."

Dylan shifted awkwardly and tried to push the woman off his lap, but she laced her arms around his neck and clung.

"It isn't what you think, Kiffany!" he cried. "There's been a mistake."

"I know! I knew it was a mistake when we broke up. I just

love you so, so much, sweetums!"

Dylan let out a strangled gag as Kiffany covered his face with kisses.

"Brooke, I could use a little help here!" he managed in between kisses.

"I think you've met your rescue quota for the day, Dylan," Brooke said, idly munching potato chips. "I think I'm going to sit this one out and just enjoy the show."

Dylan glared at her, and she just popped another chip in her mouth.

"Kiffany," Dylan said, wriggling so much that Kiffany's bare legs shot up in the air like two chopsticks. "I need to tell you something."

Not seeming disturbed at all, Kiffany managed to land her legs in the same position they'd been before, draped around Dylan's leg. "Yes, sweetums?" Kiffany said, backing off to give him a little air, but still keeping her arms secure around his neck. By the eager look on her glamorous face, she looked as if she fully expected him to declare words of love and devotion.

Dylan tilted his head toward Brooke. "Kiffany, I'd like you to meet Brooke Hutchins—my girlfriend."

Brooke choked on her chip, it's crispy ridges lodging in her throat. Coughing, sputtering, and gagging for the next thirty seconds finally brought a little relief. She grabbed her soda and took several swallows to clear her airway. Then, with a hoarse voice, she squawked, "I am NOT his girlfriend!"

Dylan raised his eyebrows expectantly, and Kiffany looked at her with trepidation, as if not knowing what to think. Dylan had forced her hand, and now there was nothing she could do except rescue him from the Barbie on his lap.

After taking another sip of soda, she spoke, raspy threads still lining her voice. "Let's see, your name is Kiffany?" Removing the list from her purse again, she ran her finger down the names. "Kiffany Kline?"

Kiffany nodded.

"Oh, yes, I remember you," Brooke said, recalling her last delivery of the day. "I delivered a bouquet of flowers to your office by accident yesterday. I'm a florist, and there was a huge mix-up where orders from the past year were repeated. I'm really sorry, but the flowers you received weren't from Dylan. They weren't from anyone. It was an accidental order."

Kiffany slid off Dylan's lap. Standing, she readjusted her skimpy red dress and then tucked her heavily highlighted blonde hair behind her ear. She looked at Brooke coldly, even though tears were pooling in her eyes. "I don't believe you," she hissed. Then turning to Dylan, her expression turned to pleading. "Why are you doing this, Dylan? Why torture me by sending me flowers and then pretending that you didn't? Please just stop with the jokes and take me somewhere we can get caught up." After sending one last glare Brooke's direction, she cuddled back up to Dylan.

Dylan shot out of his chair as if he'd just been doused with ice water.

"Kiffany, I'm telling you the truth. See, you can look at the list yourself. These were all of the deliveries that went out yesterday. Here is your name. You see the date? These are all of Dylan's orders from the past year, and every person on this paper received a repeat order yesterday."

Kiffany grabbed the paper out of Brooke's hand. "All of these women got flowers from Dylan yesterday?"

"Y-Yes," Brooke replied hesitantly, not liking the sudden look of anger on Kiffany's face.

"Destiny Montague?" she burst, her hand shaking as it held the paper. "Celeste Davenport? You sent Shauna Waterson flowers, too? Shauna, really? And Destiny is a conniving, back-stabbing... How could you send those women flowers?"

The little tableau had long since attracted the attention of everyone in the small sandwich shop. But now they all seemed to lean forward, watching with breathless anticipation the scene that seemed straight out of a soap opera.

"Well, I didn't actually send them flowers yesterday," Dylan clarified, seeming lost in how to calm her down. "Well, I did, but not intentionally."

Brooke stood as well. "Kiffany, it was very much my fault—"

The sound of Kiffany's hand slapping across Dylan's face sucked all the air from the room. An eerie hush fell for the beat of several seconds.

Then Kiffany gritted out, "I want nothing to do with a womanizer who would send flowers to Shauna Waterson!" Holding her head high, she marched out of the sandwich shop, her red high heels clicking sharply against the tile.

Less than ten seconds after Kiffany's exit, Dylan whispered. "Come on, let's get out of here."

Brooke grabbed her list of names off the floor where Kiffany had crumpled and thrown it. Then they hurriedly gathered their trash from the table and threw it in the trash can on the way out. Brooke felt Dylan's touch at her elbow in an almost protective gesture.

His feet moving rapidly, she saw him scan the whole area. She knew he was watching for Kiffany, but she was nowhere in sight.

"I don't think she quite understood," Brooke said worriedly, longing to reach up and wipe away the angry red mark from his cheek.

Dylan shook his head. "No, she didn't. But that isn't surprising. Don't let it bother you. You can't reason with someone who is irrational."

Reaching a crosswalk, Dylan's hand moved from her elbow to the small of her back as they crossed.

"Three days," he said, holding up three fingers. "I dated Kiffany for three days. We went on one date and had a nice time. However, she seemed to have a bit of a love you/hate you attitude toward me, so the next day, I sent her flowers, hoping to smooth her already ruffled feelings. That was a mistake. She became intensely attached to me, and by the next day, I couldn't take it. I bailed, completely terrified of Kiffany's 'Fatal Attraction' type mentality."

They entered an office building and headed toward the stairs.

"So it isn't surprising that she reacted the way she did," Dylan said with a sigh. "I don't know that we could have handled it any differently. Rational thought isn't her strong suit."

"Wait a minute," Brooke said, stopping on the stairs. She'd suddenly realized where they were. "Isn't this the way to Kiffany's work?" She distinctly remembered this office building and the eye doctor's office on the second floor. This was where she'd delivered Kiffany's flowers just yesterday.

"Yes, that's why we need to hurry," Dylan urged, taking a couple steps without Brooke. "Kiffany is still on lunch break, so we need to do it before she gets back."

"Do what?" Brooke asked, completely mystified.

"Talk to my girlfriend."

Brooke shook her head. "Your girlfriend? You mean, your *current* girlfriend?" Brooke had no idea why she'd never considered the possibility of him having a current girlfriend, which was silly of her. With as many exes as he had, it would be more shocking for him to not be dating someone. But, for some reason, the thought of Dylan in an existing relationship bothered her.

"Yes, and I need you to talk to her," Dylan insisted. "The only order that was not filled yesterday was the one that I'd actually wanted! I'd ordered roses for my current girlfriend, and she never received them. From her texts, I gather that she's heard of at least some women getting flowers from me yesterday, and she is not happy about it. So I need you to explain that she was actually the only one who was supposed to get flowers from me!"

Feeling dazed, Brooke followed Dylan the rest of the way up the stairs, as if on autopilot.

But at the door to the eye doctor's office, she once again found her voice. "Wait a minute. Your current girlfriend works in the same office as Kiffany, your ex-girlfriend?"

"Well, kind of," Dylan admitted reluctantly. "Come on, we need to hurry."

He pushed the door open for Brooke, and she went inside the office. Dylan hurried to the front desk and called to an older woman standing by the copy machine at the back. "I need to speak with Dr. Stevens."

"Your girlfriend is the eye doctor?" Brooke whispered fiercely.

"Yes," Dylan said, sending her a look that said he had no idea why this information was significant to her. "Dr. Monica Stevens."

"I'm sorry," the lady behind the desk replied. "The entire office is on lunch. She isn't available right now."

"Oh, I'm not a patient," Dylan explained. "Can you please just tell her that Dylan Masters is here?"

While the woman was obviously not happy about her task, she headed back into the recesses of the office.

"You are dating your ex-girlfriend's boss?" Brooke hissed, as soon as the other woman was out of hearing range. "Isn't that wrong?"

"Well, it is when you put it like that!" Dylan said with irritation. "I went on one date with Kiffany. One. I don't think that earns her the title of 'ex-girlfriend.' What was I supposed to do? Not date anyone else who might know the woman I went on one date with several months ago?"

"I don't even see Monica Stevens on the list," Brooke said, inspecting the list of accidental orders for the hundredth time. She smoothed out the wrinkles on the paper as if she could find the missing name in the folds.

"Of course she isn't," Dylan snapped. "I already explained it. You managed to send everyone flowers, but didn't fulfill the order I actually placed."

With an awful feeling in the pit of her stomach, Brooke realized Dylan was right. If Monica was on the list, then flowers would have been delivered to her. The basic problem was that her name should have been the only one on the list. Instead, there was an abundance of the wrong orders from the past year.

Brooke felt like an idiot. She knew Dylan had already explained the mix-up to her, but she hadn't understood. This whole time, she had been so focused on her list and fixing all of those accidental orders. It didn't even occur to her that some of Dylan's orders may not have been on the list at all.

It made her want to cry. It really did seem like she'd not gotten a single order correct yesterday. She closed her eyes briefly, trying to stay in control and not let the tears escape.

"Brooke," came a soft voice. The anger was suddenly gone and instead there was a gentleness that urged her to open her eyes. "Brooke, I'm so—"

"Dylan, why don't you come on back, and we can talk in my office," came a pleasant-sounding voice.

Brooke's eyes popped open to see a pretty brunette with glasses and a white lab coat.

"Thank you, Monica," Dylan said. With a slight touch to the small of her back, he urged Brooke ahead of him.

Down the hall, Dr. Stevens opened a door and let them into a small, but nicely furnished office. A rich, wood desk stood on one end of the room against a backdrop of heavily laden bookshelves. A long couch took up the wall on the opposite wall.

As soon as the door shut behind them, Brooke held out her hand, "HI, I'm Brooke Hutchins. I'm the florist at Crossroads Floral, and yesterday we had a series of mistakes, one of which affected you." With the threat of Kiffany arriving back from her lunch break, Brooke wanted to make the apologies quickly and get out of here. She had no more desire to film another episode with Kiffany than Dylan did.

"I'm Monica Stevens," the doctor replied, shaking Brooke's hand firmly.

Quickly, Brooke continued. "Yesterday, Dylan Masters

placed an order for a bouquet of flowers to be delivered to you. However, there was a mix-up, and the orders that were printed for delivery included every order from the past year instead, excluding yours. I don't understand how it happened, but I do know numerous women received flowers from Dylan—flowers that he did not order—while the one woman he did order flowers for, did not receive them. All of this mess was entirely my responsibility, and my fault. I am trying to make personal apologies to everyone affected. I am so, so sorry for the confusion and that you did not receive the flowers intended for you."

Monica nodded. "Thank you for explaining, and for your apology. I heard that there had been some mix-up with the local florist. I saw people talking about it on social media, and then I read the statement from Crossroads Floral that accidental orders had been sent out. But I didn't know I was affected by the mistakes. Nor did I realize that Dylan had been affected, or that the women I'd heard who received flowers from him were not actually intended recipients."

Brooke's heart fell. She didn't know that Helen had made an official statement about yesterday. With the number of errors and the likelihood that the small town rumor mill would be running wild, it certainly made sense. But Brooke also knew that any statement Helen made would not present her in a favorable light.

"So are we good then?" Dylan asked. "Can I still pick you up around 7:00 tonight?"

Monica nodded and smiled. "Of course. And for my part, I'm sorry I jumped to conclusions instead of asking you or doing my own investigation."

Dylan reached for Monica's hand, and Brooke turned for the door. While she hadn't minded watching Kiffany's one-sided advances of affection, she had no desire to see Dylan and Monica be affectionate. "I'll wait for you at the front of the office," she said hurriedly, not even sparing a glance back as she opened the door and exited.

Brooke breathed a sigh of relief as she headed back down the hallway to the reception area. For the first time all day, one of her apologies had gone quickly and smoothly, with no drama. And she was so very thankf—

"What are *you* doing here?"

The strident voice instantly froze Brooke.

Kiffany was back from her lunch break.

CHAPTER 10

B rooke wet her dry lips nervously, "Umm… well… I had to see Dr. Stevens," she finally answered simply.

"Oh," Kiffany answered with a possible hint of relief. "You mean, you were here for an eye appointment?"

"Well, no." As much as she'd like to lie and give Kiffany what she'd like to hear, Brooke just couldn't do it. "There was another mix-up with a floral order, and I had to make an apology to Dr. Stevens as well."

Obviously deep in thought, Kiffany came into the office more from where she stood at the door and then headed around the corner to stand near her desk. "Oh, you mean Dr. Stevens also received flowers that no one really ordered?"

Brooke could tell this was just going to go from bad to worse. The best course of action was to not really give Kiffany any more answers or information, but to just leave.

"You know, I think I'll just—"

"Dylan?" Kiffany's voice sounded strangled.

Brooke turned around to see that Dylan had stepped out of the office and now looked like a deer caught in the headlights.

"What…?" Kiffany stammered. Then a light of fanatic hope dawned in her eyes, and she stepped forward. "Oh, Dylan! I didn't know if you'd come find me after the sandwich shop, but it means so much that you did!"

Dylan stepped back and held up his hands before Kiffany could throw herself into his arms again. "Kiffany, I wasn't here to see you. I came with Brooke to see Monica. One of the order mistakes yesterday at the florist shop involved her as well."

When Dylan stepped to avoid Kiffany's advances, the view of Monica standing behind him stopped Kiffany in her tracks.

"Oh," Kiffany said, obviously thinking. Then her face clouded over, and she gritted out. "You mean she got a bouquet from you as well?"

Brooke stepped up, placing a calming hand on Kiffany's shoulder. It was her mistake, she should be the one to explain. "Dr. Stevens was supposed to receive an order yesterday, but it wasn't delivered. It was my mistake, so I came to make the apology, and Dylan accompanied me."

With her hand at the back of Kiffany's shoulder, Brooke felt the other woman's sharp intake of breath. But her shoulder never sagged in the release of that breath. Instead, Kiffany held it in. Brooke watched as, with her eyes fixed on Dylan, the model-like face took on a shade that matched her lipstick.

"You mean, the flowers that I got from you were actually supposed to go to Dr. Stevens?" she finally burst out.

"No!" Brooke said quickly, letting her hand fall helplessly from Kiffany's shoulder. Knowing she needed to explain everything before Kiffany developed any more misunderstandings, she flung out the truth, simply trying to make Kiffany understand. "Dylan ordered flowers for Dr. Stevens. But everything got screwed up, and all of his ex-girlfriends received flowers. But the original order, the one for Dr. Stevens, was never delivered."

Kiffany glared at Brooke. "You mean that she isn't your girlfriend?" She turned her glare Monica's direction. "But *she* is?"

"I don't know that we've made things official," Dylan said hesitantly, glancing at Monica. "But, yes, we are dating."

Kiffany let out a shriek and ran back to her desk.

Feeling like it was all her fault, Brooke stepped in between Kiffany and Dylan. Holding up her hands, she spoke in a soothing voice. "Please just take a deep breath, Kiffany."

"So these flowers were supposed to go to *her*," she raged. "Fine! You can have them!" Her hand swung down to grab the flowers out of the vase. But she misjudged the distance, and the force of the impact sent the vase crashing into a wall.

It shattered, sending shards of glass everywhere.

Brooke cried out and jumped back, covering her face with her arms.

Everything fell silent for the space of two solid seconds after the crash. Then Kiffany burst into tears. "I'm sorry! I didn't mean to break it!" she moaned.

Brooke slowly took her arms from her face, seeing Kiffany collapse into her office chair in a sobbing mess.

"Brooke, are you okay?" Dylan said urgently, coming up quickly behind her.

"I think so," she said, still feeling a little dazed as she turned to face him.

Dylan's eyes flew wide. "Monica, she's hurt!" he said. Before she realized what was happening, Dylan swung her into his arms and easily carried her down the hall, back to Monica's office. He carefully laid her on the couch.

"Monica, get me something to clean her up with!" Dylan said, flinging the order over his shoulder.

Brooke reached her fingers up to her forehead. Dylan turned back around and snatched her hand away, but not before she saw the red smear of blood. With the sight, it was as if her body realized it was hurt, and Brooke suddenly felt pain.

"Here you go," Monica said, bustling in with her hands full. "I have some washcloths, antiseptic wipes, antibiotic ointment, and bandages. Unloading the supplies beside Dylan, she then bent over Brooke for inspection. "It doesn't look too bad. Not too deep, and I don't think it will require glue or stitches. It's really more of a scratch. But any kind of cut right there is going to bleed a lot. Do you want me to take over, Dylan? I can get her bandaged up pretty quick."

Her words brought Brooke great comfort. She'd wondered if she was completely cut up from the glass, but maybe it wasn't so bad. She really wished they'd give her a mirror.

"No, thanks," Dylan said, already using one of the wash clothes to apply pressure to Brooke's forehead. "I've got it. I think Kiffany probably needs your attention more right now."

Monica sighed. "I think you've got the better job."

She left, and Dylan silently kept the washcloth in position. Brooke looked up at him. He was so focused on her wound that it left her free to inspect him without him noticing. His gray eyes looked cloudy with concern, and his jaw flexed with tension. Some of his dark hair waved over his forehead as he bent over her, and she had the strange desire to reach up with her fingers and push it back.

After a couple minutes of silence, Brooke asked, "So are you a doctor, too, Dylan Masters?"

Dylan blinked and glanced down at her. "No, but my mother is a nurse, which really means I'm just as good." He lifted the cloth and then reported. "It looks like the bleeding has stopped." He moved to find a bandage.

"May I have a mirror before you bandage it up?" Brooke asked.

Brooke could tell he didn't want to, but nonetheless, he stood and retrieved a small standing mirror that looked as if it belonged in the optical department.

He handed it to her then watched her worriedly as she sat up and brought the mirror to her face. A cut about an inch and a half in length ran along her hairline on the right side of her forehead.

"I'm sorry," Dylan whispered. "Apparently every relationship I've ever had is quite dysfunctional, and that isn't your fault or the fault of any accidental bouquets. I should have never tried to make you take care of my mess."

Brooke nodded. "Thank you. I appreciate you saying that, but it was my mistake that caused all of the crazy to shine through." She looked at the cut one more time and handed Dylan back the mirror. "It isn't too bad," she said, willing herself to believe the words. "It probably won't even scar." Her words caught in a little hiccup as she tried desperately to control the burning behind her eyes. She would not cry. She would not cry.

"Brooke," Dylan said, squatting down to the couch so he faced her directly. When she still refused to look up at him, he reached out and gently tilted her chin up.

"Please don't," Brooke whispered. "If you look at me, or touch me, or say anything, I'll start crying and won't be able to stop."

"Would that be so bad?" Dylan asked gently. "You've had a pretty rough day. I think you're entitled to a few tears."

Brooke shook her head and squeezed her eyes together so the tears wouldn't escape. "I can't," she managed brokenly.

"And how is our patient?" Monica called cheerfully reentering her office.

Dylan's hand dropped from where it had cradled her chin, and he reached for the bandages.

"Almost done," Dylan answered. "Do you have any pain meds, Monica? I'm sure this cut is starting to cause some pain."

Brooke was so grateful Monica had shown up when she did. With the doctor's presence, Brooke was able to gain control and not melt into a full breakdown. *Just make it to tonight*, she told herself. As soon as every apology was made, she would shut the door to her apartment and let it all out where nobody could hear her cries.

Monica retrieved some over-the-counter pills and a bottle of water from her desk. "Kiffany has the glass all cleaned up and is anxious to make an apology to Brooke."

Seeming not to have heard Monica, Dylan looked Brooke in

the eyes and said, "I'll try not to hurt you."

Maybe it was the sincerity in his eyes. Maybe it was the slight fear, as if he really was scared that he would do exactly what he intended not to. But Brooke got the feeling that, whether intentional or not, his words covered a lot more than a bandage.

Gentle fingers applied the ointment, and then the bandage. After pressing the adhesive down firmly, his fingers left her face. "All done," he announced.

Brooke immediately moved to stand. She really wanted to be out of this office. The sooner she completed all of her tasks, the sooner she got to go home and sob the whole day out.

"Careful," Dylan warned, moving quickly to wrap his arm around her waist. "You might be dizzy."

"I'm fine," Brooke assured.

But Dylan remained at her side, his hand protectively at her back when they went out the door and down the hall. Monica followed.

As if finely tuned to Dylan's touch, Brooke keenly felt every time his body even slightly brushed hers and every second his hand rested at her back. She also felt its sudden absence when, just as they exited the hall, Kiffany looked up from her desk, immediately rushing forward, and threw her arms around Brooke in a fierce hug, thereby dislodging Dylan's hold.

"I'm so sorry," she sniffled, pulling back slightly.

Kiffany's eyes, as well as her puffy nose and the rest of her face, were all red from crying, and it wasn't a very good look for her. Her makeup was smeared all over, and she had the look of a child who had been caught in a transgression.

Trying to be subtle, Brooke stepped back to gain a little distance between them and decrease the risk of a repeat hug.

"I didn't mean for the vase to break," Kiffany explained, her eyes tearing up again. "I just got so upset that I wasn't thinking or being careful. You know, maybe you really shouldn't use glass vases at the florist shop. You know, for safety reasons. Plastic vases can be just as pretty. And it would just take one person who broke a vase to be upset enough to file a lawsuit against you." Kiffany shrugged. "It's just a suggestion to think about."

Brooke felt Dylan stiffen beside her. The angry growl was soon to follow. "Kiffany, I don't think—"

Brooke reached down and grabbed Dylan's hand beside her. The instant her hand touched his, she felt his jolt of shock, and he stopped talking. She gave his hand a quick squeeze, hopefully further cementing his silence.

"Apology accepted," Brooke told Kiffany simply.

Kiffany smiled, the lines on her forehead relaxing in relief. "I really hope you weren't hurt too bad. Dr. Stevens told me it should heal just fine. Even so, is there anything I can do to help make it up to you? Maybe I can buy you a cup of coffee sometime?"

Brooke shook her head. "How about you just send me some flowers sometime?"

Kiffany paused, her face clouded in confusion. Brooke saw the instant she got the joke, and Kiffany let out a giggle. "Maybe I'll do that! But I'll have to be careful to make sure it gets to the right florist!"

Feeling Dylan's eyes on her, Brooke turned toward him. His face shone with a mixture of awe, admiration, and a little bewilderment. Realizing that her hand still rested in his, she gave a little tug. "Let's go."

"Dylan, can I speak with you?" Monica said. "It should take just a minute."

At her voice, Dylan dropped Brooke's hand as if it was hot.

"Sure," he said, stepping back into the hallway with Monica.

Brooke went to the front waiting area and sat down on one of the chairs. She flashed a weak smile at an older woman with glasses sitting in another chair. But noting the woman's open curiosity, Brooke averted her gaze. Since the woman couldn't have missed Kiffany's apology, Brooke figured they'd already provided her with enough show for an afternoon visit to the eye doctor.

About ninety seconds later, Dylan returned. He started for the door and then turned and walked back to the front desk. "Kiffany, listen carefully. I have no interest in a relationship with you, nor will I ever. I will never intentionally send you flowers or call you. Any pleasant look on my face is not directed your way. I am sorry if I have hurt you, but that wasn't my intention. I wish you the very best and hope you find someone who will love you and make you happy. But it won't be me."

Kiffany nodded. "I understand."

With that, Dylan hurried for the door without another backward glance.

Once back to Dylan's car, Brooke sank down weakly into the seat and shut her eyes for a brief moment. Dylan got in and started the engine.

Taking a deep breath, she opened her eyes. "Who's next on the list?" she asked bravely.

"No one," Dylan replied. "We're done. I'll take you back to the florist shop."

And suddenly, the words she had longed to hear all day felt terribly flat.

CHAPTER 11

"**N**o, Dylan," Brooke replied firmly as he pulled out onto the street from the parking lot. "We are not done. I want to get all the names checked off the list today. I need to."

Dylan blew out an exasperated breath. "I'm not going to take you to another name on the list and put you in the crossfire between me and one of my exes! It just isn't worth it. And I'm not okay with you cleaning up any more of my ugly dating history."

"Then maybe I should do it by myself," Brooke said, with sudden inspiration. "I think the women are reacting more to you than to the fact that they got a mistaken delivery of flowers. If I just go to them by myself and explain the situation without you, then they will have no one to get mad at."

"You're not going alone," Dylan said stubbornly, as if his statement ended the discussion.

"You really don't have any say in it, Dylan," Brooke said casually. Instead of anger, she had opted for the soft, easy you-can't-make-me attitude. "I have the names and addresses of where the flowers were delivered. I'll just make a visit to each and get it done without you."

"Absolutely not. I don't want you going alone."

Brooke turned her body away from him, pretending to be engrossed in the view. But really, she was working on not launching into a tirade. She held her silence, wanting to make it as uncomfortable as possible for him. It didn't matter to Brooke what he wanted or thought. As soon as he dropped her off, she could take her car to handle the final apologies without Dylan.

The silence stretched from seconds to minutes. Brooke watched the buildings of Crossroads pass and idly thought how nice the downtown area was looking. Many of the older buildings looked renovated and sported new paint. Instead of old and tired, their little town was taking on a cute and quaint look. She'd already heard that more tourists were starting to come through town and visit the little shops. The mayor and city council were working on some other projects that would hopefully draw more of the tourist business to Crossroads as well.

With close access to recreation and a great small town atmosphere, Brooke was happy to see Crossroads healthy and thriving, but she really didn't want too many people to come and figure out what a great place it was to live! A new Community Center sign caught her eye. She turned, but couldn't see any of the details fast enough, but it looked as if an old fire station had undergone some significant renovations. She made a mental note to ask her mom about it. She was on several committees and stayed current on what was going on in the community. She was so well known that it seemed like every person she ran into usually came with a bit of gossip to add to their "hello."

Dylan's sigh interrupted her sight-seeing. "Fine," he said, his exasperation evident. Apparently, he couldn't handle the silence any longer. "I'll get you the numbers. If you insist on making apologies, you can call instead of go in person."

Brooke looked at him, thoroughly incredulous. Had she just wasted her entire day? "I thought you said you didn't have their phone numbers!"

"I don't," Dylan insisted. "But I have my old cell phone bills. I know when I dated who and should be able to figure out their numbers if I look at my call records."

A little surprised that he was willing to go to that work,

Brooke nonetheless replied, "That would be great. Thank you." She looked at the now-crumpled paper in her hand. "It looks like there are several more names on your list that haven't been contacted yet, plus the local orders I need to call for Helen. I know she already notified them of the mistakes, but I need to call and make personal apologies."

"I may not be able to get them to you for a couple of hours," Dylan said cautiously. "After I drop you off, I have to run by the bank, and then I'll have to go home and do my research. Will you still be at the floral shop this evening?"

"No, I'm hoping that I can just pick up the order info and make the calls from home," Brooke said, worry lining her voice. "I really don't want Helen looking over my shoulder and critiquing the word choice in my apology. Would you mind dropping the phone numbers off at my apartment? I can give you my address."

Dylan nodded. "I can do that."

Suddenly remembering Dylan's plans for the evening, Brooke asked. "Do you think you'll be dropping by before or after your date with Monica?" If he didn't bring her the info until afterward, she may not have time to make the calls tonight after all.

"I'm not going out with Monica tonight," Dylan said. "You should have the numbers with plenty of time to make your apologies this evening."

"Maybe I misheard," Brooke said, confused. "I thought for sure that you said you'd pick her up this evening."

"We were supposed to go out," Dylan said. "But she canceled. That's what she called me over about right before we left."

"Oh." Brooke tried to talk herself out of asking more questions, but she couldn't quite manage it. Mostly, she was worried that it was somehow her fault. "Is she still upset about the flowers? I thought she'd taken the news very well, but maybe not."

"No, she didn't cancel because of the flowers. She canceled because she broke up with me."

Brooke couldn't hide her sharp intake of breath. "I'm so sorry! Now my mistakes have really ruined things for you!"

"It isn't your fault," Dylan said firmly. "At least not in that way. Monica wasn't upset about the flowers, and that isn't the reason she broke up with me." Dylan paused as if searching for the words to explain. "She just said she didn't want to waste our time when it was clear to her that we weren't going to be more than friends."

"I'm still sorry," Brooke said sympathetically. "You've not had a very good day. Ending it with a breakup couldn't be pleasant."

Dylan shrugged. "I'm not upset about it. Monica knew I wasn't attached to her, which was I guess the problem. I wasn't serious about her, and I wasn't going to be. In this case, the flower fiasco was a good thing. I think it made Monica realize that she didn't want a relationship that had no possibility of getting serious. And in the long run, it was probably a good thing for me as well."

Dylan pulled into the parking lot of Crossroads Floral and parked beside Brooke's car.

After wanting to be out of his presence all day, Brooke was suddenly reluctant to leave him. She sat for several seconds, trying to choose words and decide if she even wanted to speak what was on her mind.

For his part, Dylan waited patiently, seeming to realize she was struggling with something.

"Can I ask you a question?" she finally managed.

"Go ahead," Dylan said without a hint of trepidation. "You've seen just about every skeleton in my closet already today. You may as well. I think you've earned it."

"Why do you date so many women?" she asked in a rush.

Dylan was slow enough in responding that Brooke worried she had offended him.

"I don't intend to date so many women," Dylan finally responded. He spoke slowly and seriously, as if taking time to give her an honest answer. "I don't like to do things by myself. I don't have any family to speak of, especially in this area, and most of my guy friends are already married. I ask a girl out for fun, but pretty soon, she's upset because I'm not pledging my love to her or getting serious fast enough."

"But you send them flowers," Brooke said, not letting him off the hook easily. "That's a romantic gesture, especially for someone who doesn't want a serious relationship."

Dylan nodded, as if considering her point to be valid. "I usually send flowers about the second week I date a woman. Flowers are something romantic that doesn't necessarily say 'I love you.' And it usually satisfies them for another couple of dates. Then, either I can't stand them, or they are fed up with me, and we break up."

Feeling a little braver, Brooke surmised, "Then you need someone to do something with, ask another girl out, and the cycle starts over again?"

"Pretty much," Dylan answered tiredly. "Except they often invite me out. Sometimes it seems the women of the greater Crossroads area have an unwritten contest to see who can snare Dylan Masters. They all want to submit a resume, and then get mad when they don't get the job."

Brooke laughed. It was pretty amazing at how clearly Dylan understood the situation and his role in it. His words echoed what Celeste had told her earlier in the day.

"I probably should have given up long ago and just quit dating," he admitted with a grimace. "A psychologist would have fun analyzing why I keep trying. I don't enjoy being a Casanova. I don't like the attention or the reputation. And yet, I can't help but find another girl when the next weekend rolls around. And the really sad thing is, I'm not even looking for love. I'd like to get married someday, but I thought falling in love would eventually happen without me doing gymnastics to make it. And I've never found a girl I've felt romantic enough to want to get serious about."

"You've never been in love?"

"No. Shocking isn't it?" he said, wiggling his eyebrows. "Don't get me wrong, I've felt romantic toward women I've dated and had several relationships that lasted six months. But they never progressed beyond the initial romantic attraction to something deeper. Believe it or not, I really am cautious and try not to lead any women on. In fact, when I go on a first date, I usually have a standard speech on how I'm really looking for friendship. If something else develops, that's great. But my primary goal is friendship. Every woman I've dated has nodded, smiled, and said she completely agrees. Then, three weeks later, she's ticked off at me that I'm not in love with her."

"And yet you still try. Over and over."

"Isn't that the definition of insanity? Doing something repeatedly while getting the same results?" Dylan shook his head. "Maybe I'm not a complete lost cause. This whole fiasco with the flowers has made me realize that maybe the problem with my dating life is more me than them. I don't intend to lead them on and hurt them, but in retrospect, many of the flowers I sent probably did just that. I've dated probably hundreds of women and fallen in love with none. That tells me I should probably do some serious thinking. Maybe I should take a dating hiatus for a while, or only date a woman I have a strong romantic connection to and feel I have the potential to be serious with."

"Well, if my little mistake can reform Dylan Masters, maybe it wasn't a total loss," Brooke couldn't resist teasing. "I guess I'd better go try to do more damage control from that little mistake. I doubt everyone will find a personal epiphany worth the cost of accidental flowers."

With her hand on the door handle of the Porsche, the day flashed back over itself. Dylan wouldn't even speak to her at first, and now she realized how special it was that he had opened up to her. "Thank you for talking to me," she said almost shyly.

"Of course," Dylan said. Getting out of his own door, he hurried around to open the passenger side.

Brooke stepped out, and her gaze caught on his. She couldn't read him, and that, in itself was fascinating. She watched emotions she didn't understand spark like lightning in a gray storm. And in turn, those sparks seemed to produce feelings that she didn't understand in herself.

Dylan flashed a smile. "I'll see you later."

"See you," Brooke answered simply. Then she resolutely left Dylan's stormy eyes and headed to the door of the shop where she was sure Helen would have a long list of unpleasant tasks waiting.

CHAPTER 12

*P*lease, Lord! *I'm not sure* how much more I can take! Brooke prayed as she resolutely dialed the number for the next order on the list. She was back at her apartment, but had yet to have a break. After walking in the door, she had immediately begun calling the long list of local and online accidental orders and making personal apologies. While the calls were going relatively quickly, with none of the drama involved with Dylan's orders, it was humiliating.

She really believed Helen had only consented to let her make the calls from home because the older woman was too angry to stand her presence. After fielding calls from customers and those who were simply curious, as well as managing the public outcry and social media, Helen's temper was even worse than in the morning.

Brooke stopped her pacing and sat down in the straight-backed chair at her small table. Her hand shook with anxiety as she brought the phone up to her ear. This was one call she especially did not want to make.

Though Brooke knew she'd just have to repeat the call later, she silently hoped no one would pick up the ringing phone. Maybe she could just make the apology on the answering machine and leave her number if they wanted to call her back. Since it was after business hours, maybe…

"Hello. Somners Funeral Home."

Brooke cringed. Propping her elbow on the table, she leaned over to wearily rest her forehead against her hand. "Hi, this is Brooke Hutchins from Crossroads Floral. I just wanted to call and personally apologize for the order that was mistakenly delivered yesterday."

To her surprise, the man on the other end laughed. "That was quite the accidental order! It's not every day that we get a bouquet that was obviously meant for a bachelorette party, delivered to a funeral! I think there was even a piece of lingerie attached!"

Brooke shut her eyes, her face turning red even though no one was there to see it. "I'm so sorry! I wasn't the florist who put together the bouquet, but I did see the instructions. It sounds like the florist who did fulfill the order had even more fun with it than the instructions outlined!"

A knock sounded at Brooke's front door. Trying to stay focused on her conversation, she got up to open the door while the funeral director gleefully gave her a thorough description of the bachelorette party bouquet.

She swung the door wide to find Dylan. In one hand, he held a list paper-clipped to his phone bills. In the other hand, he held a sack of Chinese takeout.

Brooke motioned him inside without granting him a second glance, and then returned to her seat at the table. She heard him rummaging around with the food, but paid him no mind, focusing instead on her task. The fact that the man she was talking to, presumably Mr. Somners, was painting a vivid description of a lingerie-laden bouquet made her cheeks a little too rosy, and she didn't want to make eye contact with anyone, especially Dylan!

Finally having a turn to speak after she was given a very clear understanding of the way the lace draped over the flowers, Brooke explained, "I know that there were two orders for Tracey, Oregon, and one of the addresses was deleted by accident. So both orders— one for a funeral and one for a bachelorette party—were mistakenly delivered to the single address, which happened to be the funeral home."

Mr. Somners laughed again. "I was wondering what happened! Sounds like it was a far too easy mistake to make! But it certainly provided us with some great entertainment today! I have to say, this was one of my most favorite days ever as a funeral director!"

Brooke's eyes came open. "You mean your clients weren't upset about having such an inappropriate bouquet delivered to their loved one's funeral?"

"Well, I think they were shocked at first, and some may have been upset," Mr. Somners admitted. "But then everyone saw the humor in the situation. We had a few mishaps of trying to get the bouquet out of the public line of viewing, but I think, in the end, the family found the entire situation hilarious. It was a much-needed release for a sad day. They all agreed that their loved one would have ordered the bouquet for his own funeral himself, if he'd thought of it. And there was a heated argument and rivalry over who got to take the bouquet home!"

"Oh, I'm so relieved!" Brooke said. In the back of her mind, she recognized that Dylan seemed to have no intention of simply making his delivery and leaving. Instead, he was making himself at home by finding a plate and ladling Chinese food on it.

Steadily ignoring him, Brooke continued, "I still feel bad, though, about the discomfort and drama on a day of mourning. If you are willing to give me the number of your clients, I can call and make a personal apology to them."

"Oh, no, no, no," the jolly man said quickly. "That won't be necessary at all. I ran down the problem as soon as the bouquet arrived and handled all of the apologies. By the end of the services, everyone went home with both tears and smiles, feeling like that accidental bouquet was really a blessing disguised in lingerie!"

Brooke felt tears prickle the corners of her eyes. She put her hand up to casually shield them from where Dylan now sat eating Chinese food on her couch.

Could it really be possible that some people were thankful for her mistakes?

"You have no idea what it means to me to hear that!" she finally managed.

After that, goodbyes were made quickly, and Brooke pressed the end button on her phone. She took deep breaths, trying to combat her case of the sniffles.

"Do you want something to eat?" Dylan asked in between bites. "I thought you probably wouldn't have eaten yet, so I went ahead and got enough Chinese food for both of us."

"You're right, I haven't," Brooke said, looking up briefly and flashing him an attempt at a smile. "Thank you. That was very thoughtful. I think I'll go ahead and finish my list first. I think I only have one more name. Then I can do your list after I eat."

"Then go ahead and get it done," Dylan said easily. "I wasn't sure what you liked, so I got several different things, along with some egg rolls. It will keep until you are ready for it."

"Thank you," Brooke said, already looking down at the next name on her list. Seeing who it was, her eyes slid shut, and she couldn't help the little moan that escaped. Whether conscious or not, she had left this one for last, and now she wished she hadn't. She tried to tell herself that the last call had turned out much better than expected, so this one may, too. But her pep talk didn't quite work. This was the mistaken order that had made her sick whenever she thought about it all day long. Now there was no more putting it off.

Knowing she just had to get it over with, she took a deep breath and quickly dialed the numbers before she had a chance to change her mind.

"Hello?" came the weary voice on the other end.

"Hi, is this Aimee?" Brooke asked.

"Yes, it is," the voice answered.

"This is Brooke Hutchins from Crossroads Floral. I'm calling to apologize for the bouquet that was sent to you by accident today. It was my mistake, and I am so sorry. I can't imagine how terrible it would feel to have flowers delivered from a mother who had passed away."

"I'm so glad you called," Aimee said, and her tone suddenly brightened. "Are you the one who messed up all the orders? A woman named Helen called earlier and said someone else had made the mistakes and would be calling to personally apologize."

"Yes, that's me," Brooke acknowledged. She was sure Helen said much more than that when she called. And chances were good that it was all unflattering to Brooke. "When I printed the orders, I didn't realize that the date was wrong. Instead of the orders for yesterday, we filled the orders from that same day, but a year ago. Your mother apparently ordered flowers for you last year, and that order was inadvertently duplicated yesterday."

"Yes, yesterday was my birthday," Aimee said, her voice quiet.

Brooke shut her eyes. "Aimee, I am so very sorry. I must have ruined your day and caused you so much pain. I wish I could do something to make it better."

"Oh, but you already did," Aimee said gently. "I wanted to have a chance to talk to you. Your boss, Helen was very angry when I talked to her. And I've seen all of the mean things people are saying on social media. But I wanted to thank you."

Brooke mentally braced herself for a sarcastic tongue-lashing.

But Aimee's voice stayed soft and gentle as she continued speaking, with not a trace of scorn in sight. "Mom always sent me flowers on my birthday. When she passed away from a heart attack about six months ago, I knew that I would never again receive birthday flowers from her. And I would never again read her words, 'My favorite day ever was the one that brought me you.' I guess part of grief is going through all of those 'never agains,' and it's been so hard, especially since I was an only child. Then, on my birthday, a bouquet shows up with a card from my mother, exactly as if she had sent it herself. At first, I was confused. I even felt sorry for myself that such a cruel mistake had found me, on my birthday! Then, as I was staring at the flowers, I realized that Mom had sent the flowers. She had ordered them for me last year, and if she could have, she would have ordered me some this year as well. I happen to believe that everything happens for a reason, and I think, in my case, God found a way to let my mom order me flowers for my birthday one last time."

By the time Aimee finished, Brooke was weeping. "I don't know what to say," Brooke hiccupped. "It's such a beautiful story. Thank you for sharing it with me."

"No, Miss Hutchins, I must thank you," Aimee insisted. "I know your mistakes weren't on purpose, but I also know that they have caused a lot of trouble for you. What was a beautiful blessing for me came at great cost to you."

Aimee's kind words only seemed to increase the output of Brooke's tears. Though her voice trembled with emotion, she assured, "I'm sure I'll be okay, Aimee, especially now that I know God sent you flowers from your mom. I know there are a lot of angry people, and their stories don't seem to have any positive outcome like yours. But dealing with all of that will be easier for me now because I know that in your case, the cost of my difficulties was worth the price of your blessing."

They chatted a few more minutes. Brooke found out more about Aimee's mom and Aimee herself. She was a little older than Brooke and had been through a divorce. She had no children and didn't seem to do much outside of her work as a teacher. Aimee seemed so very nice that it bothered Brooke tremendously that the woman seemed so lonely. By the end of the conversation, Brooke had managed to invite Aimee to her church. As she finally ended the call, Brooke prayed silently for the young woman and truly hoped that she could soon count her as a friend.

Brooke pressed the end button, feeling a good measure of relief. Now she just had to finish up by calling the last of Dylan's girlfriends, and she could close this nightmarish chapter.

"This looks good," Brooke said, grabbing a plate and looking over the selection that Dylan brought.

"The egg rolls are especially good," Dylan said. Having just finished the last of his food, he came into the kitchen and began washing his plate at the sink.

Brooke loaded up her plate, grabbed a fork, and headed for the couch. She just didn't have the energy left to sit at the table and eat. Spearing a piece of sweet and sour chicken with her fork, she almost had it to her mouth when her phone rang from her pocket.

She brought it out and answered, "Hi, Tylee."

"Hi, Brooke," she answered, her normal cheerful tone quite subdued. "How are things going?"

"I'm almost done with the apology calls," Brooke reported. "For the most part, they've gone better than I expected. I just have a few more of Dylan's orders, and then I'm done."

Tylee sniffled. "I'm so sorry, Brooke! I feel like it's all my fault! With all the accidental orders and the way you're getting blamed for everything, I wouldn't be surprised if you hate me!" The young woman's sniffles were approaching the level of sobbing.

"Tylee, it is not your fault," Brooke said firmly.

But before she could comfort any further, Tylee jumped in. "But I'm the one who spilled the coffee and printed out the wrong orders!"

"But I was the one in charge!" Brooke insisted. "Helen should have never left us in charge without giving us the passwords and training we needed to manage the orders. And I should have carefully reviewed the orders before giving you the okay to print. I really don't know what I could have done differently about the online orders. Helen left me with no way to reprint them and no way to contact her, so I did the best I could, which was apparently a very lousy job that included plenty of mistakes. But the point is, everything you did was accidental. I'm the one who should fully take the blame because I was the one responsible. You were there to assist me."

Despite Brooke's words, Tylee continued to cry. To make matters worse, she noticed that Dylan was paying very close attention to her conversation and was looking at her with open curiosity from where he now perched on one of the chairs at the dining table that stood between the kitchen and living room areas.

Trying to block him out, she focused on deciphering Tylee's words through the sobs.

"I know you don't want me to feel bad," Tylee blubbered, "but you weren't at the shop today to hear all of the calls. And the way Grammy talked about you was awful!" The hiccuping sobs were making it increasingly difficult for her to speak at all. "I did try to talk to her... I want you to know that I tried... I told her I was the one who spilled the coffee. And printed out the wrong orders. But she wouldn't listen... Said it was your fault... I even told her I was the one who got her password... But I don't think she even believed me!" Tylee's last words ended in a wail.

Brooke sighed. Self consciously glancing at Dylan, she saw that he had apparently lost interest in their conversation and looked to be making a phone call on his own cell.

Realizing this might take a while, Brooke set her plate of food beside her on the couch and prayed to find the right words to say to her friend. "Thank you for trying, Tylee," she finally managed, "but I didn't expect the truth to make any difference. Listen to me, I don't want you to worry about it. I will be fine. There is nothing you can do, and I don't want you torturing yourself over something that you can't change and isn't your fault to begin with."

It took several more, long minutes to calm Tylee down to the point that she could breathe normally again. Every once in a while, movement would break her concentration, and she would look up to see Dylan talking on his phone at the other side of the room. Mostly, he was pacing. Occasionally, a hand would run through his hair or stroke his jaw as if he were involved in his own rather serious and stressful conversation.

Eventually, Brooke was able to sign off with a relatively calm Tylee, promising to see her at work the next morning.

Brooke felt the threat of tears again as soon as Tylee's voice fell silent. She wasn't done yet. Tylee's call had cost her, and now she didn't have the chance to relax and eat before finishing up with Dylan's orders. If she didn't make the calls now, it would be too late to get them done. Looking at her plate of food regretfully, she made herself stand and go look for Dylan's list on the counter.

She found it and picked it up to read the list of three names. Deciding to start with Audra, she lifted her phone to dial, but a persistent tapping on her shoulder stopped her. Turning, she found Dylan with one hand still holding the phone to his ear. With his other hand, he pointed to the phone and mouthed the word "Destiny!"

Startled, Brooke looked down at the list and then back up to him. "You're talking to Destiny?" she mouthed back.

Dylan gave an exaggerated nod.

Brooke pointed to the list and then back to herself. "I'll call Shauna," saying the words with her lips, but allowing no sound to escape.

Dylan shook his head no and pointed to himself

Brooke didn't know if that meant that he had already called Shauna, or that he intended to call her himself.

Brooke pointed to the last name on and waved it emphatically.

Dylan once again adamantly shook his head. But this time, he took a step forward and took the list from Brooke. Folding it up, he stuck it in his pocket. Then, taking her hand, he led her to the couch. Releasing her hand, he pointed to her plate of food.

His message was clear: she was not to call anyone else; she was to eat. Brooke may have argued with him and insisted that he let her make the apologies, but she was just so tired, hungry, and relieved that her muscles seemed to give out. She was sprawled on the couch before Dylan had to say anything on his end of the phone conversation.

Picking up her plate of food, she ate and idly listened to Dylan's conversation. The food was long cold by this time, but it didn't matter to Brooke. It tasted wonderful. The conversation he was having didn't sound overly dramatic, but every time he tried to sign off, the woman seemed to launch on another topic. Dylan actually did very little talking. Finally managing to end the call, he immediately dialed another number on his phone, not even sparing a glance Brooke's direction.

Brooke finished her food, washed her plate at the sink, and headed back to the couch. With more than a little anxiety, Brooke used her phone to check social media for the first time that day. Of course, she immediately found the post from Crossroads Floral about the issue with the accidental orders. Though her mind screamed not to do it, her finger pushed the button to read the comments. The unkind words blurred in front of her teary eyes. Comment after comment either poked fun or angrily suggested that the florist responsible be fired. From what she saw, none of those people had been directly affected by the accident, yet they all offered harsh and ready opinions about what should be done. There was not a single comment that was positive or sympathetic to the person responsible.

Brooke's phone slipped from her grasp, grabbed by another set of fingers. Startled, Brooke looked up to see Dylan frowning down at her with her phone in his possession. He then placed another object in her hand instead. It was a remote control. Pointing to the TV, he clearly pantomimed that she should watch TV instead.

Not having the energy to put up a fight, she obediently turned on the TV, but she watched Dylan instead. For this call, it sounded like the woman on the other end was crying while Dylan tried to comfort. He was careful to not get too personal or give hope of a future relationship, but it seemed like this second round of breakup was a difficult one. And the poor man looked plenty miserable.

Tears overflowed her eyes as she realized he was doing it for her.

He was making the calls that she should be making. She had been the one to mess up his order. She should have been the one to explain the mistakes and issue an apology. But he was talking to his ex-girlfriends and explaining things so that she wouldn't have to.

Though she wasn't thrilled about him confiscating her phone, she also realized that he, again, was trying to spare her more pain. She was sure he'd seen her face as she'd read the posts and comments. It was one of those things that she couldn't bear to watch, and couldn't bear to look away.

It was a strange feeling to have someone look out for her and to do things to try to protect her. And it was more than enough to push her weary emotions over the edge. Unfortunately, once the dam had been breached, there was no going back. Her mind lost track of Dylan's conversation and the scenes playing out on the TV, and instead, it replayed the events of the day. Every embarrassment, every awkward moment, every difficulty paraded through, ending with a detailed review of every word of criticism that she'd just seen on the screen of her phone.

Tears silently streamed down her face in long trails, and she let them. She made not a sound, and there were no sobs. But she couldn't hold it in anymore.

She wasn't really aware of when Dylan noticed her tears. All she knew was that he was suddenly sitting on the couch beside her. He still had his phone up to his ear with one hand, but he wrapped the other arm around Brooke's shoulders and pulled her close in comfort. Eventually, he must have successfully ended the call, but by then Brooke's eyes had slid shut, tired of the burning tears. The last thing she felt before sleep stole her away was gentle fingers catching the remaining tears on her face.

Some time later, she stirred, lifting her head to find it nestled against Dylan's chest. She blinked. Right where she had lain was a wet spot on his shirt, and she, unfortunately, didn't know whether it was remnants from her tears or drool.

"Shhh," Dylan said.

She realized she'd awoken when he'd tried to carefully extract himself from his position as her pillow.

He stood from the couch, but then bent back over her. His

hand gently stroked over her forehead. "It's okay. Just go back to sleep. It's all done. All the calls have been made."

"Thank you," she murmured, already back to half-asleep.

With one last touch to her cheek that, in her sleepy state, felt suspiciously like a caress, he was gone.

CHAPTER 13

Helen hung up the phone and glared, yet again, at Brooke. "If I had an order for every time I answered the phone and it was someone from the media or just a curious nobody wanting to gawk at our predicament, I would be a wealthy woman."

"I'm sorry, Helen," Brooke said, her fingers pausing in their ministrations to the roses in a large vase. "If you want to direct all the media requests to me, I'm sure I can manage and answer their questions. That way you won't have to deal with them."

"No!" Helen spat. "*You* will not be talking to any newspapers, or news stations, or radio stations, or bloggers, or who else may call! I will handle it. And the sooner everyone understands that we won't be talking about the fiasco, the sooner it will stop being talked about. People will forget quickly, and we can move on."

"But if I could just explain to people what actually did happen, then maybe they would be more understanding and sympathetic," Brooke ventured.

"Absolutely not! I am a professional, and as such, I have not released your name. Despite your deplorable actions, I intend to keep it that way. All the public needs to know is that a mistake was made."

"But Helen, it's Crossroads, everyone already knows that Brooke Hutchins is the florist at Crossroads Floral. And they are saying horrible things about me, and the shop in general. If I just came out and explained—"

"I said no! You can only make things worse! We are the laughing stock of the town, and you are the court jester! We are not going to give them more fuel to work with. We'll have enough trouble dealing with the decrease in orders from the scandal. We can't take any more. It ends here."

Tylee spoke up from where she stood at the counter getting the cards ready for delivery. "Actually, Grammie, we seem to have more orders than usual today. What is that saying? The one about bad publicity not really being bad? Or maybe it was good publicity outweighing the bad? I don't know. It's something about publicity." Tylee's forehead wrinkled in confusion.

"I did not ask for your input, Tylee!" Helen fumed.

"'There's no such thing as bad publicity.'" Brooke supplied helpfully.

Tylee's face brightened. "That's it!"

"That's enough!" Helen shrieked. "Both of you get back to work. I did not ask your opinion, and I certainly don't need it. I am the one in charge. If anyone asks you questions about the orders from yesterday, you direct them to me. I will not have either of you creating a bigger mess for me to deal with. Your lips are zipped, do you understand?"

Both Brooke and Tylee nodded, but Brooke's fingers trembled as she added baby's breath to the bouquet of a dozen roses. If she was not permitted to defend herself, she had very little hope of any redemption in the eyes of Crossroads. She was sure that Helen, a well-respected woman in the community, had already painted her the villain and would only continue to do so. The more she thought about it, the more certain she was that Helen wanted to handle all information about the incident because she wanted to be able to abstain from any responsibility in the matter. If she could blame it all on Brooke and prevent her and Tylee from talking, then no one would know her part in the matter. She would just readily repeat the story that while she was away at a funeral, mourning a dear relative, Brooke let chaos reign in the flower shop and, out of sheer stupidity and carelessness, sent orders to the wrong people.

"Brooke, I need all of those orders completed in the next hour. If we want to earn back our good reputation, we need to start by having Tylee make the deliveries early. Brooke looked at the list in front of her with great apprehension. Tylee wasn't exaggerating when she said there were more orders than usual. She had been steadily working on arrangements since she arrived hours ago. Even at her most productive, Brooke didn't know how she could finish so many orders with such a deadline.

But she knew it would do no good to complain, so she merely nodded and grabbed another vase for the next order on the list.

The bell over the door jingled. Leaning over, Brooke took a peek at the door, then quickly drew her head back, hoping she hadn't been seen.

It was Dylan.

The memories of last night instantly inflamed her face. She still had no idea how long she had lain on Dylan's chest with his arm cuddled around her. Her memories of him leaving were hazy, she had no idea what time that had been. She had fallen back asleep on the couch, only to awaken some time later. At 2:30 in the morning, she got a shower, brushed her teeth, and then crawled into bed.

"Mr. Masters, how may I help you today?" Helen greeted, her voice sickly sweet. "Do you have a special lady friend we need to send flowers to? I think it only right that, after the trouble from yesterday, this order be on the house."

"Thank you, Mrs. Garrison," Dylan replied politely, "but I won't be placing an order today. I actually need to speak with Miss Hutchins. I'd like to follow up with her about yesterday."

"Are there more apologies she needs to make?" Helen asked warily. "Did she not complete the tasks you asked her to?"

"Oh, no," Dylan assured. "She handled everything much better than I'd ever hoped. I'm on my lunch break from work, and

I merely wanted to give her an update on some of the orders we didn't have a chance to discuss yesterday."

"Oh, well that's fine," Helen said, though she obviously wasn't too happy about it. "She's working in back. You can go talk to her while she works."

"Thanks," Dylan replied.

For a few frantic seconds, Brooke considered whether she could make a run for the restroom or hide under the counter without being seen. But she knew she couldn't waste precious time hiding, so she would have to be brave and face Dylan. She just hoped his lunch break was a short one.

"Hi, Brooke," Dylan said, coming around the divider and flashing her his signature Dylan Masters smile.

"Hi," Brooke replied, barely looking up from the mini irises she was arranging in a vase.

"I wasn't sure that your warden was going to let me have visitation." Keeping his voice low, Dylan glanced over to see Helen busy at the phone.

"Yes, it is a busy day," Brooke replied simply. Deciding to forgo any small talk, she pushed him to get to the point. "Is there anything I can help you with? Did you need me to make any more calls?"

"No, I don't," he said. "You were pretty tired last night, so I just wanted to make sure you understood that it was all taken care of. All of the recipients of my orders have been contacted and issued an apology. It took some doing, but I think overall, there are no hard feelings."

"Thank you," Brooke said. Her fingers paused on the flowers as a wave of emotion caught at her, weakening her attempt at staying professional. "I know you didn't have to do that, but you did it so I wouldn't have to. And I very much appreciate it."

"You're very welcome." Dylan came closer. She could feel him just behind her, and for half a second, she longed to lean back into him and feel his arms wrap around her. "Brooke, I came to see how you are."

She jumped at the touch of his gentle hands on her arms.

"I'm fine," Brooke said, willing himself not to react. To not feel the electricity shooting from his warm hands, the gentle wisp of his breath against the back of her hair, the call of warmth emanating from the presence behind her. "As I said, it is a really busy day. Helen's received lots of calls about yesterday, but mostly it's just people who are curious. I really think I'm fine. I—"

"Brooke, can I take you to dinner?"

Dylan's words immediately cut off Brooke's babbling as well as just about every thought in her head. She turned around and looked up at him, trying to read his face. "You mean, like a date?" The question popped out, and, as much as she wanted to, she couldn't snatch it back.

Dylan looked at her with an amused grin. "Yes," he replied. "I'd like to take you on a date, Brooke."

"I thought you were swearing off dating for a while," she, turning back to her flowers and, obviously agitated, working with jerky movements. "I guess that didn't last long. It hasn't even been twenty-four hours, has it?"

"I believe I said at the time that I would allow for some exceptions," Dylan said, his tone more guarded.

Brooke was so scattered that she couldn't recall any of the exceptions Dylan was referring to. Everything was a heart-pounding blur, and her over-riding emotion was panic. Unfortunately, Brooke did not respond well when afflicted with such overwhelming emotions.

"I'd like to say I'm flattered, but that's not true." Her erratic movements knocked over some greenery, and she bent to pick it up. "At the rate you're going through the women of Crossroads, it shouldn't be surprising that it would eventually be my turn."

Brooke didn't know where the words were coming from. Even as they spewed from her mouth, she thought them terribly rude and hurtful. But she was stressed beyond reason, and Dylan's request had sent her emotions reeling so that she couldn't separate stress, attraction, anger, embarrassment, frustration, and everything else she had experienced in the past few days. At the moment, whether she intended to or not, Dylan was wearing the target for all of it.

Dylan held up his hands, as if in surrender. "Brooke, I think you are misunderstanding me. And I don't want to talk to you about it here. Can I at least meet you somewhere after work so we can talk?"

"No, Dylan," Brooke said flatly, and she turned to face him squarely for the first time. "I don't want to be one of your playmates who does fun things with you so you don't have to be lonely, and I don't want to be another tally mark on your dating record."

For once, she could clearly read Dylan. She saw the confusion and the hurt. But instead of backing off, she continued the attack as the words kept coming, with each phrase she said being worse than the previous.

"If you really need someone to date," she continued, "I can compile a list of names, and maybe even the phone numbers, if I check my cell phone bill. In fact, there's one right over there. Tylee is one of those who has admired you for a long time and would very much like to submit a Dylan Masters application. Feel free to pursue other opportunities. I definitely won't be applying."

They were words that would later torture her with regret. She'd just taken everything he'd done for her, everything that he'd opened up and shared with her, and with a cruel twist, used them to stab him in the back.

By the time her words stopped, a mask had fallen over Dylan's face. Showing no emotion whatsoever, he nodded and said. "Maybe I'll do just that. Thank you for your time. I will let you get back to your work."

Then he left.

In shock, Brooke looked down at her shaking hands. What had she just done?

As if on autopilot, her fingers returned to the work of arranging, completely unaware of her turmoil. She heard Dylan's voice talking to Tylee, but she couldn't bring herself to even attempt to eavesdrop. Maybe he really had taken her suggestion seriously and asked Tylee out.

At the idea, Brooke had to put both hands on the counter and breathe deeply through the nausea. The only coherent thought that entered or exited her mind with any coherence was the same phrase, over and over.

What have I done?

What have I done?

Brooke wasn't even aware of when the bell over the door jingled with Dylan's departure. After a while, Brooke's shock paired with a nice little coping mechanism called denial, and she was able to push everything in her mind aside save for the pretty flowers she was arranging in a bouquet. She worked quickly, and her focus was only interrupted once, when Tylee came over to match the cards with the bouquets.

After working quietly for a few minutes, the younger woman whispered, "I can't believe Dylan Masters asked you out! And I really can't believe you said no!"

Brooke didn't respond but lost focus enough that she changed her mind about five times on whether to use daisies or carnations in the bouquet she was working on.

Eventually, Brooke made it through all of the orders, and she sent Tylee on her way for deliveries. Helen even left the shop for a while on some errands, leaving Brooke some quiet with which to clean up, take stock, and prepare her purchase orders for next week. When Helen finally returned, Brooke was ready to call it a day.

"Do you need me to deliver some of those other orders?" she asked, pointing to the assortment of bouquets still sitting on the counter. "Tylee must have run out of space for all of the deliveries. I know you wanted to get them out early, but it looks like Tylee may not make it back in time for a second round."

"No, that's fine," Helen said crisply. "I'll take care of them."

Brooke nodded and handed her boss the set of completed forms she had been working on. "Here are the purchase orders and list of supplies I will need for next week. The large number of orders today depleted our stock some. I'm a bit nervous that we won't get some supplies in time before we need them. I can probably run over to the supplier in Brighton Falls tomorrow if you want."

"No, that won't be necessary," Helen answered.

Brooke hesitated. "So should I put an asterisk by the ones we need more so that you can get them yourself?"

"No, I think we will manage just fine ourselves."

Brooke looked at Helen, the tone of the older woman's voice giving her an awful premonition. There was an almost sadistic gleam in her eye, as if she was taking a moment to truly savor what she was about to say.

"Your services will no longer be needed, Miss Hutchins," she said formally. "I will make sure we have the supplies we need from now on. It is no longer your concern."

"You are firing me?" Brooke asked in shock.

"Well, if you want to term it that, then yes. You're being fired. I prefer a gentler phrase like 'being let go.' I have a reputation to consider, and the public is demanding there be some kind of retribution for the orders yesterday. It was just too big of a mistake to not be termed incompetence and treated as such. I want to be able to report that the problem was eliminated and there is no chance of the person responsible having any influence on orders again."

Brooke opened and shut her mouth several times, not even knowing what to say. "But you have orders and no florist to fulfill them," she managed. Her voice sounded weak, but she had to ask. Helen had no ability in flower design whatsoever. Had she thought through the ramifications of what firing Brooke would mean, or was she still just reacting in anger?

"I already had you create all of the orders we currently have scheduled for the next few days," she said with a condescending smile. "I'm sure they will keep fine until then. That should give me plenty of time to hire a new florist. If we have more orders that come in between now and then, I'm sure Tylee and I can manage to put a few flowers in some vases."

So she had thought things through. That's why she insisted that Brooke fulfill a crazy number of orders for today!

Feeling as if there was nothing more to say, Brooke turned to get her purse.

"I'm not completely heartless," Helen said to her back. "I do appreciate the work you've done for me for the last few years. I also realize this will put you in some significant financial constraints, especially since it is unlikely that anyone in the area will be willing to hire you with your reputation. So I'm willing to offer you a small severance package, even though I'm not legally bound to do so. All I ask is that you agree to sign this nondisclosure agreement, and then the check is yours."

Brooke slung her purse over her shoulder and shut her eyes. *Please, Lord!* She prayed, though she didn't even know what kind of request to make of the Almighty. She didn't want to play Helen's games. She didn't want to sign any kind of nondisclosure agreement in order to get a check, but she may not have a choice.

Walking back to Helen she accepted the offered paper with two checks paper-clipped to the top, and she read every word. Basically, if she signed it, Brooke would not be allowed to speak to any form of media about yesterday's events and the mistakes with the floral orders. Helen was trying to ensure that Brooke wouldn't be able to reveal the full truth of what had happened and wouldn't have a chance to ruin Helen's reputation.

"The first check is the amount owed for the work you've done through today," Helen supplied. "The second check is your severance pay, should you decide to sign the agreement."

Brooke really wanted to hand Helen back the agreement unsigned, without even looking at the check. But, with bills to pay, she didn't feel like she had the choice. She peeked at the check. It wasn't a huge amount, but it would give her enough money to pay for her rent for next month, which would hopefully give her enough time to find another job.

Brooke stared at the paper for ten long seconds. Feeling like she was backed into a corner, she snatched the pen Helen was offering and signed the agreement before she had the chance to change her mind. If paying the rent cost her pride of not being able to defend herself, then that's what she'd have to do. As tough as it was, she would rather not be homeless, even if the cost was that she was the newest town villain.

Helen accepted the papers, and then removed both checks and handed them to Brooke. "Goodbye, Brooke. I assume you can let yourself out? I have work that I need to attend to."

Without a word, Brooke turned and left. The happy little bell above the door jingled as she left, completely oblivious that Brooke felt like Cinderella whose dress had just been torn to shreds by her step-sisters. Brooke was good at floral design, and it was something she enjoyed doing. But everything she'd worked so hard at had just been destroyed and ripped from her, leaving her bare and in shock, with all her hard work in tatters.

She made it to her car and sat down in the driver's seat. She even shut the door, locked it, and put the keys in the ignition. But she couldn't turn the key. With both hands gripping the steering wheel, she slumped over it as great, wracking sobs coursed through her body.

She had no idea how long she sat there. But it was long enough that her eyes swelled up puffy, and short enough that the sobs were still wreaking havoc when a persistent knock sounded on the window.

Startled, Brooke looked up to see Dylan standing at her window, his eyes filled with compassion.

CHAPTER 14

B rooke managed to unlock the car doors, but she couldn't do anything else, not even look at Dylan.

Instead of opening her door to talk to her, he came around to the other side, opened the passenger door, and slid into the seat. The next thing she knew, strong arms wrapped around her and pulled her close. With her back heaving with great, shuddering sobs, she couldn't breathe, let alone object.

"I'm so sorry, Brooke," Dylan whispered.

"She fired me!" Brooke hiccupped out.

"I know," Dylan murmured. "But it will be okay. I know it doesn't feel that way right now, but I promise things will get better."

Over the next few minutes, Brooke gradually calmed down. She didn't know if it was more because of Dylan's continued soothing words as he stroked her hair with gentle fingers, or if it was just because she ran out of tears. Her sobs lessened to where they were just a shuddering catch in her breathing, and she became aware of the discomfort of the gear shifter digging into her hip as she leaned over it in Dylan's arms.

Coming to her senses, she pulled away and wiped at her eyes. "How did you know?" She asked, her voice still raw from crying so hard.

"Tylee called me," he answered. Though he allowed her to pull away, he kept her hand securely in his. "Apparently, Helen called Tylee to tell her she'd let you go and that she needed her to hurry back to help close the shop. Even though Tylee was very upset, she still managed to call me when you were fired, just as I'd asked."

"Wait, you knew I was going to be fired?"

Dylan nodded. "Sort of. I didn't have any inside information, but from hearing and watching Mrs. Garrison and the comments in the community, I was fairly certain you would be fired. With her anger level and the fact that she's never bothered trying to defend you to anyone, it seemed like you were the scapegoat. Firing you after you got her through the worst of the fallout seemed the logical next step, at least in her mind."

"And you asked Tylee to call you when that happened?" Brooke kept her gaze on their clasped hands. She still didn't understand why he was here.

"Yes, I did," Dylan said, his gaze steady. "On my way out of the shop earlier today, I stopped and told Tylee what I thought was going to happen. Helen was busy on the phone. I gave Tylee my number and asked her to please call me as soon as you were fired."

"Why would you do that?" Brooke asked, looking at him in complete confusion. Why would he care, especially when she'd treated him so terribly?

"I thought you might need a friend," he said simply.

Brooke paused, her throat constricting with emotion. "Thank you," she said finally, feeling a few more tears escape. "I really appreciate it." Feeling ashamed of her behavior this morning and ashamed at her out of control emotions, she dared not look at Dylan. Even when he gently squeezed her hand, she kept her eyes averted.

Wiping hastily at her tears, she reached for her phone as an excuse to release Dylan's hand. Her finger swiped the button, and the time came on the screen. "Oh no! I need to go now or else I'm going to be late!"

"Brooke, you aren't in any condition to drive," Dylan protested. "Let me drive you where you need to go. Then you can either pick up your car later, or I can come back for it."

Brooke hesitated. She didn't want him to drive her, but she also didn't want him to launch into an analysis of why she was unfit to drive. And she most definitely didn't want her swollen, watery eyes that she could barely see out of to be a topic of conversation.

"Come on, Brooke," Dylan persisted. "I don't have anything else to do. Let me be your chauffeur. Where do you need to go?"

Brooke's eyes filled with tears again, and her face crumpled. "I have to go to church!" she sniffled. "Isn't that terrible that someone who claims to be a Christian and goes to church talks to anyone the way I talked to you today? I'm a pretty lousy example of a Christian!"

Dylan laughed and cupped her wet cheek with his hand. "No, I don't think you're a lousy Christian; I think you're a real one. I don't pretend to be the authority on Christianity, but I do think that everyone makes mistakes. And I don't think being a Christian disqualifies you from that."

Brooke tried to steady her breathing. "I really am sorry about the way I treated you earlier. I was rude and said some very hurtful things. My only excuse is that I was really stressed, and that isn't much of an excuse at all."

"You're forgiven," Dylan said simply. "I know you were stressed, and I shouldn't have asked you then. I was just worried because if you got fired like I suspected you would, then I would have no way to contact you. I don't even have your phone number. But I guess that doesn't matter much now. Everything worked out, and I got the job of your chauffeur! Now hop out and let's go take my car."

Brooke got out and followed Dylan to his silver Porsche. Sliding into the passenger seat, she asked, "Are you sure you don't mind taking me to church? I'm in charge of a children's craft for tonight's service."

"I don't mind at all," Dylan said, starting the engine. "In spite of what you may think, I'm not a complete heathen. My grandmother was a devout Christian."

They kept the conversation blessedly light-hearted as Brooke directed him to the church. As he pulled into the parking lot, Brooke yanked down the overhead mirror and tried to fix the damage to her makeup. She did the best she could, cleaning the mess up and adding a little powder, but it was woefully inadequate, and she couldn't hide the fact that she had been crying.

Giving up, she got out of the car.

Dylan met her as she stepped out, saying, "Look at me."

Brooke's eyes swung to his, and she held still as he gave her face a thorough inspection, his eyes gliding over her forehead, cheeks, eyes, nose, and then lingering on her lips.

"You look fine," he declared finally. "But you are a little pale. If you want, I can say something to really embarrass you and add a little color to your cheeks."

"No," Brooke said quickly. "I don't think that will be necessary."

Briskly she turned and began striding toward the church while Dylan followed.

"I offer other options as well," he said to her back. "Options that I'm sure I would find very enjoyable."

Brooke couldn't stop a laugh. He had spent an extra long time with his gaze on her lips!

Putting a finger to her lips to silence him, she sent a chiding look over her shoulder. "We are going to church!"

With an overly innocent expression on his face, Dylan asked sweetly, "Rain check?"

Laughing and shaking her head, Brooke led the way through the front doors of the church.

"My part with the kids is at the very beginning during the worship service," she explained. "Then they go to their other activities, and I am free to go to the sermon. You are welcome to go into the sanctuary. Do you want me to meet you there when I'm done?"

"Can I just come with you and be your assistant?" he asked, his face boyish and hopeful.

"Sure," Brooke said, leading the way to the children's area.

Entering the room, she quickly got busy, taking Dylan's offer of help seriously.

"We made these last week," she said, picking up a pile of small colorful papers. "Now the kids will trace around a leaf pattern and then cut out their leaf. Then they need to think of one thing they are thankful for and write it on the leaf."

Dylan picked up one of the papers and held it up to the light. "Are these coffee filters?" he asked curiously.

"Yes, they are," Brooke confirmed. "The kids colored them autumn colors with markers. Then we sprayed the filters with water, which made the colors blend together. Aren't they pretty? I just love the way they dried."

It also gave her an insane amount of pleasure to know that this large stack of coffee filters would be used for a purpose other than coffee. She almost felt as if she'd won at least one battle against "Team Coffee," and it felt good!

"So how do you want me to help?" Dylan asked.

Brooke handed him a stack of colored coffee filters. "We will both need to help the kids with the tracing, cutting, and writing. We have a large range of ages, and some are not yet very skilled with scissors. After the leaves are finished, I will put them all together in an arrangement that we can hang at the window in the church entryway. The colors should look really pretty with the light shining through."

"Sounds like a great idea," Dylan said.

With the arrival of the children, they quickly got to work. Soon, happy conversation mingled with the sounds of scissors and the scratch of markers. Brooke looked up from helping a little boy with his scissors and just about fell over with laughter. Dylan was seated at a table with a bevy of little girls around him. They all smiled up at him, vying for which one would get his help next.

Taking pity on the outnumbered man, Brooke went over to the table. "Ok, ladies, I think several of you are old enough to manage scissors without Mr. Masters' help. How about you cut your own leaf out and then show him what a good job you did?"

Finding this acceptable, several girls began cutting out their leaves with the utmost care. Brooke helped out at the table for a few minutes longer, discreetly watching as Dylan's big hands used a pair of child-sized pink scissors to carefully cut a leaf out of a coffee filter. Then he handed it to the blonde named Stella beside him.

"Can you write 'pig' on it?" Stella asked sweetly.

"Pig?" Dylan asked. "You're thankful for pig? I could write bacon if you'd rather. I'm pretty thankful for bacon myself."

All of the girls at the table laughed.

"You're silly!" Stella grinned. "'Pig' is the name of my cat!

Dylan laughed and picked up a marker. "'Pig' is pretty easy to spell. Don't you want to write it yourself?"

"You write so much prettier than I do," she said with a sweet look sent his direction. "Just write P-I-G right in the center. Oh, and can you make a heart for the dot on the 'I'? I like those."

Dylan obediently did what he was told, even carefully drawing a miniature heart above the 'i' in pig.

The little girl grinned up at him when he handed the leaf back, and Brooke's heart melted.

She cleared her throat and busied herself collecting completed leaves. "Remember, write only one thing on each leaf," she instructed. "We have plenty of leaves, so if you want to write more than one thing, then you can make as many leaves as you need."

Turning back to the other tables, she heard one of the little girls ask in a loud whisper, "Are you Miss Hutchins' boyfriend?"

Brooke just about dropped the scissors she was holding.

Pretending she couldn't hear a thing, she continued cleaning up scraps and distributing scissors and markers where needed.

"No, I'm not," Dylan said simply.

"But do you want to be?" the little girl persisted.

Brooke coughed on her sudden gasp.

"She's really nice," the girl continued. "And pretty."

"Yes, she is," Dylan answered. "And, yes—"

"Alright, children!" Brooke called, not wanting to hear Dylan finish that answer. "It's time to get ready for your other activities. I think you have some songs and a Bible story lesson still to do. Let's pray together and then line up."

Pausing to check to make sure everyone had their heads properly bowed, Brooke prayed, "Dear, Lord, thank you for letting us have this time together and for all the blessings you give us. Help us to be thankful and to know that all good things come from You. In Jesus name, Amen."

"Will you be here next week?" a small voice asked.

Brooke looked over to see a little brunette, about 6 years old, talking to Dylan.

Dylan bent down to talk to her. "I don't know, but probably not. I just came to help Miss Hutchins today because she wasn't feeling well. I sure had fun helping you make leaves, though. Thanks for letting me have the pretty red one you made."

The girl looked troubled. "But if you ask Miss Hutchins to be her boyfriend, and she says 'yes,' then you'll have to come help her again next week, right?"

"Jaycee, I'm not scheduled to be your teacher for next week," Brooke spoke up gently. She couldn't stand it if the little girl was disappointed. It was better to let her know now that there was no possibility of Dylan or her being at her class next week. "You'll have a different teacher for a while. I think I'll be back with you after Christmas."

The little girl's bottom lip puffed out in a pout. Then, suddenly, she brightened. "Oh, good! That should be lots of time for you to become Miss Hutchins' boyfriend. Then you'll have to come with her!"

Before Brooke could close her mouth and come up with a coherent response, Jaycee skipped off with a wave to join her line that was leaving the room.

"You can charm girls at any age, Dylan Masters," Brooke said, shaking her head in amusement.

"Not true," Dylan disagreed. "I can't charm every woman. How old are you, by the way? I'd just like to know, for future reference, what the magical age is at which my powers have no effect on a woman."

Brooke laughed, but quickly set to work straightening the classroom before she left. She assigned Dylan the task of putting supplies away while she quickly put together a wreath of the leaves the children had made. She didn't have time to finish the whole thing now, but she did want to make sure it would look right. She smiled as she spread the leaves into a circle, reading what each of them had written. She carefully taped them together, hoping that tape would hold but not damage like glue might. Most of the leaves were labeled with family members, pets, or favorite toys. And of course, there was the one Dylan had clearly labeled "Pig."

Her hand paused as she found a red one that read, "Miss Hutchins." Brooke's heart warmed at the thought that one of the little ones was thankful for her. Unable to control the curiosity, Brooke flipped it over to where the child's name was supposed to be written in pencil on the back by the stem.

Just where it was supposed to be, the owner's name was clearly visible—Dylan.

It was just a leaf. A cute gesture that Dylan probably hadn't intended any other eyes to see. But it flustered her greatly. He hadn't done it to tease or show off. He couldn't have known that she would even see it.

She remembered him thanking someone for giving him a leaf. She just hadn't realized that her name would hold center stage of what he was thankful for.

Glancing at the time, she realized she would need to finish the wreath later if they wanted to make it in time for the sermon.

"What do you think?" she asked Dylan as he approached, his tasks complete.

"I think you're amazingly creative to make something that beautiful out of coffee filters," he said readily. "And I think it will look even more gorgeous with the light coming through it on the window."

Brooke carefully moved the wreath to where it would be safe on a counter in a corner. "Doing any kind of art project with coffee filters is an improvement over their intended purpose."

"Good to know you aren't on friendly terms with coffee," Dylan said, following Brooke out of the classroom. "Wasn't it coffee that spilled all over your original orders? It sounds like the animosity is mutual."

Brooke led the way down the hall and into the sanctuary. It wasn't a large church, but it wasn't especially small either. With most of the chairs already occupied, Brooke gladly found them seats in the back corner. She sincerely hoped they wouldn't attract too much attention. She didn't need the curious glances and speculation about the man Brooke Hutchins brought to church.

As soon as they were seated, the pastor finished his announcements and began the sermon. Brooke listened carefully, trying to tune everything else out. It was a relief to focus on something other than her own problems. However, she couldn't quite abandon an occasional nervous glance Dylan's direction. While she was concerned that he would be uncomfortable, he seemed very interested in the message. He didn't even glance her way as he leaned forward slightly in his chair and kept his eyes fixed on the pastor.

The sermon used the story of the woman at the well as a text and focused specifically on John 4:13-14. Brooke listened carefully to the words:

Jesus said to her, "Everyone who drinks of this water will be thirsty again, but whoever drinks of the water that I will give him will never be thirsty again. The water that I will give him will become in him a spring of water welling up to eternal life."

It was a good reminder to Brooke that she should not be getting her main satisfaction in life from her job. That kind of satisfaction was too fleeting. A few mistakes and one bad day and suddenly you're out of a job and your satisfaction level drops to nonexistent. Instead, she should be focusing on God and finding satisfaction in Him and in the work He would have her do, which would be a satisfaction that wasn't fleeting but eternal.

Thirty minutes later, the sermon was over, the last prayer had been given, and Brooke and Dylan were walking back to his car with Brooke feeling very successful that they had managed a quick exit without being waylaid by curious fellow parishioners.

"I'm hungry," Dylan said. "Why don't we go get some dinner."

Brooke shot him a wary look. "It won't be a date, right?"

"Of course not!" Dylan said. "I'll even let you pay for your own food if you want, though anyone who had a day as bad as you deserves to have her dinner paid for."

"Okay," Brooke said. "But let's go somewhere where we can get food fast. And thank you, but I'll pay for my own." She really didn't want this to in any way resemble a date, even though it wasn't easy to combat the anxiety that popped up at the thought of spending her now-limited supply of money.

As they got in the car and Dylan pulled out of the church parking lot, Brooke couldn't help but notice the slight smile on his face. And she realized that despite everything that had happened, Dylan was ending the day exactly as he'd wanted.

He was taking her to dinner.

CHAPTER 15

"**I** enjoyed the sermon," Dylan said conversationally after their beverages were delivered to their table at the restaurant. They had already placed their orders with the friendly, fortyish waitress named Trish.

Surprised that he was so open to talking about church, Brooke replied simply. "The pastor usually does a good job with his message."

"It all reminded me very much of my grandma and attending church with her and my grandpa." A shadow floated across his face.

"Did you go to church often when you were young?" Brooke asked.

Dylan nodded. "I went every Sunday I stayed with Grandma and Grandpa, and that was sometimes up to a year at a time."

"So it sounds like your grandparents had a large part in raising you," Brooke surmised.

"Yes, they did," Dylan replied. Then, with a brief pause, as if collecting himself before diving into deep water, he continued, "My dad left before I was born. I have an older sister, but she has a different dad. My parents were never married, and while Dani's dad had visitation and saw her frequently, mine wanted nothing to do with me. So when Dani went to see her dad, I went to see Grandma and Grandpa."

"I'm sorry!" Brooke said, a little caught off guard that Dylan was sharing. It was quite a difference from when he wouldn't say anything to her just yesterday when they first set out together. "That must have been tough!"

"Not really," Dylan shrugged. "I actually liked staying with my grandparents more than I liked being home, especially when Mom had a new boyfriend. She married a few other times when I was growing up, and it often just became easier to leave me with Grandma and Grandpa than to make me miserable staying with a new dad who didn't particularly like me and probably wouldn't be around long anyway."

Trish brought their food and laid their plates in front of them. Their choices had been relatively simple. Brooke ordered a club sandwich, and Dylan had a cheeseburger. But they both looked good.

Brooke hadn't been in this little café in years. She didn't often treat herself to a meal at a restaurant, and her last experience here hadn't been enough to even earn a two-star rating. Brooke looked around, thinking of the changes since she'd been here last. She'd heard that the building had been purchased by a new owner and that the café was under new management.

From what Brooke could see, they had made some vast improvements. The yucky gray and orange speckled carpet had been pulled up, and it looked like there had been hardwood underneath. With a new finish, it had a beautiful rustic look to it. The chairs, tables, and booths had all been replaced as well. Even the counter that ran along one wall looked new. With fresh white paint on the walls, blue gingham curtains, and cute, rustic décor, the café had a very country kitchen feel and had gone from scary to charming.

Tasting her sandwich, she was pleased to find a great difference in the food as well. Instead of bland, her sandwich was full of flavor. Even the French fries we good—hot and salty, just the way she liked them.

After a few minutes of eating quietly, Dylan seemed content

to let the subject of his personal background drop, but Brooke was afraid that if she let the door close, she'd never be allowed in again.

"I was very close to my grandma too," Brooke finally offered. Dylan had already shared so much. Maybe it was her turn to offer something personal as well. "It's still hard for me to think of her being gone."

Dylan's face was uncharacteristically drawn and sad. "I miss both my grandma and grandpa. Things haven't been the same since they've been gone. Maybe that's one of the reasons I date so much—to escape the loneliness of losing them."

Dylan swirled one of his fries in ketchup but didn't bring it up to his mouth. Instead, he gazed out the window that lined one side of their booth, his face thoughtful. "The sermon tonight kind of hit home in that respect. It reminded me of Grandma and Grandpa and sitting between them on a church pew every Sunday, but it also made me wonder if I've been searching for satisfaction in the wrong way. Like maybe I'm trying to find water in a dry well, or in a place that will always leave me thirsty."

"I thought of the same thing," Brooke admitted. "But in my case, I think I've been trying to seek satisfaction from my job."

Dylan let out a humorless laugh. "I don't think you're quite in my league, Brooke. If I'm being really honest, I'd admit that for most of my life, I've been worried about ending up like my mom, jumping from one relationship to another with no lasting happiness or attachments, just a roller coaster of highs and lows. Looking at my life now, that's kind of what I do! While I've tried so hard to not be serious and hop from one "in love" feeling to the next, I've not let anyone get close and actually have the same end result of being alone, dating lots of women, and finding true satisfaction elusive."

"I think that's kind of the point of that Bible verse," Brooke said thoughtfully. "The search for satisfaction and happiness is an issue that everyone struggles with, just maybe not in the same way."

"And for me, maybe what I'm truly looking for isn't a woman after all."

Brooke nodded, though she was lost on what to say. It did funny things to her heart to hear him talk about such deep topics. While she was pleased that he seemed to be coming to terms with some of his issues, hearing him almost swear off women left her very confused.

She supposed that she could launch into presenting the gospel, but if Dylan had been in church like he said he was, then he likely already knew everything she could tell him. And he also seemed to be doing a more than adequate job of self-diagnosing and thinking things through.

"I don't know you well, and I won't pretend to know all the answers," Brooke said slowly. "Honestly, I'm just as messed up as you are, just in different ways. The point of life has to be more than just the pursuit of things and a happiness that dies when you do. I want the kind of life that prepares me for something even better. I have faith in God and believe that my salvation through Jesus Christ and my relationship with Him are what matters most. Though I'm not always good at it, my greatest happiness comes when I am pursuing God, seeking to please Him, and letting Him work through me in ways that bring Him glory."

Dylan nodded. "That actually makes a lot of sense. If you don't mind, I may tag along with you to church a few more times. Do they usually have services at night like this?"

"Yes, they do," Brooke said. "I can even save you a seat. And I'm sure the pastor can help answer any questions you may have and give better advice than I ever could."

"I don't know about the advice part, but I may decide to drop in on him sometime." He folded up his napkin and looked at his watch. "Are you ready to go?"

Brooke nodded and scooted to the edge of the booth. Seeing their waitress, she lifted her hand to hail her. "Can I please have my check?"

"Oh, it's all been taken care of, honey. Both you and Mr.

Masters are good to go."

"Dylan!" Brooke protested. "I told you not to pay for my food!"

"Oh, he didn't, honey," the waitress assured. "This one is on the house. The restaurant owner owes Mr. Masters a few big favors, so he likes to treat him to dinner on the house every once in a while."

Brooke's gaze went from the waitress to Dylan and then back again. She didn't want to appear rude, but she really believed that the man across from her had just played her! "Well, can you please tell the owner thank you?" Brooke said, knowing she needed to gracefully accept the generosity. "The food was delicious."

"I sure will!" Trish beamed proudly.

While heading for the door, Brooke whispered to Dylan, "Why do I get the feeling that you knew I wouldn't have to pay for my meal when you chose this place?"

Dylan shrugged, an overly innocent expression on his face. "It's not a date, remember? You can't blame someone for using a little creativity, taking advantage of a little good luck, or a combination of the two!"

Dylan held the door for Brooke, and they exited the café.

The cool air hit Brooke in a rush, and she hurried to zip up her jacket. While pulling her hood over her head, her hand touched the cut on her forehead from yesterday.

Her wince didn't go unnoticed.

"Does it still hurt?" Dylan asked.

"Yes, but mostly just when I knock it," she said, not wanting him to be concerned.

"If you want, I can bandage it up again to help protect it," Dylan offered. "Are you sure you want me to take you back to your car at the floral shop? I can take you home and bandage you up. Then I can pick you up in the morning to get your car."

"No, but thank you. I'm fine to drive now, and I think my owie is fine too," Brooke assured with a smile. Dylan's protectiveness was rather endearing. "I took the other bandage off because I didn't want to attract attention today. I also thought it would be good to give it some air."

Dylan didn't say anything else, but she could tell that both the car and her cut still worried him. Reaching the Porsche, he opened the passenger side door, and she slipped inside with a little shiver. It sure felt cold for November.

When Dylan got in on the driver's side, Brooke asked, "Didn't you say your mom was a nurse?" She recalled his expertise with patching her up yesterday, and she was trying to match up what he'd said then with what he'd told her in the café about his background.

"Yes, she still is," he said, turning on the heat before heading out on the street toward Crossroads Floral. "Both she and my sister live in Arizona."

"Are you going to get to see them for Thanksgiving?" Brooke asked curiously.

Dylan grimaced. "No. My mom is going to my sister's house, and I'm not really welcome."

Brooke looked at him with raised eyebrows "That seems harsh."

Dylan shrugged. "Not really. I wouldn't want to go there even if I was welcome. My sister is married, and I don't get along well with her husband. I mostly object because he is a jerk who doesn't treat her well. It's better for everyone if I stay away."

His words didn't set right with Brooke. In fact, his situation sounded pretty terrible. "So what are you doing for the holiday?" she asked with concern. "Do you have any other family that you're going to see?"

"No, both my grandparents have been gone for several years now," Dylan answered. "Without a dad, and with my mom's quite colorful relationship history, there isn't really any other family to speak of. I'll probably just stay home and enjoy the day off watching football."

It was a short drive back to where Brooke's car was parked in the Crossroads Floral lot. Dylan pulled in beside her car, but instead of getting out right away, Brooke sat there, thinking about what he'd just said. Though his words seemed horribly sad, Dylan didn't seem upset about it in the least, which made her wonder how many Thanksgivings he had spent alone in front of a football game.

"Why don't you come with me and have Thanksgiving dinner with my family?" she asked impulsively.

Dylan didn't answer right away, but stared at her in surprise, as if waiting for her to immediately retract the offer. "Are you sure that's what you want?" he finally asked.

"Yes!" she said eagerly. "I have a huge family, and yet my mom still makes so much food that we have leftovers for days! I want you to come. I wouldn't be able to enjoy the dinner at all if I knew you were alone with a bag of potato chips instead of a turkey!"

Dylan spoke slowly, "Well, I guess I can come if you're sure your parents won't mind. Maybe you'd better ask your mom first."

"I will ask her, but I know for sure that she won't mind. I also know that she would very much object to you spending Thanksgiving alone." In fact, Brooke knew that her mom would be quite upset if Brooke didn't manage to get Dylan to agree to come!

"Well, if you're sure, then I'll plan on it," he said, the white of his smile catching the glow from the streetlights.

"Great!" Brooke said. Then she reached out her hand. "Can I borrow your phone?"

"Oh, you don't have to call her now," Dylan protested.

"Can I please just borrow your phone?" She held out her hand insistently.

"Where is yours?"

Without speaking, Brooke simply wiggled her empty hand.

Giving up on understanding, Dylan unlocked the screen and handed her the phone.

After a minute of pushing buttons, Brooke handed it back to him. "Now you can call if you want to talk to me. You won't need to ambush me and ask me out on a date to do so."

Dylan grinned, his eyes sparkling in the dim light from the parking lot.

"I'll call."

"You'd better," Brooke said, opening her car door. "You have no idea how much my family will enjoy the fact that I'm bringing Dylan Masters to Thanksgiving Dinner!"

CHAPTER 16

"**M**om! Dad! Brooke brought home a *boy*!"

Brooke turned to Dylan. "I did warn you about my family, right?"

Dylan looked a little wide-eyed as he followed Brooke through her parents' front door, through the living room, and into the kitchen.

"Ok, everyone!" Brooke called as soon as they came into view of the group clustered in the kitchen. "This is Dylan Masters. He is not my boyfriend. We are not dating. We are friends. And I invited him to have Thanksgiving dinner with us. End of story."

"That doesn't sound like the end of the story," Brooke's brother, Dallas, said. "Why is it that we are blessed to have Brooke's friend-but-not-boyfriend share Thanksgiving dinner with us? This isn't exactly normal Brooke Hutchins behavior. When was the last time Brooke brought a boy home?" Dallas turned to his siblings. "Five years? What was his name?"

"Jake," Sydney said. "I think it was Jake."

"No, it was Andy," Geneva said with certainty. "But you're right in that it was about five years ago."

Sydney shrugged. "Well, I guess you'd know, Geneva. You were the one who—"

"Dylan's family lives in Arizona," Brooke interrupted. "He

didn't have anywhere to go for Thanksgiving, so I invited him here, which is a decision I am beginning to regret."

"I think she also felt bad for having screwed up my order at the floral shop," Dylan supplied. "I figure this must be part of her penance."

"Now there's the story!" Dallas said eagerly.

"Tell us more about how she exactly 'screwed up' your order," Geneva said, propping her elbow on the counter and leaning against her hand, as if greatly interested. "I heard about some kind of mix up, but this sounds a bit juicy!"

"That's enough!" Brooke's mother, Lydia, said softly, but with a tone that instantly gained all attention. "Leave Brooke and her friend alone. Dallas, go see if your dad needs help checking the turkey on the deep fryer. Geneva and Sydney, finish getting the table set."

Though still sending glances of amusement Brooke's direction, while Brooke shot back glares, her siblings obediently went to their tasks.

Turning to Brooke, Lydia said, "Brooke, honey, wasn't there another friend you said you'd be bringing as well? We have plenty of food."

Brooke shook her head, thinking about the conversation she'd had just yesterday with Aimee, the woman who had accidentally gotten flowers from her deceased mother. "No, I asked Aimee, but she decided to go out of town to her aunt's house for Thanksgiving. So she won't be coming."

"Well, I am glad you could make it, Dylan!" Lydia said cheerfully. "You will have to excuse Brooke's brother and sisters. She is the youngest in the family and gets the teasing and babying from everyone. Just be thankful all of my children aren't here at once!"

"How many brothers and sisters do you have?" Dylan asked, under his breath.

"Six," Brooke replied. "But don't worry, it looks like you'll only have to deal with three. Trust me, half of them aren't nearly as difficult as *all* of them!"

Lydia turned back to the kitchen and called over her shoulder, "Brooke, could you please mash the potatoes? You always do such a nice job."

"That's me," Brooke said quietly, "the great potato masher."

"Dylan, would you mind going out to the deck and asking John how much longer the turkey will be?"

"John is my dad," Brooke supplied. "Tall with gray hair. You can't miss him."

"Thanks," Dylan said with a hint of amused sarcasm. "I don't think I could have figured it out without the description."

"I aim to please," Brooke said sweetly.

Dylan turned to his task while Brooke drained the potatoes and began mashing. Out of the corner of her eye, she watched her mom. Lydia Hutchins carried herself regally. While she often saw that same quality in her sisters, Brooke felt it had missed her particular set of genes. But, feeling awkward wasn't the only way she was different from her mom. Lydia had short brunette hair and was small in stature. She was cute, but with her taste for finer things in life, her beauty translated more to sophisticated. Brooke, however, was taller and blonder, like her dad. And sophisticated was not a word that would ever be associated with her. Though she may not have inherited her mother's physical characteristics or her social grace, Brooke really hoped she could at least resemble her in her kind, generous, and welcoming personality.

"Dylan seems like a nice man," Lydia said casually as she checked on the rolls in the oven.

"Please don't get your hopes up, Mom," Brooke said. "I am not interested in him romantically, nor do I intend to be."

"And why is that?" Lydia asked pointedly.

Startled, Brooke stammered a bit in responding, "Well, he isn't a Christian, for starters."

Lydia nodded and pulled the nicely browned rolls from the

oven. "That is a good reason. I certainly wouldn't want you to date or get attached to someone who wasn't a Christian. I just worry that you always have a reason for not letting anyone get close. It's almost like you're afraid and don't want to take any risk with your heart."

Brooke sighed and turned on the mixer. With the loud noise, she bought herself a couple minutes to respond. She had hoped that her mom's interest in her love life would slow down after her brother, Israel, gave her the first grandchild. But it hadn't. Her only consolation was that her mom probably did the same thing to her other siblings as well. Five single adult children offered plenty of fodder for meddling.

Brooke turned off the mixer and stirred the potatoes by hand. "I'm sorry, Mom, but I lost my job and my reputation in the community. Now I have no job leads and no way to pay my bills. I think my life has enough risk at the moment without a relationship."

"Sweetheart, I really wish you'd call Uncle Wayne and talk to him about that," Lydia said.

Brooke stifled a groan. Though she had successfully managed to change the subject from her love life, she didn't know this new subject was any better. "Mom, I don't know what good talking with Uncle Wayne would do. I certainly don't want to relocate so I can be his employee."

"But he's in the business, Brooke," Lydia insisted, her knife pausing as it cut through an apple for the fruit salad. "At the very least, he can give you a listening ear. He may have some advice for how you can help your reputation in the community."

"The potatoes are done," Brooke said, refusing to respond to her mom's suggestion. "It looks like everything else is ready, too. I'll go round up everyone else to wash their hands."

Then she left before her mom looked up from the fruit salad.

Ten minutes later, everyone was seated at the table, piling food on their plates after saying the blessing.

"So, Dylan, what do you do?" Geneva asked, passing him the

bowl of mashed potatoes from directly across the table.

Instant anger flared up in Brooke. She knew that tone of voice. Geneva wasn't just being friendly. That overly sweet tone meant that she was flirting. And there wasn't anything Brooke could do about it. She had already, very specifically, revoked any claim on Dylan, which meant it was open season as far as her sisters were concerned. And Geneva was gorgeous, and a doctor—exactly Dylan's type.

"I'm an investment banker," Dylan replied simply. "What about you?"

"I'm a doctor," Geneva answered, her perfect white teeth flashing in her flawless porcelain face as she smiled. "I finished my residency in Brighton Falls this past spring."

"Nice," Dylan smiled back. "Though I wouldn't have guessed you were a doctor."

"Yes, apparently I don't look the part," Geneva said, laughing. "I usually have to bring a nurse with me when I'm meeting a new patient just so she can verify my credentials."

"I doubt you get any complaints from your male patients, though," Dallas said, joining the conversation. "Once they figure out you're a real doctor, they probably want to see you for a paper cut!"

Geneva laughed. "I do pretty good triage on paper cuts!"

"You should talk, Dallas," Sydney said. "One of my friends mentioned that some of the department's more regular offenders were specifically requesting you to do their questioning. She said one lady, who was being arrested, asked if you could be the one to put her in handcuffs!"

"It's an occupational hazard of being so hot," Dallas said, wiggling his eyebrows. "But I'm sure Dylan knows all about that."

Geneva smiled craftily. "Now that you mention it, what kind of investments do you offer, Dylan? I may be interested in some of the *long-term* variety."

Brooke choked on her turkey. She coughed, her face turning

red as she gagged. Her dad pounded on her back, and Dallas looked like he was ready to hop up and give her the Heimlich.

Finally, getting the meat out of her throat, she took a swig of water, washing it down.

"Are you okay, sweetheart?" her mom asked worriedly.

"I'm fine," Brooke managed hoarsely.

Unfortunately, the incident managed to put all eyes, and attention on her.

"Brooke, I have a favor to ask," Geneva said, her focus momentarily swayed from Dylan. "A friend of mine is having a baby boy, and her baby shower is in a few weeks. Do you think you can make one of those cute diaper cakes for me to give her?"

"Sure," Brooke answered. "If you let me know if they have a theme, maybe I can work it in. I'll call you next week to talk about what you want and how much you want to spend."

"Good!" Geneva smiled. "That's a relief. I think they really like sports, so maybe you could work that in. I'm so glad I won't have to pick something out. I love having a creative sister. It gets me out of so much shopping!"

"Brooke, Mom says you're looking for a job," Sydney said from on the other side of Dylan. "I have a few contacts in the interior decorating business in Brighton Falls. Do you want me to check if they have any openings? I'm sure I could get you an interview."

Before Brooke could respond, Dallas jumped in. "This whole losing your job thing could actually be a great opportunity for you, Brooke. You should give London a call. Just think about it. She could probably get you some kind of decorating job in Hollywood. That would give you some great experience and look impressive on a resume."

"That's a good idea," Lydia said enthusiastically. "We're going to call London and wish her a 'Happy Thanksgiving' anyway. Why don't you ask her about a job?"

"Maybe Brooke doesn't want to leave Crossroads," Brooke's

dad, John, said, his forehead wrinkled with worry.

"Well, if she doesn't, she could always do something other than interior design," Sydney said helpfully. She turned to Dylan and placed her beautifully manicured hand on his forearm, "I'm sure you get a lot of traffic through your bank, Dylan. Have you heard of any place that was hiring? Brooke would be great at something that involved childcare. I'm not sure any medical or business office would hire her with her recent history of messing up orders, but she wasn't making a whole lot at Crossroads Floral anyway. It shouldn't be too difficult to find an equivalent-paying job that doesn't require education or experience."

Brooke stood suddenly, dropping her napkin onto her plate. "Thank you all for your concern. I appreciate your offers of help, but I would very much prefer to find my own employment. Now, if you will excuse me, I think I need some fresh air."

Brooke hurried for the patio door, exiting quickly to the backyard. Lifting her face to the soft breeze, she let the air cool her hot cheeks and eyes. She took great, deep breaths, working to calm her frayed nerves and the cornucopia of emotions filling her to overflowing.

She knew her family meant well. She was the baby of the family, and they wanted to help. Her siblings were so used to working to protect her that it usually didn't occur to them that she was a competent adult, capable of finding her own job and making her own decisions.

And Geneva was just a flirt. She would never intentionally hurt Brooke. Most of the time, she wasn't even conscious of her flirting tendencies or how irresistible a picture she made with her long blonde hair and dark, fluttering eyelashes. If Brooke thought about it too much, she might even conclude that Dylan and Geneva might be a good match. They were quite similar in that Geneva dated a lot for fun, but seemed to struggle with serious relationships.

But Brooke didn't want to think about it.

Sydney was a different story. Sydney usually knew exactly

what she was doing. Every phrase or gesture always had some purpose. And the fact that her older sister had very deliberately touched Dylan's forearm made Brooke think that Sydney was playing some kind of game. Brooke doubted she was actually interested in Dylan romantically. More than likely, she had picked up on the fact that Brooke felt some kind of attraction toward Dylan, and she was playing an angle to try to make Brooke jealous. Sydney wasn't mean; she was just gifted in the arts of reading and manipulating people. And of course, in Sydney's mind, she always had their best interests in mind.

Seeing a few remaining fall flowers in her mother's flower garden, Brooke grabbed a pair of clippers from the garden shed and began picking and arranging a bouquet. Though they were past their prime and a little dry, Brooke still found them pretty. Immediately, she felt the stress ooze out of her as she did a simple task she loved.

Picking a few sunflowers, she then set the clippers down and stuck them in the middle of the strawflowers she had already picked. She held the bouquet out and looked at it, examining it from all angles.

A shiver raced through her body, and she realized that she would need to return inside soon. Had she planned on making a quick escape from Thanksgiving dinner, she would have grabbed a jacket.

"Are you cold?" Dylan's voice came from behind her.

She turned.

"I hope your mom doesn't mind, but I saw this blanket and grabbed it off the couch. I knew the temperature was pretty cold out here, but that breeze makes it worse."

Brooke's eyes caught on Dylan's and she swallowed. How she wished the man didn't take her breath away nearly every time she looked at him. He was entirely too good-looking. Seeing those eyes reflecting the gray of the sky and his hair ruffling in the breeze did not help her calm down at all.

"Thank you," Brooke said, gratefully accepting the blanket.

Dylan helped wrap it tight around her shoulders, which triggered even more shivers.

"I'm sorry to just leave you there," Brooke said. It seemed like all she did was apologize to Dylan, but yet again, she hadn't done right by him. In some respects, she had jumped out of a pool of piranhas and just left him there to fend for himself.

"No worries," he said simply. "Your family isn't anything that I can't handle. They are actually entertaining. I like them. I never had a family like yours. I understand why you left, but I also understand that they love you very much."

"Yes, I know," Brooke said. "Sometimes, though, I feel like a little kitten that everyone likes to love and snuggle so much it's suffocating. With six brothers and sisters, I think there may be such a thing as 'over-loving.'"

Dylan nodded. "Those are pretty flowers," he said, looking at the bouquet in her hand.

"Yes," Brooke agreed. "They are probably the last of the season, which always makes me sad. But come spring, Mom and I will plant her flower garden again. We enjoy doing it together. She knows how much I love flowers."

"So what are your favorite flowers?" he asked.

Brooke was surprised. Not only did he sound genuinely interested, but she didn't know if anyone had ever asked her about her favorite flowers before. She thought about it, and finally answered quietly, "I love all flowers, but my very favorite are ones that I can't plant or even buy."

She looked up at him with a sad smile, and he waited for her to explain.

"My parents have always loved to travel," she said, sitting down on a bench that sat in the middle of the dried flower garden. Dylan took a seat beside her. "My dad was a CEO of a large company in Brighton Falls. He is mostly retired now, but he is still on the board and does consulting. He's always done traveling with his job and still does. For instance, my parents were in Europe until last week."

Dylan took a seat beside Brooke on the bench, momentarily causing her to lose her concentration. Brooke shifted, trying to give him as much room as possible so their bodies didn't touch at all. At the slightest contact, Brooke could feel the electricity, even through the blanket.

Not wanting him to know his effect on her, she continued speaking, "Growing up, my mom would frequently travel with Dad for work. Then when he had vacation, they would also travel. Since I was the youngest, it was often easier to leave me with my grandma when they traveled. My older siblings didn't get left as much. As they got older, they would travel, too. But I liked staying with Grandma, and it worked well for both of us. Since my grandfather had died before I was born, having me stay with her gave Grandma something to do and kept her from being lonely. Grandma lived in California and had the most beautiful flowers in her front yard. She had these hydrangeas that were in just about every shade of blue you can imagine. She also had big bushes of bright pink bougainvillea right beside her front door."

Brooke looked at Dylan and smiled. "Those are my favorite flowers."

"I understand why," he said with an answering smile. "Grandmas always have the best flowers."

"At this point, I'm sure part of their allure is their inaccessibility," Brooke admitted thoughtfully. "I can order hydrangeas and even bougainvillea, but none of them live up to the memory of hers. After she passed away, my dad's family sold his mother's house. I haven't seen it in years. The flowers probably don't even exist anymore, but they sure do in my mind. And they are beautiful."

Brooke looked at Dylan, and he looked at her. Suddenly she noticed a slight rosy tinge to his nose. "Oh, my goodness! Dylan, you're cold! Here, this is a warm blanket. I can share."

"Are you sure?" he asked.

"Of course!"

And since neither one of them seemed to want to go inside to the nice, heated house yet, Brooke opened her blanket, and Dylan huddled close, wrapping it from her shoulders around to his.

"I think that's a lot better," he said, looking down at her, his face mere inches from hers.

Brooke barely managed to nod. She definitely felt warmer, and it likely had everything to do with his proximity.

"I do have a few questions for you," he said seriously.

"Okay," Brooke said cautiously. Was he going to ask her more about flowers? Those she could handle.

"Is your full name Brooklyn?"

"No."

Dylan waited.

Brooke really hoped he would just move onto his next question, but he wasn't going to let her off that easily.

"So…" Dylan said slowly, "your brother is Dallas, and your sisters are Geneva and Sydney. Did I hear your other sister is named London?"

Releasing her breath in a rush, Brooke spoke quickly. "My siblings are Israel, Camden, Dallas, Geneva, London, Sydney, and me. Since my parents have always loved to travel, it was my mom's idea to name all of their children after places. London and Sydney are twins, and after they were born, Mom and Dad thought they were done. But I was a surprise. Mom wanted to name me Brooklyn, but Dad didn't want to. He'd always liked Brooke, with an 'e' on the end. Mom wouldn't hear of it. After all, they already had six children named after places. You can't exactly have one that is different. When Mom had me, it was a rough recovery, so Dad filled out the paperwork for my birth certificate. When I was about six weeks old, my birth certificate arrived, and Mom discovered that her baby wasn't actually named Brooklyn. Dad had named me Brooke Lydia Hutchins, hoping that if he put Mom's name as my middle name, then he would be forgiven. Needless to say, my mom wasn't happy, but I've been 'Brooke' ever since, though sometimes Mom calls me 'Brooklyn' just to aggravate

Dad."

Dylan grinned. "That's a great story!"

Brooke shrugged. "I've had that question a lot growing up, but I've never been sad I'm not 'Brooklyn.' I'm proud my dad got to name me, and it actually fits me more to be different from my siblings. After all, I'm quite different from them in about every other way as well."

"What do you mean? I can see the family resemblance between you and your sisters. You're all beautiful."

Brooke couldn't stop the slight grimace. It would have been a better compliment if it had been given on an individual basis, instead of listed in the group of beautiful sisters. Now all she could think about was that Dylan thought Geneva and Sydney were beautiful. Which they were. But still.

"I'm not like them," Brooke said, shifting uncomfortably. "All of them are quite successful. They are brilliant. I never got bad grades, went to college, and I don't exactly consider myself stupid. But I'm not on their scale. While I majored in Interior Design, they studied Criminal Justice, Medicine, or something equally impressive. Now they are actually doing things that make a difference while I am an unemployed florist."

"Come on, Brooke, it can't be that bad," Dylan said, obviously thinking she was exaggerating. "Just because you are different, or more creative, doesn't mean that you aren't equal or just as capable of making contributions. I know Geneva is a doctor but isn't Dallas a police officer? That's a relatively normal profession."

Brooke laughed. "Dallas is a police officer the way that Mozart played the piano! He has a doctorate in Criminal Justice and is a professor at a university in Brighton Falls. He helps out with the police department here in Crossroads and consults on investigations around the country because he likes doing fieldwork. Trust me, my family does a great job of pretending to be normal, but they aren't!"

"So what about the others? Like Sydney. What does Sydney

do?"

Brooke shrugged. "Your guess is as good as mine on that one. Nobody knows what Sydney does. That's kind of the point. She was recruited into the military right after high school, but for some reason, she didn't stay there. I think she got some kind of specialized training. If you ask her what she does, she will tell you she's a consultant and describe the assignment she's currently doing. Last I talked to her, she said she was working at an art museum. Once she said she was doing consulting work at a construction company. What she says always sounds completely normal, but I have serious doubts that it is. Just be careful if you ask her about anything. After one conversation with her, you'll swear she can read minds. She'll know more about you than you do!"

"And the others?"

"Israel is the oldest. His background is business, and he is a big-time CEO, like dad. He is the only one who is married. And he and his wife have a little girl. Camden is a computer genius. I don't know exactly what he does, but it's something big and with computers. London is pretty successful in Hollywood as an actress and screenwriter. They were all busy with their responsibilities and not able to make it for Thanksgiving. I'm not sure yet if they will make it home for Christmas."

"All of those do sound impressive," Dylan admitted.

"It really isn't just that they all have good jobs and are successful," Brooke explained. "It's that they are exceptional. Geneva isn't just a doctor. She is a *gifted* doctor. They all are gifted. Except for me. I'm just normal. It isn't as if I resent them. I don't. I just feel different and wish I could make some kind of contribution to the greater good, as they do."

"So now I understand why you don't want them to help you find a job," Dylan said.

Brooke nodded. "I don't want to ride their shirt-tails. I want to do it on my own."

"Brooke! Dylan!"

They looked up to see Brooke's dad leaning out the back door. "Are you ready for pie? Come on in!"

"Did I mention that my mom is *gifted* at pie?" Brooke said seriously.

Dylan threw his head back and laughed. "Well, in that case, let's hurry in before your exceptional brother and sisters eat all of the exceptional pie!"

Standing up, Dylan put his arm around Brooke to hold the blanket in place and hurried back to the house. As they stepped inside, Brooke set her flower bouquet on the table, took the blanket off their shoulders, and began to fold it up. But Dylan's hand stayed at her back in a comfortable pressure. Though Brooke didn't want to admit it, she liked it way too much.

Before they even made it to the table, a smiling Geneva handed Dylan a piece of pumpkin pie smothered with whipped cream.

Dylan's hand fell from Brooke's back as he accepted the offered pie with a delighted smile.

Feeling a little lost, Brooke retrieved her flowers and withdrew to find a vase. After all, tired fall flowers with just 'Brooke,' in no way compared to exceptional pie with 'Geneva.'

CHAPTER 17

"**B**rooke, that looks amazing!" Geneva gushed excitedly. "Just bring it in here, and we'll put it on the table with the other gifts."

The heavy diaper cake was straining her back, but Brooke managed to make it to where Geneva had cleared a spot on the table. The instant Brooke set it down, multiple women began admiring it.

Brooke was proud of it. She thought it was one of the best diaper cakes she'd ever made. Going with the sports theme Geneva had mentioned, Brooke had made a layer for basketball, one for football, and one for baseball. Each layer held a coordinating sport onesie along with a few other accessories for decorations, like socks and spoons to match. For the centerpiece at the top, Brooke had used small ball toys, such as what a young child would like to play with.

"Hi, Brooke," a voice said.

Brooke turned around to find her friend Kate. "Hi, Kate. Are you here for the baby shower?"

"Yes. Cassandra is a friend of mine. I'm so happy that she's getting a little boy! And it looks like she'll have a great turn-out with a lot of nice things. And it's such a nice venue for a baby shower. I haven't been in this building since they remodeled. It looks great!"

Brooke looked around, her eyes skimming what had once been an old fire station, but was now a beautiful new community center. What she liked best about it was the details that still gave it that old fire station flavor. The sliding pole still stood in the corner, and much of the brickwork was intact. The floor itself was a tile that resembled rustic wood. Pictures of old fire engines were set on the walls, but most of the other décor was left open so that people could rent out the space and decorate to suit their needs. In this instance, blue and white ribbons lined the railing above, and a large number of balloons floated from where they were secured at the tables.

"It really does," Brooke said. "What a great asset to the community this will be."

"Yes, I'm so glad they've invested in the downtown area again," Kate said thoughtfully. "I think it will really make the difference in Crossroads. We're really seeing an upswing in interest in the area, even at the post office."

Kate paused and looked at a large clock in the corner. "Do you want to go get a seat? I think things will start soon. It looks like they've moved all the chairs into a circle."

"You go ahead, Kate," Brooke urged. "I can't stay. I just came to drop off the diaper cake for Geneva. Cassandra is her friend."

"You made that diaper cake?" Kate asked. "Brooke, you could totally sell those!"

"The thing weighs a ton," Brooke said. "I'm not sure there would be much of a market for diaper cakes in Crossroads, and it would cost way too much to ship the things for online orders."

"You might be surprised," Kate said. "If you think about it, companies ship large boxes of diapers to people all the time. If you drop by the post office, I can give you a break down of the cost and weight limits for shipping. It's just an idea, but I really think it could work!"

"Thanks, Kate," Brooke said appreciatively. "Maybe I'll do that."

Kate worked at the post office, so Brooke thought she would surely know about shipping. If she thought it was doable, maybe it really was something that she should look into.

Brooke enjoyed making diaper cakes, wreaths, and anything creative like that. She'd never really considered that she might be able to sell them online. But now that she thought about it, an idea began to bloom of an online florist shop that carried more products than just flowers.

Brooke started for the door, but Geneva stopped her. "Thank you for bringing the diaper cake," Geneva said. "And for doing such an awesome job with it."

Brooke smiled. "No problem. I'll just put it in the sister bank and remember you owe me a big favor."

Geneva smile turned sly. "Well, you know I like to pay any debt in advance. I'm pretty sure you already owe me, so this will make us even."

"What are you talking about?" Brooke asked, thoroughly confused. She couldn't think of a single thing Geneva had done for her recently.

Geneva raised herself up as if making an important announcement. "You'll be happy to know that I did a thorough investigation of Dylan Masters. My verdict is that I approve. Go ahead and snatch him up as fast as you can."

"What are you talking about?" Brooke said, quickly becoming upset. Then that upset turned rapidly into an awful foreboding. "Geneva, what have you done? I told you I wasn't interested in him. And I *never* told you to investigate him!"

Geneva waved her hand as if Brooke's objections were an annoying fly. "You didn't have to say anything. Both Sydney and I saw the way you looked at him, and the way he looked at you. So Sydney handled the background check, and I handled the more subjective part of the investigation."

"And how did you do that?" Brooke asked with great alarm. She wouldn't put it past her sisters to do something that would completely humiliate her, all in the name of protecting her.

"Don't look at me that way, Brooke!" Geneva said, rolling her eyes. "I just flirted with him. I even managed to get his number at Thanksgiving. Then I called him a few times in the past couple weeks. The result? Absolutely nothing. He is most assuredly not interested in me. I employed my best flirting techniques. I even asked him out, and he refused. He hasn't even answered my last couple calls, and I think he might be avoiding me. Isn't that great?"

"Gen, do you have any idea how psychotic that sounds?" Brooke said, fighting the urge not to laugh at her outright.

Geneva looked confused. "Well, I did it for you! And the good news is that he isn't the type to cheat on you. He wouldn't take the bait at all. Doesn't that make you happy?"

Brooke threw her hands out in exasperation. Was Geneva not hearing what she was saying? "It might if he was my boyfriend. Or if I was interested in him romantically. But he isn't, and I'm not! I hate to be hard on your ego, Gen, but I doubt that I was the reason he wasn't interested in you. Dylan and I are not together, and I've made it clear to him that I won't even go on a date with him."

Geneva looked quite troubled. "But that's sad, Brooke! You know how Sydney is, and she was certain that he was quite enamored with you! You should at least give him a chance!"

"You do know the reputation of Dylan Masters, right?" Brooke questioned. There was no way any woman could live in the area and have not at least heard of its most eligible bachelor.

"Yes, of course," Geneva said, restlessly pushing her blonde locks away from her face. "I've seen him around town, and a few of my friends have dated him briefly. But I also know he doesn't look at other women the way he looks at you. Maybe he's changed."

"Maybe not," Brooke said, her doubt apparent.

"And you're not willing to take the risk and find out," Geneva stated flatly. It wasn't even a question. It was a diagnosis.

"No, I'm not," Brooke confirmed.

"Living your life in fear seems like a sad way to do it,"

Geneva's soft words were casual, but they carried a strange tension. Though she appeared almost distracted, glancing over at the other ladies finding seats in the circle, Brooke got the impression that she was greatly troubled by their conversation.

"Maybe," Brooke said, not bothering to try to analyze Geneva's issues. "But I've been burned before."

Geneva actually flinched. "Yes, I know," she said, her voice low and her eyes not meeting Brooke's. "And now you'll have to forgive me for attempting to do penance for that mistake."

"Is that what your Dylan Masters investigation was about?" Brooke asked with sudden clarity. "Gen, it isn't something that I am upset about. It was long ago, and I'm very thankful now that I didn't end up with Andy. You kinda did me a favor."

"I understand that." Geneva finally met Brooke's gaze. "I also understand that you haven't seriously dated anyone else since then. So there's no way I can't feel that the fear keeping you frozen, unable to take a risk, is at least partially my fault."

"Gen—"

"Thanks for the diaper cake, Brooke," she said, breaking eye contact. "It looks like the party is getting ready to start. I'd better run."

Brooke sighed and reluctantly turned to the door. She hadn't realized that Geneva carried around such guilt where she was concerned. She honestly didn't have hard feelings toward her sister, and wished there was a way to make things better. But she didn't know what to do or say. The only thing she did know was that this wasn't the time or place.

She had almost made it to the front door when a figure stepped out from one of the side hallways and headed to the door a few feet ahead of her.

"Dylan?" she called, recognizing the broad shoulders and dark hair.

Dylan turned. "Brooke!" he said, obviously surprised to see her.

"What are you doing here?" she asked.

"I was here about some business with the community center's manager," he answered. "What about you?"

"I was just dropping off a diaper cake for a baby shower. Geneva wanted me to make one as a gift."

"Oh, I think I remember her asking you at Thanksgiving," Dylan said.

Brooke nodded, but then was at a bit of a loss of what to say. Finally, she jumped in, "It's good to see you. I thought I'd run into you at church, but I haven't."

"Oh, I've been there," Dylan said. "But my schedule changed and I've been going to a different service. I even stopped and met with the pastor last week."

"That's great!" said Brooke.

But then Dylan didn't say anything else.

And she didn't feel like she could ask anything else. If he didn't want to share, then it would be rude to press him.

Dylan shifted from one foot to another, as if he didn't know what to say either. He really seemed uncharacteristically lost. Dylan had called her a few times since Thanksgiving, but they had all been rather awkward conversations where he had simply asked about her job search.

The silence stretched between them, and with it, the tension grew taut as well. It all mystified Brooke. They had talked so easily at Thanksgiving, and even before that. So why was everything suddenly so difficult?

She could think of only one reason.

"Well, I guess I'd better—"

"Dylan, do you have a minute?" Brooke asked suddenly. "I need to talk to you."

"Sure," he replied.

Wanting to get out of the way of the front door, Brooke led the way to the right and found a small seating area that was apparently designed as a large coat closet. Racks lined the walls, but in the center were some chairs, a table, and a lamp turned on low. Though some coats were hung on the racks, the area was empty, the only movement coming from little twinkle lights strung high on the walls in preparation for Christmas. The entire effect was charming, and Brooke even detected the smell of cinnamon, likely from the bowl of pinecones sitting on the little table.

Before they even fully entered the room, Brooke turned to Dylan, wanting to get it over with. "Dylan, it appears I need to apologize yet again. I just found out that my sister, Geneva, had some mistaken impressions and has possibly been pestering you. I apologize for her behavior. She was trying to watch out for me by testing your loyalty. The good news is that you passed and were apparently not interested in her advances at all. The bad news is that it means absolutely nothing since we are not, nor have we ever been together, and you are completely free to date whomever you please."

Dylan laughed, a loud, happy sound in the quiet closet area. "Well, that explains a lot! I guess I should be proud I passed her test!"

Brooke just shook her head. "I don't think it was much of a test since there was no reason why you couldn't flirt or go out with her. My only hope is that maybe it'll bring her ego down a notch to know that there wasn't really another woman that you preferred. You just didn't want her."

"Well, that may not be true," Dylan said hesitantly.

Brooke's heart leaped in sudden anxiety. Was he really interested in Geneva after all?

"I actually do prefer another woman, but the other statement you made isn't true either. You said I was completely free to date whomever I please."

Brooke looked at him blankly, unable to read his facial expressions in the dim light. "Of course you are!" she protested.

He inched forward, looking down at her while his gaze searched her face. "You tell me, Brooke. Am I free to date who I want? Am I free to date you?"

Brooke's mouth went dry, and her heart pounded. She shook her head and whispered, "No, not me."

"Why not?" he asked softly. Slowly, as if mesmerized, he took her hand and entwined it with his. Then he held it up as if admiring how perfectly their hands fit together.

Brooke didn't want to answer. She didn't want to tell him the truth, but the words came out of their own accord. "You will hurt me," she said with a half sob.

Dylan looked confused and then, suddenly, his face cleared. He reached out with his free hand and tilted Brooke's chin, so her eyes met his once more. "Did someone hurt you, Brooke? Is that why you don't have a boyfriend?"

In spite of herself, she nodded. Dylan seemed to have the ability to extract secrets Brooke would rather keep. Though her head was telling her to keep quiet, her heart did the talking, answering every question he breathed with complete honesty.

"What happened?" he asked gently.

"Every boyfriend I've ever had seemed to tire of me very quickly. I went to a party once with my first boyfriend. When it was time to go, I went to look for him and found him making out with one of my best friends. The only other relatively serious boyfriend I've had was named Andy. I took him home to meet my family. He and Geneva really hit it off, and she started flirting with him terribly. I thought it was just Geneva being Geneva. Then a few days later, Andy sent Geneva to break up with me. She tried to be nice, saying that they never intended to have feelings for each other. She even said that, though she really liked him, she wouldn't date him for my sake, if I didn't want her to. But what could I do? He was crazy about her. Who wouldn't be? So Andy and I were over, and he dated Geneva for a few months. I think he wanted to get serious, and she didn't. So they eventually broke up."

Dylan's jaw worked with tension. "I'm sorry that happened to you."

Brooke shrugged. "I know Geneva still feels bad and has a lot of guilt over it, even though I don't have hard feelings. It wasn't her fault that he liked her better. It hurt at the time, but I got over it."

"Only now, you won't give any other man the chance to hurt you again."

"You'll hurt me, Dylan," she whispered. "I know you will. You'll tire of me quickly, just like the others. You'll send me flowers at the two-week mark, just like the others, and then never again because you'll realize I'm not what you want."

"But, Brooke, you aren't just like the others." His eyes were an intense gray storm, and Brooke had no doubt that he meant every word.

But he was wrong.

"In some ways, I'm not like them," Brooke admitted. "I'm not a judge, or a beautiful cowgirl, or a model, or a doctor. I'm nobody special. Eventually, you'll realize that, and you'll leave for greener pastures and someone who isn't so ordinary. You won't intend to hurt me, but you will. Only unlike the others, my heart won't be able to take it."

"Brooke, you don't know any of that!" Dylan said. "You're just speculating on all of it and speaking through fear. What must I do to get you to trust enough to take a chance on me?"

"Dylan, there's nothing you can do. I won't date you. I can't. I'd have a hard enough time dating a man who didn't have your track record. I just can't be one of the broken hearts in your wake."

Dylan's eyes slid shut. Ironically, in her efforts that he wouldn't hurt her, she had instead hurt him.

Brooke whispered, "Dylan, I still like you. I like talking with you and being with you. I don't want to lose that. I will be your friend, but nothing more."

Dylan's eyes came open and his gaze locked with hers. Reaching up, he gently caressed her face, his touch feather-soft. "I don't know that I can be your friend, Brooke."

His face came closer, his lips hovering mere inches above her own. Brooke felt the pull of attraction drawing them together. Her lips tingled in anticipation, longing for the touch of his on hers.

"Leave now, Brooke," Dylan whispered brokenly. "If you don't, I will kiss you as long as it takes to make you forget that you don't want to be mine. Leave now and don't look back."

Brooke's eyes instantly slid shut, breaking the contact. Then she did the only thing she could do.

She left.

CHAPTER 18

"**B**rooke, sweetheart, can you come to the phone?" Brooke's mother called across the kitchen. "Uncle Wayne wants to talk to you."

Brooke shot her mom an irritated look, but she accepted the phone. Leave it to her mom to arrange things to get what she wanted. After all, Brooke was fairly certain that her sister, Sydney, came by her gifts of manipulation honestly.

"Hi, Uncle Wayne!" Brooke said as cheerfully as she could muster. "Merry Christmas!"

"Right back at you!" he greeted. "I heard you had some trouble over there in Crossroads. Some of your flower deliveries headed the wrong direction?"

Well, at least it was a relief that Uncle Wayne didn't specialize in chit-chat. He got right to the point, which was good. She didn't want to have a long conversation. Dinner was almost on the table, and she didn't want to miss any of it. Her older brother, Israel was here with his wife Marissa and two-year-old daughter, Chloe. Dallas and Geneva were here as well, though her other siblings couldn't make it. Brooke wanted to enjoy the time with her family as much as possible, especially with her niece. And she definitely did not want to be stuck on the phone, no matter what her mother devised.

"So you've been talking to Mom." It was a statement. Brooke

never had to wonder how family members knew the details to her life. Lydia had always been close to her family. Just because her children were now all adults did not mean that Lydia's mother or siblings heard any fewer details about their lives. Brooke sighed, "Yes, there were some mix-ups, but I think everything is straightened out the way it should be now."

That wasn't the complete truth, but she didn't want to be on the phone all day spilling her guts to Uncle Wayne. Though Uncle Wayne owned his own successful shop and she knew he'd lend an understanding ear, it had been over a month now. Though the Crossroads gossip mills had eventually found different fodder, things weren't the same, and Brooke had given up that they would ever return to the previous normal. She still had no job, and her money was nonexistent. She seriously doubted Uncle Wayne could change any of that, despite his well-meaning intentions.

She hated the thought of having to borrow money from her parents or give up her apartment, but if something didn't happen before the new year, then she would have no choice. Her desperation was also urging her to take her siblings up on their offers of using their connections to get interviews. But while her head argued that she shouldn't feel bad about it because it was just good networking, her stubborn streak still demanded that she do it on her own.

So she kept turning in applications, even though the fact that she hadn't even gotten a single interview made her feel like a complete loser. The only explanation as to why nobody would give her a chance was that they hadn't forgotten the mess with the floral shop. She didn't feel like she was disliked in the community, except by Helen, of course, but she did still notice the whispers. And though she had applied for every kind of job she could, even as a manager at a fast food restaurant, no one seemed interested in hiring her. With her intelligence and competence in question, Brooke didn't know that anyone in Crossroads would ever take the risk of having her as an employee.

"I heard you got canned over it," Wayne said bluntly.

Brooke sighed. Apparently, Mom didn't let any detail escape her report. Brooke would have preferred that the news of her being fired not be sent along the family grapevine, but it was obviously too late. If only she could have just said Brooke was 'looking for other work!'

"Yes, I did," she admitted. "But I'm putting in applications, even in Brighton Falls. So I'm sure I'll find something soon." Brooke's tone sounded way more optimistic than she actually was. Hopefully, Mom would give her some leftovers from Christmas dinner. If not, then she would have to eat a lot of Ramen noodles this week.

"I don't imagine anyone is eager to hire someone with a whole lot of accidental orders under her belt," Wayne said sadly.

"No, they aren't. It was a pretty big mess."

Brooke waited, hoping she didn't have to recount all the gory details of how she had screwed things up so badly. Chloe came toddling by with a toy phone. Looking up at Brooke, the dark-haired little elf handed her the phone and babbled something quite serious. Taking the phone, Brooke put it to her other ear and pretended to talk.

After the lengthy pause that Brooke had no intention of breaking, Wayne finally spoke, his tone bright. "Well, you're a good designer, Brooke. I'm sure you'll land on your feet."

Busy handing the phone back to Chloe and pretending the phone call was now for the little girl, Brooke still didn't respond.

Finally, Wayne cleared his throat and continued, "I need to tell you, Brooke, that I'm not really calling to offer my condolences or find out all the details. I'm sure Lydia has already filled Mom in on those if I have an interest in family gossip. I really wanted to call and thank you."

"Why would you need to thank me?" Brooke asked, rather startled at the sudden turn in the conversation.

Wayne chuckled. "I heard about your order mix-ups, and that gave me an idea to do my own order mix-up—kind of an accidental, on-purpose one."

"Uncle Wayne, you didn't!"

"Yes, I did!" he said, obviously thoroughly delighted with himself. "And it worked! I single-handedly managed to set up a couple with a little accidental delivery of flowers. Now they are together, and I expect an engagement announcement any day! The flowers finally gave them an excuse to talk to each other and figure out that they were in love, and I have you to thank! If you hadn't completely messed up your orders, I would have never heard about it and got the idea."

Brooke opened and closed her mouth, so shocked she had no idea how to respond. "You're welcome, I guess," she finally managed.

Uncle Wayne's laughter boomed through the phone. "See how everything works out for a reason? Messing up one order wouldn't have been good enough. You had to wreck things so much that it was bad enough for me to hear about it clear over here. Isn't God amazing? He let you mess things up, which allowed me to get a crazy idea, which allowed a wonderful couple to get together, just like they were meant to be!"

Still feeling a little whiplash about his reasoning, Brooke tried to find an appropriate response. Chloe started to wave her toy and complain loudly that distracted Aunt Brooke wasn't answering the plastic phone anymore. Before she made it to outright screaming, Israel came and plopped both her and her toy phone into his arms.

Still not knowing what to say, Brooke finally just voiced her thoughts. "I'm not sure you should make a habit of playing matchmaker or sending orders 'accidentally, on-purpose,' Uncle Wayne. But I'm glad it worked out for you this time."

Wayne snorted, "Oh, don't worry. I don't think I'll be pulling another one of those charades. I was sweating buckets there for a while, worried that it wouldn't work out."

Wayne paused as if thinking. Then, his voice a little gravelly, he continued, "You just hang in there, Brooke. Remember that God can take even our worst mistakes and make something good. Look for the good, Brooke. It will be there if you look."

Uncle Wayne may be exuberant and eccentric at times, but he did have a few acorns of wisdom that showed up every now and then.

"Thanks, Uncle Wayne," she said quietly. Brooke looked up to see her family seated at the table and Dallas gesturing wildly for her to come sit so they could say the blessing. Even Chloe was seated in her high chair.

"I've got to run, Uncle Wayne. Mom has dinner ready, and they are waiting for me. Thanks for the encouragement. Merry Christmas!"

Brooke hung up and hurried to the table. Everyone bowed their heads as Brooke's dad said the blessing. Dad's prayers, though not overly long, always found a way to mention everyone at the table, as well as those who were absent, thanking God for each person and asking His blessing on their lives. He still managed a beautiful reminder of what Christmas truly means and packed everything into around two minutes.

After the 'amen,' the food started making the rounds, and her dad turned to her. "No boy with you this time, Brooke?" he asked with a mischievous smile.

"No," Brooke said simply, piling a little too much salad on her plate in her distraction.

"He should be," Geneva muttered under her breath.

"Brooke, do you have a boyfriend?" her oldest brother, Israel, asked. "Why am I the last to know?"

"I do not have a boyfriend!" Brooke said emphatically.

"She should," Geneva muttered again.

Shooting her sister a dirty look, she turned back to Israel. "I brought a *friend* for Thanksgiving dinner since he had nowhere to go. A few of my siblings got a little excited and seemed to over-react to me bringing someone home. I checked with Dylan this past week, and he was going to Arizona to celebrate Christmas with his sister and mom. End of story."

What Brooke didn't say was that her conversation with Dylan

had been very brief and was the only time she'd spoken to him in the last few weeks. The two minutes on the phone had been very stiff and awkward. It was clear that the night at the community center was still very much in both their minds, and Brooke realized that she had hurt Dylan to the point that he may never want to talk to her again. It really seemed like any kind of friendship was off the table.

Thankfully, the subject shifted from Brooke to an interesting case that had come across Dallas's desk. When Chloe finished eating and got restless, Brooke hopped up from her seat and reached to take her niece to play so her parents could finish their meal.

She retrieved a little ball and tossed it to a giggling Chloe when her phone rang. She pulled it out of her pocket and answered. "Hello?

"Brooke!" came the whispered voice. "It's Tylee!"

"Hi, Tylee. Merry Christmas!" Brooke said, her voice normal. "Why are we whispering?"

"I don't want anyone to hear." Tylee paused, and Brooke imagined her looking around suspiciously. "I just had to call and let you know that Grammie just announced to the family that she is closing the shop and selling the building!"

"Really?" Brooke asked, surprised. She didn't think Helen would ever close the shop.

Losing her concentration momentarily, Chloe tossed the ball and Brooke forgot to catch it. Brooke winced as it hit her nose.

"Yes!" Tylee confirmed, her voice losing its whisper quality. "She said business has died, and she isn't making money anymore. Of course, she blames you, saying that the shop just couldn't recover after the mess you made. But I know that isn't true. The number of orders didn't decrease until you left. Then Grammie couldn't find another floral designer, so she tried to do the orders herself. They looked terrible! It didn't take long for customers to decide that they didn't want those kind of flowers. She also never could get the online order thing to work right. It's not easy trying to phone in each of your cross-country or overseas orders, especially when the florist on the other end doesn't speak English well. I'm pretty sure Grammie had her share of order mistakes too! At least it sounded that way from all the angry customers."

After the fun of hitting Brooke in the nose, just tossing the ball wasn't so entertaining for Chloe. As Tylee talked, Brooke followed the little girl to a stack of magazines and watched as she began unloading them.

"I'm sorry, Tylee!" Brooke said sympathetically. "I know that means you are out of a job."

"That's okay," she said. "It wasn't any fun after you left anyway. I really think it's time that Grammie retires and that it'll be best for everyone. It'll just be really strange that for the first time in thirty years, there will be no Crossroads Floral."

For some reason, Tylee's words sent a jolt of electricity through Brooke. *There will be no Crossroads Floral.*

"Someone's coming!" Tylee whispered. "Gotta go!"

The line went dead.

Riiippp!

"Oh, no, Chloe!" Brooke said, looking down at the ripped magazine in her niece's hand. "I'm not sure Grandpa wants his fishing magazine torn up!"

"Let her do it," Lydia said, coming into the room. "Your dad has way too many magazines. If Chloe wants to do the downsizing for him, then I think that's putting them to good use."

With Grandma's permission, Chloe used both hands and began ripping the magazine to shreds.

"Did you have a good talk with Wayne?" Lydia asked.

"Yes, I actually did," Brooke answered. "He was quite encouraging and made me remember that God has reasons for everything and can bring good out of my worst mistakes."

Lydia smiled. "I'm glad, sweetheart. You've seemed so sad the past couple weeks. I've been concerned."

"I'm having a hard time right now, Mom," Brooke admitted.

"I know I have to trust God, but I also know that I may not see the good God intends to bring out of a bad situation."

Brooke usually didn't intentionally take her mom as a confidante, but she really didn't have anyone she felt comfortable sharing with. And sometimes, Lydia would use just the right tone of voice that transformed Brooke into a little girl who needed her mom.

"You're right, Brooke," Lydia said, her gaze filled with love and understanding. "Sometimes we never get to see the 'why' this side of heaven. Sometimes it is very clear. And still, sometimes we have to look for it. I think this is a good thing for you, sweetheart. I've been worried that you're stuck, not allowing yourself to step out of your comfort zone. But now is the time. Take a risk and do something you want to do. Find your good, Brooke. Don't let fear keep you from finding the good God can give you."

Find the good, Brooke. Find the good.

It was the same thing Wayne had told her.

Then, like a curtain being drawn back to reveal sunlight, Brooke realized something. They weren't telling her to just wait and let the good find her. They were urging her to go find it.

"What happened to my magazines?" Brooke's dad entered the room to find Chloe sitting in a pile of magazine scraps.

Brooke didn't hear her dad's response. Her mind was too busy as an idea slowly began to form. At the thought, her hands became clammy, and her breath became shallow. Did she dare do such a thing?

Her mind said it would never work. It would be too difficult. She would fail and be the laughingstock of Crossroads yet again.

But her heart said she had to try.

CHAPTER 19

Brooke knew she'd made a mistake as soon as she stepped through the front door of the bank. But she resolutely made her feet move forward.

Then she saw Dylan.

He wasn't supposed to be here! It was 9:00 in the morning on December 26th! He was supposed to be in Arizona for Christmas!

Pivoting, she abruptly turned around to make a run for the door, but she didn't make it before Dylan looked up and saw her.

"Brooke!" he called.

She seriously thought about pretending she didn't hear him. If she had two more seconds, she might be able to make it.

He called her name again, and she reluctantly stopped. Even if she tried, he'd already seen her. He would either outrun or call her and ask why she had sprinted out the door.

"Oh, hi!" she said, trying to sound casual as if she just noticed him. "I was just... Why are you here?" she blurted irritably. "I thought you were supposed to be in Arizona with your family for Christmas."

"I was," he answered, looking at her curiously. "I was there last weekend, and we celebrated early. I flew back here on the 24th so I could be at work today."

"Dylan!" Brooke chided. "I asked about your plans for

Christmas, and you told me you were going to Arizona. If I'd known you would be spending Christmas day alone, I would have insisted you have dinner with my family."

"Honestly, Brooke, I knew you assumed I would be celebrating with them *on* Christmas, and I didn't do anything to clear up that misconception. I didn't really feel like I could join you for Christmas, so I may have misled you to some degree."

"Now I feel bad!" Brooke exclaimed, hating the idea of him sitting home alone on Christmas. "Why couldn't you come with me?"

Then she saw his face and stopped. He couldn't come to Christmas dinner because of her. Because there were too many uncomfortable feelings between them and because "just being friends" wasn't going to be possible for him.

Never answering her question, he asked a question of his own. "So what can I help you with? Why are you here?"

Brooke looked around at the bank, seeing the bank tellers busy and working. She obviously couldn't take time away from Dylan's work to talk, and right now, she wished she'd started with a different bank. She'd only come here because the bank had the best reputation in town, and she knew Dylan wouldn't be here!

"I need to speak with a loan officer," she said, wetting her lips nervously.

Dylan's eyebrows raised in surprise. "Is this about an existing loan or a new one?"

"A new one," she replied, tapping every ounce of her bravery to stop herself from turning around and walking out.

A wave of nerves gripped her, and she couldn't take it. This was a stupid idea. "You know, never mind. I don't want to take anyone's time. I'll just go and talk to you later."

"Wait, Brooke," Dylan said, and he reached for her. Thinking the better of it, his hand dropped to his side. "It's no problem. There's no harm in checking if you can get approved for a loan. Even if you don't, you're no worse off than you are now."

Brooke nodded reluctantly. "Who do I talk to?"

"Richard Dunst usually handles the bank loans. His office is right over here." Dylan led the way to an office in the corner, then paused with his hand on the doorknob. "If you don't mind, I usually stay to hear loan requests. Though I primarily deal with other types of investments with my job, I still monitor the total investments made by this and other branches."

Of course she minded! Just the thought of him being in the room made her feel ill. But she nodded anyway, and chirped a meek, "Sure."

Dylan led the way into the office. "Richard, I'd like you to meet Brooke Hutchins. She wanted to discuss obtaining a loan."

Mr. Dunst was an older man with a fringe of gray hair around a shiny bald head. He looked grouchy and entirely too serious for Brooke to feel the least bit optimistic.

"What kind of loan are you interested in Ms. Hutchins?" Mr. Dunst asked, getting right to the point after shaking Brooke's hand.

Dylan took a seat beside his coworker, facing Brooke.

Trying to focus, Brooke fixed her eyes on Mr. Dunst and worked to tune out Dylan's presence. Taking a deep breath, she forced herself to jump in. "I would like to purchase the Crossroads Floral building and open my own shop. I would like to get a loan in order to do so."

"What is your credit like?" Mr. Dunst asked briskly. "Do you own your own home?

"I do not," Brooke stated. "I rent an apartment. I pay my bills on time, but I'm not sure about my credit score."

Mr. Dunst shifted in his chair uncomfortably, but with his large girth, there wasn't a lot of wiggle room. "The way I understand it, the business for Crossroads Floral has been declining drastically. What makes you sure you can succeed when Helen Garrison has not?"

"I would like to offer more than just flowers," Brooke stated, trying to sound confident. "There seems to be a lot more tourists coming to Crossroads, and I would like to feature gifts, home décor, and other products that would appeal to that industry. Plus, I will get the online order situation figured out, which is something Helen just wasn't able to do."

"What products would you offer?" Dylan asked with interest.

"Besides the gift shop and handmade items targeting tourists, I'd like to feature wreaths, diaper cakes, maybe some edible arrangements that could also be purchased online and shipped. I would like to order a variety of things that can be sent as gifts or used as home décor here in Crossroads or anywhere. And of course, I would also provide all the products and services of a traditional florist."

Reaching in a drawer, Mr. Dunst pulled out a large sheaf of papers that he slid across the desk to Brooke. "We will need you to make an application that includes all of your financial and employment history. We will then assess everything and notify you in a few days as to whether you've been approved for the loan.

"Thank you," Brooke said, swallowing with difficulty at the sight of the intimidating application.

Mr. Dunst started to scoot his chair back and stand, thereby signaling the end of the interview, but he paused as if debating whether or not to say more. "If I were you, Ms. Hutchins, I wouldn't wait for our response. Go make applications at other banks as well. My initial feeling is that you will not be approved. Without a good credit history and an employment record that shows you could handle loan payments with your current skills, it will be a challenge. Of course, your application will be viewed objectively, but I will be surprised if our analysis shows that a business such as you suggest would earn enough revenue to support yourself and a business mortgage. And it certainly won't if you intend to hire an assistant."

Brooke nodded, realizing that there was absolutely no way she was going to get the loan. No matter at what angle she considered her idea, she couldn't figure out how she could run the business herself. By her calculations, she would need at least one other person who could handle the calls and at least some of the business side of things while she worked on the design side.

Standing up, she put out her hand to give Mr. Dunst a firm handshake. "Thank you for your time, Mr. Dunst."

During the whole interview, she managed to not look at Dylan. Now her eyes slid to him, and she read compassion in his gaze.

"I'll show you where you can fill out the paperwork," he said, leading the way out of the office.

Brooke didn't feel the threat of tears. She simply felt numb. Dylan led her to an empty desk, and she wordlessly sat down. A pretty brunette came by and told Dylan that he had a phone call, so he left, following after her clicking heels. Brooke seriously thought about leaving without filling out the paperwork. What was the point when she knew there was no hope that a loan would be approved?

She didn't know if it was stubbornness, desperation, or just the knowledge that she'd already come this far, but she sat there and filled every line out, despite her misgivings. Her mom didn't want her to be stuck anymore, and there was no way she could get unstuck by doing nothing. So she would try, even if she failed. When she received the rejection, maybe there would be a little comfort in knowing that at least she'd tried.

Dylan came by a few times to check on her. He didn't say anything, but looked over her shoulder at her progress, only to leave again. The bank itself was quiet, except for the annoying clicking of the brunette's shoes as she made near-incessant trips across the tile floor. Brooke wondered if all of her expeditions really were necessary, or if she just liked to hear the sharp clicking.

Finally finishing the packet, Brooke quietly took it up to one of the tellers, asking them to deliver it to Mr. Dunst. Then she made a quick exit before Dylan noticed.

Brooke spent the rest of the afternoon and all the next day filling out loan applications for every bank in Crossroads. She even made a trip to Brighton Falls and filled out a few there. She didn't know why she did it, but she had no other ideas to even attempt.

By the following day, she had exhausted all options and succumbed to tears. Not even bothering to change out of her pajamas, she spent the day in her robe, alternately watching sappy movies and blubbering into her Ramen noodles. Every single bank, credit union, and private lender had turned her down. Even after crying all day, she still had more rejections than she had tears to mourn them. She had received an emphatic 'no' from everywhere but Dylan's bank. Now, as the minute hand ticked past 5 o'clock, she knew it would be at least tomorrow before she received that final official rejection.

She tried to tell herself that at least she could rest well knowing that she had tried everything, but she must not have been very persuasive in her argument. The reasoning just fell flat with the knowledge that her rent was due at the beginning of next month, and she had no way to pay it.

Brooke's breath caught in a sob. *I just don't understand, Lord! What would you have me do?*

Brooke angrily brushed away the tears and swallowed down any further sobs. She had cried off and on all day, and it hadn't changed anything. She really should stop wishing things were different and accept her fate. After all, she didn't really have another choice.

She had come to the difficult decision that she would have to talk to her parents tomorrow. Borrowing the rent money from them just didn't seem smart considering she had no employment opportunities on the horizon. The better course would be to move in with them while her siblings tried to work their magic to get her a job, even if that job meant moving to Hollywood to pursue opportunities with her sister, London.

Brooke dejectedly eyed another package of Ramen noodles. Should she eat dinner or watch a movie first? Maybe she should just go to bed. Was 5:02 too early to go to bed for the night?

Finally deciding to forgo the noodles in favor of a bowl of popcorn, Brooke got off the couch, started the popcorn air popper, and poured in the kernels. She waited as white fluff started shooting out and into the bowl. As it came out, she doused it with a little butter and salt.

As soon as she flipped the machine to off, she heard a knock at the door.

Her heart leaped in panic. There was no way she was going to open the door in her bathrobe! She tiptoed quietly to the couch, hoping that whoever was at the door would simply assume she wasn't home and go away.

But the knock sounded again, this time more insistent.

Brooke brought her fingers to her mouth, literally chewing her nails in sudden anxiety.

Her phone rang, and she jumped almost a foot in pure startle reflex. The instant she landed back on the couch, she leaped off again, making a quick dive to grab the phone off the counter before it rang again.

Catching it in the middle of the second ring, Brooke answered with a barely audible whisper, "Hello?"

"Brooke, it's me. Come on. Open the door."

"Dylan!" Brooke yelped, letting her breath out in a rush. "Where are you? I'm not exactly available right now."

"I'm right outside your door," Dylan said, tapping a snappy beat on the door. "I know you're home. I can smell the popcorn."

Brooke bit her lip. Obviously, it wasn't going to work to just pretend she wasn't at home. "What are you doing here?" she asked, gazing at the front door with trepidation.

"Trying to talk to you! Now open up!"

"I can't, Dylan. I'm not dressed for company." Padding over to the door, she caught a glimpse of herself in the mirror. Her hair was half-way back in a messy ponytail that had started unraveling itself hours ago, and her eyes were puffy from crying. She looked scary, and there was no way she was going to let anyone see her like this, even if she had to be completely honest. "I have no makeup on, and I'm in my pajamas and bathrobe."

"I don't care!" Dylan insisted. "I need to talk to you. I need to tell you about your loan application."

"Just tell me over the phone!" Brooke said stubbornly.

"Come on, Brooke," Dylan said, tapping insistently at the door. "I am not going to talk to you on the phone when I'm standing three feet away behind the door. This is ridiculous. I'm hanging up the phone now. If you want to hear about your loan, then open the door."

The line went dead.

She really did want to know about the loan. Even though she was sure it was a no, she didn't want to wait until tomorrow to find out for sure.

Unlatching the deadbolt and turning the lock, she opened the door about two inches, just enough to peer out. "There, now you can tell me from right there."

Dylan laughed "I'm not going to tell you through the door, Brooke. Do you really want all of your neighbors to hear the details of your new business?"

"My new business? I got the loan?" Brooke swung the door wide.

Dylan stepped through quickly and shut the door behind him, as if afraid Brooke would change her mind and push him back out of the apartment.

"Not exactly," Dylan said hesitantly.

Brooke angrily folded her arms across her front. He'd just tricked her into opening the door.

"While your loan application was officially denied, I think there might be a slightly different option that would work," he explained.

His words didn't unfreeze her frosty attitude in the least, but he continued. "What if the building was purchased as an investment and you were allowed to rent it for your business? You wouldn't hold the mortgage or own the building, but getting approved to rent is much easier than getting approved to buy. I don't know the details yet, but I'm pretty sure it will be affordable, especially if you're willing to help with some of the building renovations and clean up. What do you think?"

Brooke's arms dropped. "Are you serious?" she asked, her breath catching.

"Yes," Dylan said, looking unsure of her reaction. "I know it isn't exactly what you had in mind but—"

Brooke threw her arms around him. "It's perfect! Thank you! Thank you! Thank you!"

Realizing that she was in his arms, Brooke suddenly pulled back. "Sorry," she said, wiping at the happy tears squeezing out the corners of her eyes.

Dylan swallowed. He looked pleased that he'd made her happy, but there was a sadness still about him. "Nothing is set in stone yet. There needs to be approval from a few different places, and Helen will need to sign the papers agreeing to the sale. I don't think it will be a problem, though."

"How soon can I get started?" Brooke asked, wondering how she would manage until she had some kind of income, especially if she had to pay up front for rent on the building.

"Helen wants a quick close on the property." Dylan wearily took a seat on one of the barstools as he explained. "You may be able to occupy as soon as next week and start taking orders as soon as you're able. I think we can arrange to have your rent deferred until the end of the month after you've earned some income. You're going to need some start-up money. When I get the green light, I'll have you go down to the shop and pick out any furnishings or supplies that you want from Helen. She's selling everything anyway, so it will save you some money to take over some of what she has. You will need money for that, plus you'll need a way to pay for your apartment rent, stock, and the other supplies you'll require before money starts coming in. We can probably get you set up with a small business loan that you can pay off on a monthly basis. Do you think $5,000 would be enough, or will you need $10,000?"

Brooke's mouth dropped open. "You can do that?"

"Sure," Dylan said with a shrug. "Richard wasn't right when he said the income potential of your business wouldn't be enough to sustain it. With the increase in tourism in the area, a shop like yours is necessary and will do very well. Any online business will be frosting on the cake. You have good ideas, a lot of talent, and a wide-open market with no competition. You will do very well."

Brooke looked at him, seeing the tiredness around his eyes. Though he hadn't given any clues, she knew he was the one who had made this happen. She was sure that, just like all of the others, Richard Dunst hadn't wanted to give her any kind of assistance. But Brooke could read between the lines and knew that Dylan had worked tirelessly to grant her dream. And she knew, without a doubt, that he'd done it for her.

Brooke impulsively stood close to Dylan's stool and planted a gentle kiss on the stubble of his cheek. "Thank you, Dylan. Thank you for convincing Mr. Dunst and whoever else you needed to in order to get approval. I know it wouldn't have happened without you."

Dylan opened his mouth to say something, but then he changed his mind and his eyes slid shut as if he was having difficulty with his emotions. "Please don't do that again, Brooke," he said hoarsely, finally opening his eyes and standing from the stool. He stepped away as if to get some distance. His hand ran through his hair, his tension obvious.

"I'm sorry!" Brooke said, immediately feeling embarrassed. "I know I'm yucky right now."

Dylan turned back to her, his eyes stormy, and he came back close. So close that he slowly reached out and fingered the band around her messy ponytail. He pulled it gently, watching mesmerized as her blonde hair fell loose. His fingers caressed through it separating the locks gently and watching the way they ran like spun gold over his hand.

"No, you're beautiful."

His hand dropped suddenly. "I need to go."

A myriad of emotions cascaded through Brooke. She didn't understand what this was between them. She couldn't define her emotions. One second she wanted to throw herself in his arms, and the next, she wanted to run away. The only thing she was sure of was that she didn't want him to leave.

"Do you want to stay for some popcorn and a cheesy movie?" Brooke asked, longing to delay him, if only for a little while.

For just an instant, Dylan looked as if he'd just been offered what he wanted most in life. Then he shook his head as if clearing it. "No, I can't. I need to make sure all of the paperwork is ready to go tomorrow morning. Thank you though."

"Rain check?" Brooke couldn't resist asking.

The corners of Dylan's mouth curved up in a sad smile. "We'll see."

After the door shut behind Dylan, Brooke's heart was slow to return to its normal pace. Instead, it was far too occupied beating a staccato pattern and whispering the lie that she was already more than half in love with Dylan Masters.

CHAPTER 20

"What are you doing here?" Helen gasped before the bell finished jingling at Brooke's entrance.

Brooke was startled. "I thought you knew!" she said, glancing around at the mess of packing boxes littering the store. "I was told I needed to come down and look through things to tell you what I wanted to purchase for my store."

She thought Dylan or someone at the bank would have told Helen that she was the one who would be taking over the building.

Like pressure building up in a boiling pot, Helen's face went from blank to irate in the space of about ten silent seconds. "You! I will NOT be selling a single thing to you! Nor will I consent to any sale of the building if you are involved! Where is my phone? I'm going to call this thing off right now! This is not at all acceptable!"

Panic shot up Brooke's spine, and she didn't know what to do. She thought the papers had been signed and there was no way Helen could back out. Dylan had told her that the money for her business loan was funded, the initial inspections complete, and that Helen had dotted every i and crossed every t. Brooke was to come over today and get started. But if there was some loophole...

Helen fumbled for her phone, lifting it out from beneath an empty box. Right as her hand touched it, it rang.

After her initial sharp greeting, Helen listened silently for about two minutes. It was like watching a balloon slowly deflate.

When she did speak again, she wore a smile. "Yes, I understand. It won't be a problem. We'll take care of it. Thank you very much!"

Helen pushed the end button and looked at Brooke brightly. "What would you like to see first, dear? Mr. Masters said to just make a list of what you want and let him know the price. He warned that he might dicker a bit, but that he would give a fair payment for anything you want or need. Then he will have the money funded to me from your assets."

In complete shock over the dramatic change in Helen, Brooke tried to swallow and gagged. She started coughing and couldn't manage to stop until Tylee rushed over with a cup of water.

"Are you okay, dear?" Helen asked, patting her gently on the back.

"I'm fine," Brooke finally managed, shying away from Helen's touch. She couldn't help but worry that, even though her former boss had a smile on her face, the hand patting her back might also hold a knife!

"Can I see the florist supplies?" she finally rasped out. "Maybe I can just pack them in some boxes to get them out of your way."

"Of course!" Helen said, leading the way to the back of the store. "Just let me know what you need. The furniture is up for grabs as well as any of the gift inventory. I have to say, my dear, I'm so relieved it is you who will be taking over. I wouldn't want to leave the building in the hands of an outsider, so I just think it's perfect."

Brooke couldn't help but look at the woman as if she'd lost her mind. Helen, however, didn't seem to notice and busied herself showing Brooke a wide variety of things she wanted Brooke to buy. Over the next few hours, it became clear to Brooke why Helen had a change of heart. Money. Dylan had told her that Brooke would buy what she wanted from the store. But no, she really didn't want the half-broken Christmas lights from the 1960s.

When it became clear that Brooke wasn't interested in the vast majority of her junk, her frustration and sour attitude began to show through once again.

"You only have three boxes of supplies," Helen complained. "I don't know how you expect to run a store without the necessities."

"I will buy what I need," Brooke said. "I'm really only interested in the more recent stock of floral supplies and a few of the shelves and tables."

"So you don't want to purchase any of the home décor stock?" she asked, waving her hand to indicate her eclectic assortment at the front of the store. "I would rather sell it to you at a discount than box it up to take it home to sell it."

Brooke tried not to wince at the idea. "No, thank you, Helen. Maybe you can have a yard sale and sell some of it. I'm going in a different direction with the store, so I can't really put it to use. Except for that toad right there. I want the toad."

Tylee reached down and held up the ugly toad that had caused all of the mess to begin with. "This one?" she asked, a puzzled look on her face. "Hey, isn't this—"

"Yes, that's the one," Brooke said, taking the toad from her friend and plopping it into one of her boxes. "Mr. Toad and I have a love-hate relationship, and I've decided to keep him around."

"He's bad luck if you ask me," Tylee mumbled.

Brooke just smiled. Tylee obviously didn't see what she saw. If not for the toad, the orders wouldn't have been messed up, Dylan wouldn't have insisted she accompany him to make apologies, and she wouldn't have lost her job. That certainly sounded like bad luck.

But if not for the toad, she also would have never gotten to know Dylan, Helen would never have decided to sell the store, she would have never had Dylan's help in getting approved for her business, and she would not be opening her own shop.

No, she was pretty sure she loved that little toad, and she would give the ugly creature a place of honor in her new shop—somewhere where she couldn't trip on him ever again.

The next few days passed in a blur. She ended up giving a great deal of help to Helen, spending hours and hours helping her sort and pack boxes. While the older woman never once thanked her, it was enough for Brooke that, as Tylee carried the last box out to the truck, Helen handed her the keys to the building.

"I guess I should tell you 'good luck,'" she said stiffly. "But I'll be really surprised if you last six months, especially since you refused to take any of the inventory of collectibles. Those really gave the shop flavor, and now? Well, you'll have to find out for yourself that people like to see those kinds of things in a shop. I guess we all have to follow our dreams, though. Best to get it out of your system and hope it doesn't ruin you financially."

With that touching bon voyage, Helen left to the tune of the little bells ringing overhead. The door fell shut, and Brooke walked over, reached up, and removed the bells. She set them down gently in a box of donation items, careful to make them ring as little as possible. She may get another set of bells for above the door, but it would not be this set.

She looked around at the empty shop, relishing in the silence. It was hers.

Thank you, Lord! she prayed, fully appreciating that God had used an ugly, little toad and some unfortunate circumstances to do something wonderful in her life. While she didn't expect everything to be smooth sailing from now on, she was grateful that God had gotten her this far and confident he would see her through tomorrow as well.

Mentally weighing the overwhelming task in front of her, she tried to imagine what it would look like in a few weeks. Her mom and sisters had offered to help, and she would definitely accept their free labor. But first, she needed something for them to do.

Taking out her paint samples, she walked around the shop and chose the colors. Dylan had already set up some renovations to begin as soon as tomorrow. Brooke was excited to be having new lighting and the floor redone, but she wanted to be ready with everything else as soon as she got the green light.

Satisfied that she at least had a few paint options to discuss with Dylan, she walked to the back of the shop and sat on a barstool pushed up to her working counter. She took out her supply catalogs and started making a list. She intended to place the order online for faster shipping. Then she could begin setting up her website tonight. Tomorrow she would pick up her mom, and they would go shopping at some thrift stores, looking for anything she could transform into something cute for the shop. She was also sure her mom would help make some of the decorations she hoped to design. There was just so much to do, especially when she really needed to be making at least some kind of income by the end of the month.

Brooke looked at the calendar and wondered exactly when the building rent would be due. She glanced at her list and mentally estimated the cost. Maybe she should be a little conservative and reserve enough of her start-up money to make her rent at the end of the month.

She frowned. It was rather difficult to know how to plan when she didn't yet know how much rent she would owe, or when it was due. Picking up her phone, she pressed the buttons to dial Dylan.

The only times she had spoken to him in the past week had been to discuss business. She had seen him twice to sign paperwork. But at none of those occasions had he said anything of a personal nature.

The phone rang.

"Hi, Brooke, can I call you back?" Dylan said by way of a greeting.

"Ummm… sure," Brooke said, caught off guard.

"Thanks. I'm leaving for Seattle on business in a few hours, and I'm trying to finish up a few things here at work before I go."

"Ok," Brooke said. "I'll talk to you later."

Then he was gone.

Brooke sighed and looked down at her list. She couldn't place her order or do anything else until she knew the specifics of her rent and how much money she had available to work with.

Had Dylan meant that he'd call her before he got on the plane, or after he got to Seattle?

Brooke glanced at the clock. It was still a few minutes before 5:00. Maybe she should just be brave and give Mr. Dunst a call. He would know the specifics of her arrangement with the bank. That way, she could find out and get her supplies ordered without needing to wait for or bother Dylan.

Before she could second-guess herself, she found the number for the bank, dialed it, and asked to speak to Mr. Dunst.

"Hello?" the voice cracked.

"Hi! This is Brooke Hutchins. I was just wondering if you could give me a little more information about the arrangement between my new business and the bank. For instance, can you tell me when my rent is due for this first month? Also, it would be helpful to know the amount, just so I know how much to plan for."

Brooke waited for a response but was met with only silence.

"Hello? Mr. Dunst? Are you there?" she asked as the quiet became increasingly uncomfortable.

"I'm sorry, Miss Hutchins," he finally responded. "I have no idea what you are talking about. Our bank denied your loan outright. If you have some kind of arrangement, it isn't with our bank."

"But Dylan said..." Brooke started, feeling the shock reverberate through her body.

"Oh, well that explains it," Mr. Dunst said, relief coloring his voice. "If you have some kind of arrangement for a business, it is likely through Dylan and his company directly. Dylan does investments for the bank, but he mostly deals with managing stocks, bonds, and higher end investments. I know he does own his own company on the side. Though he has bank approval for his side business, it is in no way associated with the bank. I think he deals mostly with real estate. If he told you about some arrangement, it was likely one of his deals. If you need more information, my advice is to check with Dylan."

Brooke stiffly thanked Mr. Dunst and ended the call.

Her hand shook as she pushed several other buttons on her phone and immediately dialed Dylan.

He picked up on the second ring. "Brooke, what do you need? I'm not quite done—"

Not letting him finish, Brooke jumped in. "I need you to tell me why you lied to me."

CHAPTER 21

B rooke drew her scarf up closer to her nose. She hoped Dylan wouldn't take too long. It was cold, and she didn't want to be here. But when Dylan had said they couldn't talk right then and told her to meet him at Trinity Ponds in twenty minutes, she didn't really have a choice. She knew why he'd chosen this location. It was on his way out of town to catch his flight in Brighton Falls. Since she desperately needed answers before he got on that plane, she'd hopped in her car and hurried to meet him.

Turning her face away from the slight breeze, she yanked her gloves up tighter on her hands and pulled her hat down lower. She supposed that she could wait in her car, but she had hoped the fresh air and peaceful scenery of the pond would calm her down. However, so far, it wasn't working.

She was still so very upset that she began pacing back and forth along that bank. Dylan had tricked her. Just as she was opposed to taking help from her family, she would never have accepted Dylan's offer if she knew it was a favor from him. She thought he had persuaded the bank, which she appreciated. She didn't know that he *was* the bank!

Brooke took deep breaths of the crisp air and tried to focus her attention on the flock of geese flying in a V against the leaden sky. Her feet crunched in the layer of snow that covered the ground, and she suspected that more snow was on the way.

She looked out across the pond, taking in the perfect reflection of sky in the water. It was beautiful here, and yet Brooke couldn't appreciate any of it. The area that was filled with people fishing, swimming, or boating, was now shrouded in silence, the clusters of evergreens crowding the shore seeming to be in the deep sleep of winter, like everything else, except Brooke. She was the lone divergent in the peaceful scene, and nothing she tried made her blend in just a little bit better.

She was angry.

"I didn't lie to you."

Brooke jumped at the sound of Dylan's voice right behind her. So intent was she on her own thoughts that she hadn't heard his car or his approach.

She turned. "I called the bank, Dylan. I know that they did not buy the building for my business, nor did they fund my business loan. You did."

"No, my company did," Dylan clarified.

"It's the same thing! I would have never accepted the offer if I'd known the truth. I didn't want special treatment. I didn't want anyone's help. I wanted to do it on my own!"

"Why, Brooke? Why did it have to be on your own? So you could prove that you were just as good as your siblings? To show that you should be a 'Brooklyn' and not just a Brooke?"

"That's not fair," Brooke said, her eyes instantly filling with tears. "I just…" she sniffled. "I just feel deceived."

Dylan shut his eyes. "Brooke, I'm sorry. I didn't lie to you, but I did let you believe something that wasn't the complete truth. I was afraid that if you knew that it was my company, that your pride would get in the way and you wouldn't take the opportunity."

He took a deep breath and explained. "I own an investment company. We deal mostly in real estate. We buy older buildings, renovate, and rent them out, thereby investing in an entire area. We also have a few other projects targeting community improvement, tourism, and revenue generated from those sources."

Suddenly, things clicked in Brooke's mind. "You mean, you're the one responsible for the changes in Crossroads? You're the one who has been improving the buildings and businesses and bringing more tourism to the area?"

Dylan shrugged. "Crossroads is a great community to invest in."

"That's why you were at the community center the day of the baby shower!" Brooke said.

Dylan nodded. "The community center has been a big project. It is owned by my company. I was speaking to the manager, and he was giving me an update on the scheduled events."

Brooke suddenly felt horrible. This man was a hero in so many ways, and yet she had treated him terribly. He had already brought so much good to Crossroads and the lives of its residents. "So it really is a company, not just you, who invested in my business?"

"Correct." Dylan's forehead relaxed in relief that she was finally understanding. "I got tired of seeing small business owners come into the bank, trying to save their livelihood, only to be turned down for loans. So I started my own company. I got approval from my bank, and since the investment work I do for them really has nothing to do with small-town real estate, they were fine with it. I think it's actually improved their reputation in the community because I approve many of those they do not."

"I just don't like the feeling that I owe you," Brooke said with a grimace, unable to let go of the feeling of discontent. "That I have to pay my rent to you. What happens if I'm late on a payment? It seems like business is a good way to complicate a friendship, and not in a good way."

"Listen, Brooke, it really is a company," Dylan said, a tinge of weariness coloring his voice. "I am involved early in the initial investment and the renovation, but after that, all of the billing and payments are outsourced to a separate entity that I've hired to handle them. You won't pay me directly. No one does. I don't keep track of who pays what when. If you miss a payment, I won't even know unless you tell me. It will be handled exclusively through the billing company."

Brooke nodded, thinking for the first time that this arrangement may be doable after all. "So it's all business? There was no preferential treatment toward me? You didn't make my business happen just because of our friendship?"

Dylan scowled. "There you said that word again. 'Friendship.' I really don't believe that's what we have. At least, not all of what we have. And no, I can't really answer that question because I don't know. I won't lie to you or pretend that I am not completely biased where you are concerned."

"And that's the part I have a problem with," Brooke confessed, turning away and kicking a rock toward the pond. "Now I feel like an imposter—like I don't deserve to have my own business. I wanted to do things on my own. I didn't want preferential treatment from anyone. Not from family or... friends," she finished, lamely flapping her hands down.

"Networking is smart," Dylan insisted. "And nobody accomplishes anything without help. If you insist on doing things alone, you'll be stuck in the mud forever. But if that bothers you, then I'm sure you'll find it even more disconcerting to know that I can't be one of your 'friends.'"

"I don't understand," Brooke said, turning back to him to try to read his expression. "You mean, we can't be friends since we're now business associates?"

Dylan scoffed and shook his head. "You really don't get it, do you? You have no idea what you do to me."

Brooke looked at him with irritation. She really wasn't as clueless as he seemed to think. "You like me. I get it. You wanted me to go on a date with you. I said no. Since that obviously doesn't happen very often, it seems to be driving you a little crazy. But what I don't understand is why you can't just let it go. You said before that what you really want is a friend, not necessarily a romantic attachment. That's what I'm offering, and yet you are refusing. So no, I don't get it."

Dylan suddenly stepped forward, close enough that their coats touched. She looked up to find his face inches from her own, so close that she could feel his warm breath and see the streaks of fire in his gray eyes. "I can't be your friend because every time I see you, I want you to be mine. Every time your hair blows in the breeze, I want it to be my fingers running through it. Every time you laugh, I want to be the reason. Every time your lips smile, I want to be kissing them. Every time you are upset, I want to rescue you and make it better. Brooke, every time my phone rings, I want it to be you. I am completely, hopelessly, *not* your friend."

His fingers reached out, brushing back a strand of blonde hair. Then they happened to fall on her cheek, and she leaned into their warmth.

"You say all that, and yet I don't believe you," Brooke whispered. "The only allure of me is that I'm unattainable. You could have any woman you want. *I* don't make sense."

A soft smile played about his lips, giving brief glimpses of his dimples. "Brooke, I've tried all different varieties of women, but I'm not interested in the ones with a stellar resume. I want the kind of woman who will tell me off when she thinks I'm wrong, and yet rescue me when I'm in too deep. I want someone who will take the hit for another person, taking the blame just to protect someone she cares about. Just like you did for Tylee. I want someone who is brilliant at problem solving, the most artistic, creative person I know, and who likes to help with Sunday school in her spare time. I don't want Janice, Celeste, Kiffany, Monica, Destiny, Shauna, Geneva, Paris, Athens, Timbuktu, or any other woman on the globe. I just want Brooke."

As he spoke, Brooke watched his face, mesmerized by the way lights flickered through his eyes. There was no doubt that he meant every word he said, and her erratically beating heart longed to believe it.

She steeled her heart, trying to force it to behave and slow down. "Dylan, you seem to have such a lofty ideal of me. But I would disappoint you and soon fall off your pedestal."

Dylan tipped his head back and laughed outright. "Hardly! Trust me, Brooke, I have no illusions about you. I am quite familiar with your faults. You see, your faults and I have met quite a few times already. You are stubborn, quick to anger, experience fear so strong it paralyzes you, and you have this maddening inferiority complex, especially where your family is concerned. You also don't like coffee, which I view as a definite fault as well."

"And those are just the faults you know about," Brooke grumbled. "Trust me, I have plenty more."

"And I would love the chance to thoroughly investigate every single one of them," Dylan said without missing a beat.

Brooke rolled her eyes. Then, shaking her head, she said seriously, "Dylan, you have a flight to catch. I know we can't stand here and argue all night. The bottom line is that we would not make a good match. Though I like you and won't deny the attraction, I also know that a relationship has to be built on more than that. We don't have the same core values, and because of that, eventually you would hurt me, and I would hurt you."

Dylan's face clouded in confusion, and for the first time, he seemed taken aback. "What do you mean?"

Brooke bit her lip, dreading the need to explain. "I mean that I'm a Christian and you're not. I know you're searching, and you've gone to church a few times. But you still aren't sure about that which is the most important thing in my life."

"Brooke, I'm sorry," Dylan said, rubbing his hand down the stubble of his chin. "It's like I sometimes have conversations with you in my mind, but then, when I try to talk to you, something happens and what I intend to tell you never comes out. I've been attending church and meeting with the pastor. Over a month ago, I repented and gave my life to the Lord. I think part of the reason I didn't tell you right away was that I didn't want you to think I'd done it because of you. This is a life decision for me. I got to the point that, with knowing who I was and who God was, I couldn't turn away. I'm still learning, and I'm not a perfect Christian. But I know God won't give up on me, and I won't give up on Him. I've finally found what I've been searching for. Like the Bible says, I've found the living water, and nothing satisfies my soul like it. I'm saved, and I intend to spend my life serving Him and doing as He wills. I agree that He is the most important priority, and I don't want you to be under the mistaken impression that I would have it any other way."

Brooke swallowed and looked out to watch tiny ripples make ever widening circles in the pond. "Wow, Dylan, I didn't know. I am so happy for you. I sincerely hope you find in the Lord the happiness you've been searching for."

"But..." Dylan said. "It sounds like there's a 'but.'"

Brooke sighed. "But I still don't believe we share the same values." Brooke bravely looked him straight in the eye, wanting him to understand what she was saying, because if he really heard and understood, he would have no argument left. "I would never be comfortable being your girlfriend. I see the way women look at you. It's like you're a piece of decadent chocolate cake they all want. I couldn't live like that, constantly looking over my shoulder to see if and when someone else caught your eye."

"What if that chocolate cake belonged only to you?"

A cool breeze floated by, making Brooke shiver. At least, that was her excuse.

"Come on, Dylan," she said, her frustration mounting. "Every woman wants a taste of the cake. All I have to do is look at your track record. You haven't ever had a girlfriend longer than six months. Why would I be different? The answer is that I wouldn't be different. You'd send me flowers with your name not signed, and maybe that would buy you a couple of dates. But eventually, you would tire of me the way you tire of everyone else."

His own frustration now matching her own, he responded. "Haven't you been listening. I've been saying that you aren't like anyone else! The way I feel about you isn't anything like the way I've felt about anyone else ever!"

"And how many of your women believed that same thing? I'm sure they all thought they were different too. They thought they were 'the one' for Dylan Masters. But you toyed with them and then threw them away when you were tired of them. I don't trust you. I can't trust you!"

As soon as the words fell from her mouth, Brooke realized what she'd done. She saw the pain flash across his eyes as if she had physically hit him. She instantly longed to snatch the words back and hide them away where they could never do any damage, but it was too late.

Dylan gritted out, "Look, I understand that deep down, you just don't like me. I get that you don't approve of my choices. I'm not perfect. I make mistakes and fully admit that I can't manage to like a woman longer than about three weeks. Maybe I should have given up on dating long ago. So feel free to make fun of my frequent dating or criticize me for commitment phobia. But please don't accuse me of not treating women well. I have seen way too many men who treated women terribly, and consider it one of my goals in life to never be like them. Dislike me all you want, but please don't claim I do the one thing I most abhor."

Brooke's mind flashed back to what he'd said about his mother and all the men who had gone through her life. She also remembered that he was highly offended by his brother-in-law's treatment of his sister. And she had just likened him to the villains he detested.

"Dylan, I'm so sorry," she said, reaching out and touching his arm with her gloved hand. "I didn't mean any of that. I know that when I feel backed into a corner, I come out swinging. I say things that I regret—things that I don't even mean—because I'm trying to make myself feel better."

She looked at him imploringly. "See why I just want to be friends? I hate that we are already hurting each other!"

Dylan said nothing, just stared out at the pond.

Brooke spoke gently. "Dylan, you want me to be your girlfriend. But the problem is that I could never believe that you are my boyfriend. You're too handsome, too alluring. I would see other women look at you and never feel like I could compete or be worthy of keeping your attention. I'm not that special. With all that attention, you would eventually want to move on to greener pastures, and I wouldn't blame you. I couldn't keep you forever, Dylan. Since I already know the end, I'd rather not start the beginning.

"So that's it, then? That's the core of your objection. Fear. You're afraid of caring. Afraid of loving because you might get hurt."

Brooke didn't respond. It was Brooke's turn to look away from him. She looked at the ground, at the way the snow gave way beneath her boot. She looked anywhere but at him.

"Well then, maybe you're right," he said regretfully. "Maybe there just isn't enough spark on your part. Maybe you don't feel about me the way that I feel about you. In my mind, any potential hurt in the future is worth it, if it will give me any relief from the current pain of not being with you."

Brooke shook her head. She had nothing left. He had challenged and met every argument. She had even pushed him away with her hurtful anger, and still, he came back, asking her to give him a chance.

And in the end, the fear was too much.

"Goodbye, Dylan," she whispered, turning to hurry away.

But he caught her arm. And before her next breath, his lips were on hers. She melted into him as his arms came around her. His kiss wasn't gentle, but it wasn't demanding either. It was insistent, as if he wanted to make sure she understood what he felt while also exploring what she felt in return.

And her heart met his fully. There was no hesitation. All arguments fell flat, and every reason she should turn and run scattered like the final leaves of fall. She kissed him back with every ounce of her being. It was a moment her heart had been waiting for, but one she also knew would never be repeated.

Brooke's hat fell off as Dylan's fingers buried themselves in her hair. Her response only fueled his more, and Brooke realized he may never let her go. If she just relaxed into him just a little, she somehow knew the ferocity of the kiss would mellow to be less urgent. But, if that happened, Brooke knew there would be no going back. She could not accept his love and walk away.

She teetered on the edge, longing to be his, and yet…

Brooke ripped her lips away from his.

"I'm sorry!" She gasped. "I can't. I just can't."

Then she turned and ran away, not looking back even once.

CHAPTER 22

"**D**id you see this?" **Tylee** squealed, plopping a newspaper down on the desk in front of Brooke.

Brooke couldn't help but smile. "Yes, I did. I had no idea Aimee was going to do that. She did an amazing job!"

It was early morning at Brooke's new shop, and the article Tylee was touting was one that had been in yesterday's local paper. It had been submitted by Aimee Maxwell, the woman who had accidentally been sent a bouquet from her deceased mother. Instead of an article describing the hurt and outrage of such a mistake, Aimee wrote about the blessing of receiving flowers from her mom on her birthday. She firmly believed that the mistake was not by accident and took it as a special gift from heaven. While the article did explain how the mistake had happened due to the florist reprinting the orders from the wrong year, it only served to paint Brooke in a good light. According to Aimee, it was a mistake that could have happened to anyone, and yet it was used by God to bring blessing in an extraordinary way. It was a beautifully penned article and one that absolved Brooke of any wrongdoing.

Tylee's excitement didn't die down even a little as she continued to practically dance around the room "People are talking about it everywhere, even in Brighton Falls! The newspaper says the article is going viral, and they are fielding requests from national news programs! You may even get to be interviewed on national TV!"

Brooke laughed. "I doubt it. If anyone will be interviewed, it will be Aimee. It's a lovely story and a lovely article. I am beyond thankful that she did what I could not. Maybe my reputation will be sewn back together after this!"

"I'll say!" Tylee said. "It looks like the answering machine is full, and I haven't even checked the online orders! But if any news programs or talk shows call, then I'm taking off to do the interview, even if you don't come with me!"

Brooke hadn't yet had a chance to relax and think things through since the newspaper came out yesterday, but she had a feeling that once she did, she would be in tears. God had arranged for her defense when she hadn't been able to defend herself. By signing that nondisclosure document, Brooke hadn't been able to tell anyone her side of the story, but Aimee had managed to do that by detailing the steps it took for the mistake with her bouquet to happen. Brooke had touched base with Aimee several times since their initial conversation, but the other woman seemed to have even more information than what Brooke had ever dispensed. Though her friend had mentioned nothing, Brooke strongly suspected that Tylee had been more than willing to share information with Aimee in Brooke's stead.

God had not only fit the pieces of the puzzle together to get Aimee her bouquet, He'd also miraculously given Brooke the business of her dreams and arranged to exonerate her reputation.

"What do you think?" Brooke asked, holding up a sign she'd just finished painting. She'd gotten to work early to finish it. Now, while it dried, she'd get her actual workday started.

"I love it," Tylee said.

"Of course, I ordered a large sign to face the road. It should be here in a few days. But I'll put this one by the front door."

"It really is perfect, Brooke," Tylee said happily, examining the sign from every angle. "I'm really glad you didn't just call the shop "Crossroads Floral." This is a much better, more creative name that completely fits."

Brooke smiled. "'The Out of the Blue Bouquet.' Most people won't know the history of accidental orders that got us started, but even then, it's still a cute name that fits. I like it, even if nobody else does."

Brooke reached down and lovingly brushed a stray shard off the sign. It was a simple sign made of barn wood given to her by Celeste Davenport. Brooke had painted the name with fancy black and white letters and intermingled them with tiny blue forget-me-nots. Brooke couldn't help but smile when she looked at it. The sign, and the name itself, served as a reminder that God was bringing a whole lot of good out of a bad situation.

"Now that the sign is done, we'd better get to work!" Brooke said, cleaning up her paint and brushes before walking over to the answering machine. "Are you ready?" she asked Tylee.

Situating herself at the computer with her document open, Tylee nodded. "This first time through, I will take notes and write down all the contact numbers. Then we'll listen to everything again so we can check it all before making the callbacks."

Tylee was actually quite competent if given specific instructions and the resources to be able to accomplish her tasks. She was excellent with using the computer and was an extremely fast typist.

There had been no question in Brooke's mind that she would hire Tylee to be her employee, and thankfully, her friend had immediately said yes. Brooke needed help since there was no way she could manage the shop, create the arrangements, and make the deliveries. Even with just two of them, it was going to be difficult to handle all the work, but until the shop started producing a good income, Tylee was all she could afford. She was just thankful that the younger woman had jumped at the chance of working at Brooke's shop.

The last two weeks had been busy with getting everything set up. Tylee had been a godsend and helped with all tasks, from painting, to decorating, to helping create some of their handmade products on display. This was only their third official day open.

With it also being the day after Aimee's article appeared in the newspaper, Brooke seemed to have turned from villain to hero in the eyes of the public, and their orders were piling in.

Brooke paid attention for the first few messages, but then her mind drifted back over the past few weeks, and suddenly a cloud drifted over her good mood. The only thing that hadn't gone well was the situation with Dylan. Brooke didn't even know if you could term it a "situation" because she hadn't actually talked to him since she left him at Trinity Pond. In all likelihood, her refusal had finally gotten through to Dylan, and he had given up on her and moved on.

And the really sad part about that was that Brooke had spent the last two weeks regretting her actions. Attending church had only made it worse when a disappointed little girl in her class had asked eagerly where Mr. Masters was. She hated seeing the disappointment on Jaycee's face, and she hated, even more, knowing that Dylan wasn't there because of Brooke.

With a little time and distance, she realized she had treated Dylan horribly. He had been simply asking for a chance, and though she cared about him deeply, she was too choked by fear to respond the way her heart longed for her to.

Her mind had played the "what if" game nearly constantly in the past two weeks. What if she would have stayed in his arms? What if she had done as he asked and given them a chance to be a couple?

In all honesty, she still didn't know if she could do it. There was no logical reason for her to refuse Dylan. With his faith commitment, he seemed paperwork perfect, but the fear was still overwhelming at times. She knew that her past experiences with her boyfriends, along with her inferiority issues, had left her damaged in some ways. Though she knew in her head that it didn't make sense, it felt like she was dealing with a phobia, and she didn't know that she would ever overcome it, even if she desperately wanted to.

She had gone over and over that evening by the pond, chiding herself and wishing she'd dared to do things differently. It was likely too late now. Brooke had repeatedly tried to call Dylan, but she'd never gotten a response. She knew he was traveling. From his social media posts, it looked like he had spent nearly all of the last two weeks in Seattle. She'd seen pictures of him smiling by the Space Needle, and with a happy group of others on a ferry in the Puget Sound. In a few of the pictures he'd posted, there seemed to be several women looking his way with admiration, and Brooke was sure that by this time, he'd likely found someone else who was more than willing to be his girlfriend.

Knowing that it was too late, knowing that she probably wouldn't be able to get past her fear anyway, and knowing that even if she did, Dylan would inevitably hurt her, she still let her mind drift all too often to the few moments when she was in his arms at the pond. She relived the sensations of feeling his arms around her and recognized that she had never felt more of a sense of belonging than she'd felt then. She tasted his warm lips on hers and felt an almost physical ache of her heart.

Suddenly, the message playing on the answering machine sent up a red flag that penetrated the fog of Brooke's memories. "What was that?" she asked, coming back to the present to push the stop button on the machine. Then she pressed the repeat button and listened carefully.

"Hi, this is Brittany, and, well, um… I was wondering if you could give me a call back. I was interested in sending some flowers to someone, but I kinda want it to be one of those accidents, like you did a while ago. I mean, I'll pay for it and everything, but I don't really want to claim responsibility for it, if that makes sense. Anyway, I can try to explain it better when you call me back."

Brooke started laughing before the girl could give her phone number. "Tylee, did you hear that? This lady wants me to pretend to make an accidental order."

Tylee laughed, "I heard that message the first time through, but I didn't know what she was talking about. What do you think? Can we do that?"

"No!" Brooke said, shaking her head adamantly. "I'm not going into the business of accidental orders. If Brittany wants to send a blank card or say that the flowers are from a secret admirer, we can do that. We just can't deal with accidents, either pretend or real!"

Tylee had Brooke press the repeat button one more time so she could write down the callback number, and then she announced, "Ok, Brooke, I think I'm done," Tylee said. "I'll print out your list of callbacks."

"Ok, thanks," Brooke said. "I'll get started."

She sighed and walked over to the printer to retrieve the paper. In spite of the humorous last message, she was still trying to shake off the last visages of memories to focus on the task at hand. Every time her mind drifted to Dylan, she'd wonder the same thing: Maybe Dylan was right. The past two weeks without him had been more miserable than she could imagine they ever could be with him.

Brooke picked up the paper and made herself focus enough to start calling. Midway through the list, she vaguely realized that Tylee had stopped working at the computer long enough to tell a UPS driver where to put a delivery of packages.

After getting the information for an order, Brooke hung up and dialed the first numbers of the last person on the list, when Tylee stopped her.

"Hey, Brooke? Do you have any idea what this box is?" she asked. "It doesn't seem to be from the same company or look like your other boxes of supplies." She turned the long, thin box around in her hands. "It's for Dylan!" she exclaimed.

Brooke hurried over. "What do you mean?"

"It says, 'Dylan Masters and Brooke Hutchins' in the recipient box!"

Brooke took the box from Tylee and saw that her friend was correct. She looked at it carefully as she took it over to the counter and realized it was from one of those online florist companies that do their own shipping.

She cut the tape open with scissors and pulled back the flaps to reveal twelve long stem roses and a vase well-cushioned inside. While Tylee was oohing and ahhing over the assortment of pastel roses, Brooke carefully inspected the packaging, figuring out how the company had managed to so effectively ship it.

Tylee picked up the instructions and hurried to pour water in the vase while Brooke found the card. As soon as she saw it, Brooke grinned, instantly knowing the purpose of the bouquet. A small picture had been digitally printed to go along with the message on the cardstock. It was the picture of a smiling woman with russet-colored hair and a man with glasses who looked like he'd just won the lottery.

To Dylan: Please consider this your 'in-your-face-bouquet.'

To Brooke: Thank you.

Tylee, of course, wanted all the details, which Brooke explained as best she could. But the retelling of a crazy ex-girlfriend who had managed to find her own happy ending didn't quite compare to the first-hand experience with Judge Janice Thornton.

It was a story that Celeste might actually appreciate more than Tylee. Brooke had kept in touch with Celeste since they first met in November. Even before Brooke had mentioned Janice in one of their conversations, Celeste had already heard plenty about the colorful judge from Dylan. Brooke made a mental note to tell Celeste about Janice's flowers when she visited the farm this weekend. Though she was still nervous about Celeste's invitation to go for a ride with Jezebel, she also thought that a trip to the farm and a visit with her friend might be exactly what she needed to get her mind off some memories that wouldn't leave her alone.

That, or it could remind her of when she had first gone there with Dylan.

Brooke sighed, her momentary delight over Janice's flowers now snuffed out again by her thoughts that ever magnetized to the one she really needed to forget.

So Brooke did the only thing she knew that would make her

thoughts less painful, she threw herself into work so that she would have no spare time or energy to think of Dylan. She finished her callbacks, finally calling the woman who was requesting an accidental order. After explaining the options that were available, the woman opted for a blank card. Though curious as to the story of why she desired to send flowers secretly and to whom, Brooke resisted the urge to ask and just took the information for the order.

Several hours later, Brooke looked at the clock and realized it was past lunchtime. She and Tylee had both been working hard taking multiple orders, organizing supplies, working on the shop itself, and filling today's orders. Brooke put the last few flowers in place in a bouquet and pronounced that all the orders were ready for delivery.

"Why don't you go grab some lunch, Tylee, and then you can make the deliveries," Brooke said.

"Brooke, I think we have a problem," she said, her face intent on the computer in front of her.

Concerned, Brooke hurried over to where Tylee sat at the desk. They'd already processed the online orders for the day, so Brooke didn't understand what the problem could be. Though she had a few items besides flowers available on her online shop, there shouldn't be any problem with those. Both Brooke and Tylee had taken the time to learn the ins and outs of the programs they used, and Tylee was very good with computers. So far, they had placed all non-local orders online without a hitch, and the orders from her personal shop were completely separate.

The disturbing thing was that if Tylee thought there was a problem, there likely was.

"How far out can an online order be scheduled for?" Tylee asked.

"I'm not sure what the program allows," Brooke answered, trying to peer over her shoulder. "I'd have to check, but I would guess maybe a year. Why do you ask?"

"Because a massive number of online orders have come through today, and some of them have a date as far out as two years!" Tylee leaned back to show Brooke a long list with a variety of future dates.

"There has to be some mistake. That's too many orders to come through in one day, and there has to be something wrong with the dates. Nobody is going to schedule a flower delivery that is two years from now!"

"Do you think it's possible that we were hacked in some way?" Tylee asked nervously.

"I don't know," Brooke answered, hating the feeling of dread building up in her. "Let me sit down and see if I can figure it out."

Tylee moved from the seat, and Brooke slid into her place. She took some deep breaths, trying to calm her already frayed nerves. This really couldn't happen again, could it? She had already dealt with a nightmare of floral mistakes, and the thought of history repeating itself was enough to send her to the verge of a panic attack.

"Have you looked at the orders individually?" Brooke asked.

"Not yet. I saw the large number and figured something had to be wrong somewhere."

Brooke clicked on one of the orders. The screen came up, and at the name on the order, Brooke's heart jumped into her throat.

Dylan Masters was listed as a sender.

Tylee wasn't looking at the computer screen anymore, but was gazing at the calendar with a puzzled expression. Obviously thinking out loud, she mused, "The weird thing is that each order really did seem to be placed individually. They each have a different time stamp of a few minutes apart, and they each have the note section filled out. I'd think it wouldn't be so detailed or spread out if it was the work of a hacker just trying to bombard our system. The other strange thing is that if you look at the dates, they are all two weeks apart. The first order is two weeks from today. But if the orders were placed today, where is today's order?"

With her heart beating wildly, Brooke clicked another button.

Brooke Hutchins was listed as the recipient.

The musical tinkling of the new bells over the door instantly drew both Brooke and Tylee's gaze up.

Dylan Masters walked through the door with a large bouquet in his hand.

CHAPTER 23

S ilence filled the shop as Dylan's gaze collided with Brooke's, and the whole world seemed to hold its breath.

"Ummm... I think I'm going to go ahead and take that lunch break now, Brooke," Tylee murmured. Grabbing her coat and purse, Tylee swept by Dylan at the door and managed to flip the sign to "Closed" on her way out.

Brooke stood and stepped hesitantly toward Dylan. "Hi," she whispered. Her gaze eagerly took him in, thinking that he looked better than he had in her imagination. He wasn't wearing a suit today, but a simple gray button up shirt that was left untucked from his jeans. His dark hair fell back from his forehead in a perfect wave, bringing more attention to the gray eyes that studied her just as closely as she studied him.

"Hi," Dylan whispered back. Glancing down at the flowers in his hand, he stepped forward and held them out to Brooke. "These are for you. I'm not exactly good at flower arranging. I did have them in a jar, but it wasn't very pretty, so I just wrapped them in a wet rag and then put some plastic wrap around it. I figured you could put them in a vase and arrange them the way you wanted. I'm sorry it isn't like a professional arrangement or anything."

Brooke had spent the whole time watching Dylan's face as he rambled through his explanation. He was nervous. Brooke had never seen him nervous, and that kind of fascinated her.

Ripping her eyes away, she glanced down at his outstretched hand and gasped.

The bouquet was a bunch of blue hydrangea in a variety of breath-taking shades. On one side, pink bougainvillea peeked out their bright heads.

"Are those...?" she started. But then she knew. After all, she would recognize those flowers anywhere. "Those are my grandma's flowers."

She took them in her hands, lifted them up, and buried her face in the soft blue petals. At the aroma, a thousand different wonderful memories of her grandma rushed over her. When she finally drew her face away, tears streamed down her cheeks. "Dylan, how did you get my grandmother's flowers?"

Dylan shrugged, a gentle smile playing about his lips. "Southern California was on my way home."

"From Seattle?" she asked incredulously.

Though his eyes were dancing, he just shrugged again, refusing to say more.

"But how could you do this? How did you know which house was hers? How did you get the flowers when the house belonged to someone else?"

As if realizing that she wasn't going to let it go, Dylan explained. "Geneva can be a very helpful friend to have. She gave me the address. Then I just went to the house and knocked on the door. The owners were very nice, and once they heard my story, they were only too happy to let me pick some flowers for the girl I love."

"For the girl you... love?" Though she mouthed the last word, no sound came out.

"Oh, I forgot to give you the card!" Dylan said, handing her a plain piece of cardstock bearing handwritten words.

These flowers are from the garden of someone who loved you,

and delivered to you by someone who loves you.

Love,

Dylan

He'd signed his name. The man who always left his name off his flower orders had signed his name. And not just once. Around the border, and at random spots on the card, he'd written his name in various sizes.

"Did you see my name?" he asked eagerly.

Brooke couldn't help but smile. "I almost missed it," she teased. "It's a good thing you signed it more than once."

Dylan nodded proudly. Then, after a pause, his expression turned bittersweet, and he spoke. "The answer to your question is 'yes,' Brooke. Yes, I love you. And I'm sorry, but because of that, I can't just walk away. I'm sorry that I didn't return your calls while I was in Seattle, but I wanted to wait and talk to you in person. I know you've said you don't want to be my girlfriend, and I understand that. But I also know the way you kissed me. You care about me, much more than you admit. I'm sorry I can't walk away. You're just going to have to forgive me over and over again. Though I'll give you space, I'm not going to stop trying to win you, not after discovering that you return my feelings. I know you're afraid. I know you're scared of being hurt. But if you can't be my girlfriend, can you please just let me be your boyfriend?"

Brooke swallowed. Instead of answering his question, she asked one of her own. "The orders? You placed the other orders?" She hesitantly looked up at him, meeting his gaze.

His eyes shone with sincerity as he spoke. "Yes, I did. Your website only allowed me to place orders for the next two years. I'm not going to be sending you flowers and then sending another woman flowers two weeks from now. They'll all be for you. I'm not going anywhere, Brooke. Just give me a chance. Just like you are not like your sisters, I'm not like your other boyfriends. I'm not going to cheat on you or lose interest in favor of someone else. You are the dream, Brooke, and I will spend all of my time trying to deserve you."

Taking a deep breath, Brooke finally spoke, but the best she could do was a whisper. "You say all the right things and more, Dylan. I have spent most of the last two weeks regretting what I did to you. But at the same time, I can't seem to flip a switch and turn my fear off. I believe you have the best of intentions, but I think of all of the girlfriends you've had, and I don't want to be just another on your list of exes."

She had to be crazy. The Crossroads Casanova had said he loved her, and she was hesitating. What was wrong with her?

Not to be deterred, Dylan took her reluctance in stride. "Brooke, I don't want you to be my girlfriend, I want to be your boyfriend. I'm not looking for you to satisfy me or make me happy. That comes from the Lord. But I can't imagine anything more wonderful than getting to spend my life making you happy-er. I can't promise I won't hurt you. In fact, I'm sure I will at some point. But I can promise that if you trust me with your heart, it will be worth it. Just so you know, I'm not offering you a ring or asking you for forever right now, but that is my goal. If you give us a chance, I fully intend to always belong to you, and to you only."

Brooke's eyes slid shut and she prayed. She prayed that God would give her the strength to trust and walk in the path that she believed He was opening up. Dylan truly was everything she'd ever wanted and more. His faith in God was obvious, as was, for whatever reason, his love for her.

With her eyes still closed, Brooke spoke, "I have spent my life feeling like I didn't measure up. It is completely foreign to me to hear someone like you say these things about me."

Feeling a feather-light touch to her jawline, she opened her eyes to see Dylan's face above hers, his eyes intense. Carefully, his fingers moved up to caress a slight scar, right along her hairline—a reminder of that first day they spent together. "Then I'll need to repeat them often for you until you can believe that they are true. Brooke Hutchins, I am so glad you aren't a Brooklyn. There's no one else like you. God made you exactly how He wanted, and you are exactly who I want."

Brooke faltered, looking away from the intensity of his eyes.

But as she glanced down, her gaze lit on an ugly, little ceramic toad peeking out from where she had placed him behind the door.

Then, with a deep breath, she looked back up at Dylan and smiled. "I've thought a lot about the past few months—how we were accidentally brought together. If I hadn't messed up your orders, then we would have never spent the day together. I wouldn't have given you the time of day, and you would have never known I existed. So..."

Brooke paused for the beat of several seconds, gathering her courage. "*What if* I reached up to give you a hug and thank you for the beautiful flowers?" While holding her flowers in one hand, she acted out her own words, reaching up and wrapping her free arm around Dylan.

Looking up at him, she continued to speak, trying to communicate her heart. "I know you went out of your way and went through a lot of trouble for the flowers, and you did it for me. *What if* I told you how much they mean to me, and how I feel that they are the most beautiful, most special gift I've ever been given? Then *what if* I went to kiss your cheek and missed?"

Standing on her tiptoes, she slowly went to plant a gentle kiss on his cheek but found his lips instead. The touch was electric. It was sweet, it was passionate, and it was completely full of joy.

Drawing back to get a breath, Brooke spoke again. "After a kiss like that, a girl might completely forget herself. She might confess that, though she tried so hard to prevent it, she'd fallen completely in love. And though she's scared stiff..."

Brooke swallowed with difficulty but held Dylan's gaze steady. "Dylan Masters, will you be my boyfriend?"

"A thousand times 'yes!'" Dylan laughed. Picking her up off her feet, he swung her around.

Finally setting her down, he whispered mischievously, "Now, Brooke, *what if* you just found yourself a boyfriend for at least the next sixty years?"

Then he kissed her quite thoroughly, proving that sixty years might not be quite long enough.

With one arm, Brooke clung to Dylan as he held her close. With the other hand, she still clutched her blue bouquet.

And she was determined to not let either of them go.

THE END

DISCUSSION QUESTIONS

S uggested discussion group questions for *Out of the Blue Bouquet* by Amanda Tru.

If not for the toad…

Would the coffee have been spilled? Would the flower orders have been messed up? Would all of the other stories have happened? Would Brooke and Dylan have met and spent the day together? Would Brooke had been fired? Would Brooke have been able to open her own store? Would Dylan have come to salvation? Would Brooke and Dylan had fallen in love???

I have long felt fascinated about how God uses the inconspicuous, and often difficult, circumstances as catalysts to get us where He wants us. Several years ago, if my husband had not seriously injured his back and had two surgeries, would I have ever seriously started writing? Maybe not. After all, it was that uncertainty that motivated me to write a book in six weeks and first take the risk of publishing.

If you turn a different direction, take a different step, is the end result the same?

Many times we don't know the why behind our difficulties, and sometimes the why we can see just isn't good enough. I've lived through some horrible, heart-breaking experiences, and sometimes I get to see something good come out of it, like me becoming an author after my husband's temporary disability. However, in some instances, the benefit of a difficulty in no way feels like it is worth the heartache. For instance, it is difficult to see any good when you lose someone you love. But, I don't think we have to see the scales balance here on earth. I'm told that God vastly tips the scales in your favor when you leave this life behind. For now, to see a little of God's work in difficult circumstance is often enough to strengthen my faith. And even if it is small, I will treasure any redeeming aspect to an awful experience.

When we get to heaven, I wonder if we will be able to see the other side of our life's tapestry. Here on earth, we can only see a bunch of multicolored threads that look quite random. Maybe, if we use enough imagination, we can follow a few of the threads to see the outline of a something bigger. But when we get to heaven, I think we'll get to turn that tapestry over. We'll see that all the mess of threads was really God weaving together a beautiful piece of art. Maybe you've tripped over a lot of toads. Maybe you can't yet follow the threads or see the why behind any of the difficulties in your life. But rest assured, God is making something beautiful. My prayer is that this book gives you enjoyment but also makes you think. Hopefully, the following questions will give you a different perspective and lead you to understand God's redemptive work in your trials, accidents, and mistakes. May you recognize God's hand weaving your life to be pleasing to Him.

For if not for God, all our toads would just be toads.

1. Discuss the title of the book and the set. What is the significance of "Out of the Blue Bouquet?" Have you experienced any out-of-the-blue bouquets in your own life?

(Genesis 50:20 And the story of Joseph in general!)

2. What did you think about how the stories were all interconnected? Did you catch how each book tied into the last? Can you see any spiritual significance to the theme and the way the stories worked together?

Romans 8:28, 2 Corinthians 4:16

3. "Out of the Blue Bouquet" is based on the huge mistake of multiple flower orders being sent to the wrong people. Brooke would certainly classify it as the biggest mistake she'd ever made. What is the biggest mistake or accident that has happened to you?

Brooke had a very long journey, but she did eventually see good things that came from her mistake and the nightmarish circumstances.

4. What were the good things that happened to Brooke because of the toad and the resulting mayhem?
2 Corinthians 4:8-12

5. Give some examples of some good coming out of bad in your own life.
Romans 5:3-5, 1 Peter 1:6-9, James 1:2-4

6. Brooke takes the blame for Tylee, even though it was Tylee who knocked the coffee over. Was she right to protect her friend? Do you see any correlation to Christ in her actions?
John 15:13

This story contained several examples of how someone's trial can be used to bless someone else. Identify some instances in the story where Brooke's mistake actually turned out to be a blessing to others.

7. Do you have any examples in your own life where your struggle or trial has inadvertently blessed someone else?
Mark 10:45, Matthew 5:16, Galatians 1:24, Isaiah 61:3

Attending church with Brooke made a big impression on Dylan. The text for the sermon was John 4:13-14.

8. How did the sermon and the verses affect Dylan? How did they affect Brooke?

9. How about you? Is your satisfaction coming from God or do you struggle with seeking it elsewhere?

Psalm 16:11, Philipians 4:11-13, Isaiah 58:11

10. What was your favorite part of this book or the set as a whole? Did anything make you think or cause you to view your life in a different way? What?

If you are doing this study with a group, please share with each other the trials that you are currently facing and pray together that God will bring good from your encounters with toads and help you see the out of the blue bouquets He is arranging.

MORE BOOKS
by Amanda Tru

Find the latest information and connect with Amanda at her website: www.amandatru.com

Yesterday Series:

Yesterday

The Locket

Today

The Choice

Tomorrow

The Promise

Forever (coming soon)

Tru Exceptions Series:

Baggage Claim

Mirage

Point of Origin

Rogue

Brides by Mail Series:
(Written with Cami Wesley)

Bride of Pretense
Bride by Request
Bride of Regret

The Secret Bride Society Series:

The Secret Bride Society

Christian Romance:

Secret Santa
The Random Acts of Cupid
The Assumption of Guilt
The Christmas Card

Clean Romance:

The Romance of the Sugar Plum Fairy

Children's:

Under the pen name J. Lasterday

Dog the Dragon Series:

The Dragon's Escape
The Cabin Boy's Treasure
The Great Expedition (coming soon)

ABOUT

www.amandatru.com

Amanda loves to write exciting books with  plenty of unexpected twists. She figures she loses so much sleep writing the things, it's only fair she makes readers lose sleep with books they can't put down!

Amanda has always loved reading, and writing books has been a lifelong dream. A vivid imagination helps her write captivating stories in a wide variety of genres. Her current book list includes everything from holiday romances, to historical, to action-packed suspense, to a Christian time travel/romance series.

Amanda is a former elementary school teacher who now spends her days being mommy to her four young children and her nights furiously writing. Amanda and her family live in a small Idaho town where the number of cows outnumbers the number of people.

Amanda loves to hear from readers! To receive notifications about Amanda Tru books and upcoming Crossroads Collections, please sign up for Amanda Tru's newsletter.

Newsletter:	Newsletter Sign-up
Website:	www.amandatru.com
Email:	truamanda@gmail.com
Facebook:	facebook.com/amandatru.author
Twitter:	@TruAmanda

Out of the Blue Bouquet

PERSONAL NOTE

Dear Readers,

Thank you for reading our *Out of the Blue Bouquet*, Crossroads Collection 1! We hope you enjoyed each individual story as well as seeing how they all wove together into a larger story that got tied up in a nice bow with the final book. Isn't it amazing to think of how God can use even one accident to affect so many lives? In this case, tripping over an ugly, little toad set off a chain reaction that involved the worlds of five different authors. That coffee spill sure created a lot of chaos and resulted in a lot of blessings!

This is a unique set of books, with each story fitting together like a puzzle piece with the final book. Since all of the stories have a point of intersection, we call it a Crossroads Collection. If you enjoyed this collection, please help spread the word, write a review, and/or recommend it to your friends. Also, if you would like to be notified of new and upcoming Crossroads Collections, please sign up with Amanda Tru's email newsletter below. She is excitedly organizing more of these multi-author sets of this type and will notify subscribers when the next one is released.

We pray our stories gave you enjoyment, touched your heart, and even made you think. We wish you the best and hope that God fits together the puzzle pieces of your life, arranging your trials of today into bouquets for tomorrow.

Sincerely,

The Out of the Blue Authors:

Hallee Bridgeman, Alana Terry, Carol Moncado, Chautona Havig, & Amanda Tru

Newsletter Sign Up:

http://eepurl.com/ZQdw9

www.ingramcontent.com/pod-product-compliance
Lightning Source LLC
Chambersburg PA
CBHW032248020726
47495CB00001B/19